THE NORDIC TRANSLATION SERIES

*Sponsored by the Nordic Cultural Commission
of the governments of Denmark, Finland,
Iceland, Norway, and Sweden*

HAVOC

HÆRVÆRK
Translated from the Danish by Carl Malmberg
With an introduction by Børge Gedsø Madsen

HAVOC

by Tom Kristensen

THE UNIVERSITY OF WISCONSIN PRESS
Madison, Milwaukee, and London, 1968

01592017

ACCRINGTON

Published by the University of Wisconsin Press
Madison, Milwaukee, and London
U.S.A.: Box 1379, Madison, Wisconsin 53701
U.K.: 27–29 Whitfield Street, London, W.1

English translation copyright © 1968
By the Regents of the University of Wisconsin
All rights reserved

Originally published by
Gyldendalsk Boghandel Nordisk Forlag A/S
Copenhagen, Denmark
Copyright © 1930 by Gyldendalsk Boghandel Nordisk Forlag A/S

Printed in the United States of America
By Kingsport Press, Inc., Kingsport, Tennessee

Library of Congress Catalog Card Number 68–14037

Beware of the soul and cultivate it not,
for doing so can be a form of vice.

CONTENTS

INTRODUCTION

For many years Tom Kristensen has been recognized in Denmark as one of the great figures of contemporary Danish literature, but he has been little known outside of Scandinavia. Fortunately his major fictional work, *Hærværk* (*Havoc*), has now been made available in English. The translation of this novel, one of the best written in Scandinavia in the twentieth century, should arouse world-wide interest in Tom Kristensen and stimulate the translation of more of his works in years to come.

Tom Kristensen was born in London in 1893, but in 1896 his family moved back to Copenhagen, where the boy grew up, the first sixteen years in very strained financial circumstances. In 1911 he passed his *Studentereksamen*, and in 1919 he received his master's degree in Danish, English, and German. His literary debut took place in 1920 with the publication of the volume of poetry *Fribytterdrømme* (*Dreams of a Freebooter*). These expressionistic poems with their violent eruptions of color effects and captivating exoticism immediately made Tom Kristensen's name known in Denmark. The poet's world view in this first book is expressed perhaps most characteristically in the poem "The Land Atlantic," in the famous opening line: "The world has become chaotic again." Impressions of life as chaotic, meaningless, and absurd have always haunted Tom Kristensen, and he is undoubtedly the most articulate exponent of this philosophy in modern Danish literature. His feelings towards the chaos of existence seem to be ambivalent; the chaotic absurdity can be frightening, but it can also stimulate artistic creativity. Tom Kristensen must have appreciated Nietzsche's famous remark, "You must have chaos in you to be able to give birth to a dancing star."

Kristensen's first novel, *Livets Arabesk* (*The Arabesque of Life*), published in 1921, continued the expressionism of *Dreams of a Freebooter* in prose form. In its description of the gradual disintegration of the personality of the main character, Dr. Baumann, the novel foreshadowed *Havoc* and Tom Kristensen's portrayal of Ole Jastrau. *Arabesque* is defined by Tom Kristensen as "meaninglessness expressed artistically," and this is a description which fits *Havoc* as well. The 1920's also saw the publication of a second novel *En Anden* (*Another,* 1923), dealing with the quest for personal identity, and three collections of poetry, *Mirakler* (*Miracles,* 1922), *Paafuglefjeren* (*The Peacock Feather,* 1922), and *Verdslige Sange* (*Worldly Songs,* 1927). In 1926 appeared the work which many Danish critics consider to be Tom Kristensen's best, the colorful, artistic, travel book *En Kavaler i Spanien* (*A Cavalier in Spain*). During this period Kristensen also wrote numerous book reviews for the liberal newspaper *Politiken*.

In 1927 Tom Kristensen temporarily left his position as reviewer at *Politiken* and isolated himself in the northern part of Zealand. For several years he had been leading a rather hectic life in Copenhagen, and apparently felt that he needed to get away from the temptations of the capital to concentrate all his efforts on his next book. It was known that he was working on a major novel about the Copenhagen newspaper world, and publication of the book was awaited with considerable excitement. When *Havoc* appeared in 1930, it created a sensation and a good deal of indignation. The novel has been described correctly as the "explosion" in Tom Kristensen's work.

In *Havoc* Tom Kristensen has described in painfully vivid detail the desperate alcoholic self-destruction of the literary critic Ole Jastrau and at the same time has written a fitting epitaph for the Lost Generation of the 1920's. When the novel was published, Tom Kristensen stated that he hoped that *Havoc* was "a courageous book . . . that describes the process of spiritual disintegration which I think is characteristic of the bourgeois and esthetic Copenhagen of the 1920's."

Ole Jastrau, Tom Kristensen's *alter ego,* finds himself living a life without values or meaning. He is bored and restless with his "beautiful and banal" wife Johanne, and their marriage is dissolved in the course of the novel. Intellectually, Jastrau is wooed by both Communism and Catholicism, but their dogmatic complacency repels him. He finds the watered-down radicalism of his newspaper *Dagbladet* equally uninspiring. Finding nothing and no one to believe in, Ole Jastrau is a man without convictions or opinions. He merely drifts. His one desire is "to go to the dogs slowly and quietly."

In the bizarre company of the brutish Communist poet Steffensen, the syphilitic servant girl Anne Marie, and the prostitute Black Else, Jastrau proceeds on his sinister odyssey of going to the dogs. His alcoholic decline gradually becomes a hell of endless and senseless repetitions. The Catholic priest Garhammer had told him that hell is known by its repetitions, and Jastrau comes to realize the truth of this statement. Recurring moods and symbols haunt Jastrau in his gradual deterioration. *"Ecce homo,"* he thinks bitterly on various occasions, as he looks at himself in mirrors during or after drinking sprees. At other times he comments on his situation with the casually indifferent line "Peter Boyesen salutes all good fellows!" which he first saw scribbled on the wall of his detention cell. After drinking bouts he often wakes up in strange hotel beds and finds himself gazing up into ceilings that seem as desolate as his philosophy of life. On some of these occasions the rain is pouring down endlessly, ominously, roaring down the gutters and drains of the hotel as Jastrau himself goes down the drain in a flood of alcohol.

In the course of the progressive disintegration of his personality, Ole Jastrau is highly conscious; he is intently observing and studying the various manifestations of his own dissolution. Some of the moods that emerge regularly from his subconscious during his drinking spells baffle and distress him. In the Copenhagen bars in the company of prostitutes, Jastrau is often overwhelmed by the feeling he is Christ. However, towards the end of the novel, Jastrau has become skeptical of his Jesus fantasies. He comments, "But then there was a good friend of mine who made me realize that of course Christ couldn't be anything but a reminiscence from my school days and consequently of no interest to me. For I wanted to arouse a creature—or a mental image—that came from deep inside the aquarium. A stalk-eyed fish with armored head and sharp joints and edges."

In his alcoholism, Jastrau at certain moments, often to the accompaniment of strident jazz music, experiences a sense of infinity. "There's always a feeling of the infinite about anything in a state of decay," he explains to Steffensen. Towards the end of the novel, after one of his many binges, he feels that perhaps, after all, there has been a philosophical purpose to his boozing. He says, "Sometimes I imagine I have a philosophical purpose. I've wanted to get at the meaning of things—my own opinions, for example. I've wanted to find out what's behind them." To which his friend replies, "Yes, and there was lust and drunkenness, wasn't there?" In another conversation Jastrau states his purpose in a slightly different way: "There is something I want, and when I drink I sometimes feel for a moment that I've captured it Liquor is the only substitute for religion. . . ."

Everything in *Havoc* is seen through Jastrau's eyes or refracted through his consciousness, and it is a tribute to Tom Kristensen's art that throughout the novel he succeeds in communicating Jastrau's private emotions and thoughts to the reader with compelling immediacy. The pace of the novel quickens as Jastrau's familiar world dissolves around him, and in many passages the reader shares with Jastrau the dizzying feeling of the infinite in all decline.

When *Havoc* was first published in 1930, many reviewers expressed their disappointment in the novel. They found it embarrassingly confessional and too much of a *roman à clef* with venomous portraits of Tom Kristensen's colleagues at *Politiken*. Many critics found fault with the book's composition which they condemned as amorphous and rambling. The view that *Havoc* is poorly composed has long since been abandoned, especially after the thorough analyses of the novel's technique by Aage Jørgensen and Hanne Marie Svendsen. Today thoughtful readers have no difficulty in perceiving that in his portrayal of Ole Jastrau's private hell of repetitions, Tom Kristensen has deliberately employed a highly sophisticated technique. As the novel opens, Jastrau is approached by a beggar with a hideous, ravaged face and finally gives him money to forget him. He felt that "he had paid for the right to turn his back on the man." At the close of the novel, it is Jastrau who sees himself in the role of this beggar, as he receives money for the ticket to Berlin from his drinking companion, the "inevitable" Kjær. Jastrau draws the parallel with the opening scene quite explicitly when he remarks, "Kjær, do you know how it is when one day you're in good spirits and you meet a beggar with a hideous ravaged face,—a person who's really in need—and then you give him money so you can be free to forget him, and so your day won't be ruined?" Kjær straightens up and replies, "You—you do have—an oddly magnanimous way of saying thanks." As Hanne Marie Svendsen writes, "The book closes like a circle." One is tempted to say "like a vicious circle." However, the gloomy subject matter of the novel is frequently relieved by humor and by the charged artistic energy of the style, especially in the vivid descriptions of Copenhagen scenery. This has been well noted by the Danish author Klaus Rifbjerg in an excellent article on *Havoc* in *Politiken*, March 25, 1960. Rifbjerg wrote, "The book is a proof that the morbid may incite to great zest, that humor, vitality, creativity may arise from degradation, from chaos."

Havoc was Kristensen's last novel. He resumed his activity as a lyrical poet and in the 1930's and 1940's developed into one of Denmark's leading literary critics. He wrote a great number of illuminating interpretations of Scandinavian writers and also of such internationally famous authors as James Joyce, D. H. Lawrence, T. S. Eliot, Hemingway, Faulkner, O'Flaherty, and others. A selection of his best critical essays was published in 1946 under the title *Mellem Krigene*

(*Between the Wars*). In 1936 he published the excellent collection of poetry *Mod den yderste Rand* (*Towards the Farthest Horizon*), which includes his moving commemorative poems for his friend the explorer Knud Rasmussen and for the parachutist Emilie Sannom who died a violent and tragic death. The following years saw the publication of additional collections of poetry: *Digte i Døgnet* (*Occasional Poems,* 1940); *Den syngende Busk* (*The Singing Bush,* 1949); and *Den sidste Lygte* (*The Last Lamp,* 1954). Tom Kristensen's most recent poems are more subdued and quiet both in tone and style than his expressionistic poetry of the 1920's. In the same way, his travel book *Rejse i Italien* (*Travel in Italy,* 1950) is more simply and less artistically written than the earlier explosive *En Kavaler i Spanien.*

Now in his seventy-sixth year, Tom Kristensen is universally respected and admired in Denmark, in fact in all of Scandinavia. Like Strindberg, about whom he has written with insight, he is a complex, elusive artist, impossible to sum up in an easy formula. In some respects Tom Kristensen has been ahead of his times. Long before the word "absurdity" became fashionable in Europe and America, he had given incisive analyses of the absurd in life in some of his expressionistic poetry and in his novels. *Havoc,* his magnum opus, is not only a book about dipsomania and pub crawling. It is just as much, and perhaps more so, a novel about the person Ole Jastrau who, through no fault of his own, is compelled to live in a world where all moral, religious, and philosophical values are in a state of flux. *Havoc* is also a candid picture of the 1920's by a highly sensitive and reflective writer who has had the intellectual courage and integrity to describe the modern world as he sees it—chaotic, meaningless, and absurd.

Børge Gedsø Madsen

University of California, Berkeley
August, 1967

A KRISTENSEN BIBLIOGRAPHY

BY TOM KRISTENSEN: A SELECTION

Fribytterdrømme (*Dreams of a Freebooter*). Copenhagen: Lybecker, 1920. (Poetry)

Livets Arabesk (*The Arabesque of Life*). Copenhagen: Hagerups Forlag, 1921. (Novel)

Mirakler (*Miracles*). Copenhagen: Gyldendal, 1922. (Poetry)

Paafuglefjeren (*The Peacock Feather*). Copenhagen: Hagerups Forlag), 1922. (Poetry)

En Anden (*Another*). Copenhagen: Hagerups Forlag, 1923. (Novel)

En Kavaler i Spanien (*A Cavalier in Spain*). Copenhagen: Hagerups Forlag, 1926. (Travel book including some poetry)

Verdslige Sange (*Worldly Songs*). Copenhagen: Naver, 1927. (Poetry)

Hærværk (*Havoc*). Copenhagen: Gyldendal, 1930. (Novel)

Kunst, Økonomi, Politik (*Art, Economics, Politics*). Copenhagen: Naver, 1932. (Literary criticism)

Vindrosen (*The Compass*). Copenhagen: Gyldendal, 1934. (Short stories)

Mod den yderste Rand (*Towards the Farthest Horizon*). Copenhagen: Gyldendal, 1936. (Poetry)

Digte i Døgnet (*Occasional Poems*). Copenhagen: Gyldendal, 1940. (Poetry)

Mellem Scylla og Charybdis. Samlede Digte fra Tyverne (*Between Scylla and Charybdis. Collected Poems from the Twenties*). Copenhagen: Gyldendal, 1943. (Poetry)

Mellem Krigene. Artikler og Kroniker (*Between the Wars. Articles and Essays*). Copenhagen: Gyldendal, 1946. (Literary criticism)

Den syngende Busk (*The Singing Bush*). Copenhagen: Gyldendal, 1949. (Poetry)

Rejse i Italien (*Travel in Italy*). Copenhagen: Carit Andersens Forlag, 1951. (Travel book)

Den sidste Lygte (*The Last Lamp*). Copenhagen: Gyldendal, 1954. (Poetry)

TRANSLATIONS INTO ENGLISH

"In a Japanese Railway Carriage" and "The Vanished Faces." Two short stories from *Vindrosen* (*The Compass*). In *Modern Danish Authors,* edited by Evelyn Heepe and Niels Heltberg. Copenhagen, London, Chicago: The Scandinavian Publishing Company, 1946.

"Diminuendo." Translated by Charles Wharton Stork. In *A Second Book of Danish Verse*. Princeton: Princeton University Press for the American-Scandinavian Foundation, 1947. (Poem)

"The Slow Spring." Translation by Martin S. Allwood and Knud K. Mogensen of "Det langsomme Foraar." In *Modern Danish Poems*. Copenhagen: Høst og Søn, 1949. (Poem)

"The Disaster." Translation by Lydia Cranfield of "Ulykken," from *Vindrosen* (*The Compass*). In *Contemporary Danish Prose*. Copenhagen: Gyldendal, 1958.

ABOUT TOM KRISTENSEN

Frandsen, Ernst. *Aargangen, der maatte snuble i Starten.* 2d ed. Copenhagen: Gyldendal, 1960.

Halvorsen, Erik. "Tom Kristensen." In *Danske Digtere i det 20. Aarhundrede*. New expanded and revised edition by Frederik Nielsen and Ole Refstrup. Copenhagen: G. E. C. Gads Forlag, vol. II, 1966.

Højberg-Pedersen, Regin. *Tom Kristensen.* Copenhagen: Gyldendal, 1942.

Johansen, Niels Kaas. "Tom Kristensen." In *Danske Digtere i det 20. Aarhundrede.* Copenhagen: G. E. C. Gads Forlag, 1951.

Jørgensen, Aage. "Studier i Tom Kristensens Roman *Hærværk*." In *Danske Studier*. Copenhagen: Schultz Forlag, 1962.

————. "Hærværk i Pressen." In *Perspektiv, Det danske Magasin.* Copenhagen: Hans Reitzels Forlag, March, 1963.

Kristensen, Sven Møller. *Dansk Litteratur, 1918–1952.* 4th ed. Copenhagen: Ejnar Munksgaard, 1956.

Svendsen, Hanne Marie. "Efterskrift." In Gyldendals Bibliotek edition of *Hærværk*. Copenhagen: Gyldendal, vol. II, 1964.

See also the Tom Kristensen bibliography in *Dansk Skønlitterært Forfatterleksikon, 1900–1950.* Copenhagen: Grønholt Pedersens Forlag, vol. II, 1960.

PART ONE

Caught Between Doctrines

The telephone rang again.

Chapter One Ole Jastrau, who was stretched out on the couch reading, laid the book aside without closing it. Out of indolence he did not put it on the table, but on top of a stack of uncut review copies, the smooth, new backs of which towered up from the floor like the wall of a new building. It was the spring literary crop waiting to be criticized in *Dagbladet*. He never put review copies on the table; the only things that belonged there were the shiny, black telephone and the crude, swarthy, Negro fetish.

He lay back on the couch again, adjusted his facial expression to soften his Mongoloid features and make himself look a bit more pleasant, and finally reached for the telephone with a feeling of abhorrence.

"Ole Jastrau speaking," he said, reclining comfortably on his back. It was a pleasant way to talk over the phone. One could imagine himself floating horizontally through space. "What's that? The society for what—? Oh, you want me to make a speech? About what? But I don't have a thing on my mind worth talking about—not a thing, I assure you, Herr Raben."

He stared up at the white square of the ceiling. It was as blank as his own outlook on life. Only the reflection of a lampshade agitated by a slight draft drifted aimlessly about with the spectral movements of a jellyfish—or of a human mind. How big and empty the ceiling was! "Philosophy? Ha ha! What are you driving at? Oh, *Lebensan-schau-ung!*" He tossed both legs in the air in an outburst of hilarity.

"Look what Father's doing!" The shrill, boyish voice filled the room, and a little round head with blond curls peeked over the edge of the table. A clear bubble hung from one nostril. "Look what Father's doing with his legs!" In the enthusiasm of the moment the bubble burst.

"Quiet, Oluf! Quiet! No, I'm afraid not, Herr Raben. To tell you the truth, I don't have the time—damned if I do! Am I going over to the paper tomorrow night to listen to the election results? All we could do

3

over there would be to laugh at ourselves. My God, we Radicals will be swamped! Yes, you can depend on that. Go out and vote? Who, me? No thanks, I can't be bothered."

Just then the front doorbell rang.

"Now there's somebody at the door, so I'll have to hang up. I'll say good-by now." He put back the receiver. "Oh, go plumb to hell!"

"Prum to—ho ho—prum to!" echoed Oluf, teasingly. Oluf had trouble with his "l"s. He stuck out his round, sweater-clad belly. "Ho ho!"

The caller rang again, a tentative, cautious ring this time.

"Stay here, Oluf," Jastrau said, and went out into the hallway.

Through the frosted glass panes of the hallway door he could barely discern a figure standing far back and to the right. Another beggar, no doubt. He wondered when Johanne was coming back anyway, so he would not have to run to the door every time the bell rang. And besides, he must remember to look after the stove. If only Oluf did not run against it and burn himself. But now, the beggar. Jastrau opened the door with the feeling that he also was vulnerable to attack from the rear—the stove, the fire that might go out, Oluf, who might fall and hurt himself.

A man with a face as red as a lobster. He stood far away from the door, hunched up, meek and cringing. And what was the matter with his eyes? They looked as if every single eyelash had been yanked out one at a time. The raw flesh lay in direct contact with the eyeballs. A blinding shock—as if the corner of a handkerchief had suddenly been flicked into Jastrau's eye.

"No—no, excuse me—we don't give to strangers at the door here," he said in a sudden transition from embarrassment to savagery. He slammed the door shut so hard that the panes rattled.

He heard the man shuffle off down the stairs. But the recollection of that lobster-red beggar face was too much for him; it was as if something clammy had suddenly been flung into his face. That crafty, yet imploring look! Those eyelids bereft of skin and the red face! Would the picture stay with him for years and years? Would he remember it as a hideous sort of sunset?

He fumbled with a crooked forefinger in a vest pocket. It was a brass coin that he came up with, a two-krone piece. It was stupid sentimentality to give so much to someone who came to your door, but— Jastrau flung the door open again and ran two flights down the narrow stairway that was as dreary as if it had been at the back of the house. He had to get that apparition—that hallucination—out of his mind.

4

"Wait a minute! You there!"

The lobster-red face turned and looked up. The beggar stood a few steps below him. The eyes blinked.

"Here, take this."

Jastrau gave him the coin, then instantly wheeled about, feeling that he had paid for the right to turn his back on the man. Slowly he started back up the stairs.

But there was that staircase window again. He stopped. The pane had been smashed. What with the housing shortage, the landlord certainly was not going to spend the few øre it would cost to replace it. But there was a trace of mildness in the cold air that came drifting in. A touch of spring. As a matter of fact, were the trees not about ready to burst into leaf? It was more than he could bear to look down into that airshaft of a courtyard with its bicycle shed and uncovered rubbish cans. Yes, a cool, fresh breeze. And a person had to appreciate spring while he had the chance.

But the stove!

No sooner did this thought occur to him than the telephone rang again in the apartment. He could hear it through the open hallway door from where he stood on the stairway. No, he could not stand still for so much as a second to enjoy a bit of fresh air and a moment of peace, or to relish the breath of spring while the opportunity was his.

But he would not be a slave to that telephone! He, who needed peace and quiet so he could read, and write his reviews. He must have quiet. So, take it easy, don't go so fast, he told himself. Forcing himself to be calm, he walked slowly back up the stairs.

"Father! The phone is ringing!" Oluf had seated himself on the floor between the yellow sofa and the rococo chair with the yellow oval back. Only his head with its curly hair was visible, sticking out like a chrysanthemum. He seemed intensely preoccupied. The curls concealed some forbidden object.

"Father! The phone is ringing!" he repeated, perhaps to divert attention from himself.

"I know it, damn it!" Jastrau whispered, smiling blandly. He did not like to swear too loudly when the boy was present. But that fire! With slow, deliberate steps, as if to torment the telephone, he walked toward the big green porcelain stove.

The fire was still burning, thank the Lord! But when was Johanne coming back? She had told him that she was only going out to buy a pair of shoes. The ashes! He opened the stove door and shook the grate so that the glowing embers rained down into the ashpan.

5

The phone rang again. This time it sounded louder.

"Father! The phone is ringing!" There was a note of gloating in the boy's voice. No, it was impossible to escape one's fate. There lay the stack of review copies—waiting, waiting.

As if he despaired of ever finding tranquillity, he went over to the telephone and sullenly grabbed the receiver. He stood near the window and stared hopelessly over at the imitation Romanesque windows of his fifth-floor neighbor across the street. The white curtains were always tightly drawn.

"Ole Jastrau speaking. Oh, it's you. Fine. How are you? Well yes, thanks. I wouldn't mind that at all if I can find the time. Yes, of course. Let me see now. A week from Thursday, eight o'clock. Tuxedo? Oh, white tie. Full war-paint, eh? Wait a minute, let me write this down." He reached for a pad and wrote, "Eyvind Krog, Thursday 24th, 8 P.M."

"Yes, of course. Lazy? Do you think so? Well, these book reviews take a lot of time. Yes, one gets balmy from reading everybody else's crazy ideas. Sure—all ideas are crazy, damn it!"

How that Krog could talk! Jastrau stood gazing absent-mindedly over at the window across the street. Only once had he seen a woman there pull the curtains aside. A face as white as the curtains, and a big dark mouth with tightly-drawn lips. A plaster mask in the forenoon light. Then she had seen him and had irritably drawn the curtains again.

"No, Eyvind, there's no damn time to write poetry—"

Then Eyvind Krog went on with his chatter. For a long, long time. Jastrau's ear began to hurt from pressing the receiver against it, and he got a cramp in his hand. How this fellow Krog could rattle on! All right, just keep looking at the roof of the building across the street. The chimneys up there, standing under the open sky like cairns on a lonely plain. He hardly ever saw anyone go in there.

"No, look now, you're all wrong. You can't write poetry when you're pressed for time. You have to loaf around awhile before you write it, and you have to know that you'll be able to loaf again after you've written it. Laziness? No, that's not what I mean. Cosmic idleness—that's what one has to have time for. Otherwise you don't get any verses out of me. No, I only get that feeling after a whiskey and soda, but when I drink I can't write. A binge is a poem that won't be put down on paper. A King George the Fourth or a Doctor's Special. I get thirsty just thinking about it. What? Oh—John Haig! Ha ha—now you're talking! You can be sure I'll toss off some big ones. Yes, some cosmic highballs—that's a good expression you coined there. Einstein

6

highballs—how do you like that? Yes, damn it all, let's live in the fourth dimension. I'll be there. Say hello to your wife. Good-by. Ha ha ha!"

As soon as he replaced the receiver the genial telephone smile faded from his face and a final "ha" fluttered aimlessly through the room like a withered leaf. Wearily he leaned his hand against the window sash, and the afternoon light fell on his pudgy face. It was not yet a face that had gone to pieces, but it was tired, washed out, and a bit vapid. His lower lip protruded at times as if he had no control over it.

Why had Krog asked him about his poems?

His face became inscrutable. His features were those of a person who might develop into either a sage or an alcoholic. It was this ambiguity that gave his face its Mongoloid characteristics.

His foot brushed against the pile of review copies. He could not afford to waste time. But first he would have to light a pipe. Oh yes, he was also supposed to phone that publisher, and then there was the number that Johanne had written down on the pad. That number. Who could that be?

"The man!" exclaimed Oluf from behind the rococo chair. It sounded as if he was striking a piece of wood against the leg of the sofa.

Jastrau looked quickly over at the table. The Negro fetish was gone. That youngster simply could not leave it where it belonged. There were all sorts of other knickknacks on the tabletop, but the boy never touched any of them. The moment he turned his back, however, Oluf made off with "the man."

"Oluf! Put 'the man' back right away!"

The room became very quiet. He saw a pair of angry eyes peering at him from under the arm of the chair.

"Did you hear me?"

Oluf came slowly out of hiding, crept forward on all fours with the fetish in his paws, and stood up with difficulty. His lower lip was distorted.

"That's the boy!" said his father.

Oluf reached up and put the Negro fetish back. But as soon as he had restored it to its place he toddled off into the next room, opened the door to the little corridor that led from the dining room to the distant kitchen, and disappeared.

It was an episode that had been repeated many times. His father followed him, smiling. Sure enough—there stood the child at the farthest end of the apartment, his arms leaning against the kitchen

7

door and his face hidden in them while he cried softly but bitterly. A small boy with curly hair hanging down over his neck like a wig and little trousers that stretched tightly about his knees, crying in a controlled manner, yet violently enough so that the latch on the door vibrated.

"Now, Oluf!"

"Go 'way! Oyuf wants to cry ayone!"

The father had to laugh. It was the easiest thing to do. Nevertheless, a sense of impotence gripped him as he stood there. Already he felt himself being shoved aside by this three-year-old personality. He had a feeling of apprehension, a foreboding . . . . But no, it was better to laugh.

Then the confounded doorbell again. What was his life anyway—a farce? Must he be constantly disrupted by those two eternally ringing bells—the telephone and the front door? A man without peace in his own apartment. What was a home? A waiting room! A telephone exchange! A dooryard to hell!

It was probably another beggar.

He went out to the hallway door again. On the other side of the frosted panes were two figures, but they stood so close to the door that they merged into a single dark object with gray indistinct outlines. He opened the door.

"Hello, Ole!"

Surprised, Jastrau screwed up his eyes because it was lighter out on the stairway than in his hallway. But he did not recognize either of the callers.

"Hello," he said hesitantly.

The nearer man, the one who had greeted him, wore a soiled cap. A pair of large dark sunglasses hid his features, and a neat light-colored topcoat with raglan sleeves added a confusing note. His lips were tightly compressed as if he were sucking them in, but soon they relaxed and the mouth became larger. He had obviously been putting on an act.

"Don't you know me?" he asked in a sonorous, deep, well-modulated, ingratiating voice.

Jastrau glanced fleetingly at the other man. He was tall and stood stooped forward. A cap, misshapen by having been constantly pulled down over the forehead, gave evidence of a sloping, pointed skull. The man wore no overcoat, although it was still cold. He kept his hands in his pockets and hunched up his shoulders like a waterfront hoodlum.

No, Jastrau did not know him either. He could not really get a clear picture of him. All he noticed was a pair of glazed eyes staring at him.

8

"Well, hello. What is it you want?" Jastrau said falteringly to the one with the sunglasses.

The man compressed his lips once more and changed his expression. It was as if he had slipped on a mask. Then he laughed, and with a sweeping, theatrical gesture removed the sunglasses. A pair of dark gypsy eyes came into view, and with the outburst of laughter the lips resumed their natural appearance.

"Oh, so it's you, Sanders," observed Jastrau stiffly. There was no cordiality in his tone. What did this Communist whippersnapper want with him?

"Oh, I knew you wouldn't be glad to see me," said Sanders. "But that makes no difference, because it's we who want to visit you, and you'll just have to put up with it." He spoke with an affected air of cynicism, but his melodious voice made his words seem both earnest and agreeable.

"See, it's just as I told you," he added, addressing his companion, who hunched his shoulders even higher and let out a snort that sounded as if he were gloating over something.

"I thought you were safely behind bars," Jastrau said. Then, to match Sanders' cynical banter, he went on, "So I figured that for the time being we'd be rid of you. But now I suppose I'll have to ask you in."

"Thanks. That's not a comradely way to talk, but we'll accept the invitation. After all, that's why we came. But you mustn't let us inconvenience you. I imagine you have a lot to do," Sanders said in his winning tone. "No doubt you have to slave in true bourgeois fashion." Now there was gentle irony in his voice, and then the tone shifted suddenly to one of heartfelt sympathy: "Of course they underpay you over at that lying sheet you work for, don't they?"

Jastrau felt himself hemmed in by all of Sanders' subtleties of manner and intonation. One moment the fellow was haughty and condescending, the next he seemed to shrivel up and become a cringing suppliant. And in the process he hardly batted an eye.

"Let's not talk about that. Come on inside," replied Jastrau.

"I suppose it's customary, for all I know, to introduce people to each other in a bourgeois household. At least so I've been told. Well, this is Stefan Steffensen, the only poet we've had in Scandinavia since Sigbjørn Obstfelder. And this is Ole Jastrau, Stefan. You know—Jastrau, the fellow you've heard about, the reviewer for that lying sheet over there—the renegade, the traitor. But excuse me, Ole, this isn't the way a guest should behave—"

But Jastrau was already responding with a low, ironical bow. He

9

kept his eyes half-closed because this gave him a feeling that he was enveloping himself in a fog. With a sweeping gesture he invited them in.

Sanders accepted the invitation and walked into the living room, polite and smiling, as if expecting to meet the lady of the house. After him came Stefan Steffensen, taking long, swinging strides without regard to the dimensions of the room.

Then, while Sanders stood over near the doorway to the dining room with a genial smile on his full lips, as if on the lookout for the household's feminine spirit, Steffensen swung one foot forward in such an exasperated manner that a long shoelace came undone and whipped through the air. Thoughtlessly, he planted his foot on the seat of one of the rococo chairs as if it had been a sawhorse and proceeded to tie the shoelace in such a painstaking manner that the old chair creaked.

Jastrau cast a nervous sidelong glance at him and had a mind to get furious. Stefan Steffensen! So this was he—the poet who wrote for the Young Communist League's little organ, *The Hammer*. There was something childlike about his oval face, but his prominent lips were set in an expression of what appeared to be inexplicable wrath.

"You're a pig to have along in a drawing room." The words came from Bernhard Sanders.

To Jastrau everything seemed hazy. What was going on? Had they come to scoff at him, to behave as they had done a fortnight ago when they had tried to paste vituperative placards up on *Dagbladet's* big windows? In among the bourgeoisie and create a panic—was that the idea? No, he was still too nervous to make things out clearly, and he merely stood there, self-conscious and caught off guard in his own living room.

Meanwhile Steffensen went about making himself as much at home as possible. With unerring aim, he sent his cap whirling through the air so that it landed on one of the rococo chairs, then flung himself heavily down on the other one and crossed his legs, disregarding entirely the smudge his shoe had left on the upholstery. His hair hung down over his brow in slovenly fashion, and his forehead was so high and sallow that when seen through the wisps of hair the effect was distinctly unpleasant. There was, indeed, something inhuman about it.

Then came a commotion, and with it a sense of relief. It was Oluf who suddenly appeared in the doorway to the dining room, his belly jutting out and his yellow hair surrounding his head like a halo. A communicative little smile played about his long upper lip so that it quivered slightly.

10

"Hello, men," he shrilled. Two big quivering tears shone uneasily in his eyes as he fearlessly approached Sanders. Sanders bowed very low to the red-eyed young gentleman who bore his last tears with an air of nonchalant dignity and who was more of a host than his father. Oluf gave a deep snuffle, as if his lungs had finally composed themselves, and his smile broke out into a breathless laugh.

Was it to amuse the boy that Bernhard Sanders sat down on the edge of the couch and threw open his smart raglan topcoat? A long Russian blouse fastened with a belt came into view, and at the sight of the belt buckle a gleam of curiosity lit up the boy's eyes. The blouse was not very clean, nor were Sanders' cheeks free of dark stubble. This was remarkable in a man as concerned about his clothes as Sanders.

"What sort of a getup is it you're wearing anyway, Sanders?" Jastrau asked, slightly irritated.

"Oh, a raglan and sunglasses."

"No, I mean that Russian outfit you've got on underneath.

Sanders gave him a look of scorn.

"After all, there's nothing strange about that. It's simple and very practical. In ten years we'll all be wearing them—you too. But the raglan coat—that's my disguise."

"Well, paradoxes are something we see plenty of."

"No, no, Ole," Sanders replied sharply. "I wear the coat and the sunglasses so the police won't recognize me. I stand to get a month for this last example of disorderly conduct. There are a few such charges against me, I might add."

"You mean this business of selling *The Hammer* on the streets?"

Sanders nodded.

"Have you read *The Hammer*?"

"No."

"Then you ought to. It's among us that things are happening."

Jastrau smiled vaguely at his remarks. But Sanders continued:

"I stand to get a month in the clink, because we don't pay fines, as a matter of principle. But now we know for sure—we have connections—that we'll get an amnesty immediately if the Social Democrats win. It's as good as promised us."

Sanders spoke with political overtones. And Jastrau guessed what he was getting at. This was the reason they had come. But then they were interrupted by Oluf, who had surrendered to the curiosity that shone in his eyes. He wanted to get close to Sanders and stand between his knees. It had to do with the belt buckle.

"This is a nice boy," said Sanders with some feeling.

"Yes. He and I get along very well together," said Jastrau, smiling.

11

"But where is your wife?" Sanders turned his head as if once more trying to peek into the dining room.

"She should be here soon," Jastrau replied coldly. There was a note of intimacy in Sanders' tone that offended him. Discussion meetings. Long conversations in the university lunchroom. Calling each other "du."* Five years ago. Did this mean that they knew each other?

"I think I'll take off my coat. It's so warm here," said Sanders.

Jastrau smiled wearily.

"Yes, you might as well," he answered. "I suppose you'll stay here until the election is over tomorrow. It would be annoying to get picked up by the police tonight."

Sanders had stood up and was removing his coat.

"It's wonderful now and then to meet people who understand, isn't it, Stefan?"

"Yes," replied Stefan, as if he had just awakened. The chair creaked under his weight. "A crummy chair," he grumbled.

Sanders laughed across the room to Jastrau and shook his head knowingly as if to say that Steffensen was impossible. But his eyes glistened with malicious pleasure.

"Yes, I had an idea that I understood the purpose of your visit," Jastrau said ironically. "It means that you're going to spend the night here."

"He's very gifted," said Sanders to Steffensen.

"He was once," muttered Steffensen. Then he cleared his throat and began to recite in a fanatical and youthfully enthusiastic tone that had a unique quality of rough charm about it:

> "Mother, Madonna, and comrade in battle,
> Beloved woman and happy warrior,
> Mother of revolutions."

He intoned the words crudely, apropos of nothing and without looking at Jastrau, who cringed at hearing quoted the words of "Proletarian Woman," one of his youthful revolutionary poems.

Sanders smiled maliciously.

Jastrau made a wry face.

"Oh, that!" he said.

"Yes, it's your own youth that's kicking you in the behind, and it kicks hard," said Sanders. "And we don't have the least sympathy for

* The familiar form of the pronoun "you," used only when addressing a member of the family, a child, or an intimate friend.

you. All I can say to you is that 'Proletarian Woman' is a good poem, and the only thing the matter with it is that you wrote it."

"I'm glad that you appreciate something about me," replied Jastrau.

Oluf had strutted across the room to where Steffensen was sitting and was staring at him with interest.

"Sing some more," he shrilled. "Oh please, sing some more."

Sanders laughed loudly. Steffensen, on the other hand, regarded the boy with a foreboding look and moved his big feet as if fearful of coming in contact with him. With what seemed to be instinctive understanding, the boy turned his back and walked over to Sanders again. The belt buckle shone.

Steffensen shifted uneasily, and the chair creaked again.

"And so you want to stay here," began Jastrau. "God knows what Johanne will say to that."

The chair kept creaking. It was as if Steffensen were unable to get settled in it.

"Oh, women always have a touch of romanticism," Sanders replied confidently. "They get a thrill—goose pimples from head to toe—when they can associate with jailbirds without any danger to themselves." He savored his words. "You get sex appeal by being revolutionary. Oh, she'll very likely be shocked at first, but then— Well, you know what I mean, Ole, from the standpoint of sexual psychology. Besides, Stefan and I are quite harmless—almost housebroken."

"But damn it all, I wouldn't mind if I had another chair," snapped Steffensen. "You come and sit here, Bernhard. You have a better ass for this kind of a chair than I do."

"Why do you have such chairs, anyhow?" asked Sanders, executing a few elaborate dance steps as he changed places with Steffensen. Oluf trotted trustfully along behind him.

"Well, they reminded me of the chairs in my toy theatre." Jastrau smiled self-consciously. "You know, the king's palace in 'The Tinder Box,' and 'Clumsy Hans.' I believe that's why I bought them. So you see—"

It sounded like an apology.

Sanders' eyes flashed spitefully. They were like the bloodshot eyes of a gypsy.

"I see," he sneered indignantly. "Yes, and you'd probably also go to war because you once played with tin soldiers. And I bet you've already corrupted this little fellow here—your son—by giving him tin soldiers. Isn't that right? You have fine soldiers, haven't you—what's your name?" he asked, addressing the boy, who stood between his knees. It was the belt buckle that fascinated him.

"Oyuf," replied the boy without looking up. He was not going to be distracted.

"Oyuf! Listen, Oluf—you should always talk properly to children, you know—listen Oluf—they are fine soldiers that you have, aren't they?"

Oluf looked up at him without answering. He had no toy soldiers, nor did he understand what the strange man was talking about. Jastrau smiled maliciously.

But Sanders was not to be stopped by such a setback. His voice grew louder and more ominous, embellished with righteous indignation, until it took on an entirely uncalled-for tone of prophetic wrath: "There's nothing so irrational as the bourgeois mind. I tell you, I could take every piece of furniture in this apartment and use it as an example of how fundamentally sentimental you are—just like all the others. And what does this sentimentality cover? At worst nothing but cowardice. No, there's nothing else hidden behind your confusion. And just look at that fetish! What business does that have being here?"

"Why? What's the matter with that?" muttered Steffensen, who had picked it up and now sat twirling it between his hands as if it were a roll of putty. With a rounded hand he felt of the shape of the head.

"Well, what's it doing here among these rococo chairs, that Christian VIII sofa, and those Christian IX pictures on the wall?"

The pictures, which were commonplace enough, had come from Jastrau's home.

"All pieced together from God knows where! A present from Aunt Bine! Something to remember grandmother by! One thing and another. Picked up in an antique shop! All pretension and sentimentality. Not even honest poverty. Why, a worker's home is—"

Just then Jastrau caught sight of the boy, who had retreated away from the vociferous Sanders and stood leaning against the door and staring at him with an angry gleam in his eyes. More the master of the house than his father.

He had enough gumption to defend his home, while his father—

"So you're going to stay here tonight!" Jastrau exclaimed, rising to his feet.

Sanders stopped talking and looked up in surprise. Steffensen set the fetish back in place.

"Yes," growled Steffensen.

"That's the idea," replied Sanders, smiling and keeping his voice well modulated.

"And that makes you my guests."

"Exactly."

"Well then, damn it, you'll have to take things as you find them. Now go hang up your things in the hall and leave me alone to do some reading. I have some reviews to do. I can't neglect my work."

"All right, we'll keep quiet," said Sanders diplomatically, getting up to hang his topcoat in the corridor. "You can take a joke, can't you, Ole?"

Jastrau did not reply.

"Of course, I'm serious about what I said," Sanders went on when he returned. "But partly I was just ribbing you. I don't tell everyone what I really think, you know."

"I suppose I should feel complimented," Jastrau said sarcastically.

Steffensen let out a rude, forced guffaw.

An endless stream of scorn and sarcasm from these two youngsters. Jastrau felt that they were mocking him as if he were a defenseless old man. They were too rough for him, this pair—so aggressive that the room seemed crammed with people. When would he ever find a little peace? He should at least get one book read and reviewed today. And then, all those other books!

"Well, now wait just a minute," he said nervously. It was invariably that way—after a brief spell of rage he always relented.

Then the telephone rang.

"One of you take it and say I've gone out," he said. "It'll be the truth, because I'm going out to the kitchen to get a bottle of port."

"An intelligent man," said Steffensen, leaning forward obligingly to pick up the receiver.

Jastrau went into the kitchen and got down on his knees in front of the cabinet. The bottles stood on the lower shelf. From inside the living room he heard Steffensen's voice. Someone had called the wrong number. Finally he found the bottle he was looking for—a fifth of ruby Burmester. It was the kind with the black label and the yellow seal in the lower corner. The sight of the label alone was enough to make him feel better, and he set the bottle gently on the kitchen table.

"I want to carry."

It was Oluf's curly head popping up at the level of his jacket pocket. He wanted to make himself useful.

"No. This is nothing for little boys. You might break it."

He brought out three green glasses, held them up to the light to see if they were clean, then went in to join the others. Oluf trotted along at his heels.

Already, now that he hugged the bottle close against his chest, he felt a warm sense of reassurance. It was as if he suddenly found himself at home—he who felt like a stranger everywhere, here among his own furniture, here with his own son, yes, even with the things he wrote. But now everything around him seemed clearer, more sharply delineated. The furniture had more definite lines. He could even see his guests more clearly, more objectively. They were now individuals in their own right, persons with whom he could associate; before they had been parts of his own ego, evil spirits within him, hallucinations he could not get rid of, persecutors.

Nevertheless, he was not transformed into the master of the house; it was not a role for which he had any talent. As he placed the bottle and the three green glasses on the black tabletop and moved the telephone over onto the windowsill, he was more the boon companion who had been lucky enough to pull a coup, and his smile was at once cunning and tinged with consciousness of triumph.

"No thanks. I don't drink," Sanders protested. But he drew up his chair in a gesture of sociability.

"Aren't you drinking either?" asked Jastrau, feeling annoyed.

"Sure," said Steffensen, smacking his lips. "I'll drink," he added, putting an accent on the word "drink" that made it sound reprehensible.

"Oh, come on, Sanders. Have one glass with us." Jastrau was chagrined. "This is good port."

"Yes, but I'm not drinking, you see. It isn't because I don't like it, but when you take a socialistic view of things, the way I do, then—"

"You've never been a souse," Jastrau objected.

Sanders drew himself up, and his voice quivered with scorn: "There you go again with the old individualistic rubbish, as if the only reason a person should quit drinking is to keep himself from going to the dogs. But, you see, I'm a Communist. I feel a sense of responsibility for others besides myself. I feel a responsibility toward society, the new society, and—"

"Amen!" intoned Steffensen, who, in a preëmptory manner, had taken the bottle and filled the glasses—all three of them. Then he lifted his glass to his lips and emptied it in one gulp, without tasting or enjoying the wine.

Jastrau looked at him in astonishment for a second, then carefully raised his own glass to his lips.

"Skaal!" he said, and managed to smile as Steffensen unceremoniously took the glass intended for Sanders and quickly emptied it too.

There was something hard, almost brutish, about that face, Jastrau thought as he took another sip. He let the wine fill his mouth, then slowly glide over his tongue and down his throat so that it would leave

16

a pleasant aftertaste. But he felt disappointed because neither of the others were drinking with him.

"But this other Communist here—Comrade Steffensen—*he* drinks. What about that?" With an ironic but dignified gesture Jastrau extended the hand that held the glass in Steffensen's direction. At that moment he was master of the house, the proper host.

"Him?" said Sanders, laughing scornfully. "He's no Communist. He's a freebooter."

Just then a key was inserted in the lock of the front door.

It was Johanne returning home.

Chapter Two

"Mother!" Oluf shouted, running toward the door.

Sanders had already gotten up. Standing with his hand against the back of his chair he made a rather fantastic and gaudy picture. The yellowish Russian blouse and the shiny belt accentuated his slim athletic figure. He was the prototype of the Russian Communist.

Steffensen, on the other hand, remained seated while he stared self-consciously at one of the empty glasses.

Then Fru Johanne appeared in the doorway, looking surprised but with an air of authority about her. She was tall and buxom, and wore a pair of high-topped boots with a becoming casualness. A suede jacket and a shoulder bag with cowboy fringe conformed to the lines of her figure, which had not yet become dumpy.

"I see you have guests," she remarked unenthusiastically as her blue eyes flashed momentarily. But then her critical glance grew milder, as became the situation, and a smile formed about her sensual lips, giving a bright aura to her face, an aura heightened by the radiance of her blonde hair. A big golden blonde.

"It's always nice to have people drop in," she added, laying a package down on a chair and letting a sigh of exhaustion escape her. "But now I'd better hurry and take off my things," she went on, pulling off her long leather gloves as she closed her eyes and took a deep breath as if to dispel the impression of overburdened activity she had created. Jastrau could see by the look in Sanders' eyes that she had brought a ray of light into the room.

"I see, Ole, that you've managed to take care of your guests. Has

Oluf been quiet? And what about the stove? There are so many things a housewife has to think of."

Her last remark was addressed to Sanders, who gallantly had come forward to help her off with her jacket. Steffensen had also risen, but with difficulty. He seemed wobbly on his feet, and as soon as she noticed him Johanne's expression froze. The benign golden aura vanished, and her features grew hard.

"Yes, I remembered to look after the stove," Jastrau replied with an air of preoccupation. But now something else was wrong. What was it? Oh yes—he must introduce them. He emptied his glass and pulled himself together.

"This is my wife, and these are—my friends, Bernhard Sanders and Steffensen. From the old days. They've just come from the lunchroom at the university."

"Bernhard Sanders," Sanders repeated, bowing.

Fru Johanne extended her hand to him in a stately manner, and Jastrau noted with a twinge of pain how naturally the dignity came to her.

Toward Steffensen, who mumbled something unintelligible, she was more reserved.

"My husband's friends are always welcome in our house. But what a lot of friends he has! It seems that new ones are always turning up."

"Yes, that's right," Jastrau said as if his mind were on something else. He was wondering how he should acquaint her with the situation.

Then the telephone rang.

"Has it been ringing often?" asked Johanne. She had seated herself and was using her feet to extricate herself from the high-topped boots. When her strong, shapely legs came to view in their flesh-colored stockings they seemed suddenly naked.

"It's been plain hell," said Jastrau. Then he answered the telephone: "Yes—it's me. No—no, it isn't set up yet. Yes—I suppose I could. Oh yes, there's more than enough up in the composing room—both ten-point and eight-point. Yes, and enough for the cuts, too. There's plenty of material, but it's that review of Stefani's book. I'd like to have seen it go on the book page, but— Couldn't we run it in the main section? Stefani is constantly pestering me about it. Yes—he keeps running up to the office every single day—either that or he's on the telephone. Ha! Impossible! Yes, damn it, he looks out for himself. He'd prefer to write the review himself. Well, if that's the case, all right. Yes—all right, all right!"

18

"Do you have to go over to the paper tonight?" Johanne asked with a touch of anxiety in her voice.

"Yes, I damn well have to," Jastrau replied.

And just then as he glanced over at Sanders he caught the last trace of a malicious smile before it disappeared. What was going on here? And behind his back, too. Whatever it was, he detected only its shadow before it slipped out of sight. And Steffensen? Steffensen had a far-away look, as if he had been eavesdropping. But what had he been listening to? The telephone conversation?

"Yes, unfortunately I'm being browbeaten into it," he repeated pensively. Here was a way out. The copy editor had not been insistent. And he shouldn't leave his wife here alone with two men, both perfect strangers. Oh, for a little peace! Just to get away—down into the street where he could calm down. People didn't bother to listen to someone else talking over the telephone. Or did they?

"I can't understand all the running around you do," Johanne exclaimed in irritation. "It's getting so I never know when you'll be home. After all, you're not a newspaper reporter."

"No, unfortunately," Jastrau sighed.

"That's the way it is, Frue," Sanders said consolingly. "Being a journalist and a homebody at the same time is too much to expect—practically an impossibility." His words came so adroitly.

"Listen, Johanne, there must be enough food in the house so that all five of us can have something," Jastrau remarked casually. He had to get around to the delicate subject of their staying, and he thought it best to approach it obliquely.

Sanders was watching him closely, and there was an annoying hint of mockery in his black gypsy-eyes.

"Yes, if your friends will take pot-luck. I thought we'd have some macaroni and a couple of steaks. I could run down and get another one, and fix them up with a tomato sauce. What do you say to that, Herr—Herr Sanders?" Suddenly she stopped, as if startled by the name, and her expression became more serious, her face paler. For a moment she was unable to speak. Then the words came again, strangely impersonal words, and her pale blue eyes stared into space as she recited what sounded like a nursery rhyme: "Yes—we have beer, we have coffee, we have sugar and cream. We'll manage, but it won't be anything fancy."

"Nothing fancy, Frue?" remarked Sanders in a singsong voice. He sounded half shocked, half jubilant. "As if such a meal wouldn't be outright gluttony. After all, food isn't so very important."

19

"Hell no," muttered Steffensen. "Hunger isn't so bad—that is if it doesn't last too long."

"You may be sure that poor folks wouldn't agree with you there," Johanne said sharply, with a didactic nod. "So don't put my boots away, Oluf."

"I'm poor myself," Steffensen objected indignantly. But at the same time he accorded her a jerky bow. He did not want to lose his temper. He stared inanely down at the wine glasses. Green glasses! Green glasses! In green glasses, port wine looks like medicine, he thought.

"But Johanne, do you think we have enough bedclothes," interjected Jastrau.

"No—no." It was Sanders who spoke up. "You really mustn't go to so much trouble. I can sleep in a chair if I have to, and Steffensen can use the sofa. That's better any time than a bench down on Søndre Boulevard—"

"Or one in Frederiksberg Circle, huh?" said Steffensen, grinning. He raised another glass to his lips and tossed it off.

Johanne's blue eyes shifted in perplexity from one to the other, then came to rest distrustfully on her husband. Then suddenly she found an outlet for her emotions. Oluf was trudging off with one of her boots, and she bent over him impetuously. "Oluf, how many times do I have to tell you? Leave my boots alone." She gave him a rap on the knuckles.

"But Frue, you mustn't think we're a couple of tramps," Sanders said politely. Johanne did not hear him. Jastrau knew that she was quick to develop dislikes, but why her sudden aversion to Sanders? It had manifested itself with such startling abruptness—literally in the twinkling of an eye.

"What are we then?" Steffensen asked with a grin.

"Yes, you—you're a tramp. But I have a place over there that I call home." He nodded in the direction of Vesterbrogade.

"But you don't dare go there. You're scared stiff of the cops," Steffensen replied.

Johanne gave a start.

"Look here, Ole—I'm getting all confused. What is this all about anyway? The police? And sleeping here tonight? We don't have room for them, and you know it very well. We can't have overnight guests here."

"The police? That doesn't amount to anything. And we can easily put them up—easily, yes easily!" Jastrau stamped on the floor and felt ridiculous. "We can. We can. We can. Because we have to. At any rate, I have to. I owe it to myself." He tried to sound furious.

20

"Well then, that's settled," said Johanne, raging inwardly. She disappeared into the kitchen so abruptly that the room suddenly seemed empty.

"No—I don't like this," Sanders hastened to say uneasily. "We don't want to force ourselves on you. If it hadn't been you, Ole, whom I've known for so long, I would never have dared—"

Steffensen said not a word, but seemed to be enjoying the situation.

"Oh, you beast!" Sanders snapped at him.

Meanwhile Jastrau heard the clatter of plates in the kitchen. There was no mistaking the irritation behind the sound. A cabinet door was slammed shut.

"Wait just a moment," he apologized nervously, and went out to the kitchen.

"Listen, Johanne."

She turned her back on him, as if completely absorbed in her calculations, and did not answer.

"Listen, Johanne." He tried to be both calm and insistent.

She put the little finger of her left hand into her mouth and bit on it, for she was deep in thought.

Then she wheeled about. Her face was pale and her expression so frank that it caught him off guard.

"You're going over to the office, and then I'll be left alone here with those two!" she burst out.

"Hush, hush. They can hear you."

"Yes, and I don't care. I must say, you have some fine friends."

With that she turned abruptly and walked over to the kitchen table. She idly picked up a glass, stood for a little while with it in her hand, then set it down with a vehement bang. "No," she said. "I won't have it!"

From the rigid lines of her back and bare neck, Jastrau could see how agitated she was.

"No! I won't have it!"

Her mind made up, she leaned against the kitchen door as if to buttress her authority.

"Do you hear? I won't have it! Tonight I'm going home to my parents. And I'm taking Oluf with me."

Now her voice assumed a tone of peevish complaint. "Yes, I'm going to. And it's your fault. You're driving me out—out of my own home. It's getting so that it's impossible to stay here any longer."

"But Johanne—" protested Jastrau.

Johanne shook her head and smoothed out her hair in an effort to regain her composure.

"No, don't give me any buts. Now I'll fix something to eat, and then we'll say that unfortunately I have to leave. But—"—and now her voice grew harsh—"but things have gone too far when a person can't have any peace in her own house. And now they're going to spend the night here in the bargain. Why—if I may ask? The police are going to grab them because of those dirty articles of theirs. Don't you think I know this Sanders? I suppose you think I don't read anything, but I know very well the stuff they write in that—that smut sheet."

"After all, they're not a couple of outright sex criminals," objected Jastrau. "They—"

"Oh, no? When they write the way they do, they're not one bit better. That's my opinion. And the mere fact that you'd let them in here at all—"

Jastrau raised his eyebrows wearily.

"I wrote the same sort of thing myself—at one time."

"No you didn't. That was something different."

"I'm damned if I can see the difference. They're people who are fighting for the sake of an idea."

"An idea! Yes. An immoral idea! A fine idea indeed—that women should be the property of the state. Isn't that what they advocate? And you'd put up with a thing like that!"

"Now, now—"

"Isn't it immoral?"

"Well now—"

"All I know is that my father never would have tolerated such people inside his house—and neither would Adolf."

"Your dear brother Adolf! Ha! Johanne, don't you understand that I can't do anything else? Look, an artist who'd shut his door in the face of a friend, who'd turn away old friends because the police are after them— Can't you see that if anything is utterly impossible, that's it? Yes, even if it were a case of murder with intent to rob—"

"You mean it?"

"Yes, what do I care about the police? And in this case it's only a matter of serving a sentence in lieu of a fine because they had the courage to write something that nobody else dared to say. It's true that I don't agree with them—not entirely, that is. But I'll be damned if I can shut my door to them, feel scandalized, or take a bourgeois attitude toward them. I just can't do it. Besides, it's only for one night, because if the Social Democrats win tomorrow—and they're going to—then they'll be granted an amnesty—"

"Well, it makes no difference to me. You're simply turning your home into a cheap saloon. But when it's my family who pays us a visit, then you always get sulky! Yes, you do! Well, anyway, I suppose I'd better go down and get some more meat."

"Are you going to stay with your parents tonight?"

"Yes."

Ole Jastrau chewed nervously on the stem of his pipe and went back to his guests.

He found that they had made themselves at home. Sanders was leaning back comfortably in his chair, reading a thin book whose covers he had doubled back so far that the spine had broken. Steffensen was tapping his pipe against the heel of his shoe and letting the ashes fall on the floor.

"It's odd that you should have Sigbjørn Obstfelder's poems," Sanders said, laying the open book in his lap. "I didn't think you knew what he was all about."

To break the back of a book that way! Black fingerprints on the white pages! No, Jastrau would not answer him. Furiously he sat down in a chair near the window, as far away as he could get from the smug complacency of the others.

Meanwhile Steffensen had lighted another pipe and was now engaged in writing. He wrote on a sheaf of *smørrebrød* menus that he had filched from a restaurant.

"As you can see, we've managed to make ourselves at home," observed Sanders without a trace of irony. "So you may as well get on with your book reviewing. We won't disturb you."

"Thank you," said Jastrau.

"What? Are you being sarcastic, Ole?"

Jastrau did not reply. But with an odd submissiveness he went over to the pile of review copies and picked up Stefani's *Wherefore Hast Thou Forsaken Me?* It was the humble side of his nature manifesting itself.

Soon everything was quiet in the room. From Vesterbrogade, a block away, came the muffled rumble of traffic, and from the central railroad station the whistles of the locomotives. Steffensen's pipe bubbled. It was the loudest sound in the room, in fact the only sound. Johanne had taken Oluf with her to do the shopping.

In spite of everything, there was something cozy about the atmosphere. It was rather nice that a few friends could settle down and feel at home in his apartment. And the fact that the police just happened to be after these two made it so unconventional, so unrelated to the normal humdrum existence. He wondered if it did not have something to do with open-mindedness, with the infinite. There were, indeed, people whose outlook could be so unbounded. Unbounded, yes. But was that sort of thing conducive to coziness?

No, it was more like sitting in the cold glare of an electric light. Under such a light a person might well freeze on a winter evening. He discovered Steffensen's hard, glassy eyes staring at him. Yes—in a glare like that of a winter evening. A horde of people. The cold, blue, hazy light of the arc lamps. The asphalt pavement.

Then Steffensen shifted his gaze again and stared down at his paper.

Sanders, however, did not move, except to turn a page in Obstfeld-er's collection of poems, or to light one cigarette from the butt of another.

Yes, there was a certain coziness about it. In any event, Jastrau wanted it to be cozy. The two of them had sought him out when they were in trouble. It was youth that had come to him, the poet and critic. Yes, they were scornful of him, but wasn't that to vindicate themselves? They quickly calmed down and soon felt at home. Conse-quently, he must have the proper temperament—the boundless tem-perament and open mind that youth admired so much. Youth? He was thirty-four—no longer young. No, not young. Had it already become his turn to bow his head and listen with rapt attention?

A key turned in the front-door lock, and he heard Oluf's voice and Johanne's boots shuffling in the corridor. There they were again.

Sanders straightened up and listened with a smug smile. Steffensen only shook his head as if he had been disturbed, then went on writing.

But Johanne did not come in. She went from the corridor directly through the bedroom into the kitchen, taking the boy with her. She was scolding him.

"Now we'll soon have something to eat," said Jastrau.

"Oh, we're putting you to too much trouble," Sanders remarked.

A quick, puffing sound issued from the kitchen. The gas had been turned on.

"Oh well, it's very seldom that we see each other these days," Jastrau replied. Sanders laughed loudly. "That's the truth," he said. Again their scorn! Jastrau had to get up out of his chair. He found this small talk intolerable. Nervously he began to wander back and forth in the room. He said nothing. It was ridiculous to take their lack of manners so much to heart. Sanders read on, unconcerned. Steffensen wrote. They felt at home, but he, he—

He ran his hand disconsolately through his hair, made believe he was thinking, and paced back and forth, back and forth.

24

Finally Johanne came bustling in, a housewife now, nothing but a housewife, but perfect for the type—authoritative and handsome, complete master of the situation.

"You can come to the table now. The food is ready."

She was like a force that Jastrau could not oppose. She'll very likely get plump like her mother, he thought.

"Please sit down. I only hope you'll find the food to your liking, for quite frankly we weren't expecting company today."

How properly she said it. How alive and radiant she became here in this commonplace dining room furnished with the imitation light oak set she had brought with her from home. In the subdued afternoon light her body, her pale face, and her golden hair became suffused with a radiance as soft yet lustrous as that of a waning April day. It must be possible for her to find happiness again. And while his thoughts ran on in this fashion, Jastrau stood absentmindedly in the doorway, blocking his guests' access to the dining room. His big hulk of a body was always in the way—always one body too many.

Sanders and Steffensen entered, Sanders with an analytical look around. At least the sight of the phonograph, which stood alongside the buffet, evoked an appreciative smile. And then they sat down, Jastrau at the end of the table, Steffensen with his back to the window, and Sanders opposite Fru Johanne and the boy.

Sanders immediately moved the Pilsner away from his plate with a gentle movement.

"I'm not drinking," he said with an awkward smile.

Then they began to eat.

At first there was an oppressive silence that had its effect even on the boy. He kept turning his blond, curly head restlessly from one side to the other, all the while wanting to say something. But he had the feeling that this was a day when it was simply impossible to avoid doing something wrong, and he kept still. Yet his mouth moved, forming mute syllables.

At last Sanders broke the silence.

"You really don't think, Frue, that because the police are looking for us we're a couple of out-and-out criminals, do you?"

His somber voice drove the silence away before it.

"No, but I think you're a couple of regular street urchins," replied Johanne with a self-conscious toss of her head. Then she stared sternly across at Sanders and nodded to reinforce her statement.

"My wife takes a more rigid view of things than we do over at the paper," Jastrau remarked, laughing.

"Such juvenile pranks!" Johanne went on indignantly. "You just can't go pasting posters like that up on the wall of *Dagbladet's* building—posters with nasty expressions like 'a newspaper full of lies,' 'a member of the kept press,' and I don't know what else was on them. You simply can't do that."

"But when it is, as a matter of fact, a lying newspaper, just like all the rest of them—"

"No! The only right thing to do was to call the police. It was downright hooliganism—that's what it was. And perhaps you can tell me what these lies are that the paper prints?"

Her face was deeply flushed. Jastrau, on the other hand, leaned back relaxed in his chair, drank his beer, and saw across the table from him the shadowy figure of Steffensen outlined in the waning daylight. He sat leaning forward with his elbows on the table and stared at Johanne.

"Well, Frue, it would take quite a while to explain it in detail," replied Sanders, gesticulating with his fork. "But by and large it's a question of that damned bank failure, and who was punished and who wasn't. It's all a matter of politics, Frue, and that's something neither you nor your husband understands."

He smiled maliciously in an attempt to look as diabolical as possible.

"My husband isn't interested in politics," Johanne said pertly.

At this, Steffensen's shadowy figure began to rock back and forth, as in a singsong tone he began to recite from "The Proletarian Woman":

> "But there will come a day when violence erupts.
>   Do you know how to handle a rifle?"

"Oh, that nonsense!" Johanne said impatiently.

"Oh, Mother, isn't that funny?" Oluf burst out laughing and bounced gleefully up and down in his chair.

"You must keep quiet! Do you hear?"

Sanders poised his knife over his plate. "You see, Frue, when it came to passing judgment on the ones who were responsible, they sentenced as few as possible. Instead of cutting the meat here, they cut off only the very edge of it." He demonstrated by slicing off a tiny fragment of the beef on his plate. "They sacrificed only those who were already compromised, and everybody—the entire country—said not a word. Everybody, that is, except us. The only paper that had anything to say was *The Hammer*."

He laid down the knife and sat up straight, as if expecting a round of applause.

26

"They want a revolution, you see," Jastrau said to Johanne with a trace of irony.

"I've known that all along," she said, cutting him short.

"Because when you catch a band of thieves you should catch the whole pack of them, including the receivers of stolen goods. You must have what's called a purge. But was there any purge in this instance?"

Sanders' indignation gave him a certain grandeur. When carried away in such fashion, he knew how to seize the collar of his Russian blouse as if he were about to rip it off.

"The principles of capitalism are a breach of Danish law," he proclaimed, raising his voice. Oluf's eyebrows went up in alarm. "This is a fact—a fact that events have shown to be true. And therefore the laws must either be changed, or—or . . ." He banged his fist against the table as if to kill.

"Oh well, that's getting to be an old story," said Jastrau with a shrug of his shoulders.

"Yes. Now the journalist is talking," replied Sanders so vehemently that little Oluf again raised his eyebrows in terror. "There is nothing so unethical to a journalist as an old story. The truth bores you. The idealist is a cantankerous cuss—but one has to be *cantankerous* in this country. Isn't that true, Frue?"

Jastrau laughed. But Johanne, who had been staring at Sanders with ever-widening eyes, nodded as if hypnotized. What force, euphony, somber passion, agitational appeal there was in this man's outbursts. It made her hair stand on end. Then she came to, surprised at herself, and cast off the spell.

"So, is that what you're fighting for?" she asked.

She uttered the word "fighting" with a somewhat rapturous lilt, so that Jastrau looked at her in astonishment. Now, once again, she seemed a stranger to him. What kind of a song was this that rose from her heart? He had never heard it before.

Sanders smiled complacently and nodded.

"Yes, that—among other things. It was when the bank collapsed that we started *The Hammer*. And how we were badgered! Well, I don't suppose we could have expected anything else."

He smiled again—a bitter, experienced smile tinged with a noble weariness. Oluf smiled too—bitterness and experience incongruously reflected in a boyish face—then again opened his moist, childish lips and held them in readiness to mimic more of the expressive contortions of Sanders' mouth.

After a momentary pause to enjoy his bitterness, Sanders went on in his well-modulated narrative style.

"No newspaper dealer would handle our sheet. If one of them got out of line he was boycotted by his distributor. A neat trick, wasn't it? Then he no longer got any copies of *Aftenbladet,* and that's what he made most of his money from. As a result, we had to go out on the streets and sell *The Hammer* ourselves. And then we were arrested—for violating the street-peddling ordinance. We were fined, but we refused to pay as a matter of principle. We served our terms in jail. But why were we fined in the first place? Because members of the students' rifle club and the fascist youngsters crowded around us as we went through the streets hawking *The Hammer.* They screamed and yelled and tried to provoke a fight with us—but of course, *they* were not arrested."

While Sanders was speaking, Steffensen slowly reached out for his friend's untouched bottle of beer and without saying a word emptied it into his glass. Jastrau could not suppress a laugh. But Johanne, who had not seen Steffensen's silent maneuver, misunderstood the reason for her husband's laughter. Throughout the conversation she had felt in need of help, and now she experienced a sense of relief.

"Well, it was basically just a boyish prank," she said with an indulgent smile.

"But we went to jail for it," replied Sanders with an air of dignity.

"Yes, but only in lieu of paying a fine," said Jastrau. "And hell, that's a form of martyrdom that you share with those who are locked up down at Stockyard Square because they don't pay for the support of their illegitimate children, and other such ne'er-do-wells."

Sanders got red in the face.

"When the grown-ups won't do anything," he said caustically, drawing in a deep breath, "then it's up to the boys. I can't see any better way out of it. And they can call me a boy as often as they want to, or a youth"—here he spoke slowly and with a biting sarcasm—"one of those sincere but over-enthusiastic young people that *Dagbladet* so affectionately refers to."

He turned and regarded Jastrau with an ironic look.

"Oh, come now. One of these days you'll both be working on the newspaper with us," Jastrau said patronizingly.

"No!" Sanders snapped back.

"I'll bet you will," muttered Steffensen.

"But you're completely forgetting to eat," exclaimed Johanne. She was much more animated than usual. Jastrau could see by the way she wrinkled her brow that disturbing thoughts were passing through her mind.

"No," repeated Sanders, shaking his head with a superior smile.

Who was it he was imitating with that constant smile? For it was an imitation of somebody.

For a while they ate in complete silence.

"Yes, you will indeed," said Jastrau suddenly with a weary gentleness indicative of both resignation and disillusion. "I believe it was no longer ago than December that Editor Iversen spoke to me about you two."

"Ah—in December. But that was before we raised a rumpus out in front of *Dagbladet's* building," Sanders said contemptuously.

"Oh, that! That goes to show that you don't know us very well, Sanders," Jastrau replied with a smile. He drew back his lips and showed his teeth when he smiled. "That makes no difference at all—not a bit. As I was saying, one day I went into the old boy's office—it must have been between Christmas and New Year—and he was sitting there absorbed in speculation as to what the new year might bring, or asleep, or perhaps both. He's getting to be pretty old now, you know—an old rhinoceros who sits coughing and spitting and grunting in his corner room, so that you can't make out anything he says any more. 'Listen, Jastrau,' he said—"

Jastrau drew his hand over his smooth-shaven upper lip, as if stroking a large, overhanging mustache, and went on speaking in a listless manner and with a pronunciation that might have been called plebeian if it had not had the mark of his own cultivated personality. Sanders laughed.

"It's a strange thing about you fellows over there at *Dagbladet*," interjected Sanders. "You can't talk about Iversen without hunching up your backs, talking as if you were in a torpor, stroking a make-believe mustache, spitting in the wastebasket, and saying, 'Is that so?' or 'Bong!' " The latter expression was the editor's way of rendering the French *bon*. "You all do it."

Johanne laughed and nodded approvingly.

"It's our way of worshipping him," replied Jastrau, also laughing.

"I must say it's a fine God you worship," said Sanders scornfully. "He's Denmark's most dangerous man—and the one who does the most harm."

"That's easy enough to say when you don't know him," Jastrau replied, showing his irritation. "But anyway, the old man said to me, very likely because he was in a New Year's mood, 'Look here, tell me, is there really anyone among these younger fellows who can write?' He asks everybody that, and when he does he looks at you with a tired, questioning look. 'Yes,' he went on, 'there are of course those who write for *The Anvil*, or whatever it's called. Hee hee! They're so sore at us.' And then he gets this crafty look. 'But folks like that, who are sore—phfty'—into the wastebasket—'you must read them very, very carefully, because often I've found that it's precisely these people who are angry who can write. Take Georg Brandes and Johannes V. Jensen, for example. Hee hee! But *The Anvil*—I took an issue of it home with me the other day, and do you know what? I was badly disappointed. There aren't any of the young people who can write, at least not readably or about anything of importance.' "

Sanders' and Steffensen's laughter was so raucous and derisive that Oluf gave a start. He scowled at them and moved closer to his mother as if seeking protection. Jastrau sat hunched up as if he had a shawl over his shoulders, just the way Editor Iversen sat. Then he spat into an invisible wastebasket, and went on:

" 'Otherwise we might have opened our columns to one—or perhaps two—of them. Pfty!' "

"Mother! Papa is spitting on the floor," shrieked Oluf. "Is he allowed to do that?" He had suddenly regained his courage.

"Hush! You must keep quiet," his mother rebuked him as she shook his arm.

But the others laughed, until Sanders' expression suddenly became serious.

"Yes, we laugh. But isn't it dreadful? All opinions are unimportant. They slip into *Dagbladet* and create a ripple on the surface. Everything is utterly without importance so long as the stuff is brilliantly written. Writing—style—phooey!"

Jastrau had now assumed his nebulous smile. It gave a touch of ironic melancholy to his pudgy, Mongoloid features. He thought it a smile that was becoming to him.

"We coddle the youngsters over at our paper," he said gently, with slow, voluptuous cruelty. "We give them cushions to sit on. We give them authority—apparently, that is—before they're grown up, and then we take it away from them before it's had a chance to develop fully. Then they become mild and tractable, without any hard and fast ideas and without any character. Either that or they become chronic grumblers with a touch of insanity, and then they need no longer be taken seriously."

He wanted to continue, but then suddenly he no longer seemed to think it worthwhile. He made a weary gesture with his hand, smiled faintly, and bent over to get a bottle of Carlsberg that stood near the leg of his chair. He poured a glassful and drank it in one draught.

Sanders extended one hand like a platform speaker and directed his somber gaze at Johanne, whose lips had gone slack at seeing her

30

husband's sudden defection. She had suspected it all along, and now she knew it. What difference did it make whether or not what he had said about the paper—of which he was the literary editor—was true? Who knew what was true and what was not? But a journalist who could not defend his paper, or a man who could not defend his wife, were one and the same thing. And now this dark, handsome, ardent Sanders would strike out hard. She knew it, and was fearful. Such a dark, impassioned man—and handsome, too.

"But don't you see, Frue, that that is subjecting yourself to perdition?" he began dramatically. "If that's what's meant by growing up and becoming mature, then God deliver me from ever reaching maturity. I may be mistaken. I may be wrong in thinking that society is in such a state that some of us must sacrifice ourselves—that those of us who can see must sacrifice ourselves—but I don't think so. A society that is not afraid does not have to coddle its youth with silken pillows. But even if I were wrong, and the Conservatives and Fascists were right, then I would nevertheless rather be what I am and be an outcast than—than live the life you do, Ole. Because in any case you are wrong, however cockeyed my own views may be."

He thrust his head and shoulders abruptly toward Johanne, who flinched. It was darkness against light. "Am I not right, Frue?"

"Are they lies that I'm telling you?" bellowed Steffensen from the end of the table.

He had raised his hands to his mouth like a megaphone and was wildly parodying Curly Charles, the eccentric who stood in front of the Hotel d'Angleterre, shouting his foul-mouthed truths at the fashionable clientele of the hotel's sidewalk café.

"Are they lies that I'm telling you?" Steffensen roared again.

Sanders turned and looked furiously at his friend. Jastrau wanted to laugh, but Steffensen's voice was so gruff that he gave a start and winced. Johanne compressed her lips and screwed up her eyes, shocked at the revolutionary beast who sat sprawling at the end of the table.

And then, in the silence that followed, Steffensen without rhyme or reason bellowed it out a third time: "Are they lies that I'm telling you?" It was stupid and brutish, like an outlet for ill will and pent-up nerves—a performance that had no place in a room with civilized company.

"Mother! Mother!" Oluf cried out, moving as close to Johanne as he could. Then he began to cry.

"Damn it! It's hard to treat you like a human being," snarled Sanders, tossing his fork on the table in disgust.

31

Oluf screamed again.

Johanne got up quickly, lifted the boy out of his chair, and carried him into the kitchen. "Now there, now there—" they heard her say while the youngster whimpered.

But Steffensen only laughed uproariously, as if he might have been an ogre standing by himself at the top of a cliff and hurling rocks over the precipice for his own amusement—a reckless, beastly, and dangerous form of amusement that no one else could understand.

"It's a pity about the boy," Sanders said bitterly.

"It's a pity for all mankind," droned Steffensen with a Strindbergian note of sarcasm. Once more he burst out laughing.

But Jastrau only leaned over the table and seemed to be listening to what was going on in the kitchen.

"Hadn't we better have another Carlsberg?" he asked, reaching down toward the floor where the bottles stood.

"Yes, you're a real judge of human nature," said Steffensen with a grin. He grasped the bottle greedily and poured the beer into his glass so fast that it foamed up and ran over onto the tablecloth.

"I'm making the coffee because it's time for me to leave," Johanne announced from the kitchen.

"Yes, my wife has to go out to Frederiksberg to see her parents," Jastrau explained. "By the way, she's going to stay there tonight, and I guess that's just as well."

Sanders smiled incredulously, and Steffensen raised his glass and muttered, *"Skaal!"* His outbursts always had a strange mixture of inarticulateness and double meaning about them.

"What do you say we go into the living room and have our coffee? Then we can chat a little and smoke before I have to go over to the paper."

Jastrau got up, and Sanders politely said thanks for the dinner.

In the living room they drew the curtains and turned on the lights. In a moment Fru Johanne came with the coffee. She was the same bustling, self-assured housewife that she had been before. She excused herself in the most matter-of-fact fashion for having to leave, and then departed without a trace of animosity. And when, a moment later, they heard the front door close and Johanne's and Oluf's footsteps receding down the staircase, Jastrau went to fetch another bottle of port. He had to have one more glass before going over to *Dagbladet*.

32

Three hours had elapsed.

Chapter Three   During this period Jastrau had been sitting in his office at *Dagbladet,* an office he shared with the paper's music critic and two of its illustrious gossip columnists. Tonight, however, he had been able to work in peace. None of his co-workers had shown up to disturb him. The room was off in a corner and a story above the editorial offices where the political writers, the reporters, the cable editor, and the editor-in-chief and the copy editor worked.

Thus left alone, he had been able to surround himself with darkness. He had turned off the ceiling light. The three other desks with their bright, shellacked surfaces had not been able to distract him. The sight of the three empty armchairs had not increased his feeling of not belonging in the place—a feeling he always had to fight against. And then it had occurred—that intimate contact between the gleam of the desk lamp and the gleam of the white copy paper. A small, radiant cosmos had been created, the brilliance of which had had a hypnotic effect on him, and once more he had succeeded in writing one of those critical articles that seemed to indicate a greater talent than he actually possessed, and that in particular showed a self-discipline of which he was not master—a discipline that he owed solely to the way the paper seemed to stare at him with pupilless, omnipotent eyes.

The glistening white heaven of a sheet of writing paper.

Now he was finally finished with his review of H. C. Stefani's book, *Wherefore Hast Thou Forsaken Me?,* and he leaned back in his chair. Once more he picked up the paper and read the article through to test the flow of the words. What he really wanted to do was read it aloud. But no—to sit there all alone in the room and engage in a monologue, that he was ashamed to do. Better to mutter the words under his breath, but carefully, to make sure the style would bear scrutiny.

At last he got up and turned off his desk lamp so that the entire room was dark.

But through the windows, which the evening rain had stippled with long dotted lines, came the flickering lights from the wet square below. They cast a reflection on the ceiling, a restless, animated shimmering like that of an aurora borealis, a blending of the soft glow from the streetcars' colored lamps and the sharp beams of automobile headlights. The windowpanes emitted a dark luster mixed with a hint of light to the raindrops, and silhouetted against their smooth surface, in reverse, were the letters that spelled DAGBLADET. In the daytime the letters were white; at night they were dark. Only the "A" and the "T" were legible. A puzzling name. You could not read it quickly, but you never tired of trying to do so. Here, however, was a place where he could sit in the darkness and leisurely stuff his pipe. Should he go home now, home to rejoin the other two? His glance fell on a streetcar down in the street. He saw its dark wet roof glide by; it looked like a barge. But he did not want to go home. The Communists had requisitioned his apartment. And then to be ridiculed—ridiculed by those two youngsters! It was enough to make him furious. But take it easy, he told himself. A barge on a river. What was it anyway that happened to a person when he stood looking at a ship or the traffic gliding by? It was like a caress, like having someone reassuringly stroke your back. So take it easy now, Jastrau, take it easy.

Suddenly from over in the darkness came a knocking at the door. Jastrau hurried over and turned on a floor lamp. He was not, in any event, going to be taken by surprise while engaged in sentimental reverie.

"Come in."

The door opened slowly, and a tall man wearing a smart light-gray overcoat stepped in, raising his derby hat in an affected greeting.

"Good evening, sir."

It was Arne Vuldum, the man of letters and assistant librarian, who was renowned for not having opened a single volume of Danish fiction for the last five years. He wrote the paper's column on foreign literature.

As he stood there attired in faultless elegance, he looked like Dante's most inconceivable paradox—a depraved virgin. It was his mouth, which had such a meager, barren look. But his red hair, which hung in a glossy metallic mass over the left side of his forehead, had an impressive sheen to it, as provoking as sunlight on water, and beneath this strange lighting effect shone a pair of gray, undependable eyes. After being with him, one could never remember for very long how they had looked.

"Good evening, Vuldum," Jastrau replied with an evasive politeness.

"I'm not disturbing you, am I?" asked Vuldum, letting himself sink with an affected air of weariness into the sofa that blocked the sliding-door passage into *Dagbladet*'s lecture hall.

"What's troubling you? Money?" asked Jastrau in a tone of ill-natured sympathy.

34

"No, my dear fellow," sighed Vuldum, carefully placing on the least cluttered of the desks the derby, which the newspapermen had dubbed "St. Peter's dome" because of his interest in Catholicism. "No, I'm suffering from something worse—syntactical troubles. I've just been up in the composing room, reading the proofs of my article again."

"It's strange that it hasn't been printed yet."

Vuldum smiled bitterly.

"The proofreaders are also quivering with indignation over the paper's negligence on that score. They're really worked up—frantic. You see, I drop in every night and make some changes."

"Oh, you're too finicky."

"No, Ole, but I've lost my mind," Vuldum said in all seriousness, removing the indispensable cigarette from his mouth. "And I've gotten that way from writing in Danish. Just think how difficult it is to express anything precisely in our language. It doesn't consist of anything except barbaric bits and fragments that reflect our materialistic culture. It's completely impossible—like American English.

He stared into space, and Jastrau thought he detected the symptoms of a personality in dissolution. The gray eyes seemed fixed on a boundless horizon.

"But how are things with you, Ole, my friend?" Vuldum asked suddenly, pulling himself together. His cordiality was exaggerated. It might easily have been mistaken for irony.

"Well, I've just finished my review of Stefani's book."

Vuldum sat up attentively. The gray eyes came closer, as if Vuldum wanted to study his expression. But when Jastrau returned his gaze, they shifted and came to rest on his necktie. And there they remained.

Jastrau felt as if he were being strangled.

"It would interest me to know what you had to say about his religious aspirin," Vuldum said softly.

"Aspirin?"

"Yes. You know he's licensed as a pharmacist in Aarhus."

"Well, the lucky fool!" Jastrau exclaimed, swiveling around in his chair. Then he added, "There's always somebody who knows how to make a go of things."

"Didn't you know?" Vuldum sounded surprised. "You'll never be a real journalist. You have no private life of your own, and you don't know anything about anyone else's. But now let me have the pleasure of listening to your review of St. Stefani."

"Well, all right." Jastrau reached for the sheets on his desk and turned his back toward the floor lamp so that the light, coming over his shoulder, fell on the review. The tone of his voice was even and mild, but it would have required only a slight nuance to transform it into one of savagery.

As he sat there in the twilight, Vuldum made a nervous gesture with his large white hands, unconsciously tapping an unlighted cigarette against his palm, a gesture that became more and more subdued as he became absorbed in Jastrau's train of thought.

Jastrau began reading: "Since Herr H. C. Stefani has ventured to offer the opinion that Jesus Christ so thoroughly assumed the attributes of a mortal man that he not only let himself be carried away by fear of death—as when he exclaimed on the cross, 'My God, my God, why hast Thou forsaken me?'—but also was not above manifesting the taint of original sin—as when in a fit of nervous rage he not only permitted himself to invoke a curse on the fig tree but drove the money-changers out of the temple with a whip—why, then, has Herr Stefani not carried his conclusion further? Why has he not paid more attention to the psychological tensions inherent in the paradoxical concept of a being at once divine and human that is the most puzzling thing about the character of Jesus and assumed that Jesus now and then might conceivably have been aroused by the sight of a beautiful woman?"

"There is something attractive about Christianity, even though a person is so unfortunate as to have no religion himself," interrupted Vuldum, drawling his words. Jastrau raised his head and smiled; he recognized the attempt to imitate Editor Iversen's manner of speaking. Vuldum went on: "And I can't understand why you, Jastrau, can't refrain from baiting the clergy. It's no longer fashionable, you know." Vuldum stroked his upper lip and spat into the wastebasket, which fortunately stood close to the sofa.

"As a matter of fact, there are many good among the clergy," he continued, still imitating the chief.

"Do you really think he'll take it that way?" Jastrau asked with a trace of excitement.

"Who can tell?" replied Vuldum, smiling maliciously and resuming his own manner of speech. "Anyhow, Stefani deserves it. There is nothing that rubs me the wrong way so much as these modern interpretations of Jesus. They are a reflection of the democratic need to get on terms of intimacy with the Divinity, and they won't stop until they've managed to catch their God *in flagrante*. Incidentally, you've hinted at that very well."

"Do you think I'll get in trouble for it?"

36

Vuldum's glance rested on him for a fleeting moment. "After all, you're not under censorship here on this old, free-thinking paper," he replied, making light of the question.

"No, I don't mean that."

"What then?"

"Well, you know what I mean. Someone calls on the telephone—an anonymous subscriber calls up the old man to tell him what he thinks of his filthy newspaper. Then for a couple of weeks he greets me with a blank look whenever I run into him."

"Is that so?" asked Vuldum, again imitating Editor Iversen.

"Or an anonymous letter comes in the mail. Or, worse yet, a couple of subscription cancellations."

"Really? Do you mean it?" Vuldum inquired in the same lackadaisical tone of voice.

"And then the glass bell closes down over me and the air is pumped out. You can't preserve your personal opinions in a vacuum, you know."

"No, my dear Jastrau," Vuldum continued without altering his tone, "that I really didn't know. That's really big news. Have we had anything about it in the paper?"

Jastrau smiled and mulishly went on talking. He had to get it off his chest.

"Everything is run so leniently—and so brutally—up here. You watch your step, and then—"

"Watch your step? Yes, hee hee, I can remember one time in Rangoon—" Still the mimicked accents of the widely traveled editor.

Now Jastrau felt his thoughts congealing, as if he were about to become ill-tempered. Why should he sit there and make a confession? Vuldum was only toying with him, teasing him, imitating Editor Iversen. So he broke it off, and in a firm, monotonous voice concluded the reading of his article:

"By his lack of consistency, H. C. Stefani has in our opinion succeeded only in belittling the Savior's character. From a psychological point of view, therefore, his book may well be stamped as blasphemy."

"That will make Stefani happy," exulted Vuldum. "Ha! Vengeance awaits him! And he has a son who wants to be a poet. That's what you might call the Lord's punishment. He'll be stricken for his iniquities. But how he does deserve it!"

"A son? I don't know him."

"No, you don't keep up with things—as I remarked before. But like all the other old radicals, whether they're religious or not, he has a son who's a Communist, and who detests his father. Yes—vengeance awaits him." The gloating Vuldum raised a clenched fist.

"Stefani—a Communist named Stefani?"

"No, as a Marxist form of protest against his father, the idiot calls himself Steffensen. Stefan Steffensen—it sounds like a proletarian marching song. Can't you hear it?"

"Well, I'll be damned!" exclaimed Jastrau, letting the papers fall on the desk. "Then he's the one who with Sanders is sitting and waiting at my apartment." And now he understood. The telephone conversation. Yes, Stefani was certainly looking out for himself. He really would like to write the review himself. A trace of a smile crossed Jastrau's face, then disappeared.

"Well, I declare—do you associate with such people?" Vuldum asked in a tone of disdain. "I'm surprised."

"I don't associate with them. Otherwise I wouldn't be sitting here."

Vuldum's eyes lit up. "So that's it—you've no place to go." There was a moment's pause. "Then you must do me the honor of letting me buy you a drink."

Vuldum rose and extended his hand with an air of exaggerated hospitality.

"But only one—I can't afford more. It's so seldom that you run across a married man away from home in the evening."

Suddenly he laid a hand uneasily on Jastrau's shoulder.

"But what about your wife? You don't mean to say—"

"She's with her parents."

"Well, thank God for that! Otherwise I'd be terribly concerned. You can't just let your womenfolk be subjected to any kind of company."

Jastrau cast a sidelong glance at him. Was he being sarcastic? No, the weary, harried face was serious, the lips tightly drawn.

"It doesn't pay to have anything to do with that sort, let me tell you. What prompted those two gentlemen to pay you a visit?"

"Oh, nothing of any importance," replied Jastrau.

"All right—it's not that I'm being curious. But now why don't you run up to the composing room with your article, and then we'll go over to Des Artistes. I just have to phone Father Garhammer to break an appointment, then I'll be ready."

Jastrau quickly took out his fountain pen and wrote some instructions for the printer in a top corner of the numbered sheets. "Book page," he noted, "10 pt. leaded." For the headline, "The Man Jesus," he indicated "Cheltenham 24 pt." Then he gathered up the sheets and went out in the hallway to get the elevator. Vuldum had already gone to the telephone to ask the operator, in an amorous voice, for the number of the Catholic church.

When Jastrau came back, Vuldum had finished his call.

"So now perhaps we can go," he said.

"Yes," Jastrau answered, crumpling up the sheets of his rough draft and tossing them into the wastebasket.

They went out together.

But Vuldum was never in a hurry. He always sauntered along, even though he might be catching a streetcar or going to keep an overdue appointment. And so they walked down the dark stairway past the editorial room.

"Ah—how I like this building," said Vuldum, taking a deep breath. "It's like a home, you might say—a regular home. This is where the paper lives. Don't you feel it too?"

On the floor below he had to stop before the plate-glass window in the door and peer into the editoral room. He had to stop to enjoy the view. Jastrau let himself be smitten with the same infection.

Behind the window lay the deserted vestibule. On a table covered with green felt lay a large roll of paper and, as usual, on the table was a large roll of paper on which the news bulletins were lettered before being pasted up in the windows facing the street. On the wall to the left hung some photographs of deceased members of the staff. And in a room deep in the interior sat the copy editor, wearing his customary gray suit. He was busy at the telephone.

Vuldum turned toward Jastrau.

"Isn't it a nice home-like setting? And this is what the novelists call the hectic, pulsating atmosphere of a newspaper editorial office. Why, it's more like a quiet interior by Vermeer. Can't you just picture it? The door here like a dark frame? The subdued light in the vestibule? The table with its green felt in the foreground? And then, the room farther in a little darker? The perspective might have been done by Velasquez—one room behind the other. And there, in the farthest background, sitting in the half-darkened room under a green lampshade, is this fellow with the light shining on his face—a contemporary, smooth-shaven face. He sits bent over his work, the telephone receiver next to his ear. What's so hectic about it? Yes, I'd like to know, because I can't see it, no matter how much these modern writers make of it. I feel I'd like to just quietly walk in."

"Now don't let yourself be so carried away that you forget you've invited me out for a drink," Jastrau said.

"No, how can you think such a thing?" Vuldum laid his hand

earnestly on Jastrau's shoulder. "Do you think I can forget that I'm honored with the company of a married man whose apartment has been commandeered by the Communists?"

Jastrau gave a start. Had Vuldum seen through his distressing story? It would be a fine thing for him to repeat up here at the office in the morning. Now he would have to be careful that the whiskey did not loosen his tongue.

"Well—hardly commandeered it," he said weakly.

"Let's not hurry. Remember, I've asked you out for only one high-ball."

They went on down the darkened stairway.

But when they got down to the brightly illuminated cablegram office, the revolving door from the street was suddenly set in motion, and they saw someone coming in.

Through the revolving glass panels which refracted the light at crazy angles, they made out a tall stoop-shouldered figure. They caught a glimpse of a derby pulled low over the man's forehead, giving him somewhat the appearance of a competent butcher's helper. And that was enough to tell them who it was.

"The old man," whispered Vuldum.

A schoolboy's smile lit up each of their faces, though it was becoming to neither of them. Vuldum's features were too harried and Jastrau's were too pudgy. The effect was rather comic, like adult actors cast in the role of schoolchildren. The smiles did not suit the jaded expression in their eyes, but their lips, so to speak, were stuck with them. They did not, however, stand like a couple of youngsters with arms at their sides, each holding his sailor hat in his hand. It was a strange performance.

The man coming in was Editor-in-Chief Iversen.

As he entered, he raised his hat slightly so that a subhuman cranium and occiput came into view. His hair was gray. A big, drooping mustache hid his mouth, but never his smile, nor could it conceal the long line of his chin, so that anyone viewing Editor Iversen from the side could not help being impressed by his bulldog jaw.

The tired, disillusioned eyes rested on them momentarily. Looking into the eyes was like looking down through soap bubbles into a cup of murky water. It took a long time for the eyes to come to life. But then the old man playfully lifted an index finger, his expression became animated so that he looked twenty years younger, and he said in a slow drawl: "Well, here we have the whole literary department—in one fell swoop. I trust you're not up to any mischief."

Vuldum wanted to raise his hand in a gesture, but all that happened was that his right arm gave a little jerk. He bowed correctly. Jastrau unconsciously took up a sheltered position a little behind him.

"Well, what can one do about it?" the editor continued after a moment's pause, staring straight ahead with a blankly philosophical expression.

Just then a dark-haired man in a black coat came hurrying by. He did not, however, neglect to shout a loud greeting, "Good evening, Herr Iversen." His voice reached into the farthest corners of the hall. The tiled floor resounded with the echo of his greeting and his hurried footsteps. Duty, duty! Heels striking against the tiles.

"And there goes the radio section," said the editor pensively, staring after the newcomer as he disappeared into the elevator. "Well, what can one do about it? That's the future—the radio. At least, so folks say."

He shook his head mournfully and cast a sympathetic glance at Vuldum and Jastrau, as if sincerely regretting that it would soon be all up with both of them.

"Yes, what is there to do about it?"

With this concluding remark he smiled and nodded good-by, then disappeared up the dark stairway.

Jastrau felt crushed. It was as if a big fist had with one stroke swept all his work into the bottomless rubbish pit of history. But then suddenly Vuldum put his hand under his arm and drew him along through the revolving door. The cool air from the dark, open square struck their faces. Vuldum shivered in his big, light-gray overcoat, and laughed.

"Yes—we two poor immortals. A drink is going to do us good."

The Bar des Artistes was only a few doors down the street. It was part of a small hotel. In front of it hung a large oval sign with the words "Bar des Artistes" painted in the form of an arch like a bridge. Beneath the bridge, representing the water, was a single word: "Dancing."

The entrance was unimpressive. The door and the two windows were squeezed off to one side of the more dignified hotel entrance and a big restaurant. At night, the light also shone more brightly from the restaurant windows, for they had transparent curtains, whereas the bar was concealed behind portières and heavy draperies so that it emitted only a subdued, intimate light, little more than a gentle glow. It was the same as far as the music was concerned. Every night from the restaurant came the sweeping rush of violin music, while behind the dark windowpanes and door of the bar could be heard only the soft tones of a phonograph, muted to the level of a whisper. No one who went there need feel conspicuous. But the bar did not have to make its existence known in a loud voice, and it was not the brightly lighted, music-filled, but deserted, restaurant that accounted for the long row of cars that were always parked on the other side of the street.

For the sake of appearances, Vuldum led Jastrau past the door of the bar—it was not everyone who found it proper to go in directly from the street—and turned in at the hotel entrance, as if they were going to the restaurant. But the hall porter, who nodded familiarly to Vuldum, was in no doubt about their destination. He quickly opened a door that led from the hotel lobby into the bar.

For a moment they were deafened by the hum of many voices and the distant whining of a phonograph playing Hawaiian guitar music. Amidst the reddish glow of the tapestries and the bluish fog of tobacco smoke they suddenly felt as if they had entered an unreal world. Male customers were clustered convivially about the round tables. But not a single woman. In any event, Jastrau saw none in his first look around.

With Vuldum taking the lead, they stepped up to a brass-ornamented bar in back of which gleaming rows of bottles lined the shelves. It was from this center that all undue noise or disturbance was controlled, partly by a clock that was always five minutes fast—one of the bar's good-natured arrangements—and partly by the manager, a Swede, with a large, amiable, but wily, satyr's face as plump as the clock was round and as red as the clock face was white, an agreeable combination of high priest and innkeeper, with a girth that inspired such confidence in his customers that they found his flaccid handshake hearty, his casual remarks confiding, and his equivocal smile warm and indicative of the friendly informality so typical among those of his nationality.

He had already, at a distance, nodded to Vuldum, as if it were a pleasure to him personally to have him there as a guest. At the same time, he had almost too obviously cocked his head to one side to size up Jastrau.

He was Scandinavia's best cocktail mixer, and his name was Lundbom.

It was difficult to make one's way through the room. Some of the customers raised an arm in a kind of non-political Fascist salute, others waved or lifted their glasses in greeting. Vuldum was obviously well known in the place. "Good evening, old boy." "Well—so it's you, Vuldum." A stout gentleman with a florid prelate's face, dimples, and a cleft chin made a pompous gesture with one hand and offered them a place at his round table, where he sat shaking dice with a small,

42

balding man, evidently a shop clerk. But Vuldum only nodded in a polite but reserved manner as he went on, his cigarette held carefully in his hand. He had suddenly caught sight of a lady in a shiny black dress who, accompanied by a broad-shouldered man, sat balanced on one of the high stools at the bar. She was the only woman in the room.

Before they settled themselves on a pair of stools next to the couple, Vuldum let his gaze hover intimately over her back and shoulders. Then, as he abstractedly ordered two whiskeys and helped himself to a salted almond from the dish that stood on the counter, he tried to catch a glimpse of her profile. He had completely forgotten about Jastrau.

Suddenly, however, he gave a start. The woman had said to him, "Oh, how do you do, Herr Vuldum." There was a trace of derision in her tone. Vuldum stiffened and with an impolite jerk of his head turned toward Jastrau. At the same time he directed an indignant, questioning look at Lundbom and turned his back on the woman in obvious disapproval. But Lundbom only narrowed his small, crafty eyes and shook his head almost imperceptibly.

"Have you seen anything of Herr Journalist Eriksen today?" he asked Vuldum with a smile, in order to divert his attention.

"No."

"He was a little high last night—yes, a little high. And when he's that way, he's a bit hard to manage." Lundbom said it with a smile that was a bit confusing because it was obviously meant to be indicative of concern.

But Vuldum was white as a corpse. His red hair gave him a ghostly appearance.

"Well now, my married friend, may I have the honor of drinking to you?" he said, pulling himself together.

Jastrau nodded and drank.

"Listen, Vuldum, why do you always seem to resent the fact that I'm married?"

Vuldum looked at him in a way that seemed to indicate that his thoughts were on the couple next to him.

"I don't have anything against your being married," he replied mechanically. "In fact, I admire you for it."

Jastrau let out a loud, derisive laugh in an attempt to dispel Vuldum's preoccupation.

"No, my dear Ole," Vuldum protested, laying his hand meaningfully on Jastrau's arm. But his eyes retained their preoccupied, ill-natured expression; they were two luminous gray dots. "I honestly admire the way you keep your wife hidden. Why, I've never so much as been introduced to her, and you never bring her along to any of *Dagbladet's* parties. I admire the way you keep your private and public life separate."

Jastrau had ears only for the mechanical way in which the words came, not for their meaning.

"I can see you don't believe me," Vuldum went on. "But it goes without saying that anyone with such a conservative nature as I—at least, people say that I'm conservative—must admire you for the way you keep your wife shut up. And if you happen to be invaded by Bolsheviks, then you send her home to her parents. But look here—your two Bolsheviks are waiting for you now."

Even in his sleep he must be spiteful, Jastrau thought.

"Oh, let them wait," he replied. Why did he have to be reminded of them now? Here he and Vuldum sat together at the bar, each with different thoughts going through the back of his head. It was like a masquerade. Suddenly a saxophone solo broke forth from the phonograph, and Jastrau wanted to rock back and forth on the bar stool in time with the music—to forget, forget, forget—

"This is a good number. It's Rudy Wiedoeft, the world's best saxophonist."

Vuldum put both of his strong hands on the brass edge of the bar and tilted his stool back until it stood balanced on two legs, ostensibly to listen, but also to enable him to make a fleeting inspection of the danger that threatened him from behind.

The lady also turned her head slightly. Jastrau could see that she had black hair. A broad face. And there was something Slavic, something a bit vulgar about it. She was certainly not pretty. But he saw her for only an instant. There was animosity in her expression, and her lips were twisted in what was presumably an expression of scorn. She turned her back on them with a shrug of contempt so naïve that Jastrau involuntarily had to laugh.

"Yes, it's a nice enough saxophone," remarked Vuldum as if he had noticed nothing, "but it isn't the kind of music I care for."

"Well, let's get back to the subject we were discussing," Jastrau said. "I'm astonished by your flattery, to say the least."

Vuldum sat up straighter.

"I feel doubly pleased that my honest conviction is flattering to you in the bargain. It happens to me so very infrequently," he replied with a dexterity of phrase that made it sound as if he were quoting. But then suddenly he added cynically, without any transition whatsoever,

44

"On the other hand, I'm not glad that your damned saxophone solo made us drink too fast. Now my glass is empty."

He set the glass down with a bang on the linoleum countertop.

"Two whiskeys," ordered Jastrau.

Vuldum breathed a sigh of relief.

"Thanks," he said. "I need it, and I don't have much money with me. But shouldn't we also have a cigar? They sell one here that's called Marsmann, and it's a passable smoke."

Jastrau nodded while he thoughtfully took his money out of his vest pocket.

"That's more than enough," remarked Vuldum, taking a long look at the brass two-krone pieces in Jastrau's hand. "We can probably have another whiskey."

"Yes, so we can," Jastrau said mechanically. He was too tired to try to remember if the money was supposed to be for something else.

At that moment a meek little man clad in a short Windbreaker walked through the room. He carried a basket of flowers on one arm, and in the other hand he held out discreetly toward the customers three pink roses. There was, indeed, something pink and sanctimonious about his entire affable appearance, and his fixed, artificial smile was a good match for the roses. He looked like a private in the Salvation Army.

He went through the room and came toward them without a word. Only a suggestive movement of the hand that held the flowers. Only a politely regretful bow when he was turned down. A silent soul with flowers for sale.

When Vuldum saw him, his gray eyes suddenly became attentive and followed his movements predaciously. He turned completely around and sat with his back to the bar.

A new phonograph record filled the room with the soft sentimental strains of "Rosemarie." Several of the customers hummed along with the music. The woman sitting next to them rocked in rhythm with the tune so that her stool creaked, and Lundbom gave the cocktail mixer such an ecstatic shake that the brittle ice could be heard crunching inside it. Everything was roses. But Jastrau felt nervous—more nervous than before—for now Vuldum was bending forward. His sleek red hair hung down over his forehead, and his eyes were expressionless.

And then the inevitable happened.

The flower vendor paid no attention to Vuldum. He had eyes only for the lady, and as he came up to the bar he held out his offering with a supplicatory and humble gallantry toward the broad-shouldered man sitting next to her. And at the same moment Vuldum rose from his stool, supporting himself on its crosspieces so that he stood head and shoulders above everyone else, and in a loud voice, with every word resounding with a metallic ring, said:

"What makes you think you can come in here and sell flowers. As you can see, there isn't a lady in the place."

A silence fell over the entire room. Only the strains of "Rosemarie" kept issuing incessantly from the phonograph.

A moment later the broad-shouldered gentleman stepped away from the bar.

"Come on. Let's go," he said to his companion in a voice that trembled.

She sprang down from the stool, he helped her on with her fur piece, and without saying good-by to Lundbom, who stood speechless with concern over the possible effect of such a scene on his business, they made their way through the crowd and disappeared, while all eyes followed them.

Jastrau had been fearful that the incident might precipitate a real disturbance. He could not bear to think of it. People were so stupid when they began bickering. At the same time, he felt a needless sympathy for the flower-seller, who smiled in bewilderment and seemed to want to bow in all directions at once. How was Jastrau to know that this unassuming man owned a house in the Nørrebro section?

"Look—let me have three roses. How much are they?"

But then came a burst of admonishing laughter from the stout man at the round table: "Oh, now—shame on you Vuldum!" The shop clerk sitting next to him shook his little doll's head reproachfully.

And at the same time, Lundbom began to launch into a quiet jeremiad in a Swedish accent: "Now I must say, Herr Vuldum, that sort of thing won't do, damn it all!"

His pronunciation of "damn it all" was perfect Danish.

But Vuldum drew himself up haughtily.

"Do you know what kind of a woman that was?"

"No, Herr Vuldum," replied the corpulent Lundbom, doubling up politely in a bow. "But you seemed to know her."

"I!" exclaimed Vuldum indignantly. "No—she knew me. And let me tell you something—if you want to keep a decent bar, you can't have Black Else or any of her girl friends coming here."

Lundbom lowered his voice to a whisper.

"That's right, Herr Vuldum. I'm well aware of it. But she was with Herr Direktør Starup, and I meant to tell him sometime that women like that—you understand that the Herr Direktør is an old friend of mine, a fine person, and he drops in here every afternoon for a drink—and I would have said it to him tomorrow—"

"Well, then say it to him," said Vuldum, unimpressed.

"I will if—if the Herr Direktør ever sets foot in here again," said Lundbom, lost in gloom. "He didn't even say good-by when he left. But a person has to behave himself here, Herr Vuldum."

"I wouldn't say so at all. Not when the Herr Direktør has the poor taste to drag Black Else in here with him. What do we want her here for? After all, we have Charles the Twelfth there. What more do we need?"

He pointed to the wall at the right. Jastrau turned and saw a life-size picture of a naked woman or, more properly speaking, a woman without clothes, with her feet illogically resting on a Botticellian seashell. Her hands were ingeniously clasped behind her neck, since her arms were too short to assume satisfactorily the traditional attitude—one arm shielding the breasts and the other down where the hand could hide the pubic region. In order to make the insipidity of the picture complete, the artist had painted hair only on the woman's head.

"Ah, yes," guffawed the stout gentleman. "Our beauty—the one and only."

"We've named her Charles the Twelfth in honor of Lundbom and his native country," Vuldum said to Jastrau, disregarding the stout man's outburst of passion.

Lundbom bowed with an embarrassed smile.

"You do me too much honor—too much honor, Herr Vuldum."

"And now perhaps we can have another whiskey, my dear Ole, because I don't suppose you spent all your money on the roses." Vuldum looked at Jastrau inquiringly.

"No, but take it easy. I've never seen you get so stirred up."

Vuldum gave him a black look.

"Did you get a good look at her?"

"No—not really."

"Well, if you had you would have understood. A fat, white neck. Didn't you notice? And to wear a black dress with a neck like that! No—I tell you."

"You didn't have to look at her."

Vuldum's expression grew more intense, and he compressed his lips into a thin line.

"And did you see that mark on her arm? Can you think of anything worse than a sore covered over with powder? No, I tell you, she's a bad one—a really brazen slut. But hadn't we better talk about something else? How are your two Bolsheviks? Why are they sitting there in your apartment—waiting for daddy?"

Jastrau did not hear him. An ulcer covered over with powder. He could see it in his mind's eye, like a color-plate in a medical book. And he felt a physical repugnance. He could not rid himself of the flesh-colored, suppurative image. He made no reply.

"Oh well," Vuldum said, raising his glass to his lips.

Farther out in the room a group of the customers had gotten together in a noisy circle. A fat, old man and a tall, thin student were dancing to the phonograph music, and every now and then the fat man would give the student a shove that sent him spinning against the wall. As he did so he would shout, "Who do you think you are anyway, you snotty kid? Are you making fun of an old man?" But these angry reproaches came with the regularity of a musical beat. The two would then continue dancing until the fat man could again chime in, in time with the music, "Who do you think you are, you snotty kid?" And then another shove that sent the student whirling against the wall.

"No, things aren't really very pleasant here tonight," Vuldum said, shuddering as if he felt cold. "It's all so stupid. And just look at Kjær and Little P. over there."

He nodded sourly toward the stout gentleman and the shop clerk. Both were drunk and had been giving vent to some loud expressions of opinion.

"We could get a few free whiskeys over there if we wanted to," Vuldum added.

"Who are they—this Kjær and Little P.?" asked Jastrau. He was not at all interested. But he had to do something to dispel the lurid picture of that syphilitic sore. He had seen its likeness once in a medical textbook. Ah—there on the bar lay the three roses.

"Nobody of any importance, but each one of them can put his hands on a sack of gold. The young fellow, that's Peter Krag, son of old Krag of Kattrupgaard, so it goes without saying that he's worth his weight in gold. Ah me!"

Jastrau glanced over toward the round table. There sat Little P., the count who looked like a shop clerk, staring out into the room with a vacant expression like that of a mannequin in a shop window. The corpulent Kjær was slumped over the table, looking at his empty whiskey glass with puckered eyebrows as if about to bellow out another order.

"And Kjær—does he have money too?"

48

Vuldum nodded.

"Ah yes—we two immortals," he sighed. "Should we on behalf of the spiritual side of things go over and cadge a few drinks from them—in spite of everything?"

Jastrau shook his head wearily.

"Oh well, I got to bed late last night too," said Vuldum. "Besides, I have a civil service job, and I have to go over to the library tomorrow and write American round hand. So I think I'd better be getting home."

"I'll walk along with you," said Jastrau. "I have to go out Vesterbro a little way, too."

He paid the bill and picked up the roses. Vuldum was already on his way toward the vestibule.

When they finally got outside, the street lay dark and empty. Over at *Dagbladet*'s building, the second and top floors were lighted, but the street in front of the building was deserted. Only a bicycle lay tipped over onto the sidewalk from the curb.

"Shouldn't we go up to the composing room and have a beer?" suggested Jastrau. At home, Sanders and Steffensen were probably sitting and waiting for him, so why go home?

"No—although it's mighty cozy up there," Vuldum replied quietly. They stood peering up at the building on the opposite corner.

"Will you be there tomorrow night?"

"At the election-night doings? No, thank you. The idea makes me shiver."

"Me too."

They turned and walked slowly across the square, which at night always seemed prodigiously big, with barren stretches where the streetcars rode in the daytime, and murky darkness around the sunken "clamshell" amphitheatre in front of the Town Hall. Between Strøget and Vesterbrogade a line of people made their way over the pavement in single file, as if crossing a frozen sea.

"There are lots of people out tonight," remarked Vuldum, shivering a little in the cold.

"They're fortifying themselves for election day."

They had no sooner reached the broad sidewalk outside the Scala and the National when Vuldum stopped and stared at one of the large shopwindows, where a woman in a light-colored coat stood leaning against a brass guardrail. Her flesh-colored stockings shone white through the darkness.

Vuldum leaned forward.

"Well—so it's you," he said softly.

"Oh, good evening, Herr Vuldum," said a youthful but rasping voice.

Vuldum and Jastrau drew nearer to her.

She was not very tall and quite plump. Big shoulders. Her face was heavily powdered. But even at their distance from the arc lamps, which imparted an icy glare to the street car tracks, they could make out the dark shadows under her eyes. Her rouged lips had the effect of a heavy black streak.

"What are you doing here?"

"I'm freezing," she said, cuddling one cheek against her shoulder.

"Is that all?"

"I'm waiting to catch a fish."

Vuldum laughed and addressed a few more chivalrous questions to her, then took her arm and complimented her on its plumpness while she laughed and wriggled coquettishly. Jastrau stood and watched, and now and then encountered her shining eyes as she looked at him appraisingly.

"Well, I'm sorry, but I have to go home, you little mouse," Vuldum finally said. "But I didn't want to go by without giving you a little present."

And with that he calmly took the three roses out of Jastrau's hand and gave them to her with an elegant bow.

"Just a slight token of esteem from my friend and me. And now, good night, my dear girl."

For some reason or other this trifling scene made Jastrau feel good—this little rococo episode from the city's night life. And it was with a certain cordiality in his voice that he said good night to Vuldum near the Freedom Statue and turned down toward Istedgade.

That was where they now lay sleeping—those two.

Chapter Four   Ole Jastrau was awakened by a clatter in the kitchen.

At first he did not perceive it very clearly, but then he awoke with a start. He always did so after an evening of whiskey drinking.

The clatter continued. Cups and plates rattled. Someone was washing dishes.

"Johanne," he called out in his usual grumpy morning voice.

Then he heard heavy footsteps in the corridor leading to the kitchen, and the door opened. He had already been alarmed by the ponderous footfalls, and as it turned out it was not Johanne. It was Sanders, his face smudged and grinning from ear to ear. His sleeves were rolled up, and he had a dishtowel draped over his arm.

"What's going on here?" exclaimed Jastrau, sitting up in bed. "Am I seeing things?" He rubbed his eyes.

Sanders' expression suddenly changed—so suddenly that Jastrau could see that the change was calculated.

"What do you mean?"

"Are you washing dishes?" Jastrau asked indignantly.

"Yes, of course,"—Sanders' lips tightened in a contemptuous smile—"Is that all that was bothering you? Yes, I'm washing dishes."

Jastrau lay back in the bed again. He did not feel like coming to grips with Sanders and his shifting facial expressions so early in the morning.

But Sanders went right on in a highly moralistic tone, "When we've made a mess of things here, it's no more than reasonable that we should clean up. As a matter of fact, I've washed the floor and dusted too, and now I'm through with the dishes. And now your lordship is soon going to have coffee in bed."

"Your lordship!" Jastrau growled from beneath the covers. "Is Steffensen still asleep?"

"Yes, the beast won't get up."

"Thank God for that," Jastrau sighed in relief. "I was afraid he might be as much of a theoretician as you are."

By this time Sanders had resumed his trickster's grin.

"No, you don't have to worry about that. He's not motivated by principles."

"Listen, is he really the son of H. C. Stefani?" he went on.

"Yes," said Sanders with a mocking smile. "And it was really quite intriguing yesterday when you were talking about Stefani over the phone. You should have seen Steffensen's face."

"How the devil should I know that Stefani's son goes by the name of Steffensen? But Arne Vuldum knew it."

"Oh, so that's why you stayed away," Sanders said pointedly. "Now I understand better."

"What do you understand better?"

"This Arne Vuldum—he's a man of such fine feelings, such a sensitive man. And I suppose it must be much more interesting to be in such cultivated company than to sit and listen to our crude Communist chatter. Well, we got along all right. Steffensen drank a bottle of port, we found what we needed in the pantry, and we smoked most of your cigars. Then we read and talked a little, and Steffensen wrote some poetry. It was really a very pleasant evening. He found one of your writing pads, and the mere sight of so much paper inspired him. Afterwards we sang a few songs and played the phonograph. So we got along admirably. And today is election day, so you'll soon be rid of us."

"You could stay for lunch," said Jastrau, lifting the covers and putting his feet on the floor. He wanted to get up.

"Yes—we've thought of the same thing. But now wouldn't you rather have coffee in bed? I was just going out to put it on the stove."

Without a word, Jastrau reached for his pants. Sanders, with a supercilious smile, had already disappeared into the kitchen. What sort of a flophouse for tramps was it that his home had become? For a moment he remained sitting morosely on the edge of the bed, thinking. But no—he didn't want to think about it.

As quickly as possible he got hold of his shirt, necktie, vest, and jacket, and hurried into the dining room where it would be warm. But then it occurred to him that Johanne had not yet come home, and there would be no fire. He gave the door an impatient shove. No, this was really too much—the preposterous Sanders had thought of that too. He had laid and lighted a fire. Not only that, but he had swept up around the stove. Oluf's playthings had been put together in an orderly pile. It was all too feminine—too ridiculous. But how well it fitted in with Sanders' erotomaniac theatricalism.

Jastrau walked back and forth brooding as he slowly got dressed. Wasn't Sanders carrying things too far—being downright impudent? He stopped before the mirror in the buffet and adjusted his necktie. Wasn't he? he asked himself. Then, catching sight of himself in the mirror, he suddenly noticed how ill-natured he looked. It startled him. He saw a face with evil, Mongolian features. But then he felt flattered, and smiled grimly to himself. Could he really look so wicked? What thoughts had been running through his mind to give him such an expression? Was it a psychologically abnormal feeling of malice toward Sanders? Were there not half-grown boys who simply loved to wear women's clothes, who loved to imagine themselves as women—so much so that the very thought of it made them tingle all over?

He went to the kitchen door, opened it with a jerk, and said sharply, "So you laid a fire in the stove, too, didn't you?"

"Yes, of course," Sanders replied blithely.

Jastrau slammed the door shut. But the noise it made was more than he had bargained for. It made even him jump. That was a bit over-done, he thought. He was giving himself away completely. So he opened the door again, and said, "There's a bad draft through here. It bangs the doors shut."

"I can't understand that," came an unruffled answer from the kitchen. "There are no windows open at the other end of the apartment."

Jastrau doggedly shut the door again and slowly went into the living room. He could not take it any longer.

Sanders had put things in order in the living room too. But Steffensen lay on the sofa still asleep, a sight which made Jastrau feel some sense of relief. And, as might be expected, he lay with his big nose straight up in the air so that Jastrau could see way into his nostrils. His mouth hung open. It was as if there were three holes in his ugly head through which all consciousness had taken flight. Besides, his beard had grown so much during the night that it made him look like a porcupine. A lovely sight!

The table was littered with a writing pad and several torn-off sheets of paper. Beside it was a fresh box of cigars that they had opened. Without thinking—his mind was on his good cigars—he picked up one of the sheets and looked at it. What was this? "Like a ruffian with bloody hands," he read. Then, farther down the page, "Like a ruffian with bloody fists." It was all that was on that sheet.

He picked up another. Again the identical lines—the same variation of "hands" and "fists." Furthermore, the paper was covered with profile drawings of old men, all in clerical collars, long pencil strokes, female legs, sketches of women's curving backs, breasts, and loins, and, inex-plicably, a marabou stork.

Apparently Steffensen had been trying to write a poem. Jastrau smiled. How well he knew the situation. The idle hand, doodling on the paper while the thoughts hovered over the sheet like a flock of pigeons that refused to light.

But on the third sheet there was finally a verse.

First a stanza written in a large, clear hand, but then crossed out:

> Like a ruffian whose hands are bloodied
> After a brawl and a binge,
> I forsake my soft bed of indifference
> For a couch at terror's raw edge.

Then, farther down the page, almost in a corner of the sheet, and bearing no relationship other than the rhyme scheme to the stanza above, three more verses had been jotted down hurriedly in small script. They had seemingly been written in one unlabored flourish of inspiration, with but a single correction. And when Jastrau, his curiosity aroused, reached for a fourth sheet, there were the same three stanzas, neatly written this time, with the date and a signature added. So it seemed that the poem had been completed:

> Fear is strong as a Mongol horde.
> It is ripened by immature years.
> And each day my heart grows heavy,
> Foreseeing the continents flooded with tears.
>
> But my fear must be vented in longing,
> In visions of horror and stress.
> I have longed for the final disaster,
> For havoc and violent death.
>
> I have longed to see cities burning
> And the races of mankind in flight—
> A world rushing headlong in panic
> From God's retribution and might.

Suddenly he turned to look at his sleeping guest. He had a feeling that he was being watched. And sure enough—Steffensen's eyelids were quivering, and a narrow segment of his eyes could be seen glistening from beneath their lashes. Furthermore, his mouth was now closed.

Then his eyes opened.

"I'm confiscating this poem for my book page," Jastrau said abruptly, folding the sheet and sticking it in his pocket.

Steffensen suddenly sat up in bed.

"So! Is it good enough for the prostitute press?" he exclaimed, glowering at Jastrau.

"It isn't always the worst-looking girls who turn out to be whores," replied Jastrau.

"Well—no," Steffensen said slowly. "But let me have another look at it."

"You can look at the rough draft. The other I'm keeping—right here." He tapped his breast pocket.

Just then Sanders came in with three cups of steaming coffee on a tray, which he placed on the table.

"Look, Bernhard—he's bought my poem," Steffensen muttered. "The one I wrote last night."

54

For a moment Sanders glanced from one to the other, then said sourly:

"I wouldn't say that it's one of your best."

"No," Steffensen growled in dead earnest. "I'm afraid that there's too much opinionitis in it."

Sanders had very quietly taken a seat in one of the rococo chairs and was biting his lips. For a moment he was not with them. Jastrau had pulled up a chair and now sat bent forward, looking at Steffensen as if hypnotized.

"What did you mean by that remark—too much opinionitis?"

Steffensen made a face. Jastrau had addressed him as "De," instead of using the more informal "du." "Are we suddenly on such formal terms now—du?" he asked.

"Nonsense," Jastrau snapped. "What did you mean?"

"I meant I'm not suffering from the same disease as Sanders."

"You'd do well to pick up some new phrases now and then," Sanders volunteered. "But now drink your coffee. And you can console yourself, Ole, with the assurance that he didn't mean anything—wasn't expressing any opinions."

Seffensen's eyes twinkled craftily. "Why should an artist have opinions?" he drawled.

Jastrau stared at him as if taken off his guard. "Quite so," he agreed cordially. "Or, to put it more correctly, an artist should have opinions, although it doesn't matter what they are."

With an expression of contempt, Sanders leaned back against the oval frame of the chair which with its imposing lines added a touch of glamour to his revolutionary appearance. Like Lenin in the Kremlin.

"Let's talk about lunch instead," he said with a supercilious Marxist smile. "The truth is always concrete. What do you have in the pantry, Ole?"

"Well, there's no beer. That I know from last night," interjected Steffensen, and Jastrau laughed. His laughter had become friendly. In any event, he was now receptive to whatever Steffensen might have to say.

But he did not, of course, know what was in the house, and Sanders did. Naturally. Had he not been out in the kitchen and taken an inventory? Some head cheese, a piece of steak, and a leftover pickled herring. There were no eggs or rye bread, and then, too, they were out of beer. But Jastrau could go out and do the shopping, and Steffensen would be more than delighted to go along to carry the bottles. Meanwhile Sanders would set the table. Naturally he knew where the clean tablecloths were kept.

"Do you know where the silverware is too?" Jastrau asked sarcastically.

Sanders nodded provokingly.

Soon Jastrau and Steffensen were down at the dairy-goods store. They were now getting along in comradely fashion. Next they had to stop at the delicatessen at the corner of Colbjørnsensgade, but here Steffensen remained standing outside with the bottles in his arms and jacket pockets.

"Say," he muttered when Jastrau came out of the store, "this Istedgade is a dandy street."

"Why?"

"Because it's so long."

Jastrau was about to answer with a laugh, but then he noticed that Steffensen was gazing far down the street and that his eyes were shining. Jastrau had to turn and share the view. It was true—the street seemed endless. The forenoon sun glistened on a myriad of window-panes as if they were raindrops, and out near Enghaveplads the gray and yellow building facades rose like distant hills until they were dissolved in a shimmering haze.

"Yes. It's stupid of me not always to be able to see how pretty it is," remarked Jastrau.

"Yes—damned if it isn't like an idea—one of those that are supposed to be found in poetry," Steffensen said with a wry smile. "All this muck and rubbish here—and then the way it gets transformed by that heavenly light off in the distance." He broke into derisive laughter.

By the time Jastrau and Steffensen got back, Johanne had arrived with Oluf. The boy came running from the dining room at full speed, leaning like a motorcycle on a curve. He came to a sudden halt as soon as he saw Steffensen with his arms full of bottles, and he stood with his awkward little body still swaying as he shouted, "Oh! Look at all the b—ee—r!" The "ee" sound was so drawn out that the "r" was hardly noticeable.

Then, to Jastrau's great surprise, the lanky Steffensen bent over and invited Oluf to take a bottle.

"Can you carry it?" he muttered, winking at the boy.

Oluf reached for the bottle and began to inspect the label, while Steffensen patted him on the head and rubbed his neck the way one would pet a dog. "There, there, puppy," he said.

"Puppy? What does he mean?" exclaimed Oluf in astonishment, staring up at him. Jastrau laughed.

"Well, what can one say to a fellow like that?" Steffensen said as if to himself with a vague smile. "Here's the beer," he announced, proceeding with his long seaman's stride into the dining room and setting the bottles on the table.

Jastrau went on into the kitchen.

"No, you mustn't! Let me do it," he heard his wife say. Her voice sounded gay. And as he stepped into the kitchen, he halted in surprise. Johanne stood near the kitchen table and was trying to take a plate away from Sanders. But it was not this that surprised him. No, it was the animated play of her features as she stood there struggling for possession of the plate. He recognized it with a feeling of bitterness. It was the same glow of animation that once had dazzled him and sent the blood coursing passionately through his veins.

Her happiness at such moments had always seemed like a trick that his eyes were playing on him.

He stood stock still, although he was inwardly raging, and followed her struggle with the swarthy Sanders, whose eyes were glistening like a bluebottle fly.

And then he saw her flourish the plate triumphantly above her head as if it were a tambourine.

"Johanne," he said quietly.

She turned and looked at her husband, and suddenly the aura of enchantment that had surrounded her vanished. He stared at her for a moment as she stood there, her eyes swimming, her mouth hanging open and gasping for breath. Like a white rabbit, he thought suddenly.

"Here are the eggs and the bread," he said in a matter-of-fact tone.

But she must have been taken back, for now she began to vent her feelings in a dozen ways at once—with words, gestures, and glances. She could not find enough ways of expressing herself.

"Isn't it simply wonderful of Herr Sanders? He's washed the dishes, cleaned the house, dusted, laid a fire in the stove, made coffee, and everything. At first he wouldn't admit it, but I found him out. Did you ever see anything like it?"

Her enthusiasm was too unfettered, too breathless. It was supposed to overwhelm him, but the effect was only comical. He stood there with a faint grudging smile.

"You could never have done such a thing, Ole."

He stared at her much too matter-of-factly. It was the female in her that had been stirred. A white rabbit. The trace of a smile remained about his lips.

"But now you leave things to me, Herr Sanders. Go inside. This is no place for men, and you can just get out of my kitchen."

Laughingly, she shoved Sanders toward the door. Jastrau got a shove too.

"Out with you! Out with you both!"

Jastrau went willingly enough. But in his resentment he could not help casting a sidelong glance at Sanders. This was the way one went about achieving a conquest with a simple, unsophisticated girl. Was it possible that a wife could be so light-headed? A sudden froth of eroticism, dazzling as in the old days—but only for a moment. Then, just as suddenly, it all seemed comical. A white rabbit. Why the change? The humdrum of married life? He wondered. Was it all over?

"One, two, three, four," came a voice from the dining room.

Steffensen had seated himself in his old position at the end of the table and had placed all the bottles in front of him. "One, two, three, four, five," he counted, pointing at each of them in turn with a crooked finger, while Oluf, his chin resting on the edge of the table, watched the procedure with enthusiasm.

"One, two, four," he volunteered experimentally.

But Jastrau paid no attention to them. Listlessly he drew a chair up to the table. He had to remain apathetic. He could not, however, fail to notice the silent vague smile with which Sanders comfortably settled himself at the table. It sank into his consciousness and remained there like a hard, glistening lump of anthracite.

Meanwhile, Johanne ran to and fro in housewifely fashion, bringing on the food.

"Now we might as well begin," said Jastrau.

"But hadn't we better wait until your wife—?" protested Sanders.

"No," was the abrupt answer.

Sanders' smile was transformed into a look of insolence.

"Indeed!" he replied with exaggerated politeness.

When Fru Johanne was at last able to sit down with the others, the conversation again began to revolve around Sanders' ability as a housekeeper. Johanne was quite hilarious. "Just think," she would say in a tone of joyous incomprehension. "Just think—"

"But look here, it's no more than natural—at least for a Communist," objected Sanders affably, gesticulating with a hand that was not clean enough to match his eloquence. "In a Communist state, where everyone has a right to one room and no more, he also is under obligation to keep it in order."

"Are you back on the subject of your Communism again?" asked Johanne, laughing and giving him a tap on the arm as if she were a servant girl coyly repulsing an advance. Jastrau looked down at the tablecloth.

"Yes—always back to that," Sanders replied, unabashed. "Because, you see, it's inseparably linked with the battle for the liberation of women. Here in this capitalistic society most women's lives are sheer barbarism, you must admit."

"Yes—" she said hesitantly. "But Communism—that's something else. It makes women the property of the state."

Jastrau did not dare to look at her. Her forehead was no doubt wrinkled in thought, and her eyes pale and colorless. He let his middle finger follow the pattern in the white tablecloth.

"That's a lie!" exclaimed Sanders. "A lie that the newspapers have been paid to circulate throughout Europe. It's a propaganda lie."

At these words, Jastrau looked over at Steffensen, who seemed completely uninterested in the conversation and was opening a bottle of beer.

"Yes, but I've read in *The Hammer*—" Johanne protested.

"Have you read *The Hammer?*"

She nodded in animated fashion, and Jastrau finally looked over at her. Yes, now she looked dim-witted. He could not help smiling.

"You're smiling, Ole," she said sharply.

"Yes—because you're so keyed up."

"Doesn't your husband ever talk with you about these things?" Sanders inquired slyly.

"No, he certainly doesn't."

"I suppose he'd say you wouldn't understand," Sanders said spitefully. Then, without waiting to see if the remark had struck home, he continued in a gloating tone, "Lord! How typical of our solid, middle-class menfolk."

But Johanne disregarded the disdain in his voice and remarked naïvely, "No, as a matter of fact, he usually says that he's the one who doesn't understand such things."

"You don't say so," said Steffensen with a grin. It was the only sound that had escaped him so far during the luncheon.

Jastrau laughed at the remark too.

But Sanders raised his voice and went on vehemently, "And incidentally, is there anything more ridiculous than our highly moral bourgeois indignation over the Communists' concept of the equality of women? But the Communists didn't have to introduce the idea. It goes back much farther in history."

His words came with such precision that it seemed as if he were quoting, and Steffensen looked at him with distrust.

But Johanne only drew a deep breath and said calmly, "Ah yes—I suppose that's true."

"There's no need for me to go on," said Sanders, conscious of having

59

made his point. "I don't have to dwell on all the scandalous gossip here in Copenhagen which, incidentally, I'm not nearly so familiar with as—well, let's say you and your husband."

"No. That's one of the penalties a journalist has to pay," Jastrau said ironically.

Johanne's brows, however, were furrowed with wrinkles of incomprehension, like water ruffled by a wind blowing at right angles to the current.

"But look," she said in confusion, "at any rate, it's wrong—this that the Communists are after. I'm convinced of it."

Jastrau got up from his chair.

"Hadn't we better have our coffee in the living room?" he asked.

"As you wish."

Steffensen rose immediately and helped Oluf down to the floor. It was laughable, the way the two self-invited guests had made themselves at home. Sanders just as quickly began to make himself useful by piling up the dishes. And Johanne laughed.

In trying to get through the doorway to the living room at the same time, Jastrau and Steffensen suddenly found themselves shoulder to shoulder.

"Such a feast of ideas, what?" Steffensen drawled sarcastically.

Jastrau shrugged his shoulders.

"I suppose," Steffensen went on, "it's a sort of substitute for wisdom." Then, as if to give emphasis to his contempt, he flung himself violently down on the sofa.

"Bang!" shouted Oluf, who had come toddling along after the two grown-ups, neither of whom paid any attention to him. He ran to his father, tugged at the pocket of his jacket, and looked up at him with round, childish eyes. "Bang!" he repeated, in astonishment at the way Steffensen had precipitated himself onto the sofa.

"Yes. Bang!" Jastrau replied abstractedly.

"No, he shouldn't do it that way," exclaimed Oluf angrily, stamping his foot. "No, daddy!" Then he turned and suddenly ran into the kitchen.

But in a little while he came dashing back.

"Well, my little man—can't you stand those two out there in the kitchen either?" Steffensen said rudely, but in a friendly tone.

"He talks so loud," said Oluf, out of breath.

Simultaneously, they heard Sanders' voice from the kitchen.

"A woman is a person in her own right—not just an object to be enjoyed. Wine and women—Luther—the man-of-the-world's viewpoint."

60

"Yes, he certainly does make a lot of noise," said Steffensen, guffawing.

Oluf remained standing at the foot of the sofa, a lost look on his face. His moist lips were half open as if there were something he wanted to say—he did not know to whom, he was so perplexed.

"It's no doubt difficult to be a little man," Steffensen said comfortingly, but with a snort of laughter. He felt uncertain in the role of a gentle consoler. And Jastrau smiled sadly.

"Would you like to play with the man?" he asked, picking up the fetish.

Oluf stared at him in surprise. His eyes grew wide as two expanses of open sky and glistened in astonishment at the incomprehensible whims of grown-ups. Then they again became child's eyes, human eyes, filled with wishes and desires, and he came running with hands extended.

"But handle him carefully. You must be good to him."

It was as if he had suddenly felt compelled to make some great sacrifice for the sake of the boy—to give him something that he was afraid might be broken. For the youngster looked so much like a little outcast.

Oluf took the fetish in both hands and carried it to a corner of the room.

"The man," he mumbled, enchanted.

Jastrau stood watching him for a little while. The recollection of the two blue, uncomprehending, boyish eyes remained with him. Then suddenly he said to himself, "God knows if it was the wrong thing to do. He isn't supposed to play with it."

"Absolutely all wrong," Steffensen said with a foolish grin.

Jastrau shook his head in despair.

But then the coffee was brought in, and with it the discussion spilled over into the living room too—ardent discussion between Johanne and Sanders. Sanders' expression was set in a confident smile, befitting the experienced debater that he was. Johanne exhibited a profusion of deranged hair, flushed cheeks, and wet, glistening, mobile lips. Jastrau was swept aside into the background, where he finally found himself a chair. From this position he could keep an eye on the fetish, and that was at least some comfort. He felt a certain amount of anxiety about it.

"Isn't it crazy, Ole?" said Johanne, laughing and brushing the golden hair back from her forehead. "Isn't it insane that I have to listen to such talk here in my own house—and that I don't even get furious about it?"

Sanders assumed a stiffly revolutionary position in his chair.

But suddenly Steffensen bellowed from the sofa, "Hear! Hear! Long live the revolution!"

"You mean the destruction of everything," Sanders snarled.

"I mean the revolution, damn it!" growled Steffensen.

"There, Herr Sanders—don't you see how ridiculous it sounds, all this about revolution?" said Johanne.

"Yes, when it comes from him," was the curt reply.

"No, when it comes from you, too," Johanne insisted. "Don't you understand? Here we walk along Vesterbrogade and Strøget every day, and the very idea that a revolution is going to break out in the streets here—"

"You're right, Johanne," said Jastrau from his place in the background.

"Yes, am I not?" she exclaimed, turning in her chair, glad to receive support.

"Yes, we know all that," Steffensen broke in with a sneer. "It's something that happens only in Russia. It can't happen here in our lovely Denmark. But, by God, it can!"

"No," objected Jastrau, shaking his head gloomily. "No, it can't."

He did not know whether he wanted to go to the trouble of saying more, but nevertheless he went on:

"I've been through it. I've seen it happen. A revolution in Denmark will be drowned—in laughter."

"Is that so?" Sanders protested.

"Yes, I've seen it. It's hardly worth talking about, it's hardly worth talking about. But I know, because I was there, under the red banners—trala—lala—back in those March days when the king tossed out the Radical government."

He sat looking into space, but the others now had their eyes turned toward him. Suddenly he found the whole scene comical. An old man! Reminiscing about his experiences! And then, as if mimicking a Storm Petersen cartoon, he went on: "An old soldier—yes, yes—fought in the Boer War. A lot of nonsense!"

"No, go on. You wanted to say something." It was Sanders who spoke.

"Oh, I really don't care to talk about it. But as I was saying, I was there to help push through the police cordon in Amalienborg Plads and to shout 'Long live the republic,' in front of the palace. It was all a lot of foolishness. There was a man who climbed up a lamppost to make a revolutionary speech. 'Comrades,' he yelled, then got so enthusiastic that he flung both arms into the air, forgetting to hold onto the post, so that he just quietly slid to the ground—while a mighty roar of revolutionary laughter went up all around him."

"But those were nothing but pranks, that time," objected Sanders. "Tomfoolery in the streets."

Jastrau shrugged his shoulders.

"Maybe so. And incidentally, I heard the only shot that was fired. A blank cartridge—fired by an overzealous policeman. And I was at the demonstrations held at The Clamshell in front of the Town Hall. Oh, it was all very funny. There was a drunk who made a speech. Very picturesque. A somber crowd, light falling from the arc lamps. The chiaroscuro effect was very good. Revolutionary drama." Again he lapsed into the Storm Petersen style: "Ha, ha! A drunk—Danton—completely blotto on a slug of apple juice. In his befuddlement he yelled, 'Down with the election law—down with it! A Copenhagener, damn it, is worth no more than one-third of a West Coast Jutlander.' Then he practically fell on his face amidst the spectators. They had to stretch him out on the pedestal, and there he lay with a couple of men sitting on him, while he shouted, 'Long live the revolution!' just like Steffensen here."

The others laughed while Jastrau continued in a caustic tone that increasingly was tinged with wry humor:

"Yes—a regular street-corner parliament—a characteristic Copenhagen scene! They finally managed to subdue the drunk, but then the crowd demanded that he be heard. 'Give us the West Jutlander,' they yelled. 'Up with the West Jutlander—he's a good fellow!' God, how idiotic it was. And then I remember saying good-by to a friend of mine far out on Vesterbro—a fellow in the advertising department. It was late that night, and we said to each other, 'Yes—tomorrow there'll be a general strike,' and we looked up at the street lights. Tomorrow they'd all be out, and we rather welcomed the idea. So what happened? Not a thing. Oh yes—there was a demonstration, with the City Council at the head of the parade. Up with the king—and genial greetings all around! And the newspapers that had threatened a general strike—well—"

"Yes, including *Dagbladet*," Steffensen remarked in disgust.

"Yes," Jastrau said wearily. "During those days the Radical Liberals received their death blow. And yet, they're still around like ghosts. But what do you care about that?"

He got up, completely out of sorts.

"I don't believe in any revolution here in this country," he went on emphatically. "The Danes don't have the guts for it. Phew! I'd like to

63

write a book about the Danish national characteristics—deceptive blue eyes and blond unreliability."

"Hey-hey!" exclaimed Johanne, so that Sanders and Steffensen had to laugh.

"It's you he's referring to," Steffensen said to Johanne with a crude attempt at coquetry and an unctuous, unnatural expression of geniality. But Johanne purposely disregarded him.

"What is it you're playing with, Oluf?" exclaimed Johanne.

"The man," came the reply from the corner.

"Don't you know that—"

"I told him he could have it," Jastrau interrupted quietly.

Johanne gave him a harsh look and shook her head, as if he were an idiot.

"But I thought—" she said.

"So did I," Jastrau responded ironically.

Then the telephone rang.

Jastrau took the call. "Jastrau speaking. What's that? But how in the world does Stefani know that? I wrote it yesterday and sent it right up to the composing room. No, I can't do that. He deserves the going-over I gave him. Blasphemy—is that so? Is that what Editor Iversen thinks? Well, well! Yes—then let Eriksen write it, although I have no idea what Eriksen knows about literature. But let him do it anyhow. Yes—I'll be over soon. Yes—yes—so long now."

Indignantly he put the receiver back and began to pace the floor, while the others' eyes followed him.

"How in the devil can Stefani know what I wrote in my review? I wrote it over at the paper last night and went right up to the composing room with it. And now Stefani has already been to see Iversen and is raising a rumpus."

"He has a sharp nose," said Steffensen, grinning.

"Yes—a charming fellow, your father," Jastrau snarled. As he said it, he glanced at Steffensen and saw that his cheeks had grown pale and his expression hard. His lips were thrust forward menacingly as if they had been carved out of wood. His glance wandered distractedly from one to the other.

Was it a madman sitting over there on the sofa? Sanders and Johanne also stared at him and an awkward silence spread through the room in eerie, ever-widening waves. Jastrau remained standing without moving.

Finally, he managed to say very quietly and casually:

"I think I'd better go over and get it straight. You can come along and pick up the payment for the poem."

64

"But, the police—" Johanne objected.

"Oh, now that this is election day there's probably no danger," said Sanders. "It's probably best if we both go. Either the Social Democrats will win and we'll get an amnesty or—well—. But it would have been annoying to have been picked up just before the election. And so now, Frue, may we thank you for putting us up and say that we hope—and so on and so forth, and all that sort of thing."

He arose and made her a chivalrous bow.

"There's really nothing to thank us for," said Johanne, extending her hand.

At the same moment, Steffensen reached for the cigar box and helped himself to five cigars.

Then they left.

Chapter Five

A cold wind was blowing and Jastrau pulled his coat collar up around his ears. But he felt restless and conscious of the quickened pulse brought on by night air and broad sidewalks. Glowing red and gaseous blue neon tubes flashed like signatures written with a single fiery stroke: Scala. Blue electric light bulbs flickered mysteriously like carriage lanterns half-hidden by foliage: Marble Garden. Names in yellow lights. An electric news bulletin coursed swiftly across the top of a building, a veil of mist dragging along behind each letter. Ahead of and behind him megaphones from the several newspaper offices bellowed the election results out over the streets so that the air seemed filled with voices. It was as if invisible giants as high as houses were shouting up at the façades of the buildings.

Over in the square swarmed a dark mass of people, and the automobiles escaping from the closely packed throng ground their gears and picked up speed into Vesterbrogade as if lurching out of a mudhole. The beams of their headlights shot forward over the streetcar tracks, which were coated and glistening with gasoline. It was one of Copenhagen's more brilliantly illuminated evenings.

Jastrau had gone out after all. He zigzagged his way through the horde of people on the sidewalk out onto the pavement and over to the flagstone area in the square. It had been painfully dull at home. It was true that they were now rid of their two self-invited guests. At the supper table, he and Johanne had sat opposite one another, each feeling lonely—he chagrined over the squabble he had gotten into at the office over the review of Stefani's book, she distant and reserved, with nervous, perpendicular wrinkles creasing her forehead. That white forehead. Like an egg. Shadowy figures of men and women hurried past him. The evening glittered like black lacquer. He saw her pale forehead amidst the swarm of people. A white egg. He saw the whole scene clearly.

But in the square he got so enmeshed in the crush that he had to edge his way out.

Over his head a megaphone intoned some unintelligible sounds and ahead of him loomed *Dagbladet*'s corner building with all its windows pouring forth light.

Obviously there were many people up at the paper. He could make out shadowy figures behind the light-colored curtains that covered the lower half of the windows. They were very likely leaning on their elbows on the thick brass rods, looking out at the milling crowd. But the corner room was dark. In its window was a screen on which the election results were flashed from time to time. At the moment, it was blank—an empty gray panel.

Suddenly he heard loud laughter around him. "*Skaal!*" someone shouted. "We want beer!" And Jastrau looked up at the corner window.

He saw a big shadowy hand grasping a large, dimly discernible object move across the right side of the screen. It came to rest there for a moment. The outline was foggy, but there was no mistaking it—the silhouette of a beer bottle. Only a glimpse of it, then it disappeared. The hand had abruptly jerked it away, and again the screen was blank.

"Aw—what a shame!" More laughter. "They need something to drown their disappointment," someone behind him wisecracked.

"Are things going very badly for the Radicals?"* Jastrau asked the man beside him, as he slowly wormed his way between him and the next person.

"Yes—and how! The Socialists are winning," the man said, trying to make room with his elbow. "It's a tough proposition—trying to get through this jam."

Finally Jastrau reached the sidewalk in front of *Dagbladet* and was

---

* Names of Danish political parties are not necessarily descriptive of their rightist or leftist orientation. The Radical Liberals are somewhat to the right of the Social Democrats. The Left Agrarians and the Conservatives are to the right of the Radical Liberals. The Communists represent the extreme left.

66

able to breathe freely. Simultaneously, an automobile made its way with difficulty up to the curb and stopped before the entrance. A tall, smartly dressed man, wearing a voluminous light-colored coat with the collar drawn up around his ears so that only a billowing crown of white hair was visible, sprang out and disappeared through the revolving door. No more than a glimpse of the bare-headed figure was necessary. It was the eternally youthfully H. C. Stefani.

Jastrau stopped in his tracks. It was that review. What a lot of fuss had been stirred up because of it. That afternoon, when he and Steffensen had gone over to the paper together, the copy editor had bawled him out—yes, bawled him out! And it wasn't like him to do such a thing. But how in the world had Stefani learned what was in the review? It had not been out of the building, but had been written in his office and taken at once to be set in type.

He had his suspicions. Nevertheless, he could not bring himself to believe it. No—such a trick would be too petty, without purpose. Deep in thought, he went on through the revolving door.

"Hey—is that you, Jazz?"

Jastrau looked up, and there, halfway up the stairs and struggling with his overcoat, stood Eriksen, the little, broad-shouldered newspaperman. He had one arm stretched out behind him, trying to get it into the sleeve. "Phew! This is a mess!" he groaned, puffing so that a miasma of port-wine and beer fumes descended around Jastrau, while he continued flapping the empty sleeve. "Let me get out of here. It's unbearable up there, and I've just created a scandal." And he screwed up his weather-beaten, ravaged features so that all the wrinkles and scars that testified to a misspent youth converged.

"You don't mean to say it was you with that bottle," said Jastrau.

"Yes." And at the same time, in his befuddlement, as he tried to shake his head he began to cough.

"So now the whole town knows that you drink."

"So what?" said Eriksen, laughing. But the tears rolled down his cheeks and his face was beet-red from his fit of coughing. "It's about time I made it public myself."

Finally the arm found its way into the sleeve, and the overcoat was on. He straightened up, threw out his chest, and flung a hand out in a sweeping gesture. "You see," he said, "I made it."

Once more he crumpled up with laughter and waved his hand as if brushing away the scandal. "But look, Jazz," he went on in a more serious tone, "it's a good thing I ran into you. I've been looking for you all evening. Oh, that business about the bottle! Are you sore? I tell you, I've been looking for you all evening." He tried to grab Jastrau by the hand. "You aren't sore at me because they gave me Stefani's book, are you, Jazz?"

"No, no." And Jastrau shut his eyes and closed off all his other senses in order to avoid the overpowering stench of wine and beer.

"No, I hope you're not disturbed about it," Eriksen went on, squeezing Jastrau's hand. "Because you understand, don't you? Yes, of course you do. But you don't know Stefani. A brilliant man—in every respect. A pharmacist in Aarhus. Yes, I can tell you a lot of things you don't know about him, and even though he's written a rotten book—what of it? But even if that weren't the case—well, I can tell you a good deal."

"Have you been out to vote?" Jastrau asked ironically. "You smell like it."

"Hee hee—yes. At the Bodega. I put a big cross after Sommer's name—Sommer, the waiter."

"Well, I think I'll sneak upstairs."

"Up there?" Eriksen inquired hoarsely, pointing to the upper floors.

"Yes. Up to the lecture room to listen to the election returns. Don't you want to come along?"

"Pooh," said Eriksen, snickering into the palm of his hand. "No, I've contributed enough to the spirit of election night. Hee hee—that business with the bottle. What do you think of that? Besides, it's unbearable up there. Phooey! Every time a Conservative or a Social Democrat is elected there's great rejoicing and hurrahs and hullabaloo, but if a Radical Liberal gets in then everybody holds his nose and says 'Down with him!'"

Suddenly he grabbed Jastrau by the lapel of his jacket, drew him close, and whispered to him through a cloud of port-wine fumes.

"And this is supposed to be a Radical Liberal newspaper. Oof! It's enough to make you get drunk and create a scandal. It makes the cold shivers run up my spine. Because it is a Radical Liberal paper, isn't it?" He was getting more wrought up by the moment. "Well, it makes no difference to me. But just the same, I don't like it. You can go up and listen for yourself. But look here"—and once again he squeezed Jastrau's hand so hard that he felt the fingers crack—"you aren't sore at me, are you, Jazz?"

"No, no."

"After all, it's your material, and so you understand." Eriksen put his arms around him. "Look, old boy, I like you very much, even though you're no great shakes. But see here—a bottle up there on the

68

screen—how about that? Of all today's bottles, that's the one, isn't it? Hee hee."

"Yes, yes, yes," replied Jastrau, tearing himself free.

Journalist Eriksen had another coughing spell, and Jastrau could hear him all the while as he discreetly retreated up the stairs.

The offices of *Dagbladet* were hardly recognizable. Doors were banging on every floor. The elevators hummed incessantly. The election-night mood had taken possession of the building and altered it. The stairways swarmed with people whom one seldom saw.

Through the windows of the vestibule where the night before he had stood with Arne Vuldum—he recalled their encounter grimly—he caught sight of one celebrity after another. A well-known actor's swarthy face. A polar explorer with a beard like a Christmas elf. An art critic who looked as if he were neighing. A Radical Liberal politician's cultivated profile. An actress with a chaste Madonna-like smile, a second-hand-book dealer who resembled a long loaf of French bread. They were either sitting around in the chairs or leaning against the big round table where one of the paper's illustrators had spread out a large roll of paper and with a crayon was lettering in the election returns, which several of the notables present were regarding with uneasy expressions.

Should he venture in among them? He invariably felt shy when the paper put on its big affairs. Then, however, he did go in, nodded and said hello to several people without really feeling at ease, and felt himself saved only when he caught sight of the copy editor, who stood in the doorway of his office, looking as if he had received unexpected guests. He had a face like a bank clerk's, except that the lines in it were deeper and his eyes were exhausted from night work. A certain air of dignified weariness was his distinguishing characteristic.

Jastrau had very little contact with him. But they had quarreled that afternoon, and Jastrau was never able to rest easily until differences between himself and others were disposed of.

"Well, Ole Jastrau, have you been out and voted the right way?"

"I didn't vote."

"It's strange about you, Ole Jastrau. You don't really go along with the paper's policies."

Jastrau did not know why he never looked the copy editor directly in the eye.

"You don't, Ole Jastrau. Otherwise, you would not have written the review of Stefani's book the way you did."

"He had it coming to him," Jastrau replied curtly.

"Yes, but he's one of our feature writers. Incidentally, he's here tonight. And the book can't be nearly as bad as you made it out to be. Vuldum says that the descriptions of the Syrian landscape—of the fig tree, for example—are as good as anything out of Johannes Jørgensen."

"I didn't think that Vuldum read Danish books," Jastrau commented sharply.

"Look, there's something else I wanted to see you about. Come in here for a moment." The copy editor laid his hand on Jastrau's shoulder and guided him into his office.

"Look at this," he said, pulling out a drawer full of manuscripts and proof sheets. "Yes, Editor Iversen has suddenly ordered all proofs for the book page sent down here, and look at this poem that you sent up today and let the cashier's office pay for. This poem—well, Editor Iversen doesn't exactly think it's a thing of beauty. Tell me, who is this Steffensen?"

"Ha!" said Jastrau, laughing. "He's Stefani's son."

The copy editor laid the poem back on the desk and looked up at Jastrau in surprise.

"But it's signed 'Steffensen.'"

"Oh, that's because he hates his father. He doesn't even want to use his name."

The copy editor smiled.

"Yes, but how are our readers going to know that? Of course, his name has to be Stefani. Otherwise we're not interested in printing the poem."

"Lord knows if he'll go along with that," Jastrau said hesitatingly.

"Of course he will. You'll see to it. And then one of these days we'll send it up to be set. I can find a place for it in the main section. But you'll take care of that matter of the name, won't you, Ole Jastrau?"

He picked up the pen from his desk, crossed out the name "Steffensen" with one swift stroke, and wrote in "Stefani."

"Editor Iversen will certainly be interested to hear about this," he added, nodding enthusiastically. "But, as I was saying, you're not really in contact with the paper, Ole Jastrau, not yet. You should, of course, have voted today, and voted the Radical ticket."

"Is *Dagbladet* a Radical paper, then?" Jastrau asked ironically.

The copy editor did not answer. He began to cross out the headline on an article that lay on the desk before him. "This doesn't sound right," he said, as if to himself. Jastrau recognized it as the signal for him to leave.

So Editor Iversen had asked to have all the proofs for his book page

70

sent down for inspection. Was this not humiliating? Did it not indicate a lack of confidence in him as an editor? It was all that was needed to make his position as literary editor shaky. All it took to pull the rug out from under him was for a literary quack like Stefani to come storming in to the old man in the corner office.

He remained standing irresolutely in the vestibule among the celebrities, who were becoming boisterous. It seemed to him that they all wore big heavy overcoats. He fervently hoped that none of them would speak to him. If he had not at some time or other offended one of them, then he had touched a sore spot of one of his friends, or ruffled the prejudices of a third, and they would gladly see him humiliated. Yes, it was humiliating—this business of ordering the proofs down for scrutiny. A photograph of Bjørnson hung on the wall. He was sure that it was only because they were not contemporaries that he had never had any differences with him.

"Well, I must say you look mighty arrogant, Herr Jastrau," a voice near him said. It was his affable colleague Otto Kryger, the business editor, who suddenly stood next to him. His hawk-like nose and wide sensitive lips made him look a little like an Indian. His blue-black hair and low forehead might well have been topped by a feathered bonnet. But he was too puny.

"No I don't," Jastrau replied crossly, like an offended schoolboy.

"Maybe you're only feeling blue. But you certainly have reason to feel that way if you take the Radical view of things."

Jastrau looked dully into the dark twinkling eyes and felt no desire to make an ironical reply, although that was the accepted manner of repartee among *Dagbladet*'s staff.

"I didn't vote at all," he said languidly.

"So that's the view you take of things. Then, of course, you have to act accordingly," said Otto Kryger. Jastrau could not understand his unaccustomed friendliness.

"I voted Conservative," added Kryger in a subdued tone with a touch of mischievousness in it.

Jastrau shook his head and smiled. His expression could be interpreted as one of hopelessness.

"Yes, it's too crazy for words," Kryger went on. "But come along with me. I'd like to have a little talk with you. First I have to go in and see if there's anything for me on my desk."

Taken by surprise, Jastrau let himself be taken in tow. Moreover, he had just then seen a well-known Ph.D. stick his bald oblong head in through the doorway and then step into the vestibule. Jastrau remembered something about a subordinate clause in one of his reviews a few months earlier—a sliver up under the fellow's fingernail, so to speak—so he thought it just as well to go along with Kryger into the editorial room which the staff had dubbed The Peristyle.

But what could Kryger want with him? They seldom talked to each other, and their relationship had always been extremely formal.

The Peristyle, which like the other rooms in the editorial department was decorated in yellow, had received its antiquated name because of a square pillar or column that stood in the middle of the room. Around it had been built a large table on which always lay a clutter of the day's Copenhagen newspapers, as well as those from the provinces. And on the pillar were lettered the names of all those who had worked for *Dagbladet* at least twenty-five years. Tradition's venerable pillar surrounded by the last twenty-four-hours' news. Now and then a quip was made about it.

"Wait here for just a minute," said Kryger, disappearing into his room.

Jastrau sat down on the edge of a low cabinet and began studying the personal notices posted on a black bulletin board. A missing fountain pen—well, well. A note of thanks from a co-worker who had just been feted on his fiftieth birthday: "Please accept my—" and so on. And then—ha ha—a couple of clippings from *Dagbladet* with sections that had been heavily underlined. One of them which began with "I"—underscored in red—went on to exhibit a profusion of "I's" and a veritable blood bath of red pencil marks. The other was a fragment of an article on a philosophical theme with a badly mangled sentence in it. Two manifestations of the newsmen's reciprocal application of lynch law in the punishment of that gravest of all crimes, the writing of wretched Danish.

For the moment the room was rather quiet. But overhead there was a tramping of feet. That was up in the lecture room. And from the throng out in the square came a roar like that of heavy surf. Now and then one of the workers would go dashing by.

"Did you vote Radical?" Jastrau amused himself by asking one of them. The answer was a noncommital mutter. There was nothing interesting about this election.

Only when the reporter who covered the Rigsdag came rushing in, with his troubled features prominently displayed, was there a subdued explosion.

"Yes. What else was I supposed to do?" he replied testily.

"Ha ha," laughed Jastrau. "Listen to this, Herr Kryger," he continued as Kryger came back from his errand, "I've finally found a true Radical Liberal."

The legislative reporter did not let himself be detained, but he could not avoid hearing Kryger's sarcastic remark.

"Yes, and he's all that's left of the Radical Liberal youth movement."

Kryger sat down on the low cabinet beside Jastrau.

"As a matter of fact, I thought you too were naïve."

"Why so?" Jastrau asked in surprise.

"Oh, I don't know," Kryger replied as he settled down in chummy fashion next to Jastrau. "Incidentally, won't you have a cigar? Here, allow me. But it seems to me that your literary criticism gives some indication of it."

He cast a sidelong glance at Jastrau.

"Of my being a Radical Liberal? No, but do you know what? I've just stirred up a rumpus with one of my reviews. It was labeled blasphemous."

"Well then, you can see for yourself I was right. That's radicalism in the good old-fashioned sense of the word—anti-religious, anti-nationalist. I thought as much."

"That kind of radicalism is dead," Jastrau answered spitefully.

Kryger slapped him genially on the shoulder.

"Then we're in agreement."

"No," replied Jastrau, moving a little away from Kryger. He was dumbfounded at the fellow slapping him on the back that way, and he was growing suspicious.

After this ironic disengagement, they both remained silent for a little while. Kryger carefully clipped off the tip of his cigar, lit it just as painstakingly, and flicked out the match.

"By the way, do you think your name will ever adorn that pillar?" he asked, swinging his foot out elegantly toward the column of names. He was wearing patent leather shoes.

"No. And neither will yours. Haven't you noticed, incidentally, that the majority of them are names of typographers or other anonymous Joes? There are very few journalists represented there—people who write what they think."

"Yes, one can't help but see that," Kryger said with a smile. "And so you don't think you'll make it. I'm inclined to agree with you. As for me, it goes without saying that I won't."

"If you did, it would be an insult to the paper." Jastrau had to edge away because the neat little man was crowding so close to him.

"Why so?"

"Your articles on business, of course. They're so conservative, so very conservative."

"I find it impossible to go along with you there," Kryger replied.

Now his wide lips had come very close, and his teeth gleamed as if he were going to bite but was hiding the inclination to do so with a smile. "My articles are based on common sense," he went on. "Isn't that what you base your reviews on?"

"Yes, but a better kind of common sense than yours."

"Well then, man, you'll end up on the pillar after all."

"No, never," Jastrau said with contempt. He laughed loud and scornfully, but he felt as if all his strength were being drained out of him.

Kryger, on the other hand, tilted his head to one side and looked fondly at his quarry.

"I don't quite understand you," he purred on in a teasing manner. "After all, what you're writing about is nothing but art, and that's a field in which you have quite a lot of latitude. The sort of thing you do demands very little responsibility."

"Really?" said Jastrau abstractedly as he stared into the distance. This fastidious little man, who could become so savage and who was edging up so close to him, what was in the back of his mind? Did he not have the same distorted twist to his mouth, the mask-like expression, that so many of those up here in the editorial offices went around with and that was so appalling when one became aware of it? Jastrau passed the palm of his hand over his face as if to get rid of the impression. But it remained with him. It was his tendency to see others in terms of caricature that sometimes unnerved him. He did not want to go away now in such a frame of mind.

"Anyhow, that's the way it seems to me." What difference did it make how it seemed to Kryger? Once again, like so many times before, an atmosphere of unreality pervaded The Peristyle. Kryger continued to regard him with a searching look. These yellow walls—a color that ate into your consciousness! Weren't the walls really transparent? Would they not flutter aside like a flimsy veil in another second—just one more second? Or had he been smoking too much?

Kryger thought Jastrau had been offended.

"Now don't take me too seriously. What does it matter to the public what you think about high finance? You're a lucky fellow. Yes, take my word for it, you'll end up with your name on that pillar."

But Jastrau only looked down at his vest, upon which the ashes from his cigar were dropping. Now, again, he felt unsure of himself. Ashes falling on his vest—just as if he were a helpless old man.

"Now I don't want you to think that I have a low opinion of art. But I've never been able to understand what it has to do with a newspaper." Kryger kept slashing away at him, attacking from unpredictable directions. What was he trying to do?

"We have to make use of whatever talents we have," Jastrau protested, staring vacantly out into the room.

"Yes, and go right on using them so that the newspapers can keep up their intellectual pretensions. That's it. But take *Dagbladet*, for example. A long time ago it swung over from being a political organ to being a nonpolitical enterprise. I'm not thinking about tonight. Tonight we're all concerned with politics. But otherwise—otherwise it's simply a business enterprise."

"Yes, a business enterprise that deals in opinions," Jastrau interposed for the sake of saying something. Opinions! Something as nebulous as opinions. But why did people, too, become like shadows—ghosts—when they sold their opinions? They were all like ghosts up here, all dealing in nebulosities.

"No," objected Kryger—this ghost sitting next to him. Couldn't he understand that it was impossible for him to make contact with Jastrau?

"No," Kryger went on, "it's a business from which people can buy the opinions that they don't know they had beforehand. Isn't that more nearly correct?"

"Oh, it drives me nuts to think about it!" Jastrau exclaimed. He could no longer stand it. Was it the central heating that thinned his blood to a degree that made him see visions? He didn't know. But he did know that in this atmosphere, where it seemed that shapes and colors were about to dissolve, it struck him that all his colleagues' eyes were like pools of glue. Oh, these journalists—these journalists! His ghostly comrades. And then to top it off, Journalist Bruun came strutting by in his conspicuous light suit and riding boots.

"How did you vote, Bruun?" Jastrau called out to him.

"I voted for the future, my friends," Bruun replied with a haughty gesture. A hard look came over his face when he saw Kryger.

"You wouldn't be one of the sixteen Communists who voted in Vanløse, would you?" Kryger asked hostilely.

"That's a good bit of news. I wouldn't have thought there were that many reasonable people in Vanløse."

Disregarding his answer, Kryger fired another question at him.

"Why aren't you wearing your red star tonight? Or is it hidden behind the lapel of your coat?"

"The stars aren't shining in Denmark—not yet," Bruun said haughtily to conceal his irritation as he turned to go. But he had taken only a few steps before he exclaimed, "But they will be some day, believe me!" And when he had proceeded into the hallway he turned suddenly and shouted, "And just in case you should have any more crazy questions, Herr Kryger, I'd prefer to have you send them to me in a letter."

Finally they saw him disappear, his hindquarters swaying dramatically with every step.

"My God," sighed Kryger, leaning back against the wall, "we certainly have a well-assorted stock-in-trade here in this shop. We even keep that sort of opinion on the shelves."

"One can tell that you're in the business end of it," Jastrau said sarcastically.

But Kryger was almost vehement. His dark eyes were flashing intensely.

"It's impossible not to look at things from the economic standpoint, my artistic friend," he said sharply. "Either you're red or you're black. There are no other colors. And that pillar there is nothing but a travesty—a memorial column erected in honor of those whose coloration was a mixture."

Jastrau did him the favor of laughing. But inwardly he was boiling. It was election night. Overhead there was a noisy shuffling of feet. A farcical performance in which the guests of a Radical Liberal newspaper rejoiced when a Social Democrat was elected. From out in the square the noise continued. An election in which the people shouted in glee at the shifting names on the screen in the corner window. One could just as well have amused them by putting a pair of hands together and moving the fingers so that a shadow picture of a horse, an elephant, an eagle, a man—or one of Eriksen's beer bottles— appeared on the screen.

"Of course, you believe in art for art's sake," Kryger went on, and Jastrau nodded a listless affirmative.

"That's so nice and safe." Now what was he getting at? "It's a fine, capitalistic point of view. You can produce brilliant poems, exciting novels, travel sketches, and romantic plays when you adopt such a point of view. Then why don't you do it? It's a wonderfully irresponsible basis on which to work." Jastrau made a wry face and threw up his arms. "No, don't misunderstand me, Herr Jastrau. I think that art for art's sake is an excellent conservative point of view—"

"Conservative?" exclaimed Jastrau in amazement, momentarily aroused from his lethargy.

Kryger nodded. "Yes—and entirely safe." His smile was now impertinent.

76

"Are you serious?" Jastrau snapped.

"What else is your viewpoint as a critic?"

Would he never let up? Jastrau hated to be made the subject of debate. He wanted to take a poke at this polished little conservative runt who was baiting him by turning communistic arguments against him. "No, don't misunderstand me," Kryger repeated. Misunderstand him? Fiddlesticks!

"No, God help me!" Jastrau burst out.

"Disinterestedness. Isn't that what it's called?" said Kryger, smiling still more brazenly. "But of course, it's not a viewpoint at all. It's an expedient. Like art for art's sake. But I suppose a critic on a paper that vacillates between a political policy and what's good for its business has to resort to it." Then he went on very gently, as if slowly sticking a dagger into Jastrau's middle: "I guess you're not so naïve as I thought. It's a good opportunistic attitude. You just don't make the most of it."

Jastrau sprang down from the cabinet in a rage.

"What the hell are you—"

"Please now, don't misunderstand me," Kryger said in a mild tone of voice and raised his hand reassuringly. "I'm only sitting here and drawing conclusions."

"You mean I'm a phoney?"

"I mean you're a respectable bourgeois—just like me and every other reasonable person. You just don't realize it yourself."

"You're crazy!" exclaimed Jastrau furiously. "Bourgeois? Me? I don't want to talk to you any more. But a work of art can be art— Hell, what am I saying? I mean a piece of work can be art and be either conservative or communistic."

"Yes, considered from the professional angle. But that's not a point of view."

"What do I care about the point of view?"

Kryger also got down off the low cabinet.

"Precisely. But neither can you budge from your viewpointless point of view. It's as if you want to run off to all corners of the world at the same time—"

For a little while Jastrau remained standing still with his eyes shut. His head was swimming. He smiled wearily as he said, "Well, I guess I'll be going. I can't stand it up here any longer."

"It was nice to talk with you, Herr Jastrau."

"Yes, and to make it clear that my talents are very limited."

"Well, I wouldn't put it exactly that way."

Then, with a quick handshake, Kryger disappeared into the telegram editor's office, while Jastrau quietly went and mingled with the guests in the vestibule, the celebrities. A single one among them called out his name. He did not stop, but went on to the stairway, intent on leaving.

"Well, here you are—at last."

He ran right into Steffensen, who stood on the landing with his hands in his pockets and his cap perched on the back of his head. He looked like a jobless drifter as he stood there rocking on unsteady legs.

"I'd like to buy you a drink, now that I have some money," he said, grinning.

Jastrau looked at him and suddenly experienced again the animosity he had felt upon first meeting him.

"I don't feel like it."

"Oh, rubbish—"

"No, I'm going home."

"Nonsense. Here I've been running around looking for you. I was up there in the lecture hall," he said with a toss of his head in that direction. "Phew! I laid myself open to an encounter with my old man. And what a look he gave me! He was up there listening to the election returns. Ugh! He looked so high and mighty, sitting there staring at his pink fingernails. He was with that red-haired fellow. You know the one I mean—"

What a way to talk about his father. But there was something else that gave Jastrau a start. Stefani and Vuldum! They had been talking together. So it was Vuldum who had spilled the beans. He had thought as much. But why? Why had he done it? The other evening Vuldum had sat listening to the review with evident relish, but nevertheless—

"Let's go down and have a highball," said Steffensen.

In the Bar des Artistes the election-night mood was even more frenetic than up at *Dagbladet*. The room was obscured in a thick blue cloud of tobacco smoke, the steady hum of voices rose now and then to a tumult of laughter, and the sound of crackling ice came incessantly from the cocktail shaker. "Four highballs here!" "Bacardi!" "A small Dubonnet!" "Champagne!" And in the background, the steady droning of the phonograph—Hawaiian guitar music, a saxophone, xylophone, and a Negro chorus singing the blues—a mild but sustained anesthetic that served to provide a rhythmic background for the monotonous rounds of highballs and cocktails. And whenever the phonograph stopped, a new and unceasing sound rent the atmosphere from a ventilator—a noise that unhinged one's brain.

The room was alive with festivity, and Jastrau and Steffensen gazed out at the innumerable heads. Red and glistening bald pates. Craniums with twenty white hairs, carefully parted. Hair brushed back in pompadour style, with a distinguished sprinkling of gray around the ears. Hair with expansive bald patches over the temples. Men and more men. A solitary smooth, round, blonde, page-boy bob, so even that it must have been cut with the help of a bowl. And a single blue-black hairdo on a woman with a nasal voice. Otherwise, men. Only men. Hoarse voices and piercing cackles as from a chicken yard. And in the background, the white face of the clock and Lundbom's round, flushed, ingratiating countenance—sun and moon in the same quarter of the sky.

"My, how good it seems not to have to think," Jastrau said in a tone of relief.

Lundbom nodded to them familiarly with a gracious smile. What? Did he already know him?

Lundbom nodded again. "Good evening, Herr Jastrau—Herr Editor." He even spoke to him by name. A warm, comfortable feeling came over him, a sense of being at home. And there, at the round table, sat Kjær and Little P. How ridiculous. He had been in the place only once before. And already he had the cozy feeling of being at home.

At length they found chairs and sank submerged into the sea of people and the hum of voices as if into a big soft feather bed. Steffensen stretched out his legs and brusquely ordered whiskey, and soon two glasses stood before them, sweating and fizzing, with a subdued tinkling of ice like bells from a fairyland.

"I can't think tonight," said Jastrau.

"Why do you have to think? We came here to relax," said Steffensen with a grin.

"And I find myself thinking anyhow."

"Don't you think I know it? It's the phonograph that's putting ideas into your head."

And it was not very long before Jastrau was involved in a long political dissertation. "The Social Democrats will win. You'll see." Steffensen laughed and replied with the monotonous, one-syllable word that expressed his views on the subject. "Shit," he said, then laughed again. But all the while his eyes had a cold, glassy luster that made chills run up Jastrau's spine.

He went on, "You'll see. An election like this is an absolute waste of time." Steffensen's rigid lips twisted in a smiling grimace, but the expression in his eyes remained the same. "It doesn't make a damn bit of difference. Because it's not the Rigsdag that governs. It's nothing but a safety valve for the people's craving for power."

"U-uh, u-uh," came the voices of a Negro chorus from the phonograph. And Jastrau's thoughts continued to flow from him like long, unending strips of paper. "U-uh," sang the Negroes. "We'll have a new government, but we'll have the same old department heads." "Uh-uh, u-uh." "Damned if anyone can make out who governs Denmark, but in any event it isn't the Rigsdag."

"No, thank God," growled Steffensen. He sat slouched against the wall—an overgrown lout, almost a hooligan. Now and then Lundbom glanced at him mistrustfully.

Jastrau did not really care about being with him. He had no graces whatever. Everything was out of proportion—his forehead was too high, his teeth were so small that it looked as if he had too many of them, and the pores were too conspicuous in a nose that seemed abnormally large, like that of an adolescent boy.

But there was, after all, that noteworthy poem—a bit of arson committed by a neurotic boy. He was inclined to view him in the light of that poem.

"And isn't it strange," he went on, "that all these things I think about—all these political matters—seem so unreal to me? Including your game with the police. Yes, now you'll be given an amnesty. Isn't it strange that I seem to find far more reality in that poem you let me have than in all this other stuff? And by the way, I wanted to ask you—"

He stopped suddenly. Steffensen's face had turned deathly pale.

Jastrau followed his glance. Down at the entrance, a tall figure had thrust aside the red portières and was making a conspicuous appearance with his light-colored coat, wavy crown of white hair, and radiant, smooth-shaven smile. It was the eternally young H. C. Stefani. And behind his shoulder, Jastrau saw Vuldum's long chalk-white face and the black St. Peter's dome.

Jastrau did not want to be seen by them and ducked his head. But they came nearer and stopped right behind Jastrau's chair.

"No, it's too crowded here," he heard Stefani say.

Steffensen, on the other hand, sat directly facing them. They could not help seeing him as he sat with his head leaned against the wall so that his cap was lifted to reveal his tousled hair. Why did he keep his cap on in such a place anyway? His face was tilted slightly to one side and the light fell directly on it. The inexplicable expression of anger that was always in evidence about his lips became more coarse and pronounced, and his eyes glinted green as ice.

Suddenly Jastrau felt a finger tap him on the shoulder. He shrank into himself, but turned his head. It was Arne Vuldum's chalk-white face that nodded at him.

80

"Good evening, Ole," he said with a polite but deadly smile. "We're leaving," he added. His tone was indulgent and friendly. Then he looked across at Steffensen and pursed up his lips astringently.

H. C. Stefani nodded coldly.

Jastrau could only nod and smile vaguely. Was his smile polite enough? Or did it reflect his confusion—give him away? The sweat stood out on his forehead.

And then the two gentlemen were gone, on their way out of the place again—two tall, dignified backs. Vuldum looked as if he had been lifted high above the crowd.

Slowly they vanished behind the red portières—with a proper theatrical touch, the way a portière should be handled.

Jastrau could hear Steffensen getting his breath back. But he was pale as a corpse and his eyelids were white and bloodless.

"Two whiskeys, waiter," he said.

"Shall I take the gentleman's hat?" the little waiter inquired impertinently.

"All right," said Steffensen, disregarding the tone of voice and indifferently handing over his cap. "But let's have two whiskeys."

Then, with a serious expression, he suddenly leaned forward and, looking Jastrau straight in the eye, said brusquely: "Now, no more talk about politics. I'm here to have a good time." Then, with a sigh: "God knows I need it."

"What shall we talk about?"

"You might tell me a dirty story. That would do me some good." But his voice sounded insincere. There was something furtive about it.

Jastrau shook his head.

"Well, then I know one, and it's the best story in the world," said Steffensen. It was he who wanted to tell a story, and right away. He made a wry face. Was he being cynical or just self-conscious? One thing was certain—the look in his eyes made it clear that he was watching for something. He was carefully observing every expression on Jastrau's face.

"You see, there's this man who meets his doctor on the street. The man is embarrassed and looks down at his pink fingernails. 'Look,' he says to the doctor, 'my son is sick—he's picked up a disease.' 'Well,' says the doctor, 'nothing serious, I hope.' 'No,' the man tells him, '—it's only that—well, you understand—these youngsters don't know how to look out for themselves.' 'Well, ha ha, old boy, don't let that worry you,' says the doctor. 'Just send him up to me and we'll soon have him fixed up.'"

Steffensen related the story very naturally, as if it might have been based on fact. He had obviously told it many times before. He went on:

"But then the fine gentleman looks at the doctor for a little while and says, 'Yes, but you see it's our housemaid who's—' 'Ah, ha ha!' laughs the doctor, 'then send her up to see me along with the boy. Oh, these young people, these young people, ha ha!' And the doctor shakes his head. 'But,' says the fine gentleman, looking down at his pink fingernails, 'it's worse than that, because, you see, I and the housemaid—well, you know, it's hard to leave the lambs alone.' At this the doctor begins to roar with laughter. 'Ah, you old goat—a youngster's disease, is that what it is?' he says. But then suddenly he stops, grows thoughtful, and asks nervously: 'What about your wife? She isn't—she didn't get it too, did she?' The other man nods. 'You don't say!' says the doctor, beginning to look terrified. 'Now I'll have to say good-by. I just remembered an appointment, and I'll have to hurry.'"

Jastrau let out an obliging roar of laughter. But Steffensen was staring at him in dead seriousness, a questioning look in his eyes. His mouth hung open, as if he were afflicted with a bad case of adenoids.

"It's funny, isn't it?" he asked in an almost imbecile fashion.

"Yes, very funny." And Jastrau laughed again.

"I mean, it's really comical. A really comical story, isn't it?"

"Yes, yes. It's a fine story."

"Yes, isn't it? It seems so to me. Ha ha." But Steffensen's laughter sounded hollow.

Jastrau looked at him closely. There was something he didn't understand. Steffensen's eyes had a far-away look in them, and he stopped gaping and drew his lips together tightly. There was nothing to indicate that he had enjoyed the story. Then suddenly he asked in a voice that betrayed nervousness:

"No one could possibly misunderstand it, do you think? It's comical, isn't it? It couldn't be—be taken seriously, could it?"

"Are you always so serious when you tell dirty stories? Do you always analyze them so thoroughly?"

"Well—no," Steffensen said stiffly. "But now we'd better have a couple more whiskeys."

He took several long pulls at his drink, and with each swallow his Adam's apple shot forth like a clenched fist.

Then Jastrau thought it was his friendly duty to come up with a story himself.

But when he had told it, Steffensen's laughter sounded strangely cold and unsympathetic.

In the meantime, the commotion around them had grown more

boisterous. Some of the customers were shouting. An advertising agent and a lawyer had gotten into a quarrel, and a little waiter was scurrying around, trying to separate them with the help of one of his colleagues who looked just as boyish. The waiters at the Bar des Artistes always looked as if they had just grown out of their bellboy uniforms.

"Two more whiskeys," Steffensen bellowed.

"Hadn't we better call it a night?" Jastrau objected. But Steffensen only stared at him with a sober yet spiteful expression.

"Are you with me, or aren't you?"

Jastrau felt himself growing weary.

"Now go ahead and drink, and don't be a spoilsport," Steffensen growled.

"Yes, that's right." The remark came from a fat old man with a blood-red face who had suddenly staggered up to their table and was wedging his colossal bulk between them. A white expanse of dress shirt protruded from between his vest and the top of his pants, as if he were coming apart. "That's right. You should stop being a bore. That's what you should do." The words drooled from his thick lips. "How about a drink, boys? That's the stuff. Don't be a bore." He began poking a finger at Steffensen's chest, but staggered as he did so.

"Oh go on, you old buffalo! Why don't you look where you're going?" Steffensen exclaimed, grinning.

The two waiters came running toward them, but the old man had regained his balance. "My name is Larsen. Ladies' lingerie." His face lit up in a crafty alcoholic smile. "A dangerous line of business. Nothing for young fellows to get into. Nothing for little Buster-boy here." He flung his arms around the little waiter and tapped him on the head. "We want some highballs here," he said, brushing the back of his hand across the tabletop so that the glasses capsized and the whiskey ran out over the table. "Highballs, little Buster-boy—highballs!"

Finally his bulky frame was shoved into a chair, and he sat staring at Jastrau with moist, lusterless oyster-eyes.

"You're a tax collector," he said. "I can tell by your looks. Ho! But you look like a nice fellow. Ooh—the way you're wobbling around, Buster-boy!" The waiter was wiping off the drenched table top. "And you," he went on, turning to Steffensen, "no—you're certainly no tax-collector—ha ha—and it was you who called me a buffalo. But look—what's happened to those drinks?"

Steffensen laughed loudly.

"Are you buying cigars too, grandpa?"

83

"Now, now—no sponging young man—no sponging."

Jastrau shoved back his chair.

"I'd better be getting home," he said.

"Nonsense!" exclaimed Steffensen.

"Right you are. Pure nonsense," philosophized Larsen, the lingerie man. "Who said 'home?' We never go home—we never go home," he hummed.

At this point, Jastrau noticed Steffensen looking at him speculatively. He was still sober.

"Look," Steffensen said, "I forgot to get the key from Bernhard. I don't suppose I could spend the night on your sofa again?"

Jastrau nodded.

Chapter Six   The following morning Johanne came into the bedroom in a rage. "We can't go on letting him stay here forever. Now the Social Democrats have won, he has nothing to be afraid of."

Jastrau was looking at himself in the mirror as he shaved. His face was puffy and his eyes looked red under their heavy lids.

"No," he snarled.

"But we really can't," Johanne repeated emphatically. She was pale with fury. "Adolf is coming for lunch, and what will he think?"

"Hell, that's right. And he'll probably hang around all afternoon."

"There you go again!" exclaimed Johanne. "That's always the way it is when it's someone from my family who's coming. I tell you, I can't stand it!" She turned suddenly and walked away, slamming the door behind her.

Jastrau rinsed the soap from his face and dried it, looked into the mirror again, and shook his head. They had gotten pretty tight the night before. The election-night atmosphere. On the way home they had bought the morning papers and confirmed that the Social Democrats had won. Hurrah! "Now you're a free man, Stefan," Jastrau had said with idiotic sincerity.

Now he had to go in and see to him.

"Father! The man is snoring," Oluf said, wide-eyed, as he ran toward him when he entered the dining room. "He's going 'rr—uuu.'"

Jastrau moved the boy gently out of his way and went on into the living room.

Steffensen lay on the sofa, fully clothed and in such an unsightly, distorted position that it looked as if his legs and belly had been screwed crookedly onto the rest of his body.

"Ho there! You've got to get up," Jastrau roared, shaking him. There was an ill-natured growl, and Steffensen slowly opened his eyes. They had a glazed and baleful look.

"Look here, you've got to see if you can't make yourself look like a human being, because I'm expecting my brother-in-law."

Steffensen rubbed his eyes and looked askance at him.

"Brother-in-law coming?" he said sleepily as he made a wry face.

"Yes."

"What sort of a person is he?"

"A stockbroker's runner."

"Does he drink?"

Jastrau laughed. "Yes, he has nothing against it—when he's in the right company."

"Thanks, that's all I need to know."

"But listen to me. You've got to get shaved and cleaned up before he comes," Jastrau said with an irritated abruptness that sounded like a command.

"Take it easy now," Steffensen grunted. But then he suddenly sat up, stretched, and yawned. "Ah—we had a fine time yesterday," he said. "The only trouble was that I didn't get drunk enough." He gave a heartfelt sigh.

Little by little, Jastrau managed to persuade him to get up. He had to entice him, almost trick him, into the bedroom. Out in the kitchen, he had to set the water on to boil himself, because Johanne was busy getting the lunch ready and the only thing she had said was, "Isn't he going soon?" "No," Jastrau had said, "he's staying for lunch." Then he had to go back and practically force the shaving brush and the Colgate's on Steffensen.

"A compulsory shave," said the latter, grinning.

Jastrau kept after him relentlessly. "Now, here's the hot water. All you have to do is get lathered up." Sometimes Steffensen's glance flashed spitefully and capriciously, so that he felt he had to let up a bit. Nevertheless, he thought he detected a streak of weakness in Steffensen's rough personality. "Here's a necktie, Stefan," he said.

And so it came about that Steffensen was able to sit on the sofa, smooth-shaven and presentable, albeit a little green in the face, when brother-in-law Adolf Smith-Jørgensen put in his appearance—a neatly dressed gentleman with light-blond hair brushed back from his forehead, a ruddy face, and no eyebrows. He was, in fact, a bit too pink and white, like a little pig.

"Hello, Sister dear." He kissed her on the cheek and embraced her so effusively that her gold necklace tinkled against the band of his wrist watch. "And how are you, sonny? Can you say hello to your Uncle Adolf?" he went on, lifting Oluf into the air. "And you, Brother-in-law—hello, hello. How are things? The same as always, I presume? That's what I thought—no reason to complain."

Jastrau introduced his brother-in-law to Steffensen. "Glad to make your acquaintance. It seems to me I've heard your name before. You're a poet, aren't you?"

"No," Steffensen mumbled.

"No?" said Smith-Jørgensen, sitting down and rubbing his big, flabby hands together. "So much the better, because I don't mind telling you that I can't put up with all these poets and celebrities that one bumps into here at my sister's."

Johanne stood in the background, pale and with an ominous expression. Her brother quickly changed the subject.

"Well, sonny." He turned to Oluf, who immediately ran to him and leaned against his knee. "Well, sonny, what do you think your uncle has brought you? Can you guess?"

"Yes!" exclaimed Oluf, standing on his toes. "Chocolate."

"Right, my boy. You have a good nose, and the devil take me if you didn't come by it from your uncle. But there are many kinds of chocolate. What kind is it?"

He held a small package in the air as if he wanted Oluf to jump for it.

"A cigar."

"Right, sonny."

And he handed him the chocolate cigar with the utmost solemnity.

Then lunch was served, and Smith-Jørgensen had an opportunity to grow really expansive. He looked pompous as he sat with the green akvavit decanter poised in his hand. He exuded affability in all directions and seemed coated with a glossy varnish of self-complacency. Opposite him, his sister had pulled herself together, too. Her brother's presence made her feel better. She was mistress of the house. Once in a while she was entitled to feel happy. But Jastrau sat hunched up in his chair looking tired and dissipated, with his thoughts apparently elsewhere between every remark that was made, so that such amiability as he was able to command came in little bursts like steam from a heating pipe.

Steffensen was mute and oblivious to what was going on as if he sat alone at a table in a café. He took so little notice of the others that it seemed as if all he lacked was a newspaper to read while he ate.

"I really don't understand you, my dear Jastrau," Smith-Jørgensen said.

"What don't you understand?" asked Jastrau. A little steam-cloud of amiability—puff. He smiled. Puff.

"Well, you see," replied Smith-Jørgensen, thrusting his arms out in an elegant gesture so that the cuffs shot out from his coat sleeves, "the other day I sat down to read some of my famous brother-in-law's works, and do you know what? I found them really quite interesting, these things of yours. But what good do they do you?"

"What do you mean, what good do they do me?"

"Oh, you know as well as I do. You'll never get a statue out of them—like Goethe. Ha ha. Because while anyone who knows you might get a lot of fun out of reading them, otherwise—good Lord— what use are they? Am I right, Herr Steffensen?"

"Yes." Steffensen nodded indifferently and went right on munching on a pickled herring.

"If you made some money out of them, it wouldn't be so bad," the brother-in-law went on. "But you don't. Now it's true that I haven't studied or read as much as you." Here he tapped his forehead with a finger. "All I have is what's up here, but it tells me that you've got hold of things from the wrong end. You aren't a business man, and unless you are it's no use. You don't get ahead in the world unless you have a business sense."

Jastrau smiled. Puff.

"Yes, you smile, my dear Ole," said his brother-in-law, laying his hand on Jastrau's shoulder and looking him straight in the eye. "After all, money is a good thing. Isn't that right, old girl?"

Johanne nodded understandingly. And Steffensen suddenly shifted his position. He planted his elbows on the table, leaned his chin on his hands, and began to stare at Smith-Jørgensen as if he were a freak.

Smith-Jørgensen grew a little embarrassed. A deep, perpendicular furrow appeared between his eyebrows, as though scratched by a nail.

"I've often thought about writing, myself," he began again after a brief pause. Now he spoke very softly, and his eyes sparkled like sunlit water at low tide. "If only one had the time," he sighed. "For I know what it is that people want. They want to know something about themselves. They want to know something about the great times we're living in. They are great times, you know." His voice rose in a notice-able crescendo. "There has never been a period as remarkable as this one. Just think of our inventions. Think of our big business men. What heads they have on their shoulders! What faculties for putting two and two together! People like that aren't concerned with fantasies. Take Ford, for example. He's a philosopher to boot. Such people's comprehension embraces everything." His eyes shone. "And what do you think such people care about a poem—or even a novel? What goes on in their heads is much more exciting." He touched his hand to his forehead as if assembling his thoughts and drawing the proper conclusions. "And it's such people that we want a book about. We want a book about them—these geniuses." Here he clenched his fist and beat the air for emphasis. "A book about the fight they're waging—a fight that thousands of people live by, and that thousands are crushed by. Write such a book, and the money will come pouring in."

Johanne sat staring at her brother. She had followed his remarks, first with a narrowed, critical glance, then with wide-eyed uneasiness, as if fearful he might bog down under the weight of his rhetoric. Now that he had landed safely, with elegance, dignity, a sweeping gesture, and the words "the money will come pouring in," she glanced fleetingly at the other two. Steffensen was still sitting with his elbows on the table, and Jastrau still wore the halfhearted smile that reflected a mixture of uncertainty and contempt. In contrast to the pink-cheeked Adolf they both looked rather frowzy, she thought.

"Yes, there might be something to what you say," Jastrau replied with a sluggish display of interest. "But think of all the things a poet has to be familiar with." They were words chosen at random.

"Yes, of course, a poet should be up on things," Smith-Jørgensen exclaimed, exultant over the impression he had made. "But you're afraid of the work involved, just like all the other poets without any backbone. That's the crux of the matter. Damn it all, you don't know anything about the life that goes on around you, and by God, you deserve your poverty. What difference does it make that you have talent? No, I tell you, talent has to be put under control. I only wish I had the time—then I'd tell you what to write. I'd give you some instructions. Then, with your talent, you could sit on your fanny and put it all down on paper, and afterwards I'd look it over and correct whatever was wrong with it. I tell you, I've often thought about it seriously."

As he was finishing his harangue, Steffensen got up without a word and went to the toilet. It was apparent that he knew the direction well.

Smith-Jørgensen's smile was suddenly transformed into a ludicrous gape, and he exclaimed indignantly, "For God's sake, one doesn't behave that way when people are sitting around over their coffee!"

Johanne also shook her head.

"Say, what kind of a person is this anyway?" said her brother.

"It's no wonder you ask," Johanne managed to say with a certain amount of pique before Jastrau could answer. "But it's plain to see that he feels himself at home."

"What a lout!"

"He's one of my friends," Jastrau replied slowly, as if he had anticipated the invective.

"He's a Bolshevik, that's what he is," Johanne said loudly. "And now that the Social Democrats have won, there's no need for him to hang around here any longer. Herr Sanders had the decency to stay away today. But every morning this fellow here is sprawled out on the sofa, and there's no getting rid of him. I can't even get things straightened up in there until he gets up."

"Hush, Johanne, he can hear you."

"I don't care."

"But I do."

"Listen now—listen," Adolf intervened, shaking his head disapprovingly, "—let's not get upset." Then, in the mildest, most conciliatory voice, he went on, "I don't suppose you'd have a drop of Benedictine. Just a drop to go with the coffee—to rinse it down. A small one, you know."

With his fingers he demonstrated how extremely small it should be.

"No. They drank it all," Johanne said before her husband could speak up.

At this point, Steffensen returned and slouched down in his place.

"That's a pity—a real pity," Smith-Jørgensen sighed with a shrug of his shoulders. "No wine cellar. Then you ought to come to my house. Really, Jastrau, you should seriously consider doing that some day. For there we have liquor. The shelves aren't empty, even though I had a party the other night—a little stag party. And by the way, Sister, I'm supposed to bring you greetings from Joachim, your girlhood sweetheart."

Johanne raised her head and her expression grew rigid.

"Thanks," she said.

"He was there. And Lord, how drunk they all got—dead drunk. Afterwards we went out to the Golden Age Club. Ha ha—God knows what became of them all. I haven't seen any of them since. But in the morning Joachim and I took a cab up to Helsingør. It was a beautiful Sunday morning, a little cold, but after all I have a good fur coat. We had a quick little breakfast at the Railway Hotel, then came back and had a bath—ah, a cold shower. But you and Joachim—well, ha ha. Anyway, you have something to look forward to when you come to see me."

"Yes, you lucky dog." Jastrau benevolently flattered him with his words. "I've often envied you your wine cellar."

"Earn some money, Brother-in-law. How often do I have to tell you that? You have plenty of opportunities." As he said this, he reached for *Dagbladet*. "God knows you have opportunities when you have a steady job with an enterprise as big as this." He slapped the newspaper with the flat of his hand. "But what do you write? Book reviews. All right, but now let's see how you go about it."

He unfolded the paper. But no sooner did Steffensen hear him resume his didactic tone than with a disgruntled jerk he moved his chair away from the table and over to the window. He made no effort to hide a sneer.

"Take for example this review of Stefani's book."

"I didn't write that, but let me see it!" Jastrau exclaimed.

Smith-Jørgensen surrendered the paper reluctantly and hitched up his trousers. He looked hurt. He felt his chain of thought interrupted, and this pained him.

Steffensen's rigid profile was outlined against the window. He was listening now and mechanically twirling his pipe between his hands.

"That's strange. Damned if it isn't," Jastrau muttered as he folded up the paper. Steffensen turned his head.

"What's strange?" asked Johanne.

"Well, it's not as favorable as I thought it would be. Eriksen—he's the one who wrote it—refers to Stefani as 'the spoiled charmer.' That's a bit of sarcasm, at any rate."

Over near the window, Steffensen let out a snort of laughter.

But Jastrau merely stared into space, and his brother-in-law took advantage of his preoccupation to grab the paper again.

"What I'd like to know," he began immediately, "is why you concern yourself with such trivialities? What difference does it make whether the reviewer calls him a spoiled charmer or not?"

"It doesn't make any difference. Nothing makes any difference," said Steffensen, laughing raucously. Oluf began to raise a fuss and kick his feet against the legs of his chair.

"Of course, I don't think it makes any difference either," said Smith-Jørgensen. He was irritated by the interruption. "It might be true, but it isn't the kind of information that's of use to anybody. Reviews can be all right, I'd say, when they tell what a book contains and whether it's a good book or a poor one. But you fellows write such deep and

90

learned stuff that a cat wouldn't bother to read it. Even if you only set down some thoughtful observations, a person might get some benefit out of it. But you don't do that either. I don't know what it is you do."

Steffensen and Jastrau both laughed. But Johanne had a sensitive ear, and she was beginning to feel uneasy on her brother's behalf. She helped Oluf down from his chair and set about clearing the table, making a lot of noise with the cups.

"What I'm saying is true," her brother continued, his face flushed with excitement. "The temper of the times—what I mean to say is that everything is so unsettled these days. We're all so busy—yes we are. Our time is so taken up that there's no opportunity to have thoughts of our own—yes, that's the way it is. That's how I feel about it, and there are many others who feel the same way."

Steffensen looked at him with unconcealed amusement.

"Yes, there are many others who feel the same way—who believe that it's the newspapers' duty to think—"

"The newspapers? Think? Now, by God, I've heard everything," Steffensen roared.

"Will you let me finish?" Johanne's brother said indignantly. He looked as if he were about to explode. "And as a matter of fact, we do have some thinking journalists—homespun philosophers, you might call them." Once more his manner became mild, his voice almost gentle. "Those fellows come up with a sensible thought every day—every single day—and that's the kind of writers we need, Ole—that's the point I'm trying to make. What I mean is, that sort of thing would be something for you, something useful—useful for those of us who don't have time to think ourselves, and useful for you as well. And it would pay damned well, you can be sure of that."

After having vented his feelings, he was once again his calm, smiling, supercilious self. "But money is still nice to have, old chap," he concluded and nodded to Jastrau.

"Adolf, don't you have to watch the time? You said you positively had to leave by one-thirty," Johanne interrupted.

"Yes, confound it, that's so!" exclaimed Adolf, pulling a large, flat, gold watch out of his pocket. It was polished so highly that it shone like a sun. "It's a good thing you reminded me."

"But wait just a bit," said Johanne, getting up. "Oluf and I have to go out for a little air, and we can go with you."

Her brother wrinkled his brow. "Don't be too long about it," he complained.

Finally Johanne was ready. The leather shoulder bag with the cowboy fringe dangled at her hip, and there was an audacious gleam in her eyes, as if she were planning to launch an attack. Oluf stood beside her in a heavy brown overcoat, shoving out his belly like a little horse trader. A brown stocking cap was pulled down over his ears.

At last they were ready to go. Jastrau wore an uneasy smile. He would not feel safe until they were well out the door.

Then Johanne launched the attack.

"And so, good-by, Herr Steffensen," she said in a polite but sharp-edged tone. "It's best that I say good-by to you now, because I'm sure you won't be here when I get back."

A faint blush colored Steffensen's cheeks as he clicked his heels together and bowed to her like a well-mannered schoolboy. But all he managed to utter was a hoarse "Good-by, Frue."

The three of them left.

For some time there was silence. Jastrau and Steffensen each sat smoking his pipe.

Finally Steffensen mumbled, "There was no mistaking what she meant."

Jastrau bit his pipestem and said nothing.

Steffensen took a breath and said, "And then that horse who would like to think! A real philosopher—God in Heaven!"

"Yes, my head is still swimming. But I guess I ought to pull myself together and get something done. I'm still pooped from last night."

Steffensen grinned. "And I suppose I'd better clear out."

"Oh, you might as well stay for the time being. Johanne won't be back right away."

They moved into the living room. Jastrau took a book from the stack of review copies and began to cut the pages. Steffensen sat on the sofa, picked up one of Jastrau's writing pads, and in a moment was busy drawing profiles and writing.

Jastrau was at loose ends. His thoughts were as unsubstantial as a cloud of dust. He found it impossible to understand how Steffensen could settle down to work so easily and calmly. Could it be that he had no hangover? He sat there sketching, sketching, sketching as if in a trance. Then, with a sudden start, he would write a line or perhaps an entire stanza. Jastrau told himself that he, too, had better get something done. Concentrate on the book that he had to review. Oh, to be able to produce again! He found himself unable to concentrate. How long it had been since he himself had written a book! Now it was always someone else's book that was waiting to be read and reviewed. And there was always a bill that was falling due. Bills! Just the thought of a bill that any moment might be shoved in through the mail slot—wasn't it enough to corrode a person's spinal cord? And the bill would have to be paid. One paid a penalty for being a respectable citizen.

And there, over on the couch, sat Steffensen, a big rawboned figure who had not the faintest idea of where he would sleep the next night. He had time and space to sit in, and that was all he needed. He could sit down and write wherever he was. Here and now.

Then the telephone rang.

Yes, that was the way it always was. There stood that apparatus, right in the middle of his room, and it rang every minute of the day. And then it was good-by to all dreams and thoughts.

"Yes, hello? Ole Jastrau speaking."

He heard his brother-in-law's voice. "Listen—you must excuse me for calling—but after all it's my sister you're married to. And I couldn't help feeling—I couldn't help feeling all the time I was up there with you . . . A person has certain sensibilities, you know, and can understand things even though they aren't made plain in so many words. Do you know what I mean?"

"No," Jastrau said curtly.

"No—I don't suppose so. I wanted to have a word with you in all seriousness, but I didn't have a chance with that lout you had up there. I imagine he's still there. But I want to tell you that he has a bad influence on you. I could notice it. You weren't at all yourself today. And then I had a talk with Johanne about it, and she told me what my own sensibilities long ago led me to think. And I want to say to you that it won't do in the long run. A home is a home. And you can't have that sort of vermin living with you. You owe your wife—my sister—a certain amount of consideration. And me too. Isn't that right?"

"Yes—you're right—you're right." Jastrau's face was contracted in a bitter frown.

"Well, that's why I called. I thought I'd tell you, even though you're older than I am. It's really just between two brothers-in-law, you know. And then—maybe now I'm being indiscreet—but aren't you boozing too much? After all, you're a married man, and I'm not. And she's my sister—"

Jastrau hung up.

The phone rang again.

"Let it ring," Jastrau said to Steffensen. "It's only that horse who likes to think."

They sank back in their chairs.

But Jastrau could not pull himself together. The white pages of the book shimmered before his eyes. It was the whiskey he had drunk the day before. There was also a certain instability in the objects around him, an animation that seemed to lurk in them and then suddenly dissolve everything in his line of vision into an hallucination. No, it was impossible to sit still. He was also conscious of an insidious restlessness in his rear end that made it necessary for him to get up and pace the floor. Go for an auto ride! Something had to happen. Here, in the daylight, he had the nagging feeling of being an outcast.

"If only the sun would set soon," he sighed.

"Why?" asked Steffensen. He had obviously finished his poem, because now he sat humming a tune he had composed himself, one that was presumably meant to correspond to the length and meter of the verses he had written.

"I wish it would get dark. The darkness calms a person down. What do you say we go out?"

"Yes, let's get out of here. She'll probably be back soon." Steffensen folded the sheet with his poem on it and put it in his pocket.

A little later they were strolling diagonally across Vesterbro Passage and past the obelisk of the Freedom Statue, which shone with a dull luster the color of old chocolate. The sun hung in a glowing afternoon haze above Vesterbro's rooftops, and even though Jastrau and Steffensen had their backs to it they were dazzled by the flickering light from the automobile windshields and bicycle handlebars—a constant stream of glistening glass and nickel that blinded them just as the traffic light changed at the corner by the Wivel.

They went on into Vesterbrogade.

"You don't have to go up to the paper?" Steffensen asked.

Jastrau looked up at *Dagbladet*'s red building. He caught sight of Vuldum through one of the windows on the second floor. The sunlight shone on his red hair as on a piece of metal. There was a consuming intensity about the pale night-denizen that reminded Jastrau of a flame burning in daylight.

"Not on your life!" he replied vehemently.

And they walked along farther toward the Bar des Artistes.

When its dark-red portières had finally closed behind them, and the semidarkness and the drone of the phonograph had engulfed them, they felt as if they had been precipitated headlong into another element. To be sure, the clock hung over the bar and indicated the time. But it was another thing entirely—like a clock in a moving picture, telling time for the actors in the film rather than for the spectators.

"Ah—now the sun has gone down," said Jastrau, puffing and sitting down at one of the nearest tables.

"What'll we have?" Steffensen asked gruffly.

"Peace, peace," sighed Jastrau. "Now we'll sink deeper and deeper out of sight. It's always night here, and there's always the sound of music. You don't get a chance to feel there's such a thing as emptiness. Now we'll very quietly—and very slowly—go to the dogs."

Up at the bar sat a group of well-dressed men—businessmen who always, about five o'clock, came in for their drink. Lundbom was all smiles. He felt honored, because these were "nice people."

But the round table, where Kjær and Little P. usually sat, was deserted.

Steffensen began to stuff his pipe.

"Hi there, waiter!" Jastrau called out. "Two cocktails—French and Italian vermouth, half and half."

The little waiter with the smile of a street urchin bowed.

"Oh hell!" exclaimed Steffensen. "Is that what you call going to the dogs?"

"Slowly—I said."

Both of them lapsed into silence.

But Jastrau felt tormented. Why was he sitting here with this person who seldom said a word? He saw him in the light of his poem, of course. But he did not understand him. Spasmodically he would utter a word or two, then shut up like a stone and become impenetrable.

"May I see your new poem?" Jastrau asked.

"Oh, go soak your head."

"Go soak your head?" It was an expression that had long ago gone out of fashion. Why had Steffensen used it? Did it indicate a crack in the mask of vulgarity he constantly wore. He usually insisted on using coarse language.

The lights were turned on in the room. It was evening, evening, and Jastrau felt it as a blessed relief. Now the sun was going down. No—someone drew the portières aside, and the blue daylight spilled in. A glimpse of hurrying traffic. Six o'clock. People were coming from work. Then the portières were drawn shut again. Yes, now the sun was going down—thank the Lord. It was like the soothing effect of a beer. It calmed him down.

"Are you thinking of publishing a collection of poems?"

"I suppose I'll have to. A collection of poems makes an ideal garbage can," replied Steffensen.

They fell silent again.

But the silence grated on Jastrau's nerves. The businessmen had left with a loud shout: "So long, old chap!" They were so British! And the place seemed deserted.

"I say, Lundbom, it looks sort of empty in here," Jastrau said to the fat Swede, who had seized the opportunity to take his evening walk down as far as the red portières.

"It usually is around six o'clock. But tonight there won't be many people here—not after an election night." Lundbom inclined his red moon-face to one side and screwed up his blue eyes knowingly. "They're resting up tonight," he said.

The phonograph had been turned off. Only the ventilator hummed, and even the tobacco smoke was being sucked out of the room.

Lundbom stood and smiled at them in genial, fatherly fashion. But soon it became evident that it was difficult to find a topic of conversation. The emptiness was audible, and the sound of the ventilator took on a symbolic significance. Emptiness. Emptiness! And suddenly the bulky, awkward figure—northern Europe's most eminent man with a cocktail shaker—stood there in his own saloon looking very lonely, and his smile became one of self-conscious embarrassment.

"I think we'd better go into the restaurant and get something in the way of food," Jastrau said suddenly, getting up from his chair. There was something about that embarrassed smile, a sick man's fear perhaps, that must not be allowed to erupt. "But we'll stay in the building, so we won't say good-by."

Lundbom's fat frame doubled up in an obsequious bow. For a moment, Jastrau thought of slapping him familiarly on the shoulder. But one could never tell about businessmen. Perhaps the awkward smile had no significance.

He walked over to the restaurant, followed by Steffensen.

There was a piano and some stringed instruments. And in the music a strong element of illusion. It made a person think he was having an experience. It made him feel as if he were playing the leading role in a film. The tone of the violin was somber, imbued with a note of the inevitability of fate. And underfoot was a carpet. You made such an impressive entrance. You saw yourself life-size in the mirrors, striding across the room. Impressive. And you caught sight of your own face so often that there could be no question about your being there.

After they had found a seat near a potted palm, Jastrau had to go to the phone booth and telephone home. Why? And why did he want to lie?

It was an interview, he told Johanne. A German aviator—something about a flight over the pole. Clever of him to think of that. At the moment, he was at the Cosmopolite Hotel. That was clever, too. It was unavoidable. He could not tell when he might get home. Yes, she was right—it was pretty late in the day to be letting her know. No, he couldn't say when he'd be home. He'd pick up a bite to eat somewhere. Finally she hung up. His forehead was covered with sweat from standing in the stuffy phone booth.

When he came out into the light, his eyes seemed clouded over with a film. Was he sleepy? He had a strange feeling of remoteness. But it must be from the day before—his latest hangover.

"First we must have a couple of beers," he said. "They'll drown our hangovers."

"*Sholom aleichem,*" Steffensen muttered solemnly, his eyes sparkling.

And so they sat over their beer and food for a couple of hours. Jastrau talked, and felt better. The violin set the tone of his mood. It was first subdued, then bombastic—now sentimental and melancholy, now a lively pizzicato.

Steffensen ate and drank with gusto, grinning and responding to Jastrau's remarks with scatological monosyllables.

But deep down inside him the conversation grated on Jastrau's nerves, and he felt compelled to order liqueur with the coffee. And cigars as well. For he had to pierce this fog of unintelligibility. It haunted him. He could not stop staring at Steffensen. But it was hopeless trying to entice a soul from a stone—a stone that seemed spattered with white bird droppings.

He chewed nervously on the end of his cigar. Before he knew it, his liqueur glass was empty. Now he was drinking faster than Steffensen.

"Now let me see that poem you wrote today," he burst out suddenly, irritated and half-drunk.

"Like hell I will. But you can buy me a whiskey over at the bar. I don't feel like sitting here any longer nipping at liqueur in the shadow of these flower pots."

"You're good at cadging drinks."

They got up and strode through the restaurant. Again he was struck by the image of himself reflected in the innumerable mirrors. Steffensen with his hands in his pockets and his rolling seaman's gait. In the mirror—now here, now there. And himself, with his little newspaperman's belly and a nervous uncertainty evident in every step he took. A strange pair. They jostled each other like a couple of lovers who had gotten out of step.

The Bar des Artistes was deserted. Lundbom had prophesied correctly. People were resting up.

There was but one customer. He sat at a table near the bar and stared listlessly at a glass of Sandeman port. It was Journalist Eriksen.

"Is that you, Jazz?" he snarled between his teeth as he raised his troubled, bloodshot countenance and looked up at them. "Yes, it's you all right, Jazz. Damned if it isn't. Sit down, Jazz. I'm buying the drinks all around. And the young man with you. Sit down, damn it all! Don't mind me—I'm only drunk, as usual."

They sat down.

"What's his name?" Eriksen asked, pointing to Steffensen and peering at him foggily.

"Steffensen."

"Oh—Stefani?"

Jastrau and Steffensen both gave a start.

"No, Steffensen."

"Oh, then I must be wrong. Don't you want some port, too? Ho skipper, where's the mess boy? Tell him to bring a couple of glasses for these two strangers."

Lundbom, who was standing behind the bar, bowed and smiled.

"Right away, Herr Eriksen—right away."

"Ugh, how hideous it sounds. 'Right away, Herr Eriksen—right away,'" Eriksen jeered, mimicking Lundbom. He inched forward over the table, like a creeping animal, until his wrinkled face almost brushed Jastrau's nose. "It's hideous, I tell you—hideous. And in a little while, it'll be, 'Now I think you'd better have a taxi, Herr Eriksen.' And by then I'll really be drunk, and all my money will be gone. The mercenary so-and-so—the money-grubber!" He raised an angry quivering fist and shook it threateningly.

But soon his fury subsided, and he seemed to collapse so that his clothes hung limply on him. It was as if a full sack had suddenly sprung a leak.

"I feel so down in the dumps today," he sighed.

"He's too tragic a figure," Steffensen blurted out. "Hadn't we better move on?"

"Tragic!" Eriksen sat up, and once again the sack was distended until his coat and vest fitted him snugly. "Tragic! Do you know what the word means? But you, Jazz—you understand. You're a newspaperman—lock, stock, and barrel. Those nitwits up in the composing room! What do we have proofreaders for? People must think I'm an idiot. 'A spoiled charmer!' Did you read it, Jazz?"

"Yes."

Steffensen's eyes were now riveted on Eriksen.

The glasses of port were brought to the table.

"Well, what's all this about the spoiled charmer?" Jastrau asked.

98

Eriksen squinted at him distrustfully.

"Honestly, Jazz—what did you think when you read it?"

Jastrau shrugged his shoulders. "It's a good description of him," he said.

"No, that's exactly what it isn't." He raised a trembling forefinger and shook it menacingly in front of Jastrau's nose. "Stefani is a decent person. And my copy read 'heretical charmer.'* Ugh—it takes a lot of port to wash down a proof error like that. What must our readers think?"

Once again he sank back, limp and deflated. But Steffensen and Jastrau burst into laughter.

"Yes, you can afford to laugh," Eriksen went on from his supine position. Both his forehead and vest were furrowed by innumerable wrinkles. "But he doesn't deserve that sort of thing. He's a decent fellow—"

"Really," growled Steffensen.

Again Journalist Eriksen threw out his chest, blew himself up almost to the bursting point, and held his head high as a general's. "Yes. I'm in a position to know," he said. "I've traveled a lot by ship, and I know many seamen who've come to Aarhus and gotten free injections and all that sort of thing from him."

Steffensen remained unimpressed. He sat with his hands in his pockets and his legs stretched out in front of him.

"Damned if I knew about that," he said without showing much interest.

"There are many things you don't know."

"Well, he's my father, so—"

Eriksen's eyes opened wider. "Hmm," was all he said. Then, paying no further attention to Steffensen's remark, he said with a desperate intensity: "But you must be able to understand what I mean, Jazz. I write 'heretical,' and then up there they set it as 'spoiled.' And everything's ruined—all that work." He leaned his head disconsolately against his big fists and rocked back and forth. "Spoiled charmer— spoiled charmer! What nonsense."

Steffensen leaned over as the boyish-looking waiter went by, and said, "Listen, Arnold, we've got to have some more port."

Eriksen took his hands away from his head and directed a listless look at Steffensen. "Yes," he said.

Just then the phonograph began blaring forth a high-pitched jazz

* In Danish, *forkælede* means "spoiled"; a person accused of heresy is said to be *forkætret*.

melody, and Jastrau gave a sudden start. All his nerves and muscles were taut. "That's right, Lundbom. Let's have a little life in this empty room."

He got up and with a clumsy dance step made his way to the bar to eat some salted almonds.

"Things are pretty dull here tonight," he remarked as he sat down on the high stool and began swaying back and forth in time with the music.

Lundbom shook his head glumly and shoved a dish of olives over to him.

Jastrau sat waving his arms. Music—music. He ate olives in time with the music, and he ordered a highball so that he could drink in time with it, too, even though his glass of Sandeman was still standing on the table over where the others were. The jazz enlivened the atmosphere, made the place come alive. Something was happening. And before he knew it, he was on his feet, waltzing around with the bar stool in his arms.

He stopped as he drew near the table where Steffensen and Eriksen sat. They had put their heads close together. Eriksen's face wore an affable, attentive expression that emerged from behind the bewildering mass of wrinkles, then disappeared, only to emerge again like a moon from behind the clouds. Steffensen's hard face had an intent look about it. His eyes were glazed with an alcoholic film, but behind it they could be seen glistening.

" 'But,' says the fine gentleman, looking down at his nails again, 'it's worse than that, because you see I and the housemaid haven't exactly been strangers to each other—' "

"Ha, ha," Jastrau roared, swinging the long legs of the stool over their heads. "That's Steffensen's only funny story."

But suddenly he put the stool down and went out into the hotel's small courtyard. He did not care to hear the story again. Steffensen was a simple soul in many ways.

Out in the darkness of the courtyard there was a medley of sounds. From the restaurant came the notes of the violin and piano, from the bar the music of the phonograph, and from the kitchen the clatter of plates and utensils. The concrete pavement and the walls of the buildings augmented the volume of sound, which in a bewildering series of discords swept up through the airshaft and out into the spring evening against the starry heavens as if through a French horn. It was a big moment—a time to feel expansive. And all those floors above, all the windows, and all that had happened in those hotel rooms over the years—all looking straight out at a blank fire wall. A strange building. A person would never have to leave it.

Then inside again. A new jazz melody greeted him, and he had to resume his dance steps.

"We've got to liven things up in this empty barroom," he shouted.

"Hush—hush," Lundbom warned.

"But now suppose there were no doctor in the story—would it still be funny?" asked Steffensen doggedly. "Would it still be funny?" He was leaning over the table toward Eriksen, who looked bored.

"Do you always get so philosophical when you tell a dirty joke?" Eriksen asked irascibly.

"I'm asking you if it would still be funny."

"Yes, of course."

"But suppose the wife had not become infected?"

"Oh, go to hell! You make me tired," Eriksen exclaimed and started to get up. But Steffensen pushed him back roughly into his chair. "Suppose the wife had not become infected. Would it still be funny?"

"Yes, it would be enough to make you die laughing. Now let go of me. I want to dance with Jazz."

And suddenly he stood in the middle of the room with his arms raised. Like a Spanish dancing girl. The phonograph played on. Jazz! Jazz! Ole Jastrau stood opposite Eriksen in the same posture. Chest thrust out. Brawny arms. Flashing eyes. Like a Spanish dancing girl. Then began a self-choreographed dance between the two men in the empty barroom—a dance of jubilance and exultation that was interrupted only whenever the record was changed.

But there was a moment when gloom again descended over the room. Eriksen collapsed, his chest caved in, his vest hung in loose folds, and he sighed, " 'Spoiled charmer!' Isn't it enough to make you get drunk?"

Then a new record was put on.

Nobody noticed Steffensen order a whole bottle of port and empty it in the course of five minutes. Nor did anyone remember how the dance ended.

Little P. had sat and watched them, smiling. Where in the devil had he come from? "Excellent, maestro," he had applauded. And the inevitable Kjær had turned up, too. The perpetual sot. He had sat there beating time to the music with both hands and quietly singing a hymn.

"Blessed, blessed are those who have peace."

This much Jastrau had been aware of. Or was it a dream? There was no way of knowing or remembering.

A Spanish dancing girl!

Chapter Seven

Suddenly Jastrau found himself in bed, wide-awake.

He stared up at the ceiling with a look of puzzlement and fright. But then what he saw looked familiar. It was the ceiling of his own bedroom. The window was open. Somebody was beating rugs down in the courtyard.

Johanne had gotten up. Oluf's black iron bed also was empty. And there on a chair, hung with almost painful care, were his clothes. But he had no pajamas on—only his undershirt.

And so it had happened again. Why? He could not recognize himself. Why did he drink? No, he was not a drunkard. He had only slipped for a couple of days.

But how quiet it was in the apartment. Not a sound. It was as if all the doors were shut—all fourteen of the doors in this apartment where the rooms were so inconveniently arranged. It was distressing—this silence. The rug-beating down in the courtyard made the bedchamber seem as desolate and impersonal as a hotel room. And how terrible he felt! A fist closed around his heart and was squeezing it. He was conscious of something ominous that threatened. It lay in wait there in the apartment. Once he had drawn up a rough floor plan of the place, and the result was most grotesque; it had resembled an ungainly animal grazing, a rhinoceros with its snout down in the water, or something equally preposterous—an arrangement that could bring nothing but trouble.

But where was Johanne? Had she gone away? How had he gotten home? Had he been up to some mischief? Gotten into a fight? He looked at his hands, rolled back the sleeves of the undershirt, and examined his arms. No, there were no marks. But how had he gotten home? He had danced with Eriksen—that he remembered. He remembered the barroom with its red linoleum, its mahogany and brasswork, and the bewildering array of gleaming colored bottles on the back bar shelves. The three oval casks set in the wall, one of them with *"Boal"* stamped on it. That much he remembered clearly. But what else? Yes, Steffensen had been there, and Kjær and Little P. But no one else. He recalled that some of the workers at *Dagbladet* usually went down to

102

the bar at about eleven o'clock. Had they seen him? Or had he himself gone up to the office to sun himself and create a spectacle, the way Eriksen did practically every night? Oh, how quiet it was. Had Johanne gone?

He sprang out of bed as nimbly as an animal. His body felt unusually alive and supple. Hurriedly he drew on his pants to go out to the kitchen for a drink of water. He was so thirsty. But how strange—he had to open the door to the small hallway, and the kitchen door as well.

He saw Johanne sitting in the kitchen. She must have shut the doors—carefully and tightly—because she had not wanted to talk to him. Now she had also shut her lips tightly, and her eyes looked weary and red-rimmed from loss of sleep. And her hands lay folded in her lap—like a picture in the *Family Journal* entitled "Forsaken Girl" or "Betrayed." A sharp twinge went through him. She was putting on an act.

"Where is Oluf?" he asked, looking around the room, puzzled.

"I let the janitor's wife take him out for a walk," she replied, moving her lips mechanically. Otherwise it was as if she were petrified. Her eyes did not move. "So he could play with their little girl," she added.

Ole Jastrau had nothing on but undershirt and pants. He was barefoot. No wonder he felt humble.

"Oh, come now, Johanne," he pleaded suddenly, shaking his head. She sent him a surprised, overbearing look.

Suddenly he ran and threw himself on his knees before her, laid his head in her lap, and rocked it back and forth. "Oh, Johanne, I don't know what's the matter with me. I don't understand it. I'm not usually this way—you know that, don't you? Sometimes I get so afraid." He wanted to cry. Yes, he would cry—it would give him a feeling of relief. But his emotion was not genuine. He felt stiff and unyielding. "Oh, Johanne—you know what I have to contend with. It's here inside me—plaguing me all the time." He sighed, and a few tears rolled down his cheeks. He felt them wetting his face. But they brought no relief. The only thing that helped was cradling his head in her lap—that seemed to calm him somewhat. It was soothing to make believe he was a child. "Oh, Johanne—don't you understand? It's enough to make me go out of my mind."

He got up suddenly, went over by the door, and leaned his head against the panelling. It was incomprehensible—this agony he was going through. It was playacting, and he was playing the part of Oluf. It was a form of self-torture. It cut through his depression and transformed it into pain. He banged his head against the door and stamped like a child. Yes, Oluf, Oluf.

"Johanne—why do I have to be this way?"

Johanne got up.

"Now stop making such a fuss," she exclaimed in disgust. "He can hear it in there."

"He—he? Is Steffensen here?" Jastrau turned and faced her. "He's the one who's to blame for it all."

Johanne smiled faintly.

"Yes, of course. It's all his fault."

And she broke into a short, contemptuous laugh.

"Don't kid yourself," she said. Her voice sounded strangely cynical.

"Don't you believe me any longer, Johanne?"

"No," she said scornfully.

"All right! Now I'm going to show you something," he exclaimed impetuously. "I won't have him in the house a minute longer. I'm going in and wake him up—"

"He is awake," Johanne told him sarcastically. "I've already served him coffee." She dropped a curtsey, and broke into a short laugh that sounded crisp and clear. "He's probably sitting in there now, reading the morning paper."

"He is?" exclaimed Jastrau. "I'm telling you—not a minute longer." Barefooted, he hurried into the living room.

Steffensen was there. His face was bloated and his small eyes had a mean look. He had seated himself in the rococo chair and lighted his pipe.

"I won't have you staying here a moment longer!"

Steffensen was fully dressed. Very calmly, he removed the pipe from his mouth and looked at Jastrau. His glance took in the undershirt, the pants, and the bare feet. The undershirt accentuated the journalistic potbelly and made it appear as a ridiculous bulge.

"Yes, go ahead and scowl," Jastrau went on brutally. "I tell you this has gone on long enough. This is my apartment here—my home—and I'm not going to have it ruined, because—because—"

Steffensen got out of the chair as if he meant to butt him with his head. But Jastrau summoned up all his nervous force and glowered right back at the angry eyes that flashed with such a glazed luster.

"You're leaving now. Do you understand, Steffensen?"

Steffensen parted his lips in a soundless laugh that made him look like a horse.

104

"You henpecked boob!" he exclaimed, raising his right hand and turning the back of it toward Jastrau as if to whack him in the face.

"You're leaving now." Jastrau came a step closer.

"Watch out for your stinking toes, or I'll step on them and flatten them out."

Suddenly he grabbed up the newspaper from the chair and shouted, "Can you tell me how it happens that the name Stefani appears underneath my poem in this paper?"

Jastrau caught his breath.

"Well—you see—" he stammered.

"It's a low-down, dirty trick—a newspaper trick. My father's name! Thank you. You can go to hell!"

He tossed the newspaper on the floor, shoved Jastrau aside, and started toward the foyer.

"I forgot to mention it to you," Jastrau called out after him. It sounded like an excuse, a sudden, plaintive transition from the positive stand he had just taken.

"That's a lie! A dirty, journalistic lie!"

And the hallway door slammed so that the windowpanes rattled.

Jastrau sat down on the sofa, supported his head with his hands, and rocked it back and forth.

So this was his victory! This was the way he had vanquished Steffensen—ending up by owing him an apology. A low-down trick. But after all, it had been a case of forgetting—it had—it had.

There was no doubt as to who had suffered defeat.

Jastrau raised his head from his hands and stared at the table in front of him, shifted the fetish, tried to put things in order. Everything was all spread out. Then he suddenly noticed the rough-draft sheets that Steffensen had left lying there, with their sketches of female legs and elephant trunks. The word "Diminuendo" had been written in large letters across one of the sheets, and Steffensen had traced in some beech branches through the loops of the "D." And there, besides, lay the finished draft of the entire poem.

It was the poem he had been so eager to see the day before.

But now he didn't dare. He did not want to read it. For suppose the poem was good. It would be another defeat for him.

Oh, nonsense. He shook his head.

"You were too rough on him, Ole."

Johanne stood in the doorway, and Jastrau looked up at her. There was a set expression around her mouth.

"What do you mean by that?" he asked, irritated.

"You might have found another way to go about it. Because the way you carried on— Well, my father would never have done it, and neither would Adolf."

Jastrau drew himself up stiffly. "If I pick up my hat, it's wrong, and if I let it lie, it's wrong too. What the devil did you want me to do? You wanted him out of here, and you got him out, and now that's wrong too."

He paced back and forth, feeling ridiculous in pants and undershirt. Suddenly he exclaimed hysterically, "I can't stand it any longer! I'll go crazy—lose my mind!"

"Now, just let's not have a repetition of that scene we had in the kitchen."

Once again her girlish voice assumed a tone of mild but irritating cynicism.

Jastrau stood for a moment and looked at her through narrowed, observant eyes. His debauched face must have reflected the animosity he felt, for Johanne's eyes opened wide—big, blue eyes, pale blue behind the pink-edged lids. Quietly she said, "I think we'd better have some lunch."

Jastrau nodded and went silently into the bedroom to shave. He did so without the help of a mirror, and got a wretched shave, but he had no desire to see his face. It must have looked terrible to Johanne when he lost control of himself. He heard her scurrying down the stairs. She probably had to go out to do some shopping. He began to whistle. It would be best to get himself into a better humor.

When Johanne got back, she looked as if she had been turning something over in her mind. Jastrau could see that her face bore a different expression. Something or other had happened.

He did not find out what it was until after they sat down to lunch.

"Ole, how could we owe for six bottles of Old Carlsberg down at the dairy store?"

"What's that?"

"Yes, the woman down there said the man with the cap had just come to get six bottles for us. And he specifically said, 'For the Jastraus.'"

Jastrau looked at her in astonishment.

"When did he do that?"

"Just now—twenty minutes ago."

Jastrau shook his head. But then he laid his hands on the table and exclaimed, "Really—this is—"

"Is it possible that—"

"Yes, of course."

106

"But that's downright thievery."

"Yes," said Ole, shrugging his shoulders. "Or revenge, or whatever you want to call it."

"But Ole, something like that! It's only a beastly criminal who'd—"

"Now, now—"

"Well, what do you want me to say? Would you do a thing like that?"

Jastrau smiled. "No, I don't think so," he said. His smile was so unrestrained that he showed his teeth. "But I understand him pretty well."

"Oh, you always understand everything," she said with a toss of her head.

"Well, I understood him well enough to throw him out." His elation at his victory was a bit uncertain, and he felt his way cautiously.

"You certainly did."

"Did you hear the whole thing?"

"No, only the beginning. Then I had enough. I held my hands to my ears because I thought you were going to fight. You can expect anything from such a person."

Jastrau smiled warmly at her. Then she had not heard their conversation about the poem, and consequently she knew nothing about his defeat. He reached across the table and squeezed her hand tenderly.

"Now I understand, Ole. You weren't too rough on him." Her lips were puckered in the wry little smile that he loved. It made one feel she possessed a deep sense of irony and a certain dangerous charm. He had never actually discovered these traits in her, but there it was—that smile. And now he could once more believe in her deep, deep sense of irony.

"Johanne," he said in a voice full of emotion.

"Yes," she replied, leaning toward him and still smiling. "What is it?"

"Oh, nothing. Well, yes, there is something. Everything, in fact." He spoke softly, and all at once he said, "I'm so happy."

"That's good," she said.

"And everything seems so nice here now. But where is Oluf? Isn't he coming soon?"

She nodded. "Yes, but we're eating earlier than usual."

When she got up, he could not help following her with his eyes, observing her figure, which had not yet become flabby. Beneath the yellow dress he could distinguish the firm gentle curves that he never dared look at when she was naked, but that his hands had felt, molded, and called into being out of the night—those nights that were so few and far between because she was so reserved. Or was it that he was a bit too bold? It had been more than a month and a half since—

Reserved. A woman who shut her eyes. A woman who during the light nights let her hair slip down so that it covered her face. It was always hidden during the moments when they were nearest to each other. Or had he never really possessed her?

He got up and felt compelled to follow her, to lay his hand on her shoulder, to caress her cheek, to kiss her.

"You seem so restless, Ole."

"It's my hangover," he said with a wry smile.

"Then I wish you always had a hangover. If this is what they do to you, I could love you for having them." There was an excruciatingly erotic expression about her lips.

"My, but you're a lovely girl," he said.

"It isn't very often you notice it," she replied.

"My head certainly feels blown up, and look at my eyes. Aren't they hideous?"

"I don't mind, because now you're fit to be with."

They heard Oluf coming into the hallway.

"Where's the man who was here?" he asked, standing in the doorway with the front of his brown horse-trader's coat bulging.

"Gone. Ps-st, and he's gone!"

"Ho ho, Mother. The man's gone ps-st. Ho ho."

Jastrau lifted him into his arms and danced around the room with him. Idyllic—simply idyllic! But a hangover idyll, he thought spitefully. The idyll would not last unless something happened. A tag-end-of-a-jag idyll. A trace of self-contempt clouded Jastrau's face. But then he drew the boy close to him and buried his face in his coat, hiding himself for a moment.

"Now look, Johanne, I have a hangover today," he said gaily as he put the boy down.

"Yes, I know that," she said, wrinkling her brow as if she found him delightfully impossible.

"And for that reason I can't do anything. I feel like going places, celebrating. You're going out for an auto ride with me, and Oluf's going with us."

"Yes, but we can't afford it. The taxes and the light bill—"

"Don't bother me with such trifles. I'm going to phone for a taxi."

"But first I have to wash the dishes."

"Dishes, dishes! Damned if I know why, but that's the way it always is!" he exclaimed in a fit of irritation. "Dishwashing, always dishwashing— I do believe that's what takes the joy out of life for you women."

"It's taken you a long time to make the discovery," said Johanne with a tragi-comic expression.

"Well, I'm going to call a taxi. It isn't every day that I have such a delightful hangover as this. Look, Johanne—it's springtime, damn it!" And he stamped his foot in a burst of enthusiasm. "You'd like to go for a taxi ride, wouldn't you, Oluf?"

"Yes, daddy. Taxi ride! Taxi ride!" Suddenly he became infected by his father's zest and, singing exuberantly, he began to run around, cutting figure eights between his parents. "Taxi ride! Taxi ride!"

"I think you've both gone crazy!" exclaimed Johanne. But she did not have a chance to say any more before Jastrau had gone to the phone and ordered a cab. "Get here as quickly as you can," he said.

It was all done in such a rush. And when they at last sat in the taxi, it was with the feeling that they had hardly had time to put their overcoats on.

"Oh, it's terrible the way I let all those dishes stand," Johanne said, laughing.

Little Oluf wriggled in between them until he found a position in which he could sit like a teddy bear with his feet stuck straight out in front of him and his arms slanting down toward his knees. "There," he said with a sigh of satisfaction.

They swung across Vesterbro Passage with its Freedom Statue and on through Copenhagen's "Wild West" quarter with its bazaars and wooden shacks. They sped across bridges and followed the railway cut, a course as devious as a detour, while the lower halves of business blocks, apartment houses, and the awkward contours of the Palace Theatre flashed by.

Jastrau disparaged everything he saw. He was in an exalted mood, and for the moment Copenhagen seemed to him a city that was hopelessly snarled.

"Is it any wonder that people get drunk in a town like this?" he exclaimed with a sweeping gesture. "Or perhaps the city is this way because we're all stewed half the time. The history of Denmark is one big binge. Our fatherland has a red nose."

But his mood became more serene as they drove through Farimagsgade. In Ørsted Park, the shimmering young leaves of the trees glittered like gold. The branches extended out over the tall iron fence, and the people on the sidewalk moved in flickering light and shadow.

"Yes, spring is here—that's sure," Jastrau went on. He could not stop talking. "It's taken us by surprise again. Haven't you noticed that the trees always burst into leaf behind your back, and then you turn around and everything is suddenly green?"

Johanne nodded, and he looked at her in amazement. This was a lady who sat beside him in a blue suit and golden hair. She looked so mature. The unaccustomed comfort of the cab—even though it was one of the stripped-down vehicles that had no cruising license—gave her a certain air of distinction. She had to feel happy once in a while. He smiled sardonically.

She was pretty and a bit commonplace, he thought.

"How wonderful you look today!" he exclaimed.

She turned toward him with a smile of satisfaction.

"I'm in a good mood today, too," she said, reaching for his hand with a perfectly natural sincerity, so that Oluf found himself sitting behind a chain of hands. Swing, swing—swing and sing and all fall down—the prettiest roses all fall down, as the janitor's daughter would say. She knew so many things. Oluf leaned forward against the swing.

"You weren't too rough at all when you showed him the door," Johanne said gently. "He was your evil spirit, Ole. Why, it was impossible to recognize you." She squeezed his hand.

It was spring.

They drove along Frederiksborggade and over the Queen Louise Bridge. The broad open stretches of water shone brightly in the sunlight.

"Look, Johanne. See how the trees have leafed out on one side of the lakes and not on the other. Isn't it nice? How I like to take the trees by surprise every year."

And they looked out over the lakes with their neat stone embankments, at the trees along the shore, and at the streets and buildings behind them. How congenial—this effect of tall trees against five-story houses. There would be a place to live. A real nest. Like being a bird. Oh—humans who aspired to live like birds!

And far across the lakes, a lovely yellow background of color could be seen reflecting the sunlight—a color he had loved in his childhood. It was the walls of the houses on distant Østerbro at the corner of Willemoesgade. It was a color that one might see in a dream. That was the sort of horizon one should be able to look out on.

They had crossed the bridge and gone on into busy Nørrebrogade, then turned off and were proceeding along Fælledvejen. They had reached the suburbs. The long Nørre Allé, with its massive trees—

asphalt with a crown of light green overhead. When they bent forward and peered over the driver's shoulder, they saw the long tree-lined thoroughfare stretching out before them like a view through a telescope—light green at the periphery, and far, far away, some buildings and a yellow streetcar.

"Our streetcars are the nicest-looking streetcars in the world. Have you ever thought about that?"

"I've never traveled," she said sadly.

"But they are. Our streetcars, our policemen, our mail carriers, our mailboxes—they're elegant, distinguished looking. They have the flavor of old Copenhagen. I love them."

"One simply wouldn't know you today."

"Am I boring you?"

"No—no—not at all," she said quietly.

Once they were past the grade-level railway gate, they left Copenhagen behind.

Then long broad highways flanked by villas and lawns. Suddenly, big fields that left the view unhampered. A solitary farmhouse, one wing of which extended way out to a flagstone sidewalk. A straw-thatched roof and asphalt. Then more villas.

"Oh!" exclaimed Oluf, dreamily staring out of the window.

Out at Femvejen, they turned into Jægersborg Allé with its tall venerable trees. Straight trunks rising with an air of poise. Then more commuters' villages where the houses seemed to shove the trees out against the curbstones.

Then over a railway bridge, a monstrous mass of concrete arches, and into the Charlottenlund Forest.

"Don't you think we should get out and stretch our legs?"

Johanne nodded.

Jastrau rapped on the window with a five-øre piece and told the driver to stop the car. He told him to go on down to the beach known as The Flypaper because of the way people swarmed to it on Sundays. They marched off with Oluf between them. He looked up first at one of them, then at the other, and Jastrau felt faint at the sight of his blue eyes—a springtime faintness. Like sparkling rain puddles in which the sky was mirrored. Always so clear and bright in springtime. It was as if he were walking at the edge of them. Down there below him they were sparkling all the while.

Jastrau let his gaze wander from the boy's round beaming face up to Johanne. His eyes followed the curve of her arm, the soft contour of her shoulder, and the line of her neck, which was pleasingly plump and dazzling white. And from the pink ear lobe, at which the brisk

111

spring air was nipping, his glance traveled on to the mass of golden hair beneath her hat. It was difficult for him to look directly at her.

The tops of the trees had not completely leafed out. Against the reddish-brown and gray background of branches and twigs, the new foliage had the appearance of a strange green mist. But could it not also be visualized as so many blotches? The green was obtrusive. Why must spring always signify freshness and purity? A damp wall, a springtime forest. Jastrau felt he had to call Johanne's attention to his fleeting thoughts. "It would be amusing to argue the thesis that spring is not so beautiful as we make it out to be," he said.

"Oh, now you're about to abandon your good humor again, Ole," she said apprehensively.

"No, no. But there's an element of fraud in all this stuff about spring, and I must see to it that it's exposed."

He laughed teasingly.

Johanne's only reply was to nod her head toward the deeper part of the woods. There, on the ground, whole drifts of anemones shone like banks of summer clouds. It was precisely because the foliage had not yet shut out the sunlight that the woods had such a fresh candid look about them—not a dim, submarine luminosity or an occult, cathedral-like ambiance, but all the clarity of an open plain. And anemones were open-air flowers; they did not thrive under a roof or in concealment. They were as free and easy, as unpretentious as a kitchen apron.

"Oluf, do you see the flowers there? They're anemones," Jastrau announced didactically, as he plucked one of them.

"Yes, but look, Father—there—over there—there's a yellow anemone!" Oluf shouted, pointing.

"Right you are—a yellow anemone." Like a teacher, Jastrau pronounced the name of the flower very distinctly.

Oluf suddenly compressed his lips and scowled.

Jastrau only laughed. The transition in the boy's mood was so sudden that it was comical. Apparently he did not feel that he needed instruction. Jastrau ran over and picked the yellow flower, too.

"There you are. One white and one yellow. You're not going to get any more, because we can't plunder the whole woods. And by the way, I've never seen a blue anemone," he added, addressing Johanne.

They walked on. The road through the woods curved as they neared the white stable of Charlottenlund Castle and then led directly down to the shore road. All of a sudden they could see way out of the woods and beyond the little artificial sand beach—The Flypaper—to Middel-grund Fortress and the blue waters of the Sound.

112

Jastrau wiped his brow. He was sweating. It was all the boozing he had done the day before—that and the excitement he felt. Yes, he was aware of what was going on. He knew he could have wretched hangovers and enjoyable ones. But if they were the enjoyable kind, something lively had to happen every minute.

"Now we'll have coffee," he said as they stood outside the restaurant called "Over the Stable." The glass veranda was empty and the orchestra platform seemed to be sagging out of loneliness.

They had their coffee out of doors. A tablecloth was fastened to the table with metal clamps to prevent it from being blown away by the fresh breeze from the Sound.

"Why aren't you always this way, Ole?" said Johanne gently, wrinkling her low, arched forehead. "When you're like this, a person can stand to be with you."

"If my hangovers were always like this one, it would be a pleasure to drink myself to death. But that set-to this morning—"

"Well, it's good he's gone," she said with a sigh of relief.

"A yellow a-ne-mo-ne, a white a-ne-mo-ne," they suddenly heard Oluf say with labored preciseness, as he laid the flowers on the tablecloth. Jastrau was on the point of laughing.

"No, you mustn't, Ole," Johanne implored. He kept still.

But the curly, childish head was bent over the flowers.

"A-ne-mo-ne," the boy repeated to himself. Then he sensed he was being observed and directed a caustic glance at his father. "It's an anemo-nee," he said sharply. Offended, he picked up the flowers again, one at a time.

The trip back along the shore road was equally pleasant. There was something unshakable about Jastrau's mood. And Johanne retained her faint smile of serenity. Even though it might disappear momentarily, a vestige of it would remain about her lips. Oluf sat with his fingers clasped around the stems of the two anemones which had begun to close their petals and droop their heads.

Thus they came back to their apartment.

It had been a refreshing trip. Their clothes were permeated with the cool spring air. And once they were inside, it seemed to spread through the rooms. Even the two withered anemones, which now lay on Oluf's play table, exuded the atmosphere of spring.

Jastrau began to sing. He must certainly have his hangover remedy—a beer or two or three—before dinner. But now he read and found himself in a receptive frame of mind. He was perhaps a more appreciative reader today than he had been at any time in several months.

"It's a good thing I never write when I've been out the night before," he remarked as Johanne passed through the room. "Today it all seems good—whatever they've written. And that certainly would never do."

It was as if happiness lay shimmering even in the light that pervaded the room. It seemed woven like a golden thread through the fabric of the curtains. And as they ate, the glow from the setting sun flooded the neighboring rooftop with an unusually soft and lovely light.

Jastrau frequently had to look out the window.

And when he looked at Johanne, he noticed the same agreeable light effect. He saw everything now in terms of light. It seemed to him that her face was different, not dull and lusterless like the faces of people one has grown tired of looking at. She was perfectly lovely, was she not? As he walked by her, he noticed the crisp freshness of her dress.

No, his feeling of happiness did not abate. He remained sitting with her in the dining room. She was embroidering, and he knew she was relaxed and at ease. Oluf had gone to bed. Altogether, it made such a cozy domestic scene that he had to smile with a mixed feeling of tenderness and irony. And several times during the course of the evening, he felt compelled to walk by her and bend down to kiss her hair. Like all women, she looked beautiful and humble while being caressed. Yes—she was his.

They sat up late. The lights were turned on. Each sat at one side of the table, and every time he glanced up from his book he encountered her placid glance. Obviously it rested on him all the time, and her eyes were a deeper blue than usual. How fortunate he was to have her! In the intensity of his feeling, he came close to believing that he too was handsome.

Was it eleven o'clock? No, it was nearer twelve.

Suddenly the telephone rang.

"Oh, if only that isn't the paper calling," she sighed, laying her needlework, a wreath of blue pansies on a background of yellow, in her lap.

He went and took the call.

"Jastrau speaking."

"Is that you, Jastrau? Well, this is the lobster shift. Do you suppose you could come over here for a moment? There's something very interesting we'd like to show you."

It was Vuldum, speaking in a subdued, glum voice. Jastrau's hand began to tremble out of a feeling of impotence. All this intrigue about

114

that review of Stefani's book. Now he ought to come right out and demand an accounting, but—

"Oh, that's it?" he asked uneasily. "Can't you tell me over the phone what it's all about?"

"Yes, but you won't get much out of it that way. It's a letter that the old man has written to H. C. Stefani."

He could clearly distinguish the spurious sympathy in Vuldum's voice—a tone of deliberate exquisite commiseration intended to torment his victim.

"Yes, but can't you just read it to me?" he asked irritably. "I was just getting ready to go to bed."

"No, I can't. You see, it's nothing but some fragments of the letter that Gundersen's long limber hands fished out of the old man's wastebasket, and we need an expert to make anything out of it."

Jastrau could hear the lobster shift at work in the background.

"Yes, but listen, Vuldum—"

"Perhaps you're not interested," came the harsh reply.

"Yes, yes—"

There was a click. Vuldum had hung up.

Jastrau remained standing in the darkened room. Now he could feel how the last few days had worn him out. He felt his jaw quivering. The darkness shimmered. But the tone of Vuldum's voice stayed with him—penetrated like a thorn. He spoke to Johanne, who was still sitting in the brightly lighted dining room.

"I've got to go over to the paper."

"Who was it?"

"The lobster shift."

"Oh, you don't have to run over there on their account."

"Yes, they've found a letter in the old man's office and I have to see it. I have to. It might be very important." He stepped into the doorway, and suddenly his voice took on a tone of grievous complaint. "One can never feel sure of himself with that paper. I feel as if something is always going on behind my back, as if someone is always lurking behind me with a dagger. It's enough to curdle your spine. No, I have to go over and find out what this letter is all about."

She looked up at him.

"It's only some practical joke they're playing on you." But then, when she saw how upset he was, she added with a sigh: "Well, then, you'd better go." She got up from the table. "But see that you come home soon—not like the last few nights, right? You need a good night's sleep. Why, you're so nervous you're trembling. So come home soon."

115

She had tears in her eyes.

Jastrau grabbed his hat and overcoat, promised to get back quickly, and left.

Getting out into the street always put life in him. The cool night air and the traffic acted as stimuli. But his heart was still beating violently. Now he would have to sit staring into Vuldum's face—that inscrutable white mask. But the traffic gave him momentary relief. A line of people, trooping like a flock of geese, made their way along Istedgade over to the railroad station, following the same path as always. That meant that one of the midnight trains was about to leave. In Reventlowsgade, the long thin ribbon of electric lights from the Bræddehytte Tavern gleamed as from an illuminated garden. He half ran, half walked, with the ridiculous gait of a harassed schoolmaster who is late for a class. Vuldum! Now he would have to have it out with Vuldum. Throw the blame for it all right in his face. What kind of a filthy trick was it he had pulled on him anyway? Again, Vesterbro served to take his mind off his troubles. Theatre-goers hurrying into taxis. Glimpses of people in evening dress, bare necks with furs and flashing gems, white shirt fronts, high hats near the entrance to the Wivel. It must be nearly midnight. People in a hurry. Several young men shouting. A poor wretch out at the edge of the sidewalk, cowering and miserable. Women who walked slowly through the crowd, taking a zigzag course and discreetly blocking the passage of an occasional man. A lingering appraising glance. Silk-clad legs in sleek profile against the dark building fronts.

Yes, this time he would have it out with him. He would look Vuldum straight in the eye. But it would take a strong heart. All right—he had it. Coolness? The air was cold. Forcefulness? The streetcar tracks were so coated with gasoline that they glistened like lacquer when the beams of the automobile headlights swept over them. Yes, all this served as a stimulant. The red Scala sign was glowing. The blue lights of the Stadil shone discreetly. And high against the midnight sky squinted the veiled yellow eyes of the Town Hall clock.

Vesterbrogade at night always had the same effect on Jastrau as a refreshing shower bath. But as he cut diagonally across the square, his courage and energy dwindled. He was rushing toward an encounter with an invincible force. There stood *Dagbladet's* corner building, with its electric news bulletin flashing by like a band of fire just below the roof line. And the illuminated advertising billboard on the same building but above the dark side street, where there was also a moving-picture theatre that could easily escape notice. And right on the corner, *Dagbladet's* name in red, roman letters, as rational as the spirit of the newspaper when it expressed itself with the greatest clarity. Vuldum called this building his home.

As Jastrau entered the vestibule he saw the three men on the lobster shift sitting at the green table with Arne Vuldum. The green felt on the table and the yellow walls gave them an official look, as if they were judges, despite their newspapermen's sturdy but shabby clothing, worn threadbare by legwork. Baggy jacket pockets sprung from being stuffed with manuscripts. Ink spots from leaky fountain pens. In short, a kind of uniform. Only Vuldum was smartly dressed. But then, he frequented the lobster shift only for fun. The other three were engaged in deadly serious work on behalf of the institution.

Otherwise the editorial department was empty. To be sure, a light was burning in the copy editor's office, but he was up in the composing room and would not be back until the paper had gone to press. The light was extinguished in the editor-in-chief's office. Editor Iversen had left. Only from the sports department came a sound of coughing and an unintelligible muttering.

"It's Eriksen—as usual," Vuldum said.

"Drunk?"

Vuldum nodded and said tartly, "You were out with him yesterday. Lundbom told me he had to throw you out."

"We didn't do any damage, did we?" Jastrau asked. Already he had been put on the defensive. There would be no showdown.

"No, it didn't amount to anything—a few glasses broken, that's all," Vuldum reassured him in a superior tone.

Jastrau looked at him apprehensively.

"But this business of the letter," interrupted Gundersen, he of the slim hands. He wore black tortoise-shell glasses and had a black mustache and purplish Negroid lips. "You should be able to make it out, since you're mentioned in it."

He carefully moved some fragments of a torn-up letter across the green felt toward Jastrau. The pieces had been assembled, but not all of the letter was there.

"It was stupid of you not to find the whole letter," remarked Rostrup, who had hair like mouldy straw and half resembled a devil because there was always a boil protruding like a horn from his forehead. Every night at about twelve o'clock, after Editor Iversen had left, it was Rostrup's job as one of the lobster shift to rummage through the drawers of Iversen's desk and read whatever he found.

"It wasn't there," the third man apologized. It was Høysgaard, a gray-haired individual who was only twenty-seven. Since he was an energetic soul, he had been given as his domain not only the editor's desk, but also whatever littered the top of it, which was no negligible quantity of material. There were letters from old and new colleagues, letters from the paper's subscribers and friends, containing criticism and complaints, praise and indiscriminate abuse. All letters were read aloud for the benefit of the entire shift. "I helped him look for it," Høysgaard added.

"You might just as well have spared yourself the trouble," Vuldum said cynically. "Finding things in the wastebasket takes ingenuity— and long, slim fingers like Gundersen's."

Gundersen felt flattered. Like all the younger men on the staff, he admired Vuldum's delightfully spiteful way of expressing himself.

Meanwhile, Jastrau bent over the scraps of the letter and read:

> ar Stefani:
> thank you for your excel
>   enings. It's profound observa
> greatly, and I don't know how
>   lly; but critics I do unders
>
> But there is another th
>   son I really didn't know. It
> no more poems. I myself was
>   y ugly, and will not stand
>   rau, my literary edit
> right that he is quite young
>   wspaper's policy of letting
> I intend to

The editorial room was very quiet. The lobster shift and Vuldum stared at Jastrau in suspense and exchanged glances. Back in the sports department, Eriksen coughed and growled like an animal.

"Can you make it out?" asked Vuldum.

Jastrau raised his head, but did not have the fortitude to look at any of them. They looked like magistrates, or worse still, a board of inquisitors, as they sat at the green table and watched him undergoing torment.

"We can't figure it out," said Gundersen. His tone had a false ring to it.

"No?" Jastrau said, trying to look him in the eye, despite the fact that everything in front of him was dancing and shimmering. "Well, it says that the old man likes Stefani's book, that we won't print any more of his son's poems, and that I'll soon be through as a critic on this damned paper."

118

"Bravo—a good job of reading!" exclaimed Vuldum. "But your last conclusion—isn't that putting a rather drastic interpretation on it? All it says is that you're too young."

Jastrau stood up. It was the easiest way to avoid the pat on the shoulder that he knew was coming.

"Excuse me a minute," he said, going toward the back of the room toward the toilet.

Then, however, he suddenly decided to go on. He cautiously opened a door and hurried down the back stairway to the street.

There was no other way for him to hide his defeat. He had to flee.

When he inserted the key in the door to his apartment, Johanne opened it from the inside.

"So you did come home after all," she said tenderly.

"Yes, of course."

She shut her eyes and let him kiss her.

PART TWO

Behold the Man

It was May, a year later.

Chapter One   Ole Jastrau was walking toward the Town Hall Square through the blustery spring sunshine. Under his arm was a small package, carelessly wrapped in crumpled tissue paper.

The Parisian-boulevard trees of Vesterbrogade tossed in the wind, their gold-green foliage whipping this way and that in long graceful swells. The breeze lashed at the women's short dresses so that now they billowed out like balloons, now hugged the body closely to reveal the outlines of legs and hips.

Outside the Paraply, with its rustling ivy and laurel, he met the lanky Arne Vuldum, who was strutting along like an elegant contemplative ghost, his face white and bony beneath the stiff and proper St. Peter's dome.

"Are you on your way up to the paper, Jastrau?" he asked, raising the derby in an ironic gesture of politeness.

"Yes, I'm pulling myself together for it."

"Well then, while you're pulling yourself together, it wouldn't be amiss if you bought me a beer."

Vuldum nodded toward the Paraply's sidewalk café. And they went in behind the rustling ivy hedge and sat down at a table with a flapping tablecloth.

"I was just on my way out to see Father Garhammer," said Vuldum. He laid a book fastidiously on top of the tablecloth to keep the wind from getting under it.

"Why do you go out so often to see those Catholics?"

"To keep my sense of eternity in good working order. When you live in a boardinghouse, as I do, you need that. A bit of intellectual exercise."

"One wouldn't think you lacked that."

"No?" Vuldum looked up sarcastically. "Would you mind telling me where else I'd find it? At the library? No, there we're overcome by pedantry. Frankly, the only thing that arouses any excitement up there is a really good detective story. You should have seen us when *The Singing Bruiser* was published. The old-timers couldn't remember such a fuss having been made over anything since Ibsen's plays. And over at the paper? I don't know whether you call what goes on there intellectual exercise. Since Kryger went over to *Danmark,* there's almost nobody you can talk with. Of course, there's you. But otherwise—" Vuldum added magnanimously.

"Kryger? I've really only talked with him once," Jastrau replied with a smile.

"Ah, yes, when he was sounding you out. That was interesting. Going around trying to find out how many Conservatives there were among us whom he might get to go with him."

"The only ones he could find were Høysgaard and little Michael—"

"Yes—and me," Vuldum interrupted. "But I stayed."

Two huge glasses of beer were placed before them. The breeze ruffled the foam so that a little of it sprayed Vuldum in the face.

"We'd better get this shower under control," he said, taking a good grip on his glass. It took strong fingers to lift it.

"Incidentally, we'll see him Thursday," he went on, wiping the suds from his lips.

"Who?"

"Kryger."

"On Thursday?"

"Yes. Aren't you going out to Eyvind Krog's? He said you were."

Jastrau looked at him in surprise.

"Yes, but—"

"Oh yes, both Kryger and I are going. And now, I'll have an opportunity to see your charming wife—finally."

"I hope you won't be disappointed. She's on an automobile tour with her brother, and it might last quite a while. I'm a widower these days."

"It seems to me you play that role quite often," Vuldum said pointedly.

Jastrau raised the glass to his lips. It was large enough so that he could hide his face behind it. And when he set down the glass, he replied, "There you're mistaken. It happens very seldom."

"Oh, you married men!" Vuldum took out a cigarette, tapped the end of it on the tablecloth, and lighted it. The sparks flew.

"Won't you have one?"

Jastrau shook his head.

"There's only one trouble with cigarettes—they turn your forefinger brown," Vuldum remarked, inspecting his finger.

"By the way, what's that book lying there?" Jastrau asked.

"Oh, it's only a gift for Father Garhammer. Some of Poul Helgesen's writings. I picked it up in a secondhand shop. What have you got there?"

Jastrau smiled awkwardly. "Nothing but a picture, but I don't mind if you have a look at it." He removed the tissue paper carefully.

It was a picture of a very young woman with an abundance of dark hair. A striped blouse, very simple, pinned with a brooch, was all one saw of her costume, and the effect was almost of impoverishment. But the large dark eyes and the broad bridge of the nose gave a singular force to her expression, and a trace of bitterness was visible around the young mouth.

Vuldum compressed his lips, squinted, and regarded the picture with the air of a connoisseur.

"It's a relative of yours," he said in a tone of disappointment.

"Yes, it's my mother. I've just been out at my half-brother's to reclaim it."

Vuldum laid the picture back on the table carefully. "It's a fine picture," he said with the quiet air of an expert. His voice assumed an almost indiscernible tone of warmth. "She's dead, isn't she?"

"Yes. Many years ago."

"Do you remember her?"

"Only vaguely. I was only three when she died."

For a long time Vuldum said nothing. He had a way of sitting and thinking with his features immobile, a habit that made him look like a Florentine.

"That's not good," he said after a long pause.

"What's not good?" asked Jastrau, who had wrapped up the picture again. He did not want it lying unprotected next to beer glasses on a café table.

Vuldum looked at him. There was a note of sympathetic irony in his smile.

"Well, it's better to have one's mother live a long life, so that you can discover that she's only a woman. Otherwise, you have a difficult time of it throughout your life."

"I don't get your point."

Vuldum laughed. "I can imagine that you're a reverent lover. Aren't you really, Ole?"

"Oh, come now!" Jastrau exclaimed in protest.

"A Madonna worshipper, a knight of the Order of Perpetual Adoration. But here comes your friend, the Bolshevik. He's no Madonna worshipper, not by a damned sight. You can tell that by the dame with him."

Jastrau looked up and caught sight of Stefan Steffensen's tall bony figure. As usual, he walked with his hands in his pockets, and his jacket and pants were flapping about him in the breeze. The tops of his shoes were scuffed and had not seen polish for a long time. He saw nobody.

Behind him came a woman. How like him it was to be dragging her along after him without saying a word to her.

Jastrau could not get a clear view of her face because the wind had whipped some wisps of hair over it. She tossed her head, brushed the hair back from her forehead with her hand, and tried in vain to tuck it up under her hat. It resembled black horsehair, he thought.

But he could detect her figure as the wind lashed her brown dress and rather shabby coat. It was a short chubby figure which one moment stood still and helpless as it was buffeted by a sudden blast and the next resolutely thrust a sturdy leg forward.

Vuldum stared at her through narrowed eyes.

"Can you conceive of any young girl wanting to have anything to do with him?" he said.

But Jastrau only smiled as he watched her. Her coat had a belt that hung far down over her hips, so that seen from the back she looked ridiculously broad in the beam.

"Oh well, she's no great beauty," he said indulgently.

"A heavy-set girl, but her legs aren't bad at all."

Jastrau shrugged his shoulders as Steffensen and his woman disappeared into the café.

"It'll be a coffee and a slice of white bread for her and a bottle of beer for him," Vuldum philosophized. "What do you say we have another one ourselves? I have a krone in cash that I'll contribute to the cause."

Jastrau nodded, preoccupied. He had not seen Steffensen since he had thrown him out of his apartment, and now suddenly he clearly recalled those days that had been the prelude to a period of such great uncertainty. He was still the chief literary critic for *Dagbladet*. But for how long? He had never been involved in so many polemics with aggrieved poets as during the preceding fall. It was as if they had sensed that his position was insecure. The lobster shift had fished letters out of the wastebasket, letters from older eminent poets who gently upbraided Editor Iversen for letting so young a man do the literary reviewing. Yes, those were the days that had seen the beginning of it all.

Jastrau slowly turned his back to the wind. That always lent him strength. And Vuldum was facing into the wind.

"Listen, Vuldum," he said quietly but intently, "why did you play that trick on me when I was reviewing Stefani's book? It's done me a lot of harm."

Vuldum looked surprised. But of course he had the wind in his face. A grimace swept over it.

"But my dear Ole, didn't you understand? I hope you've never believed that I wanted to do you any harm. Why should I? If I wanted to review Danish literature, why then—"

He made a disparaging gesture.

Jastrau looked him right in the eye for a second.

"No, I've never understood it."

"But, Ole," Vuldum said gently, "why haven't you ever said anything about it? Have you really let it trouble you for a whole year? You're much too suspicious. Frankly, I don't think you like me."

There was an ironic look of understanding in Vuldum's expression.

"I do and I don't," Jastrau replied, feeling embarrassed.

"Listen, Ole, I can well understand that, in a way. But now I'd be very interested to know what it is you like about me."

Jastrau would have liked to drop the subject. He shrugged his shoulders.

"Oh, well—"

Vuldum sent him a teasing smile.

"Do you like this Bolshevik we just saw better than you do me?"

Jastrau screwed up his eyes in a nervous frown.

"Yes and no."

"Yes, you've always had perverse tastes," Vuldum commented, placing a hand on his shoulder. "And now, you mustn't be quick at repartee and say that's why you like me very well after a fashion. But here comes the beer—and it's the number one waiter himself who's bringing it. What more could we want? Isn't it a fine sight to see an older, distinguished-looking gentleman with two such huge glasses of beer—and in a wind, too? Just look at that white hair!"

"Beer!" Jastrau exclaimed with vehemence. His thoughts were on Steffensen.

After they had raised their glasses to each other and each had taken a deep draught, Vuldum sat for a long time staring down into his beer.

"You really ought to be a little more discriminating about whom you associate with, Ole," he said at last.

"What are you driving at?" Jastrau snapped.

"Him—young Stefani." Vuldum nodded toward the inside of the café.

"Him? Oh, I tossed him out of the house long ago," Jastrau said. Nevertheless, at the same time, he felt he was going back on a friend. Why did he always have a bad conscience where this Steffensen was concerned?

"So you too have discovered that he's a criminal."

"A criminal? Certainly no more so than you or I."

Vuldum threw up both of his big white hands in a gesture of innocence.

"Yes. At any rate, I never passed on a disease to a woman. I don't know what you've done."

"What are you saying? Has Steffensen—?"

"Yes." Vuldum compressed his lips.

"Where did you get that bit of information?"

"From his own father, no less."

Jastrau made no reply. He vaguely recalled something—something that tied in with what Vuldum was saying.

"It was old Stefani himself who told me about it—in a very tolerant manner, I must say. But a thing like that must be hard on a father. He indicated as much when he said to me, 'Yes—when a father has to admit that his son is a criminal—you understand how I feel,' and then there was a very significant pause."

"I don't believe it's true," Jastrau protested in a low, almost melancholy tone of voice.

"Even though his father himself told me? It was a servant girl in their own house who was the victim. And when she found it out, she ran away—utterly bewildered, miserable, and sick. Whatever became of her nobody knows. Undoubtedly she went to the dogs. But you know how it is with a girl who's a servant in a well-to-do household. Nothing is easier than for the son to seduce such a little house-mouse. It's always that kind who has to be the guinea pig. But what a mean low-down trick! He had just passed his university exam—ugh!" He made a wry face and washed down his disgust with a swig of beer.

"But I don't suppose he knew—"

"Oh, that wasn't the only thing he did. He was up to a whole series of obnoxious tricks while he was at home in Aarhus. He's a beast."

Vuldum wrinkled his nose and shook his head.

"I didn't think you were such a moralist."

128

"No, and I'm not. But there are some things that can be described only as beastly. After all, one has a certain dimly defined sense of values."

Jastrau's lips curled in scorn.

"But look, Ole, hadn't we better drink up? I have to go see Father Garhammer and give him this book. Wouldn't you like to come along? It wouldn't do either of us any harm to get up where the atmosphere is a bit cleaner."

Jastrau nodded and summoned the waiter. Vuldum made a pretense of fishing in a vest pocket for his brass krone, but Jastrau smiled and shook his head.

"Thank you very much." Vuldum got up and bowed politely.

After Jastrau had paid, they began walking out Vesterbro with the sun and the wind in their eyes.

"But, look here, shouldn't you have gone up to the paper?" asked Vuldum, leaning forward at an angle while he kept a firm grip on his stiff hat.

"Yes." Jastrau squinted into the sun. "But the books won't run away. I can get them anytime. Besides, the old man is usually there at this time, and I can't stand the sight of him any longer. If he had someone to take my place, he'd fire me immediately."

"Do you think so?"

"Yes, God knows I think so. I'm not a newcomer any more. The paper needs a change. If only I could afford to toss the whole mess right into his face."

"That would undeniably be the smartest thing to do," Vuldum said quietly but earnestly, as if he wished to plant the idea unobtrusively in Jastrau's mind. "Four or five years—isn't that about how long you've been there? That's about par for the course. Was your predecessor there any longer than that?"

"Oh, this feeling of insecurity—it's enough to make a blithering idiot out of a person," Jastrau said bitterly. "And then at the same time one is supposed to be a calm impartial critic, and incorruptible as well. What's more, you make enemies on all sides. It's worse than being seriously in love with a bitch."

They had gotten as far as Stenosgade.

"See that advertisement for feather cleaning up there?" said Vuldum cryptically, pointing up at a second-story window of a corner building. Behind the window, a mass of feathers was being whirled about constantly so the whole thing resembled a cosmic fog. "What you see there has greater significance for the priests out here than you would think. It suggests the modern scientific view of the world, they say, and then they laugh. You ought to see them. They're just like boys when they hit on something like that. But then, I don't imagine you know anything about the Catholic sense of humor. It's really quite touching."

The short street, Stenosgade, created a confusing impression until they stood before the Church of the Sacred Heart of Jesus with its tower and arched gates tapering to a point at the top. Then the street suddenly became readily comprehensible. The red church stood nudged in between the red, monastic-looking residential buildings. At the left were the rectory and school and at the right a private house that obviously had been smitten by its close contact with Catholicism and had been trimmed with a gratuitous spire. The pointed-arch motif seemed to have invested one entire side of the street with an aspect of piety.

The private Protestant buildings on the other side of the street looked drab by comparison.

Vuldum went familiarly up the stone steps to the red rectory and rang the doorbell, and through the door panes they saw a humble doorman with stooped shoulders and downcast eyes come trudging toward them to let them in.

With a saccharine smile, Vuldum asked to see Father Garhammer, and at once he and Jastrau were ushered into the parlor. Jastrau immediately felt disappointed. What had he expected? Something entirely different—bare plaster walls, ascetic furnishings perhaps. But not the oval table and the pink, gold-edged bowl for visiting cards. Certainly not the ugly, depressing hat tree that stood in a corner with its hooks bristling, as in a pub. It was all in the most banal mediocre taste, cheap and shabby, and altogether too prosaic for troubled thirsting souls who dreamt of church windows and the fragrance of incense.

Jastrau sat down, feeling uneasy and oppressed. He felt he was in foreign territory and stared almost with longing at the dark houses across the street, the everyday houses and shops, while Vuldum rummaged through the calling-card bowl, picked up the picture postcards he found there, and read them.

"A gruesome place this, isn't it?" he asked Jastrau in a tone of disdain.

Then the door opened, and in walked little Father Garhammer, wearing a long black Jesuit's gown with a broad black belt. He seemed a little lopsided and awkward as he turned to face them directly and assumed his air of authority and his smile. He had a small head. His face was swarthy, that of a man from the south, so that the smile on his broad lips was most conspicuous. It was like the smile of a boardinghouse keeper, both cordial and crafty. He kept his head bent slightly forward.

Vuldum bowed filially and introduced his friend, Editor Ole Jastrau, and Father Garhammer immediately observed, with a noticeable German accent, that he was well acquainted with Jastrau's articles.

"We don't share the same opinions at all," he said with a touch of irony from which his accent seemed to remove all sting.

"But sit down now, and tell me what you want," he said, settling himself in a chair with the air of a lady paying a visit. His broad smile beamed on them like that of a father confessor.

"Today I merely want to make you a present of a little something I found—a little gift that, incredible though it may seem, consists of the writings of Poul Helgesen. You know, the Danish Catholic of the Reformation period." Vuldum laid a book with a dark well-worn binding on the table.

"That's very kind of you," replied the priest, opening the book for the sake of appearances. "You really shouldn't have done it, Herr Vuldum. You're a good-hearted man."

Vuldum lowered his lean ghostly profile in a polite bow.

"I shall read it with pleasure," the priest went on. "And the library will be happy to have it, too. It will go into our library, of course."

But he quickly raised his dark eyes from the book and looked quizzically at Jastrau.

Vuldum had noticed the expression on the priest's face. "Yes," he said, self-consciously hitching up his trousers, "I brought my friend along so he could see how comfortably you live here. I thought it might do a proponent of progress like him some good."

Father Garhammer suddenly drew himself up straight.

"Do you believe in progress?" he asked, immediately on guard.

"Well, yes," Jastrau replied evasively. As he did so, he noticed how Vuldum suddenly seemed to get taller and to stare down at him with a look of compassion. He felt as if he had suddenly been deserted.

"Then you must also believe that the world order had a beginning in time," the priest said, speaking rapidly and clearly. He did not smile now. He was awaiting an opponent's scintillating counterattack.

"I've never concerned myself about the creation of the world," said Jastrau, laughing. Vuldum sat looking at them indifferently, without saying a word.

"But you are forced to do just that, Herr Jastrau, if you believe in progress," Father Garhammer said, obviously relishing the argument.

Jastrau looked at him uncomprehendingly.

"Yes, so you are," the priest went on rapidly, "because if a world order has existed back into infinity, then everything would by now have been brought into being. And in that case, we would now be living in a state of utmost perfection. But I certainly don't believe that is the situation." The irony in his tone was evident, and Vuldum smiled knowingly.

Jastrau cringed.

"Oh, progress is a superficial problem," he replied with some irritation. "It really doesn't interest me. I believe only in change."

"Not in the sameness of things?" Garhammer asked with a laugh that indicated surprise.

"Well, there is something to Nietzsche's theory of eternal recurrence," Vuldum broke in, casually disregarding Jastrau as if the observation were something beyond his powers of comprehension.

"Yes. Hell is an eternal recurrence," Father Garhammer conceded. Then he turned once more in his chair, like a lady, and looked at Jastrau.

"So you are not interested in progress, Herr Jastrau. Tell me, then, what are you interested in?"

It was so unreal, this mode of thinking. And it was as if the unreality spread to their surroundings. The buildings on the other side of the street became gathering rain clouds. The oval table, the visiting-card bowl, and the hat tree seemed like pieces of furniture that had been placed out on the sidewalk by the king's bailiff. There, in those chairs on the sidewalk, sat Vuldum and Father Garhammer, and suddenly it occurred to Jastrau how feminine they both were. Vuldum tall and relentless, as only a redhead can be, and the priest short and dark, incessantly biting his wide lips and greedy for a new problem without any substance to it—argument for the sake of argument. Weren't old maids the grimmest and most implacable individuals in the world?

"I'm really interested only in myself," Jastrau replied cautiously, avoiding Vuldum's cold smile. "And consequently, in psychology, too, which is the basis for an understanding of one's self. Yes, and I'm also interested in how one constructs a real world—finds reality."

While Jastrau slowly and with difficulty groped his way forward, a change came over Father Garhammer. He became more friendly and nodded in a paternal manner, as if he wanted to help him along.

"Yes, that's a difficult problem indeed," he said with a pause between every single word. His accent gave a crafty sound to everything he said, but now he was smiling all the while, a little too benevolently and condescendingly.

132

"But of course you have science to look to, Herr Jastrau."

"Oh, yes." Jastrau smiled skeptically, and his smile kindled an expression of understanding on the face of the priest, who again nodded encouragingly and went on, "Haven't you? Yes—that you have. And you also have logic."

Jastrau smiled again. He recalled his insuperable struggles with logic as a branch of philosophy. Perhaps ethics was the only aspect of the subject that he had regarded with more contempt.

"You do have logic, too, don't you?"

"Yes. Otherwise one would turn into a fool."

Vuldum made no effort to conceal a supercilious yawn. But Father Garhammer nodded like a teacher and went on slowly and earnestly.

"And so you base your reasoning on axioms that you accept, because your knowledge of facts tells you that these axioms must be correct. Yes, that's right. And so do we. That's merely acknowledging the nature of things."

Jastrau watched him with a faint, guarded smile.

"Yes, and now you're going to confront me with your dogmas—I know it, I know it."

"But isn't it simply the same thing? We accept the dogmas. We don't understand them any more than we understand the laws of nature. We accept them because our sense of coherence tells us they must be correct. We don't want to be fools—moral fools, you understand—and I believe that's a term we can apply to sinners."

The priest's face retained its indulgent smile throughout his remarks.

"But suppose I don't acknowledge the validity of logic?" Jastrau objected.

"Then you'll remain a fool."

The last remark was made with such a strange charm, and the priest looked so much like a nice old aunt as he sat there in his black skullcap with his head roguishly cocked to one side, that both Vuldum and Jastrau had to laugh.

"Yes, these problems can be very interesting," Father Garhammer said to himself, suddenly looking from one to the other of them like a pleased child. He was just as surprised at having made a clever remark, and just as pleased with himself for having done so, as Jastrau would have been had he unintentionally delivered himself of a syllogism.

"But it's logic that's at fault," Jastrau said after a short pause.

"Not my logic, Herr Jastrau," replied Garhammer. "I'm no fool." He

133

laughed again, then shook his head and repeated: "No, I'm no fool. Ha ha ha."

"In my opinion, we place altogether too much stock in these chess-game rules that we call logic," protested Jastrau. He could not, like the priest, keep on feeling delighted about how interesting such problems could be.

But Garhammer was still laughing. "Ha ha! That's your opinion. But then you're a fool." His German accent made the word sound thick and round and good-natured. "Ha ha ha," he cackled.

"But isn't it strange," he went on, suddenly becoming serious and turning to Vuldum, "that this is what makes it so difficult for us? Catholicism has a hard time holding on to women. It is too logical, and women won't have anything to do with logic. Isn't it strange?"

Vuldum smiled. "And people here in Denmark go around believing that Catholicism means gold, frankincense, and myrrh."

"Yes, that's a big mistake," said the priest.

They spoke to each other as if they were better informed than he, and Jastrau felt humbled.

But then he noticed a crafty gleam in Vuldum's eyes, and he sat up expectantly.

"Listen, Father Garhammer, there is something I have often wanted to ask you," said Vuldum with a faint smile. "Did Jesus ever commit a sin?"

"No—no, no!" Father Garhammer replied, horrified.

Jastrau felt his cheeks growing red. Was Vuldum now going to torture him some more? It was that book of Stefani's that he was referring to. But why? Why? Why tear the legs off flies?

"I was thinking of the story of the fig tree," Vuldum went on unmercifully. "Wasn't that an act of rashness?"

Jastrau looked at him, distressed and uncomprehending.

"But the tree bore no fruit," replied the priest.

"Perhaps it might have if it had been cared for."

"No," came the decisive answer.

"There's no way one could ever know," said Vuldum. He smiled hideously.

Father Garhammer did not see the smile, nor would he have understood it if he had.

"Yes, there is," he said. "The tree's time had run out. You might as well call it a rash act when God on Judgment Day separates the goats from the sheep."

"Yes, but the story of the fig tree makes it seem as if Jesus was in a bad humor," Vuldum persisted.

"But it was not a fit of temper," replied Garhammer. "It was a parable. Jesus spoke in parables usually. But here he enacted a parable—*er machte ein Gleichnis.*"

Vuldum smiled as if satisfied.

"There's a book by H. C. Stefani that made me think of that story," he said apologetically.

"Oh—that book," replied the priest, raising his hand. "It's a—a really bad book. You ought not to have written so favorably about it, Herr Jastrau," he added.

"I didn't write the review, damn it," Jastrau said vehemently. But then he suddenly turned red in the face and said, "I'm sorry, Father. I beg your pardon."

"Oh well, a colloquialism, isn't it?" Garhammer replied in a friendly manner. "But now you'll have to excuse me, for I have to leave."

He arose and extended each of them a hand.

"And thanks. Many thanks for the book, and thanks also for the visit. Come again soon."

Jastrau and Vuldum were silent as they again strolled along Vesterbrogade. Jastrau looked down at the sidewalk and sensed that Vuldum was observing him with a secret feeling of triumph.

At the Freedom Statue he wanted to turn off and go directly home to his empty apartment. He felt no desire to go up to the paper, no desire for anything.

"Are you going home?" Vuldum asked.

Jastrau nodded.

"Lucky fellow. You have a home, whereas I have to go back to a boardinghouse," Vuldum went on in a tone of utter dejection. Suddenly Jastrau saw him looking appraisingly at the same old one-krone piece in his hand.

"If only I dared ask you to loan me two kroner, I'd have enough for an after-theatre snack and a beer."

With an ironically melancholy expression, he held the krone so that the sunlight fell on it and it glistened in a woebegone manner.

"I could very likely arrange to pay the tip later."

"Unfortunately, I haven't anything smaller than a fiver."

"Well, then, allow me to be content with that."

As soon as Vuldum had gotten the money, he disappeared in the direction of the Town Hall Square. He walked erectly with a springy step, taller by a stiff hat than the crowd.

Jastrau's eyes followed the St. Peter's dome for a long time.

Chapter Two   Jastrau had kept himself shut up in the empty apartment the whole day. He had not answered the telephone, no matter how long it had rung. Nothing had been able to intrude upon him and disturb him.

But how strange it was. As long as he had occupied himself with his ephemeral critical writing, he had not been aware of the empty rooms. On the other hand, as soon as he had put it aside and pulled out a pile of written sheets, a novel that he had been working on for more than a year and had not picked up for the last six weeks, he had immediately been troubled by the emptiness of his surroundings. The fact that his wife was off with her brother on an auto trip in North Zealand, that his son was being taken care of at her parents' house, gave him no feeling of tranquility; it only made him listless. And instead of working he had lighted his pipe and begun to wander back and forth through the vacant rooms, enlivening them only with his own presence, while he smoked and hummed to himself. A self-indulgent conglomeration of dreams and thoughts, pugnacious, apprehensive, triumphant, reconciliatory.

It had already begun to get dark when he finally sat down at his desk. The dreary walls surrounding the courtyard outside the windows of his workroom were becoming lost in shadow. He doubtless should have gotten up and turned on the lights. But he put if off for some minutes longer—long minutes during which the darkness grew thicker.

He began half-heartedly to leaf through the written sheets. Yellowed sheets. In the obscurity of the room they took on a greenish tinge. The ink had an old, murky look to it. And he remained sitting, scrupulously examining the irregularities in the individual letters of the words he had written months before.

A piece of paper slipped out of the pile—a poem written by an unfamiliar hand. It was the poem Stefan Steffensen had forgotten to take with him. Only yesterday he had seen him with a young girl over at the Paraply. And he read:

Diminuendo

Tired of your embraces, feeling spent and happy,
I live but for a kiss against your mouth,
Feel your lips grow slack and your breath
Subside as you drift away into sleep.

Tired of your kiss, I caress your soft curves,
Breasts, hips, firmly with my hand,
Shape out of darkness a vase as fragile
As your body, as light as your soul.

Tired of a caress that reveals how clearly
Love's calm aftermath has softened your form,
I see your face lost among the pillows,
Borne by hair tossed like seaweed after a storm.

Tired of seeing and feeling and loving you,
I forsake your bed and your tranquil slumber,
Roam through the room and finger its objects,
Feel you here in your peaceful abode.

Anne Marie, you live in these objects,
Anne Marie, so warm and so still,
Anne Marie, now I seek coolness
In the crisp fresh air near your windowsill.

In the semidarkness the words swam on the greenish page so that he felt his eyes grow heavy. He rubbed them and wearily shoved the poem aside. He did not care to think about Stefan Steffensen any longer.

How blue the sky was above the roofs and the shadowy chimneys. What a deep expressive color. But no, he could not rid his mind of the poem. He wondered how it would sound if Steffensen read it aloud. How would his coarse, derisive voice adapt itself to the words? To be sure, there were poets who never read their own stanzas aloud, but merely handed over a piece of paper with the words written on it—an odd, silent type of person with a wild rebellious look and a gloomy countenance. Jastrau knew the type well. But was Steffensen one of those?

It was probably impossible, this evening, to shut out the mental image of him—this tall, rawboned fellow whose jacket was always pulled aside so that his hands might remain planted in his pants pockets. And suddenly Jastrau perceived three words, as clearly as if they had been held up before him in print. Where? In the air? In his memory? In any event, he could read them: *transmitter of infection.* He could make out every letter. They radiated horror and brutality. And Jastrau wondered if this was why the image of Steffensen remained so ineradicably before him, as clearly delineated as a police-record photograph of a criminal, in profile and full face, revealing even what went on behind the man's skull.

Then the front doorbell rang.

Jastrau gave a start. The bell sounded frightful there in the twilight. His heart began to pound.

He got up slowly and went out into the hallway, where it was completely dark. He could detect only a dim light through the frosted panes and a shadowy figure outside.

He opened the door, and as he did so he gasped for breath. It was a tall stooped man with his hands in his pants pockets.

"This is really strange," Jastrau exclaimed in the hoarse tone of voice that comes so easily to one standing in the darkness. "Is it you, Steffensen?"

"Yes. After all, your wife isn't at home, so I thought I might venture up to see you," Steffensen said in a peculiar whisper.

"Well then, come in."

Jastrau forgot that he had once thrown him out of the house. But Steffensen's long furtive stride as he stepped inside brought back fleeting memories.

"Did you think I'd throw you out?"

"One can never tell," Steffensen replied gently. He behaved almost like a tramp who had wandered into a better-class apartment. There was something subdued and mysterious about him.

"Do I dare sit down?" he asked, cautiously taking a position near one of the rococo chairs.

"Yes, yes," Jastrau said, laughing.

"Uh," Steffensen grunted, and sat down. "You wouldn't have a cigarette, would you?"

"I have something better—a cigar."

"That probably won't set so well on an empty stomach," Steffensen mumbled. A trace of a smile crossed his grayish face.

"Haven't you eaten today?"

"No. I haven't eaten for a long time."

"But I saw you yesterday at the Paraply."

"Yes, that was a real debauch," Steffensen said with a grin. "I can still taste the coffee and that piece of Danish pastry, and I'm nourishing myself now by belching."

Jastrau had seated himself on the sofa, where he leaned forward and watched him. It was as if Steffensen's face were divided into two parts—a dark half on the room side and a light half turned toward the vanishing daylight let in by the windows.

"Oh, you can stand a cigar," Jastrau said callously, shoving the cigar box and a match toward him.

"All right, then," Steffensen said, letting out a guffaw. There was something imbecilic about his laughter, and when he had lighted the

138

cigar the red glow from its tip revealed a clownish face still agitated by meaningless merriment.

An instant later the face was enveloped in a cloud of white smoke.

Jastrau remained sitting and staring at him in the semidarkness. How shabby Steffensen looked. His clothes were rumpled, as if he never took them off when he slept. They had crept up on him so that as he sat stoop-shouldered his chest seemed in danger of collapsing under the strain.

"Oh, how this cigar claws at my insides!" Steffensen groaned, doubling up and continuing to laugh like a dolt. "I went hungry this way during the winter, and then I had this Anne Marie on my hands besides."

"Anne Marie—who's she?"

"Oh, just a sad sack of a servant girl we had at home," replied Steffensen, making a face. "She and I live together—in a manner of speaking." He laughed again. "But it's platonic—no love-making and nothing to eat. She's got a disease, I might add, so she's not for me."

Jastrau gave a start. Suddenly he got up and went over to Steffensen. "You look like a sad sack yourself," he said, keeping his voice pitched in a mild conversational tone.

"Oh, shut up," said Steffensen, but less roughly than might have been expected. He laughed again, but this time the laughter sounded strained. "Yes, I'm in bad shape. And I'm hungry. And tomorrow we're being thrown out on the street—dead broke. Uh—what a fix I'm in! Write home and get money and motherly advice—I did that all winter in order to get by. But now it doesn't work any more. Now it's all up with that—not a krone from home. Nothing but a letter from my father—full of moralizing. I should pull myself together and blah, blah, blah. I couldn't take it, by God—not from him." He shook his head. "But why are you standing there staring at me?"

"I was just thinking that there is some *smørrebrød** out in the kitchen," Jastrau said, his eyes sparkling.

"What's that? Oh, now—" Steffensen raised his arms beseechingly.

"I was over at the *smørrebrød* factory on Vesterbrogade this afternoon," Jastrau went on. "You know, the one near the Freedom Statue—"

"Yes, yes, yes. Look, couldn't I—?"

"But it all tastes alike. It makes no difference if the bread has headcheese or smoked eel on it. So I didn't bother to eat it."

"Do you want to torture me?" Steffensen cried out, sitting up straight.

* Open-face sandwiches.

Jastrau did not answer, but merely remained standing and staring down at him with the same flashing expression in his eyes.

"Yes, perhaps that's what I want to do," he suddenly burst out as he came back to his senses. "Now I'll go out and get the *smørrebrød*."

Steffensen looked him uncomprehendingly as he left the room.

Soon afterward, Jastrau returned with several pieces of *smørrebrød* on a plate, which he placed on the table with a bottle of beer.

"I don't care to turn on the lights," he remarked.

Steffensen said nothing. Swiftly he drew up his chair, carelessly laid the lighted cigar on the edge of the table, and began to eat. Jastrau could hear him munching and could see his dark arms and only slightly lighter hands moving. He could barely distinguish the face—a faint oval patch with eyes like bits of tinsel. For now it was completely dark.

The wall between the two windows stood out like a broad black pillar against the flickering expanse of sky that lay revealed beyond the windowpanes. At the neighbor's across the way a light was burning cozily behind a rolled-down blind. But above the rooftops the sky glowed fitfully with what appeared to be a form of self-illumination like the flashing of the northern lights, waning and waxing, waning and waxing, as the electric advertising signs above Vesterbro alternately went off and on.

"You must pardon me for what I did," Jastrau said in a gentle voice that suited the obscurity in which they sat. He was sitting with his elbows on the table and followed Steffensen's motions with his eyes.

"For what?" asked Steffensen, his mouth full of food. There was a note of expectancy, of anticipation, in the way he asked the question.

"Because I—tormented you."

"Oh, is that all?" Steffensen laughed and went on chewing. "I thought you were begging my pardon for the time you let my poem be printed with the name Stefani under it. You were a real shit that time."

"That wasn't my fault," Jastrau said softly.

"Not your fault!" Steffensen made a face and drank from the bottle. "It was a dirty trick, and you can be sure I'll get even with you for it."

"I can tell by the way you sound that you're beginning to get filled up," Jastrau replied with sudden acerbity. Steffensen chuckled.

"And since you have so much to apologize for, you might loan me some money," he said, grinning.

"So that's it. You apparently don't remember that the last time you were here you got tossed out."

They sat across from each other in the darkness and could not see each other's expressions.

140

"Yes, I remember. But tonight your wife isn't home."

"How do you know that?"

"I heard it over at the Paraply. Ha! I dragged Anne Marie along with me so I could read the Paraply's menu to her aloud. That way she could imagine herself having a feast, the bitch. And then I heard your voice behind the potted hedge. You were sitting there with that red-haired fellow. Incidentally, he's tapped my old man for two hundred bucks. Ha!"

"What's that?"

"Yes, that's what I said. It was nicely done. But, as I was saying, I heard you say your wife wasn't home. Do you think I'd have come otherwise? No, not by a damn sight."

"How much do you want?"

"Forty kroner."

"Are you crazy?"

"Yes."

Jastrau fumbled for the cigar box, found a cigar and lighted it.

"Are you disposed to let me have it?" Steffensen asked, watching him closely.

"No," came the drawling answer.

"Then hand me another cigar, because now I'm in shape to smoke it."

Jastrau held a cigar out through the darkness until it touched Steffensen's hand. Then a match flared up, and Jastrau saw that the *smørrebrød* plate was empty.

"Well," said Steffensen—only his mouth and nose were visible in the red glow from the end of the cigar—"then we'll be tossed out in the morning. All right, but it's a pity as far as Anne Marie is concerned."

Jastrau said nothing, but lay back on the sofa. *Transmitter of infection!* He saw the words before him—the printed letters. Steffensen kept sucking audibly on the cigar.

"As a matter of fact, you can have the forty kroner," Jastrau said suddenly, blowing out a cloud of tobacco smoke. It billowed upward in the glow from his cigar.

The offer sounded positively insulting.

"Thanks. Let's have it then, and I'll get out of here," Steffensen said scornfully. But Jastrau turned indolently so that he lay on his side.

"No. You might as well stay. As it is, you've ruined the evening for me."

"Do you think I want to sit here in the dark and talk about the soul and stuff like that?" Steffensen protested.

"You'll get forty kroner for it."

"Get them! Ha ha. No, I'm borrowing them."

"It amounts to the same thing."

"All right. What sort of soulfulness shall we discuss?" Steffensen leaned back in his chair in a demonstration of patience.

Jastrau remained lying on the sofa without moving. But although he did not shift his position, he was now doubled up with excitement and every muscle was tense as he stared at the dark angular figure that exuded animosity.

"You forgot a poem the last time you were here," he said gently as if he wanted to steal up on Steffensen and fling something soulful in his face like a wet rag.

"Do you want that for your paper, too?" Steffensen said spitefully.

Jastrau laughed. "No thanks. Thanks just the same. But do you write many of that kind? I suppose you do," he added sharply.

"Are you perhaps thinking of helping me get out a collection of poems?"

"Well, that might be."

"Ha! That's nice of you." Steffensen grinned. "Do you think I want to be a poet and make my living by writing made-to-order verses for special occasions and that sort of trash like the rest of you? What? Do you think I'm looking for a place in the history of literature?"

"One can never tell," Jastrau replied.

"No sir! I don't want any part of the intellectual life. It isn't for me. I just don't go for it. Just look at my father."

Jastrau gave a short laugh, but Steffensen went on. Was he being aggressive or was he on the defensive? His words fell from his lips in coarse lumps. His voice was hoarse and fanatical, full of animosity, and it seemed that he was only getting warmed up.

"Yes, you do know a little something about him. He's a fine one, isn't he? Uh—what that beast hasn't ruined! All the fine words have lain in his filthy mouth as in a coffin filled with mud, and I'm damned if I can get them washed clean. It's dirty material to work with. The whole language has been befouled by our ancestors. Have you ever heard my old man quote a stanza of verse? It's disgusting the way he licks at it. A person has to create a whole new language for himself!"

"And that's just what one does, of course," Jastrau protested.

"So?" Steffensen said, making a face. "Do you writers do that? No. You take it over just as it is—all messed up by our elders—that's what you do. Language is a slut. People should never have taken up with her. No, they should never have learned to talk. That's what's ruined our lives."

142

Jastrau stared in exasperation at the dark, faceless form—an animated black mass, an arm in motion.

"What do you want to do, then?" he asked.

"Live—nothing but live. Like an animal—without words."

"And do you?" Jastrau asked tauntingly.

"No. And that's the hell of it," Steffensen replied. It was a strangely hostile way of taking someone into his confidence. "I'm bound by a chain of words just like the rest of you, damn it! But I'm sure as hell going to break it, even if it takes a crime to do it. A crime. Phooey—there's another word. They block the way to the infinite—all these stupid words—when one wants to live, that is. Because living—does that mean thinking? Does it? Or saying something? Words? Isn't it rather going for an auto ride at a hundred and twenty kilometers an hour? Or getting into a fight, or raping a girl? Why does a person have to think, anyhow?"

"Is that what you want to do?" asked Jastrau, laughing quietly. He was not going to agree with Steffensen—never. He was more inclined to annoy him, and he smiled derisively.

"Yes." Steffensen laughed too.

"Then you had better be careful that you don't land in the clink or tumble headfirst into religion," Jastrau said slyly.

"Religion? Never!" Steffensen retorted roughly, shifting his position violently as if he had suddenly found himself sitting on a stone that was about to slip loose from a dark cliff and go plunging into the night.

"I just want to let you know that religion isn't so wonderful either," Jastrau said, suddenly becoming patronizing. "Only yesterday I was out on Stenosgade, and there I met a Jesuit who had eternity up his sleeve like a card in a game of omber. But do you suppose he so much as gave a thought to eternity? He only sat there hoping for a chance to play with a really good opponent. A good card game was all he was looking for. Fortunately, I disappointed him. I don't have any feel for card games."

"I like to play well enough," Steffensen protested.

"Can you really take an ace of spades seriously?"

"Yes—if it suits my hand, that is. Just as seriously as a poem."

Jastrau got up in a fit of irritation.

"Oh, I don't want to sit here and listen to this any longer!" he burst out as crudely as if it might have been Steffensen himself speaking.

"Well, that's good. That means that now maybe I can have the forty kroner." Steffensen got up too. As they stood directly facing each other in the darkness, they both felt the full force of their strange, wanton

hostility toward each other. They felt like two hooligans who acciden-
tally found themselves walking side by side along the sidewalk. Neither would have been surprised if the other had begun to shove him
aside with his shoulder.

Then Jastrau turned on the light. The sudden glare struck their eyes
with such impact that they each began to rub them. They also rubbed
away some of their antagonism. And they could not fully understand
the charged atmosphere that had prevailed in the darkness, the purposeless, ill-defined animosity that had striven to find expression.

"There you are," Jastrau said, taking four ten-krone notes from his
wallet. Steffensen accepted them without a word, crumpled them up
casually, and stuffed them in a vest pocket.

"Shall we go now?" Jastrau said.

They had not so much as looked at each other since the light had
been turned on. Jastrau turned it off again, and they left.

Once down in the street, they found themselves unable to part.
Jastrau could not think of an excuse, and it occurred to him that he
should have chosen to walk on out the uninteresting Istedgade in
order to get rid of his guest.

But from force of habit he turned in toward the Town Hall Square.
And Steffensen followed along without giving it a thought. Up the
steps to the plaza in front of the railway station. Over to the parapet
alongside the open cut where the tracks were. And on toward Vesterbrogade.

Neither of them said a word.

It was a mild spring evening. The sky arched black and star-strewn
over Vesterbro Passage and the old railroad right-of-way with its
hodgepodge of low-roofed shops. It was a vast dome resembling a
rural sky, flanked by the waxwork museum and the group of large
structures on Reventlowsgade, which loomed up like two dark prom-
ontories. Standing beneath this wide-open expanse they both instinctively drew a deep breath of cool evening air, seasoned with gasoline
and perfume and the fetid odor of many people, to which was added
the acrid aroma of metal and coal smoke from the subterranean
railway—a slightly intoxicating draught of poisonous liqueurs that the
big city had to offer in spring.

Suddenly Steffensen stopped in front of a mysterious, portière-hung
doorway. A gilded Buddha glowed mysteriously in a narrow window.
In a voice full of wisdom, Steffensen said, "We could use a highball."

And Jastrau followed him into a very small barroom decorated in
outlandish oriental style.

Behind a semicircular bar was an altar on which stood bottles and several ugly Buddhas whose eyes were equipped with colored electric light bulbs. And forming a voluptuous center of attraction in this crude world of divinity was a pink figure of a naked woman with breasts and other appurtenances. And behind the same bar stood a bartender with a round pink head, his face wreathed in a vague Buddha-like smile as he chatted with several gaudy priestesses with breasts that rested on the bar and other charms that bulged over the edges of the stools on which they sat. A phonograph droned on discreetly over in a corner. There was an odor of dusty furnishings, and one felt enclosed in a box with a lot of old rags and discarded imitation trinkets.

There were immediate signs of restlessness among the priestesses. Dark, ardent glances. An empty whiskey glass was raised to a red feminine mouth in a gesture meant to convey an impression of unspeakable thirst—a suggestive bit of pantomime. A skirt that slipped far up above the knee, up beyond the critical point where the flesh-colored stocking left off, while the creature fidgeted gracefully on the high stool—another seductive pantomime. Paying no attention, Jastrau and Steffensen found a place to sit on a little dais where there was an octagonal table. Very oriental.

When the whiskey had been ordered, the nature of their visit was established. They had indicated that they had come to drink and nothing more. And the priestesses quickly turned their backs on them. The cordon closed ranks. A row of supple female backs, restless hips, and bulging behinds shut off the view of the bartender's pink smile.

But Jastrau and Steffensen were still in no mood for conversation. Silently, they let themselves be lulled into a torpor by the phonograph and the stuffy atmosphere. The whiskey and soda in the thick glasses had a soothing effect. Their surroundings began to take form.

"Life is so dull!" they heard a drunken voice exclaim. "We need a new world war, damn it!"

Shrill but forced laughter from the women. A "Hear! Hear!" from a deep-throated male voice in the background.

"The girls had life in them then. The whiskey flowed." There was a commotion. The drunken man almost fell out of his chair.

Then the monologue was drowned out in a general hubbub. Voices from the oriental booths along the walls. Clinking of glasses. Toasts. Little squeals. Men and women entwined in intimate embraces, almost in arabesque fashion, so that their positions seemed to fit into the décor of the place.

Then suddenly Jastrau recognized a man with a thin head of hair that gave the impression of having been carefully parted over a doll-like skull. He also recognized the faint trace of a polite smile on the childish face. It was Little P.

But what was it that Little P. had in his hand? It looked like a travel folder. He was leafing through it as he laughed in a strange manner and shook his head.

A stout man with a thick, purple nose reached out for the folder.

"I bid three hundred! Three hundred!" And the stout man held up three fingers, as if he wanted to take an oath on it.

The rest of the little auction was hidden behind the black-clad back of a waiter.

"The drinks are standing and getting lukewarm," Steffensen said.

Jastrau pulled himself together and nodded.

"It seems damned good to get away from that hole of yours over there," Steffensen went on, raising his glass to his lips.

"You could have stayed away, you know," said Jastrau, smiling and raising his glass. "But I take it then that you like this better than sitting around talking about lofty matters."

"Let's not go into that again," Steffensen growled. "If we do, we'll only get sore at each other."

Jastrau leaned back in his chair and stared at the hard gloomy face and the tousled blond hair. Yes, he looked like a rowdy. He would certainly never have been served if Jastrau had not been with him.

"Listen, you," he said suddenly, but then stopped. It was strange. Yesterday Vuldum has asked him the same question. Strange.

"What is it?" Steffensen asked.

"Why—yes, why don't you like me?"

It was ridiculous. Sentimental. A need for sympathy? He saw Vuldum's sharp features before him. That sterile mouth.

"Yes, why don't you?" Jastrau repeated.

Suddenly Steffensen's eyes assumed the same glazed whitish luster as before, and his lips grew rigid in an expression of inexplicable anger. They were thrust forward in defiance.

"Because I thought you were a genuine rebel. But let's not talk about that now," he added imploringly, collapsing again.

"Yes, let's talk about it now," Jastrau said softly. He wanted to get the better of him. "You thought I was a genuine rebel."

"Yes." Again Steffensen sat up straight. "That's what we need. We've never really had any. And then I met a soft, pudgy bourgeois bogged down in family life and all that."

"But I was good enough for you when you needed money," Jastrau went on, still in a friendly tone.

"Yes, why not? When the bourgeoisie has a sentimental need to

146

subsidize art, then let them shell out. But let's not talk about it now."

Once more his voice had a pleading note in it, and he lifted his glass and nodded deferentially to divert attention from the subject.

"You're not drinking," he said in a friendly manner.

Jastrau drank.

"Three hundred and twenty-five is the bid," came a voice. "And not an øre more."

"You ought to take it, Little P.," came a woman's voice. "For my sake, you ought to take it. You mustn't go away—for my sake, Little P."

"What is it they're up to?" Steffensen asked, nodding toward Little P.

"I haven't any idea."

"Look, we've got to have another highball. I'm buying."

"You?" Jastrau asked in surprise. "You haven't any money."

"Oh, no?" Steffensen grinned, pulled the four crumpled ten-krone notes from his pocket, and tossed them on the table. "I put the touch on a bourgeois boob for these—ha ha!"

"Yes—but Anne Marie—"

"What do I care?"

"But you'll be thrown out on the street tomorrow."

"Then I'll simply move in with Sanders."

Jastrau wrinkled his brows, but Steffensen went on: "Sanders is all right. If he has money, then the other fellow has money too. A person can live at his place. His door is never locked. I've been there when as many as five of us were sleeping up at his hole-in-the-wall. We put up there—lived there for a week. He's the only genuine Communist in the country. Let's drink to him. Waiter! We need more whiskey. That's the way you ought to be. Like Sanders."

"And Anne Marie? Will you take her along up to his place?"

"Damned if I know. What do I care?"

At that moment a wave of exultation engulfed the entire barroom. The girls leaped down from their stools and swarmed out onto the floor. And the bartender in his white jacket squeezed his way out from behind the bar and joined in the jubilation. Men and women alike got up from their tables.

"Three hundred and fifty! Three hundred and fifty! Little P. is going to stay! Hurray!"

Little P.'s pale face appeared above the heads of the customers. He bowed smilingly in all directions while the rejoicing continued.

"Oh—Little P.!" a woman shrieked. "So you're not going away."

Little P. raised his arm in a silent gesture and waved a handful of crackling bills in the air.

"I'm buying a round for the whole house," he shouted in a thin voice. It was very difficult for such a puny person to measure up to the level of the enthusiasm and adulation that surrounded him. "I'm buying! Drinks for the house!" he squeaked.

"You did all right, getting that ticket for so little," someone shouted to the merchant with the purplish nose.

"A deal is a deal," grunted the merchant. "I have a son who can do with a trip to Canada."

"What's it all about?" Jastrau asked the bartender.

The bartender gave him a moist, Buddha-like smile.

"Oh, Little P. has sold his ticket to Canada, that's all. He was supposed to have been on the train an hour ago."

Gradually peace was restored to the room. The customers found their places again. The merchant soon left.

Little P., on the other hand, walked around the room accepting congratulations, an irremovable smile on his anemic lips. The men clapped him on the shoulder. The women kissed him on both cheeks as well as square on the mouth until, crumpled and dazed as a fashion model subjected to a roll downhill but still smiling, he stood before Jastrau's table.

"What? Is it you, maestro?"

Jastrau, infected by the general enthusiasm, embraced him cordially.

"You're staying, Little P.! Just think, Steffensen—he's staying. He's not going away. He's staying."

"Yes, I'm staying," replied Little P., unable to account for Jastrau's outburst of joy. "You see, there's no clock in this barroom, so the train got away without me. But, maestro, I'm sitting over here with a charming young lady. I'd be very happy if you'd move over to my table."

Jastrau let himself be easily persuaded. And Steffensen lumbered along after him. His face was set in a frown.

A little Frøken Caja with a heart-shaped mouth. She became downright frightened when she saw Steffensen's shoddy, dirty clothes. But there was also an oval-shaped Herr Dieterding with a soft voice, and she took shelter behind him. And a Frøken Bubi with a flushed face and heavy breasts. She kept leaning forward over either Little P. or a cocktail—a murky mixture with an egg yolk swimming uncomfortably around in it. "It looks like an abortion," Steffensen managed to remark. Thereafter he was allowed to drink in peace without being bothered by the women around him.

The drinks were kept full. The damp checks accumulated on the

148

table. Little P. smiled at everyone and shifted the three hundred and fifty kroner into his left hand each time he had to take a drink, then back to the right hand when he had to pull himself together. He looked as if he intended to take the money to bed with him.

"It's nice that I'm staying," he peeped now and then.

Then the oval Herr Dieterding permitted himself to express some opinions about literature. And Jastrau drank several highballs on behalf of the opinions.

Steffensen emptied the glasses that were placed before him and made himself noticeable only by his presence.

But it was a mobile company. People floated about like clouds. Now a few men would appear, jovial individuals who sang "For he's a jolly good fellow," then several women who leaned closely over Little P., whose childish smile became more and more lost in his disintegrating features. People crowded closer and closer.

Jastrau, however, inhaled deep draughts of this fragrance of human proximity and felt happy. A woman's fingers ran up his thigh as if playing a piano. Oh, there was no emptiness here. A woman's silk-covered breast brushed against his nose and pressed against his eye, shutting off his vision. Oh, the fullness, the exuberance of it. Fullness, abundance—that was all that was eternal. That and the proximity of human beings. Closeness to human beings. The only thing worth living for.

But Steffensen only sat there, lonely, in the midst of the gathering, and drank. Drops of sweat rolled down his unnaturally high, pale forehead.

"Why do you hate me?" Jastrau burst out, touching glasses with him.

Steffensen waved his hand aloofly.

"But why? Why?" Jastrau repeated.

"Nobody here hates anybody," intoned Little P. in his paternal, yet infantile, manner.

"Why should one hate anybody?" seconded the oval Herr Dieterding.

And then the human proximity came on in waves until it was like a sea, an element in which it was natural to embrace each other. Friendship. Oh, that precious feeling. Whiskey. Whiskey. Immerse yourself in whiskey and have faith in your friends—unlimited faith. Jastrau's arm was around Little P.'s shoulder. They sat on the high stools with their backs to the bar and stared as if hypnotized at women dancing with each other—oh Sappho!—at flesh-colored legs and dapper shoes that flashed across the carpet in surely executed dance steps, heels in, heels out, acute angles, obtuse angles, the toes cutting innumerable incessant figures.

And the two young girls passed the little red tips of their tongues over their painted lips and signaled to each other.

"It's nice that I'm staying," chirped Little P.

But it was no longer the polite Little P. who now clung amiably to him. Now it was two soft, restless girls. Not the ones who were dancing. Two others. And there was a stirring of female hips, female breasts, hands, and knees.

"Oh—one gets to be a person here with you," Jastrau exclaimed, hugging them both. "One gets to be more than a person."

But why didn't that one there—that one there, Caja—kneel before him and anoint his foot? From an alabaster vase. With spikenard or some other perfume. Why this waste? And then wipe it dry with her long hair. Ha ha. No, with her short, her wiry, her bristly bobbed hair.

Feminine warmth. Human warmth. One is a friend of man when he holds a woman close. Is he not? He becomes—the son of man.

Girls. Women. Much shall be forgiven. For his love was so great.

Whiskey—forever and ever.

He found himself standing in semidarkness. Poor light. In a toilet down in the basement. He washed his hands. Why did his hands always look as if he had been crawling about on the ground? And then he caught sight of himself in the mirror. Pudgy. Pale. Puffy, crimson lips in a sallow face. Dark hair plastered against his forehead.

A man. Behold the man! Your damned Mongolian mug! *Ecce homo!*

Chapter Three

"There's a high-class fellow in there next to us— a theologian."

The voice was gruffer than all the others in the confusing chatter. Remnants of dreams and indistinct memories drifted away, and then Jastrau lay in the darkness, awake. There was a pain in his shoulder. His legs were askew as if he had fallen and remained lying in an awkward position. One ear and cheek felt strange. They seemed to be pressed against something hard and flat. He twisted around to get into a more comfortable position and discovered he had his clothes on. They seemed loose around the back of his neck, and he felt a draft under his collar. Where was he?

A wooden bunk. A sloping block of wood, covered with oilcloth, for a pillow. He had something over him that felt like a horse blanket.

150

"Are you awake, theologian?" he heard the voice say. It came from the other side of a wall.

Jastrau muttered something and felt around with his hands. They easily reached to the floor. It was stone.

"Pretty swell accommodations here, what? But expensive as all hell. Now tell us—what did you do?"

Jastrau snarled.

"All right, cut it out. You needn't get snotty. You were stewed, and so was I. But what the hell—as long as you didn't slug a cop it doesn't matter."

"Oh-h-h!" someone else behind the wall groaned.

"Yes, you're really in trouble, but why did you have to do it?"

"Oh-h—my nose!" came the moaning answer.

"Ha ha. What's the matter? Can't you find it?" asked the talkative one.

"Ye-s, but damn it, it's all out of shape. If only I could see if it's bleeding."

"Ah—ha ha."

"Yes, damn it, it's easy enough for you to laugh. Ouch! Ou-ch! They beat me up all over."

"You could have stopped before they clobbered you, God damn it. And hitting a cop—they'll give you the works for that. Just ask the chaplain next door."

"I'm not a minister, confound it!" Jastrau shouted in exasperation as he sat up. He had no idea where he was. A narrow beam of light came in through a grated window above the head of his bunk.

"What the hell are you then, since you lie in your sleep jabbering about Jesus? Damned if I thought anybody except ministers did that. And here I lay listening quietly, all the time thinking to myself that that's how ministers sleep. Listen, you with the rubber nose, this fellow next door says he isn't a minister. What the hell is he, then? Whatever he is, he's a pious so-and-so."

Dark as it was, Jastrau was aware that he was blushing. He could feel a sickening flush creeping over his cheeks. He had been lying here in the lockup prattling in his sleep about Jesus. He cowered back in his bunk again. He did not want to think. But what did it all mean? Where was—who was it? Ah yes—Steffensen. Yesterday. Little P. And he had been talking in his sleep about Jesus. As a glimmer of recollection dawned on him, he felt slimy all over. In a barroom with two girls in his arms, and then that warm, erotic feeling of benevolence toward the girls. Slop! Jesus among the whores. Well, that was the faith of his childhood filtering through. A muddy trickle it was—polluted with

whiskey and bawdiness, and a tepid mixture of sentimentality, human-
itarianism, and Christianity as well. *Ecce homo!*

And he could not sleep. His entire body was contaminated. His
clothing constricted him, and there was a voluptuous sensation of
pressure. Should he ask?

"Listen, you in there," he shouted toward the wall. "Where can a
person urinate here?"

"Ha ha, you can tell he's an educated fellow. All right, I'll tell you.
There's a hole in the floor, and you can piss into that."

Jastrau got up and felt his way through the darkness with his feet.
Where? Where was it? As he inched forward, he felt a cool draft on
his hind quarters and was aware that his pants were slipping down.
He grabbed them and hitched them up and felt his shirttail creeping
up under his vest. What was this? His vest. Buttoned wrong. And his
suspenders—where were they?

This was disastrous. Where were his suspenders? He must have
sunk low indeed, to be standing there and losing his pants.

Then he remembered. They took the suspenders away from everyone so they would not hang themselves in the cell. At least so he had
heard. But he had never thought about what it signified. His necktie
was also gone. His pockets were empty. No knives. No sharp instruments. The vein in the wrist. Such preposterous things did happen.

Jastrau cringed. He shivered as he accomplished his mission. There
he stood, his shirt creeping up behind and his pants still slipping
down. It was impossible to regain his composure. He felt crumpled.
Tossed onto the trash heap.

"Well—that helped, didn't it?"

Jastrau did not answer.

"You could at least say thanks, couldn't you?"

But he made no reply. He was thinking of his suspenders. That
anyone had dared take them from him—tamper with him in such a
way and then leave him to himself with nothing to hold up his pants!
Shivers ran up and down his back. Shame. Indignation. Futile rage.
The pants kept slipping down.

He felt his way carefully with his feet. Yes, there was the bunk.
Nothing but a raised step. He flopped down on it. It was difficult to
shiver on such a hard surface. It was impossible to hide his head with
such an oilcloth pillow or to conceal himself under the short horse
blanket. Should he take off his shoes? One thing he knew—he wanted
to lie down. That way his pants stayed in place. Oh, if he could only
fade out of the picture, fall asleep.

In the cell next to him they kept talking. Should he try to be pals with them? Make some crude remark on their own level? Yes, that would be just lovely. Feeling the spirit of Christianity welling up in him as he sat wedged between two girls in a bar and experiencing a sanctimonious sense of comradeship in a jail cell. Slop!

Just then he became aware of a reddish light and heard a rustling of keys. He raised his head. Yes, someone with a light was coming down the stairs. He could see the light through the grating. A grated door. As in a cage. One could stand outside and look in at the animals.

"Oh, couldn't I get a drink of water?" someone groaned in the next cell.

"Yes, just wait a bit," a gruff voice answered.

Meanwhile, a key was inserted, the grated door swung open, and the man with the light approached him. The light dazzled Jastrau so that he had to rub his eyes. He could distinguish only the shadowy outlines of a large man.

"Well, have you managed to sleep it off?"

"Uuhh."

Jastrau raised himself on one elbow like one of the damned in hell. He recalled a picture he had seen—Jesus in the kingdom of the dead. There it was—Jesus again. Why was everything so obscured in a fog of impurity?

"Yes, we had a bad time with you. We couldn't get you to tell us who you were. Not a word out of you. But we have to have your name. You see, we have to phone the national registration office before we can let you go."

Jastrau gave the necessary information.

"But tell me," he said, "what did I do?"

"I don't know. Nothing very serious. But that fellow in there"—the shadow behind the light nodded toward the wall—"it will go hard with him. As usual, it's this liquor—this liquor. Why can't people drink moderately?"

He stamped on the stone floor in indignation, so that the light wobbled and the square, dimly illuminated room began to rock.

"Carousing and tomfoolery," he said impatiently.

Then he shuffled off again, rattled a tin cup, and went into the next cell.

"Well, I must say you're a pretty sight," Jastrau heard him mutter in a shocked tone of voice. "What do you think your mother would say if she saw you now?"

"Ha ha. With that schnozzle? Damned if she would be able to recognize him."

"What's that? Who asked you for your two cents' worth?"

"Nobody, God help me—nobody."

The cell door was slammed shut, and the light disappeared up the stairway again.

The sound of the lock turning in the door and the receding rattle of the bunch of keys made Jastrau feel desperate. Prison noises, they were. And at the same time a wave of inexplicable anger surged through him. He was imprisoned. He alone. Everybody had deserted him. Steffensen. All the others—the waiters, the bartender. They had let him down. Otherwise he would not have found himself lying here. It was cowardly of them. But perhaps it was he who had left them. Perhaps they did not know where he was. All the same, it was cowardly. He would get revenge. And suddenly he felt convinced—yes, there was no doubt about it—that the police had been rude to him. Hadn't they? Otherwise, why would such a feeling of indignation be welling up out of his subconscious? They had been stupid. He knew them, the lubberly beasts! How often had he not witnessed their contemptible insolence toward a drunken man? The way they suddenly grabbed the culprit by the arm and barked, "Come on now, get a move on!" Yes, he knew how it was. He had seen it so often. And, of course, that was the way they had treated him. If only he could remember it—remember exactly how they had behaved. It would be enough to send him into a fury. But it was all darkness—nothing but darkness. Nothing to remember. Nevertheless, that was how it had been. And they would be exposed—yes, they would. He would not let himself be removed from his cell. He would refuse—yes, refuse—to let himself be turned loose. They would not be allowed to get out of it so easily. He would remain there where he was. He would be obstinate about it. And there would be a scandal. An investigation. An uproar in the newspapers. It was certainly not very comfortable there. But what of it? It was a fine thing—lying on a wooden bunk. It was good for a person. One became hardened by it.

He was imprisoned. The thought was like something constricting his brain—like cords being drawn tighter and tighter around it.

Should he get up and begin pacing the floor of the cell? The prisoner's march. Wasn't that what it was called?

Then he noticed the gray wall. Had it grown so light? He made out a small, cheery pencil scrawl: "Greetings to all good fellows from Peter Boyesen." And beside it, a heartfelt observation: "Always drunk. Always drunk."

It had the effect of a ray of sunshine on the bare wall. It was like a fat man's smile. Take it easy now, Jastrau thought, take it easy—the whole thing is really quite comical—a joke. Greetings to all good fellows from Peter Boyesen!

Jastrau stared at the writing with a feeling of affection.

Greetings to all good fellows from Peter Boyesen!

What a lilt to the words. Such a nice, quiet lilt. A little drunken exclamation maybe. Always drunk. Always drunk. No, that he did not understand. It might have been written in exultation. Or perhaps in penitence. But it too had a lilt to it. It was a genial, singing wall.

Again there was a rattling over by the door. No light this time. Ah—the day was dawning. Why did his thoughts take such a poetic form? The day dawning.

"You can go now," said a voice.

And from the next cell: "Uh—the lucky dog!"

Jastrau cheerfully got up, but his pants immediately began to slip down about his knees. He had forgotten about them. He stuck his hands into the pockets to keep himself together. But his composure had vanished. He shuffled across the floor like a bum. Up a stone stairway through semidarkness. Into a large empty room. Some windows looked out on a courtyard where there was a yellowish-gray light. A dreary morning light.

Behind a counter sat a bearded man in a police uniform, glancing at a typewritten sheet of paper.

"Herr Editor Ole Jastrau."

Jastrau stood before the counter, cringing. It was his pants that kept insisting on falling down. He felt guilty because they had taken his suspenders from him. And he was ripe to be photographed for the rogues' gallery—profile, full-face, with a description underneath the picture—because he had no necktie.

"Your things are in there behind the screen. You can go now."

"But—but—" Jastrau could not bring himself to ask questions.

"It wasn't anything," said the bearded sergeant. "Nothing to amount to anything—just disorderly conduct. Nothing much. You can pay the twelve kroner at the penalty office on Monday. No, it wasn't anything."

It was impossible to tell whether the repeated "It wasn't anything" signified disappointment or reassurance. The beard was disarming, but the man's gaze was as empty as the room with its counter, desk, and police posters on the wall. All a matter-of-fact morning dreariness.

Jastru went behind the screen and found his suspenders and crumpled hat. In the hat lay his watch, fountain pen, wallet, a few letters, some Hungarian coins that he kept as good-luck pieces, and his money in a sealed envelope. Three kroner and seventeen øre was the notation on it in black ink. Was that really all that was left? He wondered how much money he had had when he left the apartment with Steffensen. The police had found three kroner and seventeen øre on him, but—

It was strange to see the contents of his pockets lying there. There was something indecent about it, as if his soul or his innermost secrets had been shaken out into a hat. In quick succession he stuffed the Hungarian coins into his left vest pocket, the money into the right, placed his fountain pen in the left breast pocket, the watch in the right, got his soul into working order with its parts arranged as they should be, then raised his hat almost imperceptibly to the sergeant, walked across the room and down some steps, stood for a moment feeling faint and disoriented in a large doorway where there was a draft, did not know whether to turn to the right or left, spied some buildings to the right, framed by the doorway, recognized them despite the strange frame in which they appeared, and slipped out into the early morning as casually as if coming out of Copenhagen's monumental courthouse was an every-morning occurrence for him.

The sunlight was brilliant, but the houses still looked gray.

A moment later he was walking along Strøget. But this morning it seemed as if something were wrong with the buildings. They were not really where they belonged. And yet, he knew them well, knew them as they appeared at virtually every hour of the day—at six o'clock in the morning when the Town Hall Square lay flooded with light before the entrance to dark Frederiksberggade, at twelve when the sun was directly over the street and bareheaded office workers ran across to a café during the lunch period and hatless shop girls dashed out to do their own shopping, at four when the strollers along Vesterbro had the glare of the sun full in their faces or beating down comfortably against their backs, at six when the light was more subdued and the swarm of cyclists was at its thickest, all on their way home to the suburbs, and then at evening and at night when it was as if Jastrau could read the hour by the tempo of the crowd and the brightness of the lights. But at eight o'clock in the morning—the hour it was now—everything seemed foreign to him. He was not familiar with things as they appeared in the forenoon light; the shadows fell differently. The office workers came cycling into town. He had been dumped out into the morning rush hour. He looked at their faces, fresh from a good night's sleep but still expressionless. One cyclist after another rode by him. They gave the impression of wooden figures or gray shadows on a film, not yet animated to the point where they were actually alive, not yet filled with blood. How drab the world was, despite the glow of the morning

156

sun and the flashing silvery-blue reflections from the bicycle handle-bars. The intense light had an eerie effect. Even the brightest scene can seem dismal when one has been on an all-night spree. The light seemed morbid.

He nodded a greeting to a youngish member of the Rigsdag who rode by, an energetic gray cyclist with a wooden face. He returned the greeting politely but with an air of abstraction—a mask saying hello to a mask. But perhaps it was the recollection of the unpleasant jail cell, the feeling of degradation that still rankled him, that made him regard the sunlit morning thoroughfare with all its gray human throng as something unreal, an empty wasteland. What did people know about him? Did they know where he had come from? And what did I know about them? Everything was disguised. What he saw was a curtain with pictures of buildings, shops, show windows, sidewalks, pedes-trians, and bicyclists—a curtain drawn in front of reality.

When he got home to the empty apartment, he at first felt a sense of relief. Now the door was closed. No one could come in. The rooms were a big mask he had put on to hide his existence. And Johanne would not be home until the next day. That was fortunate. He would be able to sleep it off. It was not yet time to meet face to face. But there was the picture of his mother, that very young woman, and the one in a gilded frame of his boy with his moistened hair combed ridiculously down across his forehead. They stood on the bookcase, both of them, staring at him. They were faces too, and there was no way of knowing what they might see. He had to turn them toward the wall. For the moment they were more real than his absent wife.

His wife! He could get a good long sleep before she came. He could relegate the whole thing into the background. To be sure, his body still ached from lying on the wooden bunk. It was still present in all its unyielding hardness. And there was still a strange feeling about his back, as if he did not have suspenders on.

He wandered aimlessly around.

What a noise a door can make when it bangs shut in an empty apartment! Out in the pantry there was nothing to eat. There was a very little bit of coffee in a tin. But how was it now that one went about making coffee? Ah yes, then the coffee bag would have to be rinsed out and all that. No, he simply wasn't up to it. There was some butter in a paper, shapeless and runny because it had stood in the sun. A few slices of rye bread lay crumbled and dry on a plate. A knife he had used to butter bread with the day before still littered the kitchen table, along with a couple of dirty plates with eggshells and the remains of a herring on them. How conspicuous these inanimate objects were. Disorder and chaos. Persistently they forced themselves into his consciousness, and persistently he had to combat them, hold them down. And he could not—no, he could not—pull himself together enough to make up his mind whether the struggle was worth the trouble.

He picked up a piece of the dry rye bread and began munching on it. It was ridiculous. In a four-room apartment the man gnaws on a crust of bread. Was it because of laziness? No—it was that the world was so full of insuperable difficulties.

Go to bed. The light in the bedroom was dazzling. Forenoon light. No soothing shadows on the unmade bed, the crumpled sheets, the pillow with the two-day-old imprint of his head. Nothing soothing anywhere—not even down in the courtyard. Somebody was beating rugs there, and the sound of every blow bounced back and forth between the building walls as it rose toward the rooftops. Things assumed such a harsh, clear aspect during the forenoon—so clear that it would be a fateful mistake to look in the mirror.

Should he shave? No—the mirror. *Ecce homo!* No! On the other hand, he found himself able to take off all his clothes and let a wet sponge glide coolly over his entire body. This immediately made him feel farther away from the lockup. It was as if he had washed it away.

Naked, he crept into bed. Even though it was unmade, the effect was soothing. Down under the feather comforter. Shut out the dazzling sunlight that tormented him into the inner recesses of his soul—the glaring light of a hospital room. And now to disappear completely.

But down in the darkness he immediately became aware of a flickering, as if his eyelids were twitching nervously. Was he lying in a ship's bunk, watching the light reflected through the porthole by the waves play on the ceiling? Yes, that was the way it seemed behind his closed eyes. But they were not white undulating waves that constantly seemed to wash over him; they were a golden bronze. And unfamiliar flowers seemed to be drifting on the water above him—incessantly.

He grew so restless that he had to rub his neck. His hand became drenched with sweat. Now he could feel it. The sweat actually dripped off his hand as he mopped his forehead. It felt as if his index finger had been dipped in sticky water. And it got worse yet. Sweat! Sweat! But that tormenting restlessness in his back was still worse. Was he lying on a torture rack? It was impossible to lie still. Besides, a feeling of vertigo was lurking in the back of his head. Something had fastened its grip on his neck. It was impossible to remain where he was.

158

The next thing he knew he was standing stark-naked beside the bed. Naturally he had forgotten to draw the blinds and of course a young woman was leaning out the kitchen window across the way. Well, that was her affair. Greetings to all good fellows from Peter Boyesen. Peter Boyesen greets all gay girls. A fat man's jovial smile. That was how life should be lived.

Back into his clothes. Should he shave? No, he would leave that to a barber. Three kroner and seventeen øre. He would have to get an advance. The towel was wet after he had dried his forehead with it.

But some beer—that was it.

A little while later, he was sitting in a dive that he seldom frequented. He sat at a small square table near the window so he could look out into the street through the transparent curtains. And every time a woman walked by in the sunlight he felt a violent surge of excitement. He could not avoid following her with his eyes. If she had a good figure and shapely legs, then it was utterly disconcerting. It sent him into a frenzy, and he noticed how his lips went slack. But if there was no grace in her movements, if there was anything the least bit ridiculous about her, he felt a sense of relief.

And so he had to drink. It calmed him down. Perhaps it was only an illusion, because when he drank beer the sweat evaporated from his brow. Over at the counter, the waiter was apparently calming himself in the same way.

But it was an empty world. A billiard table, a blackboard with some figures written on it with chalk, a rack of cues, a spittoon, sand on the floor, all like a stage set after a performance—lifeless and without meaning.

Suddenly the waiter caught sight of the figures on the blackboard and went and erased them.

"Oh, that bitch," he mumbled.

This was all that occurred.

Jastrau suddenly made up his mind that he did not want to stay longer, for the waiter was purple in the face, and a slight tremor of his thick lower lip suggested that he might express himself in greater detail concerning the female in question.

Jastrau got up, paid, and left.

Out in the street, however, it was as if a veil had been drawn aside. Now he no longer observed the women through a curtain. Still, he could not—simply could not—refrain from watching their legs, from indulging in fleeting fantasies, from stopping and turning to look. It was as if he were suffering from a disease that he could not hide. From behind the curtain, he had watched uneasily, reluctantly, and now here in the street he had just as little control over himself, despite the fact that everybody could see him. He discovered female legs at long, long distances, far down a side street perhaps, and then he would have to stop to watch. He might suddenly turn into the side street and take up the chase. There in broad daylight. Zigzagging along through the streets. It was intolerable—like a nightmare, but lacking the mollifying haziness of a dream.

He had no inkling of how long he roamed about that section of Vesterbro. It seemed he could not get away from it. So many women came hurrying along the street about whom a man couldn't be wrong. But each one was carrying a jug of cream or a box of coffee cake. And there were other women as well. Yes, he might well make a mistake. Young housewives. Servant girls with a shopping basket, or a jug of cream. A coherent world, and people with many purposes in mind. While he—here in the glaring daylight—still had the night in his blood and was preoccupied solely by night's one prime desire.

Nevertheless, there was a dream-like element in all this reality. Otherwise, why did the tall drab buildings become invested with such significance for him? Their walls seemed to become transparent, and the rooms inside were filled with the same indistinct stuff that dreams are made of. He could not help examining them curiously. Furnished rooms and more furnished rooms—small hotels. The words had a magic power, like letters that one remembers while waking from a dream. And curtains. Majolica pottery. Everything was symbolic. He could not tear himself away from this quarter with its notorious rooming houses. No, the beer was no help against this form of disquietude. Was it that the damned whiskey altered one's personality? A lustful warmth flowed through his entire body. There—a pair of flesh-colored stockings in a doorway. He had to stop. No—go on. It was insane. He went on. He passed the doorway. A werewolf who had slipped out into the light of day.

Up on Vesterbrogade, the streetcars glided quietly along with a low hum, yellow and prosaic, the sunlight flickering in their big windows, and their staid passengers sitting erect and shoulder to shoulder. It was a world he could not make his way into, as clear as an image reflected in water, but a world he could not enter. People hurrying here and there. And if he retreated back into that other world—the one it seemed he had just come from—he discovered that it was already deserted and desolate. If he went into a low dive, it turned out to be empty. They were cleaning the place up. If he sauntered into a better bar—the Orient or whatever it might be called—it was a mistake. The colored tinsel, the Chinese lanterns, and the portières looked tawdry and covered with dust. The waiters rubbed their eyes sleepily, yawned, and seemed out of sorts. Everything there was so overdone.

And so he decided he would rather keep walking along Vesterbrogade. To be sure, he had to walk at a pace different from that of these daytime people. His feet were sore from all his wandering about. But if only he could keep himself from being enticed down the next side street by a glimpse of a silk-clad leg far, far away on the sidewalk or cutting across the street—a flesh-colored symbol of hope that beckoned him from, say, way down near Halmtorvet. If only—

Once the sun went down, he knew there would be peace again. Evening would bring recovery. But that was still many hours away, many sunlit hours, and he had to keep trudging on through them, driven by anxiety and restlessness. He wondered if that was the way things were when one had committed a crime. Was it like a guilty conscience? But he did not have a guilty conscience. It was a physical phenomenon—all that whiskey in his system. That was the trouble. But it was confoundedly like a sickness of the soul.

Jastrau got himself a shave in a barber shop that he picked at random. He edged himself into the chair, but did not look in the mirror. *Ecce homo!* When he leaned back to let the barber scrape his chin, he again noticed the sensation of emptiness and vertigo in the hollow of his neck, but nevertheless he had to keep from moving. It was nearly impossible. His heart began to thump. Then he experienced that unpleasant fantasy that many modern men go through—a neurasthenic form of terror. It was the sight of the long, lethal razor glinting in the sunlight and the indulgent way the barber smacked his lips that filled him with apprehension. Luckily, he escaped unscathed.

Afterwards Jastrau went up to *Dagbladet* and drew an advance of a hundred and fifty kroner. A dark-haired young man opened the ledger and glanced obliquely at the account. "Are you starting this now, too?" he remarked in a mournful tone. Whereupon Jastrau raised his own voice a sniveling octave higher and became ashamed of himself when he heard how unnatural it sounded. But he did get the money.

Then once again he was home in the deserted apartment. A bill had come from a fire insurance company. He might just as well go and pay it at once. Then it would be over and done with.

He stood for a moment with the bunch of bank notes in his hand. Thoughtfully he riffled through them as if turning the pages of a book, then suddenly went and placed a hundred kroner in a drawer and slammed it shut. Turning on his heel, and with the rest of the ten-krone notes dangling casually from his hand, he went out the door, down the stairs, and was on his way.

Then there was the insurance company's office. The glare of sunlight through the big windows. Glass. Glass. Glass. Typewriters glistening. The office girls' hairdos, that gleamed like halos in the sunshine. The gleaming white pages of the account books, over which the light danced like a bluish liquid flame. And the bright luster of the waxed floors. Shiny, glaring surfaces. A complicated perception of space, as in a cabinet of mirrors. And everything in full swing, with a movement that could only be sensed, not felt or seen. He paid the premium on the policy with a feeling that a part of his self was groping around in a new dimension.

How his brain was whirling!

Should he go now to the Bar des Artistes or some other place where there was a salutary dusk at four o'clock in the afternoon? The portières close behind one. Gone is the sun. The noise of weekday traffic is far away, as unreal as the sound of stage props being shifted behind a lowered curtain. The tempo of things is altered. A phonograph plays a slow, subdued fox trot. The tinkling of glasses. The crunching of ice in the shining shaker. Cool atmosphere. The hum of the ventilator. People relaxing.

But he knew if he went he would stay for ten hours.

No, he was reasonable and went instead to a temperance restaurant to get something to eat. Naturally, the restaurant faced the courtyard, and with its pillars and balcony resembled a clubroom in a country town. Here there was no conversation. Instead, people read the newspapers. They all looked like solid citizens with no nonsense about them—hard-working young people with uncomplicated minds, clear eyes indicative of sobriety, pale noses, and dark suits too short in the sleeves. Young girls with hairdos and school insignia, or with their hair parted in the middle. Industrious girls, with opinions. And with sensible shoes. Ladies with long watch chains and curly hairs protruding from their chins. Pince-nez glasses. A distinct air of morality. And no sunshine. No reflections from mirrors. No embellishments. Nothing but a clean, neutral light.

Should he wait there until the sun went down?

He read all the papers. He drank rather too much of the tax-free near beer—more than was seemly in such a place. He drank it off in large draughts. And when he ordered another bottle with his meal, he smiled at the waitress as if being in a temperance restaurant was a great joke. But she did not understand.

Nevertheless, he managed to sit there for a long time, and this was fortunate, because if he went out on the street it would be too easy to run into people he knew, and in that case he would too easily fall into free drinks. It would be unavoidable. There was always someone out there volunteering to set them up.

When he finally left, the outlines of Vesterbrogade's buildings were fading in the twilight.

Couldn't he go home now, draw the blinds, and lie down and sleep? His feet were so tired. He felt weak and exhausted. It seemed that he was dragging one foot after the other and that his knees were buckling. But there was twilight in the eyes of the women he saw. The sound of the traffic lingered so long in the air. There was space and noise. A subdued sound of effervescent laughter came so comfortingly from the throng of people ahead of him.

He passed a woman in a brown suit. She was standing at the edge of the sidewalk. The shoes beneath the light-colored stockings were primly placed—one right next to the other. She had a certain air about her. Was she propositioning him?

He turned and went back, brushed closely by her. Their eyes had hardly met. But he had a feeling of inevitability. He must go ahead with it. And it had to be her. He was not going to trudge on any farther. Otherwise—yes, he was sure of it—he would walk until his feet were black and blue, staring at women and deciding first that he would, then that he wouldn't, and walking on and on until ready to collapse. It had to be her.

He nodded to her, then slowly walked on and turned the corner.

As he did so, he brushed by her closely. He looked down at her. Yes, she carried herself well. Her features were broad and rather vulgar. But her dark eyes had depth.

"Well?" she said softly.

"How much?" he asked, staring straight ahead.

"Ten," she said in the same quiet voice.

He nodded, and they quickened their pace.

Now he could not possibly turn back. It would be too ridiculous. There she was, walking along beside him and keeping in step with him. The decision had been made. The common tempo of their steps had a fateful significance, he thought. The same withholding of the breath as when one looks at the second hand of a clock and realizes the significance of every sweep of the hand.

They exchanged a few words about the weather, but otherwise they were strangely silent and remote from each other.

"Do we have far to go?"

"No, it's right nearby. I'm staying with my sister."

Why did they always surround themselves with an aura of family life, these women? It was one of those respectable remarks that were so typical. Perhaps it represented their ideal.

He could not help smiling. But then he suddenly looked at her. He should at least know what she looked like. She had black hair. Prominent cheek bones beneath her eyes. Her mouth was broad and firm, but the nose was plebeian. It seemed that he had seen her before.

"You look familiar to me," he said.

"Me? No. I don't live here in town," she replied casually.

They stopped outside of an old building with stone steps and a cellar-way. On the somewhat elevated first-floor level was a stamp dealer's shopwindow before which, as a boy, he had stood on tiptoes to look at the wonderful stamps from Bosnia and Herzegovina at the risk of tumbling into the cellar. One encountered memories everywhere in this city, he thought to himself. It was annoying.

"Come on, then."

And she hurried on ahead of him.

He watched her back as she went up the stairs. He might as well take an interest in what she looked like. His face felt flushed. Yes, he was excited, but at the same time so indifferent that it was almost depressing. She had a full, white neck. Yes, he was sure he had seen that before.

She lived in one of the old Copenhagen apartments with small square rooms and low ceilings. On the door was a nameplate: "E. Kopf, Pharmaceutical Graduate." That was puzzling. But inside everything was obvious enough. A sofa was placed diagonally in one corner. Everything, the wallpaper and the transparent curtains, had small-patterned designs. A picture of a woman in an Empire-style dress and a man reclining blissfully under a tree in nature's lap hung on the wall. Of course, it had a gilded oval frame. Oval!

"Well, this is where I live," the girl said.

"It's very nice," Jastrau replied, looking around. He was touched by the oval picture. But as he looked at it he was interrupted.

"Let's say fifteen. Then I'll take off everything." He knew it was a stock professional request.

He nodded.

After he had undressed, he noticed a string of amber beads around her neck. In the dim light admitted through the curtains, their cool, yellow color had a meliorating effect against the dull skin, somewhat as in a dream. She insisted on keeping them on, and Jastrau did not object. The bit of ornamentation made it easier to regard her as attractive. And for fifteen kroner he thought he was entitled to a little attractiveness—be it ever so little. He found her body nice and smiled at her. But it was a smile compounded of ardor and distress.

"My Lord, man, you seem to be embarrassed. I wouldn't have thought it," she said, laughing and giving him a playful twitch on the ear.

Chapter Four

Today Johanne would have to come home, because that night they were to attend a party at Eyvind Krog's. A full-dress affair—so late in the season. Almost the early part of summer.

But Jastrau was not able to think so far ahead. Johanne was coming. He had been alone so long. It was impossible to think beyond tenthirty. By that time he would be sitting in Dr. E. Rambusch's waiting room. And then—

He walked along Strøget at a brisk pace, maintaining an erect carriage, but his face was flushed. And it was odd that he should recall that episode with Vuldum in the Bar des Artistes. Her broad, Slavic features—that was what he remembered. How was it now? Yes, a little, humble man in a skimpy jacket had come into the barroom with a basket of flowers. And three pink roses clutched in his hand.

"What makes you think you can sell flowers here? As you can see, there are no ladies in the place."

It was as if he could hear Vuldum's contemptuous remark right there amidst the swarm of people on the sidewalk near the Bernina. Each word rang sharp and clear, although it had happened more than a year ago.

A black dress. A fat white neck. A bit plump, in any event. Yes, it was she. It was she. What was it Vuldum had called her? Black—black something or other. Over on the other side of the street, under the linden trees in front of the Church of the Holy Ghost, Jastrau involuntarily began to walk faster.

"Can you think of anything worse than a sore covered over with powder?" Wasn't that what he had said? Was Vuldum walking by his side? He thought he heard the words, the tone in which they were spoken, and he remembered his feeling of physical revulsion. Oh, if only it was today that Dr. Rambusch had office hours. Because it must be she. It was she. Black—Black Eva or Ellen—

Yes, it was she.

And suddenly he became so apprehensive that he could hardly get his breath. He gasped there in the sunlight. Ah—such lovely weather. Patches of sunlight on the pavement. The white bird-droppings that made the sidewalk look as if it had been sprinkled with lime. The sunshine. But it only tormented him. And that evening he would have to get into formal dress and engage in conversation. Drink and detention in the lockup, girls and the doctor and a fine, all hidden behind a white shirt front. *Ecce homo!*

Outside the house where Dr. Rambusch lived—it was discreetly tucked away in a side street—he looked cautiously around before going in. Oddly enough, all the windows in the adjoining buildings had a dull, unwashed look. It was, as a matter of fact, the rear of a row of impressive Copenhagen office buildings. They were politely turning their backs, and no one noticed him as he slipped in.

How fortunate! The doctor was having office hours, and a sign saying "Open" hung on the door. Inside the waiting room, which was drab and dreary, there was but one sun-tanned man who sat leafing absent-mindedly through one of the large supply of old issues of the *Family Journal*. He had a blue anchor tattooed on the back of one hand.

Jastrau tried to regard him as disinterestedly as he could. A muttered acknowledgement of each other's presence remained stuck in each man's throat, so that it sounded like a grunt. Jastrau went and hung his hat on a many-pronged hatstand.

An ugly and forbidding hatstand stood bristling there in the corner as in a pub, much like the one in the parlor at Stenosgade. Yes, there was one of these hideous monsters wherever people went to seek help, like an old-fashioned instrument of torture, a wheel set upon a stake.

There was always the threat that the sentence would be pronounced, and with a barbaric, medieval severity. Of what use, then, was the modern spirit of humanity? None—none whatsoever. Everywhere, people sat around ugly tables, with nothing but calling-card bowls and old issues of the *Family Journal* to comfort the eye while they waited—waited.

A door opened and a doctor in a white smock appeared. From behind him the sunlight streamed into the waiting room, momentarily dissipating the semi-obscurity. The seaman got up and went in—to what? The darkness closed in again. And Jastrau himself? What would he be going in to in a little while? Nothing could be definitely established at the time. He was aware of that. But luckily, preventive measures could be taken. How expensive stupid actions could be. One ten-øre bill foolishly spent whisked the next one away just as senselessly.

166

And then the door opened again. The seaman had a perturbed expression as he went by. Now it was Jastrau's turn.

He was a florid man, this Dr. Rambusch. He looked freshly scrubbed and pink-cheeked in his white smock. His light-blond eyebrows gave him a roguish appearance.

"And you?" he asked, holding his scrubbed hands up to the light that came through the window. "What can I do for you?" The business-like question immediately seemed to give Jastrau a feeling of reassurance. Now it would all be simply an impersonal, professional transaction that would soon be over.

"Well—it was just a stupid indiscretion."

"The usual thing—yes, of course. How long ago was it?"

"Yesterday."

"Well, then you came in time. We'll soon get rid of the Bolsheviks. Now, won't you please go in there and lie down on the couch of joy?"

And with a wave of his hand, he ushered him into a small room with a glass bench.

"Yes, that sort of thing is stupid," Jastrau said more or less to himself as he lay down.

"Ah yes," replied the doctor casually as he rolled a little wad of cotton on a thin stick.

Next, Jastrau felt a brief, corrosive pain.

"Always wise to put up with a little smarting while there's still time," the doctor remarked, smiling. "I've never known people to come back and complain of anything after this treatment."

Everything was sunshine again. It was all so routine.

As he went back to the dark waiting room, he was followed by a beam of sunlight and a doctor in a smock so white that it had nuances of yellow and blue, and it seemed as if he had been purified by a stream of light. He completely forgot that the hatstand resembled an instrument of torture. Taking his hat, he went away with a feeling that was almost merriment.

Greetings to all good fellows from Peter Boyesen.

The sunlight dappled the leaves of the elm trees in Kongens Nytorv. In the distance the buildings had an airy look, and their colors stood out clearly. It was still forenoon. The sidewalks seemed fresh and fragrant. The windows in the buildings sparkled. And how relieved he felt. Now and then a little twinge of pain shot through him, and he straightened up as he walked. It was only something to laugh at. Greetings from Peter Boyesen! Wasn't that the way a person should take things? A fat man's radiant smile.

But think of it—he had lain there in his cell chattering in his sleep about Jesus. How long ago it seemed. Here in the sunshine it seemed a very long time ago—a dark episode out of his past. But why had the thought of Jesus begun to haunt him? Was it his visit to Stenosgade? No, it could not have been the swarthy little man who juggled ideas like knives—a kind of scholastic circus act. Had that made so deep an impression on him? No. Certainly not. And yet, perhaps. Had that dark-skinned priest cast a shadow over his thoughts? It was strange how everything took fast hold in one's consciousness. Nothing was forgotten—nothing. But—greetings from Peter Boyesen—

In a mood of singular euphoria, Jastrau strolled along Strøget, took a shortcut through some side streets, arrived at the newspaper office, went in a door and up a back stairway.

And suddenly it struck him how reluctantly he was entering the building. Now he felt like another person, at once more sluggish and more irascible. The present, actuality, reality were so inconstant.

It was dark in the vestibule and The Peristyle. After the brightness of day outside, it was like coming into a twilight. Only the door to the editor-in-chief's office stood ajar, emitting a broad band of yellow light. Inside someone was coughing.

Jastrau went around behind the counter and was bending over to pick up some review copies of books that had been put aside for him when the door opened wide and Editor Iversen's tall, stooped figure appeared.

"Well, if it isn't Jastrau," he exclaimed at once, staring at his paper's reviewer with a preoccupied air. "I thought you had gone abroad—to Morocco."

Jastrau leaned self-consciously against the counter. He sensed something subtle about the remark.

"No, Herr Editor, nothing like that," he replied politely.

"Well, I really thought you had," the editor drawled, staring vacantly out into the room. He seemed like a ghost there in that mortuary darkness after the sunshine outside. "Some place down among the Negroes, I thought. We never see anything of you up here at the paper."

Now Jastrau knew what he was getting at. He was to be made invisible. It was the most propitious way of letting him know that he was in the doghouse.

"It's impossible to get the literary page to press," he protested irascibly. "It's been lying up there in the composing room for more than three weeks. The copy is just gathering dust."

He was brought up short by a brief, stabbing pain.

168

"For more than three weeks—do you really mean it?" the editor asked with a lethargic show of interest as he stroked his mustache. "Well, that's a long time. And just think—now we're going to have a radio supplement every week—every week," he repeated dreamily. "That interests people." Suddenly a trace of a smile appeared behind the drooping mustache, "It even interests the paper's business manager. He listens to the radio—hee hee! As long as there are sound waves in the air, he's completely crazy about it."

He remained standing and staring at the floor. His tall, stooped figure shook with merriment.

"Hee-hee—he thinks they're advertisements streaming in—from the angels."

He looked at Jastrau, and there was a naïvely philosophical expression in his old, gray eyes.

"But there's a future in it."

And with a jerk he brought himself up erect.

"Anyhow, you ought to see to it that the literary page gets printed. Well, now—a pleasant journey to Morocco.

Slowly he disappeared into his corner room again. But for a long while afterward his presence could be felt in the atmosphere of the half-darkened room. Like a beast of prey, he left a scent in the air, a rank, ominous odor. It was impossible to get rid of it. Indignantly Jastrau shoved the books under his arm. His job on the paper would soon be over. That was what it meant. But he had, of course, known it for more than a year. Why did it have to be dragged out so long, keeping him on tenterhooks? He went out through the revolving door.

Didn't anyone ever get fired from this paper?

And this was the way things had stood for a year. Even as recently as the previous fall, during the busy book season, he had entertained some slight hope of getting his feet on firm ground. But after New Year's, the situation had again become as hopeless as ever—articles that lay for months without getting printed, hung on the spike, as the expression was, ideas that crumbled away, arrangements that came to nothing.

He thought for a moment of going into the Braeddehytte tavern and ordering a lunch with an ice-cold *snaps* to go with it. But then he remembered that he had to be careful with his money. He bought a couple of eggs, a few slices of rye bread, and a quarter of a pound of butter from the dairy store in the building where he lived, and went upstairs to a frugal noonday meal.

So there he sat. It was strange how a plate, a knife, and a fork messed up a table when it was not a woman who had put them there. No matter how neatly he tried to spread the tablecloth, it looked like a makeshift job.

A window stood open. The sun shone on the neighbors' windows with their everlasting curtains. Curtains. A naked woman with a string of amber beads. Now Johanne must soon be coming home. Everything would slip into place as soon as he had seen her face and could tell that he had not given himself away. But he did not know whether he was strong enough. And tomorrow Oluf would come. That was good, because over by the window stood his play table, cluttered in such meaningless fashion with a couple of mechanical dolls, a duck on wheels, and a clamped box. In the long run the things there could be dangerous. Inanimate objects like that with expressions. If they lay there too long untouched they might easily get religion and turn into symbols and mascots. In a corner stood a big, dangerous-looking birch rod of the kind that children used to wake up their parents on Shrove Monday, with a cut-out picture of a Christmas elf adorning its top. It could make Jastrau feel positively bashful. A good thing that Oluf would come home tomorrow and toss all the stuff onto the floor.

Through the open window he heard a noise. An automobile door slammed shut. And from the deserted street came a clear voice: "Well, good-by then, Sis." It was his brother-in-law, Jastrau thought scornfully without moving from the table. But then he heard another voice, tender and lingering: "Good-by, Frue, and thanks for your company." The blood rushed to Jastrau's head. Yes, he recognized that ingratiating voice that seemed to curl itself about the ear and tickle it. It was Joachim Michelsen. Her girlhood sweetheart. She had not mentioned that he would be along on the excursion up to her brother's summer house near Tisvilde. No, she had not.

Quietly he put down his knife and fork, and stared—stared over at the neighbors' white curtains. They became like flames in daylight, and without his being aware of it they flamed up in his thoughts. They became his thoughts.

"Well, so there you are," exclaimed Johanne. She stood before him, fresh and red-cheeked. A hat that resembled a hood fitted tightly over her hair and ears, so that her face had a bare look. Her eyes had watered in the wind during the automobile ride. The reddishness, the rabbity characteristics were quite conspicuous.

Jastrau sniffed, inhaling the fresh air that emanated from her clothing. It cooled him off for a moment.

"Well, how did things go?" Johanne went on, taking off her hat, so that her hair lay about her head like an unruly golden haze.

"Oh, all right."

She spoke with such a cool aloofness. The look in her eyes gave the impression that she did not yet feel really at home in the room.

"How dreary and dusty it looks here." She looked around like a stranger while Jastrau sat leaning forward and watching her. "Things certainly do need straightening up here." "Ah, yes," she added, yawning and stretching her arms, "so here I am, back to the old humdrum existence."

"Are you bored already?" Jastrau asked in a tone of bitterness.

She turned suddenly and faced him. That tight-fitting jacket and her unruly hair. Yes—a real amazon.

"Right away you start making a fuss." There was a trace of vulgarity in her voice, and a cynical tightening of the lines of her well-rounded chin betrayed her annoyance.

"Wasn't it rather lonesome up there?" he asked, watching for her reaction.

"Why? We had a phonograph along while we were down by the water. That way one never gets bored."

"No, nature is wonderful," Jastrau drawled ironically.

A sharp little pain shot through him.

"Oh, you're unbearable! And you aren't making things any easier now!" she exclaimed. "But now I have to go in and phone Oluf. I'm not a completely unnatural mother."

Was she putting on an act? Were they walking around in the same room, with their faces close to each other, yet each wearing a mask? And unable to get away from each other? She had not mentioned Michelsen—not a word about him.

"Oluf wants to talk to his father, too," she shouted from in beside the telephone.

He got up languidly and went in.

"Hello, Oluf," he said pleasantly into the phone.

The boy's cheery voice came so clearly through the receiver that it sent a chill up Jastrau's spine.

"Hello, Father. Where have you and Mother been all this time?"

"We—we're here—at home," he replied. The voice was like a thin ray of sunshine in a dark damp cellar.

"Look—let me talk to him!" Johanne burst out aggressively, and took the receiver. Some cheery sounds came bubbling through it, but Jastrau was not able to make out the words.

He went back into the dining room and sat down where he had been before. Across the way the white curtains blazed. They cast a bright reflection into the dark, north-oriented room.

Curtains. A naked woman with a string of amber beads. But nothing was real any more. The boy's voice over the telephone. That was unreal, too. But there was that little corrosive pain—a stinging sensation.

Johanne went on talking in the living room. Now it was undoubtedly his mother-in-law who was on the phone. What were they talking about? The set-up in the brother's house. The view out over the water. Too cold to go in swimming. But she did not mention Joachim Michelsen's name.

He grew more and more depressed.

At last she finished talking and came in and threw her clothes on the play table.

"Incidentally, I had an unexpected visit," Jastrau remarked.

"Well, that was nice. Who was it?"

"Steffensen."

"Who did you say?"

"Steffensen—the Communist."

"The one you threw out of here!" Johanne exclaimed sharply. "You didn't let him in, did you?"

"Yes."

"You are about the most spineless character—" She did not finish the remark, and suddenly her tone of voice changed. "Then you've been drunk," she said.

"Well—"

"Yes—you stammer. But don't you think I know it? That youngster has a bad influence on you. I could see it plainly the time he was here. And you—a grown man! To let yourself be led astray by a boy."

She began to pace the floor in indignation.

"You've been drunk again, Ole. You might as well admit it."

"No—I'll be damned if I have," he answered gruffly.

"He's your evil spirit."

"Nonsense."

And suddenly he rose and burst out: "Instead of making ridiculous accusations against me, you might better give some thought to the fact that we have to go to a party at Krog's tonight."

Why did he not toss Michelsen's name at her? Why did he beat around the bush while he became more and more spiteful? A capricious spitefulness it was.

"Furthermore, I can let you in on a secret," he went on vehemently. "Pretty soon we're going to have to cut down our expenses. I've had a clash with Editor Iversen. Yes, I've had a dandy time here while you've been stretched out on the beach. Do you hear?"

172

But she only increased her pace, back and forth, back and forth. Every word he said made her walk more rapidly or provoked some violent reaction from her. She snatched up the napkin from the table, slapped it angrily against the door, against the wall, against the chairs, while she kept moving about, faster and faster, without saying a word.

"I'll soon be fired over there—do you hear?" he yelled.

"That I can easily believe," she replied ruthlessly. With a toss of her head she went into the kitchen.

Jastrau, on the other hand, sat down in the living room and began to cut the pages of review copies, so that the white motes of paper-dust fell like snowflakes on his trousers. What he really wanted to do was leave, but he realized that this would be unreasonable. He would only have to return, because they had to be at Krog's. They could not back out this time. They had to go, simply had to. And he in full dress, despite the fact that he felt so seedy.

Was it self-reproach that he felt? It was a feeling of uncleanliness, that's what it was. Very simple. It was not penitence, but fear of behaving like a free individual, being the person he was, and shouting it to the four winds. That was what tormented him most.

And then that slight disgusting pain.

And getting into full dress.

The hours slipped by. Johanne came in and looked into the money drawer.

"By the way, the fire-insurance policy is paid," he said.

"Couldn't that have waited?"

He did not answer her.

About six o'clock the tension increased. Now it was time to change clothes. The silence between them was broken in many ways. "Where is that collar button, now?" "Do you think I can wear champagne-colored shoes with that dress?" "What dress?"

The questions were asked hastily, and the answers were not always exactly soft-spoken as they dashed from room to room, looked at themselves in the mirror, combed their hair, brushed their clothes. The whole business had such an air of unreality in the strong sunlight that beat down on the opposite neighbor's roof. Going out in full dress in the daylight was like a masquerade. He felt like a waiter. Seeing Johanne in the black dress with the bold yellow pattern made it seem as if they were getting ready for a carnival. The snakeskin, as Jastrau called it.

"How do I look in it, Ole?"

"Wonderful. Thunder and lightning."

But he did not tell her that she looked a little too provocative in it.

Nevertheless, she did. Didn't such a dress give her a suggestive, come-on look? Swelling curves. Full breasts. Legs clearly outlined beneath the tight skirt. Everything about her spelled danger. A strangely untamed creature.

"Wonderful," he repeated, and suddenly felt self-conscious. There was a force here that he was not master of, a femininity, a sensuality that had not been subdued. Why was everything between them so drab?

He was still inexperienced, he thought, and she was mature.

A little later they sat in a taxi and rode out along Vesterbrogade. Jastrau already felt the sweat on his forehead.

"There's something nonsensical about giving a party at this time of the year," he remarked, gazing out at the reflection of sunlight glistening on a myriad of bicycle handlebars.

"But after all, it's your own fault," said Johanne. "He postponed it, and all on account of you."

"Well, yes. But I can't endure tails and white tie when the sun is shining."

"You're so sensitive."

"Yes—I'm sweating."

The taxi drove up in front of a villa in Frederiksberg, or rather a large ugly house that was much too big for the grounds around it. Several large chestnut trees cast so much shade that the grass in the mouldy earth looked sickly.

A little gentleman in evening clothes stood at the gate, blinking nearsightedly behind his pince-nez spectacles.

"Well, so it's you. At last—at last. Finally I've succeeded in tearing you away from the family hearth. But with you for a wife, Frue, even a pirate would become a homebody. Yes, who would have thought it of you, you old revolutionary fool. But welcome to you both. The Einstein highballs aren't ready yet, but there are chilled cocktails— really ice-cold—little Eskimos, ha ha ha. But here comes another taxi. More guests. God knows who it is."

He squinted his eyes and leaned forward. His pointed wolf's nose sniffed the air.

"Hello, Krog, and thanks for asking us to come."

A gentleman of medium height in evening dress and an open topcoat came toward them from another taxi. His expression was at once listless and arrogant. The listlessness was apparent even in the whites of his eyes.

Behind him came a little lady in an evening wrap pulled high up

174

around her neck. She fidgeted as she walked and looked as if all the while she was trying to hide her pointed nose.

There were introductions. It was Judge Asmussen and his wife.

"We'd better be going in!" exclaimed Krog. "We look like a crowd, and if we keep on standing here we'll risk a fine for disorderly conduct, won't we, Judge?"

Jastrau gave a start and looked nervously at the judge. Did he know anything? The judge was wiping his mouth with a handkerchief.

"I need whiskey, my dear Krog," he said. "I haven't tasted a drop since yesterday."

"Oh, you always have to brag about what a drunk you are, Asmus," protested his wife. She raised her nose in Johanne's direction. "We really don't have a drop in the house, you know. Except when we have company, of course."

"That's a lie, damn it, Strik," the judge said, laughing hoarsely. "I love to get drunk, and if I know Krog I'm sure he's taken my depravity into account."

They went in through the gate together.

"I love booze, let me tell you," Asmussen went on, addressing Jastrau and taking a vise-like grip on his arm.

Fru Krog, a sluggish creature with dark hair arranged in Madonna style, received them cordially with a limp handshake. A mirror in the hallway. Of course, one couldn't help seeing himself in it. *Ecce homo!* Jastrau straightened his shirt front and looked at his altogether too familiar sallow face. He knew what lay hidden behind it.

The others swarmed about him. Combs, powder puffs, and lipsticks lay in a jumble on the console in front of the mirror.

Finally, they made up their minds to go in. As they opened the door from the dark hallway, the afternoon sun struck them full in the face and dazzled them. The low mahogany bookshelves along the walls sparkled. An upright piano stood in shadow, and against it, dressed in evening clothes, his face chalk-white and his back slightly arched, leaned Vuldum. He was chatting with a small lady with a Madonna hairdo who was seated on the piano stool—Fru Krog's sister.

A slim gentleman with a somber, ominous expression and a reddish scar on one cheek rose from an armchair in which he had been sitting and staring meditatively at one of his patent-leather shoes.

Vuldum screwed up his eyes appraisingly, caught sight of Jastrau to the latter's discomfiture, and went on with an objective scrutiny of Johanne before he greeted them.

"Now we're almost all here," exclaimed Krog, rubbing his hands

175

together. "We're only lacking Kryger. But it'll do us good to wait. Our appetites will be so much the better. Come here, Jastrau, and let me show you this edition of Plato that I just got hold of."

"How he does brag—that man," Vuldum remarked in a loud voice.

Krog smiled self-consciously.

"I'm envious," he confided.

"No, Krog—why should you be envious? I don't collect books, I only read them." Vuldum turned chivalrously to the lady again. "It's really a bad habit. But I happen to be bone-lazy, Frøken, and I read a great deal."

His words passed lightly over the lady's head, and he sent a look of disdain down at her hairdo.

"You look like a Helena," he remarked apropos of nothing, as if merely letting his words fall into the part of her hair.

"Who?" she asked, giving a start of surprise and blushing.

Jastrau heard no more of the conversation. He stood there, feeling awkward and embarrassed, thumbing through the German edition of Plato with its pages white, unsullied, and untouched.

"I'm reading him in the World Classics Library," Krog said with enthusiasm. But at that moment he was interrupted.

"Listen, Krog—soon I'm going to be having food fantasies!" exclaimed the slim gentleman with the scar. It was Agner Raben, who held the position of secretary in the municipal court.

"Yes, me too," replied Krog. "But now I'll order the cocktails. Besides, Kryger will soon be here." He disappeared into the dining room.

"Yes, bring on the liquor," said the judge, laughing hoarsely. "We lawyers are always thirsty."

Over near the window, the women had gathered in a little group. The afternoon sun cast a glow of light about their party dresses and placed nebulous halos around their hair and down alongside their bare arms. There was so much bare flesh here. The married women resembled young girls, as the current fashion demanded. Their dresses fitted them tightly and covered only the area from the breasts to the knees; they were pliable, scintillating sheaths drawn over their bodies, as simply cut as paper-doll dresses, nothing but rectangles with openings for the neck and arms.

"Do you suppose we might manage to split up this bevy of beauties?" suggested Krog, who had come back to the room. "Who's the brave one? How about you, Jastrau? You're a ladies' man."

Jastrau smiled wearily.

"Yes, because I can't stand it when the women bunch up together, can you, Vuldum? But wait—here comes the man who can do it."

The door opened as he spoke. A youngish lady with restless gray eyes stepped in. She was dressed in gray silk—an animated, sparkling gray. And her eyes blinked as they encountered the sunlight.

She led the way. But with an air of resignation and humility that had become a habit she stepped aside for her husband, the diminutive Kryger with the blue-black, glistening hair and a flashing smile that revealed a set of white teeth. "Hello, everybody."

Everything perked up. A mysterious, flashing energy seemed to radiate from the newcomer.

"And now we can have the cocktails," Krog shouted.

Everybody stood up. There was a general stir. People wove in and out among each other. A servant girl in black, with a white cap and a little white apron, came in with the gray-gold cocktails on a tray.

"How are you?" asked Vuldum, who now happened to be standing close to Jastrau.

A sharp, stinging pain.

Jastrau smiled uncertainly.

"Silver nitrate," he whispered suddenly.

Vuldum looked at him for a moment. Then he dilated his nostrils, bent over, and began to laugh without making a sound.

The cocktail shook in his hand.

But the next instant Jastrau regretted his gratuitous frankness, for Vuldum was looking at Johanne with a clouded, unfathomable expression.

"And now we can go in and sit down," Krog announced.

Chapter Five

The evening had worn on until it was late. In the dining room things had been cleared away. A phonograph stood in one corner amidst a heap of records and intoned a sentimental jazz tune. But only a single couple glided quietly and intimately across the floor. It was the glum Raben and Fru Krog's younger sister.

All the others were gathered in the living room where the silent piano stood. The table was filled with glasses and bottles, large siphon bottles, square whiskey bottles, and port and madeira for the ladies. Judge Asmussen sat on the sofa, his face flushed and his arm around Krog's shoulder as he laughed.

"We don't seem to be drinking. *Skaal!*" he bellowed.

Fru Asmussen, Fru Kryger, and Fru Krog had closed ranks in a confidential little triangle and were chatting in lively fashion about the beach hotel at Skotterup. For the moment, they had been left in peace by the elegant, agile Kryger, who had attached himself to Jastrau.

"Well, old fellow," he remarked smilingly and slapped Jastrau on the knee. "Still just as radical as ever?"

"I'm not interested in politics."

"Then you're just as harmless as ever."

Jastrau was in no mood to resume a discussion that was a year old. Ever since that time, the memory of it had lodged in him like a splinter and tormented him. Now and then, he glanced across to a dimly lighted corner where Vuldum sat engaged in conversation with Johanne. She was obviously enjoying herself. Occasionally she would bend forward and laugh so that her blonde hair shook. Vuldum was very likely being witty and a bit familiar. He sat leaning back, with an arm resting casually on the back of Johanne's chair.

Jastrau shifted uneasily in his chair. Why had he been so candid with Vuldum?

"My point of view is honest enough," he said, addressing himself to Kryger. There was indignation in his tone. But was it not because of the way Vuldum's eyes were expertly appraising Johanne's bosom? Over there where the light was so dim, everything was blurred, and it seemed as if Joachim Michelsen's features blended disquietingly with Vuldum's, although the two in no way resembled each other.

"Don't misunderstand me," replied Kryger with a warm smile. "I'm not accusing you of dishonesty, but of blindness."

"Even if I were not with *Dagbladet,* I'd feel the same as I do."

"But you *are* with *Dagbladet*. And that means that you're a respectable member of society, just as I am."

"Oh, you argue just like a Communist!" Jastrau replied vehemently and took a big swallow of whiskey.

But at that moment he detected an uneasy look in Johanne's eyes over in the dimly lighted corner. Vuldum had laid his hand on her shoulder. Yes, Jastrau saw it clearly. And Johanne? She had seen him looking at her and then shifted her position suddenly so that Vuldum's hand fell limply away.

"Why don't you come in and dance?" came a voice from the doorway. It was Fru Krog's lively sister with the Madonna hairdo. Raben's figure could be seen behind her in the dark room between the lighted dining room and the living room, where the rest of the company sat.

Johanne had moved away from Vuldum. But would she have done so if—if—?

178

Fru Kryger drew up her gray head and said in answer to the inquiry, "Oh, they're drinking and talking politics."

"That's a lie, damn it," exclaimed the judge, laughing as heartily as he could. "We're drinking right enough, but we aren't drinking enough."

"You sound like a philosopher," said Vuldum.

"Yes, ha ha."

"Well then—*skaal*, everybody!" shouted the little host so loudly that one might have taken him for a broad-shouldered hulk of a man.

They all raised their glasses. But Jastrau felt another stinging reminder. After all this time. He was not being allowed to forget.

"Oh, by the way, Judge"—again it was Fru Krog's sister who spoke—"I completely forgot to thank you for the other day."

"Yes—that's right," Fru Krog summoned up the energy to say.

Asmussen laughed. "Yes. Everything's nice and cozy down there at the courthouse, isn't it?"

"At the courthouse? Can a person get in there?" asked Fru Kryger, her eyes lighting up. "That must be interesting."

"Yes." The judge laughed so that his little, round belly bobbed up and down. "Do you know what I showed the ladies, Fru Kryger?"

A cold shiver ran down Jastrau's spine.

"No, what?" asked Kryger, sitting up politely.

"The lockup."

There was a pause for a second.

Then, from his corner, Vuldum burst into loud laughter that had a startling effect on the others. Jastrau took a firmer hold on his glass and laughed along with the rest.

"The lockup," repeated the judge slowly, gloating over the interest he had aroused.

"But unfortunately there was no one in there," came a feeble feminine complaint. It was Fru Krog with the Madonna hairdo.

"My, how ferocious you are, little Frue," Vuldum observed in a caressing tone as he moved nearer. "A melancholy little beast of prey." And then his well-modulated words were drowned out in the general laughter.

But this time Jastrau did not join in, so nervous and disconcerted was he by the turn the conversation had taken. He concealed his feelings by drinking.

"Beast of prey!" replied Fru Krog with blasé indignation. She was also a little flattered. "But there's really nothing to see when there isn't one of those drunken rowdies there who's imprisoned."

"Imprisoned!" objected Krog. "That's a strong word."

"Well—arrested, then."

The three lawyers in the group broke into loud laughter. Vuldum smiled understandingly.

"But how can you say that, Anna?" exclaimed the sister, who felt no bewilderment at the nuances of Danish legal terminology. "It was unpleasant enough as it was—that little dark room and the two bunks and those dreary bare walls."

Four wrinkles of compassion appeared on her brow.

"You must really excuse us, but unfortunately we haven't yet got the pictures hung up," said Raben cynically, shoving his grinning face forth from the dark room.

Loud laughter. Jastrau cautiously edged his chair away from the others.

"But we'll have pictures there yet," bellowed the judge, his face a deep red. "They'll be there—along with our humane administration of justice. You can be sure of that."

"And beds with innerspring mattresses," seconded Vuldum.

"And female servants," Krog snickered, peering around nearsightedly in all directions.

"Yes, as a matter of fact, we treat them too well," said the judge, seizing hold of the conversation again. He spoke with a professional air. "It's really an out-and-out rest home."

So that was how they felt about it. And here he sat, Editor Ole Jastrau, in tails and white tie.

"But just the same, I'd like to see it sometime when there's someone in there—ah, yes." It was Fru Kryger's singsong voice, and she lifted her shoulders voluptuously as she spoke.

"Well, well," sighed the judge in mock resignation, while Raben laughed. "Then I don't suppose I can do anything except invite the entire company for an inspection tour of our jail cells—sometime when there are animals in the cage, mind you."

Jastrau got up quietly. Here among this group, he suddenly felt like a person in disguise, like a sober fool at a carnival. Had he believed that he belonged here? Why did the memory of the two hooligans who had been locked in the cell next to his suddenly become so warmly intimate and pleasant? Was it there that he belonged—down at the lowest level of existence where things were so nice? Did he want to go to the dogs? He wanted to—yes, he had to. The thought gave him a wholesome feeling—a sense of liberation. Then he could reveal himself as the person he was, get on intimate terms with himself.

"We'll take you at your word," Fru Kryger screamed in an outburst of joyful hysteria.

"Yes, yes—of course. But then I'll have to have everybody's address or phone number," said Asmussen, laughing. "Raben, my dear secretary, you'll have to note them down."

While the others laughed, Raben sat down at the table and began to write in his notebook. Everyone was elated, and they all crowded around him. Johanne poked her head over his shoulder and made sure that he got all the addresses correct.

Jastrau stared at her and felt his anger rising. She too was going around in a mask. Yes, she was. It was only that she wore the mask better than he. He, in full-dress clothes and possibly with disease germs lurking within him, venomous, thread-like organisms that in an instant multiplied as rapidly as people did over a period of a thousand years. Nevertheless, he was just as good as the others, as good as any of them despite his sudden fear and fit of shivering, and it was unfair that he alone of all these people should feel shabby and unclean in every way, he alone—

In self-righteous indignation he poured himself another strong whiskey and soda.

"A stiff double, what?" said Kryger, laughing.

Jastrau sent him a macabre nod and took the glass away from his mouth.

Just then Asmussen's hoarse laughter cut through the chatter. "But look here, ladies and gentlemen," he said, "—what shall we do if there happens to be a prominent animal there in the cell, ha ha?"

"But decent people don't get locked up there!" exclaimed Krog's sister-in-law naïvely. The remark suited her Madonna coiffure.

"Really?" said the judge.

There was a fresh wave of laughter, and then everyone began talking at once.

"What do you think about Dr. Harren?" Raben asked ironically.

"And Engineer Ivan Kramer," trumped Krog.

"Attorney Tingslev," Vuldum said quietly but incisively, going Krog one better.

Was that really how it was? Jastrau drank and smiled at the same time. Greetings to all good fellows from Peter Boyesen.

"Professor Geberhardt," yelled Krog, his pale eyes popping behind the spectacles.

"No. Now I must protest!" exclaimed Kryger vociferously. He got up from his chair. "He wasn't guilty of anything like that—"

He looked around at the ladies, who were enjoying themselves immensely.

"That's right, by God. He's one of the contributors to *Danmark*. I'd completely forgotten that." And Krog laughed exuberantly.

"That's not why I'm objecting," Kryger asserted, waving his hand in an imperious gesture. "He has broken with us and gone to Berlin."

"What's that?" exclaimed Vuldum with evident interest. His gray eyes shone brightly.

Kryger nodded.

"But the university? What about it, what about it?" Krog stammered in his perplexity.

"He'll no longer be teaching business science."

"This is really sensational, damned if it isn't!" Asmussen exclaimed.

Everyone stared at Kryger, who bit his lip and smiled.

"Well, it wasn't really supposed to be announced just yet," he said circumspectly and took out his watch. "But then, it's too late for it to get into the other papers now, so it doesn't make any difference. We're printing it tomorrow." He smiled and looked relieved.

"It's really scandalous having that Bolshevik occupy a professor's chair in this country," Krog said indignantly. He pronounced the words "professor's chair" with great dignity.

"He's really a conservative," Kryger protested.

"He's a devil, he is," chuckled Asmussen.

"But why doesn't he want to—?" Krog did not get the question finished.

"That sort of thing can happen these days too," interrupted Kryger, smiling and shrugging his shoulders. "People sometimes throw up everything and don't want to go on."

Just then Jastrau set his glass down on the table with a loud thump, and several of the guests stared at him. His eyes were glazed with alcohol.

"Right," he said in a gruff voice.

"Now Jastrau is drunk," Vuldum whispered to Raben, and Raben nodded knowingly.

Johanne frowned.

But Jastrau bit off the tip of a cigar so violently that the end of it was left ragged. His eyes had a vicious, remote look.

And suddenly he left the gathering and withdrew into the dark room. Yes, he had drunk too much. The darkness flickered before his eyes. He had to calm himself. He took up a position near the window and gazed down at the empty street with its nocturnal lights.

Professor Julius Geberhardt. He had seen pictures of him in the newspapers. A face that was at once rugged and crafty-looking, disorderly hair with wisps of it sticking out behind the ears, turndown collars and that sort of humbug. A professor. Member of the board of directors. An expert on the law governing the sale of securities. An extremely troublesome gentleman whom the powers of high finance had in vain attempted to have stamped as insane. And now he had finally become tired and had thrown it all overboard, his position and his title.

Wasn't that going to the dogs?

"Are you standing here dreaming?" asked Krog, suddenly looming up out of the darkness. "A lovely evening, isn't it, even if I do say so myself." He rubbed his hands together in satisfaction. "And now we're going to have a little *smørrebrød* with beer and *snaps*."

"This about Professor Geberhardt—" Jastrau could not get it off his mind. The darkness kept flickering unsteadily. "Geberhardt," he repeated.

"Yes. My God—what a relief that is. But I have to get out in the kitchen. A host has his duties."

A relief! So that was the way they felt about it. Jastrau screwed up his eyes. A relief! One of the few men who fought against the disintegration of capitalism and the political structure. But troublesome. He disappeared from the scene, and my God, what a relief!

A slight smarting pain again made itself felt, like a devil whispering something in his ear. But now it no longer reminded him only of a ridiculous escapade. It signified something revolutionary. He was made of different stuff than the others there that evening. Chaotically, his thoughts took shape as a revolt against all dissembling and hypocrisy. He drew himself up straighter. That slight prophylactic pain was a mark of distinction. He was more honest than—

The company went in to the *smørrebrød* table, chattering about all sorts of nonsense. But Jastrau's eyes were screwed up and full of malice. His silence was conspicuous. Johanne glanced uneasily at him several times.

There was *smørrebrød* with herring, and there was *snaps*. Perhaps that would help.

The conversation was strained, a bit unstable. When the guests had drunk a *snaps*, only one, their faces suddenly relaxed. Yes, after the whiskey, the *snaps* was a help. Relaxed lower lips, glistening eyes, headstrong opinions.

And what were they talking about? Professor Geberhardt. Everyone expressed himself strongly.

Nevertheless, things seemed to get a little out of control when Jastrau put in a few heated words:

"Damn it! There's no freedom of speech in this country."

It was his tone rather than the idea that was out of place. It revealed an arrant fanaticism, introduced an alien note.

And now Vuldum was again sitting familiarly beside Johanne.

"No, I'll be damned if there is," Jastrau repeated angrily, as if someone had protested. But no one had. They merely dodged the issue. Kryger shifted his chair a little farther away and surveyed him with a sidelong glance.

"Oh, now, we mustn't get into a discussion of politics again," Fru Krog complained.

"No, now we'd better go home and get to bed," said Judge Asmussen. "I can tell by your eyes, Frue." He had not touched the *snaps*.

"Already?" Kryger hastened to say.

"Oh, you never get tired, Otto," his wife interjected with a hopeless smile.

"We're not all as rugged as you, Herr Editor," sighed the judge.

"And besides, you have that important case tomorrow," said his wife, raising her nose perceptibly.

"Yes," came the feeble answer.

But when the guests finally had taken their leave and stood out on the sidewalk in the bluish light of the streetlights, ready to get into their cabs, it seemed that for the first time Kryger really began to feel expansive. His eyes sparkled.

"What do you say we go to the Golden Age Club?" he proposed eagerly.

The host and hostess stood in the doorway.

"You're indefatigable," Krog called out to him as he suppressed a yawn. "But you won't insist on me going with you. Some other time— some other time. Then I'll be up to it."

Jastrau stood leaning against one of the taxis. He was nodding a bit.

"You'll come along, won't you, Frue," Vuldum said ingratiatingly to Johanne.

But she stole a sidelong glance at her husband's tired figure leaning against the cab.

"No, Ole has to go home."

There were handshakes. Suddenly Ole Jastrau found himself sitting in a taxi. He raised his hat in a farewell gesture. Johanne sat beside him, nodding to the shadowy figures outside.

"Ole has to go home," he repeated provocatively. "Ole has to go home."

Then they drove off.

"What did you really mean by that remark?" he asked in a spiteful tone.

"That you have to go home and get to sleep," she answered wearily, settling back in the seat and drawing her wrap around her.

"I? Sleep? You probably think I'm drunk," he commented snidely.

184

"Now, now—the driver can hear us," she said in a low tone. It sounded almost as if she were hissing at him.

"It's remarkable how generous you are."

"What do you mean by that?" she asked, sitting up with a start.

"That you turn down Vuldum's company in order to get your drunken husband home to bed."

The sentence was spoken in a well-modulated tone of disdain, so clear, sober, and vindictive that no one would have suspected Jastrau of being drunk. His eyes were small and Mongoloid in his sallow, ravaged face.

Johanne looked at him, appalled.

"Why you're out of your mind!" she burst out.

"I saw what I saw." He leaned over with his hot face close to hers. "And I heard what I heard."

"You're talking riddles. Ooh—stop breathing in my face!"

"I heard what I heard," Jastrau went on, jerking his head away from her. Suddenly a feeling of savagery took possession of him. "I heard what I heard—yes, I heard Joachim Michelsen's voice very clearly today. Don't think you can fool me. I heard it—I—I—"

He gasped for breath. He felt his heart contracting, and a pain shot through his chst.

"No—I can't take it any longer. I won't—"

Johanne drew her wrap closely about her so that it no longer touched him. There was a space between them, but he could detect her body growing rigid. He did not look at her.

But then it came.

"Why did you turn those photographs around at home?" she asked harshly.

And in his mind's eye he saw himself as he had been there in the apartment—how, unable to rest because of dissipation and the whiskey in his system, he had paced back and forth through the rooms and suddenly felt himself tormented by the two faces, the photographs of his mother and his son, how he had had a feeling that they could see right through him, and then he had turned the pictures around.

So Johanne had noticed it.

And there she sat in the corner of the cab, pale as a corpse and unassailable. He sensed his powerlessness, and it made him desperate. Something had to happen. But he could not speak.

Suddenly he bent forward, rapped on the window in back of the driver, and signalled frantically for him to stop.

"What do you want? Have you gone completely crazy?" Johanne cried out in bewilderment.

The taxi slowed and then came to a stop. Jastrau already had the door open so that the breeze came whistling in. And then, with one leap, he was out on the edge of the sidewalk.

At a loss to know what was going on, the driver turned on the light inside the cab. Johanne sat silent and pale with the black evening wrap around her. She made not a single voluntary movement, merely rocked back and forth momentarily like a statue because the car had stopped so suddenly, and then regained her equilibrium.

Jastrau's lips were trembling. He wished that his rash act could be undone. He wanted to get back into the cab. But that triumphant silence must be conquered. He had to win this battle, and he would. A stupid conquest. What did the cab driver think? And then he reached into his pocket, grabbed his keys, tossed them into the cab. Out with his wallet too, and into the cab with it. Inexplicable. A silent, violent scene. And Johanne sat there in the feeble light, staring straight ahead like a person who was dying.

Without a word, Jastrau turned his back on her and began walking out Vesterbrogade. The glow from the arc lights, the broad, glistening, car tracks, the shadowy figures on the street corners, white legs flashing, women, and up above the roofs the blue-black night sky and some stars; he sensed the street as an extension of his soul, as a confirmation that something conclusive had occurred, as an extraordinary, incomprehensibly calming influence. Behind him, he heard the taxi start and get under way. It must be it, because there was not another car on the street at the moment. He would not turn around, but must simply keep walking. Then the taxi could catch up with him, draw up alongside the curb, and stop. And then they could talk to each other. The taxi had to come.

But the sound of the engine became fainter and fainter, and finally he had to turn around and look.

What he saw was the rear end of the cab. The taillight like a red cat's eye in the distance. It turned a corner down near Vesterbro's square and disappeared.

Disappeared.

And once again he was swallowed up by the night. Again he was aware of an inexplicable feeling of peace, a calmness of spirit, as if all his life he had known that this was the way it would turn out. Whatever happened from now on would be nothing but details—trivia. Indeed, the things that had happened during the last few days were trivia, superficial details which in themselves had no significance but which, seen in connection with other events, meant that—well, what did they mean?

186

Had he been unfaithful? Unfaithful? He could not really remember. Had it been something he had really experienced? Or only a figment of his imagination? The jail cell. Was that something he had imagined? Peter Boyesen sends greetings— An hallucination.

And Oluf. "Where have you and Mother been all this time?" A high-pitched boyish voice over the telephone, an unrealistic manifestation of reality, his living son fading away into unreality. An hallucination. For now he would probably never get to see Oluf again.

"Where have you and Mother been all this time?"

Something to set his mind on. The Golden Age Club. Ah, that made him feel better. A current of cool night air caressed his forehead. And with his topcoat flapping in the breeze so that his white shirt front twinkled and seemed to lure him on, he kept walking out toward the darkness of Frederiksberg Allé. He perceived it as a shadowy night-refuge that lay behind the bright lights around the newsstand at the Værnedam intersection.

A woman stopped. But he kept walking heedlessly, his coat flapping about him, as if hurrying along an accustomed route, farther and farther out Frederiksberg Allé with its newly planted trees, their sparse branches bristling ridiculously—outwards—outwards—like mere twigs. How nice the car tracks looked, as lovely as a bright nocturnal sky when the headlights of the automobiles speeding by plowed the darkness away from them. A long street. Endless. There was a world of space out there, out above the darkness of Frederiksberg Park and the dimly discernible yellow gatekeepers' houses flanking the castle, a wide expanse of starry sky, an atmosphere of nature and wide-open spaces.

In a low suburban building behind the trees in the garden of the Lorry glowed a little, unimpressive doorway. Only the long row of taxis drawn up beside the sidewalk revealed the presence of the night-club.

A doorman peered suspiciously through the window when Jastrau tried the doorknob, but the sight of the well-known journalist reassured him. After having produced his membership card, he slipped in past a row of friendly if somewhat skeptical observers. Was he drunk? Were they politely appraising the condition he was in? He greeted them cordially.

As he did so he heard the wail of a saxophone in beside the dance floor. Now he could calm down and stop his disordered flight, and the feeling of oppressiveness that all the while had been so marked in the region of his heart had evidently subsided. A call of the wild, a scream and a sob, perhaps a lamenting cry from out of the distance, perhaps an animal or a woman somewhere nearby. Now he could give himself up to remorse and still feel calm, for no grief was as intense as the wail of the saxophone.

Fortified by the jazz, he stood in the doorway leading in to the dance floor. A banjo broke up all worries and cares into fixed rhythms. A grillwork. The air vibrated with a melancholy born of virtuosity. A piano without pedals. His eyes reconnoitered among the dancers in the room, where the nation's golden-age poets peered darkly from frames hung on the light walls, like gigantic oval medallions. And just as he caught sight of the tall and lugubrious Raben, who here was continuing his intimate, long-drawn-out dance with Fru Krog's sister, whose Madonna coiffure rested caressingly against his white shirt front, Jastrau heard someone call out:

"Hello, Brother-in-law."

He glanced nervously down at a table beside him. There, with mouth wide open, sat his wife's dear brother, Adolf Smith-Jørgensen, flushed and looking somewhat befuddled. And sitting next to him was the blond, handsome architect, Joachim Michelsen, with his blue, girlish eyes and soft, curving lips. The blue eyes stared at him with an illusive depth as Michelsen withdrew an arm that had been resting on the shoulders of a girl in pink and rose from his chair with an air of marked cordiality.

"Nice to see you," he said in a subdued voice that sounded as if it had musical accompaniment.

Jastrau was immediately conscious of his own heavy bulk in contrast to this slender individual. A remote, gentle smile crossed his features, as it did whenever he saw a thing of beauty.

"The champagne is flowing here!" roared Smith-Jørgensen.

"Oh, how nice he is—your brother-in-law," purred a girl in brown, laying her head tenderly against Adolf's shoulder as with round leaden baby eyes and doll-like cheeks flushed with wine she looked at Jastrau. "How nice he is. Why haven't you ever told me that you have a brother-in-law?"

"Oh—a brother-in-law," said Adolf, laughing. "This place is swarming with brothers-in-law."

A fleeting smile appeared on Michelsen's lips—a somewhat sticky smile, Jastrau thought. Both of the young girls laughed hysterically.

"But this one here is so nice," the one in brown continued. "Sit down here with us, won't you?"

And Jastrau sat down with an awkward feeling of not being nice at all.

"I'm hunting for my party," he said.

188

"Where's Johanne?" asked Adolf. "Oh, the hell with her anyway. It's so seldom that we've been out on a binge together. Isn't she nice—this young one here? Her name is Gunhild."

Jastrau thought he ought to explain that Johanne was tired and had gone home.

"Oh, to hell with her." Adolph brushed his explanation aside. "I've seen enough of her in the last few days. Variety is the spice of life, isn't it, Joachim?" He leaned forward toward Gunhild, laughing. "Yes, as a matter of fact, he is nice. All brothers-in-law are."

His eyes were glazed, his cheeks flaming.

Jastrau, whose head had cleared during his walk, noticed it at once.

He could see that Joachim, on the other hand, was sober and only preoccupied with the girl in pink.

"We're all brothers-in-law."

At that moment Jastrau received a vigorous kick in the shin and let out an exclamation.

"What's the matter with you, Brother-in-law?" asked Adolf, staring at him dully and uncomprehendingly.

"Somebody kicked me."

"What? Somebody kicked you? Look here, Gunhild, are you kicking? You mustn't do that. Take it easy now, take it easy."

Gunhild protested.

"You're a peculiar girl, you are," Michelsen said in his gentle voice. "When I go to kiss you, you shut your eyes. I guess you don't know that that can drive me completely wild."

Shut her eyes. Shut her eyes. Was it a nightmare he was experiencing? Johanne. Johanne. She always shut her eyes. It was the modest side of her nature asserting itself, part of her personal feminine mystique, and here Michelsen had tossed off the remark to a girl he had met casually. Two saxophones tooted and wailed. All the other instruments joined in. A tuba's low notes reverberated through the room, filling it with compact strident sound and sweeping away all sense of spatial dimension. Away with it all!

A glass of champagne was placed before Jastrau, and he fumbled for it like a person who had been drugged.

Everything anyone said tonight had a double meaning. He was surrounded by diabolical remarks. It was driving him crazy. A persecution mania. This was what a persecution mania must be like. Everything assumed an insidious secondary significance. Every single word, no matter how trifling, was artfully devised by a devil. She shut her eyes—shut her eyes. A deep erotic secret given away.

"So here you are." A figure in evening dress leaned heavily against his shoulder, weighed him down, and put a stop to his thoughts. It was Kryger.

"I was hunting for you. Johanne went home."

"Good you came, good you came," Kryger intoned through his nose as he stood wobbling a bit. His eyes were bloodshot. "And what a lovely lady there beside you!"

"You—you're barging in on a private party," Adolf barked, raising his head oafishly.

"And what a charming gentleman you're with."

Jastrau introduced Kryger, and Adolf's obstreperousness gave way to a damp, cringing smile.

"So why don't you all join us?" Kryger went on in his lilting voice. "There are so many of us, a wonderful party with lots of women. Come along, all of you. Jastrau, you make sure they join us. Otherwise I'll forget because I'm drunk, and God knows how I love women."

It'll be a great honor, Herr Editor—" Adolf got no further, because Kryger had taken the girl in brown by the arm.

"Ah, how sweet you are," they heard him say.

The members of Kryger's party were gathered in the small room where the bar was, together with a number of unknown and dubious characters. Fru Kryger was listening not only to Vuldum, whose face was pale beneath his bright-red hair, but also to a completely unfamiliar man whose countenance resembled an inflated red paper bag drawn together at the top and tied by a small puckered-up mouth. How excited and nervous she seemed, now more provocative than the young girls who sat like a row of parakeets along the brass rail, now ladylike and austere as befitted a married woman. She seemed altogether unaware of the way her husband was buzzing about.

The scar on Raben's cheek was flaming red—a danger signal. His little Madonna leaned closely against him.

Then he found himself in a swarm of journalists, actors, business men, and other well-dressed individuals, as well as young girls. Jastrau did not catch their names. There was a man with slicked-down hair, gray around the temples.

"Quite a crowd," Kryger exulted, hauling Jastrau around by the arm.

"Where is the judge?" Jastrau asked.

Raben smiled sarcastically.

"I thought he liked his liquor," Jastrau went on.

"Nothing but idle talk," Raben replied. "All he does is talk about it."

"Ah, yes—if only that was the way with the rest of us," mused Kryger. "As far as women are concerned, too. Yes, if only one could be satisfied with talking about it."

190

Fru Kryger responded with a laugh that was altogether too loud.

Then Kryger dragged Jastrau over to the bar. "Here are a couple of thirsty gentlemen," he said.

They thrust their heads in between the row of parakeets. Jastrau felt shoulders and hairdos brushing him. He was swimming in a sea of feminine charm, a soft yielding feminity on all sides. He reached for the highball glass that stood sweating and fizzing on the bar and encountered Kryger's impetuous, licentious smile. It seemed to radiate a somber intensity. Was it really Kryger—the small, elegant, arrogant journalist?

"*Skaal!*"

All restraint seemed to have been lifted. So it was Kryger's real self that was asserting itself from behind his official mask. His eyes were bloodshot like those of an animal.

"Are you sitting here nipping soda water, you poor things?" said Kryger in a tone of endearment. "You shall have Blue Moons and Red Devils and White Ladies—do you hear, bartender?" He turned and shouted to his wife, "Watch out that I don't spend too much money!"

"He's a good fellow—this editor." Jastrau turned and saw Adolf's gaping mouth right next to his face. Deep inside the murky cavern a gold-crowned molar glistened.

Jastrau nodded. A woman's neck. Smooth white skin beneath a blushing ear. Everything was enveloped in a mantle of jazz.

He barely managed to bring his head up above the swirling sea of emotions and intoxication and reply, "Yes, Brother-in-law."

As he did so, he heard an asinine laugh.

"All of us here are brothers-in-law."

At the same time, he looked toward the door. There stood Michelsen, the handsome architect, helping his lady on with her wrap. His own coat was over his arm.

"He's a big spender," whispered Adolf, his moist lips close to Jastrau's face. "But so what? Here we're all brothers-in-law."

The place was mobbed. Not a bit of empty space. Perfume brushed his face as heavily as if it were a hand.

"If only we could be satisfied with talking about it," said Kryger, laughing and disappearing with a woman on each side of him. One of them had a morose, virtuous look about her. Jastrau remembered having seen her every time he had been in the place.

Then there was shouting and more hilarity. A jazz melody was repeated by request.

Jastrau went out on the floor to dance, a difficult undertaking. Several times he bumped into other dancers. It was too crowded, and he edged his way out of the jam. The girl he had danced with laughed. It was the one with the baby eyes.

At one of the tables sat two unaccompanied women with vacant smiles. A drunken man had come up and was speaking to them. He was swaying back and forth.

"You aren't enjoying yourselves this evening."

It was Kryger's voice. It had a nasal tone.

"Is that you? Jastrau?"

"Yes. Is this where you landed?"

"Yes. I can't stand to see all the lonely women sitting near the wall. They're not doing any business, and so I have to drum up trade for them. You're going to have a whiskey, girls—yes, damn it, you are. I can't make love to them all—not tonight. But I can see to it that they all have whiskey—that they feel happy. People—"

Jastrau interrupted and put an arm around him. "Do you feel that way too?"

"Yes, I feel that way too," Kryger replied, looking at him with glazed eyes.

But just then he caught sight of a solitary woman at another table. The tablecloth with its single coffee cup presented a dreary picture.

"Deflation," he muttered and went over there. Jastrau followed him, badly befuddled but faithful unto death.

"And here you must also have some whiskey—isn't that so, Frøken?" Kryger asked.

They sat down beside her. She was a broad-bosomed woman and bore herself with dignity, but she condescended to smile.

"Is that the way you feel too, Kryger? Is it Jesus among the whores that you're thinking of?" Jastrau burst out.

"You needn't be blasphemous."

"I'm not being blasphemous," said Jastrau, bringing his hand down on the table so hard that the glasses shook. He had completely forgotten the broad-bosomed lady. "That's the way I feel. I can never forget Jesus among the whores. The more I drink and dissipate, the closer He is to me. He is resurrected inside me in the midst of all this havoc— here, inside me—

"You should really be ashamed of yourself," said the woman indignantly.

"If only one could be satisfied with talking about it," Kryger intoned with a warm, uncomprehending smile. His black hair hung down over his forehead.

A glazed stare.

192

Chapter Six   A rough waiter jabbed the corner of a metal tray into the side of Jastrau's head.

It was as if he suddenly found himself inside a red cave. Paper festoons swirled in confusion and threatened to fall like rain from a supersaturated cloud. And at the same time a hush spread over the room. Voices faded and were obliterated, and a melancholy, continuous splashing filled the void. Outside, in the gray morning light, it was raining. The walls of a house on the other side of the street were dark from the rain.

Jastrau guzzled a glassful of bitter beer.

Two faces suddenly were visible. He was sitting beside them. A blond, square-jawed fellow with a ten-gallon hat, and a dark-haired chap with a blue stubble on his cheeks and a fleeting smile. The dark-haired one was drawing on the tablecloth with a pencil.

"It's a hell of a note how little kick there is in beer," said the cowboy, peering down at his empty glass.

Jastrau looked around in confusion. He was tired and drunk, and the liquor he had consumed in the last twenty-four hours was like so much stagnant, foul water. But finally he began to penetrate the fog. He was in an early-morning beer joint and restaurant. Yes, that was it. And in front of him, on a flat plate, a fried egg floated in a puddle of beer. So a glass must have been upset. All over everything.

"You might buy one more round."

"Yes, my friends," said Jastrau, his confusion and his cordiality merging into one. "We'll have another round. Waiter, more beer."

He laid his hands on their shoulders in a fatherly manner, but heavily, as if he were about to fall forward.

The dark-haired one nodded appreciatively.

"Because I like you—you two—let me tell you that," Jastrau went on. "Because I like your faces. They're real human faces."

"Yes, all right," the cowboy replied in English.

"Yes, they are," Jastrau's voice grew intense and hoarse. He gaped a little at them and went on stubbornly to make his point. For, after all, here he was, sitting between a couple of pimps—yes, two pimps. It seemed that he could visualize it all just like a picture, and he grew expansive. A table. Himself in the middle, dignified and paternal, fluent though drunk, and these two pimps, one on each side of him. Yes, pimps was just what they were, because otherwise the picture did

193

not have the depth of meaning, the biblical significance that he was unconsciously striving to invest it with. "Because you are human beings," he went on, "you live the life you must lead. You follow the dictates of your nature."

"Sure," said the cowboy. He spoke with an American accent.

"You have faces, you two—crafty, shrewd, depraved—"

"Ho ho," laughed the one with the dark hair.

"You have no idea how much I love you, you two human beings, for you are human beings."

"Boy, have you got a snootful!" the cowboy said sullenly.

"Jesus would—"

"Ho ho ho!" shouted the dark-haired one. "Well, here's the beer. Do you think you can shut up long enough to get some beer into you?"

Jastrau slumped over dejectedly. There was a loud snap as his shirt front buckled and crept up, giving him the appearance of having a bosom.

"You don't understand me," he whimpered.

"Sure—you're drunk," said the dark-haired one, grinning and biting on the pencil.

"How honest you are," Jastrau mumbled to himself as he stared down at the inundated fried egg.

The cowboy nodded to his companion. They got up and left, still laughing.

Then another outburst of laughter sounded from the back of the room. Jastrau straightened up.

"Aren't you going to eat that egg, sir?" asked a waiter. "Here's your bill."

Jastrau obeyed mechanically. Carefully he tried to balance a bit of the damp egg on a fork and convey it to his mouth. The yolk dripped down onto the lapel of his dresscoat.

"There's the bill, sir," the waiter repeated.

Jastrau went through his pockets. They were empty. He got up with difficulty and looked in his topcoat. Ah, yes—now he remembered. He had tossed it into the cab to Johanne. His wallet with all his money. And now, now he had to go home. Home to Johanne—and Oluf. He must. The waiter kept standing there waiting, insulting him by his very presence.

"Damned if I have any money," he muttered, and then let out a belch.

"Then I'd advise you to get some," came the rough answer.

"But the other two fellows—"

"They're gone. And besides, it was you, sir, who ordered."

"Yes, yes. Yes, yes. So it was I who ordered. But now let me alone." Jastrau slumped wearily back into his chair and directed his attention to the refractory egg.

"But there's this bill, sir."

"Yes, just let me think," he mumbled, stuffing his mouth full of egg.

The waiter disappeared, looking as if he might burst a blood vessel in his broad neck.

Jastrau sat for a while fumbling with his knife and fork. Sitting to one side of him were a couple of boisterous men in evening clothes and two young girls, and in the background, from behind some partitions, came a babel of voices and hoarse obscenities. A Swedish girl was babbling something about matches to an accompaniment of raucous female laughter.

When the noise subsided, the sound of rain falling on the sidewalk outside penetrated far into the room.

There on the table lay the bill. Jastrau reached for it, and in the dim mixture of daylight and artificial illumination that seemed almost obliterated by a ghostly rain-weather murkiness and tobacco-smoke fog he examined it and laboriously added it up.

Twenty-seven kroner and five øre.

For beer and fried eggs in an early-morning café.

"Well, what about it?" he heard the waiter say arrogantly.

Jastrau looked up at him with a drowsy wiliness.

"Is there a telephone?" he asked. He was so exhausted.

He would telephone Kryger. Yes, that was the thing to do. But would Kryger be up? So early?

He pulled himself together with a sudden effort and staggered off to the telephone.

"Yes—it's me—me, Jastrau."

"Who? What is it? Good God man, haven't you gotten home yet?" Kryger's voice sounded fresh from a good sleep. "There seems to be a lot of noise coming from somewhere behind you."

"I don't have any—any money," Jastrau said in a woebegone tone. Then, with an effort that was both comical and pitiful, he described his situation.

Kryger laughed so that the receiver rattled, and promised to come.

"Now, the money will soon be here," Jastrau said, leaning unsteadily toward the waiter. "A beer—one more beer."

"Certainly." The waiter sized him up fleetingly and then suddenly began to snicker.

And soon he came balancing a beer that was half water.

The place grew more and more deserted as the forenoon wore on.

Outside, the streetcars glided by. Umbrellas bobbed and rotated. The raindrops pelted the window and ran down the pane in long, oblique rivulets and then into the street.

Whenever anyone came in, they left a trail of water behind them far into the café.

Jastrau thought for a moment about going and standing in the doorway to let the rain cool him off. But when he put on his topcoat the waiter came hurrying suspiciously toward him.

"You're not leaving, are you?"

"No. I just want to get cooled off."

"You'd better not. You'll only catch cold."

Hopelessly, Jastrau flopped back in his chair with his topcoat on, looking as if he had fallen into it.

It was so hard to think. His thoughts turned to jelly. And now there were almost no customers left in the café.

"Well, so there you are. Ha ha."

It was Kryger, who had come dashing in.

"And you're still in evening clothes. Good Lord, how you do look! Waiter, a beer."

Kryger was fresh and lively, though his eyes were a little bloodshot from the night before.

"You must have gotten separated from us. Whew, but I'm busy! My stenographer is waiting for me at home. You know—my book on Danish industry. So let's pay up and see that you get home."

"I don't want to go home," Jastrau snarled, cowering still lower in his chair.

"Well," Kryger said with a shrug and a sudden, broad smile, "then come to my place. You can sleep on the sofa."

"No," was the obstinate reply.

"Well, what then? You can't stay here. And you have to get some sleep, man. You can't go traipsing all around town in broad daylight in this condition—and in evening clothes to boot. Ha ha—let me look at you."

He drew Jastrau's coat aside.

"Yes, you're a pretty sight. A broken shirt front. And fingerprints on it—enough to suggest a murder. Ha ha. And somebody has written something on it with pencil. Let's see what it says. Ha ha—'Thanks for the beer,' it says. No, you know what? You'd better be kept out of sight somewhere. I think I'd better plunk you down in a hotel."

Jastrau tried to look down at himself, but the broken shirt front cut off his view. He passed his hand over it.

"What?" he babbled.

At last Kryger got him outside and into a taxi. For a moment the raindrops spattered against his ears.

"Where's your hat?"

No answer.

Inside the cab, Jastrau collapsed completely.

What was it that happened then? More rain splashing on him. A sidewalk where the raindrops rebounded into the air like flashes of swamp gas. A lighted hotel door, faces with uniform caps behind a revolving glass pane, a whirring elevator. And then something to do with sitting on the edge of a bed, falling over backward and smacking his head against the wall because some idiot was tugging at his shoes. And then an attempt to choke him, and a feeling of relief as his necktie came off and a shirt was pulled over his head. A muttering and then laughter, and finally a window shade pulled down with a bang.

How long?

The first thing he was conscious of was a shiver running up and down his spine. In a bed with nothing on except an undershirt. Gray wallpaper teeming with flowers. A white ceiling of strange proportions—almost like in a storeroom. And, behind a dark window shade, the rain beating down incessantly. Oh, that everlasting sound. For a long time he had been listening to it as to a piece of ominous music in which the violins gave a foreboding of disaster. Rain, rain.

But why was it that the sound of the rain seemed to have some meaning? He could hear it splashing down in a courtyard. It came gushing out of a downspout, went gurgling through the sewers. And the sound had some meaning, some very definite significance.

With a start he jumped out of bed to dispel the ominous symbol, whatever it might mean, and found himself standing dazed in the middle of the floor in his short undershirt. There was a draft. His bare thighs felt cold. It was undoubtedly best to roll up the window shade and close the window, the hasp of which was constantly rattling.

He rolled up the shade to look out at a rain-dark sky, drenched rooftops, and the building walls surrounding a courtyard, all with closed windows and identical curtains on every floor, as if they were attired in uniform. He was obviously in a hotel. And now he recognized the courtyard. Down on the lower floor was the Bar des Artistes. So that was where he was.

He shut the window and went back. How had he gotten here? There on a chair lay his white shirt with its broken front, smudged and dirty. And what was that, written in pencil? "Thanks for the beer," it said. He scratched his head thoughtfully and vaguely recalled a picture, a scene from a Bible story, a scene so stupid that he involuntarily had to make a wry face. He was aware that he had made a fool of himself, and the thought made him cringe. Thanks for the beer!

Crestfallen and bewildered, he looked around the room. His dress coat and white vest hung askew over the back of a chair, as if parodying a cripple. They were spotted and dirty, with a long dribble of egg yolk down the lapel of the coat, a white splotch of powder on the shoulder, and some hairs left there by a woman. He tried unsuccessfully to rub off the spots. They had contaminated him emotionally, too, he thought. And his pants? They hung on the door hinge, with the fly immodestly open, and loose, empty legs. His shoes and socks lay scattered about on the threadbare carpet. Bits and pieces of him all around. He began to shiver—to feel wretched. His festive garments had become a fool's costume, with inscriptions on them as on a board fence. Thanks for the beer! Here he was, as if cut up into pieces and lying around, one appalling part of him over a chair, another on the floor. But suddenly he began to think about the pieces as a whole, and that was even more unpleasant. So that was how he had looked—a fashionable fool in tails and white tie, soiled, scribbled on, insulted. And now he had to get back into that degrading costume again, he must get back into it because he had to get home. It was his clothes which seemed to be the most humiliating thing about the entire situation.

But would it not be better to crawl back into bed and sleep, obliterate himself? For it was unbearable to think. But if he were going home, it must be in these clothes. The thought of it made him wince. And Johanne—oh, Johanne. Now she had won a complete victory. He could see her drawing herself up and growing rigid, her blue eyes flashing with contempt. But he had to get the better of her, and he simply must go through with it. And in that outfit—with writing on the shirt front and all: Thanks for the beer! Ah, Johanne, you have a sot for a husband, indeed you do. Why did he always go off the deep end when he drank? Otherwise he was quiet and steady enough, and industrious too. Was he not? His job, of course, was impossible—altogether impossible. A person could not be completely honest when he had to earn a living. But wasn't he honest, honest in his reviews? Yes, he was. He made enemies because of them. But then why did he have a guilty conscience? Because that he did. It was like some form of punishment that had assailed him from within. And he had become aware of it as soon as he had gone to work as reviewer for *Dagbladet*. He wished to God he could find out in what way he had transgressed. He had been honest, completely honest. But why, then, had he stagnated, become sterile? Why?

198

And then he had turned into a sot. Yes, he was a drunkard. Why not come right out and admit it? It had come about as a result of his confusion. When he was drunk he did not feel unproductive. Intoxication was the stuff of which poems were made, poems that had to be written, and so he escaped his punishment. But punishment for what? At the same time he made himself an object of ridicule—a fashionably-dressed fool seen in all of Copenhagen's cafés, a besmudged fool in soiled evening clothes. Oh, he could scream. He, Jastrau, a serious critic, the final court of appeal in Copenhagen's intellectual circle. After all, he only wanted to be a human being, and he had become two different individuals—two masks.

Oh, Johanne. If only that were over with. He could come dashing wildly, recklessly, into the house, take her by surprise, begin sobbing convulsively. Yes, he could say, it was true he was a drunkard. He could admit it, confess, be penitent. Penitence—ugh! Yes, he could weep, cry out, make her gasp. How deliberately he was rehearsing the scene. Was he not actually scheming? No, no, for he was really tormented. He wanted to lay his head in her lap, rock it back and forth, for he was so apprehensive, so afraid. Jealously. Joachim Michelsen and Vuldum. And so he had a good reason for drinking. Nonsense. Was it anything more than an excuse for having committed that stupid indiscretion the other day, that act of unfaithfulness that he could now scarcely remember? He wanted to rock his head back and forth in her lap, get down on his knees, prostrate himself at full length on the floor in his evening clothes, his soiled and crumpled evening clothes. Oh, that inscription: Thanks for the beer!

But what if Oluf had come home? "Where have you and Mother been all this time?" Suppose Oluf stood there in the middle of the room, staring at him wide-eyed and frightened. What then? And what if Johanne sat there, rigid and unbending? Would it not be impossible then? Why did he always behave so insanely and unpredictably when he had been drinking? He became another person. Whiskey altered a man's personality. He would not touch it any more. He would not.

So help him—he would not.

He turned over in bed and lay on his back.

So help him—

But what could bind him to it? What sort of an oath could he take? An oath to God?

He raised his arm in the short undershirt sleeve and held up three fingers. But that signified God the Father, the Son, and the Holy Ghost, and here he was, an unbeliever. No, he could not take such an oath. It was a theatrical gesture that he had laughed at so often. Then what should he swear by? What sort of oath should he take?

Place a finger on an eye and bid the devil strike him blind?

He squirmed restlessly on the bed. Why did a comic element insinuate itself into his seriousness? He would never touch whiskey again. But what oath? If there is a God, then as surely as there is a God, I will never—

If, if! It was too hypothetical. How could he find an oath that was frightful enough?

His arm was still upraised and wobbling back and forth. But now it was the flat of his hand that was held out. And that was the Fascists' salute.

An oath, an oath, an oath!

Should he swear by Johanne? Did he love her? He wondered if she had not gone off and left him after that scene in the taxi?

By Oluf, then? He squirmed again. That would be too sentimental. Here he lay in a hotel bed, clad only in an altogether too short undershirt, hand raised in a Fascist salute, and could not bring himself to do it. By my son, by my son—it would be too maudlin, like tears shed while drunk. There was no oath that was frightful enough. All words seemed to vanish into thin air.

He clenched his fist. An outstretched, bare arm with a clenched fist. It reminded him of a picture of a French war memorial that he had seen in a newspaper and laughed at. All gestures were ruined by poor art. But he was determined to swear, to take an oath. He would not give up.

"As surely—" he called out, then stopped. His loud voice sounded so silly there in the hotel room. Suppose the chambermaid walked by in the hallway and heard him.

"As surely—" he repeated in a normal tone, and suddenly the words of the oath formulated themselves:

"As surely as I'm afraid of getting syphilis, I will not drink whiskey again."

It sounded as if he were talking to someone. His voice was not loud or solemn, but quite calm. Nothing but an offhand remark.

He got up, feeling strengthened. Now he must wash and get dressed. The oath was taken. The future lay clear.

But it was unpleasant to have to get into his fool's costume again. He was assailed by disgust as he picked up each piece of clothing, held it gingerly with his fingertips, turned it about and examined it. These things were a bit of his past that still adhered to him. And he had to go home. He noticed how that thought alone set his heart to pounding. Home. Home.

Then he discovered a slip of paper lying on the table.

Have called your wife to tell her that you're sleeping in a hotel. The hall porter has thirty kroner that will take care of your room charge, food, and so forth. So in all, you owe me seventy-five.

Kryger.

As he read the note, Jastrau's heart immediately stopped thumping and he felt a sense of relief. Johanne knew where he was. Probably she thought he was still asleep. So there was no need to telephone her just yet or to go home right away. He could wait, prolong the time until the reckoning, draw it out. And she would think he was sleeping, for she knew he needed sleep.

He examined his features in the little mirror over the washstand. There were deep, oblique wrinkles under his eyes, and his face looked bloated. Yes, it was always that way. *Ecce homo.* That face of a criminal. But he did not have to shave, for he had done so the previous afternoon, just before they had left for the party at Krog's. Just dash a little cold water over his face and then put on that damned white shirt. Thanks for the beer! He caught sight of the pencil scrawl in the mirror, with the letters reversed. That way it did not look so bad, but nevertheless it was there. Thanks for the beer.

There was, however, the topcoat. He would have to put that on over the soiled crumpled shirt and the inscription. His hat? No hat—it was gone. Where? He shook his head and could not remember a thing.

And it was a strange-looking figure that walked stealthily down the stairway to the lobby, coat buttoned up around his neck and bareheaded.

The hall porter smiled behind his close-cropped mustache and gave him the thirty kroner, and then Jastrau stood hesitating for a moment in the vestibule, unable to make up his mind whether to go into the restaurant and eat a bit of lunch or go through the door to the left that led into the Bar des Artistes.

It was darker, however, in the bar. Besides, it would be easier to keep his coat on there, to make believe that he was in a hurry and would soon be on his way. Moreover, he could watch the clock in there and keep track of the time.

So reason prevailed.

Inside the bar the shades had been drawn and the lights turned on to dispel the dreary daylight. The phonograph drowned out the sound of the rain splashing on the sidewalk outside.

Jastrau walked through the room with his topcoat on. There were only a very few afternoon customers.

"I say, haven't you gone away yet, maestro?" It was Little P., whose bird-like head with its sparse covering of hair regarded him mawkishly from the depths of a big chair. As usual, he was seated at the round table near the cash register. And Kjær was there too, fat and red-faced, with his head leaning heavily forward. He was obviously engrossed in veiled thoughts, for he was staring dully down at a cocktail glass and breathing heavily so that his moist lips quivered and made a faint br-r-ring sound as he exhaled.

"Gone away? Who, me?" asked Jastrau suspiciously as he stopped. His thoughts immediately went back to the night in the lockup. They had, he remembered, been together that evening.

And just then another voice was heard from the other direction: "Oh, hello, Herr Jastrau. What's this? Hasn't the Herr Editor set out yet?"

It was Lundbom speaking in his nasal Swedish accent. His red, satyr-like countenance and watery, mournful eyes shone in a polite smile beneath the pale face of the clock over the bar.

Jastrau looked around mistrustfully and smiled affably. It seemed that he was being assailed by riddles from all sides. But how could they have any bearing on his brief stay in the jail cell?

"Yes. Didn't you go to Canada?" Lundbom went on. "That's what we thought."

"Rubbish," Jastrau replied, smiling and feeling relieved.

"Wasn't it you I sold the ticket to?" Little P. remarked dubiously. He looked completely dumbfounded.

"Rubbish," Jastrau repeated, and sat down at the table. He carefully wrapped himself up in the topcoat.

As he did so, a nervous shudder ran through Kjær's bulky, semiconscious figure. "Who's that?" he asked as if talking in his sleep, while he went on staring with glassy eyes at Jastrau. "Is it somebody who's deserving of a place at my table?"

But he soon sank back into a revery. "I'm afraid it's someone who doesn't deserve it," he mumbled as if ready to fall asleep again.

From behind the bar, Lundbom nodded a silent order to the little waiter.

"Wasn't it you who bought that ticket to Canada from me?" Little P. asked again. His glazed eyes shone with lack of comprehension.

Jastrau kept on shaking his head.

But at last a light seemed to dawn on Little P. He smiled happily at Jastrau and tapped him on the arm with his index finger.

"Well," he exclaimed, still staring, "then it was somebody else I sold it to!" He looked as if he had just solved a picture puzzle. "And here I've been going around telling everybody that you went on a trip. Hee hee."

Morocco, Jastrau thought with a start. Unconsciously, he raised his hand to his lip as if to stroke an invisible mustache. Morocco was what Editor Iversen had said. So the rumor had spread that quickly.

At that moment the little waiter came walking briskly over to the table accompanied by a big, muscular waiter from the restaurant. They made their way straight to Kjær's chair.

"Now, you must get up to your room, Herr Kjær."

Kjær lifted his drooping head. It resembled an old man's. For a fraction of a second he seemed to realize what was going on, and he nodded.

The two waiters lifted him from his chair as if he were a cripple. He staggered along between them, peering around dully with near-sighted eyes. But suddenly his eyes flashed, his cheeks puffed up as if he might be choking, and his bulky frame swayed toward the left so that it looked as if the little waiter might be crushed beneath his weight.

Jastrau gave a start, and with eyes half closed waited to see Kjær drop dead then and there.

"My cane," Kjær gasped, half swooning.

Still supporting him, the little waiter reached out for a heavy, gnarled walking stick that hung on a peg.

Kjær grasped it with an unconscious desperation, and his thick hand bulged as it closed around it. He set it down hard on the floor, drew up his colossal bulk, and began to hobble off on three legs. The waiters followed along cautiously on each side, ready to grab him if it should prove necessary, and the invalid procession disappeared.

"Herr Kjær is punctual," Little P. observed cynically in a croaking voice. "It's now four-thirty."

The thick-set Lundbom sighed from behind the bar. "Yes, yes, it's a pity, because otherwise he's a fine person."

His sad fish-eyes looked as if they were ready to pop out of his head.

"Is he drunk already?" asked Jastrau. His heart had been palpitating so that he had grown pale.

"Oh, he'll be down here again later in the evening," replied Little P. He was quite unconcerned, and waved his pale hand disparagingly. "That's the way he is every day, as regular as clockwork. But then, Lundbom's cocktails are pretty stiff. Gin and absinthe. Incidentally, won't you have one with me?"

Jastrau looked at him awkwardly. "No, I'm not drinking any more," he said, and then added, "Not whiskey, that is."

He heard himself say it with astonishment. What was this he was doing? With a feeling of dismay he sensed a deep abyss opening before him. His oath, as he had formulated it, included only whiskey, so there was a flaw in it, a crack that appeared without a sound and that grew bigger and bigger. Yes, but of course the idea had been to forswear liquor of every sort. The idea—yes, certainly that had been the idea. But the idea must have lost it's force. An oath consisted of words, magic phraseology, and whatever lay outside the scope of the words was not comprehended in the curse. Witchcraft was very pedantic.

"It's not whiskey, maestro. It's only absinthe and gin," said Little P. laughing.

"No, no. When one gets a look at Kjær—"

"Oh, Kjær. But he's a drinking man, and that's something very different," Little P. said, beginning to feel offended. "So what do you say we have a cocktail? We can play matches to see who pays."

He took some matches out of the matchbox holder and handed Jastrau three of them.

"But I have to get something solid into my stomach," Jastrau objected.

"And so do I, for that matter, maestro. Let's play to see who pays for a couple of raw hamburger *smørrebrød*.

Jastrau protested weakly. In the meantime, the little waiter had heard their conversation, and he appeared with the menu.

"May I help Herr Jastrau off with his topcoat?" asked the waiter as he bent over Jastrau's shoulder.

"No," came the unequivocal answer.

"What?" said Little P., taken aback. Then he suddenly began laughing uproariously. "Hee hee—still in evening clothes, hee hee. So that's the way it is. Then, by God, you do need a Lundbom cocktail."

Jastrau cringed before Little P.'s knowing look. Here he sat, for all the world as if he had a sign across his chest. Thanks for the beer. With a distorted expression on his face, he shifted his position so that he was not facing Little P. directly and burrowed himself deeper into his topcoat.

A moment later two cocktail glasses and their green contents stood before them.

"*Skaal.*"

How easy it was to be a coward and circumvent his oath. Was it conscious on his part? Had he been so calculating? But how soothingly it obliterated his troubles and his feeling of debasement. He forgot the crumpled shirt front, his befouled evening clothes, his fool's costume. The tension was gone, everything seemed brighter. Nothing to worry about for the next hour. And then, then he would telephone home.

"But I'm not drinking any whiskey," he confided to Little P.

Little P. smiled and held out a clenched fist. And surreptitiously Jastrau made haste to hide a single match in his hand. Then he was ready.

"How many?" asked Little P.

"Three."

"One."

They opened their hands simultaneously. Little P. had two matches in his hand, Jastrau one.

"They're yours." Little P. laughed maliciously and shoved the checks over to him.

Then they began to play for the smørrebrød.

It was much easier to gamble than to argue. "Six." "Four." "Hee hee, there I fooled you again, maestro. Now, hadn't we better taste the cocktails? Look, don't they resemble the water in the Atlantic? I'd say they do, although—oof—that reminds me of Canada." And Little P. shuddered sensitively in his black jacket.

A pleasant ambiance now. The phonograph droned on. The ventilator hummed. An atmosphere of coziness pervaded the place. A group of regular customers came in and sat on the tall stools along the bar. Broad backs, heavy around the hips. Greetings for Lundbom in Swedish. They were the insurance crowd, who always came at five o'clock. Fine people. "Hello, Charley." "Good old boy." "Have you been playing around with the girls?" "No, I'm the virtuous sort—my only vice is drinking." The last remark was followed by exuberant laughter.

Then the smørrebrød arrived, and it was necessary to give serious thought to the subject of snaps.

Jastrau leaned back, half deafened by the noise but enjoying the light-headed condition he was in. There was a shimmering luster to the brass bar fittings, the glass, and the highly polished woodwork. It was like looking at a calm sea. But storm clouds could suddenly loom up above the mirror-like surface and just as suddenly disappear. One moment he wanted to rest, let everything slide, and then suddenly he felt like swinging into action, being hostile, then friendly, and then he would suddenly forget again. It made no difference how he felt or what he did—neither thoughts or actions had any consequences. He was lifted up into another world in which the American melodies from the phonograph were the stuff of which life was made. "I'll sing a little tune."

"This is better than Canada," said Little P., feeling very much at home.

"Do you think so?" asked Jastrau, squinting at Little P., for now he was suddenly aware that he really despised this anemic count, this little pip-squeak. The only reason he sat there with him was that he did not dare telephone home. That was all. He had to sit with somebody. But he could pay him in the same coin, he could.

"Oof, yes!" Little P. shuddered again. "Because they say that over there in the Dominion of Canada a person has to work. My old man heard about that, and so I was to be deported. Oof!"

"Yes, I should say so. Oof!"

"But thank God it didn't turn out that way. Do you remember how homesick I felt that night? It struck me as soon as the taxi turned off there by the Freedom Statue. But that's so depressing, all that. Shouldn't we have another *snaps?*

"Well, all right."

"Shall we play for them?"

"No. In that case I'd rather buy them. But incidentally, I ought to phone my wife."

"Hee hee," snickered Little P. "Is it duty that's calling, as the popular saying goes?"

"Yes, it is, you little pip-squeak!" Jastrau burst out spitefully. He leaned over the table so threateningly that Little P. became frightened. "It's duty, all right, damn it. And you needn't laugh. Wait until you get married. Then you won't be able to sit here any longer and play matches for drinks. Then you'll be dragged home by the ears, my boy."

"Is that what's happening to you?" Little P. asked pointedly. He had to defend himself and strike back. But there was a worried look in his glassy eyes.

"To me? No." And Jastrau stopped, as if he was not sure whether he was unhappily married or not. "No, no. But nevertheless it's not right. No it isn't."

And then he was conscious of a feeling of friendliness surging up within him. He gew confidential, as if he wanted to caress Little P. and gain his sympathy, and the eyes grew calm in the small bird-like head as Little P. sat back and patiently began to listen.

"She's all right," Jastrau went on under a burning compulsion to confide in someone. "But, I tell you, the only ones who get any benefit out of marriage are the children; all the grown-ups get is trouble. And my wife might be all right if only she weren't married to me. That's the trouble, that's the way things are. She wants to keep house, wear fine clothes, be admired, you understand, put on parties—and I, what do I want? At any rate, not that—no, not that. And so—yes, it's the truth—I often catch myself wishing that the whole thing would fall apart, the sooner the better, before I lose my mind."

206

He spoke frantically. Saliva trickled out of his mouth. Without thinking, he grabbed the bottle of akvavit and poured himself one glass, two glasses, three glasses, and drank them.

"Hadn't we better have a whiskey to wash your marriage down, maestro?" said Little P. with a triumphant smile. But at the same time, he looked up from the table and began to stare.

Jastrau had an uncomfortable feeling that someone was standing behind him, and he turned around suddenly.

It was Bernhard Sanders, dark, tall, erect, and wearing the same stylish raglan coat that Jastrau had seen him in the year before. It was now somewhat shabby and wet.

"I thought I recognized your voice," remarked Sanders. A sarcastic smile played over his dark, gypsy-like features. His face was a replica of Lenin's well-known countenance.

Jastrau looked at him reluctantly.

"I don't usually come to fashionable places such as this," Sanders apologized with a note of scorn in his voice. "But today Steffensen got some money from home that left him feeling short-changed, so in righteous indignation he invited me in for a whiskey and soda."

He smiled with a superior air.

"Steffensen—is he here?" Jastrau peered suspiciously at Sanders. Why was he smirking so? Had he overheard the conversation? Or—yes, that was obviously it—he had learned about his night in the lockup. Steffensen, of course, had told him about it, for Steffensen must know about it. He had been with him that night.

"I believe you remember him, Little P.," said Jastrau. "I—"

"Hm-m," said Little P., showing a lack of interest and wrinkling his nose as if he detected a bad odor.

"I hope you'll excuse me a moment. I want to talk to him."

Little P. waved his hand in a tolerant gesture.

Jastrau got up, staggering a little, and went with Sanders to the other end of the room. He had to find out what Steffensen could remember—yes, he had to.

Steffensen was sitting over in a corner. He was leaning back so that his long bony head rested against the wall and his cap was tilted up. His jacket was darkened by the rain.

"Whew," Jastrau said as he sat down. "Yes, I'm on the town."

Steffensen sat up straight, looking serious. A trace of a smile lit sp his hard, glassy eyes as he took account of the way Jastrau was dressed. "Ha, wearing a dressing gown," he laughed.

Jastrau stiffened, then drew the topcoat lapels closer around his neck so that they would not see his white tie.

"Won't you have a highball with us?" Steffensen went on, laying a newspaper aside. Jastrau got a glimpse of Professor Geberhardt's picture on the page that was turned up, and suddenly he felt strangely disturbed.

"Well, I suppose Sanders is drinking highballs too," he observed awkwardly, so that it sounded like a sarcasm.

"I'm not a slave to alcohol," Sanders replied with dignity. "And I have no reason to avoid it as far as I personally am concerned."

"So that's the way it is," Jastrau said in the same sarcastic tone.

"No, that's not the way it is," Sanders went on, his voice becoming more intense. "Another consideration is that from a social point of view prohibition is the only proper thing, and when the revolution and the new order of society comes along I'm going to propose it and work to put it into effect. Naturally."

"Naturally," Steffensen said, making a wry face.

Sanders was irritated. "Nevertheless, I never go stumbling around the bars here in town and shooting off my mouth about my private affairs!" he exclaimed in his own melodious but scornful way. His dark eyes were flashing fire.

Jastrau drew himself up.

"What business is it of yours?"

"None whatsoever," replied Sanders in a tone of moral indignation. "But I can't help being in on the secret when you sit here in a barroom and sound off about it. And if you want my honest opinion, I find it a dirty business."

"What's that you're saying?" Jastrau felt dizzy. He was not clear-headed enough to understand what was going on.

"Yes, it's an indecent way to treat your wife."

Steffensen was enjoying himslf immensely.

"Did you invite me over here to bawl me out?" Jastrau was gasping for breath.

"We didn't invite you over here for anything," Sanders replied.

"Then I'll be damned if I'm going to sit here any longer."

"The honor is all ours," said Sanders, getting up and bowing ironically.

Pale with indignation, distracted, yet with a flash of painful awareness, Jastrau made sure he upset his chair with a crash as he got up and made his way back to Little P.

The little waiter came running in alarm, but immediately regained his composure.

Little P. was all smiles and welcomed him with open arms.

"We have to have some whiskey and soda," Jastrau groaned. His eyes were two thin slits.

"Shall we play for them?"

And immediately they began the match game.

But Jastrau lost every time. He was too preoccupied. From time to time he would fume with rage. That Sanders should have dared to treat him so! The muddle-headed moralist! What concern was it of his? "None." "Two." "Hee hee—none. Who can keep his wits about him in this place?" And now he had to make that phone call. God knows what Johanne was thinking. Had she been sitting at home and waiting all day long? He ought to call her. Yes, he ought to call. But no doubt his voice was too thick. Johanne would be able to tell at once that he was drunk. It was undoubtedly unwise to call just then. And reason prevailed.

"One."

"None."

"Well, you finally won, maestro. That's good."

And reason prevailed. Hour after hour passed, and later they moved over into the restaurant and had dinner, which they also played for. But the lighting there was too glaring. There were too many white tablecloths to dazzle the eyes, too many bright sober faces with clear expressions, an altogether too intense light that was like sunshine on ice and snow. Although they sat discreetly in a corner, everyone stared at Jastrau, who would not remove his topcoat.

There was no relief until they were again ensconced in the bar with its subdued tones of brown and red, its low tables, and the monotonous phonograph providing a background for the chattering customers.

Here they would have their last whiskey of the evening together.

In the meantime, the dinner had buoyed Jastrau up. He felt courageous and ready for what he had to do. Now it would happen, and when he had drained his glass he got up, had the phonograph shut off, and went to the telephone. He suddenly realized his heart was beating violently. So he was not altogether ready. But he had already made the call. Now it would happen. Otherwise nothing would ever come of it.

It was she who answered.

"Is it you Ole?" She sounded both weary and disdainful.

"Yes," he replied hoarsely.

"How could you do such a thing?" He could hear that she raised her head in angry pride.

"What, what do you mean—?"

"I know all about it."

"Yes, but what?" Jastrau began to work himself into a temper. But

209

he was sitting there in the barroom where everybody could hear him.

"No, never mind," came the mournful yet haughty reply. "We can talk about that some other time. Now I'm going home to my parents—tonight."

"Do you want—?" He cut himself short.

A loud clamor sounded from another part of the barroom.

"I can hear that you're in a bar," she said. "And yes, I want a divorce," came the answer over the telephone.

And Oluf—the boy? Jastrau wanted to ask. But the words stuck in his throat. And he stared out into the smoke-filled room and the crowd of noisy customers.

And just then, halfway down the room, greeted and acclaimed from all sides, came the inevitable Kjær, looking ten years younger from his nap. He rubbed his hand across his smooth-shaven chin and smiled.

The customers raised their arms in an ovation. Lundbom nodded in joyful acknowledgement of his arrival while he shook the shiny cocktail shaker between his hands so that the brittle ice could be heard crunching. And everything was conviviality and cheer.

"Good-by, then," said Jastrau. He did not get to ask about Oluf, because it seemed as if his voice had rusted fast from a combination of drunkenness and grief.

"Good-by, then." He got up and nodded to the little waiter. Now the phonograph could be set going again.

Chapter Seven   The forenoon was brilliant with sunshine after the previous day's rainy weather, and the buildings on Reventlowsgade exuded a fresh coolness.
Jastrau halted at the corner of Istedgade and looked pensively up at his fifth-floor windows. The windowpanes dreamily and innocently mirrored the clear sky, but the wall around them still had a clouded, ravaged look after the previous day's rain. It was a dreary north wall with dissolute old windows that reflected a wholly undependable image of blue sky.

Jastrau felt chilly as he looked at them.

He did not want to stand there any longer in his two-day-old evening clothes, the white tie that hung drooping from his collar, and the crumpled shirt front with its inscription hidden behind the topcoat. He would attract attention if he stood there bareheaded and

210

gaping. But those sky-blue window panes. What was it that had gone on behind them? Who had been there and told Johanne about him? Who? And what had he told her? She had sounded so tired, so sad, and at the same time so aloof over the telephone the night before, and it was not like her. It seemed that he had hardly been able to recognize her voice.

How strange it now seemed to go in through the door again. The yellow walls had suddenly become invested with a significance, a historical significance, and the stairway had taken on a patina of an existence that now was a thing of the past. Even the hole in the windowpane, through which the breeze had blown unimpeded for an entire summer and winter, had become something more than a symbol of neglect. It was now a characteristic feature of the premises, an artful dimple on the face of the house.

As Jastrau slowly made his way up the stairs, he could not refrain from whistling one of the jazz tunes he had heard over in the Bar des Artistes. Its rhythm had now taken hold of him because he had experienced so much during the hours that it had been droning into his ears, and he knew that it would remain with him all his life and that it would always signify divorce, the end of the life he had known. He had heard it all the previous evening until he had gone and tumbled into his hotel bed, and now he would never forget it.

When he stood in the hallway outside his door, it suddenly dawned on him that he had no keys. Sometime in the far, far distant past, he had tossed them into the taxicab to Johanne. But he went on whistling calmly. That melody—"I wonder, I wonder, I wonder"—kept running through his head. It had become an obsession with him—a nemesis that kept haunting him. "I wonder, I wonder." And calmly, as if in rhythm with the melody and with his fate, he bent over, moved the doormat, and found the keys beneath it. Johanne had been that clearheaded and prudent.

But the sight of the apartment, the rooms, the furnishings that he had lived with for a number of years, took his breath away. There stood the two ill-fated rococo chairs with their yellow upholstery. And there on the table was the black Negro fetish, probably the one that had brought him misfortune. Who could tell what dark, ecstatic African influence had through the years become identified with that piece of wood, and what powers it could exercise? And there was the shiny telephone, more forbidding than all the other things in the room. Through it he had heard his son's voice for the last time in this life. "Where have you and Mother been all this time?" And then a gurgling

211

sound as if Oluf had drowned and disappeared. Yes, he *had* disappeared. Oh—these telephones. And last night. Johanne's voice over the phone, the decisive words, and then she too had disappeared. Metallic echoes of voices, unrealities, and then they, the real persons, were gone. For what did it matter if one met them again, saw them again, talked with them? Now they had vanished and were submerged among all the people one met casually and chatted with. It was worse than death. It was a form of grief that one could not in decency weep about or wear mourning for. That sort of thing would be construed as hysterical weakness. A person was not permitted to indulge in that kind of grief because it was not decent.

With heavier steps and heavier heart he wandered through the rooms.

He passed his hand fondly over the tables and chairs, Oluf's play table near the window, the big, glittering Shrove Monday rod that stood stowed away in the corner—it was exactly as tall as Oluf himself, he remembered. Once, a long time ago, he had amused himself by measuring Oluf against it—a long time ago. And he had to, simply had to, stroke all these things with his hand and mutter something or other in a voice choking with sobs. Finally, hoarsely and under his breath, the words took form: "Good-by, all these precious things." He repeated it again and again until his throat was dry: "Good-by, all these precious things."

Even though he should continue to live among them, this would nevertheless be a permanent leave-taking, for he knew, he sensed, that soon he would not be the same person. Soon these things would not recognize him. He wondered if he would ever be able to feel sentimental about them again. Worldly belongings—that was all they were. Things that wore out, came apart, fell to pieces, and that a person ought not to get attached to at all. Worldly possessions—nothing but worldly possessions.

He sat down at the end of the table, lonely in his four-room apartment. He had not yet removed his topcoat, for didn't a person keep it on when sitting beside a ruin or in a dilapidated museum? At his neighbor's across the way, the white window curtains flashed alluringly in the sunlight, and he felt that he was sitting in a dark room that faced north, a cave through the entrance of which came a bit of reflected light.

His hand brushed against the newspapers he had in his coat pocket, and he took them out. They provided something to which he could direct his thoughts. There was *Dagbladet* from the previous day. The literary page had finally been printed, and this should have made him happy. He should have regarded it as a favor, but now it was too late. And yesterday's *Danmark*, containing the interview with Professor Julius Geberhardt and the picture of him with his wild shifty eyes, dirty-looking face, and hair so rumpled that it looked as if he must be constantly tearing at it. There, too, was the answer he had given the interviewer, that unfathomable answer: "Sometimes a person is overcome by disgust at being an active participant in this world's perverted affairs. I have been assailed so strongly by this feeling that I am withdrawing from the scene."

The words sank deeply into the pallid transparent calm, the bright glare from the neighbor's curtains, and into Jastrau's soul.

No, no, he told himself. What sort of a conclusion was it that he was arriving at in the depths of his soul as a result of these fortuitous words uttered by a complete stranger?

He shoved the chair back from the table and got up. Now something different had to happen. He could not keep on sitting there dreaming and letting erratic ideas take hold of him. But who was it that had spoken to Johanne about him? And what had the person told her? He had hardly been able to recognize her voice. She had not been her normal self. Had she not sounded as if somebody was with her? There they had been sitting—here in these rooms. And so their last, decisive conversation had been held with someone else present—he in a barroom—she, she—?

Back and forth, back and forth, he wandered. There were rooms aplenty—altogether too many. His thoughts ran in confused circles, impulses and sudden ideas popped into his head. There was no coherence to it all. Who had it been? And what? As mysterious as a murder. It gave him an eerie feeling to think that some unknown person had been here with her, in these very rooms. Because that certainly was the case. Now he knew it for a certainty. Otherwise, her voice would not have had such a note of long-suffering. She sounded that way only when somebody else was present.

In the sunlit bedroom he suddenly stopped beside Oluf's empty iron bed. The featherbed and pillow were so small, and suddenly he could not bear it because they were so small. He was conscious of a pressure on his heart, and he had to kneel down, bend over the bed, and hide his face in the child-size eiderdown. He felt that he ought to weep, but nothing came of it except dry sobs. Why was he there on his knees? It was as if he saw himself in a ridiculous situation.

Then he got up briskly and tossed his topcoat onto the made-up double bed. Yes, the bed had been made. The floor had been washed, too. She had performed her housewifely duty until the very end. Next he took off his tailcoat, necktie, and the crumpled shirt. It was a relief to be rid of that; there it lay with its blurred, derisive expression of gratitude for the beer. Now he was a free man.

Once in his everyday clothes, he felt calmer. His body found comfort in their accustomed folds and wrinkles, and his soul began to straighten out. He stuffed the fool's costume roughly into a drawer. It belonged to the past.

Now he would get to work. Some reviews had to be written for a new literary page.

But when he got back to the living room he began his restless wandering again. How was he to find peace in his study, which was as narrow and cramped as a corridor and looked out on a yellow firewall that stuck out to the right of the window like the face of a cliff threatening to topple over and crush him? There in the study everything was too barren and unmerciful.

No peace anywhere, no rest.

Back in the living room he suddenly began to move things around and tidy up. When he drew the brown portières across the doorway to the dining room and shut the door to the study this room became inhabitable. The brown and yellow colors were restful. The ceiling was a simple quadrangle. Everything bespoke tranquillity. And then with a resolute motion he went to take the photographs—the one of his mother and that of his son—but came to a sudden painful halt. They still stood with their backs out toward the room, an accusing reminder of a day in the past when, stricken with a guilty conscience and not daring to look them in the eye, he had turned them around.

The past hung like blemishes everywhere about him. It became difficult for him to go on cleaning up. No, he could not stand it any longer. There was only the phonograph in the dining room. That alone might provide some solace—one strident jazz tune after another, sentimental or cynical, but in an unceasing dance rhythm. Was there any other way of exorcising sorrow? For it had to be exorcised. He must get over his present state quickly. *I wonder, I wonder, I wonder.*

He put on the phonograph record, and then began an improvised dance designed for execution only in private—a dance that expressed his grief and his feelings about a life that now threatened to explode. The dance was a hodgepodge of a one-step, a black bottom, and a Charleston. Grief. Grief.

He felt like a demented person who with complete lack of restraint lets himself be carried away by his impromptu, awkward, meaningless

214

movements. And then the deep-throated lament of a saxophone triggered the release of all his pent-up emotion.

Jastrau screamed.

The scream echoed. He stopped, astonished at himself. The jazz melody droned on, the black record continuing to revolve, unconcerned. There was something diabolical about this mechanical movement, this mechanical outlet for grief.

Just then the doorbell rang, and he turned off the phonograph.

Who could it be? He felt his heart pound and was embarrassed because he had screamed. Had anyone heard him? Should he open the door?

The scream had sounded so wild. He was still exhausted from it.

When the doorbell rang again, he decided to open the door.

Outside stood his brother-in-law, polite and correct, with a round-crowned hat and a shiny walking stick. Behind him was a small man with a face that seemed to be set askew. Even his mustache looked as if it had constantly been exposed to a wind from the right.

"Do you have company?" asked Jastrau's brother-in-law. "I thought I heard a phonograph."

Jastrau shook his head.

"Well, then you're obviously dispelling gloomy thoughts, what? That was quite a spree you were on. But look—could I step inside? I brought a moving man along to pick up the youngster's bed."

Jastrau bowed hospitably, and his brother-in-law walked in, casting an appraising eye around as if to take inventory of the furniture. His pink, piggish face was beaming superciliously.

"You can wait here," he said to the moving man. "I'll be only a minute."

He stepped farther inside, walked into the dining room where he laid his walking stick and gloves on the table, then sat down on the chair at the end of the table.

"Yes, we have a few practical matters to discuss," he said with a faint sigh.

Jastrau shrugged his shoulders and sat down where he could keep an eye on the moving man in the living room.

"Tch, tch, tch," Smith-Jørgensen sighed again, looking straight ahead. He had kept his hat on. "So that's the way things have gone. But of course, it had to happen. I could see that with my eyes shut."

"Is that so?" Jastrau remarked, irritated.

"Yes, it wasn't so damned hard. After all, my dear brother-in-law, you do lap up the booze in great style, and I don't suppose you've denied yourself a bit of meat now and then, either." He winked at

Jastrau. "But I should be the last one to say a word about it to you—"

"Oh, cut it out now," exclaimed Jastrau. "If I must tell you plainly what's in my mind, I haven't the faintest idea why Johanne left."

As he said it he noticed, as through a fog, the moving man standing in the living room and making a face at the Negro fetish.

"You don't, really? After all, you did sit over in the barroom and complain in a loud voice about your marriage, and that she won't put up with, for which nobody can blame her. The whole town is gossiping about it."

Jastrau squirmed in his chair.

"How does she know that? Who told her? What is this—?"

Smith-Jørgensen leaned back smiling, his hands in his pockets.

"How the devil should I know?" he replied. "She came last night together with a well-mannered but impoverished young man, if I understood mamma correctly. But anyhow, the upshot of it is that Johanne won't take it any longer. She says she isn't going to be content with being your servant girl, and there isn't anything one can say to that. May I offer you a cigar?"

Jastrau had grown pale. He sat staring straight ahead. The moving man was in the act of sitting down cautiously on one of the rococo chairs in the other room. His hind quarters were not used to coming in contact with such elegant furniture. But this strange sight only fixed itself in Jastrau's memory so that he remembered it later; for the moment his thoughts were tumbling about in confusion. It could only be Sanders. But no—a Communist, a comrade? Then he must have gone directly up here from the bar. A Communist, a comrade—no it couldn't be? Absent-mindedly, he accepted the cigar.

"But to get down to practical matters, how do we divide the furniture?" asked Adolf, taking out a notebook.

"Of course, it was your parents who helped us by giving us these things."

"Yes, that's the way I feel about it too. So—"

Jastrau smiled wearily. "The books and the table I write on, a chair and a sofa—more I'll probably never have use for in this world."

"Well, then that's that," said Adolf, slapping the notebook against the table. "Incidentally, what's this? Have you been reading about the professor? What a crazy fellow he is. You can't imagine how we laughed about it down at the stock exchange."

But Jastrau had no desire to discuss the subject. "Shouldn't we get these practical matters disposed of first?" he said, putting the unlighted cigar in his mouth.

216

"You need a light, don't you? Here, allow me." Adolf lighted a match. "Doesn't it draw? Well, well—there we have it. And now I don't suppose you have any objection to my sister staying with my parents, do you?"

He said it in a conspicuously loud tone of voice, so that Jastrau could not help glancing in at the moving man. He seemed to be listening.

"No," Jastrau replied gently. "Now, I don't suppose you've hired the moving man as a witness, have you?"

He wrinkled up his eyebrows suspiciously.

"No, no, no," Adolf roared, his face growing flushed above his loose jowls. "How can you think of such a thing?"

"You'll have it in writing," Jastrau said, taking the fire-insurance policy and some other papers out of his pocket.

"Hadn't I better look after that policy?" exclaimed Adolf, making a quick grab for it.

"No!"

And Jastrau slapped his hand down over it hard.

"But the furniture—"

"There are the books, too. Now, I'll see that you get a written statement that Johanne hasn't deserted her home, which, in fact, is what she's done," Jastrau said irascibly.

"She informed you about what she was doing over the telephone."

"Who is there to testify to that?"

"There *was* a witness."

"So there was someone here when I phoned her!" Jastrau exclaimed in a rage.

"Yes."

"And you know who it was?"

"Yes."

"Who was it, then? Who was it?"

"That's beside the point," replied his brother-in-law. His watery blue eyes had a malicious gleam.

"Well, then, let me get this written statement finished." Jastrau sighed and took out his fountain pen.

"And now we come to the matter of a maintenance allowance," Adolf said harshly.

"Hadn't we better leave that to the lawyers? Otherwise we'll only get into a quarrel."

Smith-Jørgensen made a gracious gesture with his hand, so that his wristwatch sparkled in the sunlight.

"Done," he said, sighing in relief.

Thereupon he gave the moving man instructions. Jastrau sat and puffed on the cigar while the man juggled Oluf's bed.

"Damned if it wouldn't be interesting to be present at one's own funeral," Jastrau remarked with a smile.

"What did you say?"

Jastrau did not care to repeat it, but kept right on puffing.

"Well, then, I think I'll be running along," Adolf went on, politely showing his teeth. "We'll undoubtedly be meeting each other from time to time—out on the eternal hunting grounds, ha ha. And then there'll always be an opportunity for a drink together."

He slapped Jastrau on the shoulder, and Jastrau regarded the dapper stockbrokers' runner, who was so many years younger than he, with a sad smile.

"Shall I see you out?"

They both laughed politely. Out in the foyer, however, their mood suddenly changed to one of seriousness, for the door to the stairway was open, and in the doorwey stood Stefan Steffensen with his hands in his pockets. Behind him stood a shabbily dressed young girl.

"Well, I must hurry off," Adolf said with an ungracious smile. He bade a hasty farewell, as if he had not recognized Steffensen.

"Good-by, then. We'll be seeing each other."

And Adolf quickly made his exit.

"Well, that was your brother-in-law," Steffensen drawled with a grin. "Hello, there. May I introduce my friend? This is Frøken Jensen, and this is Herr Jastrau, and all that sort of thing. And the two of us would like to talk to you."

Jastrau looked into a pair of large, frightened, girlish eyes. The blue irises opened up so that they became white in their depths, imparting a strangely blurred, milky quality to her gaze.

"All right, come inside."

"Look, Jastrau," Steffensen began at once, as Frøken Jensen trotted along humbly at his heels, "—you see, Jastrau, Anne Marie and I would like to rent a couple of rooms from you. What the devil does a single man like you need all this room for?"

He waved his cap in the air to indicate how much too big the apartment was.

"Then you know—"

Jastrau took a step backward. Now it was all clear, revealed as by a flash of lightning.

"Yes, of course. But how can I help it if Sanders is such a full-blown pathological idiot with a muddled sense of Communist morality? I tried to prevent it, but he was so noble about it—it was his duty and all that sort of thing. And your lady—yes, he said your lady—was altogether too wonderful a person. She should not be subjected to such deception, and tra-la-la—"

"Stefan! You shouldn't run Bernhard down that way," Anne Marie protested in a lilting East Jutland accent.

"There, you see, Jastrau. The women think he's a noble soul."

"After all, he's helped us," she went on zealously, clenching her stubby hands nervously.

But Jastrau paid no attention to what they were saying.

He stood and stared at the two shabby figures. After all, this was youth coming to meet him, and now he felt on an equal footing with them.

For a moment, it seemed to him that unconsciously he had been struggling toward this as toward an objective.

But then he was suddenly overtaken by a fit of shivering, by a premonition of his desperate lot.

PART THREE

Forever and Ever

Chapter One   Ole Jastrau slowly tore a document to pieces and let the bits of white paper flutter away in the breeze. They floated in through the iron fence bordering Tivoli and fell like confetti into the shrubbery.

But suppose some inquisitive person took it into his head to pick up the pieces and put them together. What then? He would have learned that Editor Ole Jastrau, in a bad state of intoxication, had been apprehended on Frederiksberggade, where he had been annoying the passers-by. Did it mean anything more than that? Was it not out of a sense of habitual bourgeois propriety that he had destroyed this noteworthy document and committed it to the dusty bushes at the edge of Tivoli? He really should have kept it. After all, it was only proof that he paid what he owed. Fifteen kroner for disorderly conduct. He could have preserved it along with the postal receipt proving that he had sent the seventy-five kroner to Kryger. He might be a drunk, but he was honest. A decent editor. Well—a bit crazy.

He walked calmly toward the Tietgen Bridge. There was such an unobstructed view there after one had passed the red post-office building. A view of a dark but busy railroad right-of-way. Trains, watchtowers, long steel bridges, all blackened with smoke. And in the distance, cranes and the water. Here the gleaming sunlight came in with the off-shore breeze.

He could feel that he was no longer young. Here he had stood so often in his student days, looking out over the scene. This was what was called nostalgia. He had also often stood on the other side of the bridge and looked down on the station platforms and the tops of the railway coaches directly under his feet. There was a certain time in the late afternoon when the Berlin express departed. Now he had forgotten the hour. But then, in those days, one form of his youthful dissipation had been to stand on this bridge, in the evening air and the glare of the lights, and watch the express train go by. Youth. Memories of one's youth, it was called.

He stood there and in an imploring tone recited the long jejune lines of a verse he had never finished:

"Annihilation and inaction—both have I known.
The memories rankle like letters I never answered."

But now—

Just then a paunchy gentleman with dark-rimmed spectacles half-way down his nose walked by, peering nervously over the top of the glasses. His four-year-old son, a youngster with a hat pulled tightly down over his ears in hooligan fashion so that his head resembled a highly inflated football, had torn himself loose from his father, who was obviously afraid that the boy might run out into the roadway.

"Come here, Mogens."

"No, Father. Your hands are too hot and wet!"

Suddenly Jastrau shook himself. What was this? Had he become infected with Steffensen's hoodlum habit of fidgeting with his shoulders? He cast a frightened glance at the father and son. Yes, this boy too had a bit of trouble in walking. And the little fellow's shoes—exactly the same size. Stockings sagging. No, no—Jastrau had to look the other way again, out over the trains and the watchtowers, and over the harbor in the distance.

They would soon be passing by him. The thought sent a feeling of chill through his loins. Yes, now they were almost up to him. And then Jastrau had to look at the boy again. The same dignified carriage of his body on uncertain legs. The jutting belly. The same burly little figure.

A sting of pain every time a little child went by. What a lot of painful sensations there were. Children. They hurried by on the sidewalk and had the same agitating effect on him as a hazy red sun seen through a picket fence.

No, it was better to think of the deserted four-room apartment on Istedgade that already was in a state of dissolution. Altogether too large for him. And the two roomers who had forced themselves on him. Stefan Steffensen! Did he really like him? Yes and no. He was a person who at the moment was bound in the same direction as he, nothing but that, and so they might as well get along. And the dubious Anne Marie?

And suddenly Jastrau briskly crossed the road and went down a sloping sidewalk that led from the bridge down to the railroad station.

It was as if a cloud had passed in front of the sun—this section around Reventlowsgade and Istedgade. An out-of-the-way place right in the downtown part of Copenhagen, with hideouts and secret passages and doorways, and dark, damp, ground-floor dwellings that with their proper, respectable window curtains looked like camouflaged brothels.

There in a deep, cavern-like street he saw a green tree with its roots cramped in between the pavement, and sparrows making a commotion amidst the green leaves above. He could usually spare a sad smile for that sort of thing, but today it merely brushed his subconscious, like a glimpse of green seen far down through a body of murky water.

For it was all too crazy. The evening before, Steffensen had brought a young girl home with him. Had he done it to torment Anne Marie? Jastrau had heard it all. He had come home a half hour before in a semistupor from whiskey and tobacco, unsteady on his legs but nevertheless well aware of what went on. And then it had happened. Anne Marie had lain crying very softly, very gently. Steffensen might not have heard her, or perhaps had not wanted to hear, busily engaged as he was with the other girl. But the continuous sobbing there in that apartment, where the rooms had such a ghostly aspect in the glow of the light night, the sound of pent-up whimpering behind closed lips, had become more and more audible, demoralizing in its monotony. It had shaken her body so that the sofa on which she lay had creaked and groaned, an intolerable squeaking sound, and the upshot of it had been that Jastrau in a fit of rage had hurled a shoe against the sliding door and told her to shut up.

No, he would not put up with it. He would not have them living with him any longer. But if he chased them out now, the rooms would become limitless, and then he would go wandering around like a ghost through all four rooms as well as through the maid's quarters and the kitchen and the two hallways, through room after room, with doors leading into other rooms and emptiness behind emptiness, until he suffered a nervous collapse. He knew that was how it would be. Empty rooms were inhabited by spirits. Nonsense. But it was true. Doors opened of their own accord. The doorknob was slowly turned by an invisible hand, and then the door swung open. Empty apartments proliferated, spawned. And at last a person saw himself, in the flesh, sitting in a chair. Oh—hello, Jastrau. With the same embarrassed smile.

But he would not put up with it.

He ran up the stairway. The hole in the windowpane facing the courtyard was still there. Should he not write a complaint to the landlord? The breeze had been blowing in through that hole for a year and a half.

Hastily he unlocked the door and entered the apartment.

Steffensen lay on his sofa, smoking a pipe. They had reached an agreement that this room was Jastrau's. Its square ceiling had a calming, beneficial effect. The yellow and brown colors were as genial and lulling to the senses as a gentle rain.

"Why have you come barging into my room?" Jastrau demanded in a tone of exasperation.

Steffensen removed the pipe from his mouth and gaped at him. His face was pale.

"So that's the sort of mood you're in. As for me, I'm hungry."

"I suppose I have to feed you too. Is that the idea?"

"No. But Anne Marie in there, the hysterical girl, is hungry too. And I don't suppose you're planning to gorge yourself all alone."

Jastrau sat down heavily in one of the chairs, stared at the floor, and collected his wits.

"Not only a roof over your head, but food too," he said softly but meaningfully—then, in a sudden crescendo—"There isn't even a crust of bread in the pantry!"

"She could go out and get something."

"Who?"

"Her—in there. Instead of lying around feeling sorry for herself. Damn it, she might as well make herself useful."

"You're a scoundrel!"

The remark came suddenly. Jastrau sat up straight in the chair. Now he would let him have it. But his eyes would travel no farther than Steffensen's coarse, brutal mouth. It was set as if Steffensen were about to shout at him. Jastrau's eyes would not shift to take in the hard glassy gaze with which his adversary was regarding him—that gaze which was always incomprehensible. And then he could no longer launch his attack. To sit there staring at a man's necktie and then make a surprise attack—no, he could not do it.

But just then Steffensen's lips relaxed, and his features softened.

"Well, perhaps I am," he said gently.

Jastrau stared at the dust that covered the floor like a gray blanket and at the tablecloth that lay wrinkled in unseemly disorder about the fetish and the telephone. And, with a sudden feeling of being aboard a wreck, he capitulated. There was nothing to do except smile, for here, amidst the common wreckage, they were all naturally in need of food.

"Now I'll speak to her about it," he said softly, and it seemed that with his change of tone a ray of light came into the dismal picture. He wondered if Jesus had been given to making broad conciliatory gestures.

Anne Marie was in the dining room, lying on a sofa that had been

226

moved in there for her. To make room for it, the light-oak furniture that had been a present from his in-laws had been shoved over near the window, and the former respectable and symmetrical arrangement, with the sideboard centered along the wall like an altar and the chandelier in the middle of the ceiling, had been transformed into a pattern that seemed as bewildering and distorted as Einstein's concept of space.

Anne Marie indolently turned her broad back to him and blew cigarette smoke against the wallpaper.

"Listen, Frøken Jensen," Jastrau began.

"Frøken Jensen," she repeated, laughing and still facing the wall. Her broad back was quivering.

"Well, what else should I call you?" Jastrau apologized awkwardly.

Anne Marie did not reply. A white cloud of cigarette smoke crept up along the wall.

"It's just that—well, would you please help us get a little something to eat? We're hungry."

"Would I *please?*" Suddenly she turned around and looked at him wide-eyed. "You said *please.*" Her voice rang with loud Aarhusian laughter.

At the same time she sat up, leaned her elbows against her knees, and shook herself. Her eyes were directed at Jastrau, a bit too intensely. They had a rather wild look.

"You're really asking me so politely?"

"Yes—what else should I do?" Jastrau asked with a smile that was a bit uncertain because she was looking at him as if she might butt him with her forehead. He made a sweeping, conciliatory gesture with his hand.

"Frøken Jensen," she repeated, and then a reflection of his smile appeared on her face. "If only I had a less ordinary-sounding last name, because you said it so nicely." Then she brushed the hair away from her forehead as if she were waking up, and rose from the sofa with an air of determination. "Oh, you poor things—now I'll see what I can do."

And as she went into the kitchen she carried herself straighter than usual.

Jastrau sat down and stared at a large comb that lay on the table. He did not understand her.

When she appeared again he made a questioning gesture—a broad kindly gesture. Why broad and kindly? But just then her body again became gross like that of a servant girl. It seemed to collapse so that her breasts and hips appeared coarser. He could tell, as if it were mirrored in her figure, that Steffensen had come into the room and was standing behind him.

"There isn't a bit of food out in the kitchen," she said, staring at Jastrau as if she wanted to see no one but him.

Jastrau reached into his pants pocket for some bills, carefully smoothed them out on the tabletop first, then handed them to her.

"How did you get her to do it?" Steffensen asked when they heard her hurrying footsteps tripping down the stairs. "Usually you can't get her to do anything. She just hangs around like a dead weight, like someone who's been fished out of the water, wet clothes and all. A dead weight."

"I don't know. But hadn't we better cover the table with something? It's my wife's table," he added. He still wore the wavering, meaningless smile. It was as if it were fixed to a tether.

"Here's a newspaper." Steffensen tossed the paper over to him.

Jastrau spread it out over the table. But all of a sudden he stopped. It was that old copy of *Danmark* with the picture of Professor Julius Geberhardt and the interview. He brushed his hand over it as if it were something significant.

"This will do very nicely, especially since I don't care to use the tablecloth," he said. "Tablecloths are among the amenities of life, and besides they belong to my wife."

"This is more cozy," Steffensen growled and immediately sat down with his elbows planted on the newspaper. "But tell me, how in the devil did you get Anne Marie to toe the line?"

"You're a swine, the way you treat her."

Steffensen tightened his lips about the stem of his pipe.

"Hadn't we better drop the subject and start the phonograph going," Jastrau went on. "Otherwise we'll only get into a squabble."

Steffensen nodded stiffly.

Jastrau wound the phonograph and put on a worn record of the Revellers. It sounded scratchy at first. But soon the humming, boop-booping voices were heard—a series of onomatopoetic, meaningless sounds. Now they would swing into a sentimental refrain, a love song coming from thick, soft lips melting with passion, then they would relapse into pure harmony. The tones took on a superhuman, metallic quality. The singers' lungs had to have as much force as brass instruments. And then other voices joined in. The notes fluttered through the air, then stopped short in sudden breaks. It was all done with such an easy, almost jocular effect, a virtuosity brimming over with a beauty that one could take seriously only at his own risk. The rhythms sent impulses through Jastrau's body. He had to respond. Unfortu-

228

nately, he was a poor dancer; otherwise he would have felt happy. But his legs began to move in an awkward Charleston step—an attempt at being happy.

Steffensen sat staring into the other room, a scornful smile on his face.

"What are you smiling at?" Jastrau asked as the record came to an end.

"Oh, just those saints' images you have in there."

"What images—?"

Jastrau stopped suddenly. Steffensen was referring to the two photographs of his mother and son that he had placed on the table in the next room. He felt himself exposed. Had Steffensen been spying on him? He had been carrying on a sort of secret ritual with the two pictures. When he was alone, he made a secret sign when he walked by them.

"She was a pretty girl—your mother," Steffensen said.

Jastrau drew himself up, irritated.

"Damn it, after all, she's a woman now!" Steffensen exclaimed.

"She's dead."

"Well, then she was a woman," Steffensen said scornfully. "One can see that your ideas are deeply rooted."

Jastrau answered him by putting a strident jazz record on the phonograph.

"This one has a feeling of disaster about it," he said in order to talk about something else.

"Yes. Nonsense is something there's plenty of. But it has a good swing to it."

And then began a series of records, one after another, so that the blood rushed to both their heads. Steffensen sat motionless, biting his pipestem, but a jolly grin brushed lightly over his dour features, a kind of humorous jeer, whenever an artful dissonance filled the room.

"Beautiful logic," he muttered.

Jastrau, on the other hand, stood up and began an improvised dance. As always, it did not come off. He muffed every temperamental arm movement that he tried. The rhythm fell to pieces between his feet. And he was aware of it. He was a big man. But in his imagination, he saw himself now as a slim dancer, now as a heavy-set, cake-walking gentleman, and his dance steps alternated between abandon and awkward constraint, a most unsatisfactory performance which gave him no adequate release from the tension he felt. On such occasions, a light-footed, dancing temperament in a gross, clumsy body might at first seem reasonable enough, but then he would succumb to a feeling of dualism and despair that had to be overcome, blunted, and drowned out by getting drunk.

It was in such a frame of mind that he caught sight of the Shrove Monday rod over in the corner. It was mocking him because he had lost a son. Again everything was working up to a scream. That scream! But then Anne Marie came in with a basketful of beer bottles and packages, and while the phonograph went on blaring he sidled over to her with a dance step, grabbed a couple of the bottles, and swung them in time with the music.

"Ah, Bournonville!"* Steffensen exclaimed. "The beer-bottle tableau. Let me have a bottle right away."

Jastrau sat down, puffing heavily.

"Yes, waiting for beer is a difficult thing," Steffensen said comfortingly.

But just then the record played itself out and Jastrau had to get up and put a new one on.

"We ought to have a permanently employed record changer," Steffenen went on.

After the eggs had finished boiling and the late luncheon was on the table, Anne Marie was assigned the task of tending to the phonograph. It had to be kept going incessantly. They did not want to be disturbed by the silence of the apartment while they ate.

But now Anne Marie had grown nervous. She had a distracted look, and her face was flushed despite its basic pale, sickly look. She fumbled with her egg. Her stubby fingers, with their plebian nails, held the spoon the wrong way.

There was an uneven whirring and wobbling as the record ran out.

"The phonograph," Steffensen commanded harshly, screwing up his eyes.

"Yes, yes," she replied with a Jutland accent as she nervously got up from her chair. Jastrau had to grab the egg and egg cup, which she nearly upset, and as he did so he happened to brush her soft bare arm. Then it came to him, more emphatically than ever before, that she was diseased and untouchable. He could not help looking at her short sturdy body in the cheap dress with the leather belt that rested too far down on her hips. She was fleshy and sensual, even to her full lips which she adorned with lipstick. Otherwise she used no make-up. And this sensuous creature was untouchable.

He smoothed out the newspaper. He had to caress something with a gentle loving touch. Then a new record began playing.

* August Bournonville, nineteenth-century Danish ballet master.

230

"Well," said Jastrau, looking at his watch, "I guess I'd better get busy."

"First some beer," came Steffensen's answer. They each had four bottles standing in front of them.

Steffensen put one of them to his mouth, although there was a glass beside his plate.

"Ah yes, you have to get busy," he said, wiping his mouth. "Yes, of course, you have a steady job. A respectable critic—of the arts. Damned if I hadn't completely forgotten that."

"Otherwise we wouldn't get anything to eat," Jastrau replied.

Anne Marie nodded in a practical manner.

But Steffensen only took another swig of beer.

"Tell me, how long do you think it will be before they toss you out over there?" he asked as he set the bottle down with a thump.

A nervous glance from Anne Marie. The phonograph cut in in full force with a chorus from the brass instruments.

Jastrau did not answer. His eyes had a weary, foggy look.

"Things just can't go on this way," Steffensen continued, staring at him with eyes that were unnaturally bright.

"No, I'm slipping away from respectability," Jastrau replied in a sing-song tone. The jazz formed an accompaniment to his words. "I'm finally drawing closer to youth. I'll soon be on an equal footing with you two."

He nodded toward Steffensen. "I'm getting more like you, I am," he went on, "because I want to know what goes on inside you, what youth is, what the future holds. I want to be on an equal footing with you."

The music carried his words. He felt they were true. There was a stong element of fate in his life. Now he could feel the beer. It was freedom that he sought, the infinite soul. That was why all this had happened. Now he knew it—the jazz told him so.

"Why do you want to talk about it, Stefan?" Anne Marie protested. "You can see that Herr Jastrau doesn't like it."

"Take care of the phonograph, wench. You forgot to wind it. It's whining."

Jastrau started at the brutal tone of Steffensen's voice. The thought flashed through his mind that she was a helpless woman and that he should come to her defense. But she had already gotten up.

Then, as if by way of recompense, he let his glance roam over her head. He felt a desire to pat it. Like a sick animal that one could not help.

And Steffensen suddenly got a harsh look from him.

"Have you read this interview with Professor Geberhardt?" he asked after a brief pause.

"Don't know the man."

Jastrau smiled with a superior air and began to underscore with a fingernail a few of the lines in the newspaper.

"Well, what's it about?" asked Steffensen.

"Sometimes," Jastrau read aloud, "a person is overcome by disgust at being an active participant in this world's perverted affairs. I am assailed so strongly by this feeling that I am withdrawing from the scene."

Steffensen raised his head with a gloating smile.

"Are you withdrawing from *Dagbladet?*" he asked bluntly.

"No, damned if I am. Who told you that? I'm only reading something that it might do you good to hear."

Steffensen's shoulders shook, and soon came the sound of his affected laughter.

"Yes, you're going to the dogs all right, and whatever else you say is a lot of nonsense."

"No, no!" Anne Marie exclaimed impulsively.

"Yes, yes," Jastrau replied in a melancholy, gentle parody of her voice.

"It's a good thing you recognize it yourself," said Steffensen with a grin.

"Frøken—Frøken Anne Marie," Jastrau said without troubling to answer Steffensen, "now the record is running out."

She nodded.

"Frøken Anne Marie," she repeated quietly, trying to reproduce the tone in which Jastrau had addressed her. Now she no longer moved sluggishly. She wound the phonograph as if she enjoyed doing it.

"Otherwise you damn well wouldn't put up with the way we've forced ourselves on you," Steffensen went on, his eyes still twinkling and directed at Jastrau. "I have a nose for that sort of thing." He reached out and helped himself to another bottle of beer. "*Skaal.*" They crossed the necks of their bottles and clinked them together. "No sooner had Sanders—"

"I don't want to talk about it," Jastrau exclaimed heatedly.

"Oh, what of it? It had to happen," Steffensen muttered. "What if it was his fault that the apple cart got upset? It had to be upset anyhow."

There was an instrument that kept up a shrill, turbid refrain throughout the new record, and it sent cold shivers up Jastrau's back. It was an ominous, fateful sound.

"Yes, no sooner had Sanders told the story that he had cooked up than I was Johnny-on-the-spot." A crafty smile played about Steffensen's rigid lips. "I saw you floundering around in this big apartment—an abandoned wreck, luxurious but gone adrift. And I couldn't stand to see that, so I came aboard with the wench."

Anne Marie compressed her lips, but her eyes were glued on him apprehensively.

"And it worked. You didn't throw us out. Here we sit. I tell you, I have a nose that can smell when things are going to pot." Steffensen sounded boastful, and suddenly Jastrau was aware of how young he was. "I saw the whole picture, just like a story or a poem, or whatever the hell you want to call it. That's the way it is with me. It helps a person to look at things logically."

"So you have a nose for logic, too?" Jastrau asked ironically.

"Yes. After all, I'm not a fool," came the reply.

Jastrau stared at him. He had heard that answer and been through the same discussion once before. No, this dark north room, the sunlit wall across the way, these two individuals, the phonograph music playing incessantly, the beer bottles on the table strewn with bottle caps—no, all this was something he could not have experienced before. But suddenly the scene around him assumed clear, ineradicable form. These two faces. This famished, fanatical student—for that was what Steffensen was, that and nothing else, a demented student—and this servant girl who had no idea of what to do with either her body or soul.

And once again Jastrau sat at the end of the table and put his hands together as if about to break bread. *Emmaus!* In that position, he seemed to understand everything and put his trust in an inner light.

But Steffensen went on talking.

"Like a picture, I tell you. That's the way it has always seemed to me—as if the apartment were floating through the air." He took a swig from the bottle. "All I had to do was come in here, and everything levitated. The apartment, these rooms sailed along through the air like a flying ship, and that's the way it is now. Especially with the music—ha! And now I've gotten the idea into my head that it will all keep on floating—way up high, high up over the whole dirty mess—as long as we—we're the passengers—what shall I say?—as long as we simply let everything happen, everything. In other words, let the infinite call the tune."

Jastrau leaned forward and stared at Steffensen's pale harried features, the unpleasantly high forehead, the gleaming eyes, and the lips that seemed like those of an automaton. Yes, he was demented. The previous winter had left its mark on him. But the thought, the picture he had sketched, left an even stronger impression than the hard bitter face.

"Yes, I understand," Jastrau replied as Steffensen sat looking at him uneasily. "There's always a feeling of the infinite about anything in a state of decay."

"Yes."

Steffensen fell silent. He sat staring at a beer bottle as if he were clairvoyant.

But all of a sudden the jazz ground to a stop.

For a moment they all sat rigidly motionless. Jastrau expected a further development, and Anne Marie did not move.

Suddenly Steffensen grabbed his beer glass and flung it at Anne Marie.

It grazed her temple and crashed against the sideboard.

"How often do I have to remind you to tend to the phonograph, wench?"

Large tears welled up in her eyes.

And then things began to flicker before Jastrau's eyes. He saw nothing but the reflection from the white curtains at the neighbor's across the way.

"Just because you've infected her is no reason to mistreat her."

He heard the words. They were spoken clearly out into the room. It was his own voice. But it seemed to him that the words originated some inches away from his mouth. They materialized out of the air.

Steffensen sat motionless. The skin around his cheekbones was chalk-white, as if a death mask had just been removed from his face.

But Anne Marie had gotten up. She looked at Jastrau with eyes ablaze. She gasped for breath so that her gross body assumed a brutish posture. Her dress, that had worked up above the belt, bagged like the shirt of a man wearing a belt.

"And this is what we have to put up with. This is what we have to stand for from a person we don't know. We're poor, and we get our food for nothing, so we have to let ourselves be stepped on. No, no, no!" She gasped again. Her hair had fallen down over one eye. A deep flush had colored her throat and cheeks so that the morbid, lackluster complexion of the skin around her eyes was more noticeable. But now there was no fear in her eyes; they were large and bovine. Her whole being was poised for an uncontrollable onslaught, a blind spring, as she stared straight ahead with the wide-open gaze of a sleepwalker.

234

Jastrau got up, feeling wretched, and was going to lay his hands reassuringly on her shoulders. But she tore herself loose. Beneath the skin of her bare arms was a hint of muscles that were not like a woman's.

"Stay away from me! Help me, Stefan—protect me!" she screamed in a wild, senseless outburst.

"Oh, this is all insane," Steffensen drawled. The color had returned to his cheeks. "Start the phonograph going."

Anne Marie glanced at him quickly. With a brisk shake of her head and a sweep of her hand she got her hair back in place. But then her agitated face and trembling lips were thrust forward so prominently that everything she said sounded indiscreet, almost too intimate.

"Oh—I can't think," she groaned with her face held close to Jastrau's. He was afraid that she was going to fall against him. "I'm at my wit's end." She stared right into his face. But now her eyes were again disoriented by fear; the irises opened wide and milky and she seemed to be staring out into a fog. "I don't know anything. I'm stupid. I'm stupid. I'm stupid."

Then suddenly she took his head in both of her hands.

"But you're good," she said, nodding gravely. "You are a good person. But you don't believe I'm sick, do you? Not sick in that way. No, no, because then I'd be so ashamed of myself, then I couldn't stay here a second longer. Could I? No, of course I couldn't."

"Start the phonograph going now," Steffensen repeated in irritation.

Jastrau sat down, feeling weak.

"What are you thinking about?" he said with a preoccupied air to Steffensen, who sat stuffing his pipe.

"I'm thinking logically."

"Ha."

Steffensen's eyes were shining.

"I'm thinking that if I had been such a—a bandit, shall we say—well, what then? We're all drifting toward the infinite. Aren't we? We let everything happen. We're in tune with the infinite, aren't we?"

He stared at Jastrau with a leaden expression.

"But if that's the case, we'll have to go the whole way as far as crimes are concerned. And so what I've done—done to her—doesn't amount to anything."

"Is it true, then? Have you committed such a—?"

Jastrau was not able to finish the question, because Anne Marie let out a shriek, ran and threw herself on the sofa, and began sobbing convulsively.

"Let me take care of her," Steffensen said, getting up reluctantly.

Jastrau got up, left the apartment, and went downstairs into the street.

Bareheaded and with hands in his pockets, he sauntered over toward the Town Hall Square.

Chapter Two   Bareheaded, Ole Jastrau walked toward *Dagbladet*'s red building. That too was deserted. He could tell as soon as he looked up at the windows. In the course of one evening, it too had sunk into the sea and become unreal. And he himself drifted helplessly along like a person who had been drowned.

He still had his hands in his pockets as he made his way in the sunlight past the streetcars and automobiles over to the revolving door of *Dagbladet*'s building. He felt relaxed now, in a mood in which all events seemed to be part of a dramatic performance and in which all the people he saw were playing roles. He felt strangely free now, as if someone else had relieved him of the need to make decisions.

Up in the editorial department he nodded to the copy editor. Then he said a few kind words to the woman on duty. But suddenly he realized that he did not know why he had come there.

He wandered into the peristyle.

Eriksen was sitting in one of the small, box-like offices, making a conspicuous show of drinking a cup of coffee while he wrote an article.

Why shouldn't Jastrau lean against the door frame and watch him?

"Oh—so it's you, Jazz," Eriksen said with a grin as he spilled a few drops of coffee on his manuscript. "Uh-h—what a God damned mess—the sort of thing that happens only when you drink coffee." Exasperated, he grabbed a blotter and mopped up the drops. "What a mess on a clean sheet of paper. Now why in the devil are you standing there staring at me?" He threw the blotter on the floor. "And looking so superior?"

But suddenly he began laughing and coughing.

"Never mind, Jazz. How about shutting the door?"

No sooner had Jastrau complied than Eriksen, with a confiding smile, brought forth a glass of port from a hiding place behind a pile of telephone books and cleared his throat.

"There's none for you." He emptied the glass, emitted a satisfied

236

"Ah-h," and carefully secreted it again. "But this sort of thing doesn't ordinarily happen during working hours," he added in a tone of mounting wrath. "On my word of honor, it never happens." He turned indignantly in his chair. "Don't you believe me?"

"Yes, of course," Jastrau reassured him, and sat down.

But just as quickly Eriksen's tone became friendly again. He inclined his head to one side and blinked his triangular eyes cunningly. There was a nervous twitching of his eyebrows that reminded Jastrau of a dog.

"Yes, excuse me for not offering you any. But one has to look out for himself first, isn't that right? You know that—yes, I'm sure you understand, don't you, Jazz? You're a drunkard yourself."

"Am I a drunkard?" Jastrau exclaimed. "Well, perhaps."

"Now, now," Eriksen protested indignantly, lifting his hands and shaking a finger at Jastrau like an overwrought Jew. "You *are* a drunkard. Just be honest, Jazz. That's the best way of going to the dogs. Honesty. Don't you think we know you're a drunkard? We know everything up here at the paper. A first-class newspaper. We know you're a drunkard. We've known it for a long time. We know everything. And it won't do you any good to deny it. We know that your wife has run out on you. You're going to be divorced, you are, you old lecher. Well, you know how denials are treated here at the paper. Discreetly, of course. They get printed in small type on a back page in my 'Here and There' column—the dullest thing in the whole newspaper—something that nobody reads, and that nobody *has to* read, you understand. That's why it's part of the paper. But you're a drunkard—in capital letters. A drunkard."

He banged his fist convincingly on his desk so hard that the coffee cup rattled. The wine glass behind the phone books betrayed its presence by a faint tinkle.

Then he sat for a while and struggled to get his breath, while Jastrau stared at him. There was a hoarse, convulsive "r-r-r-u-u."

"Ah yes," he sighed. "But life has left its mark on me too, hee hee," he added slyly.

"Is that an advantage?" Jastrau asked, feeling bewildered.

"Are you crazy, man?" said Eriksen. "If it weren't for that, I'd have been let go long ago. No, life has left its mark on me, the old man in the corner room says, hee hee. My wife is in the hospital. I was a rich man once—during the war, when no one could avoid getting rich. And I've been a tramp too—after the war, when a person couldn't avoid becoming one. And it was as a tramp that I came up here with my first article. 'It might be that you're the man in the street,' the old man said.

Hee hee—he's always sitting in his office and waiting for the man in the street. I'm the last one who walked in off the street, and he'll never let me forget it—until the next one walks in. Isn't it the truth?"

The angular corners of his bloodshot eyes radiated his good fortune.

"But you—" he went on, waving a hand as if brushing Jastrau aside. "You came from the university, and that kind the old man doesn't like. He says they can't write. Hee hee. Well, so it turns out you can write. But now you're going to be divorced—and that he can't understand. A man's private life, yes, certainly. A little spice now and then never does any harm. But divorce! There's nothing you can say about it, because *he* can't understand it. There are plenty of girls, and they're all all right, each in her own way. One is tall and another is fat, so why do people have to get divorced? And I feel the same way about it."

"And then besides, you drink, you swine," he added after a pause.

Jastru sat and nodded without saying a word. Why did he feel compelled to sit there listening to Eriksen's ranting torrent of words? He did listen, however—listened as if a wish were in the process of being fulfilled.

"But what the hell, Jazz, don't let it worry you, damn it all," Eriksen continued, getting up from his chair. He laid a hand consolingly on Jastrau's shoulder, bent over until his mouth was close to Jastrau's ear, and spoke in a hoarse whisper. A pungent aroma of port struck Jastrau in the face.

"But don't let it get you down, damn it all. All you have to do is get it down to a system. Sure, they grumble about it up here, but all you have to do is pay attention to your work, show up every day and write your crap, and then close up shop at six o'clock. That's the way it is with me. It's six o'clock, and there's been a train wreck at Vigerslev. I couldn't care less I tell them. Thirty people dead. They have to die before six o'clock is what I tell them. It's six o'clock. I go and sit at a table over at Sommer's and have a nice cozy time with a bottle of port. Not the Bar des Artistes—no, not with that phonograph there. There I'd only behave like a Spanish dancing girl, and to hell with that, to hell with that. There I'd get high and probably pick a fight. No, Sommer's is the place. It's nice there. At nine o'clock I order another half-bottle. At ten o'clock I've lost track of time—everything is a blank. And at eleven o'clock Sommer puts me into a cab. Then I go home. And the next morning I'm back here in shape to work."

He straightened up and arched his chest. "Yes, I guess life has left its mark on me," he said in a more solemn tone, "but I stand up for my rights like a class-conscious drunkard. No two ways about it. After six o'clock I'm drunk. But you, you hang around a bar all day long. Now, you know I like you. Damn it all, I like you tremendously." He reached for Jastrau's hand and crushed it in his grip. "And I want to tell you—don't take so much as a single drink as long as the sun is still shining over Vesterbro."

He raised his left hand in a dramatic gesture.

"Not so much as a"—his face grew flushed—"not so much as a single drink." The red coloration of his face changed to purple. He let go of Jastrau's hand and suddenly clasped both of his own hands to his chest as he bent forward in a severe fit of hoarse coughing.

"You can go now. Just leave me alone," he groaned, almost doubled up. He waved one hand in the air and then the cough broke forth again, disrupting every word and shaking his small, stocky body.

Jastrau got up. He wanted to ask if he could bring him some water, but Eriksen drew himself up, red and blue in the face, with tears streaming from his eyes and still coughing so that a spray of saliva issued from his mouth.

"Go on now, damn it!" A new attack seized him. "I—I'm busy."

Jastrau left and closed Eriksen's door. But the hollow cough was audible even through the door—the sound of a man left alone.

The sun streamed into the vestibule from two empty offices whose doors stood wide open. But over in the corner, outside the corner room, it was dark. Editor Iversen was probably sitting in there.

Just then he ran into the copy editor.

"Have you got a minute, Ole Jastrau?" he asked, letting his somber, polite gaze rest on Jastrau.

"No, unfortunately I'm very busy," Jastrau replied as meekly as a schoolboy.

It was absolutely impossible for the two of them to understand each other. And so Jastrau felt humble. He could just as well have felt superior.

"I'd like to have a talk with you, because things can't go on this way for very long," the copy editor went on.

"What can't go on?" Jastrau asked uncomprehendingly.

"You're neglecting your opportunities up here. You know that very well yourself. Not your work. But you're so casual about your connection with the paper. You don't enter into things, Ole Jastrau, and we could make a big man of you. But you won't go along."

"Ye-s," Jastrau said slowly.

The copy editor shook his head sadly but with a trace of humor.

"And so I'd like to have a serious talk with you one of these days, as soon as possible, Ole Jastrau. And don't forget it, now," he concluded in a business-like tone. They exchanged smiles. Did they both understand in a flash how impossible it was?

"No, I won't," Jastrau replied in a sing-song voice that sounded anything but dependable. And with that he was out the door.

A big man! As if that were what he wanted. What did that have to do with the infinitude of the soul, the real meaning of things, a man's true self? To write an article every day about the intellectual life. Was that being a big man? To be in on editorial intrigues and always keep the publisher's interests in mind, to know all about the private lives of the Danish intellectual bigwigs, friends and enemies alike, to know who pulled what strings and why. Was that being a big man?

"Disgust with the perversity of the way the world is going," he said as he went down the stairs. He was talking aloud to himself, but it sounded like a quotation.

And when he stood bareheaded on the sidewalk outside of *Dagbladet* and saw the sunlight gleaming on bicycles, streetcars, and automobiles, flashing mirror-like surfaces that glided by in the flickering heat haze, saw cheerful human forms bending forward, intent on their destinations, and women with rounded calves, he suddenly recalled the darkness outside the closed door of Editor Iversen's corner room.

"I'll walk out on him—withdraw from the scene." That too sounded somewhat like a quotation.

Should he go back up there, burst into the corner room as into a torrent of sunshine and talk to the tall, bent-over figure that sat there blinking apathetically into the flood of sunlight, sunlight, sunlight? Talk to him and hand in his resignation now, immediately? And be washed up, once and for all?

He stuffed his pipe as he stood on the sidewalk. The wind whipped his hair. A blue automobile rode by. He had a feeling that a woman in it waved at him, and he nodded absent-mindedly. Who was it? No way of knowing.

He saw a man lift a little boy up into a streetcar. A little boy. No, it was evidently a little girl. That caused him no pangs. Let everything be blurred by the sunlight. A press photographer greeted him. The green leaves and red blossoms of the spindly chestnut trees twinkled in the light.

He had finished stuffing his pipe.

Should he not put it in his pocket now, go up there at once, and have it over with? Up the stairs and into the corner room? But after all, a person couldn't do that, couldn't come rushing in off the street with his hair in wild disorder, his hands in his pants pockets, and turn in his resignation. The old man would get a coughing fit from laughing, spit into the wastebasket, and wheeze in merriment. It was a serious matter, involving a contract and three months' notice. A person would have to be wearing a hat so he could take it off and lay it on the desk before the conversation began.

He would have to go home and get a hat. That would strengthen him in his purpose. Otherwise he might forget the whole thing.

With calm determination he walked out along Vesterbrogade and cut diagonally past the railway station into Istedgade. Now he would resign. And the future? Nobody knew. He allowed himself to become intoxicated over his fate and began to whistle.

But when he got up to his apartment it was strangely quiet there. He walked along the half-dark corridor, still whistling. Should he take his cap or his felt hat? So strangely quiet. The felt hat, of course. And his walking stick. A stick was good. One could lean on it, and it gave a person an air of reliability. But why was it so quiet? Had Steffensen and Anne Marie gone out? Anne Marie. He smiled and put on the hat.

Whistling, he went into the living room. Automatically, he made the secret, ritualistic sign as he passed the two photographs on the table. He had thought it up himself, or rather, the idea had come to him as a fleeting whim. The left hand diagonally over his chest. It might always serve to ward off some danger. But the dreary daylight coming in through the windows, which had not been cleaned for some time, dampened his spirits immediately without his being aware of it. A change in the weather? He stopped whistling.

Then he heard Anne Marie exclaim, "Oh, it never comes out right!" There was a sound of something hitting the table.

He pushed open the door to the dining room, and as he did so he detected an unusual odor, a mild, soothing fragrance in the atmosphere of dust and decay.

There were roses on the table.

"What's this—?" He remained standing, open-mouthed.

Anne Marie was sitting at the table with a deck of cards, playing solitaire, and Steffensen was lying on the sofa with his hands behind his head.

"An idyll," Steffensen muttered disdainfully.

"Yes, but what's the meaning of the roses?"

Anne Marie shook her head and said "Bizz-zz," to indicate a momentary lapse from sanity on Steffensen's part.

"Precisely," replied Steffensen. "But look—haven't you got some tobacco? I can't think."

"But the flowers?"

"Oh," Steffensen snapped, "I got sentimental. But my punishment came at once—like a sock in the jaw. I met my old man right out here in the street. I wonder what he's nosing around here for."

"Your father? Your father? You didn't say anything about that, Stefan." Anne Marie was disturbed and jumped up from her chair. "Oh, your father—is he coming here? I can't stand it. Why? What for? No, I can't stay here. I—I—"

Jastrau leaned on his stick and looked at her without understanding what she was getting at. Why was there such a look of fear in her eyes—a look of both fear and confusion? The corners of her mouth twitched nervously. Why?

"And now everything was about to be all right. Or pretty nearly all right." She sat down again as if she were about to collapse and let her head drop onto her arms so that her hair fell forward and lay in a thick mass down over the front of her head.

"It's never completely all right—never completely all right. I'm going crazy—crazy, crazy," she groaned.

"Stop it now, Anne Marie," Steffensen said with an impatient scowl, and got up lazily from his chair. "He didn't see me. He was probably out looking for some girl or other here in the neighborhood. That would be just like him."

As he said it, Anne Marie raised her head and screamed, screamed so that it must have been audible throughout the whole building. "And now you're going to hit me. Now you're going to hit me." Her face was flaming and she was beside herself with rage. "But—but I'll—" she sniveled, her soft lips protruding in brutish fashion. Then suddenly they went slack, and her mouth and chin became like a lump of soft dough. "No, no, no," she said, her voice sinking with each utterance, first into humility and then into a tone of supplication. "You mustn't hit me, Stefan. Don't hit me, don't hit me. Anything but that. Just don't hit me. I'll go away, leave you alone, gladly—yes, gladly."

Jastrau shook his head in embarrassment. What was it that was happening here in his room? Something wild and incomprehensible, someone else's private life pressing in on him so closely that he could smell it. And his own life, his own affairs—disappeared, vanished. The life that had gone on in this room. What life? Some words over the telephone—"Where have you and Mother been all this time?"—and then a woman's weary voice. Then it had all vanished, and now there were only these two strangers who shouted and screamed. He must not forget—

"Incidentally, he was in mourning, my old man. He was wearing a top hat." Steffensen laughed.

Jastrau still had on his fedora. He mustn't forget, mustn't forget. He had to go over for a talk with Editor Iversen, and he took a firm grip on his stick.

"You two ought to take a walk," he proposed in an even tone. "And be good to each other."

Gentle words. Like Jesus Christ. A foolish expression came over Jastrau's face.

Steffensen smiled derisively, and there was a sharp, harsh glint in his eyes. But Anne Marie straightened up with a toss of her head.

"I'm not stepping out of doors."

Jastrau was afraid of her eyes.

"No, of course not," Steffensen replied.

"And neither are you—neither are you! Suppose you should meet him!" she exclaimed, leaning her heavy body in toward the table. She gasped hysterically for breath, a sustained, ominous sound as if another violent outburst was in the making. It could be heard welling up from within.

"Shouldn't we—shouldn't we—forget it?" Jastrau said in a tone of conciliation. The Son of Man with a felt hat and a walking stick. "I'll go get some port, and then we'll forget it."

He should go over and hand in his resignation. What if out of sheer forgetfulness he should go on being *Dagbladet*'s chief book reviewer?

"Yes—forget, forget, forget," Anne Marie intoned, and sank limply back into her chair. Jastrau was taken aback by the look on her face. Feelings and expressions of all sorts were intermingled there, and her chin was grotesquely lost in the full folds of her neck.

"You must be crazy, Anne Marie," exclaimed Steffensen. "The old man can't do anything to me. And you—" he snorted contemptuously.

Anne Marie opened her eyes wide with a start and stared at Steffensen in abject terror.

"Stefan, Stefan," she whimpered.

"Oh, come now—I didn't mean it."

Steffensen's tone was strangely gentle. Suddenly Jastrau understood why the roses were there. A fragrant odor of conciliation amidst all this merciless decay.

"So now I'll go down and get the wine," Jastrau repeated, once more himself in a fedora. He was glad he had hit upon the right remedy. Just blunt the senses—blunt them. A thinking brain was a painful affliction.

"Yes, do that. I can't think anyhow," Steffensen said.

"Do you think?" Again that old hint of scorn in his voice.

"Yes, I'm right on the point of having a necessary thought—right on the point of it." Steffensen's expression had grown rigid again. It looked as if he were about to butt his abnormally high forehead against a wall, and his eyes had resumed their ruthless, glazed luster.

Jastrau went downstairs and across the street to a tobacco shop, where he bought three bottles of port and remembered at the same time that they were out of tobacco.

As he casually swung into the entranceway to the apartment again with the three bottles and the tobacco, the red-haired janitor, who was standing there, grinned cannily at him. He was a little younger than Jastrau.

"That makes sense," he said, winking innocently at Jastrau with his moist blue eyes.

"Wouldn't you like to come up with me?" Jastrau asked, following a sudden impulse.

"Thanks for the invitation." The janitor looked down at himself and grinned. He was wearing blue overalls. "I'm not one to say no—never. But can't I carry the bottles? I'm more used to that sort of thing than you are."

And a moment later he was prancing up the stairs in his rustling overalls with gay but flat-footed dance steps.

"I'm feeling better already," he said each time he reached a landing. "Oh—I sure do feel better."

But he stopped thoughtfully outside the hallway door.

"What do you think your wife will say?" he whispered.

"She's not here," Jastrau replied with a shrug of his shoulders. "She won't be back. We've separated, damn it."

The janitor gaped at him.

"No—really? And the little boy—he's gone too? Well, that's the way it goes sometimes, indeed it does, and what is there to say? The only fun a person has is what he makes for himself. But what the devil— you're not going to drink these three bottles here alone, are you? You're not as crazy as all that, Herr Jastrau, I don't suppose. Maybe you have company."

"Well, yes. But come on in."

The janitor followed him in self-consciously. In his blue overalls his gait was like that of a bear. And he was a little embarrassed when he set the bottles down.

"My name is Edwin Jacobsen, and I'm the janitor of the building here."

Anne Marie dried her eyes. She had been crying. As she acknowledged the janitor's introduction, she curtsied.

Steffensen stuck out his hand over the table and muttered his name. He very nearly upset the roses.

244

"Well, draw up a chair, Jacobsen," Jastrau said.

"Ha ha." The janitor sat down at the table and gave a little bounce of enthusiasm in his chair. "A fellow stands there in the entranceway and thinks it will be a long time until he gets a drink—doesn't even dare dream of it—and then it comes swinging right in to him off the street—three bottles, no less. Tra la la la la."

Steffensen was indifferent. When the bottles had been uncorked, he reached for one of them and placed it in front of him. His expression was blank. His eyes were watering.

But Anne Marie was mindful of domestic responsibilities and brought out the green glasses.

"So there's the phonograph, Herr Jastrau," exclaimed the janitor, grinning knowingly. "Yes, sometimes I've heard it in the middle of the night." He had to say something for he held a glass of port in his hand. "But that's all right, Herr Jastrau—it doesn't make any difference. Skaal. But it makes one feel so frisky to lie in bed and listen to it, and I can't afford to have any more children right now, so you must promise me to play it only now and then—just one record. Oh, pardon me, Frøken—I wasn't thinking about—"

"It's all right," Anne Marie quickly replied.

Embarrassed, he smiled.

"But shouldn't we play a number?"

Jastrau went over to wind the phonograph.

"Whoa now, is that any way to do it?" the janitor exclaimed, offended. "Guzzling it like that?"

Jastrau turned around and saw that Steffensen had placed one of the bottles to his lips and was taking a long swig from it. His Adam's apple protruded above his soft collar like a clenched fist.

"What a drunken lout," said the janitor, laughing. "I've seen a good many things, yes, indeed I have. But such a tippler I've only seen in Riga. He drank and then fell on his face. He wasn't a human being, but a Russian—"

Steffensen was unconcerned. He took the bottle from his lips with a deep sign and set it down heavily.

"Ha ha, what a drunken lout." The janitor laughed again and slapped his hand against his blue overall thighs.

Steffensen glanced across at him with a forced, ingenuous smile, but said nothing.

"Stefan!" Anne Marie burst out. She wanted to interfere. But then suddenly shook her head. "No, it's no use," she sighed and emptied her glass.

But Jastrau only shoved his hat back on his head and started the phonograph. He was enjoying himself. He must not forget. The record began with dissonant notes, and then the rhythm broke in. Mustn't forget. He was at last going to give notice that his contract with the paper was about up. Oh, evening star!

The reflection of the afternoon sun shone in on them through the dirty windows.

"Does the young lady dance?" asked the janitor, who gallantly had gotten up and was shuffling his feet.

Anne Marie brushed the hair away from her forehead.

"Ah, yes," she panted. "But isn't it frightfully warm here? Or am I already feeling the wine?"

"One should never drink port when the sun is shining," the janitor replied with a knowing smile. Then he led Anne Marie back and forth across the floor at a brisk but lumbering pace like a bear. Weak, unsteady knees.

"And here I was thinking there'd be nothing but meatballs to look forward to today," he babbled. "What I mean is we were having meatballs up at our place at six o'clock. But then it didn't turn out that way."

The jazz filled the room. Jastrau took some awkward dance steps and waved his walking stick in tune with the music. He should go right away. But Steffensen had silently put the bottle to his lips again and tipped his head far back.

"Drunken lout," giggled the janitor, and stopped his trotting. "But dancing does make a person thirsty."

A deep flush was discernible beneath his sunburned complexion.

Jastrau put on another record. He heard Anne Marie moan, "Oh—I can already feel it."

Then the janitor stood beside him.

"Now I suppose you'll give up the apartment," he said quietly, his eyes shining.

"Yes, I've already written to the landlord."

"And all this nice furniture, I suppose you'll sell it."

His artless eyes shone with an even sharper brilliance.

The furniture. Jastrau could not think. The furniture was so unreal. It stood there in the apartment that floated through the air, a Noah's ark with bits of wreckage from his past and liquor and dancing people whom he didn't know.

"My kingdom is not of this world," Jastrau replied.

"Ha ha," the janitor laughed confidingly. "I don't believe in God, either."

Jastrau did not answer him. He felt as if he were floating. And over in his chair sat Steffensen, already looking the worse for wear.

246

"*Skaal*," Jastrau announced. "It seems to me we're not drinking."

Anne Marie looked up at him with listless eyes and shook her head.

"I get high so quickly," she sighed, and took a firm hold on her glass with a kind of desperate courage.

"This is a dandy phonograph," the janitor remarked, giving it a pat. "And good records. It's a shame that you get practically nothing for them when you sell them. No, you don't, as a matter of fact, Herr Jastrau," he added sadly.

"Are you forgetting me entirely?" Anne Marie shouted.

"No—never!" exclaimed the janitor with a show of emotion, spreading his arms wide as he stood there in his overalls. "She's a lovely woman," he said to Jastrau with a grin, assuming a position like a bear who wanted to embrace everything, while Anne Marie flung herself into his arms.

Jastrau put his stick aside in order better to manage his drink.

"Ho," said Steffensen, laughing for no good reason. His tall bony frame shook with merriment. "A red-faced janitor in blue—ho!"

Then he muttered something and reached out stupidly for the bottle.

Another jazz record. Another saxophone. The subconscious was lifted into a dark, cloudy, never-never land in response to the deep tones. A high-pitched instrument cut in sharply, dispelling the somber mood with a clear, sharp, soulless rhythm.

"It's a fine phonograph!" It was the janitor who again stood beside him. "So often I've wished I could pick up a phonograph cheap—yes, indeed I have." He gave a subdued sigh.

"Then perhaps sometime you'll get this one, Herr Jacobsen," Jastrau exclaimed, slapping him on the shoulder.

Another record. A Negro song. A chorus. "Doo—doo-de-doo—doo. Wob-li-wob. I love you so dearly."

"Oh, Ole." It was Anne Marie who suddenly hung around his neck and pressed her heavy breasts against him. She leaned her head back and stared at him with glazed eyes and slack lips. "You don't think anything bad about me, do you? You don't think I'm sick, do you? Oh—I could really fall in love with you."

And suddenly her eyes seemed to focus again.

"Ha ha ha! Isn't it funny? Why don't you laugh? I could love you," she shrilled.

Then she pushed him away with a violent shove and stood wobbling unsteadily.

"Janitor—why don't you seduce me?"

"No, let's wait a little while, Frøken," the janitor replied, winking at Jastrau.

Anne Marie was staggering. She was dead white, and fumbled for her chair.

Just then a glass was upset. Steffensen stretched his long arms across the table for another bottle.

"Now things are getting really cozy here," Jastrau remarked. He felt a painful sense of depression and thought he was sober. But there was a movement in the room, as if a ripple of light were playing over the surface of the furniture.

"Oh—I'm beginning to feel sick," Anne Marie moaned, leaning against the chair for support. "Right here—oh, right here under my chest."

"You should lie down here on the sofa, Frøken," said the janitor. "I'll take care of her," he nodded over to Jastrau. "But get a pail right away."

Jastrau hurried into the kitchen, stopped suddenly at the sink, and began whistling a tune. It was badly off key. Then he turned around and was about to go back. But the pail. It was the pail he was after. He reached under the sink for it and tossed a dry mop rag onto the kitchen table. It was stiff as a board.

Anne Marie lay on the sofa in the dining room, pale as a corpse. Her lips drooped, her features were limp.

"No, I can't throw up," she barked at the janitor, who was fussing over her.

"Try now—just try, little Frøken," he said gently, placing the pail near the head of the sofa. "Stick your finger down your throat, little Frøken, then everything will be all right. You'll see how much better you'll feel."

But just then Steffensen got up, his face yellow and his eyes staring blankly, and grabbed the roses in the vase with both hands. He crushed the flowers between his fingers and carried the bouquet like a head of cabbage over to the sofa. The water dripped from the stems.

"My darling," he babbled, and threw the wet roses down over her. "Dar—dar—ling." He was going to kneel down beside the sofa, but then he fell down. A sound of sobbing came from his lips, as if he were about to burst into tears. And then he passed out.

"What a drunken lout," exclaimed the janitor, giving him a contemptuous shove with his foot. Then suddenly he could not keep from laughing. "Ha ha, damn it, the only fun a person has is what he makes for himself. But shouldn't we drag him in and put him on the other sofa, Herr Jastrau?"

Jastrau staggered as they carried Steffensen away. But the fedora was still on his head.

248

Chapter Three   It was getting dark in the courtyards. Jastrau lay on his back on top of the bed covers and stared up at the dim quadrangle of the ceiling, which drifted so strangely. Everything was drifting. Steffensen was right. They were aboard a ship that was sailing into infinity, into the unbounded. Through the open bedroom window came a cool breeze.

Into infinity? But did that mean drinking oneself into a stupor? Ah yes, there was something religious about drinking oneself into insensibility. All feeling of emptiness vanished. A person filled the room with his boisterous, babbling, drunken self—filled the entire room.

But it would have been good if he had been able to sleep. He couldn't. Anne Marie lay in the dining room, happily unconscious. Steffensen was stretched out in the living room, as if someone had hit him over the head with a club. He too was happy. And from the floor above came the sound of a guitar strumming incessantly. The janitor evidently had managed to digest his meatballs and was now strumming away his hangover, with dreams of acquiring a phonograph cheaply.

On the lookout for cheap loot, the red fox.

Jastrau screwed his features into a malicious frown. The janitor was going to be disappointed. This was not a wreck to be plundered, even though a four-room apartment was drifting away before wind and wave with fine furniture aboard. Oh, nonsense. It was perhaps a false suspicion. He was very decent, the red rascal. An ideal janitor, in fact. He could tolerate as much commotion in the building as anyone might make. And the more insane the commotion the better. Didn't he play the guitar? Didn't he stamp his feet on the floor up there in time to the music? An able-bodied seaman aboard this craft that was sailing on into infinity.

Yes, indeed. Either listen to music or get dead drunk. Life became so unbounded. A kind of shore leave.

But his present condition was intolerable. He was awake. Not sober and not drunk—his insides agglutinated by old, stagnant liquor that must have time to evaporate. And harassed by thoughts of a practical nature. He had to remember to hand in his resignation, had to remember to do so. Now that had been postponed because he had insisted on wearing a hat when he went to do it.

The hat hung on the bedpost.

But why? Yes, of course. He was going to resign. It was like peeling a whole layer of opinions from himself. He no longer wanted a steady job as a producer of opinions. Infinity—was that not what he was seeking? He wanted to be an infinite person, one who was initiated into the mysteries. Oh, cut it out! Now the lively music in the twilight of the summer evening was making a liar out of him again. How blue and lovely was the sky above the dark rooftops—a fascinating violet-blue. And the black chimneys so sharply outlined. Like an armored ship lying at Rheden.*

Some day it would become a poem—some day, if poems could ever again have meaning for him. At the moment they were lies. So were they evidently to Steffensen.

> Like an armored ship at Rheden—
> A cruise into impossibility—

Everything was a lie, transparent as an opinion.

Opinions? Take Sanders, that idiot. Opinions? Why had Sanders gone directly from the bar up to Johanne with his gossip? Presumably it was his opinions that had impelled him. Or was it?

But it was indecent, vile. To repeat what a person says when he is sitting in a bar that way and is drunk. One is supposedly among friends, the brotherhood of the flowing bowl. Everyone sitting there by the brass bar rail and drinking is a member of the same fraternity.

He could stay away from bars. But oh, the restfulness he found there. There was comfort and adventure combined. Why was it that he knew peace only when he sat leaning over a bar? Home. Everything gone to hell. A boy, a son. Snatched away from him only because that blabbing Communist— What business was it of his? Was he in love with Johanne? Oh, the somber, syrupy quality of Sanders' voice.

It seemed as if he could hear Sanders' excuses. Disgusting. Glib. But he *wanted* to hear them. Now he wanted to hear them. Something had to happen. And suppose, now, that Sanders' voice began to sound as if he were on the verge of tears, with a definite rise in pitch and a saccharine quality to it, and then broke down. That would be sweetest of all. Jastrau thrilled at the thought.

He must hear it. He had to have the memory of that voice breaking, nurse it and cherish it, hate it—

Steffensen knew where Sanders lived.

Jastrau jumped up from the bed and made his way through the dark rooms. The incandescent fog from the advertising lights above Vesterbro cast a faint flickering glow through the windows so that he

* An anchorage outside Copenhagen harbor.

250

could just distinguish the outlines of the furniture. Anne Marie lay in a murky huddle on the sofa. Her breathing filled the room with a profound stillness like the sound of waves washing in along a beach.

In the darkness he stumbled against some bottles standing on the floor. The noise did not wake her. And at once a feeling of gentleness came over him, as if she were a sleeping child. She should not be awakened, this sick little child.

"What is it?" It was Steffensen who had been aroused in the living room.

"You know where Sanders lives. Will you go along with me?" Jastrau said in a vehement whisper.

"What the devil do you want with him?" Steffensen muttered as he rubbed his eyes, only half awake.

Jastrau stood in the doorway to the dining room.

"I want revenge."

"You don't mean it!" Steffensen exclaimed in surprise, leaping up with a start into the middle of the room, where he stood wobbling.

"I'm still drunk," he announced.

"Will you go with me, Steffensen?"

"Yes." His voice was a bit thick.

Together they jogged down the stairway in a daze. They forgot to press the button that would automatically turn off the light after they were gone.

"I'm still drunk," Steffensen mumbled in bewilderment as he stopped short of breath in the entranceway. He leaned against the wall and passed his hand over his forehead.

"Let me see now," he groaned. "Yes, that was it. Oh-h! But first I have to have a beer—"

"Yes, you'd like that, and then we'll sit around and forget the whole thing," Jastrau growled nervously.

"No, I won't forget. We're going out and beat up Bernhard. But listen"—Steffensen moved away from the wall with a jerk—"I have to have a beer first, otherwise I won't be able to remember where he lives."

A bemused smile spread over his face.

They floundered into a small pub on Istedgade. Some workmen in blue-striped shirtsleeves stood lost in solemn speculation around a billiard table. A waiter with a purple face and white jacket appeared.

Jastrau remembered that it was this waiter he had once heard calling somebody a bitch. But what a long time ago that was.

The waiter sized them up skeptically for some time. Why? Finally he decided condescendingly to serve them.

At that moment, Jastrau happened to look at Steffensen. His eyes were bloodshot, and a drop of blood had collected in the corner of each eye. Wisps of hair hung down over his forehead.

"What a sight you are!" Jastrau observed.

"Do you think perhaps you look any better?" said Steffensen with a grin. "A rum pudding that has been stepped on.

Jastrau had no desire to look in a mirror. He was aware at once that what Steffensen had said was true. His face was sweaty. His cheeks hung loose and flabby, and he could almost feel them quivering.

"But look here," said Steffensen after they had seated themselves at a small table near the window, "are you really serious about this business with Bernhard?"

"Yes-s," Jastrau said, drawing the word out. A bright, sunny day. Women out on the sidewalk. Yes, this was the table at which he had sat. "Yes, I want to know—"

"Oh—you only want to know," Steffensen sneered, gulping down a glass of beer. "If that's all you want, I can damn well tell you about it. He did it in order to make society ripe for the proletarian revolution. You see, every bourgeois marriage that goes to hell is further proof of the eternal truth of Communism and all that sort of hogwash. Is that all you want to listen to?"

Jastrau compressed his lips in malicious scorn.

"I want to see him—the beast."

"And then?"

"I don't know. But I want to have him here in front of me and see him squirm. Because he may be a Communist, but a comrade—"

"And then?" Steffensen's bloodshot eyes assumed their glassy luster.

"I don't know what I'll do then." Jastrau gasped for breath.

"The only logical thing to do is beat him up."

"Oh, you and your logic—"

"Because it isn't enough just to talk to him, I tell you." Steffensen sneered as he uttered the word "talk," and then improved upon it. "To have a conversation with him—is that what you want? That would be just dandy."

"Now finish your drink, so we can get going," Jastrau exclaimed impatiently, and got up.

They hurried along the dark Abel Cathrinesgade, crossed Vesterbrogade with its stream of luminous traffic, an artery of fire pulsing through the night, and disappeared into the obscurity of Stenosgade. To their right in the darkness rose the Catholic church with its murky walls. A light was visible through the arched window of one of the parlors.

"Look in there—that's where they talk about logic," Jastrau re-

252

marked spitefully as they walked by. "That might be something for you."

Steffensen did not reply, but trudged along with hands in his pockets.

"Now we'll soon be there," he mumbled.

At the corner of Vodroffsvej there was a jumble of low buildings, a moss-coated summerhouse that looked like a dilapidated bandstand, some board fences, and a stretch of uneven pavement leading to a five-story building that seemed completely out of place in the surroundings, but merely erected on edge, so to speak, because of a vague premonition that some day tall buildings would be constructed in the neighborhood. In back of the house, a yard the width of an alley lay squeezed in between the building and the Svineryggen slope.

It was one of innumerable, ill-conceived "suburban spots" close to the center of Copenhagen.

Steffensen ran up the stairs ahead of Jastrau until he reached the attic, where he pushed open a door without knocking. A macabre glow of green light spilled out onto the dark stair landing, and the thick tobacco smoke that poured out was like steam from a laundry, so pallid did it appear in the strange light. And the hum of voices that they had been able to hear even down on the first floor now rose to a roar.

There were people there.

Had Jastrau expected to find Sanders alone? Had he dreamed of confronting him in an empty attic room with bare walls and the barren appearance of a place suited for a murder? He had forgotten that Sanders was never alone.

Steffensen had not stopped, and Jastrau followed him. They found themselves in a small room that gave the impression of a hole-in-the-wall in overpopulated Moscow. Here no one was alone.

A couple of sofas on which some young people were curled up and crowded together like vipers in a nest. Cushions on the floor. People there as well. Young students and workers with hair brushed back and Byronic collars of dubious cleanliness. Young girls with bobbed hair and a contemptuously independent attitude. Cigarette butts everywhere. Teacups on the floor and on the bookshelves, shoved in between the books. Some photographs of structural steel work on the walls—the modern concept of beauty—and an enormous picture of Lenin with his massive, saintly head and sardonic smile.

Sanders stood up, a solitary erect figure amidst the teeming, mobile mass that stirred like a brood of newly hatched chicks. The glow from a green-shaded lamp that stood on a low table cast his gigantic shadow on the wall so that the head was deflected at a right angle against the ceiling.

"What do you want?" Sanders asked in a tone of authority. He seemed to be standing on a pedestal of people.

"A talk with you," Steffensen replied with restraint, thrusting his pale face forward. The multitude of heads looked up, mercilessly delineated in the green light. Curiosity. And contempt as well.

"You're breaking into an editorial meeting. Is it something that concerns *Aktion*, or is it personal? I can well imagine it's personal," Sanders concluded sarcastically. Lenin's smile was doubled; it shone from many faces, and was multiplied many times over. The entire group smiled sardonically, even the women with bobbed hair.

"Yes, it's personal," Jastrau said quietly. This feeling of group participation overwhelmed him.

Sanders directed his dark smouldering eyes at him and with a wave of the hand indicated the entire editorial board. His shadow on the wall made the gesture still more world-encompassing.

"As you see, Ole, we're not alone," he said. Then he added with pointed irony: "Although, for that matter, you're not afraid to discuss your private life in public."

"Nor are you afraid to take advantage of what a drunken man says in a bar, and then go and tell his wife about it. Is that what you call comradeship?" Jastrau asked in a sudden fit of rage. The green hospital light dazzled him, reaching into the innermost recesses of his consciousness. For a moment he felt himself blinded by anger, as if by an enormous outburst of light.

"Oh, do we have to listen to this?" exclaimed a young worker on the floor as he raised himself on an elbow. "What do we care about all this gibberish? Let's throw them out."

There was a restless movement among the crowd. Through the flickering light which still shimmered before his eyes he could detect dark, ominous looks.

"No, no," Sanders exclaimed and made an admonitory gesture. His shadow resembled a statue of a naval hero. "This is Editor Jastrau, and he did me a favor once that I won't forget."

"Throw them out," someone yelled.

"Who's going to be tossed out of here?" Steffensen said as he reached out with a long arm and grabbed a student by his Byron collar. With a sudden jerk to one side, the student tore himself loose. Arms went up in an aggressive manner around Steffensen. The crowd began to stir. One of the girls put her hands to her head and cried "Oh!" Some cups rattled.

254

But Jastrau had regained control of himself.

"Stop it now, Steffensen," he said.

"I think we'd better go outside and talk alone for a little while," Sanders shouted. "But the rest of you can go on. I'll be right back."

He cast a sidelong glance at one of the editorial committee members, took Jastrau by the arm, and led him out into the hallway. Steffensen followed them with a hangdog look.

"Why in the world did you do it?" Jastrau asked as they descended the dark stairway. He had gently freed himself from Sanders' grasp, but he could still feel the pressure on his arm.

"Do what? Oh, you mean why did I go home and tell your wife about it?" Sanders cut loose with a melancholy laugh. "Do I really have to defend myself for that?"

"You've done me a great deal of harm."

"Uuh," Steffensen growled from behind them. "Go downstairs now and give each other a couple of punches instead of this drivel."

"Yes, as a matter of fact that's what we should do," Jastrau exclaimed suddenly, turning to face Sanders.

They could barely see each other on the dark staircase.

"All right, as far as I'm concerned, but what good will that do?" Sanders asked in a tone that seemed to indicate a shrug of the shoulders. And Jastrau understood. What good would a fistfight do?

"From my point of view," Sanders went on, "I don't have the slightest idea of what you want of me—not the slightest, I tell you. What is there to reproach me for? Two people, both of whom I regard highly, are wearing each other ragged in an unhappy marriage, and I—well, what shall I say—it's idiotic that I have to stand here and explain. Your wife was too good to go on living in ignorance of it—that's the whole story."

"Now we're getting somewhere," Steffensen growled sullenly. "Didn't I tell you so?"

Jastrau leaned against the staircase railing. Then he took an indecisive step down.

From up in the attic came a mumble of voices.

"But what business was it of yours, Sanders?" he asked glumly.

"Marriage—" Sanders began didactically.

"Oh, don't give me any of your theorizing," Jastrau interrupted testily.

Steffensen sat down on the stairs with a deep sigh.

"What do you want me to do?" Sanders asked ironically. "Shall we really go down and swap punches?"

"That wouldn't be theorizing," Jastrau exclaimed heatedly, trying to look Sanders in the eye. He saw nothing but a shadowy figure on the dark stairway. "It was your damned rotten nature that was to blame for it all. As soon as you smell a woman you become pathological—morbid."

Steffensen laughed approvingly.

"Well, what of it?" Sanders asked, a lilting tone of scorn in his voice. "What are you driving at, Ole? I'll freely admit that I'm pathological. Come to think of it, that's a strong word. But so what, Ole? I admit it. But then you must also admit that your marriage was unhappy."

"Was it?" Jastrau stopped. Then he suddenly burst out: "But was that any concern of yours?"

"No. And was it any concern of all the others there in the bar?" Sanders asked irascibly. "But we're going around in circles, Ole, and neither you nor I have time for that. The point I want to make is that your marriage didn't work out because marriage is a poor form of relationship between the sexes."

He leaned toward Jastrau. They stood on the stairs, engaged in discussion as if in a contemporary stage play. Above them Steffensen sat in an ungainly hunched-up position, since stairways are not made to sit on. He yawned loudly.

"And that's what I meant, Ole. Call me pathological or whatever else you wish. What does it matter? And suppose those people up there"—he gave a toss of his head—"are a bunch of nitwits, which as a matter of fact they are, what difference does it make? Because we're the ones who are going to prevail. We can't help but prevail. Sound reason indicates as much, and any fool can see it as soon as his eyes are opened to it. Lenin, he was only an instrument, he said, and I, perhaps I'm a poor miserable instrument, but I go along the same way, doing the best I can. So you see, Ole, I can't take you and your marriage seriously. I can't do it. It's only one of the millions of symptoms that indicate that we're right—those nitwits up there and I. And I can well understand that the loss of the boy is painful to you. But after all, I was only the pathological individual who broke up something that had gone to pieces anyway—because I don't suppose you suspected me of being in love with your wife, did you?"

"If only you had been," Jastrua replied wearily. He moved down a step, for now he wanted to go. Steffensen moved a step lower. He was following him in a sitting position. "Then I would have understood you better," Jastrau added.

Sanders laughed scornfully.

"Yes, of course. A bourgeois love affair with a diabolical seducer—that you would have understood. But that something is finished—that you can't understand."

"No, I don't understand anything," Jastrau replied bitterly.

"But had I known there would be trouble, then, of course, you realize that—"

"No, I don't."

"Ole—" Now there was a trace of a whimper in Sanders' voice. It rose in pitch, as if he were about to break into tears, and Jastrau pricked up his ears and listened, listened through the darkness. Through a window he could look down onto the dark pavement with its light and shadow from a street lamp.

"Ole—" The voice broke. "Are we on bad terms—then?"

"Yes."

Sanders turned and began to walk up the stairs. His footsteps had a melancholy, thoughtful sound. Then they became more hurried. He was getting back to the editorial conference, and Jastrau could tell that now his thoughts were only on it. There was a sudden hubbub of voices as the door above opened, then once more a subdued mumbling.

"We might have saved ourselves the trouble," said Steffensen, getting up from his hard seat on the stairway and stretching his legs.

"Are you any wiser than you were before?" he went on, jutting his woebegone face forth into the light from the street lamp as they stood on the corner of Gammel Kongevej. He was sober now.

"Well, yes. Yes, I guess I am," Jastrau replied, staring down the street. Something had been silently resolved. Not justly, not unjustly, but clearly and indispensably. And it had happened so calmly, as when during his childhood he had fervently placed a checkmark in a secondhand dealer's catalogue beside the name of a book he ardently wanted, and then at once the desire for it had imperceptibly disappeared. He had placed a checkmark on Sanders, and suddenly the desire for revenge had cooled. No hot, blinding fog. No impulsive, sudden fit of rage. Jastrau felt a sense of relief.

But Steffensen trudged along beside him with long, lurching seaman's steps and his cap pulled askew over his forehead.

"That was an illogical business," he muttered.

"Oh, you and your logic! Go on down into Stenosgade. Yes, we can at least see if there's still a light in one of the parlors," Jastrau said cheerfully. A feeling of joy and liberation surged through him. The summer night was luminous. The lights shone brightly.

They turned into Stenosgade and stopped on the sidewalk across from the Catholic church. Jastrau stretched and jumped up a bit to see if he could get a glimpse into the lighted parlor. Was it Father Garhammer who was sitting in there? He could not be sure. He thought it was a Jesuit who had his back turned toward them, but the window was too high and there was a lace curtain that frustrated his curiosity.

"Look. In there they're discussing logic."

"Yes, you've mentioned that often enough," protested Steffensen, who was filling his pipe. "But what kind of logic?"

"The logic of eternity, Steffensen. Tell me, Steffensen, do you believe in a world order that came into being at a definite time?" he said goadingly. "Or has the world order always existed? What do you say, Steffensen? You're interested in logic, so that ought to be right up your alley."

Steffensen carefully lighted his pipe.

"That's not logic," he snarled around his pipestem. "It's nothing but a stupid question that doesn't concern me in the least."

Jastrau laughed.

"That's what you think. But now listen to this. If you believe in an eternal world order—one that never had a beginning—then you also have to believe that this world we live in is perfect."

"Oh, go to hell."

"Or else you have to believe in eternal recurrence—the same thing over and over again. Isn't that right, Steffensen? And that's rather amusing to think about—that everything will be repeated eternally, that you and Anne Marie will live in my apartment on Istedgade—"

Steffensen slowly took the pipe out of his mouth.

"Have you gone off your rocker?"

"No, Steffensen," Jastrau rattled on. "Let me finish, and you listen. If the world order had no beginning, then it must have run through all the possibilities for change, isn't that right?"

"Aw—"

"And among the infinite possibilities is also the possibility of repetition, and if there is a possibility of one repetition, there must also be a possibility of infinite repetitions. Otherwise the world order has not been infinite. Tralum, tralum, Steffensen. Call it logic or barrel-organ lyricism—as far as I'm concerned you can call it what you will."

Jastrau laughed hilariously, but Steffensen would not unbend.

"And then?" he asked slowly.

"Do you believe we live in a perfect world?"

"Ha—!"

"No, you can't brush it off that way, Steffensen. Either that, or you have to believe in eternal recurrence."

"That's a hell of a thought."

"There, you see? And if you won't have it either way, you must believe that the world order had a beginning in time."

"Well, and then—"

258

"Then it must necessarily have come into being out of nothing. It was created, Steffensen, my boy. And consequently we have arrived at the concept of the Creator—we believe, we all believe, in God—tralum."

Steffensen did not reply.

He stared gloomily over at the windows of the lighted parlor and the dark, closed church. Then, as if lost in thought, he send a cloud of white smoke out into the night air.

"Well, hadn't we better go home and get some sleep, you old logician?" said Jastrau with a grin.

Steffensen nodded silently, and they walked down Vesterbrogade. Jastrau kept an eye out for women. He was in a sparkling mood. "Just look at her," he said playfully as a trim little craft sailed quietly by, leaving an aroma of feminine corporeality and perfume lingering in the night air. The darkness made the girls' eyes look big.

At Vesterbro Passage Jastrau and Steffensen remained standing on the corner of the broad sidewalk that juts out opposte Helgolandsgade like a point of land. The obelisk of the Freedom Statue rose darkly above the gleaming asphalt on which the glow from headlights and arc lamps fell, and in the distance, outlined against the blue of the summer night, were the two yellow faces of the Town Hall clocks, appearing as ovals in the perspective, and seemingly cross-eyed.

"I feel such an urge to let myself go, to go on a perpetual binge," Jastrau said with a sigh. The view over into the Town Hall Square with the few tall buildings irregularly blocking out segments of the night sky, the auto headlights darting over the asphalt pavement, and the shadowy swarm of people on the sidewalks filled him with an aching sense of longing. "But no—let's go home and sleep. I've got to look as if I've had enough sleep when I have my talk with Editor Iversen in the morning."

"About what?" Steffensen asked abstractedly.

"About the paper," Jastrau replied evasively. He did not want to make himself ridiculous. Suppose he did not, after all, hand in his resignation. They walked down Helgolandsgade toward home with a feeling of firmness of character.

"Look here," Steffensen suddenly exclaimed, "—there's an automat café on Strøget."

"Yes, but that's closed now. We couldn't get in there even if we wanted to."

"I'm talking nonsense. As a matter of fact, it isn't there any longer. A shoestore has taken its place," Steffensen said irritably. "But I used to go there so often during my first years as a student."

"Aha! Youthful memories."

"Oh, cut it out. But you see, when you sat in a certain place over by the window in that café you had a mirror behind you and another one right in front of you—damned if that sort of thing shouldn't be prohibited—and so when you sat and looked at yourself in the mirror there was an endless number of images, one within the other. Steffensen seen from in front and Steffensen seen from behind—my God, what a horrible sight! On into infinity, mind you. It's something I've often speculated about."

Jastrau laughed and swung one leg playfully out over the curb. "Ha," he said, "if it's the Jesuit that's bothering you, you can console yourself, for in recent years time has become a dimension, ha ha. Now even the Jesuits can't make head or tail of it."

Steffensen walked along, sucking on his pipe.

"You'll see. There'll be repetition—the same thing over again—even insofar as these new things that have been invented are concerned."

And in a sudden manifestation of rage, he spat on the sidewalk.

Chapter Four   Jastrau and Steffensen sat across from each other at the breakfast table. The phonograph belted out a jazz tune.

"Now the money situation is soon going to be critical," Jastrau said, thoughtfully crushing an empty eggshell.

"And you aren't doing a stroke of work," Steffensen replied.

"Are you moralizing?"

Steffensen sat and stared at him with a faint, mute smile.

Then Anne Marie came in with coffee. She put a new record on the phonograph. Her face was swollen, as if she had been crying. She looked run-down and miserable.

Jastrau smiled at her, but it was a nervous, unhappy smile that she sent him in return, and as quickly as possible she disappeared to hide herself in the kitchen.

Steffensen gulped down his coffee and said nothing.

Then they both filled their pipes.

How long could it go on? Steffensen could sit there, immovable and inviolable, for hours at a time without doing a thing. He was allowed to do so because otherwise the rooms would be empty, and in the barren apartment lay the threat of insanity. With the place empty, the feeling of degeneration would be too much to endure. Now, with people there, this feeling was tempered somewhat, as it was by the jazz from the worn and scratchy records on the phonograph. But this figure that sat leaning his chin on a hand, with a pipe dangling from his mouth, with his dirty collar and his positively malicious contempt—if he did not soon stir, make some movement, become a human being, then the feeling of emptiness would again assert itself, then he would be nothing but a lifeless object that could not keep it from asserting itself. And then hostility would break out.

"When you sit there glowering like that, what are you thinking about?" Jastrau asked in a nervous, ill-natured tone.

"I was sitting here and was about to have a thought."

The vagueness of the remark irritated Jastrau.

"You were about to have one. Does that amount to anything?"

"You bet. I'm sitting here thinking about a man with a derby hat."

"You're very amusing," said Jastrau. But why was there suddenly such a look of insecurity in Steffensen's eyes? The immovable figure had begun to stir.

"No, damn it," Steffensen said hesitatingly. "Just imagine now that one could take the lid of a human skull the way one would a derby hat, and could look in and see the thoughts. Ha—what a world! I've heard it said that thoughts were reality. Ha!"

Jastrau listened. There was a gruffness in Steffensen's voice, as if he wanted to confide in someone.

"Well, why not?"

"Yes, why not? Steffensen laughed dully. "I'm thinking of my old man, the respectable pharmacist in Aarhus. When he can't go to sleep, the old beast, he lies and figures out how a person can commit a crime without being found out. It's touching, isn't it? The bourgeois intellectual life, what?"

He was making conversation. Jastrau sat staring at him. It was simply awful, the number of teeth he had in his mouth. It was not a human mouth. But why was he talking this way? There was evidently something he wanted to gloss over. He wanted to shy away from it.

"What are you getting at?" Jastrau asked sternly in order to pin him down.

The shadow of a smile came over Steffensen's rigid lips. Then he got up with the mysterious, soundless, vagabond-like movements that Jastrau had observed in him before, and went to the door to listen to what was going on in the kitchen.

The phonograph had stopped playing. They could hear Anne Marie washing the dishes.

Steffensen smiled craftily. Jastrau kept his eyes on him. He felt no sympathy for him, but was completely caught up by his mysterious movements. He did not know what it was that had driven this son of a bourgeois Aarhus family to his present parasitic existence, and he could only guess at it. But Steffensen had not come out of it untarnished. It was plain to see that he was not spotless.

Steffensen had gone over to the sofa that Anne Marie usually occupied.

"Have you seen this?" he whispered shrewdly and lifted the spread from the sofa. A hole had been burned in it.

Jastrau shrugged his shoulders. "Well, what of it?"

"She's a slut to lie there like that, smoking cigarettes and tossing them away without watching where they land. She thinks it's bourgeois to be careful about a thing like that."

Steffensen laughed. But Jastrau only looked at him unappreciatively. Why was he being so incoherent? His pale bony face had a sinister look. His forehead seemed naked and abnormally large.

"I'd like to know if it amplifies the soul—isn't that what you call it?—to commit a crime," Steffensen went on dreamily. "Whether it really amplifies it, or if it's the same with murder as it is with drinking. When a person has one, then he wants more, and so there we are again—back on the subject of recurrence—that damned repetition. Why haven't I asked a murderer about it?"

"Are you delirious, man?" Jastrau asked. He was getting perturbed.

"No-o," Steffensen whispered cunningly and made one of his vagrant gestures to shush Jastrau. "But suppose one strangled her and then set fire to the sofa and the whole mess. After all, she gets dead drunk and lies there smoking and tossing lighted butts around, doesn't she? Who could prove anything? And as for having a bad conscience afterwards,"—he raised his voice and his eyes began to sparkle—"I'd like to know, damn it, what a guilty conscience feels like—if the feeling stays in your hands,"—he stretched out his big hands and held them up, curved, in front of him—"if your hands keep feeling her throat, I mean, or if you keep seeing her there before you. Hallucinations, you know. Or if you can't stand to see the place where the murder took place, the furniture, the inanimate objects, or—"

Jastrau followed his awkward movements, that were so much the more gruesome because they were made without a sound and were so in contrast to his customary immobility. But he could not really place credibility in what the whispering voice was saying, and he shook his head.

"I really don't have time to listen to your fantasies," he said, getting up as if he wanted to shake off the impression that Steffensen's words had left.

262

"Fantasies? No, damn it—I'm serious."

Jastrau looked at him unbelievingly.

"I have to go over to the paper," he said.

"But I tell you, I'm serious, damn it!" Steffensen exclaimed, taking a firm hold on his arm. "Can't you understand? I thought you might. Not, of course, when I think vigorously and use logic—because then you don't know what I'm talking about, or you couldn't care less. But this business of thinking in concrete terms, laying one hard fact upon another, and then, yes, then always coming up against a weak spot—"

"Listen, Steffensen—" Jastrau said. He suddenly realized that Steffensen had cracked up, and he stared at him.

But Steffensen went right on. "A weak spot, you understand, and then something has to happen. I'm forced to go ruthlessly ahead, I tell you. You don't know why, but there's a certain logic about it, a logic that's gone amok. And I must, I must find a solution—a solution that will take me out into the infinite."

"A solution to what?" Jastrau asked uneasily, glancing toward the kitchen door.

"Yes, to her—that's it," Steffensen nodded.

"I still don't understand."

"Are you curious about it?" Steffensen asked spitefully.

But then Jastrau gave up. "Listen, Stefan, I don't have time for all this. I have to get over to the paper. And you're not going to remain here. I won't allow it."

"No," came the hoarse, abrupt answer.

"You come along with me."

Jastrau tried to collect his thoughts as they stood in the hallway. His felt hat. Now he was in earnest. And his walking stick. He smiled faintly. Now he was going over to have his talk with Editor Iversen.

"Look," exclaimed Steffensen on one of the stair landings as he tugged roughly at Jastrau's arm, "I like you very much. I do, damn it, I do. But if *you* can't understand me, then I feel there isn't a soul who can."

"But what is it you want me to understand?" Jastrau asked cautiously. He suspected what it was.

"No, you can't. You're respectable like all the others, and all you'll do is laugh at me—or get maudlin."

He stood stock-still on the stairway.

"Because I am ridiculous—completely ridiculous," he suddenly burst out.

Then, without waiting for Jastrau, he went on down the stairs.

"I don't care to go with you," he said unequivocally as they went out the entranceway. Jastrau swung his stick in a show of indifference. But

Steffensen was already making his way along Istedgade. Seen from behind, he looked like a waterfront roughneck.

There was something provoking about his proletarian mannerism. It had been cultivated in imitation of some of the postwar artists and literary figures. It was a fashion.

But with Steffensen it was more than a mannerism. It was an all-inclusive protest. And it was also an act he was putting on. But was it? Jastrau had grown uneasy. If he were really serious, then there was a crime that was germinating within him. But it was simply buffoonery—yes, it was buffoonery. Jastrau let his stick strike hard against the sidewalk as he walked toward Vesterbrogade.

Wasn't it an imposition to barge in on others with one's private life and its problems as Steffensen did? Whether *he* had infected Anne Marie, or *she* him—Jastrau knew that was at the root of the trouble—did it make any difference? But Steffensen had been made an object of ridicule, and that he had not been able to bear. A typical case of a person going amok.

But then, who wasn't ridiculous? Take Jastrau himself. Here he was, having finally gotten a stylish hat on his head and a walking stick in his hand. Otherwise he would not be able to resign. The hat and the resignation went together.

Jastrau began to whistle. The benches looked so nice and comfortable beneath the trees along Vesterbrogade. Only a few customers were sitting outside the Wivel. The afternoon had not reached its high point.

The idea of resigning was by no means a new one. It had come into his head the very day he had gotten his job as chief reviewer for *Dagbladet*. Perhaps he had even mentioned it to one of his fellow workers. "I wonder when I'll get the knife in the back?" It seemed to him that he had once formulated the words. Hadn't there also been something about a thirty-year-old man in such an advanced position usually lasting four years? Had he not also quietly and cynically let such a remark escape? Of course. "So how will I manage to escape getting the knife between the shoulder blades?" Yes, he had once said that to Vuldum. And Vuldum had not reassured him—far from it. "The old men up there play us off against each other," he had said.

These four, five years. This feeling of insecurity.

Suddenly Jastrau halted. Everything looked so nice inside Tivoli. Sparrows were hopping about on the asphalt paths.

But this idea that to know and see things clearly gives one strength! Who was it that had perpetrated such nonsense? Was it not perhaps this very awareness that had made him unsure of himself and sterile as a poet? He had produced nothing in four years. Was it perhaps not this knowledge that sometime he might be thrown to the wolves, just as his predecessors had been, that gradually had undermined him? Suppose a person knew the date on which he would die. After all, he had had a wife and child—at that time. He had had to think of making a living.

Was it not also this feeling of insecurity that was to blame for the way he was now drifting? Was it not the reason for his drinking? For he did drink, didn't he? But then he smiled the same way he did when he went whizzing downward in the roller coaster at Tivoli. Well, yes, there were many reasons. And among them was the fact that he liked the taste of whiskey.

But all that was unimportant. Now he had made up his mind. How he had come to the conclusion he did not remember. He had suddenly broken through a thick growth of underbrush and found himself on a cliff overlooking the sea. Was it false romanticism? Hans Christian Andersen—The Bell? But that was the way he had felt. It was the way he felt now. To put it into words: "He walked across the Town Hall Square in the bright sunshine, whistling 'Come May, the mild month of May,' and went up to *Dagbladet* and handed in his resignation." With good and sufficient reason? Good, sufficient? He could give twenty reasons for his action.

But he could also, at this moment, ten minutes past two, on this corner outside the Paraply café, decide to remain on as the chief reviewer at *Dagbladet*.

How the sun could flash on the nickel-plated handlebar of a bicycle.

Whistling happily and yet feeling sad, yes sad, he walked across the Town Hall Square. All the buildings looked lovely and transfigured. How beautiful they were. The red color of the bricks, the Town Hall, the Palace Hotel, the Bristol. The red chestnuts. He felt as much at home there as he did in a living room—his own living room. He felt pleasantly at ease, like a familiar figure who cut across the square every day—a Copenhagener. There goes Jastrau, damn it.

Should he also take his leave of that? No, not today. But soon. And after many years he would come back and look at it with the eyes of a stranger.

Dagbladet's corner building became dear to him. Even the letters up there on the corner. They were clear, unsentimental letters. Once he had looked upon them with a feeling of awe. Now, already, their form had become a memory. He could sense it by the way they looked.

And the revolving door. And the staircase with the brightly polished railing. And the window with the view down into the asphalted courtyard that always was jammed full of bicycles. Flashing memories, all of them.

He whistled more softly. To the accompaniment of the melody he would take in these sights for the last time. Quietly he slipped into the editorial department. Very much like an everyday occurrence. The door to Editor Iversen's sunlit corner room stood open. Yes, he was there.

And there he sat in the sunshine with his long, legendary back bent forward over the desk as if he wanted to embrace it, his powerful arms extended over manuscripts and papers while he addressed the surface of the desk in a hoarse whisper. At least that was the way it looked, for the hand that held the telephone receiver was resting on the desk so that he could slouch over it while he listened or coughed a few words into the mouthpiece. His elongated animal-like skull and rugged neck were sharply silhouetted against the light. His mustache hung as if dripping from his upper lip.

Jastrau remained standing in the doorway. He cleared his throat, and one of the editor's large hands raised itself like a snake's head from the huge bulk of his body and motioned for silence.

When the conversation had been brought to a whispered conclusion, his head finally bobbed up, he hauled in his arms, sank back in his chair, and regained his normal stature. The long arms and legs assumed a discreet posture.

"Well, hee hee—if it isn't Jastrau, my literary editor!" he exclaimed in a tone of comic alarm. His eyes were lusterless. "I trust that nothing is wrong. You look so solemn—as if you were a whole delegation coming to see me."

Jastrau laid his fedora on the desk, sat down punctiliously, and leaned on his stick.

"Are you put out about something?" Editor Iversen asked with a trace of humor.

"No—far from it. But I've come to tell you that I'm resigning," he said, forming his words precisely.

The editor leaned forward slightly in order to subject the phenomenon to a closer inspection. Then he stroked his big drooping mustache, and his face took on an expression that made it look as if it had just bobbed up from a pool of water.

"Well, I declare," he muttered after a pause. "That surprises me. Isn't this a bit sudden—as far as you're concerned, I mean?"

"Not really," Jastrau replied. He now felt that he had arrived at the decision long ago. He had reached it at the very same time, five years ago, that he had stepped into the job.

"Are you resentful about something?"

"No."

266

"Is it a matter of money?"

"No."

"Well, I declare. This comes as a surprise." The editor inclined his large cranium and scratched his neck. "But now there'll be three long summer months in which you won't have anything to do," he added hopefully.

"Yes, and it's those three months I'm reckoning with. The contract calls for three months' notice, you know."

Jastrau sat there stiffly. Inside he was tingling.

Editor Iversen shifted slowly in his chair. It annoyed him that now he also had this to think about.

"But it's a long summer," he said suddenly, seizing upon a way out with a sense of relief. "A lot of things can happen, you know."

"It's no use."

"No?"

"No. Because between now and September I'll be going to the dogs, and then there'll be the fall season and all those books. No—" Jastrau shook his head in premonition.

"It's strange," Editor Iversen replied listlessly.

"I'd rather quit now and not ruin the work I've done by turning out poor stuff. I feel that I can take pride in what I've done so far," Jastrau said quickly.

"Yes, so you can," the editor replied politely. Dark patches had appeared beneath his eyes. That always happened when he felt moved during the principal speech of an evening, and Jastrau had the deepest mistrust of them. Nevertheless, his own eyes began to blink. Tears?

"Yes, your work does you great credit," the editor said as if wool-gathering, in the slow drawl that everyone in his department knew how to imitate. It sounded so honest, that Jastrau had to blink even more.

"But suppose you took a year's leave of absence," came the gentle suggestion.

Jastrau sat up straighter. He had heard rumors that Editor Iversen intended to retire within six months, and this strengthened his resolution.

"No, it's no use."

"It's strange. So you insist on leaving. But whom shall I put in your place?"

"I don't know. I haven't any idea."

"You'd do me a big favor if you would suggest someone," the editor said earnestly.

"I don't very well see how I can decide who's to be my successor—no, I don't see that," came the firm answer.

"If only you would," Iversen said wearily. The editor's listless eyes rested on him in a friendly manner. They were a darker shade than usual and there was something profoundly human in them. "If only you would decide the whole thing. More you can't ask of us. We'll extend ourselves as far as we can." He flung out his hands in a gesture of mournful irony. "And then you'd be doing me a big favor in the bargain."

Jastrau smiled.

"But I can't appoint a man to my job and then come back and toss him out again if I should take it into my head to return to normal."

The editor again brushed his hand across the lower part of his face.

"Well, I wouldn't regret it if you did that, hee hee." A sudden look of cunning came over the old man's face. "You really ought to think about it, and then, hee hee, it might be that you'd feel sorry. Shall we let it go at that?"

Having said this much, he looked content. The uncertainty had been dispelled by some sort of agreement, and this suited him best.

But Jastrau pulled himself together with a start. "No, by September I'll have gone completely to the dogs."

"Can a person say such a thing?" Iversen drawled, as if it made no sense to him. "In that case it's really very distressing."

"It's something I have to go through," Jastrau said in a lilting tone. "And in the meantime I won't be fit for anything."

Jastrau's attitude was one of irresponsibility. He swung one leg over the other and no longer had to lean on his stick.

"Well, then it really is very distressing—for me to see such a thing happening. I thought, you know, that you were on the way up—not down."

Jastrau puckered his eyebrows.

"Yes, because I hear that you're spending a good deal of time out on Stenosgade with the Catholics."

"No, that's not true," Jastrau replied emphatically.

"It did seem a bit strange," Iversen said abstractedly. "Wasn't it you? But then it must have been somebody else. A person sits up here like a father and hears about everybody, and he grows old and gets people mixed up. But anyhow, I believed it. And indeed, I could well understand it better than what you've just told me—that by September you'll have gone to the dogs, just the way I might say that I'm going up to Kregome on Thursday—hee hee."

He smiled out into space and shook his head.

"Incidentally, have you heard that the farmers now want it called Krejme because that's the way they pronounce it, hee hee?" he added.

Jastrau sat still and stared at him.

"Krejme," Iversen replied, lost in a smile.

Then he got up and walked stoop-shouldered over to a desk, opened a drawer, and took out a sheet of writing paper.

"So you want to resign," he muttered down toward the desk. "I'm really very sorry about it. It makes me feel genuinely distressed."

But suddenly he had forgotten the writing paper and walked over toward the big corner window that looked out on the sunlit teeming square.

"It looks so nice today."

The tall figure stood hunched up by the window with his hands in his pockets. "It always does, by the way. Come and see for yourself, Jastrau."

Jastrau got up. He knew it was a sign of a great favor when the editor-in-chief wanted to share the view from his window with one of his staff. To stand by that window with him was like standing on a balcony with the head of the state.

"I'm so fond of this view here," Editor Iversen went on slowly and with feeling, absorbed in a monologue. Jastrau was now standing beside him. "I never tire of it. And so I stand here so often and think that some poor boy—yes, look, there comes one down on the corner, the one with the handcart—and think that perhaps some day he'll sit in my chair. See—he's looking up here. Yes, and now it's I who am standing here. Some day he may remember that."

His voice was touched with emotion, although it might at any moment take refuge in irony. To Jastrau, however, the words seemed weighty and full of significance as the editor at the same time put his arm over his shoulder and leaned his tall, bony frame against him. Was it a human being who was revealing himself?

It was an oddly problematic, unsettled moment. Jastrau would always remember the square as it then lay spread out before him, a genial, whitish expanse slanting like the sea when viewed from the face of a cliff. And he would recall the dark, transverse column of people crossing from Vesterbrogade to Strøget, the constant move-ment, and all the bright, cheerful women. As he stood by the window, the tall, stooping editor with the dull, listless eyes and the animated square below merged into one picture representing journalism, the most living picture of all, but one with overtones of weariness and disillusion.

"Yes, I was once a boy like that. And now here I am. But for how long? I think of that so often."

There was something naïve about Editor Iversen's tone of voice when he became philosophical. One platitudinous thought abruptly followed another. When moved to emotion, he was like the readers of his paper.

"Yes, death. A person gets old, Jastrau." He looked down at him. "But how young you must be, since you are determined to go to the dogs. Hee hee. So I don't suppose you give much thought to death. I'm constantly reminded of it. Incidentally, it can be rather funny at times." He snickered, and now he had managed to overcome his emotion. But then, in order to cover himself, he added, "Despite it being so tragic. For example, yesterday I had a visit from H. C. Stefani—you know him. He was in mourning and wearing a nap hat. His wife was Norwegian, and up there they call a high silk hat a nap hat."

Jastrau suddenly grew tense under the weight of Editor Iversen's arm. Shouldn't he be allowed to resign from these five years of his life in peace? Was Steffensen's life again casting a shadow across his path? He could guess what had happened.

But the editor went on. He lapsed into an anecdote, having freed himself from tragic thoughts.

"Yes, I knew her quite well—a large woman. 'You're a fine-looking lad when you're wearing a nap hat,' she said once—we were at a big funeral. They call it a nap hat up there in Oslo. But as I was saying, yesterday Stefani came up here. He was completely upset—his wife had died—and he had her ashes with him in an urn. And you know what? The urn was in a briefcase out in the vestibule."

He stared far out into the blue sky.

"He cried—yes, he did—over that briefcase."

Steffensen's mother was dead. Jastrau envisaged her in rough outline as a big black shadow. But why was this shadow being cast over him at such a bright moment? Couldn't Jastrau be permitted to live out his own life? Now he was handing in his resignation, and he should not be compelled to think of anything else.

"Hee. Yes, it's funny when one has known Stefani—rather well. He's always had a hard time of it whenever he caught sight of a skirt, and they say she was jealous. A big Norwegian woman who is jealous in the bargain—but now he had her in a briefcase—*bon*. And then he cried. I really felt sorry for him."

Jastrau began to stir uneasily.

"Do you have to go, Jastrau?" asked the editor. "Well, then we're agreed that you'll consider it once more. You're so quick-tempered, Jastrau."

270

Jastrau looked at him. The boyish smile rippled beneath the mustache.

"No, I'm resigning today."

The editor doubled up a little, as if he had received a blow. Again there were dark patches under his eyes.

"You've always been a decent person, and I think it's foolish of you to want to go to the dogs. It would be better if you went on a trip and then came back and became a great man. But it's honest of you to want to leave rather than remain and write trash. Ha—we have enough of that."

Jastrau smiled in embarrassment. Again his eyes were blinking.

"Now I'll say good-by," he said.

"Do we have to say good-by now? We don't have to be ceremonious about it, do we? There are still three whole months during which we can shake hands. Well, good-by." And he waved roguishly.

Jastrau bowed and left the room, deeply affected.

"Ah—finally!" exclaimed a journalist who had been sitting waiting in the vestibule. It was Gundersen with the dark glasses and the Negroid lips. "It was a lengthy chat you had with the rhinoceros. What sort of a humor is he in?"

"Excellent," Jastrau said, grinning. "We stood at the corner window with tears in our eyes—both of us."

"That's fine. Let me in to see him, then."

And Gundersen knocked on the open door.

Jastrau slipped quietly away. He was so engrossed with his feeling of invulnerability that he did not want to talk to anyone. Whistling gently, he went out the door.

A faint smile played about his lips. Good-by. Good-by. The bright assurance of now being able to go tranquilly to the dogs made him tingle inside as he walked down the stairs. Down to the dogs. Good-by, good-by.

Steffensen's mother was dead. Should he tell him? No, why? Now everything was moving along smoothly. Where? Downward? And there was momentum in it.

And as he stood on the sidewalk he felt an overwhelming urge to reward himself. He had earned it. Yes, indeed. And naturally he turned to the right and went into the Bar des Artistes.

It was dim and deserted inside. Not a soul around. Nor was it later than three o'clock.

The red portières closed behind him with a subdued zipping sound and shut out the sunlight. Suddenly the day advanced several hours toward evening, and twilight set in. Far in the interior the huge array of bottles, glasses, and the bar with its brasswork gleamed like a cryptic alchemistical laboratory.

The little waiter had drawn the portières of the door leading to the courtyard a little to one side and stood bent over with laughter.

"Come and see, Herr Jastrau," he snickered. "Herr Kjær is about to yank out one of his back teeth."

Jastrau had to take a look, and out in the courtyard he saw a heavy-set gentleman in a smart gray-green suit who was performing a strange solitary dance. His movements resembled most closely those of a disabled jumping jack who could kick out with only one leg.

"What's he using, Arnold?"

"A pair of pincers, of course. We found an old, rusty pair."

And then Jastrau saw the inevitable Kjær lean his head far back, as if looking up at the little quadrangle of blue sky, and begin hopping about on one leg.

Jastrau and the waiter laughed.

Suddenly Kjær wheeled around and triumphantly waved the pincers in the air.

"Eureka!" he exclaimed as, with the sweat dripping from him, he stepped back inside. "Have you ever seen a tooth to compare with that?"

He held forth a black and bloody object with the crooked roots hanging from it.

"Why didn't you go to the dentist?"

"No," Kjær exclaimed, raising his hand in a gesture of alarm. "I'd never have found my way to one, and if I had I'd never have found my way back here. I'm no explorer."

He sat down at the round table and held the tooth philosophically out in front of him.

"You want to see it, Jazz? It has expression."

And then he held it over toward Jastrau.

"Can't you see? It looks like my lawyer."

Jastrau felt as if he were blind and shook his head.

"Then it's because you haven't had your Lundbom cocktail yet. Arnold—two of them."

And then he sighed and stared at Jastrau with his foggy blue eyes.

"Why are you looking so happy and untalented today?"

"Oh, I've fought hard for my right to go to the dogs, and today I won."

Kjær's whole body shook with soundless laughter.

"That's a lot of nonsense," he snickered. "Because it's completely impossible to go to the dogs, Jazz. A person dies first. It's just as hard as getting to Canada. Now Little P. has sold his ticket again, and he's stuck in Esbjerg."

Kjær drew out a blue envelope.

"Just listen to this. He wants to borrow money from me or from Lundbom here so he can come back. I think we'll let him have it. He's lonesome for us, the poor devil."

Chapter Five

The inevitable Kjær had become groggy, and his face was so bloated that the cleft in his chin was the only characteristic of which there was a visible trace. Now and then he would give the worm-eaten tooth that lay on the table a shove and mutter something about his lawyer. And Jastrau was silent. Lundbom's cocktails buzzed in his head, but he felt so relaxed in the twilight of the barroom. Only when the portières were drawn aside and a flash of light from the incandescent, busy street penetrated the room as from a projector did he give a sober start.

"Uh-h," muttered the slumped-over Kjær, and shook his head. His expression was bewildered. His pupils did not react. And with that egoism so typical of people who have been drinking, Jastrau suddenly found himself disgruntled with the irregularity of what was going on at the table. He got up with a vague feeling of contempt and walked slowly through the room to see if any other acquaintances had come in.

"Hello, Herr Jastrau," sounded a man's voice.

"Hello, Herr Jastrau," a woman's voice chimed in, and he encountered a pair of luminous gray eyes—the jaded, but at the same time curious, eyes of an experienced woman.

It was Fru Kryger who, with the intrepid Herr Raben, had come in for an afternoon apéritif.

"Won't you be good enough to sit down and have a drink at our table?" Raben asked amiably as he got up. Jastrau noticed that the scar on his cheek was becoming to him.

"Why yes—thanks," Jastrau said with a facetious sigh as he leaned politely against the back of a chair. "But it will have to be a very weak one." He raised his eyebrows. "Otherwise I'm afraid the result will be ghastly."

In the semidarkness of the bar, Fru Kryger's figure was like a gleam of light; her ashen hair, gray eyes, and gray silk dress were all of the same hue. Only a stormy morning seascape, with waves of icy silver

273

and a gray, glowing mass of clouds behind which the sun had disappeared could produce a similar effect.

"I dare say you live hard, Herr Jastrau," Fru Kryger remarked, bending forward toward him with a show of interest.

"A bit hectically perhaps," he replied and sat down.

"They say you do a lot of drinking," she went on aggressively.

"They also say I'm a Catholic," he answered. Why did she never once take her eyes off him?

"That I don't believe," she said, laughing. "But I don't understand how you find the time to set in circulation as many rumors as you do. You must be a regular Renaissance man. And of course you have to read all those books and review them. Incidentally, I read your reviews with great interest."

"I'm damned if I do," Raben interjected cynically. Was there already rivalry between them?

"Don't you? They're brilliantly written and always the first thing I look for when *Dagbladet* comes in the morning."

She referred to Raben as "du." So they were on familiar terms, Jastrau thought. Then perhaps her meaningful glances and ardent gestures were only a bit of coquetry intended to arouse Raben. Nevertheless, Jastrau could not help staring into her gray eyes. He suspected that beneath the gray silk dress her knees were rather bony.

"Book reviewing is somewhat subjective and vague," Raben said superciliously.

"Do you think law is more objective?" Jastrau shot back, squinting.

Fru Kryger laughed.

And when she did so, the lines in her neck indicated that she was no longer so young.

"In my dictionary, objective means the same as boring," she chirped. "When you men begin to talk objectively, then I thank my Lord and Creator that I'm a woman."

"When women have feelings and good looks, what more do they need?" Raben replied banteringly.

"Do you think so too, Herr Jastrau?" she asked quickly.

Just then three Dubonnets were placed before them.

"I don't understand women. I only have a weakness for them," Jastrau amused himself by saying as he looked deeply into her eyes. She knew that he was going to be divorced. That was why her eyes were so vivacious, and he displayed his teeth in another smile.

She laughed. "There, you see, Herr Raben—a sensible man at last. But you're also a critic."

Her laughter was consciously girlish.

"And I thought a critic was by nature more austere and scholarly," she went on, swinging her foot mischievously.

"Well, that's what I am."

All three of them laughed.

"Hm. But I really have such great respect for critics." Jastrau could hear that she was being frivolous. "And I can't understand how they know if what they write about a book is true."

Raben guffawed.

"It must be a good job, and well paid, I should think," he then remarked in an almost benevolent tone, directing his dark eyes at Jastrau.

But Jastrau felt like going on with the game. A transformation had come over him.

"Yes, it pays splendidly," he answered, stretching his legs out in front of him. "I live a carefree life. I can well afford to order three Dubonnets."

"But you make enemies," Fru Kryger interjected.

"If I didn't, how would I be able to put up with life?" Jastrau felt like a virtuoso. It made no difference what he played, as long as he was playing. "Is there anything that braces a person up more?" he went on. "I swear that nowhere is the Danish language written better than in the reviews that tear a book to pieces. It's as if you can hear the language sizzling in an article of that kind. Have you ever noticed that?"

"Yes, power is a fine thing," Raben sighed.

"Yes, power is wonderful." Jastrau laughed exultantly. Now, for the first time, he realized what an important and responsible position he had held. The thought made him feel good. He felt a desire to brag, and he stared playfully and provocatively into Fru Kryger's eyes.

"I didn't think you were so bloodthirsty," she objected.

"Bloodthirstiness, Frue,"—he thrust his lips out wolfishly— "bloodthirstiness stimulates the imagination. It sharpens a writer's language and his whole style. Take a critic's laudatory reviews and his denunciatory ones and set them side by side, and you'll see that the scathing ones are the good ones. Tight syntax that strikes home—now here, now there—subtle and smooth with amazing images, both novel and exquisitely nasty. And yet people say malice is not creative. The laudatory articles, on the other hand, are almost always limp as a dishcloth and sloppily written."

And he laughed.

"Yes, power must be wonderful," Raben said, rubbing his hands together.

But Fru Kryger leaned forward and laid her hand on Jastrau's arm. "I don't believe you mean a word of what you're saying."

"Why shouldn't I mean it?" Jastrau asked ironically. "If not, why do you think I stay at it year after year for a modest salary? Do you think it's to endear myself to those whose work I praise? Ha ha, the poets think the praise is no more than reasonable. And if I happen to praise one of their colleagues, then it's because I lack guts. No, I stay at it because the rough-and-tumble fighting is good. I like to hear Skræp sing.* That's it in a nutshell. And if I ever retire or get fired—which I hope won't happen for a long time—I want my name on the pillar up there. You know that pillar, don't you, Frue? I know that then I'll come to yearn for that sound, that very distinct sizzling in the language—Skræp making itself heard."

"You fellows aren't exactly idealists," Raben observed with a faint smile of contempt.

But Jastrau went on playing.

"There are critics who go around whistling all day long like little schoolboys when they're engaged in a squabble. Yes, there's a lot of joy and satisfaction in it."

He leaned back and showed his teeth again, and he was tingling inside. He could have sung every word he said, so little had they to do with reality. But Fru Kryger was still leaning forward and gazing at him. He could not get her to take her eyes off him. What did she want?

"You don't really mean that, do you?" she asked, pursing her lips.

"Don't I?" came the lilting reply.

Just then there was a sound of erratic footsteps, the scraping of a stick skidding on the floor, and a whispered "Have you got hold of yourself?" Fru Kryger gave a start. A stocky figure was weaving around over in the far end of the room. It looked like a scuffle.

"What—?" she managed to say breathlessly.

Then the figure approached with his arms around the shoulders of the two small tail-coated waiters. It was the inevitable Kjær, blind drunk. He would have walked right into the wall if he had not been led. Slowly and cautiously the procession made its way past their table.

"Who in the world was that old man?" asked Fru Kryger, hunching herself up as if she felt cold.

"Old man?" laughed Jastrau. "He's no more than forty-five."

And he looked smilingly over at the clock above the bar. Yes—right on the dot. It was half-past four.

* Skræp was the name given to his sword by an ancient Danish king. It sang for him with a special note when he brandished it against an enemy.

276

"Uh-h—I can't get him out of my mind," Fru Kryger said, trembling all over. "I feel positively cold."

Raben laughed.

"No, you mustn't take it that way," she exclaimed in agitation. Suddenly she looked across at Jastrau with a sharp, almost malicious expression. "Will you be that way some day, Herr Jastrau?"

"I don't think so. I'm not as regular in my habits as Kjær."

Raben slapped his hand against his thigh.

"As Kjær?" Fru Kryger repeated, and her eyes suddenly showed alarm—a quick shifting of luminous gray tones. "Do you know him, then?"

Jastrau leaned toward her with a teasing familiarity.

"He's one of my closest friends," he said.

She shook her head. "It's strange how men look upon that sort of thing. I haven't recovered yet. Hadn't we better leave? Yes, we're going, aren't we? It's so dark here."

Out on the sunlit sidewalk Fru Kryger took them each by an arm and wormed her way in between them.

"One forgets when the sun is shining," she said, laughing. "It's strange—I've always felt so nice and cozy in that bar."

"You should have had a cocktail," Raben said patronizingly.

Jastrau blinked his eyes. He felt the alcohol. Around him the traffic was a solid streaming mass. Thoughts and words were one, life a swirling rapids. He smiled to himself.

"Oh, by the way," Fru Kryger said, squeezing his arm, "the other day you wrote about a contemporary Irish book, didn't you? About Odysseus, I think it was."

"It was Vuldum who wrote about it. It was Joyce's *Ulysses*."

"Do you know the book?"

"No, but I have it.

"You have it? I don't suppose you'd let me borrow it," she said eagerly.

Jastrau looked down at her with an ironic expression.

"Do you have a strong constitution?" he asked mischievously as he looked down at her slight figure.

"A strange question to ask," she exclaimed.

"No, because it's a long, difficult book, impossible to wade through, and famous besides. You need muscles to read that book."

"May I borrow it?"

"Yes, of course."

"Well, here we are at your paper," Raben said. They were standing in the shadow of *Dagbladet*'s building. "And so I suppose we must say good-by." Jastrau did not know if it was a polite hint that he should make himself scarce, but he chose to interpret it that way.

"Yes," he said, "I have to get up there."

He said good-by. But again Fru Kryger's gray eyes rested on him inquisitively. What was the meaning of that look? Ah, good Lord—was he so interesting? Nevertheless, he could not help being attracted by this animated scrutiny of a woman of the world. He had to return her glance, smile in return, look dazed, but only for a moment.

Then he tore himself loose and pretended to go in through the revolving door—all the way around and out again. Fru Kryger and Raben had already disappeared. She still seemed to shimmer before his eyes. Was she on the loose? Raben? But forget about it. Just let the revolving door swing around. Away with everything. Say good-by to it.

There he stood a few steps above the street level and perfectly free to go to the dogs. The consciousness of it made him feel expansive. How painless everything was at the moment, simply because he could let his destiny take its course.

Now he had to go home. Home? A faint, canny smile crossed his lips as he sauntered across the square. Was it a home? A few rooms that housed him and that he was despoiling. Steffensen! Anne Marie!

A good-looking girl brightened the entrance to the Scala. Very pretty and erect of carriage. Should he turn and speak to her? Oh—all the stupid nonsense one had to utter in such a situation. He could feel that he had been living ascetically. The girls formed too conspicuous a part of the street scene for him.

Take another look at her. He smiled at a pair of girlish eyes and said, "Pss-t." All this nonsense one had to go through with. Here he was, with perfect freedom to go to the dogs, and he was not making use of it.

A fish in sunlit water. Sharp outlines of buildings and traffic. Somewhere inside his brain a cocktail glowed.

Then a woman dressed in black stepped down from a yellow streetcar.

Steffensen's mother was dead. Again something stark. There was a peculiar relentlessness about the things that were happening to Steffensen that neither could nor should be mollified.

Jastrau's lips curled in a scowl.

Why should he concern himself with what happened to another person? It was both pleasant and beneficial to sit of an evening and listen to another person grow expansive. It was like getting drunk. But

Steffensen did not grow expansive. He was as arrogant in his incommunicativeness as a puzzle. Ha ha—a puzzle? He? Well no—nothing more than a tiresome crossword puzzle that had almost been solved. And if Steffensen and Anne Marie were now sitting there at home, then—another row. Why had they chosen his particular apartment for their eternal bickering. No, he would soon have to cut loose from them. It was too unbearable.

He felt so lonely here in the shade of Reventlowsgade. He wandered close to the traffic lane and zigzagged along the sidewalk as if he felt more inclined to walk on the other side. He would, of course, be so hopelessly lost, alone, if— Yes, that was it. He must have those two persons around him, otherwise—otherwise he would have no life, nothing to live for, ha ha ha! Good Lord—couldn't he get along without them? It was too ludicrous. Steffensen. Oh yes, him he might even put up with. But Anne Marie. She was sick, yes she was. A love affair? The soft curves. A woman. Something that goes around fussing over you. Something—perhaps that was it—with an expression of fear in its eyes and—

Something that was untouchable.

That was it. His mother had died early. The sacrosanct ideal of womanhood.

An idea. Or almost an idea, a solution.

The red-haired janitor was standing in the entranceway.

"I have a buyer for your phonograph."

"But it isn't for sale," Jastrau replied sardonically.

"I thought—"

"No, no," Jastrau sang out in a teasing tone and went unconcerned up the stairs. An idea had slipped away.

Anne Marie was at home alone. Something that had an expression of fear. She sat sewing on a dress. Something untouchable.

"Do you have two dresses?" Jastrau asked jocularly as he sat down opposite her. "I didn't think you did."

She looked up at him in alarm.

"Where is Stefan?" she asked.

"Don't know."

"Are you on bad terms, then?"

"No, unfortunately."

She put the dress down on her lap and stared at him.

"Don't you like Stefan?"

At first Jastrau did not answer. He gazed mischievously but with feeling into the milky whiteness of her eyes. Why did the iris seem so milky? A weak, feminine face that looked as if it had never been completely formed. How easy it was to torment her. Steffensen's mother was dead. Wasn't this a knife to play with?

"Do you like him?" he asked abruptly.

A deep flush spread irregularly over her throat and the lower part of her cheeks, as if she had been scalded. Her lips twisted, then went slack. No firmness to her features. She was about to burst into tears.

"How can I tell?" she replied. Her Aarhus accent sounded so sorrowful, so hopeless.

Jastrau smiled gently. He did not have the heart to do anything else. "No, one never knows."

"Yes, one ought to know, but I don't—I don't know. I just don't know."

A tear glistened in her eye.

Jastrau glanced away in embarrassment and stared down at the tabletop. It was dusty. One could draw pictures on it with a finger.

"I feel happy today. Would you like to go with me to Tivoli?" he went on without a transition.

And he looked at her again. Even he could sense that his smile was insipid.

"But I don't have a dress I can wear," she exclaimed in confusion.

"You have two of them, don't you?"

"No, you mustn't tease me," she entreated him. "And besides, a servant girl—with you—in Tivoli?"

"It certainly won't be the first time I've gone to Tivoli with a servant girl," he said, laughing. The remark caused her to smile.

"I happen to feel happy at the moment," he went on persuasively, "and now you're coming along with me before I change my mind."

"But Stefan—"

Jastrau raised his eyebrows in mock concern.

"Will he be jealous?"

"Oh, he might be all sorts of things."

Jastrau laughed as she said it. "Yes, that's probably the only way to describe his frame of mind—full of all sorts of things."

Anne Marie looked at him without comprehending.

"Well, then, I'd better get myself fixed up," she said.

Jastrau could not help smiling as they went down the stairs. Her jacket and skirt were faded and worn, and the heels of her shoes run down. Around her neck she wore a mauve kerchief that looked dark and shabby. But nevertheless he felt compelled to take her by the arm, because he regretted his smile.

"Now if only you don't have a hole in your stocking," he said in a strangely ecstatic tone, and laughed.

She withdrew her arm nervously.

"No—please."

But he laughed again. "Because if not, I'll go and fall in love with you."

"I'm not going with you," she said quickly in a bitter tone.

"Nonesense."

"You'll only make a fool of me," she said timorously.

Then Jastrau laid his hand on her shoulders, turned her around roughly so that she faced him, and stared into her eyes.

"Do I look like a person who would make fun of you?" he asked vehemently. She averted her eyes from him.

"No, no," she whispered with deep feeling. At the same time a look born of experience came into her eyes, and she raised her head in a saucy manner. "You look more as if you'd like to kiss me."

And then Jastrau kissed her gently. She leaned her head far back, as if she expected a passionate kiss.

Instead their lips merely brushed each other in noncommittal fashion.

Something untouchable.

"Well!" said Anne Marie.

Jastrau remained standing there, observing her benignly. Suddenly he reached out and smoothed her left eyebrow into an even arch.

"Let's go now, little girl," he said slowly.

Anne Marie bore herself more erectly as they walked down the street.

"You're nothing but a big, fat boy," she said, laughing and looking down at the tips of her toes.

Tivoli lay bathed in the late afternoon sunshine with wide expanses of glistening asphalt between the green trees. The tree trunks were dusty and gray, and over the pathways the city's summer heat lay in a low haze, a dry, electrifying atmosphere.

"So this is Tivoli!" Anne Marie exclaimed, taking a deep breath. Her surprise lent a strong Aarhusian lilt to her voice. And it struck Jastrau that after all she was only a little girl from the provinces. Perhaps she had never before been to Tivoli, but had only heard people talk about it when she was a child.

"Have you never been here before?"

"No." And then she began to rattle on. Yes, it was an experience for her. Her father had told her about it—an enchanting description remembered from the days when he had been a soldier. Lord only knew what her father looked like. He did not have the heart to ask her what his occupation was. A laborer? And again he smiled compassionately. A hole in her stocking. Now this glowing but ominous feeling of compassion again filled him with a kind of gratification that could so easily slip into eroticism.

Should he show her Tivoli? There was the outdoor stage, built in the style of a Greek temple. Some acrobats in black and red tights that accentuated their round buttocks and rippling muscles spun around in the air, outlined against the gold and blue of the sky. Should they stand quietly in the audience and gape? He said hello to a young university professor whose violet-blue eyes were appraising Anne Marie from behind his glasses. Yes, somewhat puzzling? Jastrau smiled. And then he gently edged up very close to Anne Marie, who stood staring at the acrobats.

There was a thick crowd of spectators. Look—look! Out of the sky, a face turned toward the earth. It looked blue and blood-red, as if it were about to burst. From the man's teeth was suspended a large apparatus, consisting of a revolving wheel which flashed in the sunlight and hoops in which four acrobats—two men and two women—made swallows' nests* while the wheel whirled around.

Anne Marie was fascinated and excited.

And it seemed to Jastrau as if he saw the park in a new light. Or perhaps it was an old light, remembered from his childhood years. He and Anne Marie moved on. Look—there was the pantomime theatre with its peacock-tail curtain. They made the customary round of the asphalt paths, weaving in and out among the strolling spectators. There was the concert hall in Moorish style. People always walked slowly in this park—an easy, enjoyable Tivoli kind of saunter. And over there was the Chinese pagoda.

The buildings had not yet faded into the twilight between the trees. They stood out clearly defined as obvious imitation structures in the reddish sunset glow, and it was precisely their unreal quality that made them pretty and exciting. The Alpine landscaping of the roller coaster was altogether too colorful. The mountains were not Alps. And the colored lamps in the flower borders and along the ponds hung from what were crudely revealed as rusty iron pipes, not yet transformed into glowing flowers.

The huge illuminated arches that vaulted over the pathways and had a defoliated appearance among the crowns of the trees seemed

* Part of the acrobatic repertory consisting of hanging by the knees from a trapeze or hoop and grasping the feet with the hands.

more than anything else like a complicated croquet court for giant children.

"You've never seen my son, have you?" Jastrau said.

"No."

"Oh well, we won't go into that," Jastrau said, feeling momentarily disorganized and cynical. "He was whisked away from me over the telephone," he said jokingly. "Everything is being whisked away. But as a matter of fact, I'm very happy today. I must be sure to bear that in mind."

"Are you?" Anne Marie asked. She felt she ought to say something.

"Yes, by Jove, I am. I've committed one of my life's big stupidities today, one of the really big ones."

"Does that make a person happy?"

"Yes."

They were inside the Hall of Mirrors and saw themselves distorted in the concave mirrors. They became round and fat, and laughed at the sight. They became long and lanky, and made grotesque faces. They were endowed with long, stilt-like legs and foreshortened torsos, and long torsos and short, badger-like legs, and at last it was a real relief to see themselves in a normal mirror and shake off the distorted images. Indeed, Anne Marie became a very nice-looking girl in that mirror, perhaps a bit gross and with an unfortunately weak chin. If only her skin had not looked so sickly and sallow, if her cheeks had been flushed like those of a clerk in a dairy-goods shop, then it would almost have been a joy to walk with her. Jastrau laid his hand on her shoulder and turned her away from the mirror, and in doing so caught just a glimpse of himself in his light, finely-checked trousers and dark jacket—a combination of a Negro jazz band player and a ship's cook on shore leave, and a bit on the heavy side. Yes, that much he was just able to discern, and it was enough.

So that was how they looked.

"But now I'm in a good mood," he said softly.

It had become dark in the park. The evening sky shone blue between the dark treetops. There was an aroma of violets in the air. And in the restaurants and other establishments the lights were being turned on.

From the throng of people came a dynamic rustling that was like the sound of a forest at sundown. Polished shoes and bright eyes gleamed through the darkness. And Anne Marie walked closely beside him.

But why did he now become so confounded paternal and take her by the arm? It was the shadowy coolness of the treetops that led him to do it. It was probably also the mingling of melodies from the various orchestras that made the evening air seem permeated with a hum of insects and the murmur of voices—all the indistinct, living sounds that were audible there amidst the lights and shadows. Yes, undoubtedly the people were partly responsible too. He was doing the same as the others.

They strayed into a small rock garden where there were caves and grottos, a rococo and ludicrous bit of park architecture. But inside the caves there was the subdued red and green glow of large aquariums with fish gliding through the water. People stood looking at them in quiet fascination, their faces palely lighted by the green and red glow like anonymous poor folks standing outside shopwindows.

"Look! See the fish!" Anne Marie exclaimed in childish glee as she dragged Jastrau over in front of one of the aquariums.

Some large red fish were pursuing and snapping at each other with soft muzzles, and behind them came a swarm of small, striped perch, a teeming mass of tails and fins in rapid motion, while bubbles effervesced up through the green, illuminated water. A long eel floated with his glistening body suspended down through the aquarium like the stalk of a plant.

And a moment later, Jastrau was just as hypnotized by the gliding movements of the fish as the other spectators.

Then he gave a start. Midway in the tank was a pearl-gray fish that was remaining motionless in an oblique position with its bill-like head down at the sandy bottom. A sinister strength radiated from its unruffled composure. It was conscious of its power.

And now it was impossible to understand why he had not caught sight of it immediately. It was the center of attraction, fearsome and imperturbable. And when it shifted its eye ever so slightly, an electrical tremor ran through its body.

It was a pike.

"Why is it that I'll never forget it?" said Jastrau. And they went on.

At the Divan II, the lamps were lighted in the long stretch of arbor leading to the restaurant. There were espaliered trees and festively fluttering ivy, a mildly romantic atmosphere.

"I'm going to order lobster, and then you must congratulate me on my stupidity today," Jastrau said gaily, kicking out with one foot.

"That isn't the sort of thing you congratulate anyone for," she said soberly.

"Yes you do, because at least once a year one ought to commit a stupid act as an offering to the gods."

And then they were sitting at one of the tables, with huge lobsters and white wine between them. A cool evening breeze stirred the ivy into gentle motion. And the distant music was borne on the air like the humming of a swarm of insects, now and then like a single, fragile insect's wings vibrating close to their ears—a very subtle, delicate sound.

Anne Marie's eyes had the look of a sleepwalker's as she stared stiffly past Jastrau, seemingly all at sea.

"I can't understand—" she said helplessly, and then could go no further, as if she could not collect her thoughts.

Jastrau fondled her stubby hand, which lay on the tablecloth.

She glanced at him as if to get her bearings, as if she were just waking from a sleep.

"Would you believe it—I'm very unhappy—but—" Her eyebrows became restless. "But—I'm not aware of it right now. How can that be?"

"It's because you're with me," Jastrau replied jokingly.

Anne Marie forced a smile and brushed her hand across her forehead.

"Hadn't we better have a drink?" Jastrau proposed gently.

"Yes, of course—I'm supposed to congratulate you on some sort of nonsense," she said, staring at him. There was an uneasy look in her eyes—now observing him, now looking into the distance.

"No, on a stupidity."

"Yes, a stupidity—that was it. But I'm so stupid—I—" And suddenly she burst into laughter that was a little too loud. She gave a frightened look around and shrank back into herself.

Jastrau raised his glass of gleaming wine and smiled. Beside the red lobster shells her dishpan hands had a pale, whitish look. But he ought not to be thinking such thoughts. Concerned with aesthetics and feeling superior. She was a little, live female, she was. A sinner. Now why had that word occurred to him? Ivy, coolness, and intoxication. But that word!

He raised his glass to her.

And she nodded awkwardly.

She took such a firm hold on her glass. No grace in her movements, no ease. No flower stem, she.

And then she again became preoccupied.

"Now I'm with you," she said suddenly, but still staring past his ear out at the arbor walls, out into space. "How can it be, then, that all the while I have to remember that I'm not in love with you?"

"Now, now, now," Jastrau said in a sing-song voice, but with a tender smile.

She was looking at him with wide-open eyes.

285

"No," she said. "But—"

For a second or two she looked straight at him. For a moment there was an uncertain contact between an outer and inner light, flickering and quivering like two projector beams trying to merge.

"Once I had a friend," she went on, shifting her glance. "Her name was Agnes. She was engaged to a young man—a musician. But she deceived her fiancé with his father." She took a bite or two of lobster. "When she was with the father she loved him, and when she was with the son she loved him." She spoke rapidly now, but then she stopped for a moment and felt her way slowly: "And then it seemed to her—I mean that's what she told me—that for the first time she really felt as if she loved her fiancé."

Jastrau looked down at the tablecloth so that their eyes would not meet.

"Can that be true?" she said in a matter-on-fact but inquiring tone.

"It's probably true, if that's what she says," Jastrau replied.

He did not dare look at her. He felt overwhelmed by compassion.

"Oh—what I'm telling you is really nonsense," she said dejectedly. "I don't understand anything at all."

Jastrau reached for a slice of white bread.

"You're—" he began, but got no further because he noticed that he was crumbling the bread between his fingers—he was breaking bread. And immediately he laid the bread aside, as if it had burned his fingers. He was breaking bread! He was breaking bread! Always this pious gesture when he was drinking in the company of women. This Jesus that seemed to be in his blood!

No! No!

He screwed up his eyes and suddenly looked across at Anne Marie, stared and stared at her as if she were to blame. No! No! She looked at him, and slowly her eyes lit up with fear. She could not take her eyes off him. She was helpless, at his mercy. Her mouth fell open and her chin sagged.

"Did you know that Steffensen's mother is dead?"

It came like a slash from a knife. No Jesus here. No cloying sentimentality toward fallen women. Mary Magdalene. He ought to know how to vindicate himself.

For a moment he saw white. The gleam from a knife. And he heard the sound of his own voice ringing through the room and taking on reality. Did you know that Steffensen's mother is dead!

And at once he was filled with such remorse that it was painful. He compressed his lips and held his breath as if that might prevent the words from reaching her. But then he saw the inevitable happen. She

286

dropped her lobster fork. He let his hands fall on the table and stared at her in desperation.

"Oh, no," he groaned.

Anne Marie sat completely rigid. A deep flush spread over her neck above the mauve kerchief. Her moist lips glistened in the yellow light from the park lamp.

"So you know the whole story," she said in a whisper.

"Yes."

"Then you know that I'm sick." She was about to cry.

"Yes."

"Do you think I'll ever be well again? Oh—you know—you know so much. But that this should happen! That Hans Christian should get this disgusting disease!"

"Hans Christian?" Jastrau said quizzically. He was not being inquisitive. He was simply very unhappy. And now he had to blurt out this question, as if it were any of his business. She ought not to answer. He looked at her imploringly, but she had already begun to pour out a whole stream of confused words and emotions. Like a sleepwalker, she had stepped over the edge.

"Yes—Herr Stefani, and then me, and then Stefan. Oh, how could I help it? I came from a poor home and got a job in this high-class pharmacist's house. Fru Stefani—oh, is she dead? She didn't have an easy time of it. She was strict—but she treated me fairly. She *was* fair. She always went stamping around in big, high-topped laced shoes. It was she who nabbed Hans Christian. She always got what she wanted."

"But you mustn't tell me about it," Jastrau said, trying to keep her from going on.

"Yes—because what mustn't you think about me? But after all, I'm nothing but a stupid young girl. Stefan was going to the university. He looked just as self-important and stuck-up as he does now, but not so crude and dirty—no. And I wasn't in love with him. But he was a university student and the son of Stefani, the rich pharmacist, and one night he came into my room. I wasn't in love, not at all. I had known a chauffeur before him. But what mustn't you think of me? You're so good—"

"Nonsense," Jastrau said, turning his wine glass.

"Yes you are—otherwise you wouldn't have us living with you. I wasn't in love with him, so it wasn't right of me. I wasn't in love with Hans Christian either. Never. But he gave me liqueurs to drink, and that makes a big difference. But with Stefan—that time I had had nothing but my evening tea."

Jastrau had to laugh. "Yes," he said, "that makes matters considerably worse."

"No, no." She glanced across at him with a frightened look. "You mustn't make fun of me. And now Fru Stefani is dead. I'm so unhappy."

"Hadn't we better have some coffee now?" Jastrau suggested.

"Yes, but what do you think of me?" she exclaimed with greater intensity than before. Her eyes shone. "I had known Stefan for a month. Yes, a month. And then one evening his father brought me the liqueur. It was fine liqueur—very fancy—I can't remember what it's called, but it had a green color. Actually I didn't think it tasted so good, but I drank it anyhow because it seemed like a treat. And then it happened. But I couldn't help it, and I didn't dare tell Stefan. And oh, I suffered—you don't know how I suffered—and I didn't dare look Fru Stefani in the eye. And Herr Stefani could sit there at the dinner table and look back and forth from Stefan to me. He knew everything. And then the way he would smile. Why did he do that?"

Jastrau shrugged his shoulders in embarrassment, and Anne Marie stared at the tablecloth with a vacant expression.

"But can you understand what happened then?" she went on, as if talking in her sleep, as her eyes grew wider. The yellowish whiteness of the tablecloth was reflected eerily in them. "Can you understand that it was then I fell in love with Stefan? I couldn't do anything else. I was deceiving him—with his father—so could I do anything but fall in love with him?"

She gaped at him and added hastily, "It was certainly foolish, wasn't it?"

"No, it wasn't," Jastrau replied firmly.

"And then—no, no, I can't—" She wrung her hands. "You can't expect a woman to tell about it."

She looked over at him with her eyes flashing.

Jastrau shook his head and smiled.

"I think we should pay the bill and go," he said quietly.

"And then I got sick," she exclaimed vehemently. "This disgusting disease. Herr Stefani had been over here in Copenhagen. And when he came home, then—oh, no—do you think—no, a woman *can't* recover from it. With a man it's different. For them it doesn't amount to anything. But a woman?"

"Are you going to a doctor?"

"Oh, there's nothing that does any good. I never know whether I'm sick or well. I don't know anything about it. I'm not allowed to live like other folks. And what have I done? Was it anything so bad? Was it? Yes it was—it was wrong—but—"

288

And all of a sudden she shoved her plates and glass to one side, hid her head in her arms on the table, and began to sob.

Jastrau got up, went over to her, and gently stroked the back of her head. What should he say?

Then she raised her head with a start and seized his hands.

"But you mustn't tell Stefan that his mother is dead, because then he'll hit me again and torment me." Her lips were distorted, and her mouth opened and closed like that of a fish.

"Why do you keep on seeing Stefan?"

"It's he who—no it's—but he thinks it's his duty." She screamed the last word. "They gave me my notice—immediately—even though it was Herr Stefani, and then me, and then Stefan. They sent me packing—bitch that I am. And am I really anything else?"

She got up, brushed the hair away from her forehead, and stood there swaying her hips in a lively, provocative manner.

"Am I anything else? Am I anything else? I want to go and dance, that's what I want to do. I want to drink myself blotto. I want to—"

She stretched out her arms and threw them around Jastrau's neck.

"And you're going to dance with me all night long. You're so good—so good. You're going to dance with me. But I'm sick."

Sobbing, she hid her face against his breast.

The ivy was fluttering so festively all around them.

Chapter Six

Jastrau sat at one end of his dining room table and gazed out through the dust-coated windows that had not been cleaned from time immemorial. Long streaks left by a rain some time in the remote past looked like seaweed on the panes, and now and then the smudgy figures on them gleamed with an opalescent light.

A gleam like that of amber, Jastrau thought as his mind dwelt musingly on his neighbor's white curtains in the forenoon sun. But it struck him at once that the gleam was not like that of amber. A gleam of amber? How had he happened to think of that?

He was conscious of a sense of relief. Anne Marie was walking about the kitchen, boiling eggs. Everything was peaceful in the dark apartment. Steffensen had left and had remained away.

How dusty and dilapidated everything looked. He got up. Should he clean the place up, get rid of the clutter? That big Shrove Monday rod topped with the figure of an elf. It would have to go. But he couldn't. Not yet. There were pangs that could not be obliterated—yet. For sometime he would have to get rid of them. He stuck his hands in his pockets, turned on his heel, and went into the living room. Oluf! No, it would have to remain standing there in the corner yet awhile, that Shrove Monday rod. Then he would in any event have that sorrow relegated to a corner, a fixed and garish object. A sorrow. A Shrove Monday rod.

He could dust the room. He took out his handkerchief and rubbed the frames of the two photographs, those of his mother and his son. He breathed on the glass that covered them and polished it until it shone, and finally he put them back in place. A cryptic movement of his hand, a symbolic gesture. He had to make it whenever he stood before the two pictures, for perhaps they had the power of warding off a misfortune.

Then he sat in the rococo chair for a little while and looked at the Negro fetish. Steffensen had spoken of the apartment as a ship. A dilapidated chapel would also be a fitting description. The chapel of a religion in process of germinating out of the dusty furnishings around him, out of the stained clothing he wore like a Negro jazz-band player or a ship's cook, out of people and events. But what a sense of relief he felt. Steffensen was gone. And suddenly he realized that he and Steffensen had been confronted with a showdown, spiritual or physical. But how did things stand now?

Now Steffensen was gone.

"The food's on the table," Anne Marie called from the dining room, and Jastrau went in. He felt as if he had begun to build up something new again in a small way, one grain of dust upon another, and he smiled at Anne Marie.

"Thanks for yesterday," she said like a nice girl.

Jastrau sat down.

And as they sat there with their eggs, bread, and coffee, things became very cozy.

"We might as well be married," Jastrau remarked with a smile.

Anne Marie swallowed hard and shifted her glance in embarrassment.

"No—we won't talk about that," she said imploringly.

Jastrau laid his hand on her bare arm.

"Well, it's true," he replied gloomily. "That damnable—" he went on and then stopped. "But I could engage you as my housekeeper."

"Yes, that would be more like it—as filthy as things are here," Anne Marie exclaimed with a scornful toss of her head.

She looked over at the windows.

"How those windows do look!" she added.

290

"Oh, what of it?" Jastrau said with a laugh. "At least the birds haven't made use of them."

"No, because that means luck," Anne Marie sighed. "And luck—there's none of that here. No."

Her voice rose ominously.

"Yes, I seem to catch a glimpse of it in the offing," Jastrau said quietly as he poured some coffee. "So now you'll be my housekeeper, and I'll go over and take up my job again."

"You'll do what?" Anne Marie asked in surprise.

"I gave them notice at *Dagbladet* yesterday," Jastrau replied with a trace of a smile. "That was the stupidity we—"

"Yes, but what will we live on then?" Anne Marie exclaimed. "We—no, I mean you, of course."

"I could go over and take up the job again," Jastrau said hesitatingly. Then everything would be solved. He enjoyed the thought as a little glimmer of joy, a bit of relief.

"But a person can't do that."

"Yes, I can."

"Oh, everybody's crazy. You and Stefan—" Anne Marie shook her head so violently that her thick hair began to fall down over her forehead.

"That's right. Stefan infected me with his craziness. But now he's gone."

"Where did he go? Don't you know?" Anne Marie asked nervously. "Oh, you really mustn't tell him that his mother is dead, because then he'll take it out on me. You won't—will you?"

"No, no, but now he's gone," Jastrau said reassuringly.

"But he'll come back, he'll come back," she said in a tone of alarm. A deep flush began to flare up over her throat, and with a brusque movement of her hand she swept the hair away from her forehead.

"No, no—why should he do that," Jastrau asked, a bit exasperated.

"He'll come to get me," came the despairing answer.

"No, no."

"Oh, then you haven't understood a word I've said."

And with a violent start she lowered her head and hid it in her arms. Her shoulders shook as she sobbed quietly.

Jastrau got up and began to stuff his pipe.

"Yes, of course he'll come," he said slowly and reflectively. "But now we are two to his one. You'll see—everything will be all right."

He felt so composed and rueful as he lit the pipe.

"Now there are two of us, isn't that right, Anne Marie? Now we're Jastrau and his housekeeper. Unfortunately, we're forced to maintain a platonic relationship," he added with a faint, melancholy smile, fondling his pipe affectionately. Something untouchable. Perhaps it was just as well. Her figure was rather coarse, her lips altogether too moist. Something untouchable, unfortunate, feminine.

Anne Marie lifted her head but kept her hands raised to her temples so that at any second she could shield her eyes. A few tears glistened in them.

"And now you're going over and take up your job again," she exclaimed with a moist, bright-eyed smile. "Aren't you? You'll promise me that. You will, won't you?"

Her eyes radiated happiness.

"We-ll," Jastrau replied with a profound sigh, "I don't really know about that."

"Yes, yes—you'll do it. You'll promise, won't you? It's a promise, isn't it? And you always keep your word."

Jastrau smiled wearily.

"I think we should say I will try to do something reasonable!"

"That sounds strange.

"Yes," he said hesitantly. "It could be that I'd—yes, that I'd withdraw my resignation. It might be that I'd try to do it, but I can't promise."

Nevertheless, it was in such a frame of mind that Jastrau later went over to *Dagbladet*.

He could, of course, go into Editor Iversen's office and say that he had acted rashly. It would make him an object of ridicule with the entire editorial department. But wouldn't he also be ridiculous if he quit the job?

On the stairway he met Bruun who, in riding boots, was on his way down to an imaginary horse.

A gracious "Hello, Jastrau," a regal wave of the hand, but no questions. It was rather strange, because Bruun was not a heartless individual. He might well concern himself over his neighbor's future.

Jastrau walked into the dusk of the vestibule.

The woman on duty in the editorial office was abusing someone over the telephone. Her face was set in an expression of rage. Gundersen was leaning against the big green table. He asked if there was anything new.

"No, everything's the same as it was," Jastrau muttered philosophically, feeling annoyed as he did so.

"Have you been drinking?" Gundersen asked in a matter-of-fact tone.

But otherwise not a word. It was as if he were floating about in the empty room. Not even Gundersen, the inquisitive head of the lobster shift, questioned him. Was he wandering around among ghosts? Or was he a ghost himself?

The police reporter gave him a paternal and patronizing slap on the shoulder, then hurried on.

The door to the editor-in-chief's office stood ajar, so that a narrow shaft of light penetrated the vestibule.

The copy editor was sitting in his room, and raised his head. "Well, is it you, Ole Jastrau?" he said with casual amiability.

And from behind a closed door at the rear of the editorial department came the sound of Eriksen's hollow cough.

Everything was going along in routine fashion. No one knew that Jastrau had resigned. It was as if he had not done it. Nothing had happened. Editor Iversen had forgotten it. And he probably was sitting stooped over his desk, his walrus mustache drooping over his mouth, with a far-away look in his eyes and his thoughts in Rangoon.

From force of habit Jastrau seated himself in the chair outside the editor-in-chief's door, as if waiting for an audience. Did he really want to go in and see him? He sat back comfortably with his hat in his lap and looked around as if he were a stranger, and it filled him with a melancholy pleasure.

The woman on duty had stopped talking. She had hung up the telephone and was sitting at her desk, very red in the face. A little later a white cloud of powder drifted up around her head.

"There's no one in Herr Iversen's office," she suddenly shouted from across the room. "You may as well go in, Ole Jastrau."

Jastrau got up with a self-conscious smile.

"Damned if I'm going in there," he said in a low voice. "I was just sitting here having a nap."

"Were you out again last night?" she asked in a tone of envy.

Jastrau nodded and slipped quietly up to his room. He might just as well write that review. He had promised Anne Marie to do something sensible.

And that, then, would be his last review.

The four yellow desks shone in the sunlight. Now it made no difference that the poorest of them had been assigned to him. He no longer had any ambition. And the word DAGBLADET, with the letters reversed, was outlined in dark shadows across the patch of light cast from the window onto the varnished floor.

He composed each sentence with a strange feeling that this was a leave-taking. Yet, he could go downstairs and say that he had acted hastily. He could—yes, he could. Nevertheless, this was his leave-taking. He knew it. It was impossible to keep a subjective tone out of the article. The style resounded with it. Each word took on a double meaning. Keep his feelings in check! Be disciplined! There—that was something that resembled objectivity.

There was a knock on the door.

Jastrau quickly glanced at his watch. It was four-thirty.

"Come in."

Yes, sure enough, it was Arne Vuldum, who was just coming from the library. Looking deathly pale in the sea of sunlight that flooded the room and gleamed on the varnished woodwork. Lusterless and gray in the face. With his elegant derby hat, his walking stick, and the inevitable cigarette.

"I thought I'd find you sitting here. And I did so want to have a chat with you. Is it something exciting that you're reviewing?"

He seated himself on the creaking sofa.

"No. A translation of Renan," Jastrau replied. "I'm treating him like Papa Renan—in a filial tone, you know."

"That's as it should be," said Vuldum. "And it's the easiest thing to do."

Jastrau turned in his chair so that he could keep an eye on him. Didn't he know anything about it, either? But Vuldum's eyes did not have the gray, unfathomable, animal-like expression that they usually assumed when he was lying in wait to ambush someone. His thin lips were not compressed about his cigarette. His hard face only looked tired—very tired.

"Renan was in reality only a cruel intellectualist," Jastrau remarked.

"Only?" said Vuldum with an air of preoccupation.

Jastrau looked at him with distrust. Did he want to borrow money? But Vuldum caught his expression immediately and managed a genteel smile.

"Actually, yes," Jastrau went on. Vuldum could no longer undermine his position. He was invulnerable. Just say no to him if he wanted a loan. Perhaps entice him into doing so, and then—

"Actually, yes," Jastrau repeated in a haughty sing-song tone. "His ideal was, after all, essentially an intellectual dictatorship, cruel and relentless—not at all construed as a transitional form."

Jastrau's eyes shone mischievously.

"A spiritual and aesthetic dictatorship—I must say that's a pretty ideal," Vuldum replied, raising his eyebrows. "And a little cruelty, a little bloodthirstiness—why not? At six o'clock, when I'm sitting there at the long table in my boardinghouse, I'd relish such an idea. An aesthetic Cheka. Have you ever lived at a boardinghouse, Jastrau?"

294

"Yes. For short periods at a time."

"For short periods," Vuldum repeated slowly and spitefully. "But not for fifteen years—fifteen years."

"No."

Vuldum's expression grew sharp.

"Then you don't know what hate is. That tablecloth—I tell you! The people! That row of faces bent over that tablecloth! It makes a person sick. An aesthetic Cheka would sentence the whole kit and caboodle to death." He made a gesture with the flat of his hand, as if lopping off a row of heads. "And what a relief that would be."

"You're bloodthirsty, all right," Jastrau exclaimed with a laugh.

"Yes, it's made me vicious. You sit there and talk with this row of heads and are affable and then go back to your room, to an inferno in tasteless Skindergade style. You sit there—and read Mallarmé. Mallarmé in the most hideous of all worlds—the boardinghouse world. Huh!" He stood up, feeling cold all over. "And then, 'endlessly view the dreary chimneypots,'" he quoted to himself as he went over and stood in the sunlight by the window.

"This is apparently one of your bad days, Vuldum," Jastrau remarked.

Vuldum looked at him as if he expected sympathy.

"Yes, today I'm being visited by the executioner's apprentice—the headsman's boy, who doesn't know his trade. A miserable bungler. He was supposed to make another attempt to chop off my head, but this time the axe didn't cut through either. It's still sitting here in my cervical vertebra." He rubbed his neck as if racked by pain. "And now he's trying to wriggle it loose."

"Nicotine," was Jastrau's unmerciful diagnosis.

Vuldum smiled wearily.

"It isn't only nicotine. It's life. I swear I'd have been a different person if I'd had a room to live in with nice things around me, and not these ugly boardinghouse furnishings."

"Oh, we all live in a shabby manner," Jastrau protested. Now and then, a glimmer of opalescent light came from the streaks left on the windowpanes by the rain.

"Yes. We poor immortals." Vuldum spread his hands in a tragicomic gesture. "We who sacrifice our lives for a well-turned sentence."

He looked gloomily at Jastrau. But his long, severe face with its prominent, pointed chin did not invite sympathy. In the sunlight, his red hair shone with a pale, chilling intensity.

"Shouldn't we go out to a restaurant and have something to eat together? Then I'd escape the boardinghouse," he proposed quietly.

"I'm busy."

"I see," came the sharp reply, and Vuldum's lips tightened. For a moment there was an awkward silence. Formerly, Jastrau would have felt compelled to oblige; there would have been a tug at his heartstrings. But now it made no difference to him. He shrugged his shoulders, with a show of regret, to be sure, and he was about to incline his head teasingly to one side when Vuldum drew a ten-krone note from his vest pocket.

"Look, I don't suppose you could change this for me, could you, Jastrau?"

Taken by surprise, Jastrau shook his head.

"Well, then I may as well go. You're busy. Good-by, sir."

His words had the faint metallic resonance that Jastrau knew so well. The door closed with a discreet, barely perceptible bang. But it was a bang, was it not? And then Vuldum was gone.

Jastrau wanted to leap up and run after him. They could, indeed, have eaten together. Vuldum was tired. He needed company. Wasn't that it?

Wasn't it?

He needed someone to talk to—living as he did in that boarding-house world. He was dejected and tired. He was weak. An attack of weakness.

Jastrau got up and stood for some minutes by the window. The executioner's apprentice! He rubbed his hand against the back of his neck and had the uncomfortable feeling that it shrank from his touch. Wriggling the axe loose. Why did people never realize when they ought to help each other?

Because Vuldum had suffered an attack of weakness—yes he had. But no—Vuldum weak? No, no, that was unthinkable.

But good God! Jastrau paced back and forth. He was going to miss Vuldum.

"Damned if I won't end up as a humanitarian," he sneered half-aloud.

Good heavens! This room with its glossy, varnished floor and the four shiny desks, the radiators marred by the caps of the beer bottles that he and the other journalists had opened on them, the wastebaskets that sometimes were filled with empty bottles—a recognized characteristic of all editorial premises—and the dry atmosphere of central heating. Should he say good-by to all that? Farewell, dearly beloved telephone. A farewell poem.

He could, of course, go down to Editor Iversen right below him and tell him it was all the result of rashness. That he could do. Perhaps Editor Iversen was sitting there expecting him. And besides, he had promised Anne Marie—his housekeeper now—to do something sensible.

Suddenly he grabbed the telephone and called his home.

"Is that you, Anne Marie? This is Ole Jastrau."

Strange that he should be so formal in giving his name.

"Is it you?" came her voice. It struck him how melodious her dialect was. "Yes, Stefan has come back." She paused for a moment, and at that same instant Jastrau knew that he would not be going down to see Editor Iversen. "He's upstairs at the janitor's—drinking beer."

"Where did he spend the night?" Jastrau asked. Now his life seemed recognizable to him again.

"He slept at Bernhard Sanders'."

"Yes, of course. What a fool I am not to have thought of that!" replied Jastrau. Everything was infinite. A toast to the infinitude of the soul.

"You mustn't fix any food for me, Anne Marie," he went on. "I'll be home later. I'm doing something sensible."

He laughed. A toast to the soul's infinitude. Then a person was not faithful to his friends. Was that right, Steffensen? For faithfulness had nothing to do with infinity.

"I'm doing something sensible," he sang into the phone.

"I don't believe that," came her voice, faint and uneasy.

"No, you had better not."

"But Herr Jastrau—you promised. You said—that we were two against his one, and now I'll be alone." He heard her whimpering.

Jastrau bent over close to the telephone mouthpiece as if he were kissing her on the forehead. How afraid and unhappy she was. Tears came to his eyes.

"But I'm coming back, little girl. But later. I'm very definitely coming back."

The sound of suppressed weeping bubbled in the receiver.

"We are two together, aren't we? We are two, aren't we? I'm depending on you. I don't have anyone else, Herr Jastrau. And you're coming back."

"Yes, of course."

"I'm depending—on you."

He hung up.

But why had he said he was going home later? All he had to do was take the review up to the composing room. And then—ah yes—he wanted to gather his strength. For what? A dinner with *snaps* and beer, all by himself. Just to give his face a rest. But he must not let her down.

When he had been up to the composing room and left hurried instructions, he quietly left *Dagbladet*.

In the revolving door he met the copy editor.

"Listen, Ole Jastrau, it's a shame to take all the material away from Vuldum.

"But I haven't done that."

"Well, it seems that you have. He was in to see me a moment ago and spoke about a book—I don't remember who it was by—and I suppose he was right in feeling that he had been shoved aside.

Jastrau laughed.

"Have you ever known anyone strong enough to shove Vuldum aside?" he asked.

The copy editor smiled.

"But now remember this the next time, Ole Jastrau," he remarked and waved good-by.

So quiet and undramatic, then, was to be Ole Jastrau's departure from *Dagbladet*. He was to vanish like a ghost.

No one knew anything about it.

And he could not help smiling at the soundlessness of his exodus. The silence rang in his ears.

But now for a dinner with *snaps* and beer.

He smiled again.

He must not fail her. Not let her down.

In front of the hotel entrance next door to the Bar des Artistes, two deep wicker chairs had been placed. The hotel was pretending it was summer. And in one of them lay sprawled Little P., the one who liked to play matches for drinks. He waved a pale hand when he caught sight of Jastrau.

"What are you doing out here—in all this fresh air?" Jastrau asked.

"I'm sitting and observing life—as it goes rushing by," came the feeble voice from the depths of the chair.

"I thought you were in Canada."

"No, maestro, I got scared when I saw the North Sea. It's an ugly body of water." He raised himself up in the chair. "But look, maestro, how about slipping inside and playing matches for a gin and tonic?" He carefully smoothed out his thin hair.

"No. I need food."

"Well, maybe later then," said Little P. with a faint smile. "And in

298

that case I'll just remain sitting here for the time being and observing life—as it goes rushing by."

His vacant, glassy eyes followed a streetcar that was going toward the Town Hall Square. It was a very ordinary streetcar.

Chapter Seven   Tra la la! Yes, the sun is going down. Jastrau kicked out skittishly with one leg. Light-colored, checked trousers. A Negro jazz-band player or a ship's cook on shore leave.

Istedgade. Infinity. The houses lay so that the street looked like a long blue gorge in the last red puddle of the sunset. The fifth-story windows mirrored a violet-blue sky.

And harp music filled the air. The sounds of distant trolley cars vibrated through the summer evening. Up between the rooftops the angels sang, because up there songs resounded so clearly, so clearly:

> And where have you been, Billy Boy, Billy Boy?
> And where have you been, charming Billy?

No, it was not he who was singing. It *was* the angels. A hoarse male duet and a nasal phonograph, high, high up among the rooftops. Open windows. A breeze blowing through his apartment. A curtain fluttered outside a window.

Yes—the janitor and Steffensen. They were having a blowout. Well, well.

Jastrau sang as he went up the stairs. A summer atmosphere outside all the stairway windows. He hummed as he let himself in. Doors and walls vibrated with the singing and stamping of feet and the incessant sound of the phonograph.

> And where have you been, Billy Boy, Billy Boy?

And then he saw Anne Marie standing in the dark hallway.

"Oh, it's good you finally came," she said breathlessly and leaned against him.

"Yes, yes, yes," he sang.

"But—have you been drinking too? Yes, I can smell it," she exclaimed in dismay, giving him a shove.

"No, no, no—I've been eating," he hummed.

"And I, who thought we'd stick together," she whimpered. "You promised me. You promised me so very definitely."

She leaned against the wall, and he could discern only her eyes in the darkness. They shone like a pool of water at night.

"Little girl, little girl," Jastrau said comfortingly, and wanted to pat her on the cheek.

"And where have you been, Billy Boy, Billy Boy?" They were shouting in the rooms upstairs. Chairs were being shoved about. Then one of them overturned.

"Oh, they're so drunk," Anne Marie sighed.

Jastrau exhaled a miasma of *snaps* fumes. "Don't worry—I'll protect you," he said hoarsely. It was difficult to speak out of rhythm with the strains of Billy Boy. And then he pushed the door open, stood suddenly inside the half-darkened room, where two shadowy men were stomping around in a bearish foxtrot, jubilantly placed one foot on an overturned chair, raised both arms in the air, and let out a yell.

Steffensen shoved the janitor away and joined in, shrilly and inarticulately, and the janitor, who in his blue overalls seemed completely shapeless, resembling more closely than anything else an ogre with elephant's legs, doubled up with laughter and slapped his hands against his thighs.

"Oh, what a life," he moaned.

Three bottles of port stood on the table.

"It's your wine," Steffensen said with a grin. "I—I've sold some of your books."

"Oh, yes—the fine books," sighed the janitor. He flung open his arms, Steffensen again tumbled into them and up against his overall breast, and the clubfooted fox trot was noisily resumed in the darkness. "And where have you been, charming Billy?" Jastrau could distinguish their faces only as two yellowish ovals devoid of expression. Only their eyes shone, as if tears were glistening in them.

"They're crazy," Anne Marie whispered. She stood beside Jastrau in the folding doorway.

"And she won't drink. She's become too genteel for that," Steffensen shouted scornfully as he went on stomping through the dance. A cool summer breeze blew through the rooms.

"Yes, yes, yes," Jastrau sighed as he poured a glassful of port and raised it in a toast.

"To the infinitude of the soul—*skaal!*" he shouted. At the same moment the record ran out, so that his voice rang out far too loudly through the room.

300

"Ho ho," whispered the janitor. "This won't do."

The phonograph needle wobbled back and forth over the record, and the room was filled with a hideous noise like that of a streetcar on worn-out rails.

Anne Marie stopped it.

"Why isn't she drinking? What did you do to her while I was away?" shouted Steffensen.

"Hush, hush," whispered the janitor, motioning for quiet with his big paws.

"We've been to Tivoli," Jastrau hummed, and took a drink.

"Where have you been?" snarled Steffensen.

"And where have you been, Billy Boy, Billy Boy?" the janitor quipped in a stage whisper, and then broke into laughter. "Oh, what a life! But hadn't we better shut the window, you drunken louts?"

"No damn it—if we do we won't be able to breathe in here," Steffensen shouted.

"Quiet, quiet!" said the janitor.

"Quiet, quiet!" Jastrau repeated mechanically.

"I have a right to open my mouth if I want to," Steffensen shouted.

"You can open your mouth as much as you like, but you have to pour something into it," the janitor said in a reassuring whisper as he laid a heavy hand on Steffensen's shoulder. In the darkness their figures merged in fraternal proximity.

"Hadn't we better turn on the lights?" Anne Marie suggested from the background.

"No! To hell with that!" Steffensen yelled.

A general shushing, a whispered "*skaal*," and a silent emptying of glasses.

And then it suddenly happened that all three of them put their ivory-yellow faces together and formed a deaf-and-dumb group over in the faint light by the window. They shushed each other and held up their hands for silence, they poured and toasted with weird, soundless gestures, and opened and closed their mouths as if singing, while the sound of footsteps down on Istedgade's sidewalk reached them through the open window.

A hoarse croak issued from Steffensen's throat.

"But why isn't she drinking?"

"It's best when the girlies don't drink," the janitor explained. "Then there's so much more for those who are thirsty. Hee hee."

"But why isn't she drinking?" Steffensen repeated fatuously. "You know the reason, Jastrau."

"Let's drink in peace," Jastrau replied with drunken placability.

"But there's a reason. What have you done to her?"

"Ah-ha ha," said the janitor with a subdued laugh as he whirled completely around on one heel so that his overalls flapped and the wine in his glass splashed over.

"I? I haven't done anything," Jastrau replied. In the dim light he could catch a hint of the malicious manner in which Steffensen was squinting at him.

And suddenly, with a jerk, Steffensen shoved his face close as if he meant to butt Jastrau in the head.

"You didn't dare," he sneered, with his face close to Jastrau's.

"Hee hee," snickered the janitor. His eyes were blinking with curiosity as he stood licking the wine from his fingers.

"I dare to do everything," Jastrau exclaimed, holding his head high and looking at Steffensen with a bleary smile. "Every—thing."

Just then a door slammed with a loud bang. Anne Marie had gone out into the kitchen.

"Every—thing," Jastrau repeated in befuddlement. "You needn't laugh so scornfully."

In the semidarkness he could dimly see Steffensen's set smile.

The janitor stared anxiously at the closed door.

"Now you had better behave, you two drunken louts. Why do we have to stand here glaring at each other? Let's sit down for a while. You get so tired, standing up and drinking." And when at last he had seated himself, he sighed, "Yes, you certainly do."

All three of them sat at the table and were silent. In the darkness, none of them could see what the others were thinking. But all three of them listened.

Not a sound came from the kitchen.

"Uh, it's enough to make a person sober," Jastrau said hoarsely, and reached for a bottle. It was empty. He grabbed for another. It too was empty.

"What the hell, you can't see a thing here in the dark. This—"

Steffensen snatched up the third bottle.

"Drinks disappear altogether too easily," the janitor exclaimed philosophically.

"We have to have more," exclaimed Jastrau. They sat in the darkness and strained their eyes to see that the port was distributed impartially in the glasses.

"Is it really worthwhile?" remarked the janitor. "This is turning into a regular brawl, and after all, I'm the janitor here. I'm the one who's sort of responsible for the place." He struck his hand against his chest. Then he relaxed from his briefly asserted position of authority. His

302

overalls bagged like a flabby bosom. "But if you have money, Herr Jastrau, then—then of course I could get a little more to drink, whether it's worthwhile or not," he added in a wheedling tone.

Steffensen sat with his elbows on the table and stared into the darkness. The outlines of the furniture were dimly visible. An indistinct light appeared beneath the ceiling. The streetlights were being turned on.

"A person gets to feeling sad," he muttered.

"The phonograph," Jastrau suggested. He sat staring down at the dark wine glowing in his glass.

"I've found a buyer for it," the janitor interjected quickly.

"Nonsense."

"No, not at all. It's really a damn fine phonograph."

"Nonsense."

"Oh, stop putting on an act, Ole," the janitor exclaimed raffishly. "Is it more to drink that you need, you drunken pig? If so I'll get it right away."

He laid his big fist on the table, palm up.

"But papa has to have the dough," he said with firmness.

With a sigh, Jastrau handed him a ten-krone note.

"What's so tragic about it?" Steffensen broke in. "I'm thirsty. And Edwin—"

"Aha—you bet—a dry spot way down in my throat," said the janitor, calmly closing his hand about the bill so that it crackled. "Ah," he exclaimed when he heard the sound, and then got up.

And Jastrau and Steffensen were left alone in the darkness.

They sat nipping at their drinks.

Anne Marie opened the door quietly and came in.

"Why aren't you drinking, kiddo?" Steffensen began again.

"Now—now you must be good to her, do you hear?" Jastrau interrupted in a gruff voice.

"Are you feeling noble?"

Steffensen shifted his elbows on the table so that he turned his face toward Jastrau. His face was an indistinguishable mass in the darkness.

"I guess you didn't dare."

"Stefan!" Anne Marie screamed, and Jastrau gave a start. Her voice could be heard far down in the street.

"I tell you, you must be good to her," he stammered.

"It must be tough to be in love, and then not dare to do it," Steffensen went on, laughing. The dark, sphinx-like figure's shoulders were shaking as if he were enjoying the situation.

Jastrau suddenly stood up and banged his fist on the table so that the glasses jumped. Anne Marie grabbed him from behind.

"No, no, you mustn't fight! You mustn't fight!" she shrieked. "If you do, I'm going to leave."

"It would be better if you made some coffee," Steffensen said, laughing.

Jastrau felt taken back by the calm suggestion, and he sank back into his chair. He felt belligerent and ridiculous.

"Shall I? Shall I make coffee, Herr Jastrau?"

Anne Marie's hands fumbled about as if seeking to avert a fight between the two of them.

"Shall I, Herr Jastrau?" she repeated.

"Herr Jastrau!" Steffensen sneered through his nose.

"Yes, yes. Go ahead and make some," Jastrau replied, trying to be calm. "And you might as well turn on the lights."

There was a click on the switch, and suddenly the lights went on, dazzling them. Jastrau and Steffensen both gave a start. Only with difficulty could they look at each other. They blinked. They rubbed their eyelids. They tried to see. And their faces stood out clearly— Steffensen's tense and grayish-yellow around the prominent cheekbones, hair rumpled and hanging down over the high pale forehead, lips protruding and half-open as if set in an expression of brutal anger—Jastrau's sallow and pudgy, flabby about the jowls, eyes squinting half shut, slanting, and slightly Mongoloid. Two hostile faces, Steffensen's prepared to attack, Jastrau's lying in wait and inscrutable, but ready to take the offensive.

Anne Marie had gone into the kitchen.

"I guess you didn't dare," Steffensen began again.

Jastrau did not reply, only shifted his glance as if looking for a weak spot at which to spring.

"Because I've taken her over," Steffensen snarled, moving his face closer. "Infected her," he added with an abrupt brutality that made Jastrau see red.

And Jastrau hit back blindly. "It wasn't you who did it, but your father." Through his mind flashed the thought: His mother is dead. An urn in a briefcase.

A deep, abrupt noise came from Steffensen's throat. Jastrau had to look at him, and his glance encountered a pair of wide-open eyes. Their glazed luster was almost white. It was as if Steffensen were staring and staring without being able to collect his thoughts.

"So you know," he finally said with a sneer. "You know about it, and—" He got up with a bound, then went on, "And now you're laughing—like everybody else. Aren't you? Aren't you? It's howlingly funny."

"I'm not laughing."

"Yes, you are. Everybody does."

"No."

Steffensen sat down again with a forced and crafty smile on his lips. "Then it's because you're in love with her," he drawled.

Jastrau shook his head.

"Yes," Steffensen replied abruptly, and then uttered a brutal laugh. "But she's sick, and she'll never get well."

"You can't tell. It might well happen."

Steffensen made a face and lapsed into a silence.

For long, long minutes they sat as if frozen. True, their arms moved, their bodies continued to function mechanically, but their thoughts had come to a stop. For a second, their souls assumed solid form and cast a shadow out into the nothingness about them. Steffensen lit a pipe. He sat for a long time and toyed with the matchbox in his hand. Jastrau turned his wine glass around like an old wine connoisseur and sniffed at it as if to capture the aroma, but without appreciating it or even realizing what he was doing.

"Uh, how I hate—" Steffensen said suddenly. The words came rushing from him in staccato syllables. "How I hate—all the old—scoundrels. He took her—because he knew—I was spending the nights with her. It excited him—the old goat—to hang a pair of horns on his son's forehead. It gave him his manhood back again—otherwise he wouldn't have been able—wouldn't have been able to do anything. That smile of his—when we sat together at the table—And Mother!" Jastrau sat up straight at the words. He must not say anything. "And Mother!" Steffensen repeated. "Harsh and unyielding and sallow-complected—I take after her. Oh no—I tell you—"

He leaned his breast against the edge of the table and writhed in agony. And Jastrau exerted every effort to hold himself back. He must not say it. The urn in the briefcase. It seemed to him that Steffensen's face glowed with a strange light. Every feature became significant, as in the face of a person in a death chamber.

"Oh—I've—I've been made ridiculous forever. Do you understand what I mean? Ridiculous forever. My grief is ridiculous, laughable. My feelings—my love— Oh, damn it all! I can't get over it. I have to get out somewhere—into space—where all this will seem like nothing. Or get revenge. Revenge, I tell you!"

He rubbed his breast against the table and edged farther and farther forward. And Jastrau perceived him as an apparition, a vision—as he always perceived things when he grew sober during a drinking bout. Steffensen had drawn back his lips, baring his long, narrow teeth, and a faint flush spread over his forehead. His face was like a mask, set in a rigid grimace that was at once painful and comic, and clearly illuminated and delineated in the glare from the light-yellow oak furniture. And the furniture stood out with a weird clarity, as in a ship's salon at night when the dark sea outside foams against the hull.

"I've hurled the whole thing in his face," Steffensen went on in a low, hoarse voice. "I did—I did. His impotence. I said it to him when she got tossed out—for naturally she was tossed out—and then—then I left too. But I'll get revenge. Ah—these old scoundrels—they've made a laughing stock of us forever."

Jastrau glanced uneasily toward the kitchen door. He heard Anne Marie walking about there and getting out the coffee cups.

Steffensen had absent-mindedly opened the matchbox and was letting the matches fall onto the table.

Then the doorbell rang.

"Ah! Now he's coming with the wine!" Steffensen exclaimed with relief.

Jastrau got up and opened the door.

But it was not the janitor. It was a little four-year-old girl with a round head and round shining eyes. She stood there with a wine bottle in her arms as if it were a doll, and in her hand she clutched some money.

"Father said I should tell you that he couldn't come."

She stopped to collect her thoughts.

"And here's the money that's left," she exclaimed dutifully, giving Jastrau a two-krone piece that was still warm from the childish hand.

Jastrau took the bottle. "Give your father my regards."

But when the little one had fulfilled her mission, she leaned curiously to one side in order to see around Jastrau's legs and peer into the hallway.

"Where's the little boy?" she asked, looking up at Jastrau with sparkling eyes.

"He's gone away."

"Yes, that's what Father said too," she replied calmly.

Having established the fact, she immediately turned around and, with the help of the stair rail began to pull herself up the altogether too high steps. With each effort, her little dress was hoisted way up to her middle.

Jastrau's face twisted into a brief scowl in an effort to forget, forget.

306

"Here's the wine," he said as he stepped into the living room. It seemed to him that the Shrove Monday rod, topped by the paper flowers and the cut-out elf, shone so brightly. "But Edwin himself isn't coming back."

Anne Marie stood by the table with the coffeepot in her hand.

"Oh, I suppose his wife got her hooks into him," Steffensen said, grinning and reaching for the wine bottle. Anne Marie looked up at Jastrau for a moment. Ah—now he remembered. And he smiled tenderly at her. Yes, now they were two together. He would not let her down. They were two now, and Steffensen could do them no harm.

"What do we want with coffee?" Steffensen growled.

"You were the one who asked for it," Jastrau said. He was suffering torture. A little girl had leaned to one side to peer inquisitively around his legs and into the hallway.

Meanwhile Anne Marie poured the coffee and took her place at the table. Her mouth hung half-open. She felt insecure, and did not take her eyes off Jastrau. He nodded to her with a preoccupied air.

"Ah," Steffensen sighed when he had poured himself some wine. "Now you're going to have something to drink too, kiddo."

Anne Marie shook her head in confusion and again looked inquiringly at Jastrau. Was she doing the right thing? At the same time, she became uneasy because Jastrau reached out for the wine bottle with an unconscious impetuousness. To forget, to forget.

"Well, thank God," Steffensen said with a grin. He too, had seen how hastily Jastrau reached for the wine. He sat hunched up in his chair like a consumptive, waiting to see what was going to happen. "And so, let's drink to—what was it you said before—the intractability of the soul? Ho!"

Jastrau laughed and drank.

"But why aren't you drinking?" Steffensen went on stubbornly, addressing Anne Marie. "Why isn't she drinking, Jastrau old boy—why isn't she drinking?"

"Let her alone now," Jastrau replied. He drank apprehensively. "Let her alone now."

"All right! I'll let her alone, damn it!" Steffensen exclaimed so vehemently that a sudden spasm went through his slumped-over body. "But why isn't she drinking? What have you—?"

Suddenly his shining eyes came to rest on Jastrau's hand, which was reassuringly patting Anne Marie's bare arm.

"Ha!"

Then he took another drink and sat staring over his glass as if hypnotized.

307

They sat in silence for some minutes. Jastrau drank in feverish haste, alternately from the coffee and the wine.

"Be careful now," Anne Marie implored.

"Ye-s," Jastrau replied.

He sensed that she was looking at him with wide-open eyes full of fear, and he nodded.

"I could kiss you on the forehead," he said gently.

"Ha!" Steffensen said, laughing.

"I could. I could, I tell you," Jastrau went on. Anne Marie tried to withdraw her arm, but he held it with desperate firmness. "I could."

"Why isn't she drinking?" Steffensen said, sitting up straight in his chair.

Jastrau leaned over and kissed Anne Marie on the wrist.

"What?" Steffesen sat up even straighter. "What are you doing? Don't you know she's—?"

"Now you shut up!" Anne Marie exclaimed angrily, and rose from her chair. "Otherwise I'm going to leave."

Steffensen rummaged with the matches on the table.

"Do you want her?" he asked listlessly.

Jastrau did not hear what he said. He sat staring at Anne Marie. His eyes had become blurred.

A breeze blew in through the open window, as if they were aboard a ship.

Then Steffensen picked up some of the matches.

"We—we can play matches for her," he said.

"Stefan!"

Anne Marie did not get to say anything more, because just then she detected a glimmer of light in Jastrau's eyes, far behind their blurred exterior. And Jastrau had eyes only for Steffensen. He kept staring at him.

"Yes—you. We can play matches for her."

Anne Marie said nothing. She could not move. She stood limp and motionless like a woman up for sale in a slave market, in a state of collapse, broad in the hips, limp. It couldn't be true. Steffensen stooped over, fumbling with the matches, and far inside Jastrau's eyes was an ominous glimmer that she had never seen before.

"One of us has to test whether she's sick or not."

Who said it? Steffensen sat up with a start. Jastrau leaned over the table as if to leap at the matches. It was he who had said it. And Anne Marie screamed. She screamed. Stared from one to the other. Jastrau wanted to get up. Suddenly he understood. But a gambler's smile still played about his lips, a cruel twinkle of a smile.

She saw nothing else. She saw only the bleary, Mongoloid face. Far out in the yellowish light she sensed Steffensen sitting rigidly with bloodshot eyes, a dull, oily luster emanating from eyes that had once mirrored a soul. But she saw nothing except the Mongoloid face. And it was that in which she had put her trust!

"Oh God!" she exclaimed, raising her hands to her breast.

And then she ran. Out into the hallway. The door slammed. Jastrau stood leaning on his chair for support. He wanted to stop her. He wanted to repent. Hurried footsteps sounded on the stairway. Going up or down? It was impossible to tell.

"It's a good thing she beat it. Otherwise I'd have murdered her," Steffensen said softly.

And Jastrau gave up completely. He simply sat down.

"A good thing," Steffensen repeated while a slightly awkward smile played about his rigid lips. He shoved his arms toward the center of the table so that a heap of matches was pushed in across the tabletop.

"Now we can drink in peace," he went on, nodding his head.

Jastrau got up again.

"But where did she run off to? We ought to know—"

"It was a good thing. She—"

"But—but—"

"It was a good thing, I tell you."

"Yes, yes, yes." And Jastrau shook his head in bewilderment. "But we're crazy, man—stark, staring mad!"

"Yes—what else?"

Steffensen raised his listless eyes.

"Let's drink now." And Jastrau sank heavily back into his chair.

When they had finished the port, they poured the coffee into the glasses.

"I think Edwin and I brought some bottles of beer down here," Steffensen remarked. "Ha, Edwin!" And he blinked his eyes.

"You probably drank them."

"Yes." Steffensen shook with soundless laughter. "But we can't drink a toast with coffee—a toast to the intractability of the soul?"

"Infinitude," Jastrau corrected peevishly.

"Really? Is that where you are—way out there?"

"Now cut out this stupid jargon, because that's all it is. You—you're nothing but a student."

Jastrau put all his bitterness into the remark. His mind was clear, but not under control. His words took on an unaccustomed sharpness. And Steffensen had to dodge as if a knife had been thrown at him. For a second, his eyes flashed with hate.

"So-o?" he said, slumping in his chair.

"It's a mannerism," Jastrau said, striking again.

"The unmannerliness of the soul—what?"

"It's proletarian snobbery—all your damned crustiness."

"Hadn't we better decide it in some other manner?" Steffensen said doggedly as he swayed unsteadily and laid his fist on the table. He clenched it slowly. Jastrau had seen him do the same thing once before that evening.

"You admire your muscle, don't you?"

Then suddenly Steffensen laughed as if in reconciliation. "Damned if I ever thought coffee could make you so nasty."

"It isn't the coffee. It's the whole business. We were rough on her."

"You were lovey-dovey enough."

"Yes, you might well call it that."

"You looked so disgustingly sanctimonious."

Jastrau put his coffee-filled glass aside in surprise and stared across at Steffensen.

"Could you notice it?" he asked slowly. "It's Jesus."

"Ah—ha ha!" Steffensen laughed boisterously. "You idiot."

"It is. When I've been drinking, or when I'm with women—especially a certain kind of women—then He turns up. Here—from inside me. You know—Jesus and the fallen women, and all that—it's an obsession with me. Then I behave like him—imitate him."

"Haven't you gotten farther than that?" Steffensen said scornfully. The light shone on the jumble of empty bottles and glasses and dulled their vision.

"Farther than that? I'm speaking seriously!" Jastrau exclaimed with intense feeling.

"So am I, damn it! I'm so confounded serious that I have to have another pipeful of tobacco."

He fumbled with his pipe. It slid from his hand and fell to the floor. With a groan, he retrieved it.

"Haven't you gotten beyond that?" he repeated, out of breath.

"What do you mean?" Jastrau asked irascibly.

"I mean you're getting old." Steffensen drew back his lips. "You're the one who prattles about the infinitude of the soul. And then you haven't gotten farther than the Bible stories. Ah, yes, it's nothing but the religious lessons you learned in school that crop up, you poor boob."

"No it isn't. It's—"

"Oh, come now. No, you've gotten only as far as the Bible stories. Do you think that's being spiritual—going back to your childhood? All the nonsense they filled us with in school. It's nothing but that that crops up when we sit and drink to the intractability of the soul—and then we get emotional about it. That's being spiritual? Nuts! It's nothing but propaganda from our schooldays—all this business about the soul. Haven't you come any farther than that?"

"Yes, I have," Jastrau replied desperately. "Because this sort of life we lead is a mess—drinking and whoring around. It's nothing but a mess, and it louses up the universe. I'm going to see someone I know."

"What are you going to do?"

"I'm going. Will you go with me? All this drinking and whoring—I can't stand it any longer. Will you go with me? I know a man who can make sense—a system—out of it all. He knows everything. Will you go along?"

They looked fixedly at each other. They were at once sober and beside themselves from drinking.

"What's this about, anyway?" asked Steffensen. His face underwent a change. His features seemed on the point of relaxing, but the corners of his eyes were bloodshot.

"Catholicism—that's what I mean. There's conversion in the air. I'm going right into the church. They're looking hard for converts down there in Stenosgade. Will you go along, Steffensen? I know a man who has the whole universe figured out—everything neatly in order. And so we'll get converted now—right away, tonight. We'll walk right into the church, right into it. Will you go along?"

"Well, now—" Steffensen said quietly.

"No, you're not going to slip out of it. We're going now. This place isn't fit to stay in. Look at the mess here on the table. It's filthy. And so we stood right up from the feast and went and got converted. And you're going with me, aren't you? Then we'll get everything straightened out."

"Yes," Steffensen said quietly. He was making a pledge. A pale radiance was visible about his face.

A mild current of air swept through the room, a breeze as gentle as that stirred up by a ship's own movement.

They were sailing along through violet-blue space.

"Ha ha," Jastrau laughed gaily. "And what a commotion in the morning. Converted! What will your dear father say?"

"My father!" Steffensen drew out the words, and suddenly swept his hand through the air as if catching a fly. "Then, by Jove, I'll have gotten the best of him! With all his new-fangled religious orientation. Ha—we'll crush him, I tell you."

They were remarkably clear-headed as they lurched down the stairs. It was a moment of clarity. Their movements were swift and animal-like, following the rhythm of their thoughts. They were in unison with it. And they made no sound as they went. Merely two silent creatures hurrying through the nocturnal streets, ready to leap into infinity, intent upon an eternal settlement.

"And so—we go straight to the church," Jastrau said, gesticulating enthusiastically. He ran half a step ahead of Steffensen, with his body turned obliquely toward him.

Steffensen nodded silently as he shuffled along hastily beside him with the kind of thieves' gait so often seen in that quarter. Swiftly. Swiftly. The lights gleamed clearly in the obscurity of Istedgade.

"Won't they be asleep?" Steffensen muttered as if to himself.

"No, Catholic churches are always open at night. You know that, don't you? And that's the way it should be, for suppose a person goes and gets converted—suddenly." Jastrau spoke quietly but with intensity. "There are people who have gone into a church and experienced God all of a sudden."

They did not stop at the little pub. It was not a time for deliberation, but for action, and that at once. Abel Catherinesgade. Dark irregular facades, as if the buildings had been wrongly placed. Viktoriagade. Subdued music in the Café Fatty. Vesterbrogade with its bright lights. And then they were there.

Stenosgade lay dark and uninviting, as if it were only a disreputable side-street. Outside the church was a low iron fence. But all the gates were locked. The church lay brooding behind big closed doors, protected by a fence, just as if it were somebody's residence. Strangely enough there was no threatening sign: Dog unleashed after six.

Steffensen jerked furiously at the iron gates. "What's this?" he growled angrily. "When we want to get in? Is this a respectable institution?"

"Don't worry," Jastrau reassured him. His thoughts flashed through his mind like lightning. "We'll talk with Father Garhammer."

But Steffensen stood with his hands in his pockets, looking maliciously up at the big dark church that towered into the night and eternity. A dark spire sailed along between the stars.

"The kingdom of God is afraid of thieves and robbers—at night," he growled contemptuously up at the dim, inaccessible structure.

"We'll get them to open up, you'll see," Jastrau said.

And with animal-like haste they scrambled up the stairs to the janitor's residence and rang the bell.

They could hear the bell ringing through the empty hallways and staircases.

"Again!" said Jastrau, and rang once more, violently and persistently. "You'll see—we'll wake them up." And he rang again. Why didn't they come running in there? The place should have been swarming immediately with dark figures of monks in flapping gowns, with angels, devils, and Jesuits. Couldn't they hear that something was up? Like a thief in the night. The end of the world. Or a fire. A catastrophe. The bell rang and rang.

"They're apparently afraid of the dark," Steffensen muttered. He stood back and leaned against the railing.

Finally they heard slow, shuffling footsteps. A key was inserted in the lock from the inside, and the door was cautiously opened partway. A pale, frightened face appeared in the opening and stammered something unintelligible in a foreign accent.

"We'd like to talk to Herr Father Garhammer," Jastrau said politely with his hat in his hand and leaning close to the door without thinking of the liquor on his breath.

The janitor's nostrils dilated, and there was a sudden glint of fear in his eyes.

"Who—who shall I say is calling?"

"Editor Ole Jastrau. From *Dagbladet.*"

The door was hastily closed. The key was carefully turned in the lock. And the shuffling footsteps retreated into the distance along the tile floor of the hallway.

"A shut-up building," Steffensen growled. "And here we stand."

"Yes, but just wait—just wait," Jastrau whispered insistently. "And you mustn't back down now. We'll go right in. We'll be converted tonight. Why not?"

There they stood on an ordinary Copenhagen street, wanting to take the leap into eternity. It was almost impossible to stand still.

"Isn't he coming?" Steffensen asked impatiently.

Finally they heard the dragging footsteps once more, and the door was opened again, even more cautiously than before.

"Father is asleep," came a very subdued whisper.

"But—but—." Jastrau gasped for breath.

It was as if the night had come crashing down about them.

"What the devil—is God's house locked up at night?" Steffensen exclaimed savagely. Jastrau did not hear how violent the muffled words sounded. He was not aware of any blasphemy, but only of a door being closed noiselessly, of the sound of the key turning in the lock, of being excluded when he had expected to be admitted to the infinite.

"I won't stand for this," Steffensen went on. "I'll make their ears hum." And he rang again and again.

It was like striking out in blind fury at a stone. What good would it do if all the priests were awakened? They would only lie abed and listen. It does no good to strike a stone, even a stone with a soul.

"But—but Catholic churches *are* always open at night. They *are* open. Come on, Steffensen."

They ran back down to the iron fence. Jastrau climbed it with difficulty. He was too fat, and for a moment he was impaled on the iron pickets. "I think I've ripped my pants," he groaned. A feeling of debasement. A person tore himself to pieces on the threshold of eternity, ripped his breeches. A cool breeze on his behind. And one became ridiculous, a laughingstock, here at the very portals of the All Highest.

But Steffensen was already over the fence. He ran around like a man possessed, like a monkey in a cage. He tugged at the big main doors and the smaller side doors, cursed and threatened and roared.

And at last Jastrau also got over. A breeze fanned the inner surface of one of his thighs. And he too had to try the doors. Perhaps Steffensen did not know how to open them. Oh, those stone piers! They hindered their movements, made it impossible to leap back and forth. They had to twist and turn, hop up and down. And pound they must, since the doors would not yield. With nothing but their fists, when what they should have had was a battering ram. Pitiful—as useless as children's hands against a wall of rock. And no echo of their commotion from inside the church. No one in there could hear the noise. All was a dead silence. Their vain attempt at conversion, their impotent assault on infinity met with the same dark silence.

And then Jastrau hurt his fingers and they began to smart. Ridiculous of him to hurt his fingers, but there were wrought-iron projections on the doors—hard, angular projections. They were armed, those doors.

"Look, Steffensen," Jastrau said spitefully, giving up the attack, "I know a bar that's never closed at night."

"All right."

And they climbed back over the fence. The breeze blew through the hole in Jastrau's pants. "I know a bar that's open all night," he repeated slowly in a voice filled with scorn.

Steffensen was like an animal. He ran back and forth on the sidewalk. "Come on! Come on!" As he said it they passed a small display case in which the *Nordisk Ugeblad,* a weekly paper for Catholic Christians, was pasted up. Steffensen swung one leg back at it. An acrobatic performance. A manifestation of unbelief on one leg. And with unerring aim, his heel crashed through the glass.

Jastrau did not stop. He was moving altogether too fast. No sound

314

they made reached inside the church. He barely heard the pieces of glass tinkle against the sidewalk, but he was completely preoccupied with his new gospel of bitterness.

"Come on, Steffensen. I know a bar that's never closed."

And Steffensen followed him obediently.

Chapter Eight

"Don't turn on the lights," Jastrau groaned as he sank down on the sofa.

The reflection from the advertising lights above Vesterbro drifted like a yellowish fog into the dark living room.

"It's recurrence—the whole business," Steffensen scoffed. He sat stiffly and ill-tempered in one of the rococo chairs.

But Jastrau closed his eyes as if racked by pain. He could feel his whole body quivering like the floor of a machine shop—a big, soft mass that trembled incessantly. His heart throbbed like a dynamo, and the blood, like rhythmically intermittent streams of yellow and reddish light, pulsated through his veins from deep inside the darkness of his chest out to the very edges of his eyelids. The flowers on the wallpaper floated along the surface of a sunlit brook while he lay on the bottom and with eyes shut stared up through the rippling water. Thus everything was transformed, and his nerves became visible to him as pictures. His sensitivity was of a supernatural order. He could even perceive the chemical processes going on in his intestines, tentatively and cautiously at first, then with a sudden rush, as if the functions each time had to pull themselves together for the effort. He lay on a glowing grill.

"Recurrence, I tell you," Steffensen repeated.

"Now stop being a Catholic," Jastrau moaned with his hands covering his eyes. "We've given that a try, you know."

"Recurrence, I tell you. Hurrah, hurrah! And have a drink," Steffensen sneered. "And good morning, old boy. Have you had fun?"

"Oh, cut it out!" Jastrau exclaimed as he writhed back and forth on the sofa.

They had been drinking for twenty-four hours.

"What a conversion!" Steffensen said, and then fell silent.

"But it seems to me—" he said a little while later. He did not finish the sentence, but got up with difficulty and began to roam around through the rooms, muttering as he went. Jastrau heard him rummag-

315

ing around in the bedroom and uttering short grunts. There was a sound of glass clinking.

"Here they are—the janitor's beer bottles. The ones we forgot about."

Steffensen had returned and set the bottles down hard on the black rococo table.

"Now we'll drink these, and then go to sleep."

Jastrau opened his eyes and saw Steffensen's tall dark figure stooped over the table like the shadow of a wolf on a cliff. He was supporting himself on two beer bottles as if they were a pair of front legs.

Jastrau raised himself on the sofa with a sigh. With the effort, a glimpse of a universe with a foggy milky way rushed through his brain. Then his hand closed around one of the bottles.

A cool and soothing liquid flowed through him. The glowing coals beneath the grill were extinguished.

A deep groan came from over by the rococo chair.

"Recurrence," growled Steffensen. Now he was sitting there again. "It's nothing but recurrence. How do you do? Gin and tonic. And we were the ones who wanted to bust right into infinity."

"Yes. What a bit of luck that we didn't get there," Jastrau said with a grin. He felt of the rip in his pants.

"Luck, did you say?" Steffensen asked irascibly. The bottle glistened in the reflection from the advertising lights as he straightened up in his chair.

"Yes, just think if we had been converted." Jastrau shuddered and took a drink. "It gives you a crummy feeling just to think about it."

"Look here now—really!" Steffensen exclaimed in a threatening tone, and moved as if to get up. He sank back again with a thud.

Jastrau did not answer. It was something he did not grasp. Steffensen was paralyzed from the effects of old stale liquor, but there was something decisive about his manner. He seemed to have made up his mind about something.

"Look here now—really!" Steffensen went on in a tone of fury, his words coming in fits and starts. "You're like my father. You both have this business about Jesus, and at the same time you don't have it."

"Rubbish," Jastrau snapped back wearily, trying to brush the conversation aside with a wave of his hand. But Steffensen went on unmoved. His voice became sharper and sharper.

"Well, never mind the oldsters. They're senile. Let them have their regrets about the pickle they've gotten the world into. But you senile fools in your thirties—you're impossible—damn it!"

"What's the matter with us?" Jastrau asked, bending forward. The

316

darkness floated about him, tinged with phosphorescence. The indefatigable Steffensen would not let him alone. "What's the matter with us?" he repeated, watching Steffensen closely and lowering his forehead to attack.

"With you and the others like you? You don't want to think things through," Steffensen snarled, waving the bottle in the air so that a bit of beer slopped onto the rug with a muffled splash. "Ha," he laughed, "you want to swindle your way through—a little sympathy, a little justice, a little understanding for everyone concerned."

Jastrau was about to leap to his feet. But then came a remark that was like a flash in the darkness.

"All the while you've wanted to understand me. Instead, you should have thrown me out—the second time as well."

And Steffensen dried the neck of the bottle with the palm of his hand and drank noisily.

Jastrau sat blinking at him with a nervous smile. Then he bent still farther over the table, as if closing in on the dim hostile figure in the chair across from him.

"You should remember that you're an object of ridicule—forever," he said slowly and insidiously.

"I? I?" Steffensen exclaimed sharply. "But, damn it all, I'm not sentimental—the way you are about those."

And at the same time he took one of the brass beer-bottle caps and threw it over at the table where the two pictures of Jastrau's mother and son could be dimly seen like luminous spots in the darkness. The bottle cap struck the glass so that one of the pictures slid down onto the tabletop.

Jastrau let out an incoherent yell.

"You can be glad the picture didn't fall off the table."

"What can I be glad about?" Steffensen said, laughing and tossing another bottle cap. It landed in the corner by the stove. "Sentimentality," he continued, getting up out of his chair. "His mother and his son! Ha—images of saints. A chapel. I'll—" He reached out for the pictures with a shadowy arm, but at that instant Jastrau flew up from the sofa. His voice was shrill:

"I guess you don't know that your mother is dead."

There was a sudden silence. Jastrau and Steffensen stood opposite each other in the darkness and could feel each other's breath. Their eyes were flashing. But otherwise they were like two belligerent figures who could not read the expressions in each other's faces. Each had his hands extended as if the next moment he meant to grab the other by the throat and choke him.

"Is Mother dead?" Steffensen moaned as his hands sank to his sides. "It isn't true, is it?" he added hastily and savagely. "It can't be true! Although the old man— Ah, that was the reason he was in mourning when I saw him down on the street here. And you didn't tell me? You've known it all along, and you—you—"

He rushed at Jastrau so unexpectedly that both of them fell against the table, overturning it. The telephone slid to the floor and a metal disc tumbled out of it. Steffensen, hard and raw-boned, was by far the stronger. But Jastrau rolled cautiously around with the sharp table edge cutting into him. A fist grazed his cheek so that he could feel it burn. In a rage, he kicked out at some legs. Then he kicked again and leaped up with a howl. It was a table leg that he had struck.

Where was Steffensen? A groan sounded from between the table and the sofa. Then something grabbed him around the legs and began hauling itself up. He felt as if he were being drawn through a narrowing barrel hoop. But he would fix him. A clenched fist descended through the darkness, striking a shoulder. It did him good to throw a punch. Who was it that dared to come here and lay waste to his home? A chapel. He would give him a chapel down there in the darkness. Yes, indeed, it was a chapel with ruins and saints' images. One saint's image. Take that! Right in the face. Another blow, then still another.

A piercing pain in his thigh. Jastrau screamed and tried to tear Steffensen loose. A big, black, gigantic leech that rose from the floor and was indistinguishable from the rug, the darkness, and the sofa, a shapeless creature, but one that would not be shaken loose.

Steffensen had taken a firm hold with his teeth.

Wild with fear, Jastrau shoved at the dark head down below, screamed and screamed and screamed, and kicked out with his legs. A creature without form. A warm animal body. Darkness with teeth.

And suddenly Steffensen stood before him, drawn up to his full height.

"My mother!"

A hoarse inarticulate bellow. The voice exploded so that it was beyond recognition.

There was nothing to do but rush him so that he could not bring his long muscular arms into play. They lurched about through the dark room. A chair creaked. There was a tinkling of glass. Now the large table with the two pictures on it was upset. Desecration of the saints. Was this any way to behave? To destroy everything, to trample everything? Wanton destruction. Havoc.

They reeled out into the hallway, intertwined and groaning. Jastrau braced his stomach muscles, which were soft and flabby, and let himself fall forward with his body's full weight so that Steffensen had to give way—give way before the heavy quilt that smothered him and restrained all his movements. And then suddenly Jastrau found a point of support for his heel. A wall behind him. And that gave him strength, invincibility. It was an Archimedean point. With a bestial and all-embracing force, Jastrau took hold of Steffensen by the shoulders, the whole man between his hands, and pushed him against one of the panes in the hallway door. Steffensen's head went through. The pieces of glass fell tinkling onto the staircase.

And at the same instant, Jastrau put his arms around his enemy and with a feeling of apprehension and horror let his hand glide caressingly over his neck. He felt an intoxicating friendliness well up within him, as well as grief, compassion, and fear that Steffensen might have been injured. He expected to see his hand wet with blood.

"You aren't hurt, are you, my friend?" he exclaimed gently, leading Steffensen back into the large room so that he would not again succumb to temptation and without any reason shove his head through the other pane in the hallway door.

Steffensen was dazed and confused.

Again and again Jastrau passed his hand over Steffensen's neck. "You're not bleeding, my friend," he rejoiced ecstatically and kissed him on both cheeks. Fervently he took Steffensen's head between his two hands. Friendship and good feeling. Old, old, friendship that transcended all understanding. And then, suddenly, a wave of resentment again, and he gave him a resounding slap in the face.

Then Steffensen drew himself up so that Jastrau reeled backward. Steffensen now had space around him. Jastrau's stout body, his all-embracing arms, his weight no longer hemmed him in. He had room to swing, and he struck only one blow. Hard and direct, right on Jastrau's chin.

Jastrau fell backward and plunged down through darkness.

There was a shower of glass fragments, a thin drizzle. A voice sounded uncertainly through the darkness. Then there were two voices. They fluttered in the air like two birds quarreling. And someone ran across the floor in bare feet.

"Drunken louts!"

And just then the lights were turned on.

"Drunken louts!"

Jastrau regained his senses for a moment and blinked. The room was floating in a sea of reddish light, and over near the light switch stood the red-haired janitor with nothing on but a shirt. He looked angry.

"Behave yourself!" he snarled at Steffensen.

Then they began wrangling again.

The red light faded into a fog.

"Shall we haul the carcass over on the sofa?"

Jastrau felt himself being lifted into the air.

"Ouch!" And the janitor grinned. "It isn't easy being a barefoot dancer."

Jastrau surrendered to the desire to sleep.

"Dancing on broken glass, so to speak—hee hee," came the sound of a voice.

And then again the patter of bare feet before the darkness and silence closed in around Jastrau.

PART FOUR

And All Suns Are Darkened

Chapter One

The telephone rang again. Ole Jastrau opened his eyes. Yes, the telephone had rung once before. It had rung in his dream.

He reached for it from force of habit. The table stood there. But the telephone lay on the floor. Oh—yesterday's brawl. He remembered the sound of glass, unpleasant as the crunching of sugar between the teeth. Now, in the forenoon light, the chairs lay overturned and the door to the hallway stood open. He could see the big star-shaped hole in the gray frosted pane, and the noise from the hallway came all the way into the room.

He groped for the receiver with his hand. He did not want to think. No, he didn't.

"Ole Jastrau speaking," he said into the mouthpiece while he remained lying on his back. The daylight hurt his eyes.

"It's Vuldum you're talking to. I'm calling from down here in the library because it's urgent."

The voice was indistinct. Now and then there was a rattling in the telephone mouthpiece.

"Talk louder," Jastrau replied in irritation.

"It's your little tour de force down in Stenosgade that I'm referring to."

"Louder."

"I can't speak louder," came Vuldum's faint voice. "There must be something wrong with your phone. But there are such wild rumors going around about your attempt to get converted that they've even reached me. The entire Catholic beehive is buzzing."

"Ha ha! They need a pick-me-up down there," Jastrau laughed.

"You mustn't take it that way, my dear Ole. Remember, they're Jesuits, and they're thinking of making something serious out of it. That's why I'm not losing any time in—" An unclear rattle drowned out the voice.

"I can hardly hear you."

"What the devil is the matter with your telephone? I can hear you clearly. But you ought to forestall them."

"Who? What?"

"Them—down there in Stenosgade. It seems there was a pane of glass broken."

"Well, what of it?"

"You ought to go down and apologize to Father Garhammer, and then pay for the glass."

"Oh, go fly a kite!"

"Well—now I've warned you," Vuldum said slowly. "But I can imagine that this would be good material for the scandal sheets. Remember, they're Jesuits you're dealing with. The chief reviewer for *Dagbladet* attempts to get converted, a pane of glass gets broken—it's not altogether dull stuff, and they wouldn't set it in small type."

Jastrau laughed. He had a sudden feeling of emancipation. How trivial it all was. Now nobody could touch him.

"It could jeopardize your position on the paper, and after all that isn't any too good now."

"All right, let it jeopardize it," Jastrau said, laughing.

"Well, it was for your own sake that I called. But now I have to get back to the reading room. So good-by. Now I've told you about it, and it seems to me—yes, it's my opinion—that you absolutely must go out and apologize to Father Garhammer. Anyway, we'll discuss it later. Good-by now."

"Good-by, and thanks for your thoughtfulness," Jastrau replied ironically. He was invulnerable now. Everything that formerly had tormented him over at the paper, everything that could weaken or undermine his position, was nothing but a voice drowned out now and then by a rattling sound, a faint, faint voice in a wrecked telephone receiver. Nothing, nothing could hurt him any more.

He laid the receiver back on the floor and got up. So Vuldum still had no inkling that he had resigned, that he had finally crossed the divide. It was almost funny. No one was capable of doing him any harm. Their good advice, their warnings, their malice, their intrigues—nothing but indistinct voices in a cracked telephone receiver.

And the reality of his present surroundings, the overturned furniture, a broken chair back, the shattered panes in the hallway door—could he take them at all seriously? So many things can be smashed to pieces around a person that he ends up finding it comical. Wasn't there something at Tivoli called the Fun Kitchen, where for twenty-five øre one was permitted to smash the chinaware?

Here was the point at which Steffensen became a lunatic.

But it was at this point that Jastrau was strongest.

He wondered how Steffensen was. Had he left like Anne Marie? Was the devastation now over?

324

Jastrau felt a smile forming on his lips. Canny was the word for such a smile. And he walked into the bedroom. A strong morning sun was shining in there.

Steffensen lay sprawled across the double bed, fully clothed. The sun shone on his blond hair, giving it a golden, childish look. He lay with his mouth open, snoring.

Jastrau stood for a moment observing his rigid features. There was nothing puzzling about them now. Angry lips. Many small teeth. An altogether too high forehead, serving as a cover for a logic gone amok. Unshaven he was, too. Collar stretched tightly over his Adam's apple like a dirty bandage on a clenched fist.

An object of ridicule. Forever.

Jastrau picked up his shaving things and went back to the living room. He lathered his face. He walked back and forth in his undershirt, pants, and bare feet. Where was Anne Marie? He used the shaving brush with vigor. Ah—that bewildered little girl. His suspenders dangled about his legs. He was a gay devil. Now she was very likely running about the streets and alleyways. He began to scrape one cheek in front of the mirror. And so probably she was going to the dogs. He made a shaver's grimace and was aware of a smile coming over his twisted lips. A canny smile it was called. He was invulnerable.

Just then the hallway doorbell rang, and he shifted one leg irritably. He felt a breeze. The Catholic rip in his pants. How would he get it sewed up?

He turned around.

It was a lady who stood peering aghast through the large star-shaped hole in the door pane. He could see part of her face. A pair of bright piercing eyes. And she had caught sight of him, too. Consequently, he would have to go to the door. But one cheek was smeared with white lather, he had on only an undershirt and pants, the latter ripped, and who could tell that the rip was the result of a spiritual conflict? Nevertheless, he would have to go to the door. Who was she?

He opened the door, and his razor dripped soap as he raised it in a gesture of surprise.

"No! Is it you, Fru Kryger?"

It was she. She stood out on the landing, dressed in luminous gray. But her eyes were wide with alarm, almost unseeing, and she was leaning forward as if at any moment she would fall against him.

"Then this *is* the right place." She blinked, and the searching gray expression returned to her eyes. "Yes, your name is there on the door plate, but—"

Jastrau bowed politely and smiled. The soap was drying and puckering up his cheek.

"Yes. I must ask your pardon, Frue. As you can see, I live in a state of siege."

"So I see," she replied, drawing a deep breath.

"Do I dare invite you to visit the ruins?" There seemed to be a flickering in his brain. There was sunlight on the stairway, and long bright shafts of it were reflected by Fru Kryger's gray dress.

"Well, I almost don't know whether I dare," she said with a smile, and then suddenly laughed. "Wouldn't it be better if you shut the door and handed me that book—the one by Joyce—out through the hole there?"

"It's too thick—the book. If you want it, you'll have to venture in."

Slowly Fru Kryger stepped inside. She put her foot cautiously forward, as if walking on a quagmire, and looked around, completely at a loss and helplessly alone, and when she stopped in the middle of the room she stood with her feet close together, looking down in front of her as if fearful of being contaminated. The overturned chairs, the pictures littering the floor, the bits of glass, the bottles and beer caps filled her with alarm.

"How this place does look!"

"Yes. A conversation took place here," Jastrau replied, gallantly flourishing his razor as if it were a fencing foil. There is a type of smile that is called canny.

Greetings to all good fellows from Peter Boyesen.

"Is it *so* difficult for a man to live alone?" exclaimed Fru Luise, looking at him inquiringly. "Are you menfolk like this?"

Jastrau sat down on the sofa, passed his hand self-consciously over his face, and got his fingers sticky from the solidifying soap.

"I must finish shaving," he said hurriedly. "If you dare to stay here alone, I'll be through in a—"

"Yes, I dare to, all right," she replied with mock bravado. "But I won't deny that I feel a bit like a lion tamer."

She stood erectly as she smiled.

Jastrau took all his clothes—shirt, collar, jacket and vest—rolled them into a bundle, and tossed it into the dining room.

"There. Now I'll be back in a jiffy," he said. Had she seen the tear in his pants—that degrading tear? There was nothing so humiliating as a hole in one's pants. Yes, there was too—suspenders. To be without suspenders. At least, he had them on. They dangled behind him like a ridiculous tail, and he grabbed hold of them, blushed deeply, and whispered, "I'll be right back." Then he shut the sliding doors behind him and was alone in the dining room.

He shaved hurriedly as he restlessly paced the floor. Now if only

326

Steffensen didn't wake up. He went over to the bedroom door and listened while he shaved. No, he was still sleeping. Jastrau could hear that. But he could also hear his own heart thumping from overexertion. Oh, if only he had a Pilsner! And she, Fru Kryger? He heard a chair being righted in there. She should not do that, damn it all. She should not straighten things up, get domestic. But he had better finish getting ready. Out into the kitchen to wash so as not to wake Steffensen. Put on his shirt and collar. Vest and jacket. If only he didn't have that rip in his pants. What should he do? He would have to go out to the hallway and put on his light topcoat.

He would have to invite her for a walk.

Wearing the topcoat and his felt hat, and with James Joyce's fat novel under his arm, he went back in to Fru Luise. She was sitting in one of the chairs, which now stood where it belonged. He noticed that the pictures of his mother and son had been placed on the table, and he smiled gratefully. But at the same time he felt a twinge go through him. He saw a flash of light on the glass that covered the picture of his son. It was cracked.

"It's so dismal here," he said nervously. The light from the crack in the glass seemed to pierce right through him. "Hadn't we better go out?"

"Yes, by all means," Fru Luise replied, and got up. "Oh! There's the book. Yes, I can see it's a big one."

On the stairway they met the janitor, who was carrying some boards. When he caught sight of Fru Luise, he blinked at Jastrau with his blue eyes.

"I'm just going to slap a few of these boards up over the door to cover the hole. Otherwise anyone can walk right in or out, so to speak. Isn't that so?"

Jastrau nodded.

"And I've phoned for the glazier. I'm a janitor, ha ha, but I won't cause you any trouble."

And with a snicker he went on up the stairway with the boards.

"Where shall we go?" Jastrau asked when they were down on the street. All the while he could feel her gray eyes resting on him.

"Oh, wherever you wish. I have plenty of time. My husband is away, you know."

"Isn't it fun to be a widow for a change?"

"I'm a widow all the time as a matter of fact," she said bitterly. Suddenly the lines of her mouth tightened and she assumed the wizened expression of an old lady.

Jastrau looked at her earnestly, but then she shifted her glance.

"Shouldn't we go to Frederiksberg Park?" she exclaimed abruptly. She pronounced it "Fresber Park," and moved her lips like those of a baby. "Shall we? Yes, that's what we'll do. Yes, come on!" And she seized his arm eagerly. But she did not look at him.

"Frederiksberg Park," Jastrau repeated slowly. He wondered if Oluf might not be playing there. His wife's parents lived in the neighborhood. There was a crack in the glass over the photograph. Like a flash of lightning. And it had struck him.

"Yes, let's do that," he said with a sigh, feeling that he was surrendering himself to his fate.

Amidst the forenoon traffic on Vesterbrogade he made a few missteps. It was as if the sidewalk under his feet insisted on opening up, leaving him to step out into empty space. He removed his hat and nervously passed his hand over his wet forehead. But then he went on talking—incessantly, in order to forget his giddiness. Ah—a Pilsner would soothe him.

"You'll never get this book read," he teased her, tapping the volume of Joyce with his hand. "It takes a set of directions to get through it."

But Fru Luise walked primly and calmly along at his side. She was very quiet, and Jastrau was afraid that she would suddenly begin to ask questions. He knew that then they would pour in on him, intelligent as sparkling water, and cast their reflections so far into his self—that dark cave—that he would have to expose himself, give himself away. The gray dress shone, the gray eyes gleamed and brushed him for a long moment, then went dull again, as if she were shutting herself in and thinking again, thinking again, while she calmly and in a consciously matter-of-fact way kept in step with him.

Frederiksberg Allé was prodigiously wide, like the view out over a sea. There were no car tracks—only an asphalt surface. And he had never before thought about the fact that car tracks made a street narrower. Now, however, he sensed it. At the moment, he yearned for car tracks.

And the entrance to Frederiksberg Park! With its yellow walls and yellow gardeners' quarters and iron grillwork in the style of the eighteenth century. When one entered this park, he felt himself in a miniature European kingdom. The illusion of monarchy that pervaded the yellowish atmosphere of the place seemed to embellish it. And the statue of that simple man, the promenading autocrat,* seemed to greet them so convivially.

"Denmark," Jastrau remarked jovially, without apparent reason.

* King Frederik VI (1808–39).

328

"Yes, and I like it," Fru Luise replied.

"But then, you're married to a conservative man."

"Are you making fun of me because you've slipped the bonds of your marriage?" she asked. Jastrau thought she sounded querulous. "Do you have it any better in your state of siege?" But then she quickly added, as if fearing an answer, "Though perhaps you have."

Jastrau sensed that he should not pursue the subject farther.

Then they turned into the pathway at the left. The massive green crowns of the trees breathed coolly above their heads, and from between the park's venerable tree trunks Josty's little restaurant in Greek temple style, gray and idyllic, and with a stamp of pagan false piety about it, seemed to entice them.

But in front of the Josty, the gravelled space between the two rows of summerhouses was swarming with children. Baby carriages were being rocked back and forth incessantly with one arm as with the other the nursemaids raised their coffee cups to their mouths. Many baby carriages, and always the same creaking movement. How full of children the world was. Two small boys kicked gravel in onto the flagstones so that it sounded like the lapping of waves against a beach. Behind the trellises of the summerhouses, children were playing peek-a-boo. A little girl's round face with bangs popped out from between the leaves like a Japanese doll. From the table surfaces came the faint, metallic patter of the house-sparrows' claws as the birds tamely and fitfully hopped about looking for cake crumbs and sugar. All of these sounds merged into one, and suddenly Jastrau felt overwhelmed by them as by a tidal wave of grief. Children!

Feeling strangely careworn, he invited Fru Luise to step into the restaurant.

"Wouldn't it be better if we sat outside?" she objected. "The sunshine is so lovely."

"No, no, no," he replied dejectedly. He did not want to state his reason. He simply led the way inside and found a table as far, far away from the children as possible.

"I'm sure you'll pardon me, Frue, if I order a beer." He sat opposite her and with a weary irony gazed into the deep, gray eyes. "Like all drunkards, I must have my morning bottle of beer to calm me down."

"Drunkard! Now I dare say you're bragging." She looked at him with a twinkling smile and drew the thick book by Joyce toward her.

"No. That's certainly all I am."

"You're a critic too—and a good critic at that."

"No. That's certainly what I'm not. I'm a drunkard."

Fru Luise laughed.

Just then coffee was placed before her and a beer before him, and she looked ironically at the green bottle. The contractions at the corners of her mouth were those of an experienced woman. "What does it matter if you're a drunkard? What is a drunkard?" she suddenly said with mock irritation. It was as if she suddenly had decided to obtrude herself into his life. But he lifted his glass with its foaming head and drank, and felt a melancholy tranquility come over him.

"I want to be at ease with myself," he said, "and observe what comes to the surface from deep down inside me." Far off in the distance he heard the noise of the children playing, and he felt he had to be candid with her. From across the table, those gray, intelligent feminine eyes were staring at him. "Fru Kryger—Fru Luise—may I call you that? You know these caves that you see in aquariums, don't you? The ones with a dim green light and with red and green fish darting forth, and bits of seaweed that seem to want to swim out. That's how I want to be, and that's the way I am when I drink."

"But you don't have to drink in order to do that. We can all be like that," she replied.

He smiled.

"But then, when you see something unexpected, a fish with a head like a beak and a body sharp as a knife, or perhaps more like a file, and with wicked eyes—the sort of thing you never believed yourself to be like."

"Then you go out into the daylight, and the creature is gone."

"Is it?"

"Well, I suppose not. But you forget it."

She sounded so certain of herself. She clenched her nervous hands as if she wanted to pound them against the table, and her words came twice as fast as his. He spoke very slowly, now and then in a nasal tone, and with a slight Copenhagen accent.

"Don't you think, though, that it's quite funny to see such a creature?" he asked.

"No."

"But I do. And it seems to me that it's the only thing that really is funny."

"But that doesn't have to make you a drunkard, and you aren't one either," she said, almost as if brushing the subject aside.

"Yes, for some inexplicable reason it does. Because I see creatures I've never set eyes on before. One of them blinks his eyes, and an electric shock goes through me. Recently, I've experienced Jesus in this way."

"You were speaking of animals," she said with a touch of irony.

"All right, then let's say forms or mental images, or whatever you

330

want to call them. As a matter of fact, Christ is often symbolized by a fish, isn't He? And so I caught sight of Him, His form stood there immovably before my mind's eye—and that's why I have a hole in my pants," he added in a desperate attempt at a witticism. He had just shifted his leg and noticed the humiliating draft on his thigh.

"Are you crazy?" she asked bluntly, staring at him uncomprehendingly. She was becoming uneasy.

"No, but I'm not a critic. So there was the figure of Christ, blinking at me," he said, laughing. "But then there was a good friend of mine who made me realize that of course Christ couldn't be anything but a reminiscence from my school days, and consequently of no interest to me. For I wanted to arouse a creature—or a mental image—that came from deep inside the aquarium. A stalk-eyed fish with an armored head and sharp joints and edges. Do you know how it is when a person strikes himself on the eye in order to see visions—flaming visions?"

"You want to get back to your work," she replied quietly. She compressed her lips as if she understood.

"No," he said firmly.

"But, for goodness sake, what is it you want then?"

"There is something I want, and when I drink I sometimes feel for a moment that I've captured it. Liquor is the only substitute for religion, shall we put it that way—just for fun?"

"You want to forget—that's it," she remarked with conviction. Jastrau could tell that she had been a student as a young woman.

"Yes—ideas, opinions, and all such trivia. And then on the other hand I don't know whether everything I'm sitting here and telling you isn't fiction—because I'm simply a drunkard, thirsty. In other words, an excuse."

He raised his beer glass and toasted her banteringly. Fru Luise had appeared to be understanding, he thought. That would not do.

"I want to sit around comfortably, drinking, and at the same time fancy that I'm working hard. A bit of seaweed that thinks it's a fish," he added in a slow drawl when he had finished his drink. "Waiter! Another beer."

"What you need is a love affair," she exclaimed with the voice of experience.

Jastrau looked at her and laughed. "Ah yes. As a matter of fact I almost had one the other day. And that was a strange fish—that feeling. It was practically invisible—wouldn't take shape. And then it turned out that a friend and I played matches for her."

"You did what?"

Jastrau took some matches from the container on the table and in a matter-of-fact way explained the rules of the game, while Fru Luise's eyes grew wider and wider. She sat up very straight as if scandalized, and Jastrau could see how thin she was. It struck him that despite her intelligent banter she was essentially quite dull.

"And you did this to a woman with whom you were in love?"

"Yes. That, you see, is the question. Was I in love with her?" he replied slowly. "You see, Fru Luise, every normal person wants to experience that feeling and to have it take its usual form, the way he has read about it and has seen others do. He will call it love and behave the way a person in love behaves. But I want such a feeling to take a unique form—not become just a love affair. That's a cliché. Do you understand?"

"No."

"But it ended in a farce, don't you see? It ended with us playing for her with matches. And as a matter of fact, that's how it was with my religious experience. That ended in disorderly conduct, too. It ended as a farce. Do you understand?"

"No."

"Don't you realize, either, that I've resigned from *Dagbladet?*"

Fru Luise leaned forward over the table.

"What did you say? You're no longer a critic?" she asked with feverish excitement.

Jastrau shook his head.

"But how are you going to make a living?"

"Naturally you ask me that question. God knows how often I'm going to hear it now."

"Yes, but why did you do it?" she asked in agitation.

"Yes. That's the question. Perhaps, Fru Luise, it's your husband who's to blame for it. He told me one election night that I was a good conservative critic. What he said, in effect, was that aesthetics preserves the illusion that there is freedom of thought in the country."

"Freedom of thought—but we do have that."

Jastrau shook his head.

"No, it's an illusion. A person can think whatever he wants to about aesthetics, ethics, and I don't know what else. But if he has opinions that encroach on economics, then the freedom no longer applies."

"But your opinions have nothing to do with economics," Fru Luise protested. Her gray eyes wavered uneasily as if she was recoiling from the argument.

"No, not yet—not yet. As I've told you, I have no opinions. But if—"

"If, if!" She shook her head.

"Yes, if some day it should occur to me that this and that is right and this and that is wrong, and if my opinion were contrary to that of the economic powers that be, then—"

"No, no, that's really too ambiguous," Fru Luise said with a sigh. "When people talk about economics and capitalism, they get boring—all of a sudden."

Jastrau smiled and went on unconcerned.

"I believe that it's this 'if'—that it's the possibility, or the thought of the possibility, of being forced that has driven me away from it all."

"And I, who thought I was sitting here with the chief reviewer for *Dagbladet*, the well-known critic!" she exclaimed with droll despair. Her voice had a singsong quality.

"Yes, and then I turn out to be a simple, ordinary man who has made a slight attempt to plumb the depths of the soul and find the meaning of absolute freedom. And for now I've managed to become a drunk."

His tone was at once ironic and melancholy, and Fru Luise had to look up and smile. Then, with sudden animation and assurance, she extended her hand to him across the table. He took it hesitantly, and she squeezed his hand gently—a gratuitous expression of confidence.

"I was just about to get furious with you," she said. The tender smile remained on her thin lips. "But I can't. No, I can't. I see this drunkard before me, your close friend, that apoplectic in the Bar des Artistes. And I see your apartment. Broken furniture and bits of glass. And you tell me that you and another man drew lots for a woman. But then it becomes something else when you talk about it. It's as if you were discussing a theory."

Jastrau's lips curled in a sneer. But she tugged at his hand.

"You must get away from that apartment, do you hear? You mustn't go back up there to all those rooms. Where are you going to eat tonight? Come home with me. Yes—my husband—" She laughed. "Ah yes, he certainly has it better than he deserves. But you ought to come—you should. Instead of sitting up there in your apartment. Uh, how dismal it was! Or instead of going to a restaurant, you—you incorrigible drunkard."

He promised to come.

When they parted a little later he stood at the park gate and watched her retreating figure, the luminous gray dress, her agile legs. His eyes could follow her far down the avenue. The thinly-leaved, newly planted trees afforded a broad view.

Then he wanted to turn around and go back into the park. There was a playground over at the right in the northern corner, and perhaps Oluf was playing there.

Slowly he lighted his pipe. The stream of people was more concentrated here near the exit from the park. Suppose Oluf now appeared on the scene. There were so many children. Suppose he did. People sauntered by slowly, the way they walk in a park. A child's play wagon screeched. It could be Oluf's.

And suddenly he saw himself with new eyes.

Frederiksberg Park! It was a park for children and lonely pensioners. And in the evening it was frequented by the young people. There they sought each other out in the darkness along the asphalt pathways.

This he had always known.

But was it not also a park for divorced men?

Didn't they steal out here to catch a glimpse of their children? Didn't they stand, lonely and decorously, at the edge of the play area? They did not go any closer. They did not disturb the children at play, but held themselves under rigid control in order not to betray themselves with a sentimental wave of the hand.

A park for divorced men.

He studied the people going by. But divorced men are not so easy to distinguish in a public park. It is much easier to see them in a barroom.

There were also people seated along the two long rows of benches that were called "the traps." He looked along the rows. But suddenly he had to shift his glance because it had fallen on a pair of dark bird-like eyes that fastened themselves curiously on his hands and the awkward way he held his pipe. The bird-eyes twinkled, and the sunlight flashed on the spangles of a bonnet over white hair, so that it seemed that a score of dark curious eyes were watching him. An old lady, clad in black.

Ill at ease, Jastrau turned on his heel like a soldier. Now, he felt, the old lady would observe his decisive maneuver with interest. But he did not want to be spied upon. And he left the park.

In towards town.

Suddenly he called a taxi on the avenue and rode to the Bar des Artistes.

Chapter Two

Jastrau and the inevitable Kjær sat opposite each other in the semidarkness of the Bar des Artistes, both of them dull and listless. The ventilator hummed incessantly as it sucked up the blue tobacco smoke.

334

"Nice to have you staying here, Jazz."

Kjær raised his broad, puffy prelate's face and directed his groggy eyes toward him.

"Yes, thanks," Jastrau grunted. "I had a date with a woman yesterday—at noon—and then I went and forgot it."

It was stuffy in the dimly-lighted room, while outside the afternoon sunlight was brilliant.

"One forgets everything—one forgets everything," Kjær puffed, waving his hand.

His body shook with soundless laughter, so that his chair creaked.

"But I can't forget, Jazz, that finally I've seen the beginning of a white mouse. It happened yesterday out in the lobby. It was running around underneath the hall porter's feet. 'Chase it away,' I yelled. 'Chase it away.' And then he laughed—the uniformed beast."

Suddenly Kjær exploded with laughter.

"It's eyes weren't open yet—that little mouse. But that will come. 'Give me time, give me time,' it squeaked happily and wiggled its little ears," Kjær went on in a singsong voice. 'All in good time, all in good time," he intoned again while he beat out the measure with a smoking cigar.

"All in good time, all in good time," Jastrau chimed in.

"But we won't create a disturbance." Kjær raised his hand admonishingly, so that his arm shot out from his clean blue shirtcuff. As always, he was well dressed. No sign of disintegration. No ashes on his vest, no necktie that sat askew, no shabby collar. Nothing gave him away except a prematurely aged face with hollows and loose skin and brown liver spots.

"My life's purpose has always been to be a quiet, heavy drinker, and that I've achieved."

He fastidiously tapped the ashes from his cigar.

"Look ahead, but never back," he hummed as he stared listlessly deep into Jastrau's eyes while in a hoarse voice he went on singing and again waved his cigar in a sweeping, rhythmical gesture like a baton.

"Look ahead, but never back. What the heart desires,
Perhaps will someday come to be."

"Yes," he continued with a faint, remote smile, "as a matter of fact I've written verses, too. It was twenty-five years ago, when I was still slim."

"We're no longer that," Jastrau sighed down into his whiskey glass. They were having a profound twilight conversation in the middle of a summer afternoon. They had both drunk long and heavily the night before.

"We—we!" the inevitable Kjær snorted. "After all, you're nothing but a young man who should keep his trap shut and listen in reverence. At your age I was a director and producer at Charlottenborg, and a copy-editor. But one gets tired of being so talented. And what does it lead to? Vanity. And now I've seen the beginning of a white mouse."

He spread his big, well-groomed hands in an ironical, defeatist gesture of resignation.

"All talents don't get you that far," he added with a sigh.

"Look ahead, but never back. What the heart desires—"

And Kjær's hoarse, halting song rang out through the subtle twilight atmosphere of gleaming bottles and brasswork, creating its own mood, like a drunken man's solo tenor coming from the distance in a deserted street. But then a gabbling, nasal voice cut in.

"I thought I'd find you here, brother-in-law. Ha ha—I thought so. And why waste time? Think logically and act accordingly. If people have to drink, then they have to drink."

And Jastrau was bowled over by a friendly clap on the shoulder that caught him completely off guard. It was Adolf Smith-Jørgensen.

With somber mien, the inevitable Kjær leaned ominously over the big round table. His bleary eyes flashed with a singular malice in the melancholy blue atmosphere.

"I forbid this man to sit at our table!" he exclaimed, pointing a complaining finger at Jastrau's brother-in-law, who in consternation took a step backward.

"Pardon me—pardon me, for breaking into your party. But may I introduce myself?"

"No!" thundered Kjær. "Plebeians don't interest me."

And Kjær quietly began to busy himself with his whiskey, as if the intruder had left.

But Jastrau got up listlessly, staggered a bit, and followed his brother-in-law over to another table.

"Bad company, bad company," muttered the inevitable Kjær, shaking his head while he stared down at the table. "Extremely bad company, my dear Jazz," he added, nodding at the matchbox container.

"Well, I declare. What a boor!" Smith-Jørgensen exclaimed indignantly.

"Is there something else you want to tell me?" Jastrau asked dully, raising his head.

"This is really too much," his brother-in-law went on, laying down

336

his gloves, derby, and walking stick. But gradually he calmed down. "Well, let's forget this barbarian. We certainly do have other things to talk about. We ought to see about—if not the divorce—then in any event about a separation, and apparently you haven't thought about that, not really, that is, have you? Ha ha, you're an amiable bounder."

"Do I have to think?" Jastrau asked, collapsing wearily.

"Johanne hasn't seen as much as an øre from you, and that won't do. We must have it arranged legally. Haven't you had a letter from Johanne's lawyer?"

"Lawyer?" Jastrau repeated apathetically.

"Yes, of course she has a lawyer. We must get this worked out along clear lines. That's always been my principle."

"Clear lines?" Jastrau said.

"Is it physically impossible for you to see clear lines today?" Smith-Jørgensen exclaimed with a supercilious laugh.

"Ha ha. But now listen to me. Johanne must have four hundred kroner within the next few days. Can you get that through your muddled head?"

"Four hundred kroner? Yes, I have that much—up at the paper. Sure—I think so. And when I've drawn it out—when I've drawn it out—then—then there won't be anything left."

His brother-in-law shot him a quick glance.

"Can't we go up there and draw it out now?" he asked in a business-like way.

"Draw, draw, draw," Jastrau muttered. But then suddenly he drew himself up and said, "All right, draw it out and be damned."

"Yes, but—" His brother-in-law drummed nervously on the table with his fingers. "You can't go up to the cashier in this condition."

Jastrau sank back in his chair again, so that his chin rested against his chest.

"No, I certainly can't," he mumbled down at his necktie.

"But look here!" Adolf exclaimed, slapping the palm of his hand against the table top so that the glasses jumped. Both Jastrau and Kjær gave a start. "The cur!" Kjær growled, sagging heavily against the table.

Jastrau's eyes blinked in alarm.

"You frightened me, damn it," he said. "But I agree with you. We must—we must get this cleared up. Yes, we must, we must, we must—"

Adolf's round cheeks puffed out dangerously, and his lips grew thin and compressed.

"Now I'm going," he said menacingly. "I don't have time for this sort of nonsense. And so you'll have to excuse me if I and Johanne's lawyer take hold of this thing in our own way. Speaking of lawyers, what's your lawyer's name?"

Jastrau looked at his brother-in-law through blurred eyes and then burst into a giggle.

"Yes, God knows what his name is."

"Oh, you're intolerable. But—you'll—hear—from—me! And incidentally, while we're on the subject, what about that fire-insurance policy?"

Jastrau tittered and shook his head.

"It's expired."

"That's a lie."

Jastrau shrugged his shoulders and shook himself.

"He says it's a lie, he says it's a lie," he remarked, laughing.

And with brisk, springy steps, with the derby on his head, the walking stick in hand, and the tapering fingers of his gloves bristling in all directions, Adolf Smith-Jørgensen marched toward the door, a picture of noble and righteous indignation.

The move took Jastrau by surprise.

"Say hello to Michelsen," he managed to call out.

At that moment, subdued Hawaiian guitar music began to issue from the phonograph over in the corner. The little snub-nosed waiter, who had been standing silent and motionless behind the bar had, with a certain feeling for the amenities, set it going.

And once more Jastrau staggered over to the inevitable Kjær.

"Jazz," said Kjær reproachfully, raising his broad head from out of his lethargy, "you mustn't do that, you mustn't do that."

Jastrau grunted irascibly.

"He was far beneath your level, Jazz. A person has to be particular."

And once more the broad head drooped.

Jastrau groaned. Suddenly he felt as if he would explode with the heat. The dusky atmosphere tormented him. He could not recapture the feeling of coziness.

"I want to get out," he said.

"I want out, I want out," Kjær hummed.

"Let's get a taxi and take a ride," Jastrau proposed.

Kjær shook his head. Wrinkles of anxiety appeared on his forehead.

"No. I'm staying here," he said, raising his hand slowly in a disparaging gesture.

"No. You're coming with me."

"No, no."

"Yes."

Kjær's large frame squirmed uncomfortably.

338

"But I don't want to, damn it," he said.

"Have you seen the woods this year?" Jastrau asked stubbornly.

"I don't want to."

"But you must!" shouted Jastrau.

"What do I want with the woods? They're only green."

"This year they're blue."

Kjær's eyes widened in amazement. "What are you saying?"

"Yes, yes, the wine-blue beeches."

"You're drunk, Jazz."

"I want you along. I do, I do."

"Arnold," said the inevitable Kjær, turning slowly in his chair, "should I go along with this drunken gentleman to the woods? He sees blue beech trees."

"Yes, I think you should Herr Kjær. A little fresh air, you know." And the waiter waved his hand politely.

"All right, then," Kjaer exclaimed with a groan. He stood up in all his solemn majesty. "If Arnold says so, then, damn it, I'll have to go into the woods."

A little later, they walked through the room arm in arm, humming softly. The portière was drawn aside so that the sunlight exploded around them. Out on the sidewalk, they reeled for a moment and rubbed their eyes. The people walking by looked remarkably clear-skinned, but their faces were tightly drawn. They took too short steps, these people, and they did not swing their arms as they walked. Besides, they swerved out of the way. Jastrau and Kjær were left with plenty of space around them, as well as too intense sunlight.

Finally they sat in a taxi.

Arnold stood in the doorway of the bar. The uniformed hall porter stood in the entrance to the hotel, and behind the windows were several grinning faces, eager to witness the beginning of the journey to Charlottenlund. Kjær waved his hand in a broad gesture of acknowledgment. His fedora sat low and askew over his forehead.

"Uh," he said as the taxi turned into Farimagsgade. "Strange buildings, what? I don't really like it."

But the park flashed by at their right. The tree branches stretched out over the tall iron fence, and beneath the leaves the passers-by moved restlessly in the flickering light and shadow.

And Jastrau began to be aware of things. The breeze whistled about his forehead. They were in an open-topped taxi. He suddenly discovered that his hands were dirty, as if he had been crawling around on the ground.

But just then Kjær was thrown over against him. They were swinging into the Frederiksborggade crossing. Kjær's hat rolled off onto the floor, and he leaned forward with a groan to retrieve it.

"Oh, oh," he sighed from below. "Isn't there anyone who sympathizes with me? There! There it is."

Jastrau managed with difficulty to help him back into the seat, and once more the hat was placed askew over his forehead.

"Are we going to Canada, over to see Little P.?" asked Kjær, and then he laughed in bewilderment.

Now they drove over the Queen Louise Bridge. On both sides of them stretched the lakes with their neat stone embankments. Far away in the sunlight a charming yellow coloration was discernible, a color that Jastrau had loved as a boy. It was the buildings on distant Østerbro, the corner properties at Willemoesgade. The color was so lovely, like something in a dream. That was the way the horizon should shine.

"Where is Little P.?" Jastrau asked, straightening up in the seat again. From deep within his memory the color glowed like the recollection of a joy he had known long ago, and he found himself preoccupied and lucid at one and the same time. He did not understand the double nature of the feelings that were part of this auto ride, this experience. There above the houses on Nørrebro was the real sunshine, today's sunshine, but beneath it glowed the rays from a bygone sunshine, radiant and full of sentimentality.

"Old Little P. came and got young Little P., and now he's on his way to New York with him—ha ha. But Little P. will come back to the Bar des Artistes, that I know for certain." And Kjær nodded so vigorously that his hat nearly fell off again. "He'll come, yes. For what's he going to do in a wild, uncivilized place like America—among a lot of bar-fly Indians?"

A greenish tinge came over his face, and he shuddered. They drove out along Nørre Allé, with the huge tree trunks like pillars on both sides of them, while ahead the branches met to form high tapering arches. The color was like sunlight coming through stained-glass windows.

The inevitable Kjær groaned deeply.

But in Jastrau's world the long avenue was like a telescope, green on its inner side, while in the round aperture, far in the distance, were some buildings and a yellow streetcar that happened to be passing by.

"Our streetcars are the best looking streetcars in the world," said Jastrau, thinking at the same time that blue suits were flattering to blonde-haired women. But the inevitable Kjær did not hear him. He

sat with his hands folded over his fat belly and his hat over his right
ear while he sang:

> "Think when once the fog has vanished,
> Think when once the fog has—
> When once the fog has vanished,
> Think when once the fog has van—ish—"

"Oh!" he sighed deeply as they rode out past the houses on
Lyngbyvej. He pushed off his hat and mopped his wet brow with a
handkerchief. "Oh, Jazz, thank God! I thought we were in church,
Jazz." He laid his hand heavily on Jastrau's knee and drew a deep,
labored breath. "I can't stand such excitement." Then, with sudden
intensity, he asked, "What—what time is it?" He was blue in the face,
as if about to suffer an attack of apoplexy.

Jastrau pulled his watch out of his vest pocket and looked at it.

It was four-thirty.

And suddenly he could see before him the angle of the hands of the
clock at the Bar des Artistes, and he could see the procession—Kjær
with his unseeing eyes and swaying colossus of a body, and the two
small tail-coated waiters, both leaning in against him to keep him in
equilibrium.

"It's three o'clock," Jastrau replied, drawing a breath of relief when
he saw the inevitable Kjær straighten up with renewed strength.

"I thought I was in church," he repeated with half-open lips, gaping
and smiling in bewilderment. "But where are we going, Jazz? I'm
thirsty."

Jastrau waved his hand at the road ahead. And they drove rapidly
on under the railway grade-crossing gates and out toward the open
country which soon became a residential area. A long straight road lay
ahead.

Now and then they heard the rustle of a treetop above their heads,
now and then a streetcar whizzed by close to them, leaving a long-
sustained singing in the trolley cable as the breeze raised by the car's
passing blew down on them in the open taxi.

"It's—it's like drowning," gasped Kjær, who still sat with his hands
folded over his ponderous belly. His breath came in jerks. "It's more
than a person can stand," he groaned. "It's disgusting all this fresh
air. If only I were back at the bar again."

He laid his hand imploringly on Jastrau's shoulder. "Why did you drag me out here? I don't care anything about seeing the woods." He stamped his foot in rage and went on monotonously, "I don't want to see the woods. I don't want to see the woods."

Out at Femvejen, they swung into Jægersborg Allé with its tall, majestic trees, and when their green crowns began to cast back a wave of sound over their heads Kjær involuntarily ducked his head, folded his hands, and hummed:

"Think when once the fog has vanished—no, no, of course—they're trees." He put both hands up to his face. "They're trees, but—it's like being in church. They're trees."

At the restaurant at the edge of the Charlottenlund woods Jastrau rose up in the seat.

"Stop here."

A yellow anemone! Yes, they were both crazy. A yellow anemone! An obstinate boyish voice from out of the remote past, when life had been different.

"Well—there are the woods," Kjær moaned, laboriously rising from the seat. "Shouldn't we go in and have an absinthe?"

He remained standing for a moment on the sidewalk and let his eyes wander over the edge of the woods and the dark-green treetops. The broad road, flooded with intense light, cut into the forest. Then he shook his head in bewilderment and with a smile took Jastrau by the arm.

"*Allons enfants de la patrie*," he hummed, and they marched on into the little restaurant.

They gulped down their first absinthe in silence.

"I've never seen a blue anemone," Jastrau suddenly sighed. He felt a boundless grief, a grief that could never be allayed.

Kjær's eyes were blurred as he let them wander around the dining room. It had an air of provincial elegance.

"Neither have I," he replied with equal melancholy. "Nobody has. A blue anemone. What are you driving at? What did we have to come out here for anyway?" he whined. "Why, Jazz? After all, I'm not much of a traveler any more. I'm old and tired." And he supported his sparsely-haired pate with both hands as he stared down at the table-cloth.

"What business do I have in strange places?" he groaned.

"I've never seen a blue anemone," Jastrau repeated, and drank the second absinthe. "What shall I do about it?"

Kjær raised his head and looked at him with unspeakable sadness.

"But enough of this," Jastrau exclaimed with a sudden display of energy. "This place is unbearable. And now I'm going out to visit a

342

lady—that's what I'm going to do. Keep a date—that's what. And you're coming with me. Yes, you are. You need a change."

"No, no women," Kjær replied quietly. "You must promise me that." He sighed deeply. "It was bad enough with the trees. I thought I was in church." He sputtered with laughter.

"But you must!" Jastrau's arms were flailing about, and he spoke so loudly that his voice rang disconcertingly through the empty room. "You must!" He pounded the table. "Now I'm going to call her up. I must get this damned, repulsive blue anemone out of my head."

And with an unaccountable zeal he got up from his chair and found his way to a telephone located on the back stairway of the restaurant.

"Hello. This is Ole Jastrau."

He almost fell against the telephone.

"Is it you, Herr Jastrau? I thought you were going to let me down," came Fru Luise's voice.

"Never!" Jastrau gesticulated with exaggerated force so that he had to hop sideways like a starling on a ridgepole in order not to lose his balance and stumble back against the telephone.

Fru Luise laughed skeptically.

"I'm out at Charlottenlund with a friend."

"It wouldn't be your friend who came to see about the door panes, would it?" she asked in mock alarm.

"No, no. He's a gentleman, one of the most genteel persons I know, and we're coming to see you."

He shut his lips tightly. Now he had luckily gotten through that sentence without stumbling, and he drew himself up so energetically that he had to take a step backward, and then another, as far as the telephone would reach.

"But my goodness! Who is he?"

Jastrau came close to the telephone and spoke earnestly.

"A gentleman," he said intently. "And—and we're coming."

"Well, all right," came the resigned answer. "But when?"

"In just a minute."

"From Charlottenlund?" Her voice sounded as if she had misgivings. "Oh, all right then."

"So we'll be there."

And Jastrau hung up immediately. But then he remained standing, staring at the telephone. He really ought not to go back into town to visit Fru Luise, should he? No, he shouldn't. If he went there with Kjær— Well, Kjær was a gentleman. He certainly was. But hadn't they had too much to drink? That damned blue anemone! But he had promised her he would come. It would be impolite not to do so. And

343

the day before, he had forgotten. Impolite. Unforgiveable. So he would have to make amends—and go.

Kjær was having his third absinthe.

"So are we going to the woods?" he asked abstractedly. He muttered as if his lips were stuck together.

"She's waiting," exclaimed Jastrau, downing the fresh glass of absinthe.

Kjær did not understand.

"She? She? A woman?" He smiled drowsily. "Yes, Charles the Twelfth is waiting. Yes, let's go. King Charles, the young hero, there she stood—" He broke off his subdued singing and finished his drink.

Slowly they tottered out to the taxi. The afternoon sun shone on the road so brightly that their eyes hurt. A white hotel on the other side of the road stood deserted and gleaming in the sunlight.

Jastrau told the driver to take them to a street in the Christianshavn section.

"And no trees," Kjær whimpered.

The driver shook his head, but Kjær leaned forward toward him.

"Yes, no tree-lined avenues, do you understand? You must avoid the avenues with trees. My head won't stand it."

Jastrau crawled into the taxi and sank into the seat. Green treetops in sunlight. A glittering blue sky. White houses. And a storm was brewing. A whirring sound around them. And then they put out from land. The pleasant feeling of movement when a ship begins to pitch. Far, far away. It is cool at sea.

> Master Jacob! Master Jacob!
> Are you sleeping? Are you sleeping?
> Don't you hear the bell ring?
> Don't you hear the bell ring?
> Ding–dong–ding.
> Ding–dong–ding.

Gray fronts of some houses. Old-fashioned houses with thick walls.

> Master Jacob! Master Jacob!
> Are you sleeping? Are you sleeping?

It was the inevitable Kjær's hoarse voice. He waved his chubby hands while he sang, and now and then Jastrau felt a shove. "Don't you hear the bell ring? Don't you hear the bell ring? Ding—dong—ding. Ding—dong—ding." The big, puffy face with its bloodshot

344

eyes and blue and green blemishes bent over him, lighted up with a reddish tinge from the afternoon sun, and the damp corners of his mouth glistened. "Master Jacob!"

Jastrau felt a cold shiver zigzag down his spine, as well as a pain in his shoulder caused by the distorted position in which he had been lying back in the seat. Kjær continued to sing in lively fashion, and beyond his head Jastrau caught glimpses of old, brown, house gables that hovered oddly in the distance. A fresh breeze and the sound of gently lapping water aroused him, and he straightened up.

A canal with green water. The dark-green color impressed itself deeply in his consciousness.

"So here we are," he lisped as he crawled freezing out of the taxi, supporting himself against it and feeling his way. The sidewalk whirled, a house with ugly blue-gray walls flickered before his eyes, and he had to support himself against the taxi again. Then finally there was something broad and solid to lean against. The inevitable Kjær, thick-set, portly, and strenuously maintaining his composure, stalked off holding Jastrau by the arm. The street door gave way before their combined weight. Two heavy bodies. They lurched in onto a staircase and floundered and fumbled about until they ended up at a railing.

"Phew!" Kjær groaned. "I have to think for both of us."

"Like hell you do," Jastrau wheezed as he hauled himself up by the railing. "There, there!" He pointed at a door with a nameplate on it. Otto Kryger's name. "Go ahead and ring. Or shall I?" He staggered away from the railing and over toward the door, got his foot in under the doormat, and sank to his knees as he reached up and rang the doorbell.

The door opened at the same time, and Fru Luise's gray silk dress shone in the dark hallway. Her face grew rigid and in an instant took on a lean, oldish look. Only her gray eyes were unnaturally bright, as if she had a fever.

"This is a crazy business we've let ourselves in for," muttered Kjær, who had leaned up against the wall. He wanted to raise his hand politely to his hat but gave up and let the hand fall helplessly back.

"Luise, Fru Lui-i-se," said Jastrau on his knees while he pitched forward so that the door could not be closed. Fru Luise stepped back in horror, placed her thin hands against her breasts, and gasped.

"But—but—" She sounded as if she was sobbing.

"Yes. This is altogether wrong, Frue," came Kjær's voice, and once more he made an unsuccessful attempt to remove his hat. His hand dangled.

But then footsteps sounded on the stairway above. Someone was on the way down. A look of fear flashed across Fru Luise's face, and her eyes lighted up wildly, as if she were trying to look up the stairway and see through to all the floors above.

"Come on, man! Help me!" she whispered vehemently to Kjær. "Oh—what if someone should see us?"

She bent over, seized Jastrau by one arm, and tugged at him. Kjær lurched forward and got Jastrau's feet disengaged from the doormat, shoved them inside, then followed them in. The door slammed shut behind him. They stood in a dark hallway, breathing heavily but feeling relieved. The footsteps passed by outside.

"But what am I going to do with a pair like you?" Fru Luise sighed. Jastrau tried to get up.

"This is altogether wrong, Frue," Kjær said consolingly.

"Wow wow! Wow wow!" Jastrau barked fatuously, crawling on all fours. "I'm a dog. Wow wow! Wow wow!"

"It's altogether wrong, Frue."

And suddenly Fru Luise broke into laughter—a strange, fluttery sort of laughter. "How completely crazy!" she exclaimed. "And—and what luck! I let my housemaid go for the afternoon."

"A dog. Wow wow!"

"It's wrong, Frue—all wrong."

"No, it's funny." Her eyes had opened wide, and they remained so while she laughed. "How funny—and crazy. Yes, crazy. But he can't lie there like that, barking."

"No, he can't. No, he can't." Kjær muttered.

"Wow wow!"

"Ha ha." With a child-like gesture Kjær raised an index finger. "And in the green woods. Fido learned that w–o–w always means wow."

Fru Luise bent over and grabbed Jastrau by the arm again, and now Kjær stooped over too. With difficulty they got Jastrau on his feet and led him in through a sunny dining room in which a smorgasbord had been set for three.

At the sight of the gleaming *snaps* glasses Kjær instinctively came to a halt.

"No, we must go on into my husband's study," Fru Luise commanded. Then she attempted to laugh, but the laughter turned into a groan under her burden.

"I'm sorry," Jastrau sniveled. For a second he had a flash of lucidity. The green canal. He remembered that. They opened a door and helped him to a couch.

346

Chapter Three The morning light shone down from a strange ceiling, and in the white glare three black men popped up like goblins out of a jack-in-the-box. They had no arms. And the black Jesuits' robes in which they were clad grew larger and larger until the three lean drawn faces hung over Jastrau, staring at him with dark squinting eyes.

And then all three of them spat, so that the air around them glistened with the droplets.

Jastrau felt his heart being constricted. It pained him, and he sat up. The men were still standing there. It seemed to him that the long robes came together at the bottom, like three branches merging into one tree trunk. But that was not the reason his heart beat so violently. It was the malice which the three ash-gray faces, with their creases and wrinkles revealed—a caustic, ascetic malice that knew no bounds, the essence of evil in triune monkish form, tainted by piety and contempt—a pale devil in the shape of a Jesuitical hydra.

The lips that had spat were still open and drawn taut, and he was afraid that once again, once more they would spit so that the air around them would glisten. But he would not give in. His heart pounded. He would not give in. And he stared steadfastly at them, stared and cried out because his heart hurt so. And then the faces faded, the black robes became transparent, and everything assumed concrete form. Two black bookcases. One of them he viewed from the side. And between them, a picture of a young pale-faced man with a distinguished oval face and dark ecstatic eyes—a reproduction of one of El Greco's idealized male figures.

Jastrau drew a deep breath of relief. His breast heaved and fell. Where was he? A new fear assailed him. The jail cell! No, no. A strange ceiling. He was afraid of it, hardly dared to look up at it, it made his heart pound so. Where was he? Where? A canal with green water. "Master Jacob. Master Jacob." He remembered, and his whole body began to tremble. Here he lay on a strange couch, fully clothed. He even had his shoes on.

And once more he let his glance wander over the menacing white ceiling. Over by the window the light was pouring in. Brilliant reflections undulated fitfully across the ceiling with the serpentine suppleness of water.

A door opened, and a pale, slightly-built woman with an almost boyish figure, dressed in pink pajamas, stood in the doorway. She looked at him with wide-open eyes.

"Why did you scream?" she asked breathlessly.

He sat up and peered at her through the morning glare. There were bags under her eyes, and her face was swollen from lack of sleep. The skin over her cheeks and neck sagged like that of an old woman.

"Did I scream?" he asked, and a smile passed over his lips. He could feel that his lips were dry and burning, and he was aware of an itching that bespoke a growing stubble of beard. He rubbed his hand awkwardly over it and smiled again, a canny, desperately ironic smile.

Fru Luise's breast was heaving violently beneath the flimsy pajama top.

"Oh, you scared me so," she moaned as she caught her breath.

"I simply had an hallucination," Jastrau replied with the same fixed smile. He spoke as if hallucinations were an everyday occurrence.

And just then Fru Luise looked chastely down at her pajamas.

"And here I am," she laughed, "standing stark naked in front of a strange man." There was an odd quiver to her laughter.

"Compromised!" she exclaimed, bringing her feet and the legs of the pink pajama pants together. He suspected that her legs were skinny and her knees sharp.

"Well!" He drew the exclamation out. But she had concealed herself behind a portière so that only her head, with its ash-gray, rumpled boyish hair, protruded. As she stood there she broke into loud shrill laughter.

"This is wild," she said in a high-pitched voice.

"Is it?" Jastrau asked apathetically as he raised his eyebrows and looked down at his soiled hands. That was the way hands always looked the morning after—the skin grimy, the fingers stained with nicotine, the nails black. He could smell them; it was an odor like that of dusty old clothes. "I just think it's ludicrous," he added.

"Really now, you don't mean that!" she exclaimed. "And you have the nerve to put it that way! Ludicrous! Don't you consider me and the position you've placed me in?"

Jastrau glanced up and stared into her flashing gray eyes, stared so long that a faint blush spread over her powdered face.

"Yes, that's exactly what I'm doing," he said, compressing his lips in irony. "For you it's ludicrous. As for me, I don't have to care."

"What do you mean by that?" she asked impetuously, stepping halfway out from behind the portière. The neck of the pajama top had fallen aside, and in the glow from the pink fabric one of her breasts, which had come to view, shone with a fresh and youthful charm, and

348

the dark nipple caught his glance and fascinated him by its disproportionate size, so large was the brown aureola surrounding it.

"I mean I have to leave," he said. He got up and walked toward the door.

But she stepped in his way.

"No. You must tell me what you mean by 'ludicrous.'"

And with a wild, distraught expression she looked him squarely in the eye. Her expression was much too intense. The skin around her chin looked old and wrinkled. And he wanted to cup his hands, take her gently by the arms, and move her aside, but one of his hands slipped in against her breast. Was it she who had thrust her breast forward? Through the thin pajamas, he felt softness and warmth, a slender female form, and he saw her breast, fresh and youthful in a glow of morning sunlight through pink cloth. And it was this glow of youth and morning that welled up in him like a dream. He seized her, kissed her. Her lips remained motionless. They gave no indication of proficiency. But the expression on her face was resolute—that of a married woman. And he lifted her up and carried her to the couch, while her dilated eyes stared and stared and were so large that they seemed to take in the entire room in its morning radiance, as well as the window and the houses across the canal.

She was animated and much too hasty, devoid of real passion. She exhibited no emotion, only movement—no understanding, only experience. And so it became not a fusion but an encounter, without ecstasy or synthesis of feeling.

And she jabbered. "My, how wild!" There was nothing wild about it. "Do you love me? Tell me." She stroked the back of his neck fitfully; it was like the wing beats of young birds. "Oh, you barbaric creature!" She rubbed her cheeks against his so that the stubble-growth of beard crackled. "And you're unshaven, you wild man. And all you want to do is get drunk." Her voice rose to a frenzied pitch and she laughed. "Oh you—fierce and unshaved—oh you, you—"

"Now it's probably not at all so ludicrous," Jastrau said, and went over to the window. Rose-red morning clouds drifted across a pale blue sky. Clouds that seemed to reflect the glow of Fru Luise's pajamas. The houses with the old-fashioned gables on the other side of the canal stood with their colors revealed, brown and yellow, soft as skin, and red as if transparently suffused with blood. Fru Luise's breast.

"What are you thinking of?" asked Fru Luise. She was applying face powder.

"I'm only being quiet," he replied. "I'm only being stupid," he heard someone say clearly. Every word came from a voice he did not

349

recognize, so it was very likely his own. An auditory hallucination.

"Ah yes," Fru Luise sighed from over on the couch. She was coloring her mouth with a lipstick. "Passion—that's life." And she laughed. He could hear that she was exerting herself to be hilarious. "Life is so many-sided. 'Drink until your head swells,' as your friend said." And she struck her hand vigorously against the couch.

"What happened to Kjær?" Jastrau asked. He was still standing by the window, looking out over the canal.

"He took a taxi."

Suddenly she stood behind him, flung her arms around his neck and hung squirming on his back.

"But Ole, he was that old sot we saw in the bar. I was so afraid, and now I'm so happy, so happy. He was polite."

"He always is," Jastrau managed to say. Her arms were practically choking him.

"And drunk as well," she laughed, and once again suspended herself along his back with her legs thrust out behind her so that he almost toppled over. "But I did get so frightened. You crawled around on all fours and barked, and I was furious and laughed because I didn't know that you were my Great Dane—mine, mine. Do you always scream in your sleep?"

And then she snuggled her head in under his arm.

"Squeeze it, squeeze it!" she cried out, her voice muffled in his clothing. "I've always had too many brains, and I don't want it that way any more. Squeeze it to pieces, do you hear?"

He squeezed her head gently, but then all at once found himself beginning to tremble. The three malicious faces. It was the trinity of wickedness that he had beheld, the essence of evil. And now? He was a friend of Otto Kryger. It would be impossible to look him in the eye any longer.

"Oh, you," he said disconsolately, letting his hand glide caressingly over her head, which he still held tightly under his arm. Half-strangled, she laughed into his jacket. Her ash-gray bobbed hair hung down, bristling like a dust brush. He went on, "It was a real bit of stupidity, this."

Immediately she withdrew her head.

"What do you mean?" she asked savagely, and stood before him. She had been too liberal with the lipstick, so that her mouth had a hard, ruthless look. Dry, thin lips covered with red.

And he looked down at the slight female figure in the pink pajamas, passed his eyes over her as she stood there in front of him, and thought that there was nothing appealing about her figure—no soft, gentle curves.

350

"It was a stupid thing to do," he repeated, looking into her eyes. They were gray and weary.

But deep within the gray eyes something dark stirred—a look of understanding. She became herself again, and once more her eyes were those of a woman of experience. She looked at Jastrau's corpulent figure, his broad unshaven face, his weak disillusioned mouth, and eyes that already shone with distrust, bloodshot as they were. She looked at his cheeks and at the creases of flesh under his chin. The entire lower part of his face was dissolving into a shapeless mass despite the fact that he had originally had a forceful chin. The tumefied face of a drunkard. Drink until your head swells.

And she laughed and nodded. "Yes, so it was," she said.

It was an uneasy, nervous laugh, and suddenly she turned her back to him. Her head with its rumpled bobbed hair was lowered as if she was thinking.

"Now you must go, do you hear?" she said as if to herself.

"Go?" he asked in a hoarse voice.

She was still standing with her back toward him, and she nodded in a determined manner.

"Yes, yes. I don't want to see you any more," she said firmly.

She was about to slip away from him. So soon. Should he seize the initiative and consolidate his conquest? When he had been drinking he was equal to a conquest. But was conquest the word for it?

"Yes, I suppose that's best. Well, good-by then, Fru Luise, and—" He stopped. "And, thank you."

She whirled about in surprise. A broad smile spread over her features, and she burst into laughter.

"And so you thank me. There's nothing to thank me for, sir." And suddenly she let her hands fall to her sides, twisted her lips in an expression of wistfulness, and shook her head. "It was nothing. You had better go, and—no, no, it was I who was looking for the big experience. No, no—good-by now. Say good-by to a little wife who is disregarded and neglected. Good-by—go now. Say good-by to your friend's wife. Go! Don't you hear me?"

And she ran over to the couch, flung herself down on it, and buried her head in a pillow.

"Yes. Now I'm going," he said.

She did not sob. She only hid her face.

And Jastrau walked quietly and thoughtfully toward the door.

He left.

Down at the corner of Torvegade he lighted a pipe. The streets were empty and bright, with the multiple colors of the stonework blossoming faintly in the pavements and on the building fronts. A solitary truck gardener's wagon from Amager rumbled along with the horse and driver enveloped in an atmosphere of morning grumpiness. The horseshoes clattered sedately, and the echoes took their time about resounding from the walls of the buildings.

Jastrau walked slowly toward the Knippel Bridge. He leaned his head back, as all morning ramblers are in the habit of doing, let his gaze follow the lines of the roofs outlined against the pale blue sky and the reddish clouds—Fru Luise—smiled and observed the reflections of the day's brightness in the highest windows. All the fifth floors were as empty and glittering as soap bubbles. Curtains and potted plants and all signs of humanity had vanished behind floating films of moisture, obliterated by the luster of the sky mirrored in the windowpanes.

But he did not want to think.

He rubbed his hands together, so that he got a feeling of being himself, and sauntered on calmly. He noticed how tender his feet were, and trod gingerly on the sidewalk. Now and then he took a resolute step. He was himself.

The verdigris-coated dragons entwined around the steeple of the stock exchange! There were many delightful sights to be seen in the morning, all clearly revealed and each a joy in itself. And the morning air was so still that the smoke from his pipe rose in a straight, undispersed column.

He had achieved a conquest with a woman. Did that enable him to see things more clearly? A bright morning did. The first time he had been with a woman, he had stood and looked up at the tops of the trees along Rahbeksallé. That too had been a morning sky, but darker. And the façades of the houses, standing out white in the early dawn. The same clearly discerned emptiness. A fifth-story windowpane mirroring the brightness of the summer sky.

Højbroplads lay deserted, tawny and inviting as a sitting room. Why did he want to walk along Strøget on his way home? It was pleasant and had a true Copenhagen atmosphere. Strøget was part of a morning stroll.

A friend's wife. But wasn't it hysterical? Otto worshiped strange gods. Didn't he deserve it? It was a punishment that had long awaited him.

And the pigeons cooed on Strøget's rooftops. A glimpse of a photographer's studio window. A faint shadow over the street, transparent and brown. The fronts of the buildings and the sidewalks glistened. And the constant rolling sound of pigeons, as if the courtyards behind were swarming with them. Now and then a noisy flapping, followed by a procession of wings and white feathers through the air.

352

The cooing was like that of pigeons in empty palaces. In the deserted palace courtyards. Copenhagen on an early summer morning.

But over toward the right on Nytorv was the courthouse with its colossal pillars, a yellowish-brown temple, and behind its walls was the jail.

Cold shivers ran up his spine.

He was wearing his suspenders. His pants stayed up. But there were many forms of humiliation. It was lucky that he had gotten the hotel chambermaid to sew up the rip in his pants the day before—the Catholic rip, a wound sustained in a spiritual battle. How long was it since he had been home on Istedgade? It had been the day before yesterday, when the janitor had come dragging the boards up the stairs to nail them over the holes in the panes of the hallway door. How long ago that seemed! In the meantime he had come to know Fru Luise.

"*Dagbla-det! Dagbla-det!*" he heard a voice shouting from out of a dark ravine that emerged into the Town Hall Square, where the buildings lay in a pale haze. Frederiksberggade.

When he encountered the newsboy he did not buy a paper. Strange. He wanted to break himself of the habit of feverishly grabbing for any paper that still bore the smell of the rotary press.

And then across the sunlit, enormous Town Hall Square. A pale-faced girl came sauntering around the corner by the Paraply. He knew her by sight. He wondered if she were the one who up at the editorial room was known as The Whistle. There was another who was called The Face. It wasn't she.

And finally he stood with sore feet outside the entranceway in Istedgade. Why hadn't he gone to a hotel? Why? Steffensen was probably lying up there asleep, as if it were his apartment. Had Anne Marie returned?

As he opened the heavy outer door, he shut his eyes. He was so tired, and the darkness seemed filled with fire and smoke. A flaming unrest that lurked within him.

"Hee hee—good morning." And before him stood the janitor with red-rimmed eyes and two beer bottles protruding from the front pockets of his overalls. "No, it isn't easy to be up in the front lines." He was lurching.

Jastrau nodded.

"Now we can go along together a few steps—up the stairs, as the saying goes. Company makes the way shorter."

"I'm tired."

"Yes, I ought to get a little shut-eye too before tomorrow—which incidentally is today. I've been talking politics fluently with the baker, you might say. He's the one who'd like to buy your phonograph, but damn it, Jastrau, I want a commission. Aw, Jastrau, you drunken galoot."

They were on their way up the stairs, which looked dusty in the morning light. The windows needed cleaning.

"Drunken lout," said the janitor, grinning and clapping him on the shoulder. "And here I've been thinking all along that you're a genteel sort and a good-for-nothing, and then you turn out to be a human being. A human being. And we're on familiar terms, right? Believe me, I made quite a commotion putting those boards up over your hallway door. Hee hee. The place looks as if there'd been a murder there."

Jastrau looked up at his door and stopped abruptly. The frosted patterned panes, the big star-shaped hole with its exploded jagged edges, and the crude boards that had been nailed up behind it so that an intruder could not reach an arm in and open the door from the inside—the crass reality of it all made such an impression on him that he caught his breath. It was havoc, all too clearly visible, and the janitor was right. It looked as if a murder had been committed behind the barricaded door.

"Nice work, so to speak," said the janitor, snickering and lurching against him.

"Is he asleep in there?" Jastrau asked, puffing for breath. He could not take his eyes away from the damaged door. It was the entrance to his home. What a home!

"Him—that lout? Yes, he's playing lord and master. Frøken Jensen is scared to death of him. He's a tough customer, and besides he comes from a good family."

"Frøken Jensen?" Jastrau asked in wearied bewilderment, turning aside and leaning against the bannister.

"Yes, the young girl who ran out on you that night. But," he went on, tottering a bit, "I can't make it, the way these stairs are heaving."

"Then we'll sit down," replied Jastrau, and sat on the steps with his back toward the disconcerting door.

"All right, then we'll sit down," the janitor exclaimed. "Phew! The battle isn't so easy. No, indeed it isn't."

Jastrau stared down at the staircase window with its little air hole, and out into the courtyard.

"Frøken Jensen—Anne Marie," he said softly. "So she ran upstairs to you?"

"Yes. Not to me that is, but to my wife, of course," said the janitor, grinning and leaning his elbows comfortably on the stair tread behind him as he stared down at the bagging front of his overalls. "But what's

354

that I see sticking out of my front pockets? Two beers—for two gentlemen. So you see, I had an idea I'd meet you on the stairway. Have one."

He yanked the caps off the bottles and let them roll down the stairs. Then he and Jastrau crossed and clinked the bottle necks, toasted, and drank.

"Look here, Jastrau," the janitor said, moaning over the neck of the bottle so that a hollow whistle sounded from down inside it, "aren't you going to sell that dandy phonograph?"

"No," came the irritated reply. "But is Anne Marie still staying with you? Is she upstairs?"

The janitor scratched his red hair.

"Anne Marie? Oh, you mean Frøken Jensen." He grinned thoughtfully. "I promised her I wouldn't tell anyone, but it isn't so easy to keep your mouth shut when you run into someone on the stairs and you're both going up to hit the sack. Ah—that bottle hit the spot. It's wonderful how beer can keep on tasting so good."

Jastrau wrinkled his brows.

"You can't possibly afford it," he said.

"Beer? No," replied the janitor, gaping at him and then suddenly inserting the bottle into his mouth, since it happened to be open anyway.

"But one manages to get what he has to have," he said, puffing and glancing at Jastrau with a crafty look in his bleary, ingenuous eyes. "Listen now, wouldn't you like to sell that phonograph—once for all?" he exclaimed suddenly, giving Jastrau a playful shove.

"I meant you can't afford to have her living with you," Jastrau said obstinately, as if trying to cut through his own morning stupor and the janitor's fanciful thoughts at one and the same time.

"No, I can't afford that either. No sir!"

"What do you intend to do with her?"

"Hee hee." The janitor slapped his thighs. "Do you think my wife would put up with it? No, then you don't know her. Besides, she's still young and frisky herself. Hell, you must have noticed that yourself. She can give a man enough to do—and one man doesn't amount to so much in that respect. Right? *Skaal!* Beer is a wonderful thing."

Jastrau drank without enjoyment. He felt listless.

"I don't understand it," he said, staring down at the stair treads.

"Damned if I do either," said the janitor with a grin. "And I can't for the life of me understand what it is that you don't understand. Is it about the phonograph?"

"I don't understand how you can have Anne Marie living with you."

355

"Anne Marie? Who? Oh, Frøken Jensen." The janitor raised the bottle in an elucidating gesture. "Well, you see, she helps my wife, and then my wife helps her to look for a job—in the help-wanted ad-ver-tise-ments. Phew, a big word for so early in the morning. And she loans her things to wear—you know, so she can look decent, so to speak, when she goes looking for a job. She's really a good-hearted soul—my wife, that is. A big heart. Big bubbies. Big hips. Big ass. Everything about her is big. Hee hee. But I suppose a person shouldn't talk that way about his wife."

Jastrau got up and looked at him.

"You're nice people," he said. He did not know if he meant it, but he felt a compulsion to be genial.

"What's that? Are you being sarcastic?" the janitor asked with a suspicious jerk of his head.

Jastrau was already on his way down the stairs.

"What do you mean? And are you leaving?"

"Yes, I don't want to sleep here," Jastrau replied, nodding over his shoulder. He had suddenly come to his senses. He did not want to see that door any longer. It was too disconcerting. Never, never would he forget it, with its broken panes and the boards nailed over them. It was as if he had seen his own life in ruins.

"You don't want to stay here with me any longer, is that it? But what about the bills? What about them?"

"What bills?"

"The glazier and the boards and everything. Did you think I was making you a present of them?" The janitor stuck his freckled face out angrily toward him.

Jastrau had already descended a few steps. Then he carefully turned to face the janitor, so stiffly and cautiously that he did not catch so much as a glimpse of the broken panes in the hallway door. The janitor was still sitting astride the stairway, his face thrust forward in an expression of chagrin.

"Send them over to my hotel," Jastrau answered arrogantly. Involuntarily the janitor drew himself up.

"All right. I'll do that."

Then he collapsed again and shut himself up in his thoughts.

But as Jastrau continued down the stairs, fragments of a muddled monologue reached his ears.

"You never know how you stand—oh, my God. Just when we're sitting here—everything nice and comfortable—then they suddenly get up on their high horse. Oh, oh, oh—what the hell! Nice people—you too. Oh, my God—such a dandy phonograph."

356

And when Jastrau had almost reached the bottom of the stairs he heard a groan and a scraping of feet. At the same time the two beer bottles came bouncing and rattling down the stairway step by step.

It was the janitor who had gotten to his feet with difficulty and was on the way up to catch a wink of sleep before morning.

With a feeling of having walked many miles, Jastrau made his way back to the Town Hall Square. At the streetcar stop in the middle of the deserted square stood a young girl in a black dress that shone like lacquer about her superb figure. In her flesh-colored stockings and tight-fitting dress, she looked as if she were in a bathing suit, glistening wet in the morning sunlight. Jastrau made a close detour around her. For a moment he was aroused. He was a conqueror of women. But her face was smeared with make-up, and her red mouth looked weary and shameless. Fru Luise had gray, intelligent eyes. It was all so remote and unreal.

Then, feeling even wearier, he made his way over toward the hotel.

Outside of it hung the large oval sign. The letters "Bar des Artistes" were painted in an arc, the way one would sketch a bridge, and beneath it in a straight line, denoting the water under the bridge, was the inciting word "Dancing."

He was home.

And with a feeling of peace, he went up to the entrance of the hotel and rang the bell.

"Have you heard about it, Herr Jastrau?" the hall porter whispered to him after he had let him in. "Half an hour ago, Herr Kjær came down fully dressed and freshly shaved, and wanted to get into the bar. He thought it was one o'clock."

The porter hid his little black mustache behind his hand and laughed.

"You have no idea how long it took to convince him that it was still morning. Ha ha. It makes me laugh to think about it. And do you know what he said? No, you can't guess. He said he'd gotten mixed up about the time because he had been to church—that's what he said—and he couldn't stand such an irregular life. He hadn't been drunk at four-thirty. Ha ha ha! And as a matter of fact, he said it was you who had dragged him off to church. Is that really true, Herr Jastrau?"

"No. We rode out to the woods. When he saw the trees, the branches and the treetops, he was afraid and thought he was in church," Jastrau replied with a tired smile.

"A-ha," exclaimed the porter, almost breaking into a discreet giggle. "You don't say. Yes, Herr Kjær is priceless."

357

And then: "Good morning, Herr Jastrau." Whereupon the porter opened the elevator door with a clatter.

Just then a streetcar rattled by out on the street.

The day had begun.

Chapter Four

Two days later, Ole Jastrau sat in the hotel's ground-floor restaurant and ate his lunch. Through the curtain he could see the glitter of sunlight high up between the rooftops, but only a pale, sickly light reached the place where he was sitting. The view of the inevitable firewall dampened his spirits, and he rubbed his hands nervously on his napkin.

It was almost impossible to sit still. Waiting for the next dish was unbearable. Now and then he would crumble a roll to bits out of impatience.

Then he raised the *snaps* glass cautiously to his lips. But the liquor in the glass quivered. It was his hands. Impossible to keep them steady. He held one hand out in front of him and observed it for a long while—thirty seconds. It was trembling.

But he had to have another *snaps*.

Kjær was certainly not up yet. He missed him. It occurred to him that he was the only person he knew. The only one. And they were apparently going the same way. But Kjær—that decayed tooth—had assets, managed for him by a lawyer. It took money to go to the dogs. To the dogs? Nonsense. Now he had collected his three months's pay from *Dagbladet*. Most of it had gone for support of his wife and child. And the rest? Should he count his money? I can't drink myself to death because I have to stay sober in order to earn the money I must have for drinks. I can't afford to drink. Or how should he put it? It had the makings of an aphorism. But an aphorism is no good until it is collapsed like a telescope. Akvavit is a medicine. And he closed his eyes as he emptied another glass of *snaps*.

"There's a phone call for you, Herr Jastrau."

A waiter bowed to him with a knowing smile. Oh, yes—the night before. Yes, indeed. He had been over here in the restaurant the night before, and in *that* condition. Who had seen him? What had he said? The waiter's smile was most omniscient. Ah yes, he was living in an atmosphere of waiters' smiles; they were crowding in on him much too closely, and they could not be driven away with a mere flick of a napkin. Like mosquitoes! And their smiles were the same as those that hovered in a swarm about the inevitable Kjær—indulgent, knowledgeable, intimate, reproachful, and admonitory.

"A phone call? Thanks," he replied as he got up.

But who would take it into his head to call him? He came to a halt in the middle of the deserted room. A Frenchman with a full white beard was in the process of wiping his mouth with his napkin. He was the only guest in the restaurant—a wine salesman from Bordeaux. They said *"Bon jour, monsieur"* to each other. They did that every day at lunch. Then they laughed: "Hee hee, hee hee."

And then the world grew half-dark and empty again while the sun shone outside behind the curtains. Always behind the curtains. People, bicycles, automobiles—fleeting glimpses of them. But who would think of calling him? It might be Fru Luise. He had not heard from her since that day. Strange. Was he becoming alienated from everything? What is it that happens to a person? The restaurant, the bar, the inevitable Kjær kept recurring. Semidarkness, phonograph music, a taste as if a five-øre piece were resting on his tongue, a feeling of repulsion at the thought of whiskey—a feeling which nevertheless abated each day—all these recurred incessantly. It was like a stream, a river flowing on. It was undoubtedly Fru Luise who had called him. And if it was she, what then? A voice from the bank of the stream as he floated by.

Floated—floated—floated. But it would stop of its own accord. He would have to write an article to get money—now—today—no, perhaps not until tomorrow. But it would stop of its own accord.

And he was able to smile craftily to himself. Canny was the word for such a smile. For this process of disintegration must automatically cease. This he knew in his innermost being; it was his own subtle, scintillating secret.

He seized the telephone receiver.

"De profundis clamo," he heard a deep voice say.

"What the devil?" Jastrau was on the point of hanging up.

"It's I—Vuldum—calling from out of the depths."

"Oh," Jastrau replied, his face clouding with weariness. Were they now going to talk some more about that broken pane of glass out in Stenosgade?

"I think it was wise of you, Ole," Vuldum went on without explanation. "You got out just in time."

"So—do you really think so?"

At last Vuldum knew. Now the editorial room was buzzing.

"But you might have told me in advance," came Vuldum's voice in a

359

tone of mild indignation. "I could perhaps have prevented a complete nonentity from becoming your successor. Now one can never tell. Some Mr. Nobody, perhaps."

"You may be right about that, Vuldum," Jastrau replied listlessly.

"It shows a certain lack of loyalty to a colleague, don't you admit that?" The voice sounded sorrowful on Jastrau's behalf.

"Yes," said Jastrau.

"Self-awareness is a good thing," said Vuldum, laughing. "But since you've acknowledged so much, perhaps you'll also admit that you owe Father Garhammer an apology. I know that he has the glazier's bill for that piece of glass. It's four or five kroner—a mere trifle."

"Am I being forced to Canossa?" Jastrau asked with a laugh.

"No, Ole. All you have to do is show a little ordinary courtesy. After all, it was I who had the honor of introducing you to each other."

"You seem to be taking a special interest in this matter."

"Let's say special as far as you're concerned, Ole. I know that Father Garhammer has been expecting you every day. He can always be seen at about four o'clock."

Vuldum's tone was subdued and earnest.

"So now you ought to think it over, Ole. You understand, of course, that it makes no difference to me."

He wants to force me to go out there, Jastrau thought as he hung up. Force me! I'm to be humiliated. Out in Stenosgade. Come cowering. Sit there in the parlor and cower in humility. Initiate me into the confessional. *De profundis clamavi ad te, Domine.* A repentant sinner, paying for a bit of broken glass. But earlier Vuldum had referred to it as a pane of glass. And the rumors. He was sure that rumor had magnified it so that it had become a church window with stained and leaded panes. But now it had again become a piece of glass. A person had to fight his way by slow degrees to get an admission of the truth.

Back in the restaurant, Jastrau caught a glimpse of himself in a pier glass, a full-size image of himself in his black tight-fitting jacket and light checked trousers, like a Negro jazz-band player or a ship's cook on shore leave. It would be good if one could form a picture of himself as seen by an objective observer. It might yield some badly needed information. But then there were those concave mirrors at Tivoli. Now they made one look fat and round, now tall and lanky. They contorted one's face into weird, ascetic expressions and endowed one first with long, stilt-like legs and a short torso, then with a long torso and short legs like those of a badger.

And weren't there concave mirrors all about you? He wondered.

How did he look to the lady near the buffet over there behind the artificial palm? The room was so dark that the electric lights had been turned on, and there she sat, fat and pale from overeating, and smiling graciously. And how did he appear to Anne Marie? The concave mirrors at Tivoli! Was she just as afraid of him as she was of Steffensen?

And Fru Luise?

Then he heard swift, energetic footsteps in the room and turned around uneasily. It was a small, dark-haired man in a smart, light-colored topcoat. He carried his felt hat in his swinging hand.

"Well, there you are. And already at the *snaps*. Ha ha."

Jastrau turned deathly pale and felt dizzy as he encountered a sympathetic, cheery smile.

"Hello, Kryger," he said hoarsely.

But Kryger sat down, unconcerned, on a chair opposite him and tossed his hat onto an unoccupied table.

"Yes, I'm busy. A beer, waiter. Yes. But nothing to eat. No. And how are things with you, Jastrau? Gone completely to hell, I dare say."

Jastrau looked at his powerful hands, the strong wrists, and the gleaming white cuffs. Those were the hands that caressed Fru Luise and many other women—lots of them.

"The wreck never founders," he replied. "It just drifts along. It gives in to the opposition."

"Well, are you in a funereal mood? That goes with the lighting in here. Incidentally, I bring you greetings from Luise. She's very fond of you."

Jastrau had to meet Kryger's glance. His eyes were dark and cordial. A broad smile lit up his face.

"The feeling is mutual," Jastrau replied.

"But I say—you look really terrible," Kryger went on, drawing his chair closer to the table. "Have you let go all your moorings?"

"Yes, so to speak."

Kryger's tie was smoothly knotted and rounded at the ends.

"Your marriage?"

"Yes."

"And the boy, too?"

"Yes."

Kryger apparently never fastened the top button of his vest.

"And *Dagbladet*? So I hear."

"Yes."

"And so you're going to start writing on your own—producing?"

"No."

Kryger had a low forehead. It was odd to be sitting there looking at it. There was a slight hump over each eye—roots of the horns.

But Kryger leaned back, returned Jastrau's glance, and exposed his teeth in a broad, ironic smile.

"What do you want to do, then? Drink?"

Jastrau quickly shifted his gaze. This aggressive cordiality made him ill at ease. Kryger looked so bright and cheerful that the effect was dazzling. It was strange that Fru Luise—

"You ought not to keep on living here. You'll only ruin yourself if you do," Kryger went on, taking two cigars from his pocket. "Have one. You ought to move in with us. I have a couch in my study."

"You have a couch?" Jastrau asked slowly. Three black figures like three branches stemming from one trunk. Three spitting faces. The essence of evil. How wild! Do you love me? Tell me! Oh you barbaric, unbarbered man!

"You sound as if you didn't believe me, Jastrau."

"Yes, I believe you," Jastrau replied somberly while he stared and stared at Kryger's hands.

"You seem preoccupied, to put it mildly. Either that or you have a hangover."

Jastrau knew that Kryger was not stupid. But could this be? Was it so easy to feel superior to a person? Yes, simply impose upon him, deceive him. Then one became superior—held the fourth position at the card game. And Jastrau looked directly into Kryger's eyes.

"What a wild look you have, Jastrau."

"Yes, I've been drinking a good deal lately," Jastrau replied. And he kept looking straight into Kryger's eyes. How easy it was.

"But things can't possibly go on this way, man," Kryger exclaimed, carefully, almost meticulously cutting the tip off his cigar and blowing through it to get the dust out. Again Jastrau's eyes grazed Kryger's forehead and his comely, smooth, blue-black hair.

"Well then, what do you want to do?" asked Kryger.

"Sometimes I imagine I have a philosophical purpose," Jastrau said. "I've wanted to get at the meaning of things—my own opinions, for example. I've wanted to find out what's behind them."

"Yes, and there was lust and drunkeness, wasn't there?" Kryger said, laughing and lighting his cigar. "Are you in love with someone?"

"No," Jastrau replied with a smile. And suddenly he dared say it. He keyed himself up for it, as if tuning an instrument. "If I were, it would be with your wife."

"You don't say," replied Kryger, opening his eyes wider. A twinkle came into them, and then he smiled ironically. "As a matter of fact, Jastrau, I don't think you know anything about love. I've never thought so."

"You don't think so?" Jastrau said provocatively with a sudden burst of laughter. "The fact of the matter is that you're right."

Kryger nodded understandingly.

"As far as I'm concerned, women fall into two definite categories—the ones a man makes love to and those he worships," Jastrau went on. He felt a compulsion to be tactlessly honest with this man whom he had deceived, lay himself open, confess his guilt, regardless of the consequences, and yet escape unscathed. "There are Mary Magdalenes and Madonnas, and it's impossible for me to comprehend the two in one woman."

"But you have been married, haven't you?" Kryger asked abruptly.

Jastrau nodded.

"What's the real reason for your divorce?"

"Well, I hardly know. Was it I who was unfaithful, or was it she?" Jastrau stared straight ahead with a vacant look. "I miss my boy so much," he added.

Kryger had taken the cigar from his mouth. He uttered a low whistle.

"And your mother?" he asked.

"Are you conducting a cross-examination?" Jastrau asked in a tone of annoyance.

"Oh no, not at all," Kryger replied amiably, almost tenderly. "I am very sorry, old boy. I am very sorry. It was just something that occurred to me as I sat here thinking, and then I forgot myself. I had no intention of hurting you—no certainly not. That wasn't the reason I came here—you likable old fool."

He inclined his head to one side and regarded Jastrau in a cordial manner. His wide, sensitive lips were as soft as those of a woman.

But Jastrau leaned his forehead against his hands, stared down at the tablecloth, and was on the point of bursting into tears. It would have been a relief to do so. But would they have been anything but alcoholic tears, a manifestation of a hangover headache, and an exhibition of undignified remorse? This was the day he was supposed to go out to Stenosgade. *De profundis clamavi! De profundis clamavi!* He would have to get it over with, get it off his chest. But when had he made up his mind to that?

He mopped his face with his hand and drew himself up with a scowl of contempt. He would have to go through with it.

"It was something else entirely that I wanted to see you about,"

363

Kryger said abruptly. His eyes were again flashing the signal for a surprise attack. "Do you think you might like to take a job in Berlin as secretary to Professor Geberhardt?"

"Secretary?" Jastrau sat up with a start.

Kryger nodded. "To the best of my recollection, you know shorthand. I remember seeing some shorthand notes on one of your rough drafts."

Jastrau sighed.

"Yes, that's right. But that doesn't mean that I have a degree in economics, and so what would Geberhardt want with me?"

"I know all that," Kryger said sharply. "But I'm in correspondence with Geberhardt, and in his last letter he asked me to get him a secretary. I'm going to talk to him over the telephone tonight in Berlin, and so I'll arrange it, because you have to get away from this damned city here. That's the main thing."

Jastrau gazed at him with a tired smile. It was indeed an awkward bit of magnanimity on Kryger's part. If only he could say no to it. Did Kryger know something? If only he could say no.

"It does present some difficulties," he objected.

"What are they?" Kryger asked, showing his teeth.

"My job with *Dagbladet*. The three months aren't up yet."

"I'll fix that. The most important thing is to see that you get out of town. All I'll have to do is drop a hint to Editor Iversen. Do you think it's to the advantage of the newspaper to have you floundering around here in this condition?"

"It looks as if I'm to be sent into exile," Jastrau said sullenly, narrowing his eyes suspiciously.

"Are there any further difficulties?"

"Yes. Lots of them. I don't know my way around in Berlin."

"Nonsense! If you have something I can write on I'll give you Professor Geberhardt's address."

Jastrau searched in his wallet and in his pockets. He had his passport, which he always carried with him, and the fire-insurance policy.

"You may as well write it on this," he said, shoving the insurance policy across the table. "I even give you leave to draw on it—decorate it." He laughed.

Kryger inspected the policy and wrote the professor's address on a section of white margin: Landauerstrasse, Berlin-Willmersdorf.

"If you use this as a notebook, it's going to look really pretty. But I take it there are still other difficulties."

"Yes, plenty of them. What about the separation from my wife? That isn't arranged."

"I'll take care of that—get a lawyer and all that sort of thing. The

364

only thing that really matters is that you get away from this destructive city."

"Since when have you become a moralist?" Jastrau asked, winking at the philandering journalist.

"Strictly speaking, that has nothing to do with the matter," Kryger said with a smile. He seemed quite unconcerned and self-assured, but nevertheless insistent. He sat erect, his diminutive body enfolded in the wrinkled summer topcoat. "And now I don't suppose there's anything else to stand in your way. Tonight or tomorrow night, the hall porter will have a message for you, and then all you have to do is hustle off and catch the express train south. It will do you good to learn something about economics, to get a little idea of what capitalism is all about. Don't you think that has just as much significance as your enchanting concern with the work of young poets?"

"Yes, perhaps just as much—but no more," Jastrau replied.

Kryger smiled ironically.

"So then it's all agreed, Jastrau, because I'm in a rush."

"But I don't have the money for a trip to Berlin," Jastrau said, provokingly interposing a new hindrance to the plan. But then, with a hurried motion, Kryger slapped his wallet down on the table. "You're quite dependable in money matters, so here's a hundred kroner."

Jastrau took the bill, folded it casually, and stuck it in his vest pocket.

"What has made you so philanthropical?" he asked in a somewhat scornful tone.

"It annoys me to look at a wreck, to use your own expression," came the quick reply. "But now I'm going, and you might as well come along with me and buy the ticket at Bennett's at once."

They left together.

But Jastrau could not take Kryger altogether seriously. Laying out the money for his trip. Such a noble offer. He looked haughtily down at Kryger's elegant little figure and smiled at the authoritative way he carried himself. And when Kryger turned for a moment to look at two bareheaded little office girls and stared at them with complete absorption, Jastrau had to laugh. Kryger's fedora was pulled low over his forehead. The two humps, the roots of the horns, were concealed.

"I hate to think of you as a benevolent person, Kryger," Jastrau said, laughing again.

"You paid me the seventy-five kroner the last time," Kryger replied. "Does that surprise you?"

"I'm not usually coddled in such fashion. But here's Bennett's. Good-by, and a pleasant journey."

They stood in a crowd of people on a corner of Strøget.

"Shall I thank you, Kryger?" Jastrau asked suddenly with a desperate cordiality. He did not dare look at him, for he could feel his eyes growing moist. It was so disconcerting, such a sham. It must be discernable. Through a glistening veil of tears he saw Kryger's modish figure and his warm, sympathetic smile. "Good-by, then, and my greetings to your wife," he said. Was he being scornful? And at the same moment he repented. It was a cutting remark—the flash of a knife in the solar haze that lay over the crowd around them.

With a wave of the hand Kryger disappeared. "Have a good trip." The sound of the words remained hanging in the air. And at the same moment a large bus came roaring around the corner. Everything was swallowed up in movement. Jastrau went into the travel agency.

A young man behind the counter came up to him. It was a question of that ticket to Berlin. But could he buy it with the money—money he had borrowed from this man, Kryger? He, whom he had sent off with a derisive kick—"And my greetings to your wife." For it was a kick, even though Kryger did not suspect it. Why had he uttered that scornful remark. "And my greetings to your wife"? Ordinary politeness? Kryger was such a little fellow, and so sure of himself. He was being noble. He deserved nothing better than such a kick in the behind. But nevertheless, no one was going to get Jastrau to travel to Berlin with that man's money. Kryger would get it back—he would! And now Jastrau would go out to Stenosgade, he would go through with it, go right through with it and get it over with, and then back to the hotel, write a couple of articles, find a market for them, get some money, and then—then—

There was no danger of running into Kryger. He had disappeared among the swarm of people on the sidewalk of Strøget.

Jastrau left the travel agency immediately, walked over to the cab stand, and took a taxi out to the corner of Vesterbrogade and Stenosgade. He leaned back in the cab and whistled. Now he would get it over with. The speed of the taxi was like the thrill of a caress running through him. Women on the sidewalk. Always women. The sun called forth their pretty faces and fine figures.

De profundis clamavi. But where were the depths? As long as one can see a pretty woman's face, a ray of sunshine penetrates the depths. Look at her—that unbelievable girl there on the sidewalk. A dark fringe of hair over her forehead and Asta Nielsen eyes. Just a glimpse of them. But he had to get out there and pay for that wretched piece of splintered glass, and then a paltry scrap of paper—paid bill—would put an end to all his Catholic whims.

If only he had that bill in his possession, had it in his wallet. All paid, all paid!

At the corner of Stenosgade he leaped out of the taxi and hurried over toward the red building.

But suddenly it seemed as if the sun had slipped behind a cloud. And he walked quickly by, way down as far as Gammel Kongevej. It was a humiliation, and he had been taken advantage of deliberately—a heathen forced to go to confession. He couldn't do it. He wouldn't. But Vuldum's incessant phone calls kept buzzing in his ears. He had to flee from them as from a swarm of wasps. If he were going to Berlin, it would have been a different matter. He could have gone, but he was not going to do so. In any event, he was not going to let Kryger help him. Kryger would have his hundred kroner back. To keep the money would be too mean a trick. And so he would have to go into this ordinary Catholic church and pay for that bit of glass.

Once again he walked along Stenosgade, this time on the opposite side. He stopped and looked over at the pointed-arch windows with their lace curtains and let his gaze wander over toward the closed doors of the church. Why had he and Steffensen climbed over the iron fence and cavorted around in front of those doors like devils on the loose? Shadows, moods that had been reduced to foam against the church walls. And now a little scrap of paper came floating back on the wave—a bill. He had seen such dirty, unclean waves laden with bits of paper.

A pale face came into view behind the pane of glass in the door. The dark eyes rested on him for a moment and then casually stared down the street.

Jastrau felt he was being spied upon. But he remained standing where he was and let his gaze travel up at the church steeple. The face had vanished.

Jastrau retraced his steps a short distance and walked back and forth on the opposite sidewalk.

He felt he was still being observed. The windows had watchful eyes. And then he made out the face again behind the curtains in the parlor. The dark eyes followed him. It was very likely the janitor. But the janitor was apparently aware that he had been discovered, for now he made himself quite visible, carefully straightened the curtain with his hand, stared up at the sky as if interested in the weather, and let his glance descend slowly over the façades of the buildings until it again came to rest on Jastrau as if by accident.

With a feeling of indignation and audacity, Jastrau stared back, frankly and unashamed—stared the man away from the window. But Jastrau could still sense the dark eyes glowing in a pale ascetic face from deeper within the room.

Why did Jastrau have to stare back? It was a childish reaction, irritation at being observed. Did the janitor know who he was? Well, if so, it was impossible, of course, to go away. Then there was nothing to do but take the road to humiliation—to Canossa.

He went across the street and rang the bell.

To Canossa! A slight, bitter, ironical wince as the words formed on his lips. A piece of glass that had splintered. A pitiable sort of Canossa. Yes, he had seen it. The Scandinavian weekly for Catholic Christians had gotten a new pane of glass in its display case. Nothing but a piece of glass, and for that he was to be humiliated. The thought tormented him. He had been forced down here. By chance? Because of Vuldum's fortuitous phone calls? No, he knew better. And besides, it was not even he who had broken the glass.

He looked dejected and out-of-sorts when the janitor came to the door. But before he could open his mouth the man said, "I'll tell Father Garhammer you're here. Won't the Herr Editor wait inside?"

The janitor's face was impenetrable, his eyes humble, his lay-brother's manner subservient. There was no trace of irony in his gentle voice. Nevertheless, Jastrau got a chilling impression of how expected his arrival was. The janitor had recognized him.

And so Jastrau sat down in the parlor. The calling-card bowl stood on the table, and beside it lay a Catholic catechism. There could be nothing impolite about opening it.

But he forgot it as soon as he saw the forbidding hatstand that stood in the corner—as in a pub—as in a doctor's waiting room—an old-fashioned instrument of torture, a wheel set upon a stake, with his gray hat that he had hung on it resembling a martyred corpse.

Yes, there was always some sentence that hung over one—a sentence with a medieval, barbaric severity about it. Of what use, then, was modern humanism? None, none at all. Everywhere people sat at ugly tables and waited for a sentence or a revelation, with nothing except calling-card bowls or back numbers of the *Family Journal* to console the eye while they waited, waited.

And was a door opening now? Was a doctor in a white smock appearing? And was the sunlight streaming into the examination room behind him?

Then Father Garhammer walked in, small and slight, dignified yet constrained in his black Jesuit's garb, and Jastrau stood up, breathing heavily. The trinity of evil. The three black figures in long black robes, but without arms. It was comforting to see the priest's hands. He rubbed them together self-consciously. It was comforting to see the priest's face. There was no movement of the lips, as if he were about to spit. Did a gob of spittle go flashing through the air? No, it was a glitter from something out in the street.

368

Jastrau looked uneasily at the priest and received a smile. There was no gleam of triumph in his expression, and if there was any wiliness it was mingled with the sympathetic look of a friendly aunt. Perhaps it was wrong for him to have come to obtain the compromising piece of paper, the bill for the broken glass, to be humble, or play a humble role, in order to get hold of it.

"It was nice of you to come to see me," said Father Garhammer, sitting down at the table. "Please remain seated."

Jastrau leaned forward over the table. He could not speak.

"How is our friend Vuldum?" asked the priest. He still wore the same smile. "He comes here very seldom and that makes me uneasy." He placed the emphasis on the "un" so that the word bore some resemblance to the German equivalent, *unruhig*.

"Well, he's phoned me several times."

"Ah, so?" And Father Garhammer smiled as if thinking of a distant friend. "I believe he's a very good and true friend of yours."

"Well—" Jastrau sounded hesitant and a little skeptical.

But the priest nodded. "Yes, I'm sure of it. *Der liebe* Vuldum. Alas, he's far too interested in *reservatio mentalis*. And that makes me uneasy on his behalf. Such an interest can be damaging to his soul."

And the priest turned to face Jastrau.

"You find it difficult too, Herr Jastrau."

Jastrau bent humbly forward.

"Yes—yes—yes," he said, and then suddenly found the right words. "No moral system can be constructed from scientific premises," he said gloomily.

Father Garhammer patted him on the hand.

"Do you know that, Herr Jastrau? I didn't believe you realized it," he said amiably.

"I've always known it," Jastrau replied in a subdued tone, but with fervent conviction. "But now I feel it, and that's worse."

"Yes, that's worse. But you try to do the right thing, that's what I think, Herr Jastrau."

Again Jastrau was conscious of tears forming in his eyes. It was the second time that day—a day of humiliation. But he exorcised them with a smile, and looked up into the priest's face.

"You know that I came here one night and raised a commotion," he said abruptly.

"Yes, I know," Father Garhammer replied with a faint smile. "You were just a bit obstreperous, let's say."

"And I broke something."

"Nothing that amounted to much, Herr Jastrau. So many things can happen when one is having a bad time of it."

"I'd like to pay for it." The words came with an almost crude note of insistence.

Father Garhammer fumbled in his cassock and drew forth a small sales slip. He was carrying it with him. And Jastrau spread the bit of paper out in front of him. Four kroner for a piece of glass, installed. A scrap of paper. And now the scrap of paper was floating back on the wave. He gazed at the glazier's uncertain handwriting, done in pencil.

"Was it only four kroner?" he asked with a note of chagrin.

"Yes, you raised a very minor commotion," the priest replied in a tone of irony that sounded both naïve and quaint in his foreign accent.

Jastrau felt ashamed as he lay a five-krone note on the table, but the priest picked it up in a practical, matter-of-fact way.

"We don't carry money about with us, but the janitor will be here right away with your change. It was good of you to come and see me. Please give my regards to Herr Vuldum. Now you must excuse me. I'm busy and have to go. But it was nice to talk with you, and it was good of you to want to pay for that bit of glass. You needn't have done so. We understand."

Jastrau rose and bowed filially.

"Until we meet again," said the priest, and left the room.

And once more Jastrau sat alone in the parlor. He rubbed his eyes and looked around.

Then he went over to the hatstand and took his hat. He walked over to the window and looked calmly and pensively out into the street, as if he had just undergone a tooth extraction.

The glazier's bill lay carefully tucked away in his wallet.

Soon there was knock on the door. The janitor came in, handed him a krone, and followed him out with a face devoid of expression.

Jastrau had nearly reached the Town Hall Square before he remembered to light up a pipeful of tobacco.

Chapter Five   It was late in the evening. The back door at the Bar des Artistes that led to the dark courtyard stood open so that a faint breeze could penetrate into the stuffy barroom. The phonograph droned on with a narcotizing monotony. The cash register rang incessantly. And Lundbom rattled the cocktail shaker with a sweeping, undulating motion that kept time with the jazz, while the sweat rolled down his round, red, satyr's face. With a smile that was now saccharine, now sour, he presided over the bar.

Midway in the summer, the place was unexpectedly experiencing a big evening with a noisy crowd of guests.

Even the inevitable Kjær, who presided at his round table, was animated. His blue eyes were dull and lusterless behind his pince-nez, but his flabby face was deeply flushed, and often he had to raise his hand in a paternal greeting.

Jastrau sat slouched back in a chair opposite him. Journalist Eriksen, who had reached the frenzied stage in which the wrinkles in his ravaged face were as tangled as those in a crumpled ball of paper, tugged now at Kjær's jacket lapel, now at Jastrau's, and confided to them alternately his outspoken opinion about everything.

"Life is the damnedest filthy mess I've ever come up against, and it's amazing that Goethe never said so in one syllable," he said.

"Yes, all the things that Goethe didn't say are enough to drive you crazy," growled Jastrau, who was lucid but in an irritable mood.

And the fourth person at the table, Copenhagen's leading second-hand-book dealer, the gigantic Mogensen with his moon-like face, who was called Bogensen because he dealt in books and was from Funen,* laughed so that his cheeks shook.

"What are you laughing at?" asked the diminutive journalist, shoving his face forward. "You look like the devil himself."

"Watch your manners, gentlemen," warned the inevitable Kjær, raising his hands in admonition. "Why use such foul language? *Skaal,* gentlemen."

But the secondhand-book dealer sputtered into his glass, and his huge body shook with laughter. All the buttons on his clothing remained quivering for a long time.

Meanwhile, farther down the room, an altercation between a lawyer and an advertising-space salesman had been smouldering. They were forever wrangling. Therefore they invariably sought each other out like a pair of mad dogs.

"Are they at it again?" Journalist Eriksen asked, turning around in his chair. "Tear them limb from limb and throw them out, Lundbom."

"Now, now, don't be so rough, Herr Eriksen," Lundbom said. He had come out from behind the bar and stood with his hand resting in a friendly manner on the little journalist's shoulder, while he kept his eyes fixed on the center of disturbance.

* A play on words based on the word *bogen,* which means "book" and Bogense, a town in Funen.

Then they heard a chair scrape against the floor.

"Now they're going to tear each other apart," exclaimed Eriksen, twitching in his chair.

But suddenly the broad-shouldered, big-jawed waiter from over in the restaurant and the hotel's uniformed hall porter stood beside the two unruly customers.

"Now, we don't want any commotion here."

"You're disturbing the other guests."

"Who do you think you are, you flunky?"

A breathless silence settled over the room, even at the round table. The square-jawed waiter and the porter had grabbed the obstreperous lawyer by the arms and with tenacious politeness had forced him out the door. For a moment all the guests were subdued.

Jastrau raised his whiskey glass to his lips with a feeling of relief.

And at that moment it occurred to Jastrau that he was not at all alone in doing so. Some impulse had seized all the customers in the bar at one and the same time—Kjær, Eriksen, Bogensen, everybody—a collective thought, an unconscious, simultaneous bending of elbows.

And with this emotion-charged display of fellow-feeling the memory of an unpleasant incident was rinsed down. The droning of the phonograph was again heard, and Lundbom once more stood behind the bar and went through his pompous, rhythmical ceremony with the gleaming cocktail shaker.

A short-lived interval of silent felicity—for now the inevitable Kjær began singing his own rhythm.

Jastrau found it more and more obtrusive.

"Peace reigns o'er town and countryside," Kjær hummed, gently waving his hand without being thrown off beat by the rhythm of the phonograph's frenetic jazz. He had no ear for syncopation.

The clash between the two rhythms had the same effect on Jastrau as seeing a cross-eyed man.

"Another round of whiskey here," he ordered.

"Now I have it! Now I know what you look like," Journalist Eriksen exclaimed with a triumphant shout as he pointed his finger right at Bogensen's face. "Yes, that's it exactly—you look like a pallid whale." He slapped a hand against his thigh.

Kjær shook his head in despair. "Pallid whale? A pallid whale? Oh, a white whale," he snickered. Bogensen's whole body quivered as if he had been harpooned. He was having a wonderful time.

But Jastrau's lips curled in a disgruntled frown.

He sat there and nibbled at a stanza of verse. It had never amounted to anything but a few simple, fleeting lines. He lacked the power of concentration, and things were not as in his young days when the words flowed forth into long poems.

> Though once I thought of sin
> As a dark and muddy deep,
> Now I know that it's a plain
> Filled with tedious things that creep.

They were still snickering, those three dissolute, bestial, faces, red and blotchy, damp with perspiration and alcohol, sagging with the summer heat. It was a sultry evening. And there was no mirror, so he could not see himself—the fourth bestial face.

"Yes, you're all right," said the colossal Bogensen, holding his whiskey glass out toward Eriksen, who sat writhing with mirth in his chair. "So are all of you—you boys from *Dagbladet*. You're all so much fun to be with. I know Vuldum too."

"Did you say Vuldum?" Eriksen bellowed indignantly. "Did you hear that, Jazz? He said Vuldum! Is he trying to insult me—this white whale from Funen, who's straight out of Revelations?"

Bogensen shook with suppressed merriment, his eyes fastened admiringly on Eriksen.

"What's the matter? Isn't he a decent chap?"

"Decent! Oh—h, you naïve, quivering old dodo." Eriksen's voice rose to a high pitch. "Buckwheat porridge." A sheer falsetto. "Bogensen-wheat porridge." But suddenly he wrinkled his brows and shook his fist in Bogensen's face. "Believe me, you miserable, gigantic tub of lard, when I say there have been nights when I've gotten down on my knees and prayed, prayed—yes, I said prayed, although that's not like me at all—prayed to God time after time to ask him if in His mercy He wouldn't soon let a streetcar run over this damned Vuldum."

The inevitable Kjær laughed softly, but Jastrau screwed up his eyes understandingly and nodded his head.

"Yes, you know what I mean, Jazz. We two are in the same boat. The fact that you've jumped overboard won't do you any good, Ole—in spite of that, you're in the boat. But Lord, how I'll miss you! I will. Because I like you one hell of a lot. You're a splendid fellow. But you're not good for anything."

His triangular eyes were bloodshot, agitated, searching.

"Jazz, Jazz, Jazz. I could cry when I think of how much I'll miss you. I miss you already. Yes, I do, damn it. I miss you like the very devil."

Whereupon he squeezed Jastrau's hand and assumed a woebegone expression.

"But this fellow Vuldum," said Bogensen, interrupting the touching scene, "is he unreliable?"

"Unreliable! Ah ha!" Eriksen shouted, gesticulating dramatically. "That isn't the word for it. Unreliable! What do you mean, you windbag? He's—"

And he clenched his fist.

"Now, now, Eriksen," Kjær admonished, directing his weary gaze at him. "Vuldum sat here at this table—at my table—this afternoon." He raised his big, jowly head authoritatively. "And I won't hear a harsh word about him."

"A harsh word! What I have to say is the truth, damn it!" Eriksen bellowed.

"I don't want to hear the truth at my table," shouted the inevitable Kjær. "It isn't housebroken."

Then he giggled.

"The truth is not housebroken, do you hear?" Kjær repeated.

"But at any rate he can be relied on, can't he?" asked Bogensen. "At least I hope so."

"Have you loaned him money, you sperm whale? Ah!" Eriksen laughed and gesticulated so vigorously that his fingers flapped against each other.

"No, I never loan anybody money. But I sold him a book on credit—the works of Poul Helgesen in Danish."

Jastrau drew himself up in his chair.

"You'll never see the money for it, you baleen whale," howled Eriksen. "Never, never. He's already sold it to one of your competitors."

Eriksen was doubled up with laughter.

The inevitable Kjær had haughtily turned aside and leaned his elbows on the table while he fixed his gaze on the life-size, insipid painting of the naked woman who had been dubbed Charles the Twelfth.

"Yes, but—but—" Bogensen sputtered, staring disconsolately into space.

"He—he's—" Eriksen began with a mighty cough. But then he was interrupted, because the inevitable Kjær had suddenly turned to face them again.

"Gentlemen," he said in a deep, hoarse voice, "he sat here at this table, and if the truth must be spoken, he writes better than the three of you put together. And furthermore, he has sat at this table."

He lapsed into a sulky silence and looked from one to the other with a dictatorial air.

374

"He has sat at this table and that should be enough. Would I rub elbows with just anyone who comes along? I, in bad company? It's inconceivable."

"Then I'm not going to sit here," Eriksen exploded. "Because I'm bad company. You can bet your life I'm bad company. You have no idea how bad. Rotten to the core."

Eriksen got up. "I want a taxi," he said. His face was crumpled and his eyebrows hung down over his eyes. "Huh!" he grunted, and shook himself. "I'm bad company, Lundbom, and so are you, you old Swedish poison-blender and corrupter of youth. A taxi, do you hear, you old devil?"

"Now, now, not so rough, Herr Eriksen," Lundbom came out from behind the bar with a patronizing air and followed Eriksen to the door.

"Yes, he was getting rough," Bogensen said with a grin, pulling a handkerchief the size of a bed sheet out of his pocket and mopping his face with it. "Don't you think I'll get the money for that book?"

"Hee," said Kjær with a wave of his hand. "Hee hee."

"I mean for the book that belonged to me—that I had in my shop."

"Well, anyhow—*skaal!*" Kjær replied, clinking glasses.

Jastrau had gone over to the bar to stretch his legs, and sat there munching on the salted almonds.

"Herr Eriksen can be very difficult," sighed Lundbom, who had returned. "He drinks more than is good for him." He inclined his red satyr's head benevolently to one side.

"Y—es," replied Jastrau, drinking another whiskey.

"But otherwise he's a fine person," Lundbom said, sighing again.

"Yes, God knows he is," replied Jastrau. "Look, can't we have a little music from the phonograph?"

Over at the round table, the inevitable Kjær and Bogensen were talking to each other, and Jastrau sat and watched them. There was material for a poem. And there was material for another one about the collection of animals in the barroom. He must get it written. Their puffy, harried faces, ready to burst from elevated blood pressure. Whew, how sultry the evening was. Another cool whiskey. Then he would slip up to his room. But it was stuffy there too. The window toward the street stood open. All the night sounds came in. The streets were noisy at night. And then the ceiling—the reflection of the automobile lights on it. The strange ceiling. When would he find a ceiling that he was not afraid of—a familiar ceiling that did not bring on heart palpitations when he looked at it? Oh, those ceilings. Ever since that apparition of the three black men, the trinity of evil. Every morning he sprang up from his bed feeling the pressure inside his chest. No, he would not go up to his room yet.

"Another record, Lundbom."

"No, it's too late now. We have to close soon."

"Another whiskey."

"All right—although it's late."

"Ah, you're a man of feeling."

"Hm, do you think so?" Lundbom nodded and smiled bashfully.

"You shall have something to remember me by, Lundbom, because I'm going to die soon," Jastrau ranted as he leaned in over the bar.

Lundbom nodded again and shoved the fresh glass of whiskey toward him.

"Yes, by Jove, you're going to have a souvenir," Jastrau muttered, and fumbled through his pockets. He found nothing. Yes—the fire insurance policy. Down in one corner was that address. In Kryger's handwriting. *Ach!* Berlin-Wilmersdorf.

Jastrau took out his fountain pen and wrote across the face of the policy:

Inscribed to Herr Arvid Lundbom
Scandinavia's foremost cocktail mixer
The master with the fine hand
from
Ole Jastrau

"There you are, you amiable old thief!" he exclaimed, handing Lundbom the policy.

"Thanks, thanks. I'll take care of it for you."

"It's all yours," Jastrau said in an offhand manner. "And now I'd like to pay up," he added, taking the folded hundred-krone note from his pocket.

Berlin-Wilmersdorf.

And he dangled his feet so that the toes of his shoes beat out a reckless, rhythmic tattoo against the polished mahogany front of the bar: Professor J. Geberhardt. Landauerstrasse 4. Berlin-Wilmersdorf.

Lundbom's pudgy hand shoved some bills across the linoleum bar counter. Money again. Jastrau could still travel. Still. Still. He went on tapping with his toes: Wilmersdorf, Berlin, Wilmersdorf, Berlin—

"It isn't time to go to bed, is it?" a lilting voice said near his ear, and he sensed Bogensen's huge figure behind him.

"No, no—far from it," Jastrau sang back as he sat with his elbows on the bar.

376

"Are you going along to the Golden Age?"

Jastrau breathed a sigh of relief and nodded. Now, as far as he was concerned, the hotel room with its blue-gray, closely-patterned wallpaper flowers, red plush chair, and sinister white ceiling could lie in wait for him—and wait and wait.

"Is Kjær going?" he asked, turning on his stool.

But the inevitable Kjær sat drunk and as if petrified at his table. Just then a waiter laid the bill down in front of him. Kjær stared at it with glazed eyes. "That—that's right," he muttered. "Six, seventy-five—eighty-eight—ninety-two. Right." He fumbled in his breast pocket for his fountain pen, failed to connect with it, then failed again. The waiter came to his help, tried the pen to see if there was ink in it, then placed it in Kjær's hand.

And with the helpless ineptitude of a somnambulist, Kjær signed the bill, put too much force into the period after his name, dropped the pen, and pitched forward onto the table with his full weight as if his walking stick had slipped out from under him.

The following day, the bill would, as usual, be presented to his lawyer.

"We're going," Bogensen said in a tone of reluctance.

And leaning amiably against each other, Jastrau and Bogensen strolled out to a taxi.

"It seems to me that Kjær drinks too much," Bogensen remarked in a subdued lilting tone of reproach as they drove through the sultry summer night. White figures floated by on the dark sidewalks, restless and happy, as if Copenhagen was unable to sleep, and toward the north there was a faint light in the heavens as if the heat had breached the sky and made an exit for itself.

"He's made up his mind about how he wants to live," Jastrau said with an apathetic grin, and leaned back in the seat.

"But you aren't drunk, are you?"

"I don't think I'm sober. But the night is heavy with a delicate fragrance."

"We'll never go home," he hummed as he inhaled the cool air stirred up by the speed of the cab.

Bogensen remained silent until they caught sight of the dark tree-tops in Frederiksberg Park. They loomed up black against the light night sky. Then he suddenly sat up with a jerk.

"Do you think I'll ever get the money?" he asked.

"What money?"

"For the book I sold to Vuldum."

"Ha—no." And Jastrau was propelled over against the thick-set, pudgy Bogensen as the taxi turned into the park and drove up to the lighted entrance of the Golden Age Club. "Ha—sure, you'll get it."

As the door opened, they immediately heard the sound of jazz music, subdued and yet gay, and Jastrau was conscious of a feeling of suppleness in his legs. He uttered a loud laugh.

"We'll never go home," he repeated.

But once inside the room the feeling of exuberance vanished immediately, and so overwhelming was the impression of emptiness and lack of activity that they felt their spirits ebb. Two lonely couples were moving tediously about the dance floor, and alongside the yellow walls, which reflected a hopeless boredom, sat unaccompanied women with weary, dejected expressions on their faces. Now and then they shifted their positions morosely and adjusted their clothing to no avail. Mannequins in a window that nobody passed. Only the music attempted to keep up the pretense that all was as it should be; but it seemed purposeless with its full tonal volume so lacking in bubble and dash. During the chorus, a couple of pitifully thin female voices were timidly raised in the empty, unanimated room, as they chirped a cheerful "Forget your sorrow until tomorrow—"

The formally attired waiters stood conspicuously posted in doorways and alcoves like so many corpses.

"I guess it's pretty dead here tonight," Bogensen said to one of them in his Funen accent.

The waiter sighed as only a waiter can. All the disgust in the world was reflected in his conventional face.

But Jastrau stalked briskly through the room, for behind him was nothing but a hotel chamber with small-patterned flowered wallpaper and nothing else—nothing except heart palpitations when he lay in bed and stared up at the strange, whitewashed ceiling.

They got a table and ordered smørrebrød, and Bogensen sank into his chair with a moan.

"And they call this a place of entertainment," he sighed.

They sat looking idly at the women. "A row of masks hung on the wall," Jastrau said peevishly, and Bogensen's huge body quivered as he broke into a snicker.

A woman with flaxen-yellow hair and a look of venerable distinction about her mouth nodded.

"Do you know her?" Bogensen asked.

"No, but I can imagine what she'll say. That she washes her hair in champagne, and all that sort of thing."

"But that's a nice head of hair she has."

"There—you can see for yourself. And that's the first thing you'll say to her, and then we'll have things started," Jastrau said sullenly. He recognized the atmosphere of the place and realized suddenly that he would not even be able to get drunk tonight. And behind him waited the hotel room. "The priest was damn well right. It's through repetition that one gets to know hell."

"What priest?"

"Oh, a priest."

"You're beginning to get pretty grim, my friend," Bogensen said with his characteristic lilt.

Just then the music stopped, and they could hear that there was, at least, one jovial group present—a few ladies and gentlemen sitting in a corner.

"They're either office clerks or pickpockets," Jastrau remarked sullenly. All the whiskey he had drunk in the last several days was stagnating in him, as stale as pond water, and he felt tormentingly clear-headed, lucid but not sober, abnormal but rational, and in a bad frame of mind.

The *smørrebrød* helped somewhat.

Then one of the women in the noisy little group got up. With her hands held to her cheeks, she cut diagonally across the floor with uncertain steps. Jastrau followed her with his eyes. Did he know her? Midway across the room she let her hands drop, shook her head, and took a deep breath. She was wearing a black dress, and over it hung a string of amber beads.

"She's had a few too many," said Bogensen. "Do you know her?"

Jastrau nodded and continued to watch her as with a sudden burst of resolution she hurried over toward the cloakroom. The world-weary waiter helped her navigate.

"She's pretty."

"Oh, yes."

"Couldn't you get her over here?"

"No. Let's sit here in peace," Jastrau replied with a shrug of his shoulders, as the piano player began to pound the keys. A little later a wailing saxophone joined in—a fresh desperate attempt to drug the customers with music.

Bogensen tried in vain to conceal a yawn.

"No, it's no use," Jastrau said regretfully. "I can't get drunk tonight. Sometimes I feel so low that I can't get drunk. For a moment there in the bar, I had hopes—"

"Then I must always be feeling low," Bogensen replied calmly.

Jastrau looked at him inquiringly.

"Because I'm never able to get drunk," Bogensen went on, lifting a *snaps* glass as his small eyes, set deeply in his fat face, lit up in a smile.

"Unfortunately, we might just as well stay," Jastrau sighed hopelessly. "But you're right—the *snaps!*"

They raised their glasses to each other and drank.

"There she is again," exclaimed the man from Funen.

Jastrau looked over toward the wall and saw Black Else, who was maneuvering carefully from table to table. Suddenly her eyes met Jastrau's, and she nodded apathetically. Then she seemed to forget again, and her expression once more became foggy. She smiled out into the room and up at the ceiling, focused her eyes on him again, and started to make her way over to them.

"I know you," she said, lifting an unsteady finger.

"Sit down here, Frøken," Bogensen said politely, getting up from his chair in all his bulk.

Black Else held a hand up to her ear and made a face. "Did you say Frøken? I'm married—Fru Kopf." And she staggered dangerously as she made a little curtsey.

"Fru head," Bogensen said as his shoulders quivered noiselessly. "Have a seat. It will be a little safer."

"I know you," she repeated dully to Jastrau as she sat down. "What are you wrinkling up your forehead for?" she went on in an offended tone as she leaned back limply in the chair. "But who's that you have with you? A fat one. Does he have money? I'm drunk as the devil. Is he a newspaperman too?"

Jastrau gave a start, and Bogensen laughed.

"Won't you have a whiskey, Frue?"

"Y—es," she replied. But then she waved her hand so vigorously that she almost toppled over. "But I—I have a highball over there too—over there. But yes,"—she nodded and suppressed a hiccup—"I'd just as soon have one here as well."

"She's nice—but sort of tiresome," said the man from Funen.

"What did you say, fatty?" She put her hand up to her ear. And then she addressed herself listlessly to Jastrau. "Is he a newspaperman like you and Arne?"

"Arne?"

"Yes—that red-headed monkey. You see, I know both of you. I'm not too drunk for that."

"She means Vuldum," Jastrau said sullenly to Bogensen. "So you know Vuldum?"

He squinted his eyes and looked at her sharply. Her cheeks were slack and there was a careworn expression about her wide, prominent mouth.

380

But she did not reply. With a shrill burst of laughter she grabbed the whiskey glass and emptied it in one gulp.

"No now—that will never do," Bogensen remarked uneasily.

"What did you say?"

"No, now listen, Frue," Jastrau said, getting up. "Hadn't we better ride you home, Frue? This will never do."

"Do you want to go home with me?" she asked, raising her head in an unconsciously business-like manner.

"No, no—we want to give you a ride home," Bogensen protested. "God forbid," he added softly.

"Do you think you're going with us?" She leaned over the table and laughed. "The fat one is not going along—uh-h, no!"

"All right, then he isn't going along," Jastrau said in a matter-of-fact but irritated tone, and Bogensen nodded. But there was a sour expression about the small mouth between his round cheeks.

Jastrau was clear-headed, energetic, and extraordinarily alert. He perceived everything in sharp, baleful contours, in a glaring white light that was disillusioning to the highest degree, and when he felt that way he could not get drunk. At such times he acted swiftly and with an exasperating crudeness—exasperating because he made it evident that nothing was worth going to any trouble for.

He got up and led her out.

Next they were sitting in a taxi. She in a gray fur piece. Outside, the park lay in a subdued morning light. All the nuances of pattern and color in the bark of the trees, the gravel paths, and the foliage were visible.

"Istedgade," she had automatically told the driver.

"Istedgade?" Jastrau repeated in surprise, and turned toward her. But immediately he realized that he could not expect a reasonable answer from her. In the natural light of day, in which the trees and houses became alive, her face took on the appearance of a mask. Small particles of powder threatened to fall away from the wrinkles around her eyes, and the two blemishes near her temples that she had rouged in order to make her face appear narrower made her look ridiculous, as if the artificial flush had been mistakenly applied too far up on her cheeks.

"Istedgade" she muttered. Jastrau began to feel perturbed. He wanted to question her, but he was sitting next to a deaf person. With the speed of the cab, the air began to fan their hot faces as they drove toward Frederiksberg Circle. Perhaps she could bring her to her senses. Why was his heart beating so violently? Frederiksberg Church loomed up like a tent against the sky.

He sat staring straight ahead. Suppose—suppose it turned out that she lived in the house across the street from him? The windows with the drawn curtains. The white reflection of the sunlight upon which all his thoughts had been concentrated, which in itself had become a thought, white and dazzling. Suppose—suppose—?"

"So you've moved."

"M-mm."

Ah yes, then those were the windows, that was the apartment. But why was he afraid? His heart? He smoked too much, he drank too much. The curtains that had shone with a white light far into his being—a white projector beam that had sought him out and come to rest upon him in his—in his grief. What was grief? But if Black Else lived there, then it all took on some significance. It was not a mere coincidence. If only—if only the devil had all symbolism.

Suddenly Black Else broke down and began to sob.

Had the cool morning air brought her to her senses? Jastrau shook himself in exasperation. A nervous fit of weeping brought about by lack of sleep and too much liquor. He would not waste his sympathy on it. Can you waste your sympathy? He knew that sort of crying. It was typical of that kind of women. That kind of women, he thought. He was far from being Jesus now. And Black Else whispered, "Oh—I'm so drunk, and I have so many troubles and so much grief. Oh, I could whip you all. What is it you want of me?"

"Now look here, all I want to do is ride you home," Jastrau said in a grudgingly comforting tone and turned halfway toward her. They were approaching the houses at the broad end of Frederiksberg Allé. They had a soft, blue-gray tone, and their windows had a sleepy look.

"Nonsense!" she said, and shook her head. Her tears, mixed with powder, slid down into the hollowed-out furrows beneath her eyes.

But Jastrau nodded in affirmation of his statement.

"Then you don't want to come home with me? Aren't you my friend?"

She leaned her head against his shoulder and began to whimper again.

"I have so many worries. They'd fill a whole novel. You could write it. I'm an entire novel in myself, let me tell you. You have no idea. But oh, I do so want to talk—talk—really talk to someone. Are you coming with me? We can talk to each other. I have a feeling we can. And I do so need to talk to someone."

Jastrau looked over at her black hair, which was being blown by the breeze. It was the window of the feather-cleaning shop that caught his glance, that cosmic haze of gray feathers swirling around as an adver-

tisement for the establishment. The corner of Stenosgade. Far removed from Jesus. A glimpse of the red Catholic church and school. A
spiritual dental clinic. And they turned the corner into Viktoriagade.

"You're not coming up with me?"

"No, no."

"So you aren't coming up. Well, I am drunk. But I would so like to
talk to someone. Then tomorrow—you'll come tomorrow. Promise me. I
need to talk to someone so badly. Ask for Fru Kopf. You will, won't
you? You'll come?"

She raised her painted face and opened her eyes. There was a
glazed film over them.

"Oh, I'm so unhappy, and you don't care!" she exclaimed. "None of
you men care about anything."

"I promise I'll come tomorrow," Jastrau replied as convincingly as
he could.

And at that moment a dark cloud passed over his soul. They were
approaching the house he lived in, and its dreary facade grew bigger
and bigger. He could not help looking up for a moment at the
windows of his own apartment. In them was reflected the morning
sky. God help me, he thought—the windowpanes are mirroring the
heavens.

"This is where I live," Black Else said mechanically.

They drew up at the curb.

Else lurched out and staggered over to the front door.

"Shall I help you?" Jastrau called out from the cab.

But she did not answer. With mechanical, unconscious movements
she got the door open and then disappeared. She did not turn around.
She did not wave. She was not aware of anything.

And so, it was the windows with the white drawn curtains.

"Drive on, to the Town Hall Square," Jastrau shouted querulously to
the chauffeur. He turned his back on the house he had lived in.

Chapter Six   Jastrau and the inevitable Kjær sat in the
two wicker chairs in the hotel lobby observing
the people and traffic passing by—individuals in
an inordinate hurry, bicycles, trucks, and streetcars. A press photographer dashed by in his small, gray car, and waved a greeting. Kjær
formally laid a hand on his pleated vest and nodded in return. "Peace
be with him," he said. Jastrau removed the pipe from his mouth.

It was practically impossible to sit still. Jastrau really did not have time to do so. He had to get an article written and see about selling it. But that could wait until tomorrow. A bicycle capsized. It was a nuisance to park it so that the pedal rested against the curb. One of the wheels kept revolving so that the spokes flashed in the light. A pretty invention. An insect!

"Herr Jastrau." It was the hall porter with the black mustache. He stood beside Jastrau's chair. "A gentleman just phoned with a message for you. He said that everything was arranged and that you could go to Berlin tonight."

Kjær turned slowly and indolently toward Jastrau with an ironical expression and whistled.

Jastrau thanked the porter, but the latter went on in a low tone of voice: "May I be allowed to present you with your bill?"

"Ha," Kjær exclaimed, laughing from his position in the other chair and kicking out with one foot as Jastrau studied the bill with an air of resignation, and then paid it.

"Are you leaving us, Jazz? Are you deserting the camp?" Kjær asked, sputtering with laughter.

Jastrau shrugged his shoulders.

"Like Little P.—ha ha. You can't see it through." Kjær leaned back in the wicker chair and gazed up at the roofs of the buildings across the street, so that the sky was reflected in his bleary eyes. There was a look of quiet wistfulness in them. "I've tried it myself, Jazz. But one invariably comes back to the Bar des Artistes. Are you familiar with the antlion?"

"Is that the name of a bar?"

"Ha, no. It's an animal," Kjær said, grinning. "It digs a hole in the sand—a hole with slanting sides so that the ants slide down into it."

"I must say you're being profound."

"No, I'm only wise, and since you won't listen to the master's wisdom, go ahead and travel to Berlin—or Canada—ha." Kjær sat there in his dignity, like a god, and laughed. "I've heard from Little P. He's become something of an explorer. He writes that he's found a bar in London—ha."

Jastrau did not reply.

"Now he's sitting and playing matches for drinks—ah yes," Kjær went on, lost in memories. "And now you're going to Berlin. But you and he will both be back. You'll come back—that I know for sure. 'And when tomorrow you return, tell me everything you saw,'" he hummed as if to himself. "You really ought to take an interest in the antlion, you know."

Just then an auto horn tooted frantically over in the Town Hall Square. Traffic outside the hotel halted, streetcars came to a stop, and an ambulance with a yellow flag protruding diagonally and flapping from its side swept by with the speed of a shiver running down a spine.

Their eyes followed the ambulance, and when the sound of its horn died away after it had turned into Nørrevoldgade Kjær got up from his chair with a groan. "I think I'll look up the antlion in an encyclopedia," he said with a sigh. Blue in the face from exertion, he hobbled on his gouty feet in to the hall porter.

But the sound of the ambulance remained fixed in Jastrau's consciousness. The accident. The shriek of a bird piercing the air. When one was dancing to phonograph music to blunt one's senses, and then suddenly had to let out a scream— Suppose it was Oluf whom the ambulance was going for. But it had driven down Nørrevold, so that could not be it. Gone. Invisible. That boy, that boy. If something should happen to him Jastrau would not know about it. There were so many dangers. Spread out his hands and protect him.

Involuntarily he extended his arms, with his hands in a grasping position, but suddenly he realized how ridiculous the gesture was. Like carrying on a distraught conversation with oneself.

Behind him he heard the inevitable Kjær puffing, and then a door slammed. Kjær had gone into the bar after his strenuous bout with the antlion and the encyclopedia. That was how it was when a person had money. When one was comfortably fixed, as the saying was. A saying.

And now all this would soon be over, almost automatically. In order to go to the dogs, a person must be able to afford it. But that article. One, at least, could be written. What was there of current importance? Nothing. What was interesting? An article could be written about summer in the big city, warm and dusty—poetic dust. Oh, rubbish! The only thing of interest was the soul, and he'd be damned, if he even knew what that was.

A *skaal* to the infinitude of the soul. The intractability of the soul, Steffensen had said, making a face. How was Steffensen? he wondered. Was he still living in the apartment? And Black Else lived across the street behind the white curtains. She was unhappy. No— dead drunk. He must not let his humanitarian feelings run away with him. That sort of softness belonged to the past, when Jesus rose to the surface from the aquarium of his soul, and he made those pious gestures in imitation of him—*De Imitatione*.

But with grasping hands. A boy stands at the edge of an abyss, and then the hands reach out, grasping. It would be the same thing.

385

Perhaps she was standing at the edge of the abyss, and then his grasping hands reached out. And Oluf—beside the abyss—then—grasping hands. Where from? Who could tell? And why? Yes, he knew why. Because he had grasped Black Else. Hands. Hands. Space is full of hands. And they imitate me. When I threaten, then all hands threaten me.

Jastrau got up. He would go over and see Black Else. His cap was hanging in the barroom.

In the darkness of the bar the sunlight still flickered before his eyes and danced between the gleaming colored bottles on the shelves. The pale, impertinent, Copenhagen face of Arnold, the waiter, protruded from behind the bar, and at the round table sat the inevitable Kjær as if enveloped in a rain cloud, dimly discernable and bending over his Lundbom cocktail.

"Well, how did you make out with the antlion?" Jastrau asked as he took his cap.

"It's a boring animal," Kjær muttered, staring down at his cocktail.

"And this is a boring hotel," he went on after a pause. "No encyclopedia. And this is a boring bar. And this is a dull cocktail."

Nothing but emptiness all around as he sat there in the dusk.

Jastrau drew the portière aside and went out into the sunny street again. A blue, transparent haze seemed to be rising from the asphalt. Or was it the dusk of the bar evaporating?

Suddenly an image of Kjær, sitting over his Lundbom cocktail like a frog, appeared with great clarity before his eyes. Yes, Kjær looked like a frog hidden in the shade.

Strange how people resembled animals.

As Jastrau passed *Dagbladet*'s building, he glanced like a stranger up at its red walls. Would they take an article from him? But no—it would go on his account. So there was no way out. He had to go to Berlin—was being forced to go there as he had been forced to go to Stenosgade by Vuldum. Black Else knew Vuldum. Yes, a flower peddler came walking through the barroom with three roses bristling from his hand. But why did Vuldum hate her so intensely? "As you can see, there are no ladies in the room."

He could hear Vuldum's voice.

"Can you think of anything worse than a sore covered over with powder?" Again the voice sounded clearly, word for word. Vuldum's voice. But had Black Else had such a mark on her arm? Was she diseased—diseased—diseased?

A movie theater on a corner. *The Scourge of Mankind*, the sign said in big letters. "A film everybody should see. Children under sixteen not admitted."

386

The sun shone down into the square around the Freedom Statue so that the asphalt lay like a polished surface, and everything seemed so open. The sunshine came pouring down.

Black letters. *The Scourge of Mankind.*

It was not to be requited with free love that he was seeking out Black Else. That much he knew. Was he being noble? Hands grasping out to help—?

He could hate Vuldum for that remark about the sore.

But if that was what he was doing, then the whole thing was so stupid, so ridiculous. Going up to see a girl in order to have a profound conversation with her! Had he, then, been expecting something else? A woman. A woman. A woman.

And he found himself in Istedgade. In the entranceway, the janitor's daughter was dancing in circles with a rag doll, and singing so that the sound of her shrill, joyous voice reverberated through the street. But he turned his back on her. Indeed, he had to turn his back, for he was headed for the door of the neighbor across the street. That symbolic business of the white curtains had to be driven from his mind. He did not like it. It was a result of nerves and alcohol. White ceilings, curtains, an ambulance, moving-picture titles—apparitions all of them. So the three black men had indeed been an honest-to-goodness hallucination. God only knew what a time the inevitable Kjær was having with his beginning of a white mouse.

He rang the bell, and an elderly woman with a faded smile and omniscient eyes opened the door. Her eyelids were half-lowered to hide her curiosity.

"Yes, Fru Kopf is at home, I do believe. But whom am I talking to?"

"Editor Ole Jastrau," he replied from force of habit.

"I'll tell her you're here."

And she slipped away as silently as a moth.

A little later a door was opened into the hallway, and the same ingratiating voice said, "You can come in. But it will be a little while, because Fru Kopf is not up yet."

Jastrau stepped into a room with polished mahogany furniture and an atmosphere of banal luxury, very gaudy and overfurnished. A broad sofa with a mass of cushions looked like a cheap Oriental dream, a sea of ease and comfort, and an oval picture of a man and a woman reclining blissfully in the lap of nature beneath a tree grazed his consciousness with a touch of familiarity. But Jastrau remained standing and staring at the drawn curtains. They commanded all his attention.

Now he had finally penetrated behind the veil of those curtains. Through a haze he caught a glimpse of his own windows across the street. How disorderly things looked over there. The curtains drawn unevenly. The windowpanes clouded with grime. He caught his breath. After all, they had once been his windows. He still recognized the curtains. Was Steffensen still living there? He should really let Johanne know that she could come and get the furniture. But a letter! It was impossible to write a letter. He was not up to it.

A red tobacco tin stood over on the windowsill. Yes, it was Craven Mixture. That was how life would seem if the soul could once liberate itself from the body—so disorderly and so wanting in purpose. The only memory that remained with him was that he had been smoking—Craven Mixture in a red tin. Now the ashes from Vesuvius could cover Pompeii. He had left a tobacco tin behind.

"Well, so it's only you," said a voice behind him. It was Black Else. The door to her bedroom stood slightly ajar, and she was looking out at him. "Fru Lund said it was some executive or other who was wearing a dirty necktie, and then it only turns out to be you. So now I'll go back to bed. Oh, I'm so tired." He heard a yawn. "You can come in if you want to."

The blind was pulled down in the bedroom so that everything lay bathed in a tawny light. But Jastrau spied a canopied bed with a lot of white bedclothing. It was elegant even though dimly discernible, and the fringed canopy came to a point at the top. Black Else's head was resting on the pillow of this princess's bed. Her features were blurred and in the dim light she looked like a girl whose forebears had been dark-skinned.

And Jastrau bowed and smiled. So such a bed was the ideal. Like the oval picture. Rococo, Oriental, out of a story book—and the essence of bourgeois respectability. He felt like a tramp.

"You've evidently become a prosperous girl since the last time," he said. But she probably did not remember the last time, even though—

"Oh yes—that time," she said, wrinkling her nose.

"I can see that the memory of it isn't pleasant," he replied in a tone of irony. He remained standing in the doorway.

"You don't think I'm the kind that walks the streets, do you? And I'm not, either. I just want to let you know that."

She sat up in bed, perturbed, almost indignant. The eiderdown slipped aside, revealing a bright red kimono.

Jastrau stared at her, unable to understand what she was getting at, and she went on, "I'll have you know that I'm a bar girl. I work in a bar, not on the street. I was expecting my husband, and I had no cognac in the house, and so—" She gesticulated and laughed shrilly. "So then I slipped. I went out on the street. I didn't have time to go

388

over to the bar and catch a fish, not with my husband due back in an hour or so. Naturally I couldn't have him come home and find me here with a man, could I? But I won't have you going around saying that I cruise the streets, for I swear to God I don't do that—ordinarily, that is," she added with pathetic agitation.

"So, it was just by accident—"

"But what do you want anyway? Oh, is it about last night?" She passed her hand wearily over her forehead. "Because I was so staggering drunk, wasn't I? I can't remember a blessed thing. How did I get home? No—were you with me? Did you come up here with me? Did I make love to you? No, I'm sure I didn't. But how drunk was I? Have a chair, whatever your name is, and sit over here and be nice. I suppose I was very drunk, wasn't I?"

"Yes, damned right you were," he replied, laughing. He found a chair and sat down near the edge of the bed.

A painful expression came over her face.

"You mustn't swear, do you hear?" she said nervously.

"Pardon me," Jastrau replied with a smile.

"But anyway—hello," she said suddenly, and extended her hand to him. "Why did you really come to see me?"

There was a decidedly cynical expression about her lips, which could signify that she wanted to laugh all sentimentality away.

"Don't you remember that I promised to come?" Jastrau said slowly.

"No," she said, shaking her head.

"Did I cry?" she asked with a sneer. "Well, thanks. Then you needn't tell me any more. And you promised to come and comfort me. That was nice of you." A little smile hovered on her lips, as if she was lost in her own thoughts.

Then she lay back against the pillow again, folded her hands under her neck, and gazed up at the canopy over the bed.

"You!" she said. "No, I don't know your name, but you're a newspaperman. Like this Vuldum." She mentioned the name with distaste.

"Yes, You know him."

"Uh—no. But will you believe it, he hates me. Oh how he hates me," she said, looking at Jastrau. "And all because one night out at the Golden Age Club I called him a red-headed monkey. 'You red-headed monkey, what a red-headed monkey,' I said. And you should have seen him. But he can go to hell!"

"Yes, one night I was at the Bar des Artistes—"

"Was that you? Then you can see for yourself. After all, he is red-headed, although he can't help that."

Jastrau caught himself staring at her arm. The kimono had slid up, revealing a muscular arm that looked too strong and powerful. And he could see a blue mark there. A finger imprint. Someone had taken hold of her too roughly.

"But look here, you—what was it I wanted to say?" Her eyes wandered searchingly up toward the bed canopy. "Yes, now I know. Why do you drink so much? I've seen you drunk so often, and it's not becoming to you."

Jastrau shrugged his shoulders.

"I just want to say to you that it's stupid," she went on moralizing. Her dark-red lips took on a naïve expression. "You can leave that to the others."

She lay there, quiet and sanctimonious, as if waiting to see the effect of her remarks. But Jastrau could not take her words seriously. He laughed.

"Well, you needn't laugh, because Vera says you're a really nice fellow when you're sober."

"Don't know her," Jastrau replied.

"She hangs out over here at the railroad station bar every afternoon. And so do I. As a matter of fact, I ought to be over there now. What time is it?"

Jastrau took out his watch and peered at it in the dim light.

"Quarter after four."

"You don't say! What a bawling out I'll get then, because I'm playing hooky."

And she laughed hilariously.

"From—your man friend?" Jastrau ventured to ask quietly. He was interested as an objective observer.

"Man friend?" She laughed scornfully. "No, and besides that's out of fashion nowadays. But I don't have a girl friend either. All the girls do. Can you understand why they care about that sort of thing?" She turned her questioning dark eyes toward him. "They don't care for men at all. It's only for the money. Oh, it's all so crazy—never catching a wink of sleep." She shook her head. "No, it's the waiter who'll bawl me out, and he has to do that, of course."

"It's evidently no bed of roses—all this."

"What's no bed of roses?"

"This life you lead," Jastrau said gently. Immediately he hated himself for the solicitude he was showing.

But Black Else looked at him mischievously. Then she drew the eiderdown way up to her nose and laughed. Jastrau felt like a missionary who made the rounds of the landed estates.

390

"You must excuse me for coming," he said gently.

"It was really very nice of you. Menfolk never keep their promises, damned if they do. There—I swore," she added respectably. "But won't you have a cup of coffee? I'll ring for Fru Lund now. Don't you think she's nice?"

"She's an angel."

The angelic Fru Lund entered soundlessly, spoke a few soft words, and disappeared.

And suddenly Black Else leaned out of the bed, drew Jastrau toward her, and whispered:

"She thinks I have a rich man friend. She doesn't know that we're no longer on good terms—my friend and I. Hush!"

"But then you'll have to—take to the streets again," Jastrau said.

"I!" Black Else exclaimed with indignation. "No, never! May I never sink so low! Rather than that, I'll—I don't know what—hang myself." And she let her tongue hang far out of her mouth, as if she were choking.

"Yes but—"

"You'll say I'm a fool, and so I am. But I'm hopping mad. Yesterday my husband showed up—that mug. He's one-quarter suicidal. He created a scene and threw himself on the floor in there, and I flung the door open so that it banged against his silly head while he lay stretched out full-length and moaning. And then I went out and drank and drank and drank—well, you know the story much better than I do."

"So you're still married," Jastrau said matter-of-factly. He stared at her as if she were some strange animal. Her cheekbones stood out prominently beneath her eyes.

"My God, yes!"

"And the man who's really your friend—does Kopf know about him?"

"I don't know what Kopf knows. Kopf is a soft-headed fool, and so for that matter is my friend—a real soft-headed old fool of a pharmacist, and I've told him so. Hush!"

Fru Lund entered silently with a tray.

"Will the Herr Editor move just a little?" she asked, placing a small table between him and the bed.

Jastrau shifted his chair, and his foot struck something that made a slight noise. Had he dropped something? He bent over. It was a leather strap, and he picked it up.

When Fru Lund had quietly floated out of the room, Black Else sat up in bed.

"God! How Jansen, the waiter, will bawl me out tomorrow," she said, laughing and quivering inside the kimono as she raised the steaming coffee cup to her lips.

"What a reckless person you are," Jastrau remarked, shaking his head in despair. "Keep this up, and you'll end on the street." And in order to give moral emphasis to his words, he hit the table with the strap.

Black Else hastily set aside her cup. "What's that? Let me see. Here, give it to me." She grabbed the strap, looked at it, and fell back in the bed with a shrill laugh.

"What's the matter?" Jastrau asked in perturbation. Suddenly he felt ill at ease. There in the sepia twilight lay this girl, who resembled a Moroccan, tossing back and forth in the bed. He could follow the violent movements of her legs beneath the eiderdown. She was the buxom type, actually coarse of build, and lacking in any intoxicating charm. But she brandished the strap in the air and followed its movements with glistening eyes.

"Where did you find it?"

"On the floor."

She laughed again and swung the strap to and fro in the semidarkness. It was as if she were playing with a grass snake. And it crackled slightly, almost inaudibly.

Jastrau felt chilled at this incomprehensible display of feminine ungovernability. She was shaken as if by convulsions, and kept laughing.

"Do you know what it's used for?" she panted.

Jastrau did not reply. He had a foreboding of shadows lurking in the brownish half-light and experienced a subdued feeling of alarm and repugnance.

"I tie the pharmacist with it," she said, and laughed again.

"The pharmacist?" Jastrau repeated breathlessly. He was being assailed by suspicions.

"Yes—my rich friend. He's old and queer—that way. He has to have it—like that, and that, and that." She swung the strap wildly, beating the air around her in a fit of ecstasy and laughter. The bed quivered, and the eiderdown resounded under the blows. "Like that, and that, and that—then he howls and screams and becomes young again. I tie his hands behind his back with this, and I have a dog whip in there. He gave it to me himself. Oh, he's crazy." And with a final savage laugh she flung the strap across the room so that it struck the wall and fell to the floor.

"Oh, it's disgusting!" Out of breath, she fell back onto the bed.

"You say he is a pharmacist?" Jastrau ventured quietly.

"Yes, and very rich. It was he who gave me all the furniture. Isn't it nice here? It's almost elegant, wouldn't you say? Have you really had a look at my living room?"

She moaned as she paused for breath.

"It's driving me completely daffy, I tell you," she sighed, pressing her hand to her heart as she lay with her mouth open, breathing audibly.

Jastrau did not dare to speak. He was fearful of having his suspicions confirmed, and a sinister shadow fell over him like a shroud—the shadow of a person he did not know, a person from chaos, from the generation preceding him. Will we all become like that? he asked himself. Oh God! He raised his hands to his head and hid his face. Is this the cursed infinitude of the soul?

"Do you understand now why I became rip-roaring mad?" said Black Else, gasping for breath. "Because then his wife died—"

Jastrau bent forward with his face still hidden in his hands.

"He came up here—dressed in black—wearing a high hat—"

Yes, that was the shadow. It was he. A distorted life. And he wrote about Jesus. *Wherefore Hast Thou Forsaken Me?*

"And then he became—well, just like a nineteen-year-old—"

Yes, Steffensen had encountered him. Yes, dressed in mourning. Steffensen had not known that his mother was dead.

"Because he was in mourning, of course—the old—"

The urn in the briefcase.

"And then afterwards he got sentimental and cried about his dead wife, and then I couldn't take it any longer, but told him off. I couldn't take it any longer—damned if I could."

Jastrau straightened up. He did not want to look at Black Else. He did not want to do anything.

"But just the same, I was a fool," Black Else said in a matter-of-fact tone, "because I haven't heard from him since. And Vera is laughing at me."

"But look," she exclaimed suddenly, sitting up in the bed, "I'm hungry. Shouldn't we go somewhere and have a bite to eat?"

"I don't know," Jastrau said uneasily. "I'm short of money—and it seems I have to go to Berlin. I don't know, but—"

He reached into his breast pocket for his wallet.

From force of habit Black Else took the wallet, opened it, removed the bills, and spread them out on the eiderdown.

"There could be more here," she said, wrinkling her nose. "But so what? I have some money, and we need food."

She handed him the empty wallet and gathered up the bills.

"You're a pal," she said as her bare legs slipped out from beneath the bed covers.

"Is that an up-to-date expression for a—?"

She looked at him without understanding.

Chapter Seven

A sound like a pistol shot—and a tinkling of glass.

Jastrau awoke in a daze, aware of complete darkness around him and conscious of the odor of a strange room. Next to him lay a naked body breathing and exuding warmth. From out of the darkness far below came the noise of a crowd. Voices shouted and echoed as in a cellar passageway. And in the background of all the voices and commotion there was a devouring sound like that of a sprint race being run through the underbrush of a forest floor. It grew louder and louder, and it was not a dream. For a moment the darkness whirled about him, but then up became up and down became down. The commotion came from the street, and the sound reached the bedroom, which looked out on the courtyard.

Black Else stirred restlessly in her sleep.

Then he heard the wail of a siren piercing the night air. The sound spread like fire through tinder and kindled a phosphorescence in his blood as he stared out into the darkness of the room and listened. The blood surged through his veins. Racing along on a bicycle, a boy with his tongue hanging out of his mouth, racing along after the fire engines.

Suddenly he sat up. There was a rustling in the next room, and at once he became aware of a thin, fiery-red streak in the darkness, as if he had been staring too long into a carbon-filament lamp. He shifted his glance. The fiery-red streak was still there. It did not shift with the movement of his eyes. It was real. The door panel must have sprung a crack.

"Fire!" he shouted. He sprang out of bed and almost stumbled over an empty port wine bottle, which went rolling across the floor. What a jolly time they had had, sitting in bed and drinking. The darkness whirled again like a globe seen from within. He managed to fling open the door to the living room, and remained standing stock still, blinded by the flickering light of long licking tongues of flame outside the window. Was there a fire on the floors below? Were they already

394

enveloped in flames—in a bowl of fire? Or was the fire across the street?

"What's the matter? Oh, my God!"

It was Black Else. Naked, she sprang out of bed.

"Fire! Fire! Help!"

But Jastrau stood in the doorway, open-mouthed and continuing to stare. The window curtains fluttered, and now and then the flames behind them seemed veiled and unreal. But his nose could detect the hot scorched odor that drifted in through the open window.

"There's a fire over at my house," he said almost in a whisper.

Suddenly the flames shot up as if they had been replenished with fuel, and he saw a spark dancing like a firefly on the curtains. Quickly he ran over and smothered it, crushing it as if it were an insect. A scrap of charred paper fluttered to the floor like a black butterfly.

"Close the window!" Black Else shouted.

He pulled the curtain aside and slammed the open window shut, but the glass came clattering out of the frame. The pane had been cracked by the heat. And he laughed. What had he accomplished? Now they were right where they had been before. The sparks could fly in and set fire to the room. A blast of hot air made him gasp for breath. His chest felt scorched. He was naked.

But then he forgot everything except the fire.

He could only gaze helplessly at the red flames, as if hypnotized. Yes, it was his apartment that was burning over there. Only now did he comprehend it fully. Something within him seemed to open up. The dining room was a sea of flames, like a blazing fire behind an open stove door. In the living room the fire alternately flared up and subsided, bursting forth like a volcanic eruption as a curtain went up in flames, then dying down only to erupt again, while the black smoke made its way out through the broken windowpanes, forcing the fragments of glass loose so that they fell away like scales. And it was with a purely instinctive, unconscious impulse that he reached for the curtain and modestly hid his nakedness behind it, as if to shield himself from the prurience of the flames.

"There's a fire over at my place," he repeated in a trance.

Black Else stood by his side.

"Your place?" she said with lack of comprehension.

He looked at her. The heat was making his eyes water, and red shadows danced before them—fiery shadows, bloody shadows. The naked female body floated upright but obliquely through purple waves, arms outstretched above its head. A greenish darkness lurked in the shadowy armpits. Black Else! Her breasts became so full in the reflection of the red light flickering on the yellowish skin. Feminine curves. Just then a tongue of flame shot up across the way and ignited another curtain—an elongated feminine arm, a demanding feminine body, supple, alluring, devouring. A raging fire. Yes—a woman.

"Your place?" she repeated breathlessly.

He stood with the curtain wrapped about him. Was it because of her that he was being modest? In the fiery glow she looked appallingly red, like meat hung up in a butcher shop. Her breasts were altogether too big.

"Yes, I live over there," he panted, meeting her eyes, which sparkled from the heat. The red fire was reflected in the tears that rolled from his eyes. Everything shone. Everything looked strange and blurred.

"Everything's burning up, damned if it isn't," he said, gesticulating dramatically with a bare arm as he stood there wrapped in his toga. "It's burning up!" he shouted jubilantly, his voice assuming an ecstatic, literary quality. "All the ships are burning."

And his ears were deafened by the noise that came from the street, incessantly as the pealing of a bell. Down there everything was gleaming. Police helmets. Firemen's helmets. Pavement and sidewalks glistened with water and had the dark-red color of mahogany. Long, gray hoses lay writhing on the pavement, with torrents of water issuing from their nozzles. And in the middle of the street stood a truck with a ladder rising vertically from it and slowly moving in against the wall of the building and the burning window frames where the flames darted back and forth like grass snakes, forcing their way through the space between the brick and the woodwork.

"What shall we do, Fru?"

It was Fru Lund's whimpering voice. She was wearing a peignoir, and her hair was an owl's nest of curlpapers.

"My God—stark naked!"

She disappeared with a virtuous scream.

"We can't stand here like this," Black Else shrieked, and ran into the bedroom. But Jastrau only turned and laughed. The room was alive with red and green light. His home, his furniture—everything was burning. Whew! The fire was reflected on Else's back. Her flesh quivered in the red glow as she ran with her ridiculous feminine gait. Slack and flabby, it quivered as she ran.

But he could not remain standing there either, naked among the strange furnishings. The hot air swept against his skin in waves. The smoke in the air was beginning to tickle his nostrils.

And coughing, he too ran into the bedroom, slamming the door behind him.

396

Else was dashing around in the dark. Jastrau heard the sound of her bare feet. The empty bottles rolled about on the floor as in a ship's cabin. He fumbled for his clothes.

"You have to get over there," she groaned.

"Why?" He laughed and stood on one leg, trying to put on his pants.

"Your furniture."

"It isn't mine."

"I never knew you lived over there."

"Ha ha, ha ha!"

"My God! What shall we do, what shall we do?"

It was Fru Lund, who stuck her head into the room. She had turned on the light in the hallway, and a narrow shaft of light penetrated into the dark bedroom. The curlpapers were silhouetted about her temples like a wreath of vine leaves.

"It's burning fine, isn't it, Fru Lund?" Jastrau danced around on the other leg. He could still feel the effects of the port.

"The curtains might catch on fire," Fru Lund lamented. "The sparks are flying right in the window."

"Yes, yes. I'll be there in a minute. Hell—right in the middle of a sound sleep!"

Black Else's voice was husky.

Then she ran out, her red kimono flapping. Jastrau caught a glimpse of it as she dashed through the shaft of light that came from the hallway. He bent over to pick up his jacket. The door to the living room was flung open again. As he straightened up, the glow from the flames illuminated the canopied bed in rosy red. Oh, cupids and angels' wings! A suffocating cloud of smoke penetrated the room.

"You'll choke!" he shouted. "You'll choke!"

Now he had his pants and shirt on. Fate had taken him by surprise while he was naked. He began to whistle.

"Why don't you come and help us, you stupid man?" Black Else shouted above the din from the street, which could be heard through the broken panes. She and Fru Lund hovered for a moment like dark shadows against the red, agitated, smoky background. His home! It was burning, burning. All the way to the ground. What a relief. What a feeling of liberation. And he went on whistling deliriously, monotonously, in rhythm with the roar of the flames as they climbed higher and higher. The two dark shadows stood balancing on chairs. Long curtain-rods dipped like the yardarms of a ship, and the curtains flapped. For a moment a constellation of sparks glittered, caught in one of the curtains, and a little tongue of flame shot forth. A scream. Then it was extinguished. And suddenly the glare from the flames

397

came garishly into the room. The curtains had been taken down, and the mahogany shone in the darkness. The furniture reflected the fire as if wine had been spilled over it.

A wild, monotonous whistling. It was burning, burning. All the furniture, everything in his home, chairs, tables, books.

It was all on fire.

There was a photograph of his mother. It was burning. There was a photograph of his son. The glass was cracked—a crack in the shape of a pitchfork. It had been jabbed into his heart. And everything was afire. Had new frosted panes been put into the hallway door? The phonograph, the rococo chairs, the Shrove Monday rod—up in flames. And the oak furniture. Ah, ha ha. It was burning, burning.

He might just as well put on all his clothes.

And the fire-insurance policy had been inscribed to Lundbom. He could have it. Yes, yes, little brother-in-law. Where is the fire-insurance policy? Tomorrow, when you read the newspaper, little brother-in-law, you'll open and close your mouth like a fish.

He kept whistling incessantly.

The two women were moving furniture. Jastrau tied his necktie carefully before a mirror in which there was a blood-red glow.

"You idiot! Why don't you help us?" groaned Else, who was standing helplessly at the head of the sofa with its inflammable cushions.

"Now—"

He did not get to say more. The words were lost in a fit of coughing. A black cloud of smoke whirled about in the midst of the flames, a belching cloud of darkness, and suddenly a thick, heavy bubble of soot and smoke forced its way out through the middle window—a black orb which at contact with the air from the street burst apart and like a broad banner of factory smoke unfurled itself, blackening the façade of the building as it rose until it concealed the roof.

Jastrau came to their aid. But he handled everything so recklessly.

"It's his apartment that's burning," Black Else said with a nod in his direction as she struggled with the table.

Fru Lund did not reply. She was in no mood for joking. She placed a bucket of water beside the window.

"Is the roof burning?" Jastrau asked. He bent forward and peered up through the banner of smoke that fluttered against the summer night's sky. Now and then a puff of whirling sparks burst forth and flickered red and yellow against the background of pale and peaceful stars while the reddish-brown smoke rose ever higher.

Then there was a hissing, seething sound. A stream of water smashed against the window frames across the street, and a cloud of white steam rose slowly from them. He could see a head with a fire helmet, a fireman on a ladder.

"No, apparently it's only my apartment that's burning," Jastrau said.

Fru Lund said nothing. But suddenly it dawned on her that it really was Jastrau's apartment that was afire. His remark had the effect of an insult, and she bridled with indignation. Furiously, she turned abruptly around and slapped a wet mop cloth against a spark that flew in over the windowsill.

"What a fathead!" she exclaimed.

Just then the doorbell rang.

Fru Lund hastened out into the hallway. It was a relief to be rid of her. They could hear her groaning.

Jastrau and Black Else coughed as they walked about the room, which was illuminated by a faint red light, now very faint because the fire was now restricted to the farther end of the rooms across the way. It was being brought under control, and from the windows with their charred wooden frames only clouds of steam and smoke issued, with now and then a whirl of sparks.

"Oh, my furniture!" Black Else moaned, spitting and clearing her throat.

Jastrau struggled to get his breath. The taste of smoke was almost closing off his windpipe.

They moved the chairs over toward the farthest wall.

"Oh, it will be so scratched up," she complained.

"Just think of my furniture," Jastrau said.

"I don't understand you at all," she replied, irritated.

Jastrau coughed.

From out in the hallway came the sound of men's voices, and a fireman entered. The masses of smoke were now so dark that the room lay in obscurity. But the fireman switched on a flashlight and let its pale beam play over the furniture.

The light came to rest on the bucket.

"A wise arrangement," he said, puffing. "They're as pesky as flies—these damned sparks."

He glanced over at the clouds of smoke.

"But now, thank God, there's nothing but smoke and the mess left by the water."

He remained standing with the flashlight lighted. They could hear him puffing like a tired horse. He was quite content to remain standing there.

"Was anything saved?" Jastrau asked. His voice was intense but unruffled.

"Not a thing."

His hand, which moved in a graphic gesture, could just be distinguished near the cone of light coming from the flashlight.

"You see—" Black Else sputtered. But suddenly a spark landed on her skin.

And then Jastrau abruptly asked in a harried, perturbed tone, "Was anyone burned to death?"

"No-o—not so far as I know," and the beam of light shifted. The fireman was getting ready to leave. Else stood clearly illuminated in her red kimono. She rubbed a foot against her bare shin.

"Well—are you quite sure of that?" Jastrau sprang toward the fireman and grasped him by the arm. His voice was ready to break, as if he meant to get cantankerous. "Are you quite sure nobody was burned to death?"

"No, but that will be investigated," came the patronizing reply, as the fireman freed his arm.

"Because anything can happen in that apartment," Jastrau went on, pursuing him.

"Yes, so it damn well seems," the fireman said, coming to a halt. He had nothing against taking a breather. "But the family over there has apparently gone away. It's supposed to be a journalist—a bundle of nerves, according to the janitor at any rate. Ha ha, the janitor must have had his toes toasted up there in his apartment, right above the fire. But I have to go. Apparently not so much as a canary bird was burned to death."

"How did the fire start?" Jastrau sounded agitated.

"A short-circuit, most likely. There's been no one in the apartment for the last couple of days—not even the roomer."

"Yes, yes. Ha ha. Are you quite sure of that?" Again Jastrau grasped the fireman's arm. "Because a short-circuit—ha ha—that's what they always say when they can't find the reason. But just imagine a lighted cigarette on a sofa spread—what about that? It lies there smouldering—what? It could start a fire—couldn't it?" Jastrau laughed wildly and tugged at the fireman's arm. "And then imagine that a murdered woman is lying on the sofa, so that she gets burned up. And then the murder is never discovered."

"Pooh!" groaned the fireman. "All this heat has made me soft in the head, too."

But Jastrau stuck his hands in his pockets and laughed. And through the darkness came the sound of Black Else's gay, relieved laughter.

"All right, it's a lot of nonsense," Jastrau said.

400

"That's my way of looking at it too," the fireman replied sardonically, and then left.

"But Ole, you're insane!" exclaimed Black Else.

"Am I?" Jastrau shook his head. "Am I? Quite possibly I am. But no—he did say that the roomer had not been there the last couple of days. No—then it didn't happen. No—perhaps not. Don't you have something I can drink, Else?"

They were standing in the darkness now. From the windows across the street now rose only black smoke, and from far inside could be seen occasional restless flames. The beams from firemen's flashlights crossed each other like swords. They could still hear the sizzling of water. Down in the street it had grown quieter.

"Oh for something to drink!"

"Yes, let's go out to the kitchen and see," Black Else said. She took his arm, half-jocularly, half-protectively. "I know how you feel. But don't you think it would be best if you went over and found out how many of your things have been burned? It must be terrible. Just think—all your furniture. But I didn't know it was you who lived over there."

Out in the kitchen she turned on the light, and Jastrau sat down, exhausted, on a kitchen chair. He sagged limply, in a state of collapse.

"But my Lord, what a lot of nonsense you rattled off to that fireman. A murdered woman on a sofa. Do you really know what you were talking about?" She laughed and opened the cupboard.

"By rights there ought to be a murdered woman there," he said with a sigh, staring at the floor. He was sweating profusely. "Oh, you've no idea of what I've been through. There *should* be a murdered woman on the sofa." His voice rose. "Yes! There was a murdered woman on the sofa—and the cigarettes—yes, it was all figured out with diabolical cleverness. They'll never find out about it. Oh, Else, Else. It's driving me crazy."

"Now, now, now," Black Else consoled him. "Drink this cognac— even though you drink too much."

Jastrau emptied the glass.

"Yes, I realize it's all fantasy. Of course it's fantasy." His voice grew calmer, rose now and then, tremulous and uncertain, but then subsided again. "Oh, I tell you, it was the queerest life we led in that apartment. It was something intangible; we were groping around with a psychological experiment. Steffensen—Stefani's son—well—"

"Do you know Stefani?" she asked frantically.

"Yes, yes." Jastrau smiled wearily and nodded. "I know him, and he

401

deserves all the thrashings you've given him—but never mind that. It's all so hopeless, so meaningless."

"When I was telling you about it, did you know—?"

Jastrau nodded again.

"Yes, but I don't give a damn. What does it all mean to me—the whole business? It's no more real than the three black men. I could see through them, and they went away. And now I'll soon be able to see through all this, and then that will go away too and there'll be nothing but black bookcases and a picture by El Greco, and then I'll look at it more carefully, and then it will go away too—the bookcases, the El Greco, and everything."

Else looked at him in alarm. She thought he was becoming hysterical.

"Look, wouldn't you like to lie down and rest?" She put her hand on his forehead. "You're so hot. You're all upset. You're sick."

"No, no." He shook his head. "Just let me sit here. So I can see the fire."

"But the fire's been put out. You should go in and lie down on my bed—yes, you should."

"I can't stand to close my eyes. I see flames. Just let me sit here. It's cool here, and the light is on. And everything is so clear in this white light. Oh, sometimes I go crazy, but just let me sit. Shouldn't you go in and help Fru Lund? There's no longer any danger."

"I think you ought to lie down," she went on obstinately.

But Jastrau's voice broke, and he began to whimper. "No, let me alone. You mustn't keep after me. It gives me a headache. Let me sit for a while—sit here alone so that—"

"All right, then I'll go." Meekly, but with an expression of slight chagrin, she shrugged her shoulders and left the room.

He could hear a subdued sound of motors far in the distance, and fire engines honking their horns. They were returning to the fire station. Then he suddenly caught sight of the cognac bottle, and with a rapidity that surprised even him he leapt up, seized the bottle, and poured still another drink.

He was in a state of utmost excitement.

With a bound he reached the door. There was no one in the hallway. Back to the kitchen table again. He emptied the glass. Back again to the door. He helped Fru Lund move some furniture. There was his hat, hanging on the hall rack. He slipped out to get it. Stole back to the kitchen again. Grabbed the cognac bottle. Went out in the hallway. Opened the foyer door noiselessly. Closed it without a sound,

402

and started down the stairway with long strides. The bottle—yes, the bottle!

He tucked it away in the inner pocket of his jacket and carefully gathered the jacket about him.

He was on the lower floor. Opened the street door. People were standing about on the sidewalk, staring up at the smoking windows. A fire engine was getting ready to pull away. It was still half dark. He could steal away close to the buildings and disappear around the corner.

He had slipped away unnoticed.

The gentle break of day. The houses were still dark. The streets lay as if submerged in bluish water, and doors and windows seemed obscured in a submarine dimness, behind which there was a stirring of invisible life. Overhead the sky was clear and bright. Morning had arrived up there, but it had not yet descended to the earth.

Odors emanated from the pavements.

Jastrau trudged along. He felt like a shadow. He trudged on—it mattered not where. He stopped at a street corner, raised the bottle to his lips, and took a swig.

He must gather his thoughts. To be alone and think. Steffensen—he had murdered her. Now he had done it, he must have done it. But it was a frightful thought. Had it given him the cold shivers? It was terrifying. Had Steffensen strangled her? Choked her? To have the sensation of a soft throat between one's hands! And a warm female body that grows limper and limper. At first a struggle, terror in her eyes. Mouth obstructed, unable to scream, because I am tightening my hands around her throat. Her head rolls back and forth. What was it like? Did her face turn blue? Did her eyes bulge, her tongue slip out of her mouth? What was it like?

Jastrau stood in the deserted street, absorbed in a gruesome pantomime, as if afflicted with St. Vitus' dance.

So Steffensen had murdered her. That animal! That beast! His eyes. That ominous glassy luster. The abnormal forehead. The teeth of a criminal—altogether too many of them, and far too small. The pale, sweaty, bony face with its brutish, protruding lips. But Anne Marie? How was it now that she looked? He could not form a mental picture of her. How was it she looked?

Jastrau closed his eyes and saw red flames.

Fire. Yes, his home and furniture. Nothing was left. Memories. Oh, let them go up in flames or—sprinkle them like rose petals. One and the same thing—flames and rose petals—one and the same. And

Vesterbro Passage lay unobstructed and clear in the morning light. The obelisk of the Freedom Statue was rose-colored granite. At times, under a certain light, there were roses in the stone. Rose petals and flames—one and the same. Did the corpse have red cheeks? The corpse? Anne Marie? No, she was alive. Of course Steffensen had not killed her. It was impossible when the Freedom Statue was rose-colored.

He wanted to turn away and go on. He did not want to enter the Town Hall Square, which lay suffused in soft, delicate shades of reddish brown. Why hadn't it burned—the entire Town Hall Square? All memories ought to go up in flames. He wanted to turn off and skirt Tivoli, go across Long Bridge and over into Amager. The countryside with its green trees would be cooling, and he needed a cool atmosphere in which to think. His lips were hot and swollen. He had no tobacco. But he did have cognac.

He stood motionless on the sidewalk, raised the bottle to his lips, and tilted his head back. All alone on a long, long sidewalk. An endless succession of concrete sidewalk sections. A ladder to the heavens that had fallen to the ground. The morning was as white as light reflected from chalk.

But yes, Steffensen *had* murdered Anne Marie. A crime had been committed. He could feel it in his bones. A major catastrophe had occurred. Catastrophe—κατά and στρέφω. Finally, finally, it had happened. Thank God! But what was there to thank God about? Jastrau walked on as if in a frenzy. It was gruesome. Bestial. Alive, then dead. Alive one second, dead the next. And it had taken place in his rooms, among the objects he knew so well—the oak furniture, the phonograph, the Shrove Monday rod had all been witnesses to it. Oluf had seen it. He—the boy—had seen it. Those figures pitching and tossing about, Steffensen's brutal yellowish hands, and Anne Marie, who had no chin. Now he remembered—she had had no chin. Why had he never kissed her on that weak chin that so revealed her helplessness. A murder had been committed, a murder of a child. Help! Help!

It ought to be reported.

I want to report a case of arson and murder—no, murder and then arson.

But had Steffensen really murdered her? Wasn't it his imagination? No. A crime *had* been committed. He knew that devil Steffensen. Hadn't he planned it, gone around watching for his opportunity, noticed how careless she was about lying on the sofa and smoking, then tossing the lighted cigarette butts aside? And the crime—that, of

404

course, was an example of the boundlessness of the soul. Steffensen had murdered her.

Otherwise the thing had no meaning whatsoever.

A cool breeze emanating from Kalvebodstrand swept over him. What was that bristling iron sphere? A morning star? A forbidding-looking gray building ornamented with two morning stars. And a sidewalk as broad as a public square.

A granite wall.

He edged farther and farther away from it. That monolithic building—how brutal it looked! It was the police headquarters. He panted for breath. Now he should go in there to a police officer and say, "Arrest me." No, he shouldn't ask to be arrested, but he should say, "There's been a fire in Istedgade—a case of homicidal arson, or so I think."

He should—but should he?

A policeman with a smug mustache came toward him, and now was the time—yes, this was the time—for him to speak up. The policeman stared at him.

"Good morning," said Jastrau, taking an uncertain step nearer.

Homi—homicidal arson. Was that the word? Yes, that was it.

"Good morning," came the gruff reply. "You're just a little high, aren't you?"

"A fine police station," Jastrau said abruptly.

"Watch out that you don't get better acquainted with it," the policeman said in a tone of truculent authority.

Jastrau drew himself up indignantly and went on.

Nasty. Overbearing. That mustache and the gruff voice. No, now the police could find out about it themselves. Now it was their affair. They could track down their homicidal arsonist themselves. Why should he help them? It would only make them conceited.

Nor was there any reason for him to report it. Who was he—Jastrau—that he should dare to report a murder? A crime? Did he know what a crime was? Did he have a moral right to report a crime? Was he going to report a crime? No, he was not going to report a crime.

That was society's job, and consequently not his. For he was not the state.

A cool morning breeze over Long Bridge. The state—that he was not. And alongside an old embankment with green trees, a moat with water that shone like pewter. Farther along, an elegant fenced-in embankment like a park. But he would go up on the decrepit part, take refuge under the bedraggled trees, and shake himself loose from society. He did not belong in fine company. The turf there was worn away in large patches. Deep furrows and paths had been worn in the embankment so that it looked like an emaciated whale with its ribs protruding. And down alongside the water was the Thieves' Walk. One did not report crimes. Just lie down here and empty the cognac bottle.

How fragrant the water and the sky. The birds moved about in the foliage. He found a patch of grass and a tree that leaned out over the moat beside the embankment. The tree made a good footrest, so that he could lie down and see the pale, blue sky. There were some restless, dark clouds. Beneath the clouds cold breezes were stirring. And he was homeless and without shelter. A flophouse for down-and-outers. That was how things could turn out.

A cold shiver ran down his spine. A down-and-outer with dirt and withered grass on his clothes. A ne'er-do-well under the open sky, and

> . . . a bottle lay beside him,
> but the brandy was inside him.

He recognized the bottle. Now the birds began to sing. He closed his eyes. Sure enough. Didn't it sound as if a copper wire were being swung through the air? A bird in a certain tree begins to sing, "Now we're getting up." Birds have bird habits. And then the sound spreads through the treetops and becomes absolutely unbearable.

But there was no cognac left.

He awoke shivering, and his heart pounded as he saw a branch of a tree over his head. He heard the noise from a trolley-car cable. Sky, trees, earth, water. The trolley car was going by on the other side of the moat. He had gone to sleep beside the Thieves' Walk along the Christianshavn embankment.

He walked slowly down to the water, rinsed his hands and face, and dried them with his handkerchief. It was disagreeable to go around for a whole day with a moist handkerchief. One's pocket gets damp. He straightened up and stretched himself. What was it that had happened? Why had he become another individual? His personality had suffered a dislocation. It was—no, not Anne Marie. He felt a pressure in the region of his heart. No, no. His heart was in the grip of a brutal fist—a fist that was compressing it as one squeezes a sponge. No, it couldn't be true. It was he who was out of his mind. If only he had some tobacco or money. But no—not an øre. Just twenty-five øre was all he needed—for some cigarettes. And there lay the cognac bottle. He held it up to the light. Yes, something inside it glistened.

One single drop of cognac can cover the entire tongue.

A moment passed. Then the fist gripped his heart again. It couldn't be true. But he had stood behind the curtains, and he had seen that anything could happen. His home had gone up in flames. All the things he had once been so attached to—to think that he had had to say good-by to them—burned. But Steffensen—it was impossible.

Jastrau could not remain where he was; he was too agitated. Nor could he just calmly walk away. Had he had money, he would have taken a taxi. He must, of course, have a talk with the janitor. Why hadn't he thought of that the night before? But could he talk to him without appearing ridiculous? Suppose it was the product of a deranged mind, sheer fabrication and fantasy? He could walk in to Istedgade. But he had no money, so he could not go into the shops, buy something, and then casually make inquiries. No, he could not make a fool of himself.

Short of breath, he walked in toward the center of town, along Vestre Boulevard, across Tietgen Bridge, and behind the railroad station to Istedgade.

Then he spied a woman in a brown dress coming out of a bakery shop with a package of pastry in her hand.

A black belt encircled her waist above her broad hips.

"Anne Marie!" he cried out, running toward her.

She turned around.

And as she did so he sank to his knees and wrapped his arms about her legs.

"Oh, thank God!" he exclaimed with a moan.

A beer truck was drawn up at the curb beside them. The driver, who was lugging a case of beer, looked up in surprise, placed it on the sidewalk so that the bottles rattled, and then began to laugh.

"Why, Herr Jastrau—you must be crazy! What will people think?" Anne Marie exclaimed, trying to tear herself away. The pastry fell out of the loose tissue-paper wrapping.

Jastrau got up hastily and stared at her with a wild look. Tears glistened in his eyes.

"It doesn't matter, Anne Marie. I'm going now."

"But look here now—"

Jastrau was already some distance down the street, and Anne Marie stood staring after him. His clothes were wrinkled. His collar was dirty. The brim of his hat was covered with dust.

"Here you are, Frøken," said the beer-truck driver, gallantly gathering up the pastry for her.

But she dared not look at him. She had a feeling that he was shaking his head very expressively, and she heard a soft-spoken remark:

"Off his rocker."

Then she ran into an entranceway and burst into tears.

Chapter Eight

For several hours Jastrau had been lying and staring at the small-patterned flowered wallpaper as he listened to the rain splashing down in the hotel courtyard. Now and then he turned his head and watched the raindrops rolling down the windowpanes in long rivulets with the same dogged sluggishness as the thoughts coursing through his brain.

He did not want to get up and put on his clothes. What could he say to the hall porter? He had no money. Actually, he was swindling the hotel by appearing there without an øre and ordering a room. That was what he had done about eight o'clock that morning. But everything was a swindle when one had no money. He did not even have a right to be there in that small, shoddy hotel room.

He was hungry. His belly was shrunken. There were so many things to think about. But they all lay in a heap of ruins now—all the things he should be thinking of. He was famished. But he could not bring himself to do it. Go down and speak to the hall porter? That hall porter with his hand discreetly poised in front of his mustache? How could he ask him if he would get one of the waiters to step out into the lobby? He did not want to discuss the situation inside the restaurant. And then enter into negotiation with him—for food on credit? The thought was repulsive. The distrustful look in waiters' eyes always remained in one's mind. No, he could not bring himself to do it yet.

The rain fell steadily, a dark, descending pall outside the windowpanes, and with the same somber monotony his thoughts grew more depressing. He was a drunkard. Consequently, he ought to feel despair. He ought to lose heart. The rain kept falling, spattering in the courtyard, and the monotony of it made him feel so helpless that he could not even raise his hands. It was the same thing over and over—a constant recurrence. It was hell. Lying on his bed, he floated down through the darkness of hell, and hell too resounded with an eternal, ceaseless movement like the rain—a moving curtain of gray, slanting rivulets and a murky twilight that percolated through everything.

He wondered what time it might be. A little while before he had heard the Town Hall clock strike the half hour. But which hour? Should he reach his hand out toward his vest, which hung over the back of a chair, and look at his watch? Should he?

He gave a start, and his hand stopped in mid-air.

Something heavy bumped against his door with a noise like thunder. There was a scraping and lurching out in the hallway, a noise which because of its indefinite character had a disagreeable effect and invested the ceaseless rain and the continuous, perpetual semidarkness with an even more melancholy quality. There was a sound of ponderous, uneven steps, a walking stick came down heavily against the floor, striking it each time with a loud thud as if the tip would explode, and then several short, tripping footfalls could be heard vainly trying to keep in step with the heavy thumps. An apoplectic groan added a sinister note to it all. It was the invalid procession going by out in the corridor.

So it was half-past four.

And Jastrau heard the door of the room next to his being opened. The inevitable Kjær gasped for breath in an ominous, agonized manner. Then he heard Kjær's ponderous bulk being rolled over on the bed as the snickering waiter began to pull off his clothes.

It was half-past four.

It was as if the rainy atmosphere had grown darker and the darkness more distressing. Ghosts of ill-omen were lurching about in the hallway. Or they lay in ugly rooms beneath ceilings that brought on heart palpitations. And one of them was hungry. Jastrau was hungry.

Oh, couldn't he wait a few more hours? He could hear the water running in the roof gutters, areaways, and drains outside. Or could he not at least fall asleep and not wake up until morning? By that time perhaps the weather would have cleared, and under a bright sky hope would manifest itself like a song in a sunny courtyard. Tomorrow he could perhaps wangle a lunch. That was easier. During the forenoon there was no one in the restaurant, so it would be less embarrassing to deal with the waiter.

His home had burned.

He sat up, as if the thought of the fire had roused him. His home had burned. He had not said a word about it to the hall porter that morning when he had taken a room, and the porter had believed that he had been on a binge the whole night long. His home had burned. Something might be said about that, and about the fire-insurance policy that he had inscribed to Lundbom. But it belonged to his wife. Ah yes. But nevertheless, couldn't some dodge be managed with it so that he would get a respite—for a few days.

He had to get up. A few days respite. Then he could write a series of articles—

But then there was a knock on the door.

Should he make believe he was asleep? Who could it be? Whoever it was, it would be disagreeable. Suddenly the door opened. He had forgotten to lock it. And Otto Kryger entered hastily.

"Good heavens!" he exclaimed when he saw Jastrau in bed.

"What do you want?" Jastrau asked in a tone of exasperation.

"I want to send you off to Berlin, my dear fellow, and that immediately." He shook his head, laid his wet topcoat aside on the little sofa, and placed his wet hat on the table. "But I see by the paper that your apartment has burned. What about that? Did you have it insured?"

Jastrau sat up in bed and watched him with a sardonic expression. Kryger's self-assured gestures were laughable, and his beaming, precipitate friendliness was unbearable. Was Otto Kryger a decent sort? Decent? Ha ha. He was a cuckold. And so decent that it made a person indignant.

"Did you have it insured, I'm asking you?"

"I made Lundbom a present of the policy," Jastrau said with a faint, canny smile that hovered senselessly over his unhappy, harried features. There was a trace of dementia about it.

"Has the policy been renewed?" Kryger went on.

"Of course. Do you think my gifts are worthless?" was the scornful reply.

Kryger looked at him. Jastrau's swollen face, his screwed-up eyes, his generally run-down appearance, combined with his stubborn, unyielding attitude and supercilious smile, made Kryger uneasy. It was indeed a disconcerting sight. Jastrau was sitting up in bed with his rumpled shirt in disorder and his hair a mess, his slovenliness revealed down to its innermost depths, more an animal than a man.

"Well, I'll get hold of that policy, don't you worry," Kryger said.

"So-o?" Jastrau replied scoffingly, having thus been declared incapable of handling his own affairs.

"But why haven't you gone to Berlin, man?" Kryger sat down in a chair and crossed one leg over the other.

"It's lucky I didn't go. If I had, you wouldn't know where the policy was."

Kryger lowered his eyelids and disregarded Jastrau's mocking tone. It sounded so scathing, so jarring, that Kryger did not want to recognize it. If he gave in to that mocking, Mongoloid face that peered at him so malevolently through the rainy twilight, then Jastrau would turn into an imperturbable, irremovable hulk, a lunatic prophet sitting up in his tousled bed with the eiderdown humped about his knees.

"Well then, have you spent the money on booze? Because you understand that Professor Geberhardt is expecting you, and I don't want to let him down."

But Jastrau did not reply. He sat staring vacantly into space through the darkness of the room. Suddenly, in a faint, singsong voice, he began:

"Then crime's consuming fire flares up
With a blue and gaseous flame—"

"What?" Kryger shook his head in exasperation.

"Yes, it may sound trite. And it may be that you're right," was the unexpectedly mild reply.

"Look here now, we're talking about realities," Kryger exclaimed harshly. "Hadn't we better keep to them?"

"Very well." Jastrau bowed politely from the bed and managed a foggy, subservient smile. "So we'll keep to the realities. I don't have money to pay for this room, so at this moment I could be locked up for cheating the hotel."

Now his voice was hard and factual.

"You're being hysterical," Kryger exclaimed.

"Perhaps." Jastrau laughed. "But I'm hungry."

"Haven't you any money? Where's it gone? At least you have the ticket. You did go into Bennett's."

"I went into Bennett's, that's right," Jastrau replied, raising a forefinger ironically. "But that doesn't mean that I bought a ticket. I went into Bennett's, and then I went out again."

"But what about the hundred kroner?"

"Can't last forever when a person needs women and liquor and other luxuries."

Jastrau closed his eyes ecstatically and sat swaying back and forth in an aggravating manner.

"Whew! You're hopeless!" Kryger groaned.

Jastrau did not answer him. But the swaying motion continued, incessantly and monotonously as if he were a demented patient, and the impression was heightened by the rhythmic spattering of the rain against the concrete down in the courtyard.

"Damn it all! This I can't stand!" Kryger shouted in vexation, and sprang up. "Now, you're going to get your clothes on, and then we'll go down and get something to eat. Perhaps that will bring you to your senses. Incidentally, here's a letter for you. It was lying down at the desk."

He tossed a letter over to Jastrau on the bed.

"Now you read that letter, which I hope doesn't make you lose your head entirely, and then get into your clothes and meet me down in the restaurant. In the meantime, I'll speak to Lundbom about that insurance policy."

Kryger issued his orders in a firm, clear voice, irked as he was by Jastrau's disconsolate rocking back and forth. Fortunately, the intolerable motion had now stopped. The letter had an effect. Kryger slung his topcoat over his arm while Jastrau nodded in a preoccupied manner and stared at the letter. The writing on the envelope was in a large, clumsy hand.

"Do you follow me?" asked Kryger.

Jastrau nodded again and opened the letter. It was brief, and all it said was:

Dear Jastrau: Hear that your apartment has burned. Haven't been there for three days. So it wasn't I who set fire to it. Wanted you to know that. Father Garhammer asks me to give you his regards.

Stefan Stefani

"Say—I don't suppose you'd have a cigarette," Jastrau managed to call out before Kryger had gone out the door.

A package of cigarettes sailed through the air.

"Anything hair-raising in the letter?" Kryger asked.

"No." Jastrau fumbled for the cigarettes.

"Thank God for that." And the door was closed.

Jastrau was out of bed immediately. He lit up and inhaled the nicotine, went over to the bed again, spread Steffensen's letter out on the eiderdown, and read it once more. Stefan Stefani? Why in bloody hell had he signed himself Stefani—his father's name? What had happened? Oh, he could not think just wearing a shirt! But Stefani! Why had he reassumed the name he despised? Jastrau reached for his shorts and socks. There was a hole near the big toe. All his clothes at home in Istedgade had burned. And the books. Some part of the insurance money must go to him. Consequently he was not a swindler and a hotel-cheat. Nor could he go to Berlin before the business of the insurance was settled.

But *Stefani!* The letter was signed Stefan Stefani. Ha! And the greeting from Father Garhammer. Father Garhammer asks me to give

412

you his regards. But Steffensen did not even know Father Garhammer. "Asks me to give you his regards." It sounded as if Father Garhammer had been sitting across the table from Steffensen while he had been writing the letter. What did it mean? The mystery must be cleared up. And his shoes were muddy. Mud from the Christianshavn embankment. He must ring for the bellboy and get them polished. And he must have a brush for his clothes. He was not a hotel-cheat. There must be some money coming from the fire insurance.

He phoned and got a brush.

How dreadful the back of his jacket looked. Stefan! Stefan Stefani! He must have ground his elbows into the earth, they were so filthy. But Stefani! Why Stefani? And his hat! The entire brim was crusted with dirt. And besides, Father Garhammer—Father—Garhammer!

Suddenly Jastrau tossed hat and brush up against the wall. It couldn't awaken the inevitable Kjær in the depths of his slumber. And of course—to think that it hadn't occurred to him before—Steffensen was on the point of being converted. Pooh! He too had to find the way to *his* infinity, there were no two ways about it. *Sub specie aeterni.* Conversion had lurked in Steffensen's face that last crazy evening they had been together. What else could that tense, determined mask that he had assumed signify. Of course. A convert. And how like the Catholics it was. A son of the renowned Stefani. They could use Steffensen with a name like that. Ah yes, with his father's well-known name. Propaganda. Three cheers for publicity in the name of piety. O-oh! Jastrau stuck his entire head into the wash basin and puffed and snorted. The water felt good.

Of course Steffensen had leapt into a conversion. Logic. Eternal recurrence. And now he could assuage his wounded vanity with the thought of infinity, cool it off as Jastrau was cooling his head in the wash basin. Pruu-u-u. *Sub specie aeterni!*

Sub specie aeterni nobody is ridiculous or everyone is ridiculous. Now Steffensen had found his way home.

Jastrau flapped the towel as he dried himself. How that religion suited Steffensen. Absolute and uncompromising. A religion. Jastrau sat down and laughed loudly. Alone in his dreary hotel room.

Now Steffensen had taken a position. Now he could find use for his fists—strike out with them. Was it his youthfulness?

Carrying things to an extreme—orthodox, unswayed by sentiment.

Was it his youthfulness?

Yes. And his boundless vanity.

And Jastrau himself? No, he was no youth. He was thirty-five years old, and an old man. He had a belly. It stuck out noticeably when he stood in pants and shirtsleeves. There was a suspicion of a bald spot at the back of his head. And within this incipient corpulence resided his soul.

Soul! Soul! Soul! He glanced at himself in the mirror and discovered a dark shadow of sprouting whiskers. Yes, he recognized that face. *Ecce homo!* Behold the man. But wasn't it a lie to maintain that he had sought for the spiritual? He with his Mongoloid features? The infinitude and intractability of the soul?

Anyway, what had come of it?

A ruined marriage and a lost job. Here he was. Brawling and broken windowpanes. Tawdry seduction and infidelity. Ridiculous conversion and a home gone up in flames. Hallucinations and havoc. And *Ecce homo!* Was it a man who stood here? And whiskey, whiskey, whiskey!

> I have longed for shipwreck and disaster,
> For havoc and sudden death.

Steffensen's poem from out of the past, a long, long time ago.

Jastrau breathed more freely. A few words set to rhythm had relieved him. Now he could finally go down to the restaurant.

In the lobby, he handed the hall porter the key with a casual air.

"It seems you had a fire, Herr Jastrau," the porter snickered.

"Don't bring up the subject. However, the insurance—" His smile hinted at a large, reassuring amount of indemnity, and the porter bowed.

Although it was summer, there were many customers in the restaurant. The rain had driven them in. The electric lights had been turned on early, too, in order to dispel the gloominess of the weather, and a piano and violin drowned out the splashing of the rain.

Kryger had found a place over near the window next to the hotel courtyard. He sat studying the insurance policy.

"Well, I see that Lundbom hung onto it," said Jastrau, laughing.

Kryger looked up and wrinkled his brows.

"You look rather déclassé," he remarked.

"Yes, my collar, my collar," Jastrau repeated nervously as he sat down. "I realize that it isn't altogether clean. But then, I lost all my clothes in the fire."

Kryger stopped a waiter and asked for a menu.

"Now we'll eat, and then—then we'll have to see if we can't make some order out of all this Babylonian confusion," he said.

"Yes, I suppose I'll have to stay here in town until the insurance—"

"Well, that's what you think." Kryger showed his teeth. "No, you're

414

going to Berlin to be a secretary and learn something about economics and finance—about realities, to put it briefly. They're good sound subjects."

Jastrau did not want to smile. It was easy to feel superior toward a man who had humps on his forehead—the roots of antlers. And that man talked about realities. But why yield to such a cheap feeling of superiority?

The roast was served, the *snaps* poured, and Jastrau stared at Kryger's forehead, stared stupidly at it in order to blot out a cynical thought. Finally, in order to get his breath he had to—simply had to—ask:

"Why do you really want to help me this way?"

Kryger directed his dark eyes toward him, and a smile appeared on his wide, sensitive lips. There was a pronounced irony in the smile, yet it was cordial.

"Quite frankly, because my wife likes you."

Jastrau nearly choked on his *snaps*. It burned and scorched his throat. And as he coughed, he felt himself blushing.

"Now, now—not with that expensive *snaps*," Kryger joked. When Jastrau had finally calmed down, although he still had tears in his eyes, Kryger went on, "Because I must confide to you that for some stupid reason or other my wife seems to have faith in you, and I've been influenced by it. How could I help but be?"

"I see," Jastrau muttered. He could not look Kryger in the eye.

"However, I don't know," Kryger continued. "I've loaned you a hundred kroner, and now I suppose I'll have to loan you another hundred. And you must admit that you're not the safest bank I could put my money in. But as I said, Luise believes in you, and what won't a person do when confronted with such a touching display of confidence by a member of the fair sex? As a matter of fact, she won't be satisfied until you're in Berlin. That's the way she is."

He made an expansive gesture with one hand to indicate that he himself had given up trying to solve the riddle.

"Furthermore, as far as I personally am concerned," he added, "I can imagine that under Geberhardt's social and economic tutelage you might come to your senses."

"And become aware of the realities and turn into a conservative," Jastrau went on sarcastically.

"Ah yes, may God grant that," Kryger sighed. "Then at least I'd have saved a man from perdition. Incidentally, are you reading my articles?"

"No, I abhor business and conservatism."

"You abhor them? Good Lord!" Kryger threw up his hands pathetically. "So that's the sort of a monster I'm helping. Ah yes. But incidentally, this meat tastes good." The sudden change of subject was not without a conscious note of sarcasm.

"Yes, you believe in the realities," Jastrau replied in the same tone.

"Yes." And Kryger sipped at his *snaps*.

But a glint of mischief had come into Jastrau's eyes, and he leaned closer to Kryger.

"I remember that you once asked me about my mother," he said slyly.

Kryger ignored the tone of voice and looked at him with concern.

"Oh yes, so I did," he replied apologetically. "But it was certainly not my intention to hurt you, I can assure you of that."

"You wanted to show that I was a poor lover," Jastrau went on, speaking still more slowly.

"Let's forget about it," Kryger replied with a nervous flick of his hand.

"And you wanted to indicate an Oedipus complex, didn't you?"

Kryger sighed. "Yes, yes, yes. I regret what I said—I assure you I do."

"You mustn't." Jastrau lingered over his words. "You mustn't do so. But now you're going to solve a riddle."

"Where do you think we are? In school?" Kryger asked. His teeth were gleaming.

Jastrau laughed. "Now listen to this," he said. "A man is put to studying economics."

"The most important subject of all," Kryger interrupted.

"His mother died when she was twenty. Consequently he never knew her—but he worships her. But he knows that she was a woman of the proletariat—in the true and most hopeless sense of the word." Jastrau's voice had become serious, and it quivered with intensity. The glint of mischief had vanished from his eyes, and he sat as if hypnotized from staring at a distant fire. And now Kryger's eyes sparkled. He knew what Jastrau was getting at.

And Jastrau went on incisively: "Now, economics is as objective as anything can be, isn't it? Figures and realities. Or am I mistaken? Isn't it more objective than poetry? And now I ask you"—here Jastrau uttered a loud laugh—"does such a man become a conservative or a Communist?"

"It's to be hoped that he doesn't become a radical," Kryger replied with a wave of his hand.

Then he emptied his glass and refilled it.

416

"A nice complex that, indeed," he went on. "Nevertheless, I'm going to risk sending you down to Professor Julius Geberhardt. I believe in you," he added, shrugging his shoulders. "And why do I believe in you? Because my wife believes in you. And why does she believe in you? I dare say because it's downright, scandalously idiotic. So you're going to be compelled to go to Berlin."

"But I haven't any money."

"Yes, but I'll loan you some, and for the second time. I suppose because that's shockingly idiotic, too."

"But I don't care to go tonight. And the insurance—" Jastrau replied languidly.

"We'll talk about the insurance after we have our coffee."

"All right, but I'm not setting out tonight," Jastrau said with a sluggish obstinacy.

"And what that means," Kryger said with a feigned air of jauntiness, "is that I again have to risk a hundred kroner, and right here in this dangerous place to boot, next door to the Bar des Artistes." He stared at Jastrau for a long time, but suddenly he grasped his glass and became suave and resilient. He was now acting as he did at the big parties—with an air of urbane detachment. "If it isn't delightfully idiotic, then Luise is not the marvelous female she is. So, *enfin,* let's drink to her—to Luise."

Taken aback, Jastrau picked up his glass. A fog floated before his eyes. Kryger's black eyes sparkled. Did he know what the situation was? Was he being sarcastic? Was his obligingness an ironic form of revenge, a quiet attempt to remove him from the scene?

Something had to be said. Jastrau stared at the elevations on Kryger's forehead. Who was the stronger of the two—the horned stag or the Mongoloid? Some remark had to be made.

"A toast to private initiative," he said.

"And now we have to get to work," Kryger said, laying a notebook on the table. For the next few hours they compiled a list of Jastrau's belongings that had been lost in the fire. Kryger wrote them down.

Now and then they sipped at a whiskey. It was a subtle way of getting revenge. Jastrau lighted a fresh cigar. If it was indeed revenge. Helping him and getting rid of him.

Wasn't it a fight between the horned stag and the Mongol?

No, it was no fight. Kryger was gently easing Jastrau out of Copenhagen. That was the entire battle.

And Jastrau recalled that election night when they had sat together up in the editorial room across from the pillar with the names on it, and Kryger had been fishing for conservative sympathizers. Or hadn't he been fishing? Every human being was like a prism. It should be possible to measure the goodness that radiated from it. The refraction of light could be measured.

"My Lord, it's eleven o'clock!" Kryger exclaimed, looking at his watch. "That means I have to get up to the paper. Well, I have it all down here. And I'll turn the policy and this list over to the lawyer. I have your address in Berlin. So now there's no more for us to do."

He got up and tucked the notebook meticulously away in his inner pocket.

"And so good-by. Oh yes, that's right—" Again a smile crossed his face. Jastrau noticed now that it was the face of an Indian—the low forehead, the prominent nose, the blue-black hair. The smile was not sincere. It was erotic, and its brightness reflected cruelty. "Here's the new loan." He shoved a hundred-krone note across the tablecloth. "For God's sake, don't thank me for it. And give my warmest regards to dear Professor Julius."

Jastrau got up laboriously and extended him his hand.

"Don't you want me to greet Luise—for you?" Kryger's black eyes shone for a second.

"Yes, take her my greetings."

"And now don't drink up the money."

Jastrau did not reply. He stood fumbling with the hundred-krone note. Should he give it back to him?

"When the insurance is paid, you can take out the two hundred," he said.

"Why, yes—that's right. So I'm protected in the bargain." Kryger laughed, waved his hand, and strode away through the restaurant. Over near the piano, he turned, waved once again, and disappeared.

Jastrau sat down, rested his elbows on the table, and stared at the money.

Then he folded it, stuck it in his vest pocket, and went out to the men's room.

He turned on the water faucet, the water rushed into the basin, and in its swift stream he could distinguish the sound of music. The notes resolved themselves into those of a violin, and suddenly Sinding's "Rustle of Spring" was dancing up and down in the bubbling jet of water. He could not help doing a tap dance on the tile floor. The white porcelain washbowls, the mirrors, the towels, the glazed brilliance of the fixtures lighted up the room as if for a festival. For now he had money in his pocket. Now he had a right to everything—the violin in the stream of water, the music in the café, the phonograph over in the bar. Now he possessed it all, this comfortable humming house. For how many hours? How did he know? That morning he had lain out there on the bare ground like a tramp, and tonight all the music, all the lighted windows, the cozy dimness of the bar, the crunching sound of ice in the cocktail shaker were his, his, his.

How much did a ticket to Berlin cost? He had no idea. But there was plenty of money for yet another night.

His collar was not clean. He was not cleanshaven. But he was the man he was.

Keeping in step with the music and in a quietly jubilant mood—what was the subdued, fatalistic waltz they were playing?—he slipped quietly through the restaurant, out into the lobby, and through the door to the Bar des Artistes.

The phonograph hummed. The soft lights and the reflection from the reddish-brown walls had a soothing effect. And behind the gleaming bar stood Lundbom with his deeply flushed face, flourishing the shiny shaker with long, undulating motions.

"Good luck with the fire insurance," someone yelled. And Jastrau smiled.

Lundbom nodded graciously from far in the distance.

Oh, that comfortable, cozy bar. The brasswork, that always was reminscent of trolley cars and long rides, or of machinery which the public was not allowed to get close to. The high stools which ought only to be occupied by Negroes in stars-and-stripes pants. The salted almonds which whetted the thirst—gratis. The wet drink checks. The multicolored cocktails. And the life-size picture of the naked Charles the Twelfth, a discreet reminder of the other pleasures to be had.

"Those whom the good Lord loveth never shall meet for a final farewell," intoned a subdued, hollow voice. The inevitable Kjær was seated at the round table, singing. He beat time briskly with his hands. He was rejoicing because now his solitcde had been broken.

"Ah, Jazz, I've been waiting for you. But I knew you'd come."

And Kjær spread his arms in an all-encompassing embrace.

"And now one of these days Little P. will come back. We'll get together, we'll all get together. 'Those whom the good Lord loveth—' "

Jastrau sank into an armchair and drew a breath of surprise.

"Arnold, bring me a whiskey so I'll have something to hold on to. Is Little P. coming?"

"Yes, yes, yes, because his mother is on her deathbed. Little P. and Old P. hadn't gotten any farther than Liverpool, and now they're coming. Little P. is coming by plane."

The inevitable Kjær was jubilant. "He's coming by plane, Jazz. He's coming by plane. The trumpets sounded retreat."

Kjær gazed at Jastrau with bleary eyes. A contented prelate's smile hovered about his lips, and the cleft in his chin gave him a roguish look.

"It's a joyful evening tonight, Jazz. And I hear that your arson worked out well for you. *Skaal, skaal.* And congratulations. Yes, something had to be done. It was a splendid idea to set fire to it all—a good old farmer's trick. Good luck with the indemnity."

There was nothing to do except raise his whiskey glass in acknowledgment and drink. Over at the bar, Lundbom wrinkled his face up into a satyr's smile and nodded. Everything was warmth and comfort. Everybody wished him well.

"It was a good thing I kept the policy," Lundbom remarked.

"Yes, you honorable old rascal," Jastrau replied with a hilarious shout. "We must have more whiskey, more whiskey, more women."

"No women," groaned the inevitable Kjær, raising the palm of his hand in alarm. "Positively not."

"All right, but whiskey then, whiskey."

And once more he was sitting at the round table, with Kjær holding court opposite him in all his majestic bulk. Here, and here only, could be found a peacefulness that was not of this world. The ventilator rumbled above their heads, the back door stood open out to the dark courtyard and the splashing rain, the red portières fluttered gently in the damp breeze, and over in the corner the phonograph droned out "No More Machines for Me—"

"To you, the only gentleman in the world—*skaal!*" Jastrau exclaimed ecstatically.

But Kjær immediately set his glass aside, raised his head high, and tried to make his dull eyes flash.

"That's backbiting, my dear Jazz," he said sternly.

"Well, then in any event—*skaal!*"

"Yes, that's something quite different," Kjær replied, and drank. Then for a little while he sat smacking his lips. "Something entirely different," he said pensively.

"But after all, it's up to me to judge," Jastrau objected.

"No," was the harsh reply. "There is but one gentleman in Denmark, and that is H. C. Stefani."

"That's as if to say—"

But Kjær raised his head, as if demanding silence. "It's as I say, young man. One time—he demonstrated—that he was a gentleman. If only I could remember it. It was on a certain occasion, and it will probably come back to me, but I forget—forget." He had collapsed again and was gesticulating in a gloomy manner. The stamp of authority had vanished from his expression, and a helpless, quizzical look came into his eyes. "But I know that he's a gentleman," he added firmly.

Jastrau smiled skeptically.

"Do you know him, then?"

"No, but—"

"Then how can you—" Kjær stopped and shook his head. "Young man, young man—you sit there with a distrustful smile. With a smile like that you can kill a good man's reputation. And Stefani is a good man. Because once when I was young—I was young and slender then—once when I was young, as I told you, he proved himself to be a gentleman. But I can't remember it—I can't. But do you doubt me? Do you dare to doubt me?"

He struck his clenched fist against the tabletop with a loud bang.

"Mark my words, Jazz! Stefani is a gentleman, because once when I was young—no, no—"

And suddenly he put his hands up to his head, pressed them against his temples, and began to whimper.

What was it that made Jastrau shiver? He got up. It must be the damp air coming from the courtyard. He shut the door.

"Oh, what becomes of it all—everything that once happened? It disappears—slips away—"

Jastrau's gaze fell on Kjær's bleary blue eyes. They peered out from his bloated face, seeking help, and a foolish smile attempted to conceal his impotence.

"But now Little P. is coming. This is going to be a joyful night. He's coming by plane."

Jastrau rubbed his hands together. It was as if he could feel earth under them. The Christianshavn embankment. Now he was conscious of the dew-soaked ground and the worn, sparse grass. Back to the earth. One has to be buried sometime.

And there was an unreal light in the barroom. It was an hallucination seen through a red haze, while the impression of earth and grass was realistic. Was he lying on the Christianshavn embankment at that moment, down by the Thieves' Walk, and dying? With the phonograph droning on? Or playing in the trees? Among the sickly-looking leaves?

Another whiskey. How realistic the check looked.

"Ah yes, it takes all sorts of things to make a world, but in any event, *skaal*," the inevitable Kjær said with a sigh.

It was good to be drinking. But why had Jastrau gotten that feeling of dirt on his hands? Couldn't it be rubbed off?

"It all slips away—ha!" And Kjær shrugged his heavy shoulders disconsolately. "I can't remember." He waved his hands despairingly. "If it weren't for Charles the Twelfth hanging up there, I'd have forgotten what a woman looks like. But now I can at least remember."

He snickered.

But it was as if Jastrau had sunk into a quagmire of despair. He sank lower and lower. Simply in order to be sociable he said "Ha," and took a drink of his whiskey. It tasted like ground water.

"And I was married, Jazz."

"Just as we were."

"And then she was unfaithful. Her name was Esther. Or else I was unfaithful. I can't remember—it all slips away." Kjær stared hopelessly out into space. "Ha ha," he tittered, "both of us were undoubtedly unfaithful, but it doesn't make any difference. It's all slipped away. Everything has slipped away."

"I'm also separated from my wife." But then he stopped. An uncomfortable feeling that he was only echoing Kjær rose up in him and made him hold his tongue. And then she was unfaithful. Or else it was I who was unfaithful. But it made no difference, because now he lay on the Christianshavn embankment and was dying. And his final hallucination was a reddish haze, the Bar des Artistes. Lundbom's red face, the sun setting, the gleam of the cocktail shaker, the water in the moat beside the embankment.

But he could not see right through that hallucination.

No. Voices and the general hubbub constantly assailed his ears. Someone broke into song, and he shut his eyes. It was the inevitable Kjær, who was singing in his husky voice:

"I looked but at the past. For me life lost its savor.
Then through my soul rang out so comforting a song:
Look ahead but never back. What the heart desires,
Some sunny day perhaps will come to be.

Where life's spring gushes forth, there lie my thoughts.
Where life's tree blooms, there bloom my thoughts anew.
Look ahead but never back. What the heart desires,
Some sunny day perhaps will come to be."

The voice rose in volume, resounding through the room, and Jastrau lay stretched out on the bare ground.

"Hush! You're annoying the guests."

"Shut up, you Swedish heathen. When the true Christian spirit—the

422

Grundtvigian spirit—awakes in me, I want to air my feelings, you Swedish cannibal."

The hallucination persisted in all its clarity. Lundbom kept shushing the inevitable Kjær, who obligingly switched over to a silent song, opening and closing his mouth without a sound. But the earth on his hands. Was it real? In his pocket was a real handkerchief. It was damp, and the pocket was moist. There were graves with ground water in them.

Again the hoarse voice sounded and grew louder:

> "But if the soul has all it longs for under the sun,
> Then there are still other suns and other stars.
> And all suns and all stars are darkened—"

"Hush now! Be quiet and behave yourself, Herr Kjær. Do you hear?"

Epilogue   Jastrau and the inevitable Kjær sat in the two wicker chairs near the hotel entrance and watched the bustle of traffic. For some strange reason everyone seemed to be in a hurry.

With their swollen, red-veined faces they looked like two stuffed animals.

Jastrau was casually whistling a tune.

"Give that hideous melody a rest," Kjær exclaimed in exasperation, dropping cigar ashes on himself.

Jastrau stopped his whistling.

But Kjær fidgeted in his chair. He brushed himself off, shook the bottom of his coat, snorted, and emitted a groan.

"I can get so worked up. And listening to that tune—"

"What tune?"

"Good God!" Kjær exclaimed in despair. "You have no idea what you're whistling, but just sit here very calmly and me all worked up. It was the Internationale, Jazz—the Internationale."

Jastrau gave a start. He had not realized what he was doing. But what did it matter? Was it anything more than a sentimental melody arising out of his subconsciousness? Emotional communism? With a feeling of irritation, he squirmed about until he was again comfortable in his chair. Emotionalism always ended with broken panes of glass—at a cost of four kroner.

"I have to go to Berlin," he announced across to Kjær.

Kjær stirred in his chair and laughed. "And Little P. is coming today. Coming today. They come and go, come and go. Only Kjær remains."

"But I don't have any money."

At once Kjær lapsed into silence. He sat motionless, his head drooping and his lips sealed, while Jastrau squirmed in his chair, troubled, embarrassed, desperate.

"I don't have the price of a ticket."

"Yes, I heard you."

"Will you loan it to me?"

424

Quickly—quickly! Now he had said it. But the silence was ominous. The noise of the street traffic bore in on them.

"I hadn't expected that of you," Kjær replied with an indignant sidelong glance. "You disappoint me, Jazz."

"I'm not rich," Jastrau said spitefully.

Kjær half turned his back on him.

"This is a sorry busniess, Jazz. You'll only drink up the money."

Jastrau let out a loud laugh.

"All the same, Jazz, it's a bad business." And Kjær stirred a little as if a shiver was running down his spine.

"I say!" he called out suddenly to the hall porter.

The porter's polite mustache protruded from behind the counter.

"Can you send one of the bellboys over to Bennett's for a ticket to Berlin?"

"Are you going away, Herr Kjær?"

"No—damned if I am. That's certainly a gruesome thought. But I'd like to have such a ticket. I collect them."

A little later a bellboy stood before Kjær while he received his instructions and the money.

But as the boy was about to run off, Jastrau called out after him.

"What is it now?" Kjær asked irritably.

"Look, I'd just like to see those ten-krone notes. Just let me see them. It could be that they're counterfeit," Jastrau exclaimed.

Hesitantly, the bellboy handed him the money.

"Are you crazy?" Kjær burst out, and started to get up.

But Jastrau sat with the brown ten-krone notes in his hand. He merely wanted to look at them. These were the wretched shinplasters that Kjær didn't dare trust him with. Should he tear them up? He stared and stared at them. A head of Hermes in an oval. And three lions with crowns on their heads.

"Have you gone completely crazy?"

And with a weary gesture Jastrau handed the money back.

Kjær shook his head.

"Are you getting soft in the head, Jazz?"

"I just wanted to see the money. I wanted to see the money."

"Oh."

And a little later:

"Kjær, do you know how it is when one day you're in good spirits and you meet a beggar with a hideous, ravaged face—a person who's really in need—and then you give him money, so you can be free to forget him, and so your day won't be ruined?"

Kjær straightened up in his chair.

"You—you do have—an oddly magnanimous way of saying thanks."

425

Published in

THE NORDIC TRANSLATION SERIES

FROM DENMARK

H. C. Branner, *Two Minutes of Silence.* Selected short stories, translated by Vera Lindholm Vance, with an introduction by Richard B. Vowles. 1966.

Tom Kristensen, *Havoc. Hærværk,* translated by Carl Malmberg, with an introduction by Børge Gedsø Madsen. 1968.

Jacob Paludan, *Jørgen Stein.* Translated by Carl Malmberg, with an introduction by P. M. Mitchell. 1966.

FROM FINLAND

Hagar Olsson, *The Woodcarver and Death. Träsnidaren och döden,* translated by George C. Schoolfield. 1965.

Toivo Pekkanen, *My Childhood. Lapsuuteni,* translated by Alan Blair, with an introduction by Thomas Warburton. 1966.

F. E. Sillanpää, *People in the Summer Night. Ihmiset suviyössä,* translated by Alan Blair, with an introduction by Thomas Warburton. 1966.

FROM ICELAND

Fire and Ice: Three Icelandic Plays, with introductions by Einar Haugen. Jóhann Sigurjónsson, *The Wish* (*Galdra-Loftur*), translated by Einar Haugen. Davið Stefánsson, *The Golden Gate* (*Gullna hliðið*), translated by G. M. Gathorne-Hardy. Agnar Thórðarson, *Atoms and Madams* (*Kjarnorka og kvenhylli*), translated by Einar Haugen. 1967.

Gunnar Gunnarsson, *The Black Cliffs. Svartfugl,* translated by Cecil Wood, with an introduction by Richard N. Ringler. 1967.

FROM NORWAY

Aksel Sandemose, *The Werewolf. Varulven,* translated by Gustaf Lannestock, with an introduction by Harald S. Næss. 1966.

426

Tarjei Vesaas, *The Great Cycle. Det store spelet,* translated by Elizabeth Rokkan, with an introduction by Harald S. Næss. 1967.

FROM SWEDEN

Tage Aurell, *Rose of Jericho and Other Stories. Berättelser,* translated by Martin Allwood, with an introduction by Eric O. Johannesson. 1968.

Karin Boye, *Kallocain.* Translated by Gustaf Lannestock, with an introduction by Richard B. Vowles. 1966.

Peder Sjögren, *Bread of Love. Kärlekens bröd,* translated by Richard B. Vowles. 1965.

OTHER TRANSLATIONS TO COME

427